ONE TUESDAY MORNING

TWO BOOKS IN ONE

BEYOND TUESDAY MORNING

Books by Karen Kingsbury

Redemption Series, coauthored by Gary Smalley
Redemption
Remember
Return
Rejoice
Reunion

The Firstborn Series
Fame
Forgiven
Found (summer 2006)
Family (sfall 2006)
Forever (spring 2007)

September 11 Series
One Tuesday Morning
Beyond Tuesday Morning

Women of Faith Series
A Time to Dance
A Time to Embrace

Where Yesterday Lives
When Joy Came to Stay
On Every Side
Oceans Apart
A Thousand Tomorrows

Forever Faith Series
Waiting for Morning
Moment of Weakness
Halfway to Forever

Red Gloves Series
Gideon's Gift
Maggie's Miracle
Sarah's Song

Children's Titles
Let Me Hold You Longer

A Treasury of Miracles Series
Treasury of Christmas Miracles
A Treasury of Miracles for Women
A Treasury of Miracles for Teens
Treasury of Miracles for Friends

KAREN
KINGSBURY

#1 BESTSELLING AUTHOR

ONE TUESDAY
MORNING

TWO BOOKS IN ONE

BEYOND TUESDAY
MORNING

ZONDERVAN®

GRAND RAPIDS, MICHIGAN 49530 USA

ZONDERVAN.COM/
AUTHOR**TRACKER**

ZONDERVAN®

One Tuesday Morning/Beyond Tuesday Morning
Copyright © 2006 by Karen Kingsbury

One Tuesday Morning
Copyright © 2003 by Karen Kingsbury

Beyond Tuesday Morning
Copyright © 2004 by Karen Kingsbury

Requests for information should be addressed to:
Zondervan, *Grand Rapids, Michigan 49530*

ISBN-10: 0-310-60651-9
ISBN-13: 978-0-310-60651-2

Published in association with the literary agency of Alive Communications, Inc., 7680 Goddard Street, Colorado Springs, Colorado 80920

Interior design by Michelle Espinoza

Printed in the United States of America

06 07 08 09 10 11 12 • 10 9 8 7 6 5 4 3 2 1

ONE
TUESDAY
MORNING

DEDICATION

To Donald, my prince charming. When I wrote about Jake Bryan, I was writing about you—a man whose love for God is the heartbeat of all he does, all he says. All he is. I thank God that you are that kind of man, and that I am blessed to call you mine. I pray that our days together will always be the light they are today, and that I will continue to follow your lead, as you follow Christ's.

To Kelsey, my little Norm, our precious teenager. The other day I remembered a time when you and Katie and Jentry were walking into kindergarten together. You were just the way I've made Sierra to be in this book—long golden curls and a smile that left a mark on everyone it touched. The beautiful thing, honey, is that you're still like that. I love that you are a one-in-a-million girl. You are the laughter in our home, Kelsey. I love you always and forever.

To Tyler, my special boy. Watching you grow up I am often moved to silent awe—not an easy place (especially if you ask your dad). Handsome and tall, eyes set firmly on the goals you have for tomorrow. How many ten-year-olds want to star on Broadway, produce Hollywood films that are pleasing to God, and still write novels as a hobby? We all know the answer. Tears fill my eyes when I look to the day—dangling out there in the not-so-distant future—when the theme to *Annie* won't play constantly in the background. But for now, I'm savoring every note, memorizing every crazy thing you say and do, and knowing that God has a special plan for you. And remember what you mean to me. I'll always love you, always believe in you, always pray for you ... my oldest son. Hold on fast to Jesus, buddy. He knows the way from here to there.

To Austin, my miracle boy, who's gotten so big this past summer. Just a few more months and our time together will be over, little one. In the fall you'll join the whirlwind with the others—off to school. But for now you and I still have what feels like endless mornings of give-and-go on your plastic indoor basketball hoop. "Make it higher, Mommy ... I'm Michael Jordan, remember?" Yes ... I remember. And when you score seven goals in a soccer game as you did last week, I know without a doubt that God is smiling at you. Was it five years ago that the doctor rushed you into surgery and told us there was something wrong with your heart, when he told us you might not live to see your fourth week of life? Even the doctors are amazed at how well you are now, how you have not a trace of the heart problem you suffered back then. Lucky, they say. Very lucky. But we know the truth, don't we, MJ? God gave you back to me, and I am grateful for every single morning. I love you, Austin. Always and always.

To EJ, my first chosen son. You have grown in leaps and bounds since coming to live with us from Haiti. We thought we were going to bless you by giving you a place in our home. But that wasn't how it worked out. The blessings have been all ours ... watching you go from a frightened, helpless child to a self-sufficient, articulate little boy. God is the one who brought us together, and I pray you hang on to Him every day of your life. He has huge plans for you, son. I love you, EJ.

To Sean, my happy silly-heart. You are so easily pleased, so happy to be here. I remember when you told me that one day you'd get a job and save up some money. "So I can give it to you, Mommy ... for everything you and Daddy have done for me." What I told you then is the same thing I want to tell you now. Just love God, Sean. Nothing would make me happier in the years and decades to come than to watch you love God the same way you love Him now. Don't forget about all the gifts He's given you ... I love you, Sean.

To Josh, our gentle giant. You are easily the fastest boy at school, the strongest in any game you play. Yet watching you is like watching an adult among children—you have that same gentle quality, that patience and kindness. I see it especially when you play with Austin, letting him win and even more, letting him think he's won. That takes a special type of confidence, a rare gift. You can do whatever you want to in life, Joshua. God has blessed you that greatly. Always remember that your abilities come from Him ... and know that I love you forever and ever.

And to God Almighty, the Author of Life, who has—for now— blessed me with these.

ACKNOWLEDGMENTS

A book of this magnitude does not come together without an enormous amount of research and assistance. For that reason, there are several people I must thank before getting into the story of *One Tuesday Morning*.

First, a humble thanks to the firefighters across the nation who courageously do their job on our behalf; and especially to the brave members of the FDNY. I have used a fictitious New York station in this novel, and also a fictitious Engine and Ladder company. But the truth is it could have been any of those in Manhattan and the surrounding areas. A special thanks to FDNY Press Secretary David Billing for helping me with determining fictitious Engine and Ladder companies, and for helping me accurately depict certain FDNY details. Also a heartfelt thanks to firefighter Brian Baum and dozens of others who lent priceless insight and accuracy to this novel. I count you among my heroes and friends.

As in the past, I want to thank Dr. Bryce Cleary for helping me have a true picture of the medical side of what my characters went through in *One Tuesday Morning*. You are my honorary doctor, and I enjoy giving you cameos in the stories that grow in my heart.

Thanks, also, to my editor at Zondervan—Dave Lambert. I am blessed beyond measure to have the privilege to work with you in this novel. The book it is today is proof that you are gifted in what you do. In that same vein, a thanks to the others at Zondervan, and especially to my amazing cover designer—Kirk DouPonce of Uttley-DouPonce Designworks. I've said it before, and I'll say it again. People judge a book by the cover, and I can only pray the story measures up. You are amazing!

A thank-you to my agent, Greg Johnson. There isn't enough space here to adequately thank you for all you do, Greg. I treasure our friendship, trust your judgment, and easily leave my career in God's hands and yours. I'm still grateful beyond words for that CBA luncheon when Terri Blackstock told me about you. Nothing has been the same since.

Thanks also to my special friends—the ones who encourage me and pray for me. Sylvia and Walt Walgren, Anne and Ron Hudson, Vicki, Joan, Kathy, Melinda, John, Robyn, Rick, and many, many more. Please keep praying, friends. I need you now more than ever. A special thanks goes to my family as well for understanding the extra hours I put in on this novel. I believe the end result has been well worth it . . . and I look forward to the time we'll have together in the coming weeks. You guys are the best!

And, of course, a special thanks to my parents and my sister, Tricia, for helping me down the stretch while I edited *One Tuesday Morning*. I am grateful for your servant hearts in helping me through what would otherwise have been an impossible time.

Finally, a special thanks to God for giving me the story of *One Tuesday Morning*. When I wrote the last page, there were tears on my face, and I raised my hands upwards. Because a novel like this one could only have come from Him.

A NOTE TO THE READER

To write a novel rooted in truth, an author must take certain liberties. I did that with *One Tuesday Morning*. Certain events—for instance the funeral of the unnamed probational firefighter detailed early in the book— were changed for the purpose of the story line. In reality firefighter Michael Gorumba, twenty-seven, suffered a heart attack and was remembered on September 1, 2001, at a St. Charles Catholic Church service in Staten Island, not on September 2, in Manhattan as my novel depicts.

Other such changes to true events occur in a minor sense only.

For the most part I've tried to write my novel within the confines of the tragic reality of the events that took place around September 11. *One Tuesday Morning* does not pretend to be a novelization of the tragedy that happened in Manhattan that terrible day. Too much of what took place with the terrorist attacks is not covered in this novel for that to be the case. Rather, I drew from hundreds of firsthand accounts, news stories, personal interviews, and other research. In the process I created a story that truly could've happened, given the multiple cases of amnesia caused when the World Trade Center collapsed.

One Tuesday Morning is my way of grieving through all the events of September 11.

Out of respect for the New York City Fire Department and the real heroes who fought and in many cases died on September 11, I've created for the purpose of this novel a fictitious fire station, along with fictitious Engine and Ladder companies. Any similarities to actual FDNY firefighters or fire stations is purely coincidental.

ONE

SEPTEMBER 2, 2001

There were too many funerals.

Jamie Bryan locked eyes on the casket anchored atop a specially fitted slow-moving New York City fire truck, and that was her only thought. Too many funerals. So many that this one—like those before it—was steeped in tradition: the haunting refrains from fifty bagpipes, the white-gloved salute, the lone bugler sounding taps, the helicopter passing overhead. Jamie knew the routine well. Hundreds of dignitaries and several thousand uniformed firefighters lined Fifth Avenue outside St. Patrick's Cathedral, the same way they'd done five times already that year.

A sad melody lifted from the bagpipes and mingled with the early September wind.

"I hate this," she whispered without moving.

Her husband stood a few inches away, tall and proud, his blue uniform pressed crisp, right hand sharply at attention near his brow. He squeezed her hand. No words came, no response to her statement. What could he say? Funerals were part of the job. Sometimes ten a year, sometimes twenty. This year was the lightest yet. Only six so far—six men like Jake who went to work for the FDNY one morning and never came home.

The funeral music swelled, and Jamie Bryan could feel the walls, feel them growing and building within her. The first bricks had been with her since the beginning, back when she first considered marrying a New York City firefighter.

Back when she and Jake Bryan were just twelve years old.

"I'm never leaving New York City." They'd been playing tag with neighbor kids outside his house one day that summer. Everyone else had gone in for dinner. "I'll be FDNY like my daddy." Certainty shone from his eyes as they made their way onto his front lawn. "Puttin' out fires and savin' people."

"That's fine for you." She'd dropped to the ground and leaned back on her elbows. "When I grow up I'm gonna live in France." She stared at the hazy humid New York sky. "Artists live there."

"Oh yeah?" Jake flopped down beside her. "Before or after you marry me?"

She lowered her chin to her chest and raised her eyebrows at him. "What makes you think I'd marry you, Jake Bryan?"

"Because . . ." He twisted his baseball cap and shot her a grin. "You love me. And you always will."

That had been it, really. They didn't date until high school, but after that summer Jake Bryan had been the only boy for her.

"What do you see in him?" Her father peered at her over the top of his newspaper the day after her eighteenth birthday. "He'll never be rich."

Jamie had rolled her eyes. "Money isn't everything, Daddy."

"But security is." Her father let the newspaper fall to the table. "You'll get neither from Jake."

Anger had flashed like lightning across Jamie's heart. "How can you say that?"

"Because." Her father had rested his forearms on the table, his expression softer. "It's a tough job, fighting fires in New York City. The danger's always there, Jamie, as close as the next call." He gestured in the direction of Jake's house. "Look at his mother. She lives with the danger every day. It's in her eyes, part of who she is. That'll be you one day if you marry Jake Bryan."

Her father and Jake's were both Staten Island men, hardworking New Yorkers who made the commute to Manhattan every day. But the similarities stopped there. Jake's father, Jim, was a fireman, a chaplain who always had something to say about God or the importance of faith.

"What good thing has the Lord done for you today, Jamie?" he'd ask, grinning at her with piercing blue eyes that would light up the room.

Jamie was never sure how to answer the man. She had no practice at giving God credit for the good things in life. Small wonder, really. Her father, Henry Steele, was an investment banker who had built a small financial empire with nothing more than brains, determination, and self-reliance. At least that was his explanation.

Their family had lived in the same house where Jake and Jamie and their daughter, Sierra, lived today. In an elite section of Westerleigh, not far from the Staten Island Expressway and the ferry ramps. The sprawling two-story colonial had a finished basement and a built-in pool in the backyard. Back then Jamie and her sister had been friends, just two years apart and living the charmed life of summer beach parties and winter vacations in the Florida Keys.

All of it compliments of Henry Steele's hard work and ingenuity. God got no credit at all.

"A man doesn't need anyone but himself," he would tell Jamie and her sister. "Religion is a sign of weakness." Then he'd shoot a pointed look at Jamie. "Of course, when a person fights fires in New York City, faith might be a necessity."

And so Jamie waited month after month for something terrible to happen to Jake's father. But in the end it had been Jamie's father, not Jake's, who died the tragic death. One evening when her parents were driving home from the ferry, her father lost control at the wheel, careened off the road, and wrapped their car around a telephone pole. By the time paramedics arrived at the scene, both her parents were dead. Jamie was twenty that year, her sister, eighteen.

Their parents carried a million dollars' life insurance each, and a lawyer helped the girls work out an agreement. Jamie got the family house; Kara got a full ride to Florida State University and stocks. They were both given enough savings to last a lifetime, but no amount of money could stop the arguments that developed over the next few years. An ocean of differences lay between them now. It had been five years since they'd spoken to each other.

Three years after the death of her parents, Jamie remembered her father's warning about Jake's job as she stood by and watched him graduate with his fire science degree. Weeks later he was hired by the New York Fire Department. The next summer Jake and Jamie married and honeymooned on a Caribbean cruise, and since then Jamie hadn't been more than a hundred miles from the East Coast.

But she no longer wanted to travel the world. Sights from a dozen exotic countries could never rival the pleasure she felt simply loving Jake Bryan.

"You don't have to work, you know . . ." Jamie had mentioned the fact to Jake just once—a month before his first shift with FDNY. "We have enough money." Jake had bristled in a way she hadn't seen him do before or since.

"Listen. Fighting fires in New York City is part of who I am, Jamie. Deep inside me." His eyes held a hard glint. "It's not about the money."

The bagpipes stopped, and a sad silence hung in the air.

A bugle cry pierced the quiet morning, and the lonely sound of taps filled the street. Jamie stared at the coffin again. The dead man had been a proby, a probational firefighter still serving his first year with the department. This time deadly smoke, fiery flames, and falling ceiling beams weren't responsible.

The man's engine company had simply responded to an auto shop on fire. For several minutes the proby worked a massive hose reel at the side of the engine, then he climbed back into the cab. His buddies found him not long afterwards, slumped forward, dead of a heart attack at twenty-seven years old. Just five months after graduating top of his class.

He was the fourth fireman to suffer a fatal heart attack in ten months.

The bugle rang out its last note, and in very little time, the sea of blue began to break up. Jamie and Jake held hands as they made their way back to his pickup truck and headed home to Sierra.

Sierra . . .

The image of their four-year-old daughter filled Jamie's heart and for a moment dimmed the deep ache there. Sierra had Jake's blue eyes and Jamie's trademark dimples. No one knew where Sierra had gotten her blonde silky hair, but she was a beauty, inside and out. Days like this, Jamie could hardly wait to hold her, to soak in the warmth and hope of her precious laugh. The girl had held both their hearts captive since the day she was born.

Jamie stared out the truck window.

Manhattan smelled of warm bistros and cabbie exhaust fumes. It didn't have a downtime. The sidewalks teamed with people as much now as they would on a weekday. She keyed on a couple about the same age as she and Jake, dressed for business, walking briskly toward some lower Manhattan destination. The two exchanged a smile, and for a fraction of a second, Jamie wondered, *Do they know about the dead fireman? Do they spend time pondering the fact that men like Jake are willing to die for their safety?*

Jamie shifted and slipped her hand into Jake's. *Of course they don't. Unless they know a firefighter or police officer, unless they regularly attend the funerals, why would they?* She leaned back in her seat and looked at Jake. The silence between them was heavy, and words didn't come until they hit the ferry docks.

"When's the last time you had your heart checked?"

Jake glanced at her. "What?"

"Your heart." She swallowed and tried to find a neutral tone. "When's the last time you had it checked?"

"Jamie . . ." Understanding flooded his eyes. "I'm fine. There's nothing wrong with my heart."

"I'd rather have the doctors decide."

"Honey, heart attacks are part of life." He worked his fingers a little more tightly between hers and kept his eyes on the road. "Not just for firemen."

She stared out the window again and let the air ease from her lungs. Did he always have to read her mind? Couldn't she keep even a little fear to herself? He would never be honest with her as long as he knew she was afraid. Every time he sensed her concern, he had the same answer. *Not me, Jamie ... I'll be careful ... nothing'll happen ...* And now this. *There's nothing wrong with my heart ...*

They pulled into line at the Whitehall terminal and inched their way onto the ferry. When they'd driven up as far as they could, Jake slipped the truck into park and faced her. His voice was a gentle caress. "I'm sorry."

She turned to him. "For what?"

"For the funeral." He bit his lip. "I know how much you hate them."

A cavernous pit of sorrow welled within her, but she wouldn't cry. She never did, not in front of him, anyway. "It's not your fault."

"You could stay home next time." He reached out and loosely gripped her knee. "Lots of wives do."

"No." She gave a quick double shake of her head. "I'd rather go."

"Jamie ..." The ferry gave a slight lurch and began to move across the harbor.

"I *would*." She gritted her teeth. "It reminds me what I'm up against."

"Come on, baby." A chuckle sounded low in his throat, one that was weighted in empathy. "When are you going to stop waiting for something bad to happen?"

"When you work your last shift." Their eyes met and desire stirred within her. They'd been married nearly a decade, but he still moved her, still made her want to hold on to him an extra minute or two every time they came together.

He leaned over and kissed her, the slow passionate kiss of a love that didn't happen in spurts, a love that colored every page of a life they'd written together. He moved his lips along her cheekbone toward her earlobe. "Ten years is too long to worry."

"Nine."

"Nine?" He drew back, and his little-boy expression almost made her laugh.

"Yes. You're almost thirty-six, Jake. You said you'd retire at forty-five like your father. That's nine years."

"Okay, nine. It's still too long to worry. Besides . . . I love what I do." Without waiting for a response, he worked his fingers up beneath her rayon blouse and pressed his thumbs against her ribs. "Almost as much as I love you."

She squirmed and couldn't contain a giggle. "Stop it!"

"Anyway, you're worrying about the wrong thing." He tickled her once more, and when she twisted free, he held his hands up in surrender.

"Oh yeah." She caught her breath and straightened her shirt. "What am I supposed to worry about?"

"Beating me at tennis."

"Okay." She forced a sarcastic laugh. "I could try to worry about that."

"What? Is that arrogance in my fair damsel's voice?" He stifled a grin. "You beat me in three sets last week, and now I'm no challenge? Is that it?"

She let her head fall back and she laughed, this time without reservation. "Okay . . . I'm worried, Jake."

"Good. And don't forget—today's Sierra's first lesson."

"Here we go." Jamie could feel the sparkle in her eyes. "She's four, Jake."

"Martina Hingis was probably four when she picked up a racket."

Jamie's laughter rang through the cab. "You're crazy."

"About Sierra, yes." Jake's smile faded some. "I don't know what I'd do without her." He took her hand. "Or you."

"Me either." She settled against the door of the truck, still facing Jake. "Sierra's perfect, isn't she?"

Jake stared out at the harbor, and his eyes grew distant. "Being a dad has given me these feelings . . ." He angled his head. "A love I can't describe."

Jamie smiled, slow and easy. The cry of the bagpipes faded from her memory, and one by one the clouds of fear lifted, breaking up like morning fog over the water. Jake was right. Worrying did no good. Especially when every day held so much life for their little family.

"Come on." Jake opened his truck door and motioned for Jamie to follow. She did, and the two of them walked to the front of the ferry, found a quiet spot against a railing, and turned to face the receding New York skyline.

"It's breathtaking every time." She stared past the Statue of Liberty and lifted her eyes to where the World Trade Center towered over the rest of lower Manhattan. "You've been on every floor, haven't you?"

"Of the Twin Towers?" Jake squinted and gazed up at the tall buildings. "Probably. Jammed elevators, chest pains, faulty wiring in the office coffeemaker."

"And the bombing." She lifted her chin and studied his face. "Don't forget about that."

"Yeah." He lifted one shoulder. "But the fire was out before we got there."

"Still . . . it was scary. I remember it like it was yesterday."

"The towers are safe, Jamie. Stairwells run down three sides." He narrowed his eyes and looked back at the buildings. "It's the old warehouses and abandoned factories. Those are scary."

"I know." She gripped the railing behind her and studied the city again. After a moment she shifted her gaze to him. "I'll try not to worry so much. Okay?"

He slipped his arm around her and kissed the top of her head. "Okay. Besides, who of you, by worrying, can add an hour to his life?" He paused. "That's from the Bible."

Jamie let the comment pass. Letting go of her fear was one thing. Claiming some sort of help or understanding from an old leather-bound book of ancient letters was another. But to say so would only upset Jake. And the day was too beautiful, their time together too short for that.

"I love you, Jake Bryan." She slid her arms around his neck, letting herself get lost in his embrace. "I'm sorry for being afraid."

"I know." He kissed her again, this time more slowly. The ferry was less crowded than usual, and they had privacy in the place where they stood. When he pulled away, he searched her eyes. "I'm not going anywhere, Jamie. God and I have a little deal, a secret."

"Is that so?" She tilted her face and batted her eyelashes at him. "I don't suppose you'll share it with me."

"Nope. But I can tell you this much. God isn't finished with me yet." He brought his lips to hers once more. "And He's not finished with you, either."

They held hands as they returned to Jake's truck and climbed back inside. Fifteen minutes later they pulled into their tree-lined neighborhood and the same familiar street where they'd grown up. This was home. The quaintness of the island, the way she knew every front yard, every family that made up this part of Westerleigh.

The old house was gray now with white trim, but it was still much the same as it had been when Jamie grew up there. They pulled in the drive, and the moment they walked inside, Sierra ran to them, her eyes lit up.

"You're home!" She stretched her hands up toward Jamie. "Oooh, Mommy. You look pretty."

"Thanks, baby." Jamie swung her up into a hug and nuzzled her cheek against Sierra's. She smelled nice, like baby powder and maple syrup.

Jake paid the sitter, and when she was gone, the three of them moved into the living room.

"Did you and Daddy go to church?"

The question poked pins at Jamie's good feelings. Before she could answer, Jake came up alongside them. "Hey, little girl." He took Sierra into his arms. "How was your morning?"

"We had pancakes." Sierra rubbed noses with Jake and giggled. "Did you and Mommy go to church?"

"Sort of." Jake twirled one of Sierra's curls around his finger. "It was a special church meeting for one of the firemen at Daddy's work."

"Oh." Sierra searched his eyes. Her golden hair shimmered against her blue T-shirt. "Did he do something good?"

Jake tilted his head and hesitated long enough for Jamie to read his heart. "Yeah, baby." He pursed his lips and nodded, and Jamie felt the familiar ache from earlier. "He did something real good."

Sierra brought her chin to her chest and placed her hands on either side of Jake's face. "Is Mommy going with us *next* Sunday?"

Jake gave Jamie a quick smile. He never pushed her, just left it open. In case she ever changed her mind. Jamie cleared her throat. "Mommy has her painting class next Sunday, sweetheart."

"Oh." Sierra blinked at Jake. "But you'll take *me*, right, Daddy? Two times a month?"

"Right, honey."

"Because Mrs. Ritchie looks for me two Sundays at class time."

"Yep. Mrs. Ritchie won't be disappointed. You'll be there next week for sure."

"Goodie!" Sierra jumped down and made a quick wave in Jamie's direction. "I'm gonna check on Brownie. She sleeped in my bed this morning."

Brownie was their faithful lab. Eight years old and graying around her jowls, she was wonderful with Sierra and didn't mind wearing baby bonnets. The two of them were best friends. Jamie watched their daughter scamper off, and a thread of guilt sewed itself around the perimeter of her soul. She looked at Jake and gave him a crooked smile. "Thanks."

"For what?" A lazy grin tugged at the corners of his mouth. He crossed the room into the kitchen and poured himself a glass of water.

She followed, her voice quiet. "For not making a big deal out of the church thing."

"I'll never push you, Jamie." He took a swig of water and studied her. "You know that."

"Still . . ." She felt uneasy in a way she couldn't quite pin down. "It means a lot."

"No big deal." He set the glass down. "I'm gonna change clothes. Tennis in half an hour?"

She leaned against the counter and felt her gaze soften. "Okay."

"You over the fear thing?"

Jamie smiled. "For now."

It wasn't until she went upstairs to change that she caught sight of the mirror and stopped short. Who was she kidding? The worry wasn't gone; as long as firefighters were dying it would never be gone. They had Sierra and each other and a life sweeter than she'd dared to dream. Jake's job loomed as the single threat to everything that mattered.

Sometimes where Jake and Sierra were concerned, Jamie felt like a little girl again, building sandcastles on the beach, desperate to stretch the day, to make the sunny hours last as long as she could. Jamie could still see herself the way she'd been on sandcastle Sundays, giggling and skittering back and forth on the sand, chasing back the waves, believing somehow she could stop the tide from claiming her precious creation.

But in the end the waves would come. Always they would come. And when they did, they would wash away all she'd built. There hadn't been a single thing she could do to stop them.

Her father's long-ago words came back to her. *Look at Jake's mother. She lives with the danger every day. It's in her eyes, part of who she is. That'll be you one day if you marry Jake Bryan.*

Jamie leaned closer and scrutinized her eyes. Her father had been right all along. When had her eyes stopped being the light-filled carefree speckled brown of her childhood? Now they were dark and deep, and they'd taken on a new color, one that bore an uncanny resemblance to that in Jake's mother's eyes. The same color Jamie had seen in the eyes of a dozen other firefighter wives.

The color of fear.

TWO

Laura Michaels whipped around and ran smack into a giant mouse.

She shrieked, but the sound was lost among the roar of a hundred happy children. Taking a step backwards, she ran her hands down the rat's furry arms. She looked both ways to make sure none of the kids were watching. Then she leaned close and whispered in a loud voice. "Are you okay?"

The mouse nodded, and his oversized plastic head bobbed up and down. He lifted his paw and pointed to the melting ice-cream cake on a nearby table.

Laura gasped. "The cake!" She raked her fingers through her straight blonde hair and glanced at her watch. Seven o'clock. Eric should've been there an hour ago. She managed a smile and aimed her words through the mouth of the giant mouse so whoever was inside could hear her. "I'll get the boys and be right back."

The mouse nodded again and wandered off to another table.

Josh had wanted to celebrate his eighth birthday at Chuck E. Cheese's, and Laura and Eric had easily agreed. Laura could pick up an ice-cream cake, and the restaurant would take care of pizza and drinks. Josh and his friends would entertain themselves for hours, and there'd be nothing to clean up.

"Get there at five-thirty, and I'll be right behind you," Eric had promised earlier that afternoon. "No later than six."

It seemed doable. The restaurant was at the west end of the San Fernando Valley, just ten minutes from Eric's office in the heart of Warner Center. At first the afternoon had gone as planned. Six young guests had arrived at the Michaels' Westlake Village house and ridden with her thirty minutes on the Ventura Freeway to the pizza parlor.

But five-thirty had become six, and the boys had eaten their pizza with no sign of Eric. When they were finished, Josh and his friends fanned out into the game gallery while Laura snatched glances back at the front door. An hour passed, and without Eric, she had no one to help her round up the boys. Now she was standing guard over a melting ice-cream cake and leftover pizza balanced precariously atop a pile of unopened birthday presents.

This is crazy . . . where is he?

Her silent words were more introspective than prayer, and Laura didn't wait for a response. She peered through the maze of children looking for any sign of the boys. Forget the cake and presents; they'd be fine without her for a few minutes. She took a few hurried steps toward the arcade area when suddenly she felt a hand on her shoulder. She spun around. "Thank goodness you're—" The sight of Eric's brother stopped her short.

"Where's Eric?" Clay Michaels leaned against the table and locked eyes with Laura. Clay had attended a small college in Missouri and had returned to Southern California a few months ago. He was a police officer, and he idolized his older brother.

"You've got it all, Eric," Clay had told him a few weeks ago. His tone had been light and not completely serious. But the admiration he had for Eric was evident. "You're a great husband, great father. The perfect guy with the perfect family."

Laura hadn't had the heart to set him straight. Besides, if he lived near them long enough, Clay would get a clearer picture of Eric soon enough. Times like this one were bound to expose Eric for what he was—a corporate climber with eyes for nothing but whatever lay at the top of the ladder.

She managed a quick smile. "He's . . . he's late."

"For Josh's birthday?" Clay's eyebrows rose a notch. "What's keeping him?"

The same thing that always keeps him, Laura thought. "Work. He's probably on his way."

"Where's Josh?" Clay snagged a piece of pizza from the pan and moved it off the stack of presents. "Looks like the cake's about to give out."

Laura shifted her gaze and stared hard at the mass of children in the arcade room. "He's in there somewhere." She looked back at Clay. "He's with six eight-year-olds. Could you get him?"

"Sure." Clay set the pizza down on a plate, grabbed a napkin, and headed toward the other room. "Be right back."

Laura watched him walk away. She'd had mixed feelings about Eric's younger brother since their days as classmates in grade school. Clay was kind and gentle, with blonde hair and a square forehead that made people wonder whether he and Eric were really brothers. Her feelings for the two men had always been as different as their looks. Laura had fallen for Eric the moment she'd met him. His confidence and ambition, the sure way he held himself. Clay had been her friend; Eric, her first love.

Her only love.

But since Clay's return to Southern California, Laura had to wonder. Had she picked the wrong brother so many years ago? The thought was crazy, really, but still it lay there on the doormat of her heart. Laura watched Clay as he made his way through the arcade searching for Josh. Clay wasn't the financial success that Eric was, and he didn't have Eric's striking looks. But what did those things matter, really? Clay could make her smile as easily as he could swing Josh up onto his shoulders. The man taught Sunday school at the church they all attended, he sang in the choir, and even though he'd been back just a short while, he'd already taken part in two workdays at the Los Angeles homeless mission.

Why couldn't Eric be that way? And why couldn't he be as attentive to Josh as Clay had been these past few months?

Laura let the thought pass. Maybe it was time she and Eric saw the counselor again.

It was something they'd done every few years for the past decade, and they were about due for another round. Nothing permanent ever came of their sessions. Laura would talk about how she felt distant, unloved, ignored; and Eric would explain that his job needed him if he were ever going to make something of himself. They'd hash it out with the counselor for ten or twelve weeks and make promises to change: Laura, that she'd be more understanding; and Eric, that he'd look for ways to spend time at home.

The changes never lasted more than a few months.

Clay was heading toward her again, Josh and his buddies in tow. Josh jogged ahead of the others, gave Laura a quick side hug, and stared at his cake. "Why didn't you tell us it was melting?"

"I didn't want to leave the—"

"Where's Dad?" Josh stared across the restaurant toward the front door and back at Laura. Disappointment settled in around the corners of his eyes. "He didn't come, did he?"

Clay stood with Josh's buddies a few feet away. His eyes met Laura's and she saw confusion there. The fact that Eric hadn't made it to Josh's birthday was a shock to Clay. Laura bit her lip and moved her gaze to Josh. "He'll be here, buddy. He's running late."

"I'm hungry!" One of Josh's friends wormed his way to the front of the pack. "That's my favorite cake."

"Okay, guys." Laura summoned a smile. "Take a seat and let's sing."

Clay anchored himself beside her while she led the boys in an upbeat off-key version of the birthday song. When they finished he nudged her elbow and leaned close enough so that only she could hear him. "I'm worried about Eric." He reached into her purse, pulled out her cell phone, and handed it to her. "I'll cut the cake. Go call him."

* * * *

Eric Michaels was surrounded by Koppel and Grant's top planners, four men and two women who collectively orchestrated multimillion-dollar deals each day for high-stakes investors and major corporations around the world. The planners worked on commission, and each had already earned six-figure bonuses that year. The meeting was a brainstorming session about which pharmaceutical company's potential earnings most outweighed the risk of investment in the current market.

They were two hours late with no sign of reaching an agreement.

"My gut says go with Amgen." Paul Murphy stood and paced to the window. The sun was setting, and the sky over the San Fernando Valley was streaked in orange. "They're working on that Lou Gherig's cure, and insiders say they're developing a genetic response to a broad range of cancers. They're the ticket."

"If we're talking gut, I'd say Chiron's a better choice. Their numbers are up the past few weeks, and they've got a cancer cure on the table."

"Listen." Eric leaned back in his chair and tapped his pencil on his notepad. "Our clients don't pay us to go with our gut." A sharp sigh escaped him. "New York wants our decision first thing in the morning." He looked around the room. "We can't afford to be wrong."

"We've been right three out of the last four times." Murphy spun around and paced back to the table. He was a heavyset man, and the veins near his temple made distinct blue lines on either side of his forehead. "What do they want? We can't see into the future."

"With ten million dollars riding . . ."—Eric met the eyes of the others—"we better learn how." He hesitated. "Allen says one more mistake, and they'll consider closing us."

"Close the LA office?" Murphy's mouth hung open. "Allen's crazy."

"Murphy's right." One of the two women at the table leaned forward, her brow pinched. "Investors won't work with a planner whose only office is in New York. West Coast players are too important."

"I know that, and so does Allen. But let's remember one thing." Eric stared at the ceiling for a moment. He loved this, loved the banter back and forth and the clients waiting breathlessly for their decision. The outcome of this meeting would influence the way fortunes were made or lost. That kind of power was heady in a way that never lost its allure. He looked at his peers once more. "In this business everyone's replaceable."

From a small pocket inside his leather briefcase, Eric's cell phone rang. He stared at the bag and suddenly he remembered.

Josh's birthday.

It was today, wasn't it? Yes, September 4 ... that was the day. The boy was eight. Eric shot a look at the clock on the wall and grimaced. Seven-thirty. What time had he told Laura he'd be there? Six o'clock, or was it six-thirty? Either way he was late. The phone rang again, and Eric glanced around the room. All eyes were on him. He reached into the bag, grabbed his phone, stood and held up a single finger. "Be right back," he mouthed the words.

Then, with the phone still ringing in his hand, Eric moved quickly across the room and slipped into the hallway. In one motion he extended the antenna, flipped the phone open, and lifted it to his ear. "Hello?"

"Eric?"

"Laura?" The background sounds were so loud Eric could barely hear her. He braced himself for what was coming. "Are you at the restaurant?" There was a pause and Eric hesitated. Maybe she couldn't hear him. "Laura?"

"I'm here," she said, exhaling hard, disappointment in her tone. "Of course I'm at the restaurant. We've been here for two hours. The pizza's gone, the tokens are spent, and Clay's helping Josh cut his birthday cake."

"Clay?" Eric swallowed, desperate to buy some time. At least his brother had remembered, which meant Laura wasn't handling the party by herself. Still ... Eric was the boy's father, and they had just one child, after all. He pressed his thumb and forefinger into his temples. How could he have forgotten? "Is Clay helping you?"

"Yes." She paused long enough to make him nervous. "He likes being a part of Josh's life."

Eric wiped a thin layer of perspiration off his forehead and cursed under his breath. "I can be there in fifteen minutes."

Laura said nothing.

"Fifteen minutes, Laura. I mean it."

"What happened this time?" Sarcasm filled in the spaces between her words. "Did you forget?"

"Of course not." His answer was quick and sounded like a lie even to him. "We had a decision to make, an important meeting. I was in charge, Laura. I couldn't just walk out. New York needs our answer by tomorrow."

"Tell that to Josh."

"Look . . ." He felt trapped and his heart rate doubled. His associates were only a few yards away behind the closed office door, so he kept his voice quiet. "We're wasting time. I'll be there in fifteen, Laura. I swear."

"No, Eric. Forget it."

"Why?" He made a weak attempt at sounding indignant. "You'll be another half hour. I could get there for the end of it, at least."

"You wouldn't."

"Fifteen minutes, Laura. I promise. I'll be there in—"

"Stop." Laura raised her voice and just as quickly dropped it again. "We both know you won't be here in fifteen minutes." Her voice broke and she hesitated. "I'll make something up for Josh, tell him it was out of your control."

"It is, Laura. That's not a lie."

"Spare me, please. Meetings can be rescheduled." She dropped the sarcasm, and a tired sadness filled her voice instead. "It's Josh's birthday."

Eric swallowed hard. He could hardly tell her the truth, that until her phone call he hadn't given the boy's birthday a single thought. "You're right." He steadied his tone. "I messed up. Tell Josh I'll make it up to him this weekend."

"With what?"

"With . . ." His mind raced. "With a trip to the beach. Tell him I got him something special, something we can only use out on the water."

"The beach?" Laura sounded doubtful. "This weekend?"

"Or next at the latest."

"You'll be in New York this weekend."

"Right, right." He made a fist and pounded out a series of light staccatos against the doorframe. "Next weekend, then. Tell him it'll be next weekend for sure."

"Fine." Laura's tone told him everything her words didn't say. She was tired of his excuses, his absence at home, the way his heavy work schedule left her a single parent so often. They were feelings that came up every now and then, feelings that sometimes sent them to a counselor for help. But no matter how crazy his work schedule became, no matter how often they made appointments with a counselor, the result was always the same.

Laura would understand.

She might not have been happy about it, but she would understand because ultimately she had to. His job was their single source of income, and it cost a lot to run a household like theirs. They could talk about family or faith coming first in their lives, but the truth was everything else revolved around his work schedule. And it would until he was named president of the company.

When that day came, he would make up for a lifetime of missed birthdays. Or at least that was the plan. And until then Laura would have no choice but to go along with it. The silence between them was too long to be anything but intentional. Eric rolled his eyes and focused on a vent in the hallway ceiling. "Laura?"

"What?" Her voice was quieter than before, defeated.

"I'm sorry." He took a step back toward the meeting room. "Tell Josh for me."

"Good-bye, Eric."

"Hey . . ." If he didn't need to leave for Josh's party, then they might as well finish their discussion about Amgen and Chiron. It could take hours the way things were going. "Don't wait up for me."

"What?" Her anger was quick and intense.

Eric held his breath and kept his voice low. "The meeting could last until after ten. If I finish up, I can go in late tomorrow and maybe have breakfast with you and Josh." He gave her a chance to respond, but she said nothing. "Josh'll be in bed by the time I get home, anyway."

"Fine. Good-bye."

"That's okay, isn't it? Wouldn't it be better to get the meeting—"

There was a click at the other end, and after a few seconds, the phone went dead. Eric closed the phone and stared at it for a moment. Fine. Work was easier when she was mad at him. It gave him another reason to stay late at the office. He steadied himself, then returned to the meeting room. A discussion was under way about the reality of Chiron's discovery in the cancer field. Before Eric joined in, he slipped his phone back into his briefcase and pulled out his palm pilot. In the notes section, he jotted down, "Buy Josh a boogie board."

Then he checked his weekend calendar. His flight to New York was first thing Saturday morning. That would give him Sunday breakfast and lunch to connect with Allen and a handful of execs from the New York office. Monday and Tuesday would be booked solid with meetings on the sixty-fourth floor of the World Trade Center.

One of the most powerful places on earth.

Ideally he could buy Josh the boogie board tonight. That way he could give it to him over breakfast. Where had he seen one recently? Eric stared at his palm pilot and tried to remember. Then it came to him. The Albertsons near the freeway. Every now and then the grocery stores carried beach supplies—even boogie boards. And last week Eric had stopped in for an orange juice, and there they were, stacked in a pyramid near the front of the store. Fortunately, the place was open until eleven on weeknights.

Eric snapped the pen into the side of his palm pilot and slipped it back in his briefcase. Perfect. He would stop by the market on the way home, buy the boogie board, and surprise Josh the next morning. That ought to make up for missing the boy's birthday party. Besides, Clay was there. He'd help Laura get the presents to the car and make Josh feel special.

That was all that mattered.

Someone had shifted the conversation back to Amgen, and Eric listened for a moment before cutting in. "There're five other pharmaceuticals that need our consideration." He opened the portfolio on the table in front of him. "Let me read you some of their statistics . . ."

The meeting wore on hour after hour and didn't wrap up until ten-thirty. Disclosures had been made by each planner at the table, and finally they agreed that Amgen was their best bet. Put the money on Amgen and you couldn't lose. They were right this time. Eric could sense it.

The moment they were finished, Murphy reached into his portable file and pulled out a single piece of paper. "I almost forgot. Allen wants us to divide up a list of new investors before we call tomorrow."

A series of collective groans sounded from the others. "We should've done that tonight." Eric folded his arms and frowned.

"It's too late." Murphy returned the paper to his file and closed it. "Let's meet for breakfast tomorrow at the café downstairs. Seven o'clock." He looked at the others. "Does that work?"

There were nods of agreement from around the room as people reached for their palm pilots and day planners and penciled in the morning meeting. The group dispersed and headed for their private offices where some of them would spend another hour working their computer files.

Eric walked to the parking lot with Trish O'Reilly, the newest member of the team. They were halfway to their cars when Trish slowed her steps and cast him a long look. "Who was on the phone?"

The question caught Eric off guard.

He made it a point not to get into his personal life at work. But something about the late hour and the relief of having wrapped up the meeting made him feel like talking. Or maybe it was simply the fact that he wasn't looking forward to going home and facing Laura. He stared past the parking lot lights to the sky beyond. "My wife."

Trish stopped walking and crossed her arms. Her bag hung from one shoulder, and for the first time Eric noticed how young she was. Not more than twenty-seven, and not bad looking.

She narrowed her eyes and said, "How do you do it? Keep her happy with all the hours you put in here?"

"Well . . ." Eric remembered Laura's tone from earlier. "It's not easy."

"I know." Trish let her gaze fall to the asphalt parking lot for a moment. When she looked up, a certain vulnerability filled her eyes. "My husband filed for divorce yesterday."

"Wow." Eric set his briefcase down and slipped his hands in his pocket. "I'm sorry."

A single tear fell onto Trish's cheek and she dabbed at it.

"Hey . . . it's okay." Eric felt suddenly awkward. "You'll find someone else." Without knowing why exactly, he moved closer and hugged her. Not an intimate embrace, but the sort of loose hug people gave at funerals when they didn't know what to say.

Trish stayed in his arms for several seconds and then pulled away. "I'm sorry." She sniffed. "I didn't mean to lose it." Her eyes met his again. "I love working here, really I do. But sometimes I wonder how any of us can do both. You know, have the dream job and the perfect home life."

"It's all about sacrifice." Eric took a step backwards and reached for his briefcase again. "My wife likes the life we live, the house, the trips, the cars. She doesn't complain very often." He pictured Josh and his buddies enjoying themselves at the pizza parlor. "Sometimes I miss out on the family."

"Sounds like you have it figured out."

"Yeah." Doubt nibbled at the heels of Eric's conscience. "I guess."

Somewhere in the distant places of his mind, Eric wondered if Trish was interested in him or merely looking for a friend in light of her personal troubles. Either way, he wasn't interested. He didn't have enough time for Laura and Josh, let alone a diversion like Trish. They talked for another few minutes, and then Eric nodded toward his car. "I better get going."

"Yeah." Trish gave him a sad smile. "Me too. See you tomorrow at breakfast."

"Tomorrow . . ." Eric's voice trailed off. He'd promised Laura he'd go in late tomorrow and share breakfast with her and Josh. Now he'd have to leave earlier than usual. Why hadn't he thought of that when Murphy brought it up? He could have insisted they stay late tonight rather than meet so early in the morning. "Seven o'clock, was that it?"

"Yep." Trish took a few steps toward her car. "Hey, Eric. Thanks for listening."

"Sure." He moved toward his new model black Mercedes. "Anytime."

Five minutes later he was driving by Albertson's supermarket when he slammed on the brakes. The boogie board! He backed up, pulled into the parking, and sent a hurried look at the time on his dashboard. Two minutes after eleven. *Be open, come on, guys.* He sped into a spot near the front, slammed the gearshift into park, and raced up to the double doors. A teenager in a white smock was mopping the floor inside.

"Hey . . ." Eric banged on the window until the teen looked at him. "Open up. Please! I have to buy something."

"Sorry." The boy shook his head. He stopped sweeping and moved a few steps toward the doors. "We're closed."

Eric banged again. "It's an emergency." No pimple-faced kid was going to tell him what he could and couldn't do. "Get your manager!"

The boy disappeared and returned in less than a minute with a short, frazzled man in a rumpled shirt and tie. The man came up to the doors and shouted at Eric. "The registers are closed for the night. We open at seven tomorrow morning."

Desperation surged through Eric. He couldn't come home empty-handed. Not after missing Josh's birthday party. His hands shook as he reached into his pocket and grabbed his wallet. Fumbling with the flaps, he opened it, yanked out a hundred-dollar bill, and waved it at the manager. "It's an emergency. Please!"

The man eyed the bill and looked around. The teenager was gone, no doubt sweeping some other part of the store. In a sudden motion, the manager slipped a key in one of the doors and opened it just wide enough for Eric to slip through. "Look." He took the hundred dollars and gave Eric a frustrated shake of his head. "You have two minutes."

Eric glared at the man. *Two minutes for a hundred bucks?*

He took off into the store, mumbling under his breath. If he needed more time, he'd take it. He crossed the store and made his way toward the boogie board display. It took him thirty seconds to realize it had been taken down. "Hey!" He barked the word, and it echoed across the line of empty checkout stands.

The manager appeared, impatience working its way into the wrinkles around his mouth. "You ready?"

"Where're the boogie boards? You had a hundred last week."

"It was a promotion. Shipped the last of 'em back yesterday."

Eric gritted his teeth and glanced around the store. What else would a supermarket have for an eight-year-old boy? He moved quickly through the store and decided on a tall red birthday card and an oversized bar of chocolate. He paid the manager and was back in his car in two minutes.

One hundred and four dollars for a card and candy.

When he pulled in the garage a half hour later, the house was dark. He crept into the house and turned on the light over the stovetop. In the dim glow he grabbed a pen from the junk drawer and opened the birthday card.

Dear Josh . . . sorry I missed your party, but guess what? You get to help pick out your present the weekend after I get back from New York. A boogie board! Won't that be great? I'll teach you everything I know, and we'll have a great day. Happy birthday, son. Take care. Dad.

He put the card into its envelope, sealed the flap, and wrote Josh's name across the front. Then he propped it up next to the candy bar in a place on the counter where Josh would see it the next morning.

Laura was already asleep, so Eric crashed in the guest room rather than wake her. He tossed and turned most of the night, wondering if they should have gone with Chiron over Amgen and whether the execs at either pharmaceutical actually had their hands on a cancer cure.

By six-thirty the next morning, he was back on the road headed for the breakfast meeting at work.

THREE

The jet ski was flying fifty miles an hour over the harbor.

Beneath another unseasonably warm, clear blue September morning, Jake felt his wife bury her face against his back. He loved how her body felt as it came against him, loved the way it made him feel bigger than her, stronger. Like she needed him—if only for a few minutes on the open water.

It was September 7, the day they'd looked forward to all week.

Once a month he had a Friday off, and as long as the weather allowed, they would end up just off South Beach down at the water. Most years saw them putting the jet ski away by now. But not this September. It had been the most beautiful fall Jake could ever remember.

This time Sue and Larry Henning had come with them, and the two couples were taking turns watching the kids splash along the shoreline. Sierra's best playmate was the Hennings' daughter, Katy. The girls were both four, both a year away from kindergarten. Larry and Sue also had a six-month-old, but he was spending the day with his grandparents.

Good ol' Larry. The man had been Jake's best friend since high school. They went through fire science together and joined the fire department the same month. It took a few years to wind up at the same station, but for the past six years, they'd both worked in downtown Manhattan, Engine 57.

Larry's knees weren't what they once were. Too many years of football—both in high school and for the FDNY team. But he never missed a chance to hit the water with Jake.

"Flying across the water for an hour," Larry often said, "is worth a week of icing my knees."

Jake turned the jet ski in a gradual arch, and he felt Jamie lay her head to the side, letting the chilly water spray her face. He knew what she was thinking because she'd told him a hundred times. She loved being out on the water with him, loved the speed and the feeling of their bodies working together with the machine.

She leaned up close to his ear. "My turn."

He nodded, cut the engine, and spun in a tight circle. With grace and ease he swung his body around hers and took the backseat. At the same time she slid forward into the driver's seat, and he gave her ribs a playful poke. "Hey ... don't kill us."

"Come on, ya big chicken." Jamie laughed and shot him a glance over her left shoulder. "A little speed never hurt anyone."

Jake loved the teasing in her voice, the way her eyes danced. He brought his hands up and covered his eyes. "Tell me when I can look."

She let her head fall back as she kicked the engine into high gear. At work Jake had the more dangerous job. Jamie was a stay-at-home mom, after all. The most dangerous thing she did was cook dinner.

But when it came time to play, Jamie's thrill seeking knew no limits.

Jake perched his chin on her shoulder and watched her spot a cruiser a hundred yards out. "Hold on!" Jamie's voice faded in the roar of the engine as she opened the throttle and headed toward the boat's considerable wake. Jake peered over her shoulder and watched the speedometer climb past fifty ... fifty-five ... fifty-eight ...

The move had Jamie's signature all over it. Here she was— terrified deep down in some private cellar of her heart that he would get hurt fighting fires—but more than willing to risk both their lives on a simple day of fun. He let his hands fall to Jamie's narrow waist. Her wild streak had always been there, even back when they were kids.

The other football players wouldn't have considered dating Jamie Steel. "She's a beauty, don't get me wrong," Larry had told Jake the fall of their sophomore year. "But the girl would make a better safety than half the guys on the team. If I made her mad, she'd kick my behind."

Back then, Larry had probably been right.

Jamie had been point guard on the basketball team, catcher for the softball squad, and a state champion in the javelin throw. The school records she set back in the late eighties stood to this day, as far as Jake knew.

After high school, when their dating grew more serious, Jake would take her for walks around Wolfe's Pond Park. Always after a few minutes the same stretch of dirt road lay out before them, and Jamie would tap him on the shoulder. "Race ya." And with that she'd be off, sprinting with everything in her to the end of the road.

It always took Jake a few seconds to kick into gear, but a number of times, Jamie actually beat him. Fair and square. After the race they would walk to a nearby tree and fall onto the ground beneath it, gasping for breath. Once when they lay there that way, Jake studied her and shook his head. "What're you runnin' from, Jamie?"

She rolled onto her stomach and played with a piece of grass. "You."

He remembered shaking his head, assuming she didn't understand the question. "Not the race, silly. In life. Why do you push so hard all the time? You must be running from something."

For a long time, she looked at him, her eyes deeper than the New York Harbor. "I told you, goofy."

"Me?" He cocked his head. "You're running from me?"

"Yep." She planted her elbows in the soft ground and rested her chin in her hands. "I have all this . . . I don't know, this stuff in my heart. Feelings and emotions . . . an energy, almost. Way more than I should have." She gave him a lopsided grin. "The more I use up on sports, the less I have for you."

He'd leaned against the tree that afternoon and felt himself falling in love with her. "Is that right?"

"Yes." Her eyes sparkled in the midday sun. "That way if anything ever happens to you, I won't lose myself."

There were times after that—in the first year of their marriage—when Jake tried to remind her of that conversation. But she pretended not to remember. "You hold back with me, Jamie. How come?"

"I do not." She'd look surprised, hurt even. "Everything I have to give is yours, Jake. You know that."

He would study her, trying to understand her. "Remember that day at Wolfe's Pond? You told me you couldn't give me everything in case something happened to me. Because you didn't want to lose yourself, remember? Like you were afraid to love me too much."

She would toss her dark hair and shake her head. "I'm competitive, maybe. And I worry about your job. But I'm not afraid to love you, Jake." She would frame his face with her fingertips and speak straight to his soul. "I'm not holding back, honey. Not with you. Not ever."

But she did. She still did.

It was obvious, if only at times like this, when she was blazing across the harbor with her hair on fire, frantic to outrun some unseen terror, something she was terrified would catch her if she didn't run. Jake held on to her so he wouldn't fall off the back.

If she wasn't running from him, maybe she was running from God. Jake was practically desperate for God to get her attention somehow. He prayed about it every day, but still Jamie hadn't shown any interest.

Whatever it was, Jamie was running from it. Jake was convinced. They reached the cruiser and headed straight for its wake.

"Hold on," she yelled.

They hit the wave full bore, and both of them lifted with the jet ski to catch two seconds of air before smacking down against the water and hitting the second wave. This time they nearly wiped out.

"Slow down, Jamie." He gave her shoulders a gentle squeeze. "Don't be crazy."

She eased up on the speed and did a wide turn. "What time do we need to be back?"

Jake looked at his watch. "Five minutes."

"No problem." She took aim for the cruiser's wake once more and hit the throttle, sailing out of it in a perfect angle toward the shore. "I'll get us there in three."

Jamie lowered her head and gave it as much gas as she could, shooting them across the harbor at unbelievable speeds. Jake wasn't worried. They both could swim, and Jamie was too keen a driver to let anything bad happen on the open water. But as he leaned against her, savoring her naked back against his chest, he knew he would never quite connect with her the way he wanted to, the way she was capable of connecting.

Not as long as she was running.

He gazed out at the city skyline and the wispy clouds beyond. *God, if she's running from You, please ... catch her. She's so afraid ... afraid of loss and change and death. Afraid of You. I don't know what else to do, God. Help her stop running ... Whatever it takes.*

A seagull swooped low a few feet from them as Jamie cut the engine and eased the jet ski up onto the shore. Sierra and Katy came running, their knees and ankles covered in sand.

Jake kissed the back of Jamie's neck. "Nice ride."

"Thanks." Jamie was breathless, her cheeks red. "I could've gone on that way forever."

Jake smiled, but her words left a pit in his stomach. Whatever she was running from, it still plagued her, just as it always had. They parked the jet ski and headed toward Larry and Sue, and the whole time Jake wondered about his wife. Would she run this way forever? Or would she be brave enough to slow down one of these days and let him catch her?

Not just him, but God as well.

＊＊＊＊

Jamie and Sue stayed with the girls so the men could have a run on the water together. The women moved their beach chairs closer to the shore, and within earshot of Sierra and Katy.

"I swear Katy's grown two inches since the last time we did this." Jamie shielded her eyes so she could see the little girls in front of them.

"She's taking after my side of the family." Sue reached for a can of Diet Coke. "My mother's nearly six foot."

"Lucky girl. She'll be first picked on the basketball team." Jamie leaned back. "Not like us shrimps who had to work for every minute on the court."

They were quiet then, and Sue stared out at the water after their husbands. "I love seeing them together out there." She shifted her gaze to Jamie. "They're so much alike. Brothers almost."

Jamie reached for a bottle of sunscreen, poured the warm white liquid into her palms, and worked it along her forearms. It felt hot and wonderful against her skin, erasing the deep cold from the ride across the harbor. "I like them working the same shifts." She glanced at Sue. "They look out for each other."

"Larry says Jake would never let anything happen to him on the job." Sue chuckled. "Like Jake's somehow bigger than life."

"Jake feels the same way about Larry." Jamie set the sunscreen down in the sand. "They're quite a team."

"Like twins, separated at birth." Sue cast an easy grin toward the spot where the men were picking up speed and heading out for deeper water. "Even if they look nothing alike."

Jamie took hold of the armrests and stared out at the horizon. Sue was right. The men looked like polar opposites. Jake six-two, lean and built with short dark hair and blue eyes. Larry moved like a tank, two hundred pounds of muscle on a frame that was barely five-nine in his work boots. His skin was covered with the kind of freckles that usually accompany his shade of red hair.

Jamie shook her head. "You should've seen them in high school. Mo and Curley all over again."

"I bet."

"Larry, the wild one ... sensible Jake, the voice of reason." Jamie dug around in the bag beside her, found a white visor, and slid it onto her head. A breeze washed over her, and she breathed in the ocean air. "You can't believe the crazy things they did back then."

"Like what?"

Jamie closed her eyes for a moment and grabbed at one of a hundred memories. "Like the time Larry convinced the football team to run lines down here at the beach at midnight."

"Midnight?"

"Yes." Jamie raised an eyebrow. "In winter." She chuckled at the memory. "The guys had icicles hanging from their hair before Jake rounded everyone up and told them to meet back at the school."

"Hmmm." Sue looked back out to sea, and Jamie followed her gaze. The men were just a dot on the distant horizon. "I wish I could've been there."

"It seems like you were around back then." From a few yards away, Sierra waved, and Jamie waved back. "You met Larry in college, right?"

"Our junior year. Third meeting of the campus Bible study."

Something about the words soured Jamie's mood, and she fell silent for several minutes. Usually, she let it pass when Larry or Sue or even Jake brought up anything religious. But here, now, she felt suddenly compelled to ask. She turned to her friend and cocked her head. "Is it really that wonderful?"

Sue's face went blank. "What?"

"Church . . . Bible studies . . . you know, the God stuff." Jamie's words were slow, thoughtful. "It's kept your attention all these years, but why? What's so great about it?"

"Uh-oh." She wrinkled her nose. "Jake's pushing you?"

"No." Jamie laughed even as the tension built within her. "He hasn't done that for years. He knows better." Her tone grew serious again. "I just wonder, I guess. Why bother? I mean we have so little time together as it is. Why spend Sunday mornings in some old building singing songs?"

Peace washed over Sue's face, and she took a sip from her pop. "It isn't about the building or the songs." There wasn't a trace of criticism in Sue's voice. "It's about coming together and declaring as a group that you believe . . . that you desperately need a Savior and that the week wouldn't be the same without taking time to say so."

Doubt blew across the barren places of Jamie's heart. "You actually want to be there?"

"Yes." Sue's expression was sympathetic. "You should give it a try someday, Jamie. One Sunday wouldn't hurt."

Jamie bristled at the idea. "If I believed in God, I'd go."

"Oh." Sue waited a minute before responding. "You still don't believe?" She motioned toward the girls. They had built a sand-castle and were digging a moat around it. "Even after having Sierra?"

"Meaning what?" Jamie didn't see the connection.

"Kids. The miracle of life." Sue shrugged. "If anything convinced me God was real, it was holding Katy for the first time. There she was, a part of me and a part of Larry, all knit together perfectly. Only God could do that."

For an instant Jamie understood.

She'd felt that same sense of wonder the first time she held Sierra. Every time she'd held her since then, for that matter. But it wasn't God she was sensing. It was life itself. As Sue had said, the miracle of life. Jamie dusted the sand off her ankles and met Sue's eyes. "If there is a God . . . why doesn't He put out fires before our guys have to fight them?"

A sigh slipped from Sue's lips. "This isn't heaven, Jamie. Nothing's going to be perfect here. But even still, God's in control."

"But how do you know?" Jamie gestured toward the sea. "You and Larry and Jake talk about heaven like you've been there. But there's no guarantee. And if God's willing to let us suffer here on earth, why should I believe He has something better for me after I die?"

Sue spread her fingers over her heart, her voice barely audible above the ocean breeze. "It's a knowing, Jamie. A sureness, a certainty. With everything in me I believe in God, and I'm convinced that life here is just a shadow of what's to come. Earth is like a giant waiting area." She pointed heavenward. "Up there, that's when real life will begin."

They were quiet again. Jamie stood and stretched. "Sorry for the tangent." She smiled at Sue. "Not exactly relaxing beach conversation."

Sue worked her eyebrows together. For an instant Jamie wondered if her friend might say something to refute her statement. But instead the lines eased on Sue's face and she set her Diet Coke down on the sand.

"Any time, Jamie. If you ever wanna talk about God, I'm here. Okay?"

"Okay." Jamie crossed her arms and studied the water until she spotted the distant jet ski. "Didn't see you at the funeral Sunday."

"No." Sue drew a deep breath. "I'm not much for fire department funerals."

"But God's still in control, right? Even when a twenty-seven-year-old proby reels out a fire hose and falls over dead from a heart attack?"

Sue's eyes grew wide and Jamie chided herself. Her tone had been cold, almost biting, but she hadn't meant it that way. She wasn't trying to argue, just prove a point.

"I'm sorry." Jamie reached out and touched her friend's arm. "You don't have to answer that."

"No." Sue cleared her throat. "I want to answer you." She bent forward and hugged her knees to her chest. "Yes . . . God's still in control, even at a proby's funeral. Somewhere, somehow, God has a plan in all of it. Even if we can't understand that plan right now."

"So God's in control . . . and you trust Him completely, right?" Jamie was baffled. This was the very reason she struggled with the notion of God. Because if there was a God, He wasn't fair. Some people lived untouched by tragedy into their eighties and nineties, while others—people like her parents or the proby—died tragic deaths with babies and loved ones waiting back home. "Even in death?"

"Yes." Sue's voice was full, passionate. "Even in death."

"Okay . . ." The argumentative tone was gone from Jamie's voice. In its place was a question that came from the depths of her soul. "Then, why don't I see you at the funerals?"

"Because . . ." Sue stared across the beach at Katy and Sierra. When she answered, it seemed to come from the very deepest places in her soul. "Because I can't bear to think that someday God's plan might include a fire department funeral for Larry."

FOUR

SEPTEMBER 7, 2001

Laura pulled out of her driveway and turned her car toward the setting sun. It was a fifteen-minute drive to church, and she was grateful for the solitude. A handful of women were getting together to box up supplies they'd collected for an orphanage in Haiti. The church's college group was going to Port-au-Prince in a few weeks to paint the main building. The supplies would go ahead of them as part of an outreach.

Laura was on the planning committee.

Temperatures had spiked across the San Fernando Valley again, and that night as she made her way down the hill toward Thousand Oaks Boulevard, it was still ninety-two degrees. Laura rolled her window down and rested her arm on the door.

Originally, Eric had agreed to work with her on this project. But he hadn't had time once so far, and tonight's meeting was the last before the outreach. In the past Laura had gone to church angry, clenching the steering wheel, wondering the whole evening long why her husband wasn't with her.

But not this time.

Since his fiasco with Josh's birthday the other day, the two of them had barely spoken to each other. Tonight he was staying home with Josh, spending time with their son for the first time all week. Laura was grateful for the time alone. She turned right and settled against the back of her seat.

She knew what she was supposed to do. Go to church and help pack the supplies for Haiti, then come home and talk to Eric, tell him it was time to call a counselor. But this time the whole routine felt pointless and tiresome. They weren't kidding anyone anymore, not the people at church, not Josh, not God. Not even each other. Why make an appointment for counseling if nothing was going to change?

Laura squinted behind her sunglasses and flipped down the visor. If only she had the guts to throw in the towel, turn the car around and storm up the drive, find Eric, and demand a divorce. It was the only thing that would set either of them free at this point.

God . . . help me.

The silent cry came from the depths of her soul and made the corners of her eyes sting.

Daughter . . . I am with you . . . I know the plans I have for you, plans to give you a hope and a future and not to harm you . . .

The Scripture came as easily as Laura's next breath, the same way it always had. Since she was adopted as a young teenager, she'd clung to the promise, believing that God truly knew the plans He had for her. Believing they were good. But what place did the words have in her life now? Good plans and hope? A future? The loveless routine she shared with Eric was hardly that. And what good could possibly come from their life together?

Then, like the streaky lines across the summer sky, the answer came. Josh, of course. Josh was the good that had come from the two of them. Back from a time and place when she and Eric had loved each other more than life itself. And Josh was the one who would pay the price if she asked for a divorce.

She turned her car into the church parking lot, pulled into a front row space, and turned off the engine. For a moment she sat there, letting her head fall against the steering wheel. No, she couldn't divorce Eric, not ever. He hadn't done anything wrong. He'd never cheated on her or slapped her or called her a bad name. He'd rarely said an unkind word.

The familiar sting in her eyes grew stronger. She whisked her sunglasses off and tossed them on the seat beside her. As she did, a tear fell on her jean shorts and made a tiny wet circle on the denim. She'd been looking forward to the time alone, but not so she could break down. This was no time to cry. The committee would be there in five minutes, and the next few hours would culminate months of planning and collecting. Their efforts would help dozens of children in Haiti have food and medicine and school supplies.

So what was the problem? Why did she feel like her world was falling apart, like a part of her heart would never breathe again?

Laura wiped her eyes and sniffed twice. The answer was obvious. It wasn't what Eric had done that made her miserable, it was what he hadn't done. What he'd stopped doing somewhere along the trail of years. Whenever it was that he'd stopped keeping promises, when he'd stopped taking her on dates or spending a few moments with Josh.

With Eric she shared little more than a functional business relationship. None of the love and passion she'd hoped to find by marrying the man, none of the magic they'd shared in their first few years together. But those weren't grounds for divorce—not even close.

She gripped the steering wheel. *God . . . there's no way out. Give me something, a sign, a reason to believe it'll get better one day.* She was trapped in a prison of pretense and promises, and unless Eric had a change of heart, her sentence would last a lifetime. Because being president of Koppel and Grant wouldn't be enough for Eric; neither would making a million dollars. There would still be one more deal, one more meeting, one more corporate account to conquer.

And those things would always take precedence over her and Josh.

She wiped her eyes and lifted her head just as she heard footsteps come up along the side of her car.

"Laura?"

She jerked her head up, and there, standing just outside her car door, was Eric's brother, Clay. "Oh, hey." As quick as she could, she grabbed her sunglasses and slipped them back on. She managed a smile. "You scared me."

Clay leaned closer and rested his forearms against the roof of her Escolade. "You're crying."

"No." A plastic laugh forced its way across her lips. "Just a long day."

He cocked his head and studied her. "You sure?"

"Yes." She sniffed again. "What're you doing here?"

Clay nodded over his shoulder to the church building. "Picking up a packet for Sunday school." His grin was easy. "Second grade starts a new unit this Sunday." He hesitated. "You here for the mission meeting?"

Laura nodded. She was grateful for the chance to collect herself. Clay knew her too well to be tricked, and the last thing she wanted was for this to be the moment when Clay finally understood the truth about her marriage.

Clay took a step back and leaned against a van parked next to Laura's. "Isn't Eric supposed to be with you?"

"He's too busy. Couldn't make the meetings."

"Oh." Clay hesitated. "What about Josh?"

"Eric's with him." She forced the corners of her lips up again. "Just the two of them."

"That's good."

Laura drew a slow breath. "How was work?"

"No car chases all week." He grinned at her. "Must be some kind of record."

Laura's gaze fell to her hands. She hadn't seen Clay since the pizza place, and she needed to thank him. "Hey, about the birthday party ..." She climbed out of the car, shut the door, and leaned against it so that she faced Clay. "Thanks for showing up. It meant a lot to Josh."

"Eric should've been there." Something just short of anger flickered in Clay's expression. He locked onto Laura's eyes a beat longer than necessary. "It's a pattern, isn't it?"

For an instant Laura had the strange urge to defend Eric. He was her husband, after all, and his work schedule had been this way since long before Josh was born. But she couldn't do it. Clay was right. Eric wasn't around enough, it was that simple.

"Yes. For a while now." She looked at a spot on the ground near her feet. *No tears, God. Please. Not here, not now.* "He and Josh barely know each other."

"He's crazy." Clay clenched his teeth and let the air ease through them. "He works so hard he doesn't know what he's missing."

Laura looked at him and tried to read into that last sentence. She wanted to ask exactly what he meant, whether he was talking about Josh or her. But she knew better. There were certain lines in-laws didn't cross. Even if they'd been friends since high school. She found Clay's eyes again. "It could be worse."

"Yes." The depth in Clay's eyes looked suddenly more pronounced. "Eric's a good guy, but ... well, maybe his priorities need a little rearranging." Clay shrugged. "He should've been at the party."

She nodded, and Clay seemed to sense that the conversation was hard on her.

He leaned his head back and stared at the pink and orange sky above them. "Josh had fun ... that's all that matters."

An image flashed in Laura's mind. Eric holding court with his colleagues at Koppel and Grant, waxing on about the virtues of one stock over the other, while Clay played air hockey with Josh at Chuck E. Cheese's. That didn't make Eric a bad guy, exactly. Lots of fathers worked too many hours, and she should be grateful Josh had someone like Clay. But instead of feeling grateful, her soul ached at the impossible situation she was in.

Clay strained to see her eyes. "Talk to him, okay?"

"Okay."

Then without saying another word, he pulled her into a hug, the kind they'd shared a thousand times before, but one Laura needed more than air. "I'm here for you, Laura. For both of you. Don't let anything crazy happen."

Laura slid her fingers beneath her glasses and wiped at an errant tear. "We won't."

"Good." He drew back and patted his hand against her cheek. "You're my two favorite people in the world."

She sniffed and pulled away, reaching into her car for her purse. "I know."

"Come on." Clay took a step toward the church. "Everything's gonna be fine."

Three hours later Laura pulled into their driveway. Something about seeing Clay, hearing his optimism had lit a spark in her heart. Maybe it wasn't too late. Maybe they could get counseling again and make real changes this time. If they'd loved each other once, then somehow, someway God could lead them back to that place, right?

She was about to step out of her car when she noticed something strange. A car sat parked in their driveway, and Laura stared at it, confused. It was nearly ten o'clock on a Friday night. Who could've been visiting at that hour? She grabbed her things and headed inside. Josh was sitting at the dining room table writing something, and next to him was Jenna, their baby-sitter.

Laura froze in place, trying to make sense of what she was seeing. "Hello, Jenna." She hesitated. "I expected to see Mr. Michaels."

The teenager smiled and slid an eraser across the table to Josh. "He got called into work." She pointed to a stack of notepaper. "Josh and I were doing a little multiplication."

Laura set her things down and made her way slowly into the dining room. The moment she saw Josh's bloodshot eyes, she knew. Eric had done it again, made a promise and then broken it without a second thought as to how it would affect Josh.

Anger trampled over Laura's optimism, and she held her tongue. She wouldn't talk about their troubles in front of Jenna. Laura pulled her wallet from her purse. "What time did you get here?"

"Just before seven." Jenna tousled Josh's hair and gave Laura a knowing look. "He's had a hard night."

Just before seven? Laura could've strangled Eric. She'd left for church at six-forty-five. That meant she hadn't been gone ten minutes when he called Jenna and headed off for work. Laura ordered herself to stay calm. "Did he say when he'd be home?"

"Actually . . ." An uneasy expression filled Jenna's face. "He was gone by the time I got here. He said it was an emergency."

"You mean . . ." Laura's heart skipped a beat and then slid into an unrecognizable rhythm. "He left Josh alone?"

"Just for a few minutes. I told him I'd be right over, so he put a video on for Josh." Jenna directed her next sentence toward the child. "You were right where you were supposed to be, huh, buddy?"

Josh nodded and cast Laura a look that was part anger, part unspeakable sorrow. Laura gave him a weak smile. "We'll talk in a minute, okay?"

He hung his head and stared at his paper.

Laura motioned for Jenna to follow, and the two of them moved across the house toward the front door. When they were alone in the foyer, Laura sighed. "Was Josh crying when you got here?"

Jenna kept her voice low. "Sobbing." She frowned. "Poor little guy. It took him half an hour to calm down."

Laura's blood moved from hot to boiling. She paid Jenna and stood there, staring at the tiles that made up their entryway. The fury inside her was so strong she couldn't move. How dare Eric do this? After what had happened on Josh's birthday . . . and with a trip to New York tomorrow morning? Her anger became rage. Maybe she should drive to Koppel and Grant's offices and tell Eric it was time. A separation was the only way to stop the damage to Josh.

But that wasn't possible, not now anyway. Not with Josh sitting defeated and brokenhearted in the next room.

She exhaled slowly. *God . . . get me through this. How can I love Eric and hate him all at the same time?* She returned to the dining room and found her son at the table. "Josh?" Without making a sound, she took the seat beside him and reached for his hands. "What did Daddy tell you?"

Huge tears welled up in Josh's eyes, and he barely lifted one shoulder. "It was a special meeting. A 'mergency." Josh sniffed and ran the back of his hand beneath his eyes. No doubt he wanted to be strong in front of her. The sadness, the disappointment, was simply too great. "He said he'd make it up to me when he comes back from New York."

"Well . . ." Laura clenched her teeth. It was the same thing Eric always said. "He is extra busy before a trip, Josh." The words were purely for Josh's sake. So the child wouldn't hate his father. "I'm sure he wanted to stay."

"Sometimes I think . . ." Josh twisted his face, and a sob sounded from deep in his chest. "He doesn't even like me, Mom."

"Josh!" She pulled the boy close, silently cursing Eric for everything he'd never been to the boy. "That isn't true. Your father's a very busy man. Just because he isn't home much doesn't mean he doesn't like you." She soothed her hand down his back and felt his small body jerk and twitch as he began to sob. "He loves you, buddy. Really."

"If . . . if he loves me, why didn't he come to my birthday party?" Josh grabbed three quick breaths. "And why did he leave me all alone tonight?"

Laura's heart throbbed. She had no answers for her son. She wanted to tell him he was reading his father wrong, that the man hadn't always been this way, and that come next week things would be back to normal. But as far back as she could remember, this series of missed moments and broken promises was the most normal thing either of them knew.

"Next weekend—" She stopped herself. What about next weekend? Would Eric even remember his promise to take Josh to the beach, to buy him a boogie board, and play with him on the shore all day? Why would he? Surely, there'd be a dozen meetings to follow up the trip to New York. And someone's stock performance was bound to put Koppel and Grant in a tailspin. It happened every time. Eric might still have the audacity to make promises to Josh, but Laura couldn't bring herself to repeat them.

Her son was staring at her, his eyes puffy and red. "Next weekend what?"

Laura pulled back and sat straighter in her chair. "I was thinking of the beach."

"You know what?" Josh pulled one leg up and hugged his knee to his chest. "I don't like the beach. I want a basketball so Dad could take me to the park to shoot. Like the other dads."

Several times that past summer, Josh had gone to the park with his friends and their fathers, and even with Clay once. The gym was open all day Saturday, and local fathers and sons had adopted the place. Josh had mentioned it to Eric three times at least, but Eric was either busy at his computer, or going over a list of documents, or about to make a phone call. He'd wave Josh off and nod quickly. "Sure, son . . . you bet. One of these days we'll go to the park and shoot hoops."

But it had never happened.

A minute passed, and Josh's crying subsided. He dried his face once more, stood, and kissed Laura. "I'm going to bed. Tell Dad I'll see him next week."

"I love you, Josh."

"You too." He started to walk off, then stopped and turned around. "I wish Uncle Clay was my daddy. That'd be so cool."

Laura's remaining resolve crumbled like ancient pottery. "I'm sorry, Josh."

"That's okay." He slumped forward a bit. His chin almost touched his chest as he walked off. "G'night."

She listened while he made his way up the stairs toward his bedroom. When the door closed, she grabbed the cordless phone from the wall and dialed Eric's office number. A young woman answered on the third ring.

"Hello?" Her voice was perky.

Laura wanted to scream. "Eric Michaels, please."

"Eric . . . let's see." She covered up the phone to muffle her voice. "Someone tell Eric he has a phone call."

Eric? Who was the girl, and what was she doing there after ten on a Friday night?

A minute passed and Eric picked up the phone. "Hello?"

"You left Josh *alone?*" Her tone was a pinched mix of shock and controlled fury.

"Laura, let me explain." He paused a moment too long.

"No." She huffed. "You're too late. Your son went to sleep in tears, Eric."

"Look, I don't need a guilt trip. I feel bad enough."

"Oh, I can tell." She raised her voice. "What could be so important you had to leave our son alone, Eric? What?"

"A teleconference from New York, that's what." He hesitated. "The minute you left, Murphy called wondering where I was. The call was scheduled for seven-thirty."

"That's ten-thirty New York time." Laura gave a short laugh. "Even a man like Allen couldn't possibly keep hours like that."

"What's that supposed to mean?"

"It means after a while the stories get old." She took the phone into the living room and dropped onto the edge of the leather recliner. "Who answered the phone?"

"Here?"

"Yes, there. Whoever she was she called you by your first name. I thought secretaries had more class than that."

"Her name's Vicky. She's not a secretary. She's Murphy's assistant, and she's happily married. None of us are formal with the assistants." His tone was condescending. "Does that answer your question?"

"Look, Eric . . ." The conversation was going nowhere. "I don't care if President Bush was calling you, Murphy could've handled the teleconference." She huffed. "Josh needed you tonight. It took Jenna half an hour to calm him down."

"That's ridiculous. He's old enough to—" Eric stopped himself and paused. "I passed Jenna on my way out of the neighborhood. He wasn't alone for three minutes, Laura."

"Okay, so you had your phone call. You could've come home."

"Things came up." He let loose a long sigh. "You know how it is before a trip. Don't do this now, Laura, please."

Suddenly, she could feel Clay's arms around her, hear him reminding her not to do anything crazy, and that everything was going to be okay. But Clay was wrong. Everything was wrong, for that matter. What was happening to her? When was the last time she'd read her Bible or prayed about her relationship with Eric? Everything that ever mattered was unraveling like a half-knit sweater, and she couldn't think of a single way to stop it.

Worse, she didn't want to stop it.

When she spoke again, the fight was gone from her voice. "I'm going to sleep, Eric. When you get home from New York we need to talk."

"Talk?" For the first time that night, the slightest hint of fear spilled over into his words. "Don't overreact, Laura. You know how busy I've been."

"Yes, I know. Josh knows too." She closed her eyes. "That's why we need to talk." Her voice broke, but she did her best to cover it. "We can't go on like this, Eric. I can't."

Silence hovered between them, then Eric's tired sigh sounded over the phone line. "You're right. I get back early Thursday afternoon." His voice was kinder than before. "I'll come straight here and take you to dinner. I promise, Laura . . . things'll slow down. I'll make it up to you and Josh. Give me a chance."

Normally, Eric's promises melted her, even though he rarely made good on them. But tonight she was too tired, too hurt to care. "Good night, Eric."

He hesitated. "Plan on dinner, okay?"

"We'll see. I have to go."

They hung up with no declarations of love or assurances that the other would be missed. Laura returned the phone to its place on the wall and tried to remember the last time Eric had told her he loved her. Two months? Three, maybe? Was this the man she'd thought would rescue her from a childhood of sorrow and abandonment? The man she'd thought would share her dreams of happily ever after?

And what about Josh? Eric had never once told the boy he loved him, even after she confronted Eric about the issue back when their son was four. Not one time.

"You love him, don't you?" They'd been finishing up dinner, and Josh had gone out back to play.

"Josh?" Eric had looked surprised. "Of course."

"Then tell him. A boy needs to hear that from his father."

Eric had dismissed her with a wave of his hand. "That's ridiculous. My father never said it to me."

"Your father wasn't a Christian."

"Maybe I'm not either." The moment he'd said the words his face had looked stricken. "I . . . I didn't mean that."

But he had meant it, of course. Eric hadn't been to church with her since the stillborn death of their tiny daughter a year after they were married. At the time Laura had thought the loss was infinitely harder on her than Eric. Until one afternoon when she came home to their small apartment and found him in the baby's bedroom, sitting in the rocking chair they'd bought at a garage sale.

It was the only time before or since that she'd seen him weep.

"Why, Laura?" He'd been utterly broken, his usual confidence shattered. "Why would God take her?"

"He didn't take her." Laura had knelt between his legs, gripping his wrists and trying her best to help him understand. "It's just one of those things."

"No, it's not." He squeezed his eyes shut. "Because I'm still in school and God didn't help us and no one'll give us decent medical care. Otherwise she would've lived."

In some ways Eric was right. A nurse at the hospital told them that their baby's death had been preventable. With ultrasound testing they could've worked on her before she was born. But without insurance, the test hadn't been an option.

Even now—so many years later—Laura could see that time in their life as a dividing line. Until then Eric's faith had been stronger than the San Gabriel Mountains. Solid and unmoving. But that night as Eric wept, something hardened in his heart. Not long afterwards he stopped going to church, stopped talking about God's will or referring to Bible verses.

Several times Laura talked to him about it. "This is because of the baby, isn't it?" Eric would only shake his head and give brief, terse answers. "The baby wasn't meant to be."

"Then why, Eric? What's happened?"

Once when she asked him, he locked his gaze with hers and waited a moment. "We lost that little girl because I couldn't give you the very best care." He gritted his teeth. "Life's about making your own way. And believe me, Laura, I'm not leaving that up to God. Once I get started, you'll never have to worry about medical care again."

Eric had kept his promise. By the time Josh was born, they had the best insurance, the best doctors in Southern California. But in the years since, he'd become a driven businessman who didn't share his family's beliefs, and who couldn't muster up the words to tell his son he loved him.

Laura got undressed, slipped into a nightgown, and eased herself between the cool sheets. Eric would be up into the wee hours of the morning, packing, checking last-minute details before leaving. He'd stay in the guest room, no doubt, so she wouldn't hear from him again until Thursday.

As she fell asleep she tried to feel sorry for herself, but she couldn't. Her marriage was dying, and she and Eric were both at fault. Yes, he'd been difficult to love. But how hard had *she* tried? Why hadn't she said something the first time he slept in the guest room? And how many years had it been since she'd surprised him with a weekend getaway or a special date night?

What was it the Bible said? That little foxes were the ones that spoiled the vines? How many little foxes had she allowed in since Josh was born? Laura rolled over. Only one memory could replace the missed opportunities filling her mind.

The memory of a long-ago yesterday, back when Eric Michaels couldn't wait to leave college and race home to be with her. Once, a lifetime ago, they'd been lovers. But now—in a way that seemed almost sudden—the branches of their love had become completely barren.

And spring didn't feel like it would ever come again.

FIVE

SEPTEMBER 9, 2001

Sierra looked like a princess.

Jake gave a low, appreciative whistle and leaned against the hallway wall. "My goodness." He grinned at her. "I bet you're the most beautiful girl in all of New York City."

Her eyes sparkled. "Really, Daddy?" She did a twirl, and her pink and white skirt fluffed out around her knees. "Mommy bought this for me so I'd have a pretty church dress."

"You found the perfect one." He played with a strand of her hair. "Curlies today?"

"Yes, please." She batted her eyelashes at him. "Susie's daddy never curls her hair."

"Susie?" Jake crouched down so he was eye level with Sierra. "From Sunday school?"

"Yep. Her mommy lives in New Jersey, so her daddy brings her." Sierra brushed her nose up against his. "Just like me and you!"

"I see." Jake gave a slow, thoughtful nod. "But he doesn't curl her hair, is that right?"

"Right!"

Jake puffed his chest up and planted his fists at his waist. "Then that makes me Super-Daddy."

"And Mommy's Super-Mommy." She giggled. "Know why?"

Jake felt his heart melt, the same way it always did in the presence of his small daughter. "Why, sweetheart?"

"Because," she held her chin a bit higher, "Mommy bought me a church dress. Susie's mommy didn't do that."

"Well . . . then you're right. Mommy is Super-Mommy."

Sierra leaned close, placing her nose up against his. "Butterfly kisses?"

"For my best girl!" He rubbed his nose against hers, then turned his face and blinked in time with her so that their lashes brushed up against each other three times. Butterfly kisses were part of their morning routine. He stood up and caught another strand of her hair. "Go play in your room. I'll call you when I'm ready to curl, okay?"

She clasped her hands, her blue eyes wide and innocent. "Horsie ride?"

She could have asked him for the moon, and he'd have broken his neck to get it. Something about her sweet spirit and fresh-faced beauty had that effect on him. He had no idea how he'd survive her wedding. "Okay, pumpkin pie . . ." He turned around and bent over. "Hop aboard."

Sierra's giggle rang out again, her laughter playing across his soul like music from a favorite song. She climbed onto Jake's back and gave him a gentle tap with her heels. "Giddyap!"

Jake reared his head back and made a few realistic snorting sounds. "Where to, Princess Sierra?" He used a deep voice, the one he always used when he was the horse and Sierra the rider.

"To my palace!" She patted his head. "You should grow your hair long, Daddy. Horsies are 'posed to have long hair."

"Sorry." Jake whinnied and began galloping down the hallway toward Sierra's room. "This horsie has to keep his hair short, princess."

"That's okay, horsie," she said, then leaned close and kissed the back of his head. "I still love you."

Jake rounded the corner and pulled up sharp next to Sierra's bed. "Your palace, dear princess."

Sierra slid down and did her best impression of a royal curtsy. "Thank you." She patted Jake's head once more. "Do you like my pretty dress, horsie?"

Leaping and pawing the air like a wild stallion, Jake gave three exaggerated nods of his head. "Who made you so pretty, Princess Sierra?"

The princess persona faded. Sierra tilted her face, brought her lips together, and gave him a guileless smile. "Jesus did." Her voice fell to a whisper. "I'm gonna read my Bible book, Daddy. See you in a few minutes."

Jake pranced around in a small circle, then back down the hall toward his and Jamie's bedroom. He took his shower, dressed, and found his razor in the cupboard beneath the bathroom sink. As he shaved, a sadness settled in his gut. Why couldn't Jamie miss her painting class and come with them? Just once?

He ran the blade over the angles of his face. *God . . . how long will this go on? How long until she sees the light and wants what Sierra and I have?*

Remember, my son, I began a good work in her, and I'll be faithful to see it through.

Jake froze, his razor poised beneath his right cheekbone. He'd felt similar nudges almost daily in the past month. Responses from somewhere inside him, all with a similar message so clear it was almost audible. And the silent whispers in his soul always brought about the same memory. He and Jamie at the Young Life high school summer camp the summer after he graduated. Jake couldn't exactly remember what they'd learned that week, but whatever it was, Jamie had felt it.

Felt it all the way to her soul.

When the camp leaders asked people to come forward if they wanted to live for Jesus, Jamie was one of the first campers on her feet.

Before they came home, she explained her feelings to Jake. "For the first time life means something. Like I don't have to worry that something bad's going to happen. Because God has it all figured out."

Jake had been certain that Jamie's decision would be life-changing. His own decision—made back when he was eight years old—certainly had been. Instead, she had questions from the beginning. Questions and doubts and an immediate return to the aversion she'd always had regarding faith and church and God in general. A few years later, her skepticism had been fueled by her parents' tragic deaths.

And by every firefighter funeral since.

For Jamie, a huge chasm lay between belief and unbelief, and there was simply no bridge great enough to span the gap. No bridge except God Himself. And as time went on, Jamie wanted less and less to do with God.

This, then, had become the crux of Jake's prayers for his wife. That God make good on the promise that constantly echoed in his mind. That He might complete in Jamie that faith that began two decades ago at summer camp. Jake moved the razor down his chin. And every time he prayed for her, he'd been given a reassurance, a knowing, that felt heaven-sent. No doubt about it. Not only had God *heard* his prayers for Jamie, He was going to answer them.

Soon.

It was this knowing that convinced Jake he and God had a deal going. That Jake wasn't going anywhere, that his body wouldn't be the next one paraded in front of five thousand uniformed firefighters. Not when God was on the brink of using him to turn Jamie's lifelong doubts into the sweetest devotion.

She was already changing. After all, she'd cared enough to buy Sierra a new dress. Jake straightened and examined his face for missed spots. Yes, Jamie cared. Just not enough to come to church with them. She'd left an hour earlier for breakfast and tole painting with a few of the firefighter wives. Twice a month on Sundays they met, giving her an excuse for two out of every four Sundays. The other two were family days, Jamie had decided. Time to hike or bike or play with the jet ski.

"God can't expect you to spend every weekend in church, can He?" She'd joked with Jake about the subject a dozen times. But the bottom line was clearer than the sky above the city this past week. Jamie didn't want to go. And she didn't want anything to do with God.

Still, she'd bought Sierra a church dress.

That was better than the way she'd reacted a year ago when Jake started taking their daughter to church. He could still hear the frustration in her voice when they first discussed the issue.

"It's not right to fill her head with fairy tales," she had lowered her voice to a whisper so Sierra couldn't hear her. "She doesn't need make-believe stuff about a God who"—she waved her hands—"who might not exist."

Jake had stayed calm, his voice as quiet as hers. "What would it hurt? She'll draw pictures and sing songs and learn how to pray." He took gentle hold of her shoulders. "Is that so bad, Jamie?"

"Yes." She stepped backwards and planted her hands on her hips. "It'll only disappoint her if something bad happens and . . . and God turns out to be just another fantasy."

"What if He isn't?" Jake had kept his distance, allowing her the space to process what he was saying. "What if God's real, Jamie. Do you really want to keep Sierra from knowing about Him? Just two Sundays a month?"

In the end Jamie had agreed—on one condition. "Don't bug me about it, Jake. I'll find something else to do those Sundays, but leave me out of it."

Her words still stung, but she'd come a long way since then. For the past few months she would ask Sierra about Sunday school and listen while their daughter repeated her Bible story. Twice in the past month she'd even said she might attend Christmas service with them this year.

And now the pretty new dress.

Jake plugged in the curling iron and caught a glimpse of his simple gold wedding band. He loved her more than words could ever describe. Yes, Jamie's day of reckoning with God was coming. If his sense of the Lord's timing was right, it was coming soon. He slipped into a pair of new jeans and a pullover shirt.

"Sierra!" He leaned toward his open bedroom door. "Beauty parlor's open."

"Goody!" She came running, all giggles and bouncing thick blonde hair. He never tired of her, never stopped marveling at the wonder of her life. She was only one day old when she first gripped his fingers, and he hers. In the days since, he'd yet to let go.

She wrapped her arms around his legs and hugged him. "I thought you'd never open."

Jake patted her head. "We beauticians have to shave every now and then, you know."

Sierra came to him and framed his jaw with her little-girl hands. "Mmmm. Nice and smooth. Mommy likes it that way."

"That's what matters." Jake grinned.

"Yep." Sierra nodded. "Mommy says she likes her men clean and shaken."

A chuckle simmered in his belly, but he stifled it. "You mean clean shaven?"

She thought for a moment. "Yep, that's it."

"Okay, young lady, turn around." Sierra did as she was told and faced the mirror. Jake took the curling iron and expertly wrapped it around an inch-wide section of her hair. He caught Sierra watching him in the mirror. Her smile faded some, and her mood seemed more somber than before. He held the curl in place. "What's wrong, sweetie?"

A small frown creased her brow. "I think we should pray for Mommy."

"Okay." Jake released the curling iron, and a single ringlet cascaded down Sierra's back. "How come?"

"Because, when Mommy bought me my pretty dress, she asked me about church."

"She did?" Hope grabbed hold of Jake's heart as he sectioned out another piece of Sierra's hair. "What'd she say?"

"She asked me if it was fun, and I told her yes. It was the funnest thing in the world." Sierra was careful to hold still. "Then she told me a secret. Just between me and her."

"Really?" A secret? Jake tried not to seem too anxious as he slid the curling iron from Sierra's hair and watched a second ringlet fall alongside the first. "Can you tell me?"

Sierra gave a dainty shrug. "I guess so."

"Okay then . . ." Jake gathered another section of Sierra's hair. "What did she tell you?"

"Well . . ." Their eyes met in the mirror again, and Sierra's looked deeper, wiser than her years. "She said sometimes she wishes she could go to church with us."

"Really?" Jake swallowed and released another curl. He forced a light tone. "Then why doesn't she go?"

"Because she isn't ready yet." Sierra bit her lip. "That's why we need to pray for her. So she'll get ready."

Jake nodded. For a while he was quiet as he finished with Sierra's hair. Then he unplugged the curling iron and led Sierra to a chair near the foot of his bed. "C'mere, honey." He sat down and pulled Sierra onto his lap. "Let's pray for Mommy now, okay? Then we can pray for her again at church."

"Okay." Sierra smiled at him and brushed her nose against his. Then she grew serious and closed her eyes, bowing her head just a bit. Jake closed his eyes too and listened. "Dear God." Sierra's voice was small but strong. "Me and Daddy get ready for church really fast. But it takes Mommy a long, long time." She hesitated. "Please help Mommy get ready very soon. So we can all go to church . . . like a family."

Her last words caught on Jake's heart and hung there for a moment. He hugged Sierra and waited for the lump in his throat to go down. When it did, he kissed her cheek. "Good job, honey." He slid her to her feet, stood, and took hold of her hand. "I bet God's working on that one right now."

Sierra studied the sections of her hair that fell over the front of her shoulders. "It's not curly enough, Daddy."

"Well, it'll have to do. We'll be late if we do more."

"Okay." She did a little huff and squinted at him. "Do the curlies in the back boing enough?" She took a few steps in front of him and looked up so that her hair fell nearly to her waist.

"Oh yes . . . they're the boingy-est curlies I've ever seen." Jake caught up with her again. "Let's go . . . Don't wanna be late for the opening song."

They walked down the stairs, and as they rounded the corner, Sierra stopped. "We have to swing hands, Daddy. Remember? We always swing hands."

"That's right!" Jake opened his eyes wide, playing with her. "I almost forgot."

Sierra giggled, and the rest of the way to the garage the two of them swung their joined hands. When they climbed inside Jake's truck, Sierra met his eyes and grinned. "'Jesus Loves Me,' right?"

"Right!"

Then, as they did every time they went to church together, they launched into a version of the song that would make a choir director cringe. But one Jake knew he would never forget.

Not if he lived a hundred years.

Sierra was tired when they got home from church, and Jake cuddled with her on the living room sofa until she fell asleep. Then he took her up to her room, crept back down, and called his father. It was something he tried to do every Sunday.

"Hello?"

"Dad . . . it's Jake."

"Well, hey there!" His father sounded strong and bursting with life, the way he always sounded. "How was church?"

"Good. Sierra wore a new dress, and she colored a picture of Moses." Jake crossed the living room and settled in an old recliner. Brownie, their lab, trailed behind him and dropped in a heap near his feet. "She prayed for Jamie today."

"Really?" There was a hint of concern in his tone. "Everything okay?"

"Yes. She prayed Jamie would be ready to come to church one of these days."

A moment passed before Jake's father spoke. "One of these days I believe she will. She's like a frightened bird, in some ways, isn't she?"

"Yes." Jake smiled. "Afraid to stick her head too far out of the nest."

"Afraid she'll fall, when really . . . if she'd only give it a go, she'd fly. Just like the rest of us."

Jake tried to picture that—his whole family flying together in faith. "It'll happen."

"Yep."

Jake heard his father draw a slow breath and could almost see him sitting at one of the kitchen barstools, phone cord stretched across the counter as he gazed out across his ranch. His words held the relaxed tone of someone at peace with God.

"How's work?"

"Good. Had another funeral last weekend."

"Hmmm. Sorry to hear it, son. Anyone I know?"

"Nope. He was a proby, a young guy, dropped dead of a heart attack working the hose reel."

"Lot of heart attacks this year."

"Four."

"That kind of thing keeps the chaplain busy. Funerals were always tough back when I did it. Some years were bad. Twenty, thirty men lost in a handful of fatal fires. Not usually so many heart attacks."

"Makes Jamie worry about my health."

"Ah, you're fine." Jim Bryan had been one of the toughest firefighters FDNY ever had. But his voice conveyed a mixture of deep faith and gentleness. Jim gave a sad chuckle. "Besides, not one of us goes home until God makes the call."

Jake leaned back in the chair. "How's the horses?"

"Anxious for fall. Summer's been hot."

"The jet ski got a lot of use, that's for sure."

An easy quiet filled the lines for a moment. "When are you coming up?"

"Maybe next weekend. Jamie wants to get out of the city for a few days."

"I'd love to have you. We could ride all morning and later on whip up our famous barbecue chicken and salsa."

"Don't forget football."

"That's right. Starts Monday night, doesn't it?"

"At Denver."

"Okay, let's plan on Saturday morning."

"I'll let you know if anything changes." The front door opened and Jamie walked in. Their eyes met and they shared a smile. "Hey, Dad, gotta go. Thanks for the chat."

"Let me know about the weekend."

"Okay." Jake stood and headed back to the kitchen. "I love you, Dad. Take care of yourself."

"Love you too."

Jake hung up the phone and leaned against the counter. His eyes found Jamie's once more. "Hi."

"Hi." She came toward him, one hand hidden behind her back. Her face was tanned from their time on the water Friday, and she looked as beautiful as she had the day he married her. "How was church?"

"Good." He leaned sideways and tried to sneak a look at what she had in her hand. She shifted her body so he couldn't see, and his eyes met hers again. "Sierra drew a picture of Moses."

"Very nice. Never too many pictures of Moses." Jamie raised her eyebrows appreciatively, a teasing smile turning the corners of her mouth.

Jake didn't have to see what was behind her back to know Jamie was up to something. She came closer until their toes were touching.

"I have something for you."

"Really?" Jake made a subtle move for whatever was behind Jamie's back, but she took a step back and lowered her chin, her eyes big and flirty.

"Now, now. You can't peek."

Jake thought about making another grab for the gift. He loved times like this, when he and Jamie could play. "Okay." He closed his eyes and held out one hand. Almost instantly, he felt her place something cold there. "Can I open?"

"Yes, silly." A lighthearted laugh came from her. "You can open."

He did, and there in his hand was a painted six-inch ceramic figurine of a firefighter with a guardian angel poised just behind him. The details were intricate and carefully painted. No wonder she was later than usual. "Jamie . . . it's beautiful. Did you paint it?"

Their eye contact held for another beat, and she stared at him, clearly enjoying his reaction. "The little guy kinda looked like you." She grinned. "So I gave him your dark hair and blue eyes."

"And there's my angel, right over my shoulder, looking out for me."

"Yep. Let's put it where I can see it, okay?"

Jake slipped his hand along the base of her neck and wove his fingers into her hair. "Thank you." He brought her face to his and kissed her. Then he pulled away from her and took a few steps toward the kitchen sink. The small shelves on either side were part of the cupboards, the place where Jamie kept knickknacks they'd gathered over the years.

He set the painted statue on the lowest shelf to the right of the sink. "There." He stepped back. "That way we can see it whenever we're in the kitchen."

Jamie tucked herself against Jake, just beneath his arm. She studied the figurine again. "Do you think it's true?"

"What?" Jamie wore a white tank top, and Jake ran his fingers along her bare arm.

"The guardian angel part." Jamie lifted her eyes to his. "Do you think it's possible?"

"Of course." Jake smiled at her and kissed her forehead this time. "I don't go out the door without an angel bigger than that hanging right beside me."

"I hope you're right." A fine layer of tears gathered in Jamie's eyes. "Because I've kinda kept a secret from you."

"A secret?" Was she going to tell him the thing about wanting to go to church, about almost being ready, the story Sierra shared with him that morning? He let his eyes take in everything about her. "What secret?"

"The secret that I need you, Jake Bryan." Her voice fell to a choked whisper. "I couldn't bear it if something happened to you."

"Ahh, Jamie." Jake wrapped his other arm around her and pulled her into a hug. She was always like this after a firefighter funeral. But for some reason, the one last week seemed to bother her more than the others. "Nothing's going to happen to me, honey."

"It better not." She muttered the words against his neck. Her tears fell on his shoulder and left a wet area on his pullover.

"It won't." He drew back and kissed her, more slowly this time. "I promise."

They stayed that way awhile, Jake kissing her, savoring the feel of her in his arms and believing with all his heart that the words he'd told her were true. Sure, fighting fires in New York City was dangerous. But for that matter, so was driving and walking and breathing. No bad thing was headed Jake's way, he was sure of it.

After all, he and God had a deal.

Six

September 10, 2001

The pace had been crazy since Eric Michaels stepped off the airplane at La Guardia Saturday afternoon.

Many of Koppel and Grant's top clients sensed that recent downward shifts in the market might be a precursor to something bigger. Dozens of them were demanding reports on safer stocks, technology and pharmaceuticals, defense and service sector holdings. Eric hadn't worked his way to the top by being wrong. In fact, his track record on investments was practically unmatched in the business. But in a sluggish market like this, Eric worked fifteen hours a day either researching or developing instinct. Weekends were no different.

It was Monday, and so far his day was like any other when he was in Manhattan. Up at five-thirty, three miles on a treadmill in the hotel basement, weight lifting for another twenty minutes, followed by a quick shower and a light breakfast. The entire time he was mentally calculating which segments of which portfolios could be diversified or sold for the purchase of a single stock.

Thoughts of Laura and Josh were relegated to the flight home on Thursday.

Koppel and Grant's New York office was located on the sixty-fourth floor of the World Trade Center south tower. The company leased space from an insurance company and kept a staff of just fifty-six people. The smaller the overhead, the more profits at the top. That was R. Allen Koppel's attitude. And Allen ran the company, no question about it. Robert Grant III had passed away two years earlier. His name stayed on the company stationery, and no one had taken his place.

Eric hoped someday the position would be his. Koppel, Grant, and Michaels. Or even Koppel and Michaels. Either way it had a certain ring to it, a ring that kept Eric up at nights even when he had to be back at the office in a scant five or six hours. Yes, Koppel ran the show. But since Grant's death, Eric had become increasingly important to the firm. The decisions they would make that week had more money riding on them than any they'd made in so short a time. That's why Eric was in New York: Koppel needed him.

And the knowledge of that felt better than anything Eric could imagine.

At eight o'clock sharp he stepped off the elevator at the sixty-fourth floor, turned right down one hallway and then another, until he came to a heavy walnut door with a brass plate that read "Koppel and Grant." Eric stared at it for a moment and caught his reflection in the polished metal. *There I am . . . right where I belong. It's my company . . . and one day the sign will say so.*

He breezed inside and walked past the secretary.

She looked up briefly. "Mr. Koppel's in his office."

"Thanks." The secretary was new, but Eric never broke stride. Secretaries at Koppel and Grant were paid modestly and expected to keep busy. Overtime hours were part of the job. Secretaries who didn't like the work conditions were replaced. Eric visited the New York office at least once every six months, and he rarely walked past the same secretary twice.

He spent the rest of the day with Allen, crunching numbers and making decisions about the portfolios of a dozen top clients. Sometime after eight o'clock that evening, Allen pushed back from his desk.

"That'll do it for today." A grin spanned the short distance from one side of Allen's face to the other. "Lets go meet some women."

Allen was thin and wiry, a diminutive man who ate little and drank less. He was fifty-three, and Eric figured the man weighed maybe a hundred and twenty pounds with his designer suit, dress shoes, and leather portfolio. He was so thin his shoulders and elbows looked knobby even through his clothes. The three wives he'd married and divorced had been nothing more than short-term mistresses, because his first love was without question Koppel and Grant.

But each of the wives had cost him, and Allen didn't intend to make the same mistake a fourth time. Allen and Eric spoke on the phone several times each week, and apparently Allen had become quite the player in the Manhattan nightclub scene. Allen was aware that generally speaking, women dated him for his millions. When they realized he wasn't interested in sharing his last name, most moved on. Allen had already complained that he hadn't had a date since August.

"You with me on this, Michaels?" Allen stood up and slid several folders into his briefcase.

"You're serious?" Eric studied his boss for a moment. "We have another hour at least."

"Nah." Allen waved his hand at the paperwork spread out across the desk between them. "We got further than I thought." He smiled again. "Besides, the work'll still be here tomorrow."

Every now and then, Allen did something like this. Surprised Eric and showed a side of himself less machinelike than usual. A side that was almost human. Eric shrugged. "I'll go." He raised one eyebrow. "But no women, Allen. I'm married, remember?"

Allen made a brushing motion with his hand and frowned. "Marriage never lasts. Besides, with a face like yours, women'll line up."

"No women, sir." Eric gave his boss a crooked grin. "But I'll take dinner."

Allen thought about that for a moment. "Okay." He sighed. "I'll change your mind while we eat. Where to?"

"Your choice."

"Well, then . . . Windows on the World, my boy. What else is there when you work in the World Trade Center?"

The restaurant was at the top of the World Trade Center's north tower, more than a hundred floors off the ground. The two men made a point of having at least one power lunch or client dinner there every time Eric was in town. This would be somewhat different, since no clients were involved.

An elevator led them to the ground level, where they walked next door and took another elevator up to the restaurant. The maître d' led them to a table against a wall of windows, and Eric slid his chair as close to the glass as he could. Darkness had settled over the city, and a sea of twinkling lights spread out before him. The view couldn't have been any better from an airplane.

"Amazing, isn't it?" Eric looked out and realized once more the incredible height of the Twin Towers. The two buildings stood like a couple of giants. Redwoods among a forest of saplings.

Allen ordered sautéed mushrooms and a two-hundred-dollar bottle of Chardonnay. He waited until the waitress had served them each a glass before speaking again. "You're looking good, Eric. Taking care of yourself."

"I try." Eric settled back in his chair and sipped the wine. He drank only for appearances, at times like these. Never for any other reason. He couldn't afford for his mind to be anything less than sharp. Eric set his glass down. "Still running and lifting."

"Good." Allen leaned forward. "You need to stay fit, Eric. You'll be head of the company one day."

A burst of adrenaline raced through Eric's veins. "Yes, sir ... I hope so." It was all Eric could do to stay in his seat. He'd always believed that one day the position would be his, but Allen had never come out and said so. Not until now. Eric took a slow, deliberate swallow of wine and managed an appropriate smile. "I'd like that."

Allen winked at him. "Don't get me wrong. I still have a dozen good years left." He leaned his forearms on the table. "But you'll take over one day. No one else is close."

Eric didn't know what to say. The waitress appeared with their mushrooms and gave them each a small plate. Her demure smile conveyed more than an interest in their dining pleasure, and Eric noticed she lingered near him a little longer than necessary. They made small talk for a minute or so, then she took their order and turned back to the kitchen.

The moment she was gone, Allen raised an eyebrow. "She's crazy about you." He whispered the words. "Give her your hotel number when we're done."

"Now ..." Eric chuckled and shook his head. His many years of marriage to Laura actually baffled his boss. Eric helped himself to three mushrooms and flashed his gold wedding band at Allen. "Laura wouldn't like that too much."

"Ahh, Laura would never know." Allen pushed his chair back and crossed one leg over the other. "Besides, look at you. Handsome, fit. Women fall all over you every time we're out together."

Eric raised a single eyebrow. "The same way they've done for you."

"They want my money. Nothing more."

"And they got it—at least a fair amount of it if I'm not mistaken, sir. Isn't that right?"

It was Allen's turn to laugh. "You have me there." He gestured toward the kitchen. "But women like that would be happy with a single night's entertainment, Eric. You're thousands of miles from home." He took two mushrooms and cut into one of them. "Who would know?"

Eric was trying to think up an answer when something caught his eye.

At the table adjacent to theirs along the window, a family was being seated. A businessman, a woman who must've been his wife, and two children. A boy and girl about the same age as Josh. The woman helped them get seated and then tied a bouquet of red and white helium balloons on the back of the girl's chair.

A birthday party. Like the one he'd missed a week ago for Josh.

Allen was saying something about the oil companies and the impact an embargo could make on a host of reports the next quarter, but Eric wasn't listening. He was caught up in the drama unfolding just behind Allen at the next table.

The couple sat side by side, their elbows on the linen table-cloth, hands linked in a way that showed off the woman's wedding ring. The children were busy with their menus, and the man whispered something to the woman. Whatever he said, his wife giggled and kissed him full on the lips.

Just then the young girl looked up and clucked her tongue. Eric could barely make out her words. "Mom, you guys act like teenagers." But instead of looking bothered, the woman kissed her husband again and said something Eric couldn't hear.

"Eric? You listening to me?" Allen finished his first glass of wine and poured a second.

If it was like other meals they'd shared, Eric doubted he'd finish it. One and a half glasses was his usual stopping point on the rare occasion when he drank.

"Absolutely, sir." Eric snapped to attention. "Every word."

"As I was saying, the prospects of an embargo may be slim, but those Arab nations are a finicky group. Back in the eighties when ..."

Again Eric tuned out. The family at the next table was holding hands now, their eyes closed, heads bowed. The birthday girl did the praying. Eric strained to listen. "Lord, we're thankful for all we have. For Mom and Dad and for each other. I pray we have as much fun together this year as we did last." She paused. "Oh, and thank You for the food."

Eric averted his eyes so they wouldn't see him staring. He nodded his agreement to Allen and focused once more on the family. Distractions didn't usually affect his business conversations. But the family's interactions were spellbinding, as though Eric were seeing them unfold on a movie screen.

The man reached across the table and took hold of the girl's fingers. "Happy birthday, honey." He patted her hand and grinned at the boy beside her. The boy puffed out his chest, his voice a little louder than the others. "Don't worry, Dad. I might be younger but I'll look out for her. When the boys come calling ... I'll be ready."

"Here you are." The waitress was back, and Eric jumped a little in his seat. She set a plate of roasted chicken and vegetables in front of him, and shrimp for Allen. Then she stepped back, made direct eye contact with Eric and held it. "If there's anything else I can do for you, let me know."

When she was gone, Allen pointed his fork at Eric. "See . . . I told you. Whatever you want, she'll do it. She's yours, Eric. Did you take a look at her legs? You're crazy if you pass this one up."

Eric picked up his knife and fork, and for the first time in years, he thought about praying. Not out loud the way the family beside them had done. But quietly, in his heart out of thanks for all God had done, all Eric hadn't thanked Him for in the years since the death of their unborn daughter.

But the moment passed quickly.

It was too late for casual conversation with God—even words of thanks. He and God had parted ways long ago, and Eric doubted they'd ever make amends again. Besides, he was doing pretty well without God. Second in command for one of the most powerful financial groups in Manhattan, with the presidency looming just a few years away. A better house, car, and savings account than anyone his age had a right to.

And all of it a direct reflection of his own hard work. If anyone deserved a vote of thanks it was him, not God.

The family at the table beside them finished eating and left, while the meal Eric and Allen shared lingered another half hour. When it was finally over, Allen paid the bill, and Eric finished his third glass of wine. More than he'd had in months, years even. His head buzzed, and a warm feeling crept over him as they left the table.

Eric was careful not to look at the waitress as he left the restaurant. He didn't want to give her the wrong idea, because the truth was, he hadn't the slightest interest in her. Laura was his wife, and he wouldn't go out with other women behind her back. He might not have had the best relationship with Laura, but he wasn't about to complicate his life with an affair. Nothing about the idea appealed to him. He'd talked about it with Murphy at the Los Angeles office once a few months ago.

"Ever notice how the things you lust after change in a job like this?" They'd been waiting for the elevator late one night.

"Yeah." Murphy huffed. "You got that right."

"Used to be love and sex." Eric had narrowed his eyes. "Now it's power and money. Success. And you know what?"

"You like it better?"

"I do." Eric had been incredulous about the fact. "The things that make life exciting are within my control, no one else's. I like it that way."

The conversation played again in Eric's mind as he and Allen rode the elevators down a hundred floors to ground level. Outside, Allen hailed a cab and grinned at Eric. "How 'bout some nightlife?"

It was after ten o'clock and Eric was tired. Maybe it was the wine, but he couldn't stop thinking about the family he'd watched earlier. "No, sir. I'm turning in." A cab pulled up, and Eric flagged down another driver ten yards down the street.

"Okay, then. Two cabs it is." Allen stepped into the backseat. "See you tomorrow. Eight o'clock."

"Yes, sir." Eric's cab pulled up as Allen shut the door of his.

Back at his hotel, Eric thought about turning on the television but decided against it. He hated TV, hated the way it wasted his time. And tonight he couldn't have focused if he'd wanted to. Not because of the wine. But because images of the family at the restaurant kept running through his head. The way the woman's eyes sparkled as she kissed her husband, the gentle way he touched his daughter's hand. The humor and closeness and determination to pray even in a public place.

Had he and Laura and Josh ever been that way? The picture of a loving, well-adjusted family? Had Laura ever kissed him like that, her eyes aglow with the joy of simply being with him? Eric racked his brain trying to remember. Certainly they'd loved like that at some point.

He hung his suit coat up in the mirrored closet and ran his hand over it so it wouldn't wrinkle during the night. Fifteen minutes later he turned the lights off and propped himself up in bed. He wasn't tired enough to lie down, and a glow from the city filtered through a crack in the drapes. His vision blurred some, and he felt his eyes close. As they did, a memory drifted in. Laura and him in their early days, back when they were still in college. They'd both been vocal about their faith, committed to God, determined to stay pure until they were married.

It was the reason they'd walked down the aisle when Laura was just eighteen, barely out of high school. Eric had been working on his master's degree back then, and money was scarce. When his parents arranged for them to live in Eric's aunt's guest house, he and Laura jumped at the chance. The place was small, two hundred square feet tops. It smelled old and musty, and they called it "the bunker." When they weren't asleep or in class, they spent most of their time sitting outside on a weathered picnic table, him playing his guitar while they sang and talked about the future.

Back then life was simple. The memory Eric could see now was from a night like that, crickets keeping time in the distant background and a canopy of stars sparkling overhead. He could see himself, finishing whatever song he'd been singing. He set the guitar down and leaned closer to Laura. "I love to sing." He'd brought his face closer to Laura.

"Mmmm." She closed her eyes. "I love to hear you."

"Know what else I love?" He'd leaned in and traced the outline of her lips with his finger.

"The bunker?" she giggled, wrinkling her nose in a way she never did anymore.

He waited until her laughter faded. Then he framed her face with his hands and gave her a kiss that was both long and unhurried. When he drew back, he let his forehead fall against hers. "No, crazy girl. I love being with you. Everything about you." He eased back some and his eyes locked on hers. "I love you, Laura."

And suddenly the memory was playing out before him as clearly as the scene from the restaurant earlier that evening. Yes, there it was . . . Laura's eyes *had* sparkled like the stars above them. Like the eyes of the woman in the restaurant. The memory blurred some, and Eric forced himself to think. What had happened next? Something important, wasn't it? Something he'd thought about often after that night until . . . until their baby girl died and life somehow fell flat. Until some point when it had stopped being important.

He opened his eyes and stared at the dark hotel ceiling. Gradually, the rest of the memory returned, and he closed his eyes again. Laura had stood up and made a small, slow circle, glancing at everything around her—Eric . . . his guitar . . . the picnic table . . . the bunker . . . even the cracked cement patio where they'd spent so many evenings.

"What're you doing?" He'd been amused by her actions.

"I'm taking it in." She leaned her head back and breathed in deep through her nose. "Every single detail."

"Of this?" Eric had given a short laugh. "This is nothing." He stood and caught Laura in his arms. "But one day, Laura, one day I promise you'll have it all." He studied her face. "You'll live like a queen, the way you deserve to."

Laura had only smiled at him. "You don't get it, do you?"

"What?" He'd searched her eyes.

"I already do. No matter how much money we make when we're older, all I need is you, Eric. You and God." She took another slow breath, as though she were trying to bottle the moment deep within her. "Nothing in the world could make me happier than I am right now."

The images in his mind faded, and he opened his eyes again. Instinct turned his head to the clock on the nightstand. It was after midnight. He'd be going on fumes all day tomorrow if he didn't get some sleep. Yet as he lay there, still the memory haunted him. And in that moment, still groggy from the wine, his conversation with Murphy came back to him. The one about power and money and success.

How had those things replaced what he and Laura had shared that night outside the bunker? And why had he stopped playing the guitar? The soft refrains had comforted him back then, mingling with the evening breeze and giving him the sense that all was right with the world. Playing the guitar had been one way he could slow down, focus on God and the people in his life and not just the tempting, all-consuming notion of getting ahead.

That was all that mattered to him these days. Eric blinked and rolled onto his other side. Was there anything wrong with that? With thinking and acting differently than he'd done a decade earlier?

It wasn't that he wanted to forget about physical or emotional love, really. It was just that there wasn't time for those things. Back when he and Laura first married, they'd had all the time in the world. That had changed as the years went by, and it didn't make life better or worse now. Just different. Anyway, love could wait; Laura wasn't going anywhere. She and Josh would be around when he was finished climbing the ladder and slowed down some. Either when he took over for Grant or sooner, if they picked up the right accounts.

In the meantime Laura didn't want for anything. In fact, these days if she stopped and looked around the way she'd done that night at the bunker, she'd see that he'd more than made good on his promise. A Cadillac SUV in the garage, five thousand square feet of custom home in the nicest area of Westlake Village. An in-ground pool and daily maid service. Memberships to all the right clubs and, for Josh, enrollment at Westmont Academy, an elite private Christian school.

Laura might not be perfectly happy, but one thing was certain: She lived like a queen.

The fact was enough to ease Eric's mind. In a matter of seconds, his eyes closed once more, and he could feel himself drifting off to sleep. He comforted his conscience with one last fact before he dropped off. The hours he put in at work were all for Laura and Josh. And love? Love would come later.

They had all the time in the world.

SEVEN

SEPTEMBER 10, 2001

Laura was trying to keep busy.

She and Josh had spent Saturday with friends and Sunday at church. Earlier that morning she'd volunteered in Josh's classroom, worked at the library fair after school, and met up with another Westmont family for dinner. As long as she was busy, she wouldn't have time to worry about her life, or the fact that her marriage barely had a pulse.

But now, at ten o'clock with Josh asleep down the hall, Laura lay wide awake in the dark, and the thoughts came unbidden. Somewhere out there under that same September sky, Eric was sound asleep in New York City. But was he alone? He spent more time away from home every year, and Laura had begun to wonder. Their physical relationship had been infrequent and hurried for years—more a release than a show of love. Even his declarations seemed shallow and contrived. Not the kind of sentiment that accompanied a lingering look or whispered words of passion.

Laura thought about that. Passion.

That's what was missing in her life. It was the thing that made divorce so appealing—the thought that someone else out there might be able to give her the passion she so badly missed. Laura's heart skittered into an irregular beat. It had done that off and on for the past eight years. But it was worse lately, and it meant sleep would be just about impossible.

She sat up and turned on the light. On nights like this peace came from just one source. She reached into the drawer of her nightstand and pulled out her worn blue leather Bible. Eric had bought it for her as a wedding present. Laura tried not to focus on the irony. It had been a decade since Eric had been remotely interested in Scripture. Since before her first pregnancy.

The pages were soft and thin, some crinkled from use more than others. Philippians chapter four was that way—the entire section. Laura found the text she was looking for and let her eyes settle on the fourth verse.

Rejoice in the Lord always. I will say it again: Rejoice! Let your gentleness be evident to all. The Lord is near. Do not be anxious about anything, but in everything, by prayer and petition, with thanksgiving, present your requests to God. And the peace of God, which transcends all understanding, will guard your hearts and your minds in Christ Jesus.

Laura read the passage again and again. She savored the part about God's peace guarding her heart and mind, and she felt the tension leave her arms and legs. Finally, even the pit in her stomach—the one that had been there since Josh's birthday last week—unwound and faded away.

Instead of falling asleep, Laura thought about the passion missing from her life. Eric had been passionate back then, hadn't he? Wasn't that what had attracted her to him in the first place? Those early days played again in Laura's mind like a movie she hadn't seen in years. Had she only been young and naïve? Or had Eric really been in love with her, really promised her he'd love her forever?

Suddenly, from the deepest part of her heart, memories began to surface. Memories she'd all but forgotten in the years since Eric graduated with his doctorate and took the job with Koppel and Grant.

For the first time in years, Laura didn't order the memories back where they belonged. Instead, she returned her Bible to the nightstand drawer, turned off the lights, and sat there in the dark, willing back everything about Eric Michaels and a love that began the fall of her junior year at Canoga Park High School.

Laura halted the memories for a moment. If she was going to go back, she might as well go all the way. Back to the summer of 1974, when she was just three years old. That was the year Laura was taken away from her parents and placed in a foster home. Laura didn't understand it at the time, but later she was shown copies of the court records.

Her parents had operated a methamphetamine lab in the backyard of their Topanga Canyon home, and four times they'd been arrested for making and selling illegal drugs. Always they paid fast-talking lawyers and were given stiff fines and another chance. But on the fifth arrest, the judge was finished with them. The two were given twenty years to life and sent to separate penitentiaries. Their parental rights to Laura were severed permanently, and she was put up for adoption within California's social services system.

Laura's foster parents applied to adopt her, but a year later, they divorced and changed their minds. Laura lived in a series of state homes until she was seven, when a family in Canoga Park, just west of Los Angeles, agreed to take Laura as part of a foster-adopt program.

The Paige family was large and multicultural with four birth children and four adopted—two Hispanic and two Romanian. Laura was the family's ninth child, but with so many children in the house, Laura rarely received one-on-one time with her adoptive parents. They were kind Christian people, but there was no getting around the camplike atmosphere that pervaded their home.

Years passed, and Laura Paige was a freshman at Canoga Park High School when she walked into second period health class and took the only empty seat in the room. Beside her, half-hidden behind a stack of books, was a blonde boy with glasses.

He poked his head around the stack and smiled at her. "Hi. Remember me?"

Laura had felt herself blush from the roots of her hair to below her neck. The boy looked familiar, but the two of them had never talked. And the teacher had already started talking.

When she said nothing, the boy continued. "I'm Clay Michaels. We're in leadership club together. Remember? At lunch the other day?"

Before she could answer, the teacher walked up to them. His eyes were narrow and angry. "There'll be no talking in class. Not now or at any time during the school year." He boomed the words and looked directly at Clay. "Is that understood?"

Clay's face had gone red. He slouched behind the books and leveled his gaze toward the front of the room. A few guys nearby shot him silent smirks. Laura dismissed the entire incident. She'd been a shy, academic girl who ran with the smart kids in Honor Society and after-school study sessions. The kids with a life outside the social circles at Canoga Park High. She had nothing more than a passing interest in boys—even one in leadership class.

Still, they had several classes together, and by the end of that year, Laura and Clay were friends. Sure, once in a while he'd pass her in the hallway and wave. But other than that he made no attempt to ask her out or make more of their friendship. That was fine with Laura. She knew there was nothing remarkable about her. She didn't bounce around the school giggling about Friday night football games. She had no desire whatsoever to be a cheerleader. Her single goal in life was to work hard enough to earn a scholarship to a local state college. Then maybe get a teaching credential and work with children.

Boys and dating and relationships could all wait. And when it was time, she doubted she'd fall in love with someone like Clay Michaels, someone shy and awkward who had never even made her heartbeat quicken. No, she'd find someone she felt passionate about, who would dote on her and treasure her and be her very own.

Someone who made her heart stand still. And that someone definitely wasn't Clay Michaels.

Then, in the fall of their junior year, things changed.

This time Laura and Clay shared a math class, and Laura began to notice something. Clay had changed. He was wearing contact lenses, and he'd not only gotten taller, but he'd filled out. He'd never been athletic in the years she'd known him, but that year he looked like he was lifting weights. And something else, something about the way he carried himself. A confidence she hadn't noticed before.

At the end of the first week, when Clay suggested they study together, Laura's heart beat a bit faster than before.

Laura thought about it for a moment. "You mean here? After school?"

"No." The look in Clay's eyes was deeper than before. "I mean at my house." He shrugged. "I have a car. We could study together once a week, and I could give you a ride home."

"What's in it for me?" Laura was playing with him, but only in part. For the first time since she'd known him, she liked the idea of spending time with Clay Michaels. It sounded more fun than studying alone.

"For you?" Clay's mouth hung open. "Uh . . ." He broke into a quick grin. "I'll make you laugh . . . I'll sing and dance for you." His smile faded, and he tossed his hands in the air. "Ah, come on, Laura. We'll be better together."

Laura laughed at his pitiful expression. "Fine."

For eight weeks she and Clay spent Monday afternoons at his house working on math, and not once did Laura ever guess he had an older brother. The house was modest and sparsely decorated, and when Laura met Clay's mother, she was cordial but distant. Laura guessed something wasn't entirely right with Clay's family, but she didn't know him well enough to ask.

The one time she met Clay's father, she was struck by two main details. First, the man was strikingly handsome, and second, he was as nonverbal as his wife. Laura and Clay were finishing up a session of algebra when he opened the front door, hung his jacket in the closet, and turned to them.

"Clay." The man said, then he gave a single nod of his head. "I assume this is your study partner."

"Yes, Father." Clay stood and cast a nervous glance toward Laura. "This is Laura."

"Laura." Clay's father nodded again. "Nice to meet you."

"You too, sir." Laura remained seated and waited for him to approach Clay, hug him, or ask him about his day. The man did none of those things.

"Is he mad at you?" Laura whispered when Clay's father left the room and walked upstairs.

"Who?" A blank look fell across Clay's face. "My dad? No." He hesitated. "My parents have a lot on their minds."

"Is everything okay?" She hated asking.

Clay kept his voice barely more than a whisper. "They're getting divorced." He blinked, and a kind of raw pain filled his eyes that hadn't been there before. "It'll be final in a month."

"Oh." Laura bit her lip. "Sorry."

Clay shrugged. "That's okay." He managed a smile that didn't quite make it to his eyes. "Everyone thinks it'll be better when it's over."

The next week Laura met Eric.

She and Clay were working on a series of word problems when a young, handsome replica of Clay's father walked through the front door. Laura had a clear shot of him from her place at the dining room table, and her breath caught in her throat. Whoever he was, he waved at them and headed for the kitchen.

Clay caught her expression, and his smile fell just a notch. "Girls always act like that when they see Eric for the first time." He planted his elbows on the table and cocked his head. "Now, how come your eyebrows don't rise like that when I walk in the room?"

"Eric?"

"Yes." Clay set his pencil down. "He's a junior at Cal State Northridge, point guard for the basketball team, headed for USC business school when he graduates. He's also one of the top golfers at the school, and he'll have his doctorate before he's twenty-five—all of it on scholarship." Clay chuckled. "I've looked up to him since before I could walk."

They were still working on their last math problem when Eric sauntered into the room and came up behind them. "Separate those last two numbers from the rest and make it a two-part problem. Once you've got answers for each part, divide the first part into the second."

"Actually," Laura slid her chair back and faced him, "once we have answers for both parts, we multiply the answers. The solution to a division problem involving fractions is always multiplication. Even in algebraic formulas."

Eric glanced at the problem in the book once more and then back at Laura. "I'm Eric." He held out his hand and smiled at her. "I don't believe we've met."

Laura was suddenly tongue-tied. "I . . . I'm Laura Paige."

"Well . . ." Eric gave Clay a lighthearted punch in the shoulder. "If you're dating my brother, you better be good to him."

Just as Laura was shaking her head, Clay slipped his arm around her shoulders. "She is." He shifted so that his eyes connected with hers. "She's great."

"That's good." He spoke to Clay, but his eyes never left hers. "Take care of her . . . she's a good one."

Up close Eric was breathtaking, and Laura could barely focus on the conversation. Again she couldn't think of a thing to say, so she grinned like the ditzy girls at school. When Eric left the room, she slid her chair back up to the table. This time the blush felt like it went clear to her toes. The moment Eric was gone she realized something.

For just a moment, her heart had stood still.

Clay removed his arm from her shoulders and stared at her. "You like him."

Laura huffed and forced herself to shift gears. "What do you mean?"

"I mean," Clay directed his attention back to the math paper, "you like him."

"Yeah, and by the way what's the deal about us dating?"

"Well . . ." Clay lifted his eyes to hers again. "We could be . . ."

At that point Laura did something she hadn't thought of often through the years, something that stood out now as the single most vivid part of the memory.

She laughed.

Not a mean or mocking laugh, but a laugh that killed the idea of the two of them dating before it ever had a chance to take root. She still remembered the hurt that flashed in his eyes, a hurt that caught her off guard and made her scramble for something to say.

"Clay . . . you can't be serious. We've been meeting all these weeks." She shook her head. "You never said anything like that before. I . . . I thought you were joking."

For a moment she'd held Clay's expression, and she saw he was serious. That somehow along the course of Mondays, he'd fallen for her. But just as quickly, his guard was back up, and he stared at the math book once more. "You're right." He shrugged. "I'm just playing with you."

Before she left Clay's house that day, Laura went to the kitchen for a drink of water and saw Eric in the family room. He spotted her and motioned for her to come. Laura went to him, even though she felt she was somehow betraying Clay. Her heart skittered within her, and she could feel her eyes dance as she drew near to him.

When she was close enough, Eric leaned forward. "You aren't really dating Clay, are you?"

"No." She grinned. "He was teasing."

Eric leveled his gaze at her. "I wasn't." He sat a bit straighter on the sofa. "Go out with me, Laura. Come watch my basketball game this Friday."

Laura felt something strange in her gut. Why not? She and Clay were nothing more than studying partners. Distant friends at best. Still, she wasn't about to make it easy. Not for Eric or any boy. "I'm busy."

"Doing what?"

"Studying Friday night." She hesitated. "And on Saturday there's a concert at church."

"I'll take you." Eric practically jumped to his feet. "I love church concerts."

A quiet laugh slipped from Laura's throat. "Fine." She took a step backwards and told him her address. "Pick me up at seven."

"Can we go out afterwards?"

She studied him for a moment, praying her attraction to him wouldn't show. "How old are you?"

"Twenty. How 'bout you?"

"Sixteen." She smiled again. "Better count on just the concert. My dad will want to meet you before we go anywhere else."

After that weekend there had been no turning back. She was Eric's girl from the moment he picked her up for the concert. Her adoptive father approved wholeheartedly, and they spent the next two school years together. They took trips to the LA Museum and discussed the lack of evidence supporting the theory of evolution. On weekends they held hands and walked barefoot along the shores of Malibu or Zuma Beach, spilling their most private secrets and savoring their time together.

"I love you," he'd tell her. "I can't wait to make a life for you one day. A life better than either of us ever had."

Dating Eric was the most amazing experience. Laura thought she'd died and gone to heaven. Eric was everything she'd ever wanted in a boyfriend, and when he proposed to her on Christmas Eve of her senior year in high school, she didn't hesitate for a moment. Her dreams of college and teaching paled in comparison to being Laura Michaels. Eighteen might have been too young for some girls, but not Laura. She'd been born old, and after a lifetime of wanting someone to love her all by herself, Laura was sure she'd found her dream man in Eric Michaels.

Clay took the news well, congratulating them and assuring Eric he couldn't be happier for him. But something sad had flickered in Clay's eyes when he turned to her and gave her a quick hug. Something that seemed more pronounced now in the glow of so many years gone by.

But Laura never gave another thought to the passing interest she'd had in Clay in the weeks leading up to her meeting Eric. They were married that summer in a simple wedding attended by only fifty people, family and friends. But it was a day that felt ordained by God Himself. Laura floated out of the church and into the reception at a hotel banquet room.

"I can't give you much now," Eric told her later that night when they were alone. "But one day, Laura . . . one day I'll give you everything you ever dreamed of. I promise."

Laura only kissed him and looked deep into his soul. "I already have it, Eric. I have you."

The cloud of memories lifted, and Laura nestled into her pillow. Her heart felt more hopeful for the time she'd spent in the past, the memories helping her forget, if just for one night, that Eric had found another love.

The love he had for Koppel and Grant.

That night she dreamed of her honeymoon, reliving every kiss, every intimate moment. But when she woke up the next morning, it only took a few seconds for reality to set in. She wasn't eighteen and in love with the most wonderful man in the world. She was thirty-two, and her husband barely talked to her. Indeed, she wouldn't spend the day frolicking on a Mexican beach and basking in the feel of Eric Michaels' arms.

She would spend it alone in her Westlake Village mansion, surrounded by memories and dying dreams, wondering again whether she'd chosen the wrong brother.

Reality was harsh after a night of dreaming. But there was no question about one thing. This wasn't the first day of her honeymoon. It was just a day that marked nothing more significant than the passing of time.

Just another Tuesday morning in the lonely life of Laura Michaels.

Eight

Jake's Bible verse that day was from Proverbs.

Lean not on your own understanding; in all your ways acknowledge him, and he will make your paths straight.

He read the words, underlined them, and read them again. Wasn't that exactly where Jamie was at? If only she could stop leaning on her own understanding and start leaning on God. He would make her paths straight. He'd take away her fear and help her feel safe about loving him. People had misjudged Jamie over the years, taken her as unbending and cold. A person with little love to give.

Jake's cousin had thought that of Jamie. "She's so competitive, Jake. There's nothing soft about her."

But the cousin couldn't have been more wrong. Jamie had a world of love inside her, too much love, maybe. So much that it scared her, frightened her into thinking something would somehow come along to steal that love away. No, there wasn't any limit to Jamie's love. The hard part was making her feel safe enough to give it away, safe enough to stop running.

And really, it all came down to the message in that single verse from Proverbs. If Jamie would lean on God, He'd take care of the rest. In the margins next to the verse, Jake scribbled, *Jamie . . . this verse is for you, honey.*

He did that often, though he never showed her what he'd written. The first hour of his morning was between him and the Lord. He would read a little from his Bible, underline a few key verses, and jot notes in the margins. Then he'd write a page or two in his journal.

One day in the not-too-distant future, when Jamie might show even a little interest, Jake would bring out the Bible and the journal and let her read both. He had nothing to hide. The material was simply an accounting of the walk he'd shared with God since he and Jamie had married seven years earlier. It was something he looked back on every now and then as a way of charting how far he'd come, a way of remembering what was important.

Jake glanced at Jamie, cuddled up beside him, sleeping. She looked young and vulnerable, without the armor she typically wore when she was awake. In this light the resemblance between her and Sierra was striking.

He sighed and stared at her a moment longer. No question about it, he was the luckiest man in the world. A beautiful wife who just happened to be his best friend . . . and a daughter who was at least half angel. *Thank you so much, God . . . every day with them is a miracle.*

The numbers on Jake's bedside clock changed, and he tore his eyes away from Jamie. He needed to finish, or he wouldn't get to work on time. The shift began at nine o'clock, but he would arrive no later than eight. It usually took an hour for the night shift to debrief them on the incidents that had occurred while Manhattan slept.

Jake opened his journal and began to write. A restlessness stirred within him, something Jake couldn't quite define. This time he didn't make references to the Bible text and how it applied to his life. He wrote a letter to Jamie.

Dear sweet Jamie,

I have this feeling, deep in my heart, that something's about to change for me and you. Maybe it's your questions about church or the way you seem to hang on to Sierra's Bible stories a little bit longer these days. Whatever it is, I've prayed for God to touch your heart, baby. He means everything to me, and I know that one day He'll mean everything to you too. On that day, you'll no longer have to be afraid, because you'll have God Almighty to lean on. I want you to know, honey, that when you find that precious faith, I'll be smiling bigger than you've ever seen me smile. Because the thing I want even more than your love is the knowledge that we'll have eternity together.

I simply cannot bear the idea of being in heaven without you. I love you too much to lose you.

Jake kept writing until he'd filled almost two pages. Then he closed the journal, closed the Bible, and slipped them both beneath the bed. He leaned down and nuzzled his face against hers. "I love you . . ." His whispered words caused her to stir, and slowly she opened her eyes.

"Mmmm." She pulled her arms from under the sheets and caught the back of Jake's head. "C'mere."

Jake grinned. "Gladly." He positioned himself partway over her body and kissed her more fully this time. When he drew back, desire burned in both their eyes. "You're gorgeous, you know that?"

"Not as much as you." She kissed him again and moved the covers off her pajama-clad body. "Come back to bed."

"Don't tempt me." Jake could feel his body responding to hers, and for a moment he considered it. Then he kissed her once more and sat up. "I need to shower. Shift change is in an hour."

"Oh, Jake, come on." Jamie sat up and worked her hands along the sides of his naked chest. "Call in sick. It's a beautiful day. We'll play under the covers for an hour and take Sierra to the zoo."

Most workdays Jamie barely woke up to tell him good-bye, and so her request was almost too much to pass up. He eased her back onto the bed, gave her a series of kisses, and then forced himself onto his feet. "One of the day guys is sick this week." He brushed a lock of dark hair off her forehead. "Otherwise I would." He looked out the window. "Besides, the good weather is supposed to last."

"Next week, then?"

He grinned and stretched. "Okay, next week. Unless someone else gets sick." He turned toward the bathroom, his tone still filled with the passion he felt for her. "I better shower."

"Okay." Jamie exhaled her disappointment. "But, Jake, one thing."

He stopped. "What?"

"About that shower . . ." A grin filled her face. "Make it a cold one."

Thirty minutes later, Jake was dressed in his work uniform—black pants, a white T-shirt and short-sleeve buttoned-down, black socks, and comfortable dress shoes. His turnouts—the uniform he wore for fighting fires—stayed at the station near the rig. Ready at a moment's notice whenever they got a call.

He kissed Jamie one last time. "See you tonight."

"Chinese food?"

"Mmmm." He started to smile but changed his mind. "Wait . . . are you cooking?"

She giggled and placed the palm of her hand against his chest, pushing him playfully away from her. "Go to work, you big oaf. I can cook Chinese food just fine."

"Okay." He took a step toward the door and raised an eyebrow. "But keep the takeout number handy. Just in case."

Her laughter faded. "Hey."

"Yeah?" He spun around, and his eyes found hers. The connection between them was as deep as it was instant.

"Be careful."

He winked at her. "You know it, Jamie. I love you."

"Love you too."

Before he left, he stopped by Sierra's room.

She was up, moving about near her closet. So far she'd managed to pull on pink leggings and a blue-and-red-striped shirt. At age five, dressing herself was the ultimate in independence and proof, if nothing else, that she was Jamie's daughter. She saw Jake and ran to him, hugging his legs tight, and stirring feelings in his heart that made a day at the zoo sound wonderful.

He swept her into a full hug and then set her down again. "Isn't this pretty, Daddy?" She did a twirl. "Mommy says I have to pick colors that go together. Pink, red, and blue go together, right?"

Jake bit his lip. "Right, baby. Definitely." He crouched down and rubbed noses with her. "Daddy's running late, honey. See you after work, okay?"

"Butterfly kisses first." She moved her face so that their noses rubbed together, then she turned her face a few inches, and at the same time they brushed their eyelashes against each other's cheeks. She pulled back and grinned at him. "There. Now you can go."

"Be good." He hugged her once more. "And don't forget to pray to Jesus."

"Okay, Daddy. I love you."

"Love you too, sweetie." He stood and blew her a kiss.

She pretended to catch it in the air and place it over her heart. Then she blew one in his direction. Jake grabbed at a handful of air. "Caught it!" He brought his fist to his chest. "Forever and always."

"Forever and always!" Sierra clapped and jumped up and down. "Bye, Daddy."

"Bye, honey. We'll play horsie when I get home."

Jake's commute was tedious, but he could've done it in his sleep. Surface streets to the Staten Island Express. Ten minutes to the ferry parking lots. Depending on the shift, some days he'd drive his pickup into the city and park outside the station. But over the last few years he'd pulled mostly days. At this hour it would be impossible to find a spot, so he stood in the line for walk-ons and paid his fare.

Usually he preferred an inside seat because of the fog or cool weather. But this morning was particularly gorgeous. Blue skies as far as he could see and the city skyline stretching out before him like a surreal postcard. He liked the ferry, liked the way it made the commute seem less frantic.

Jake moved on and took a seat near the front.

Days like this made it easy to see why his father had settled their family in New York City, why the old man had chosen a crazy busy place like FDNY to fight fires. Manhattan pulsed with life and energy, each building in the skyline standing at attention while the activity in it raced at breakneck speeds. Every financial power in the world stepped back and watched in awe as New York City did her thing.

His father could have chosen any one of a thousand small towns across America. Places where a house fire was big news and most days were a series of paramedic runs and training drills. But Jake was grateful his father had opted for what they both thought was the greatest fire-fighting challenge of all—Manhattan.

The ferry pulled in, and Jake took a series of subway trains to a set of stairs just half a block from the station. Engine 57 had operated out of this same stone building for seventy years. His father had never worked Engine 57, but he'd split time at two nearby stations.

He entered through the station's front door and immediately saw Larry smile at him from one of the picnic tables lining the dining room wall. "You're late, JB."

The guys at the station never called him Jake Bryan. He was JB. Jake glanced at an old clock that hung over the kitchen sink. "Eight-oh-one isn't late, Larry Boy. It's fashionable."

"You're usually early."

"So . . ." Jake made his way to the table.

"Jamie kept you." It wasn't a question. Larry shot a smirk at him and stuffed half a blueberry muffin into his mouth. He followed it with a swig of coffee.

"It's not so bad, Larry Boy." Jake grinned and took a seat across from his friend. "A few fashionable mornings might be good for you and Sue."

"And a cup of coffee might be good for you." He stood, crossed the dining room, and filled a paper cup with chunky black liquid from the bottom of the coffeemaker. "Here." He set the cup down in front of Jake. "Be careful. You might need a spoon."

"Thanks." Jake lifted the cup to his nose and breathed in the steam.

Larry sat back down. "Doesn't sound like the night shift had much."

One at a time the night crew guys joined them at the tables, pounding down muffins and coffee and an occasional piece of fruit. Maxwell was in charge that day. He stood with his back against the chipped kitchen counter and called the meeting to order. "Just a few calls to go over." He glanced at a clipboard in his hands. "A car fire a block south of Forty-Second needs some follow-up. Owner says it was arson."

Maxwell touched on a few more items, then crossed the kitchen and started a fresh pot of coffee. He glanced at the guys from night crew. "Anything else?"

A few firefighters made suggestions, and another reminded Maxwell of an unfinished incident from the weekend. Conversation was comfortable and casual for the next half hour, the way it always was during shift change. The station had two probies, but otherwise the firefighters from Engine 57 and Ladder 96 had worked together long enough to be family. The station was manned by thirty-six men, enough for three shifts, and each thought of the station as their second home. During downtime they cooked steaks, cleaned the kitchen, and offered advice to whichever of them was struggling at home.

On a call they were tighter than brothers.

"You with us today, JB?" Maxwell raised his eyes in Jake's direction. "I asked which of the day guys did follow-up on the warehouse fire from the weekend."

Jake straightened himself and tried to focus. Maxwell wasn't angry, but he wanted an answer. Before Jake could think of one, Larry cut in. "JB's distracted." He snickered and poked an elbow at the man beside him. "Too much morning time with that pretty wife of his."

"Or not enough." Jake whispered the retort and at the same time turned his attention fully to Maxwell. The man was a veteran, a captain with twenty years experience in the department. Jake cleared his throat. "I worked the report, sir. No surprises. A few more phone calls today, and we should be ready to file."

Each call required a report. Some were simple and could be done minutes after a run. Others took longer and depended on interviews from outside sources or investigative work before a cause of a fire could be determined, and arrests possibly made.

Maxwell was about to say something when the rumbling of a large airplane overhead stopped him. Because of the World Trade Center, jets had to observe strict guidelines about staying away from Manhattan. To a man, the firefighters around the table looked up.

"That's too low ..." Jake muttered. But before anyone had a chance to respond, a muffled explosion pierced the quiet morning, and the ground vibrated beneath their feet.

Maxwell darted for the station door with Jake and the others close behind. The scene outside made them stop and stare in horror. Massive flames and sections of building were exploding from the upper section of one of the World Trade Center buildings. Jake stared at the billowing black smoke, and his eyes grew wide. *Dear God ... no ... it can't be ...*

Around him, for a split second, all of New York City seemed to hold its breath, as though the disaster they were witnessing was too awful to believe. Cars pulled off to the side of the road at bizarre angles, pedestrians stopped and looked straight up, their mouths open. In an instant the air was pierced by screams and shouts. Across the street two old women held each other and began to cry.

A man a few yards away looked from the flaming Twin Tower to the cluster of firefighters. "The plane ... it went into the building!" Then he began to run, unfazed by the papers flying out of his attaché case.

Jake's heart was pounding. A plane had crashed into the World Trade Center? It was impossible, the devastation he was watching too overwhelming. A fifty-foot-high ball of fire and smoke shot out from high up in the tower. It was the most horrific thing Jake had ever seen.

New York City firefighters liked to talk about the big one, the fire of all fires that would bring every one of them out of their stations to fight it. "See you at the big one" was a sentiment casually tossed about at most New York firehouses. Jake's was no exception. He squinted, unable to believe the magnitude of the blaze. How in the world had the pilot made such an error? Couldn't he have dropped a doomed jet into the harbor or struggled to land in some sort of treed area?

And how were they ever going to fight a fire that size so many floors off the ground?

An awful thought flashed through Jake's mind. What if the plane had been a passenger jet? One with a hundred people aboard? He shuddered as he realized something else. It didn't matter whether it was a passenger jet or not—either way they'd be dealing with massive loss of life. An MCI ... massive casualty incident. A fire that intense would mean the deaths of everyone on the plane, and perhaps several hundred businesspeople.

Maybe more.

These thoughts—all of them—flashed through Jake's mind in as much time as it took him to blink twice. Adrenaline rushed through his bloodstream. People were in trouble, thousands of them. Every instinct in him wanted to race down the firehouse stairs, jump into his uniform, and fly to the fire.

But before he could move, the group's silent shock was interrupted by Maxwell's voice—calm and steady.

"All right, men. Get dressed. We might not be first called, but we'll be on the list." Without saying a word, they hurried into the station garage. They were halfway down the stairs when Maxwell stopped and faced them once more. "I'm not much of a praying man, but right now every one of you should say your prayers." He gazed again at the blazing World Trade Center. "A lot of people are gonna' die today."

NINE

Terrorists.

That was the first thought Eric Michaels had when he heard the explosion.

He'd been in Allen's office rehashing the conversation from the night before when the building was rocked by first one jolt, then another. The second one was both louder and longer, and Eric almost expected the floor to crumble beneath his feet.

He and Allen stared at each other for a moment and then dashed to the window behind Allen's desk. It faced due south, and from their vantage point, the city looked like it did on any other beautiful September morning. The sky was a brilliant blue; sailboats dotted the harbor. Not a plume of smoke, not a sign of trouble, not a thing out of place. But the rumble from the second explosion still filled the building, and Eric headed for the door. *Breathe*, he told himself. *Everything's going to be fine.* None of them knew what had happened, but Eric was sure of one thing. The destruction would be huge. "Let's check the rest of the office."

Allen nodded and followed Eric, and together they burst through the double oak doors and into the plush hallway. Outside Allen's office the entire unit seemed to be in a state of shock. Some people sat at their desks, hands frozen above their keyboards. Others had walked to the nearest windows and were staring down at the city below.

Three minutes after the explosion, sirens began to sound in the distance. More sirens than Eric had ever heard in his life. Whatever it was—it was big. And Eric guessed they were probably in danger. But from what? From where? Eric continued to move ahead of Allen toward the office entrance. "Let's check the other side of the building."

Dozens of people congregated in the firm's entryway, and now they followed Allen and Eric down a series of hallways into a more open office that bordered the north side of the building. A crowd was gathered at the wall of windows, and several people had their hands over their mouths. Eric found a spot and wedged his way between two suits.

What he saw made his knees weak.

He wasn't sure if anything had happened to the south tower, where the Koppel and Grant offices were, but fire was pouring out of an entire bank of north tower windows, about thirty floors up from where Eric stood.

Behind him someone shouted. "I've got it on TV!"

Eric and Allen and a couple dozen other people crowded around the man's desk. A nineteen-inch color television screen was full of an image of the flaming World Trade Center, and a reporter in the studio was talking loud and fast, his voice-over somewhat broken up as the horrifying pictures from the scene continued to come in.

"I repeat, a passenger jet has slammed into the north tower of the World Trade Center. It is assumed at this time that the disaster was some kind of an accident, though ground control received no reports of trouble before the collision occurred."

Eric took a step back from the desk and turned toward the window once more. A passenger jet? How in the world had something like that happened? And what if it wasn't a mistake? Stunned, Eric walked the remaining ten feet back to the window edge and stared at the flames still pouring from the neighboring building. Hundreds of people had to be dead. And what about the people above the fire? How would they ever get past the inferno?

For a moment, Eric hung his head and closed his eyes. *God . . . it has to be a nightmare in there. Help those people . . . please.* As Eric blinked and took in the awful sight again, he had a distant realization. He had talked to God as though it were the most natural thing in the world. The notion produced a dozen questions at once. Why had it taken this long for Eric to break his silence with God? Why had he stopped praying in the first place? Babies died, didn't they? Had it made his loss any easier by cutting off God? And would God really hear him now, after all these years?

They were questions he'd have to answer later. Right now the entire city was in crisis, and he had to figure out what to do, where to go. Allen was talking to a man a few feet away, and Eric turned back toward the interior of the building. Nearly half the people from the sixty-fourth floor were headed for the bank of elevators. Nervous conversations took place all around him, and Eric caught bits and pieces of the closest of them.

". . . down now before something happens to *this* building."

". . . no point in staying. They'll have the whole street cordoned off if we don't get out of here soon."

"I couldn't work . . . not with the tower next to us on fire."

Distant sirens at the ground level continued to fill the air outside the building. The sixty-fourth floor had a feel of chaos, but not panic. Not yet. Certainly the other floors were experiencing the same thing.

Eric glanced around the expansive office. Most of the employees on that floor worked at the insurance company. There were easily a couple hundred workstations within view of where Eric was standing, and clearly, not all the people at them were leaving.

Allen joined him again, and they watched the pictures on TV for a few minutes. Around them, those who didn't grab their things and leave formed groups of threes and fours, and with a slow, hushed presence, they walked back to their desks.

"We're better off up here out of the way," an older man said to a group of wide-eyed women. "There's nothing to worry about."

"What if the fire spreads?"

The man shook his head. "These buildings are too safe for that. Believe me, you're better off back at your desks. You can watch the news from there. The streets will be a nightmare with all those fire trucks."

Televisions throughout the floor were on now, all tuned to the disaster. Eric glanced at his watch and figured it was just before six o'clock on the West Coast. Laura would still be sleeping, but the news would make her frantic. The only way to ease the shock was to call her himself.

He turned to Allen. "I need to call Laura."

"Good idea." Allen's face was pale, but his voice stayed calm. "I'll come with you. Someone at the LA office needs to know we're okay."

They moved quickly through the insurance company's work space back down the hallway to the office of Koppel and Grant. The secretary had left the front desk, and the place was deserted. Allen strode down the hallway toward his office, and Eric flopped into the secretary's chair, picked up the phone, and dialed his home number.

He listened to the first ring, and suddenly he had an image of the unbelievable nightmare taking place in the building next door. People would be burning alive, suffering torturous deaths. A second ring sounded, and Eric closed his eyes, trying to shut out the horrible pictures in his head. Then for the second time in a handful of minutes, Eric did something he hadn't done in years.

He prayed.

****

Laura had been awake since five-thirty that morning, unable to sleep after the vivid details in her dreams. When the phone rang she glanced at the clock, and in the early morning fog, she wondered if maybe she'd overslept. She reached for the receiver, saw it wasn't on the hook, and remembered that she'd left it in the upstairs office the night before.

It was cool for a Los Angeles morning. She hopped out of bed, slipped into her robe, and darted down the hallway. Josh was sleeping two doors away, so she kept her steps light. She found the phone on the office desk and clicked it just as it rang a third time.

"Hello?" She was out of breath as she fell back on a leather love seat against the office window.

"Hi . . . it's me."

For a moment she thought it was Clay. The two brothers' voices were almost identical, but then Clay would never have called her at this hour.

But neither would Eric.

"Eric?" He was breathless, his voice filled with an urgent tone she couldn't remember hearing before.

"Something's happened, Laura . . . I want you to listen to me. A plane flew into the World Trade Center building, the one next to the one I'm in. A passenger plane. The entire upper section of the tower is on fire." He paused. "My tower is fine." He took a shaky breath. "I wanted you to know I was safe."

"Where . . . where are you? Are you on the ground?"

"No. I'm still on the sixty-fourth floor. No one's telling us to leave." He hesitated. "I thought it was a bomb. In this building, not the other one. It was that loud."

"You can't stay up there." Laura's heart skipped a beat and then raced at twice its normal speed. She grabbed a nearby remote control, flicked on the television, and immediately saw it. The building was billowing black smoke and enormous flames. Her free hand flew over her mouth. "Oh, Eric . . . it's awful. I've . . . I've never seen anything like it. A passenger plane did that?"

"Yes." Eric was breathing fast. He must've been more worried than he let on. "The reporter said it looks like an accident, like the pilot lost control of the plane."

Laura's eyes were locked on the image of the burning tower. "An accident? Surely a pilot could figure out a way to miss the World Trade Center. Even if the plane was out of control. You aren't staying, are you?"

"For now. Most people seem to think we're better off up here, out of the way of the firefighters."

Suddenly, Laura saw something fall from high up near the burning floors of the building. Not three seconds later, two more things plummeted from one of the flaming windows.

"No! This is too awful." The reporter's voice sounded suddenly frantic. "I believe those were people you just saw falling from the building." He paused. "Falling or jumping." Another hesitation. "Yes, I've just been told those were people jumping from the tower." His voice grew quieter. "We can only imagine the horror taking place in that building right now."

Laura closed her eyes for a moment. What had she just witnessed? Frantic people hurling themselves to certain death? It was the worst thing she could imagine. "God Almighty help them." She muttered the words and struggled to exhale.

"What's happening, Laura? I don't have a TV in the office here."

"People are jumping." Her tone was soft, filled with shock. She looked away from the television. "I can't watch."

"Don't then. Leave it on, but look away." For the first time in years his tone held a hint of concern for her. "Maybe I'll leave after all. Go back to the hotel and stay there until my flight leaves. That way I'll . . ."

She was no longer listening to him. From the corner of the screen, an enormous passenger jet came into view, angled slightly, and headed straight for Eric's building. Laura jumped up, her heart in her throat.

"Eric!" She shouted his name and gripped the phone. "Look out!"

The plane slammed straight into the tower, and flames sliced across the building and ripped through at least four floors. "Eric! Can you hear me?" Laura screamed into the receiver, her words shrill and desperate. Her entire body shook, and she felt her head begin to spin. Why wouldn't he answer her? "Talk to me!"

She smashed the phone to her ear, frantic for any kind of sound from him. But there was only silence. Two seconds passed, and she heard a click on the other line, followed by a dial tone. She held the phone in front of her and pressed the Caller I.D. button. Her fingers were shaking so much she could barely press the talk button, but as she did, the phone automatically dialed the number Eric had called from.

Laura waited, unable to breathe. But instead of ringing, there was only a fast busy signal. "No, God . . . no!" She whispered the prayer as she dropped the TV remote, grabbed a quick breath, and dialed the number again. "Not Eric. Get him out of there . . . please." Again the busy signal sounded on the other end. She moved closer to the television and dropped to the floor, her eyes glued to the second flaming tower.

"No, God . . . !" Her words were muted, breathy and weak. She wanted to scream, but she couldn't find the strength. Black spots danced before her eyes, and she slipped her head between her knees for a moment. She couldn't faint, not now. She needed to find out what floors were involved in this second collision. It was possible Eric was okay. Yes, it had to be possible.

She sucked in three quick breaths and ordered herself to remain alert.

A few feet away, the reporter was shouting out the news. "A second plane, I repeat, a second plane has hit the World Trade Center south tower. We're getting word now that the United States is possibly under some type of terrorist attack."

Laura lifted her head and pursed her lips. Short breaths. She needed to take short breaths and push the air out so she didn't hyperventilate. "What floor?" She raised her voice at the television and slid closer. "Tell me what floor!"

". . . terrorists may have hijacked the planes and flown them into the World Trade Center as some kind of attack. We have confirmation now that one of the planes was American Airlines Flight 11 out of Boston and the other . . ."

The images made Laura dizzy. Sections of both towers were fully engulfed in flames, but where was Eric? She lifted the telephone receiver close to her face and thought of something. His cell phone! Why hadn't he called from his cell in the first place? Eric always had his cell phone. She dialed the number from memory.

"Answer . . . come on, Eric, answer the phone!" She hissed the words, certain that this time she'd hear ringing on the other end. But instead, a mechanical voice sounded across the line. "The caller you're trying to reach is not available or out of the service area. Please try your call at a later—"

She dropped the receiver and slapped the television. "Tell me what floor!" Her tone was loud again, almost shouting. "Where's the fire? Come on, tell me!" The sound was too low, that was it. The television needed to be louder in case they might mention which floors were on fire. She searched the carpet beside her for the TV remote and grabbed it. Her hands shook worse than before, but she managed to turn up the volume.

"... made hotter by an unknown amount of jet fuel aboard the planes." The reporter hesitated. "Reports say that the plane that crashed into the south tower was United Flight 175 from Boston. There may have been a hundred or more people on each of those passenger jets."

The news camera angle widened some, and Laura could see most of both of the towers. An idea gripped her. She could count down from the top of the south tower; figure out where the fire was burning that way. The black dots were back, but she ignored them. Walking on her knees, she came up to the television set, placed her finger on the top floor of the flaming south tower and began silently counting.

One, two, three, four, five, six ...

The image changed, and now Laura was looking at dozens of fire trucks arriving at the scene. "No! Don't do this to me." Her scream echoed against the walls. "Let me see the building!" Nausea swept over her, and she shook her head, desperate to keep herself from fainting. Three quick breaths and she brought her lips together once more. *Blow out ... God, help me blow out. I need to focus.*

The picture shifted again, and this time Laura could see a partial view of the south tower. Bringing her nose almost to the screen, she began to cry. "Eric! Where are you? ... Call me and tell me you're okay!"

Something moved outside the office. She looked up, and through her tears she saw Josh, standing in the hallway staring at her, his mouth open. He was still in his pajamas, and his eyes looked squinty.

"Mom? What's wrong?" He entered the office and studied her. She'd woken him up. Laura wiped at her eyes and sat back on her heels. Something about the boy's presence instantly restored within her a semblance of normalcy. "Josh, honey, come here." She held out her arms and waited while he crossed the room.

He hugged her, his arms tight around her neck for several seconds. Then he pulled away and looked at the TV screen. "Wow." Once more the image was of the Twin Towers, balls of fire and black smoke still pouring from the buildings. Josh studied the picture for a moment while Laura held her breath. Josh had seen pictures of Manhattan often enough to recognize it. He shifted his gaze to Laura. "Mom, is that New York City?"

Laura gulped and locked eyes with her son; then she dropped to the floor again. She had to tell him; there was no way around it. Besides, the news station had begun to replay the image of the passenger jet slamming into the south tower. "Yes." She reached out and took his small hand in hers. "Airplanes crashed into the buildings, Josh."

He looked at the television again. "Is Dad in there?"

"Well . . ." She couldn't seem to get enough air to talk, but she forced herself to say the words, anyway. "Yes, honey. He's in there somewhere."

"In the . . ." The color drained from Josh's face, and he blinked twice. Again he glanced at Laura. "In the fire? Is that where Dad is?"

"No." Laura shook her head as quickly as she could, short jerky movements as though the more certain she appeared about Eric's fate, the better off he'd somehow be. "No, Daddy's not in the fire. His office is lower than that." Her words sounded unnatural, like someone else was saying them. It was impossible to know if she was telling her son the truth or not. *Where is he, God . . . how come they won't say what floor the fire's on?*

Josh sat down cross-legged on the floor beside Laura. "That's the biggest fire I've ever seen."

"Me too." Laura wanted to scream. She wanted to run around the room and hit the walls, or call someone in New York and ask if Eric was okay. But she had Josh to think about. She pursed her lips once more and blew out two quick times. Another idea hit her. She could call Murphy from the Woodland Hills office and ask if he'd heard from Eric. Her husband was meticulously organized. Murphy's number was bound to be in the desk drawer in Eric's phonebook.

She was on her feet, grabbing the phone from the floor and tearing through the drawer. It had to be here. Her hands trembled less than before as she flipped through the letters to the *M* section. Where is it? Come on . . . Murphy . . . Murphy . . . Murphy.

There it was. Three numbers—one for work, one for the man's cell, and one for home.

"What're you doing?" Josh was watching her, his face nervous.

"Calling Daddy's friend." She managed to keep her voice calm. "He might know where Daddy is."

As quickly as her fingers could move, she tapped out the number and held the phone to her ear. Murphy answered on the second ring. "Hello?"

"Hi . . . this is Laura Michaels."

There was the briefest pause. "Are you watching the news?"

"Yes." Laura fought back the dizziness. "I was talking to Eric when it . . . when the plane hit."

"I'm sorry, Laura." Murphy's voice was stilted, unnatural. The entire conversation, the scenes from the television, all of it felt like it was happening to someone else.

"Have you heard from him? Since it happened, I mean?" As the words left her mouth, she realized how crazy they sounded. Of course Murphy hadn't heard from Eric. The phones had gone out the minute the plane hit the building. Still, she waited for Murphy's response, hoping that somehow he knew something she didn't.

"He hasn't called." Murphy waited a moment. "But he's okay, Laura. I have to believe that."

A flicker of hope ignited in Laura's soul. "How . . . how come?"

"The news said the plane entered at about the seventy-eighth floor. Koppel and Grant's on the sixty-fourth. I'd guess the fire's spread below the crash site, but our guys were down far enough. They should be able to get out."

Laura imagined Eric and Allen and the others from the company rushing for the elevator. Or maybe the elevator wasn't working. If not, then they'd be pushing frantically for the stairwell trying to walk to ground level. The notion was absurd. Sixty-four floors! Eric might be able to handle the climb down, but what about the older men and women who worked that high up. "Eric knows I'm worried. How long would it take him to get out of there?"

"One of the reporters said the evacuation was averaging about one floor every minute. So, I don't know. An hour at least."

"How long's it been?" Laura steadied herself against the desk to keep from falling. The floor beneath her feet felt like it had turned to jelly, the same way it felt the last time a minor earthquake rolled through their area. Laura closed her eyes again to stave off the nausea.

"The plane hit a little after nine." Murphy paused. "It's a quarter past right now."

Laura opened her eyes and took Josh's hand in hers as she did the math. "So sometime around ten o'clock he should be calling me. Is that right?"

Murphy was quiet. "Things are pretty crazy down there, Laura. I'd give him longer than that. Who knows, the entire phone system is probably jammed."

"But he has his cell phone, wouldn't you say? Eric always has his cell."

"Have you tried it?" Murphy sounded tired.

"Yes." Laura felt the room sway. Josh's eyes were wide now, but she couldn't do anything about it. She made a fist with her free hand and pressed it into her stomach, anything to ward off the nausea. This couldn't be happening. All of it seemed like something from a terrible dream. As though any minute she'd wake up and everything would be fine. She remembered Murphy on the other end. "What'd you ask?"

"About Eric's cell phone."

"Oh, right. I tried. The call wouldn't go through."

"So maybe closer to ten you can try it again."

"Good. Good idea. Thanks, Murphy." Laura looked at Josh, but he was watching the TV, his gaze fixed on the terrible pictures. "I gotta go."

"He's all right, Laura."

"Pray, Murphy. Do that for him, will you?" Laura had no idea if Murphy was a praying man, but it didn't matter. Right now she guessed just about everyone in America believed in prayer.

"I'll pray. Call me if you hear anything."

Laura hung up and returned to her spot next to Josh. It didn't matter how she felt or whether she fainted. She needed to get Josh away from the television. Images like the ones that had been flashing across the screen could scar a little boy forever. Especially if Eric . . .

She refused the thought. "Why don't you go get dressed, buddy?"

He nodded absently, never taking his eyes from the TV. "When are they going to put out the fire?"

"They're probably putting it out right now."

He looked at her. "From the inside, you mean?"

"Mmmhmm." Her stomach convulsed. They couldn't possibly have firefighters up that far into the building yet. The fire was clearly raging out of control in both towers. And if they didn't get water on it soon, it would spread to—

"They'll get it out, though, right, Mom? Firemen always get the fires out, don't they?"

It was the first time Laura had considered the idea. Firefighters would have water sources on the ground, but seventy floors up? Eighty or ninety? What could they possibly do to douse a fire that size so far up in the air? Josh was waiting for an answer. Laura still had hold of his hand, and she squeezed it gently. "Yes, son. They'll get it out." She leaned forward, and against everything in her, she turned off the television. "Daddy'll call in an hour or so and tell us all about it."

Laura walked Josh to his room and helped him find a pair of shorts and a T-shirt. The whole time he asked questions about firefighters and mile-long hoses and ladders that could reach up to the sky. She did her best to answer him, but she was haunted by the most awful idea.

What if the fire had spread through the stairwell? What if Eric and the others were trapped, unable to get out? And what if the flames had spread to the floors beneath the crash site. Even the sixty-fourth floor? What if an hour passed and she didn't hear from Eric?

God . . . stop my terrible thoughts. Please . . . Help me believe that Eric's okay. Be with him, guide him down the stairs and back home, Lord. I beg You . . .

Then quiet words came from someplace deep in her soul: *Lean not on your own understanding, daughter . . .*

But the words were lost in a fog of panicky questions. What if they couldn't get water up that high? What if . . .

The list would work its way through her mind and then start over again. What if the fire had spread through the stairwell? What if Eric and the others were trapped, unable to get out? And finally the worst question of all. The one that—as she made oatmeal for Josh—made her gasp for breath every minute or so.

What if she never saw Eric again?

TEN

The orders were given just before the second plane hit. All units respond to the World Trade Center except Engine 57 and Ladder 96. Those two units would be on standby, in case a fire broke out somewhere else in the city. Jake and the rest of the men at his station were frustrated about the order from the beginning.

But Captain Maxwell was outraged. He got on the phone immediately and called headquarters. "I don't care what the orders are, it's crazy to keep us here." He paced the length of the station, shouting into the receiver. "The people in that building need every available firefighter on site if we're going to save lives!"

After the south tower was struck, Maxwell became downright furious. Jake watched the man storm across the kitchen, into the dining room, out toward the front room, and back again.

Jake understood completely. For him to sit by and watch a fire of any kind was like trying not to breathe. He sat beside Larry, his back stiff, his feet tapping out an urgent rhythm. This was the worst fire New York had ever seen. No, it was bigger than that. Jake stared at the TV screen and the thick black smoke bursting from the World Trade Center. It was one of the worst disasters in the nation's history. Jake knew the numbers; they all did. At any given time there could be as many as twenty thousand people in the World Trade Center towers. If every firefighter in a twenty-mile radius showed up at the scene, they'd still be severely stretched for manpower.

It was all he and Larry and the others could do to obey the orders. But they had to wait until the call came in, so that's what they did. Jake and Larry and the other men—everyone from both the night and day shift—sat at the dining room picnic tables watching the unfolding terror on TV and waiting.

Maxwell was still pacing the floor, talking on the phone, yelling at someone from headquarters. His language was worse than Jake had heard it in a while. "Listen to me, I don't care. If someone doesn't call us out, I'll send the men myself. This is our city's single worst mo–"

Jake tuned the man out. He'd called Jamie twice and left brief messages both times, saying he'd try her again in a few minutes. She was probably at the gym with Sierra, but she should've been home by now. He slipped away from the table, snapped open his cell phone, and hit redial.

Two rings . . . three . . . four. The answering machine clicked on, and Jamie's voice sounded over the line. At the tone Jake cleared his throat. "Hi . . . it's me again. Looks like we'll get the call here pretty soon, honey. Everything's going to be okay, Jamie. I love you and I'll be home tonight, I promise. God's with me. Oh yeah, and my angel. Can't forget about him." He paused, hoping she'd walk through the door of their home any minute and pick up the phone. His throat was thick, but he kept his voice upbeat. "So, I'll see you later, all right? And, sweetheart, tell Sierra I love her."

He snapped the phone shut, slipped it in his pants pocket, and returned to his spot at the table next to Larry. The pictures on TV showed the score. The fire was getting worse. Jake leaned close to his friend and whispered, "We've gotta get out there."

"I know." Larry glanced at him. "Did you get hold of Jamie?"

"No." Jake swallowed hard. "Left a better message this time, though." He tapped his fingers on the worn wood table. "What about Sue? Did you call her?"

"Yep. She's watching it at home." Larry looked back at the television and squinted. "Scared to death."

"Wherever Jamie is, I'm sure she's panicking. Probably tearing across the island to get home. Fires scare her anyway. This one . . ." Jake shot a look at the screen. "This one will terrify her."

Larry was quiet for a moment. "Hey, JB . . ." He narrowed his gaze and kept it locked on the television. "Ever think about how hot jet fuel burns?"

"Yeah." A close-up of the fire flashed on the TV. Jake took a swig of his coffee and grimaced. "A hundred times since the first plane hit."

"What do you think those buildings can take, you know, heat-wise?"

Jake turned to Larry once more. "I'm trying not to think about it. Jamie's the worrier in our family."

"I don't know." Larry shook his head. "I've never seen a fire like that in my life. We wouldn't be breathing if we weren't worried." He looked at Jake again. "What about you, JB . . . aren't you even a little scared?"

"No." Jake clenched his teeth. His answer was quick, automatic. "My family's been fighting fires since before I was born. Fear isn't part of it."

"You called Jamie three times in five minutes." Larry lowered his head so the others couldn't hear him. "Come on, Jake, be honest with me, man. I mean, I want to get out there and fight the thing too. But I'm thinking about it this time."

Nearly a minute passed while Jake processed the idea. It wasn't fear, was it, this thing he was feeling? But then no one in three generations of Bryan firefighters had ever faced a fire like this one. A sigh came from deep within Jake. "All right." He folded his hands so tightly his knuckles turned white. They were cold and clammy. "I feel it. I keep asking myself why this fire scares me. I'm not afraid to die, so what is it?" His hands trembled just barely as he reached into his back pocket and pulled out his wallet. He flipped it open. There was a picture of Sierra from a few months ago, and one of Jamie and him taken last summer. With careful fingers he traced the outline of her face and then Sierra's. "It's this. That's what scares me."

"Yep." Larry nodded slow and deliberate. "I know."

"Back when I first joined the department, I never thought about the size of a fire or whether I was in danger. You didn't either. We didn't have wives and little girls back then." Jake returned the wallet and let his eyes meet Larry's. "But now ... we have so much to lose."

Larry didn't say anything, and for a moment they both were quiet. Jake remembered something. Six months ago Sierra pasted a photo of herself onto a piece of paper and then carefully printed her name beneath it. "Here, Daddy ... this is for you," she'd told him. "For your desk at work."

But Jake's work didn't require a desk. So he'd taped the photo complete with her printed name onto the inside of his helmet. The picture had been with him, against the top of his head, every call he'd taken since then. A reminder of why he had to be careful, why he couldn't afford a single mistake on the job.

It was like he'd just told Larry. He had too much to lose.

Larry broke the moment by jabbing an elbow into Jake's ribs. "Okay, JB, sorry. Enough of that." He managed a crooked, determined grin. "No worries about the fire today, friend. You watch my back, and I'll watch yours. We'll put out some flames, save a few lives, and get back in time for dinner."

It was their motto, the thing they'd said to each other every time they'd taken a call together. No worries. Put out some flames ...

save a few lives ... back in time for dinner. Jake returned the grin and settled his gaze on the TV.

The image switched to a harried reporter who was shouting above the sirens and chaos coming from the streets of lower Manhattan. The Port Authority had closed all bridges and tunnels leading into New York City. "The latest reports say that the attacks on the World Trade Center were definitely intentional." The man's gaze darted to a sheet of paper in his hand. "President Bush is calling it a terrorist act of unequaled proportion and—"

Suddenly, Maxwell burst into the room, his eyes wide. "Okay, men, it's our turn. Both units to the south tower. There's a control post in the lobby. We'll report there and be assigned a floor." He paused. "None of the elevators are working. We'll be walking up, so pace yourself. At this point everyone above the seventy-eighth floor is trapped and needs assistance."

The moment Maxwell stopped speaking, Jake and seventeen men seated around the two picnic tables snapped into action, racing for their respective trucks, grabbing helmets and doubling up on nearly every seat so the men from both shifts would fit. Jake stared at the picture of Sierra taped to the inside of his helmet, then he put it firmly on his head and squeezed into the backseat of Engine 57, between Larry and a guy from the night crew.

God ... be with us ... get us home safely.

I will be with you, son, always ... always even until the end.

The words were part of a verse, one Jake had memorized years ago. They flashed in his mind as the sirens on both trucks pierced the air and joined those sounding across the city. Jake steeled himself for the task ahead, for the horrific sights he would no doubt see.

This is the big one, God ... we're gonna need You.

Always, son ... I'm with you always even until the end.

Jake clenched his fists and stared at the buildings as they rushed past. He always prayed en route to a fire. It was something that came as naturally as stepping into his turnouts or finding his place on the truck. Prayer was simply part of going to a fire. And always God's peace and strength and assurance came as he prayed, giving Jake an invisible armor to go along with his uniform.

But rarely did a Scripture flash in his mind.

They rounded a corner and Jake held on. The streets were empty except for emergency vehicles, so they were making better time than usual. He closed his eyes for a moment. The Scripture was from the book of Matthew, the place where Jake had been doing his morning Bible study for the past few weeks. Comforting words, words filled with promise. Jesus would be with him always even until the end of the age.

It was the last part that seemed somehow more profound.

The Lord would be with him until the end.

Jake shifted and gazed out the windshield of the fire truck. Profound or maybe prophetic. The truck raced through an intersection, and Jake shook off the strange thoughts. He was psyching himself out, imagining warnings where none lay. This was a bad fire, but it was still a fire. And fighting fires was something he was trained to do. The dangers were the same as with any other call, weren't they? He glanced at Larry sitting beside him, but his friend's eyes were glazed over—the way they always were when he was mentally preparing himself for the call.

What had Larry said earlier about the temperature of jet fuel and the strength of the World Trade Center? Jake blinked and the questions disappeared. There was no point worrying. He had a job to do, and his body pulsed with adrenaline over the prospect. He couldn't wait to get it done. They were two blocks away when Maxwell—who was sitting in the front passenger seat of the fire truck—turned around and briefed them on the scene.

"Jet fuel shot through the elevator shaft a few seconds after both crashes." He hesitated. "Some folks fell to their deaths. Others jumped. Many of them were on fire. Falling bodies have already claimed the lives of some of our men, so watch your step."

Jake swallowed hard and resisted the urge to ask which men. It didn't matter. FDNY was a fraternity, and all of them were connected in one way or another. The losses they'd suffer individually and as a group that day would be too great to fathom. Especially with the fire still out of control.

They sped the remaining distance, turned onto West Street, and pulled up alongside another engine. Maxwell's warning could not have prepared Jake for the scene at the base of the south tower. Bodies were still falling from the upper floors, and Jake caught the expression of terror on a woman as she plummeted from the building. He looked away just as a thud echoed across the street.

The thud of her body hitting the ground.

God . . . it's a nightmare. Help those people . . . please.

He stared at the street around them and gritted his teeth. It looked like something from a battlefield. Bodies lay strewn along the pavement, firefighters scrambled in a dozen different directions, and burn victims on stretchers were being carried to an endless line of waiting ambulances and paramedics.

Anger joined the emotions raging in Jake's soul. What type of monster would orchestrate mass murder on this level? And how dare they take aim at the heart of New York City? Jake and the others piled out of the truck, grabbed air tanks, and jogged toward the lobby of the south tower.

"Watch the sky!" Maxwell shouted over his shoulder.

The men did as he said, and Jake was struck by how macabre the moment was. With so many lives at stake in the building and outside it, the jumpers had become one more kind of hazardous debris. They could do nothing to help the falling people, so they directed all their effort to avoid them. Jake gritted his teeth and jogged with the others across the street.

On the way he nearly tripped over something bulky, something he first assumed was a piece of the building. Not until he was just past it did he stop, turn around, and stare once more. The thing he'd almost fallen over was not a windowsill or a chunk of debris. It was a body, burned completely beyond recognition. In the span of a single second, Jake glanced around. He couldn't count the number of bodies lining the streets.

"Come on, JB, there's work to do." Larry was a few steps in front of him.

Jake inhaled sharply through his nose and kept walking. "Right behind you." Certainly Larry had seen the same thing he'd seen. But Larry was right. They could take care of the dead later. Right now their job was in the building, not outside it. Both of their units entered the lobby and reported in at the command post. Battalion chiefs were manning the station using chalkboards to keep track of men assigned to various floors.

Maxwell stepped up and spoke for the group. "Engine 57, Ladder 96 here. Where do you want us?"

Jake could hear the captain talking with his peers, making decisions about where they would be assigned. "We need a staging area on the sixty-first floor. We think one of the elevators there is working, and we want to use it to transport victims to the ground. Other units are on their way up to the crash site, so have your men establish sixty-one. No elevators are being used to go up, so you'll have to walk."

"Got it." Maxwell nodded and moved the group across the lobby. There were so many firefighters taking and giving orders,

Jake had to strain to hear his captain. "Everyone have air?" He gave a quick look at the line of men in front of him. Each of them had the mandatory tank, and several of them had two. A second one was optional. The weight of two would make it harder to climb, but an extra air tank could also save a firefighter's life.

Jake took two.

"Let's split up. It'll be easier to stay together if something happens." He motioned to the other captain on duty—Captain Hisel. "Take the ladder company and look for victims along the way. Have your men take any victims back to the street and the waiting ambulances." He looked at Jake and Larry. "I'll take the engine crew." Maxwell started toward the main stairwell. "Follow me."

Inside was a narrow set of stairs that would eventually lead them to the sixty-first floor. A quiet stream of people, their faces etched in shock and terror, streamed down one side of the steps. Company presidents and lowly assistants were on equal footing here as each of them continued moving, desperate to escape the burning building.

Maxwell turned around. "They want us to average one flight a minute." He leveled an intense gaze at them. "I say we average two."

Jake and Larry were behind Maxwell, and the group of them began attacking the stairs. Most of them were in excellent condition. Even with their equipment, a flight of stairs every thirty seconds would be manageable. At least for the first twenty floors or so.

At the first landing Jake realized something he hadn't before. The building was vibrating. Not badly, but it was moving some all the same, as though the entire hundred-story structure was shuddering in response to the inferno raging far above them. Of all the times he'd been in one of the World Trade Center towers, Jake had never felt the building tremble. He blinked and focused on his feet. The building could handle that type of heat, couldn't it? They kept walking.

Two floors, three, four . . . six . . . eight . . .

Jake's mind began to wander. Steel became compromised at a certain point, but in the confusion of the stairwell, Jake couldn't remember what temperature that happened at. Five thousand degrees? Ten thousand? And exactly how hot did jet fuel burn? Had anyone thought to protect these towers against that type of heat?

Once more Jake dismissed the thought and focused his attention on the people heading down the stairs. He wanted to be available if any of them had breathing trouble or needed help. He caught fragments of their conversations.

"Frank . . . hang in there, we're almost out." It was a woman, her eyes wide as she kept pace behind a heavyset man with a red face.

Maxwell heard the conversation. "What floor you people from?"

"Fifty-two." The woman stopped even with Maxwell. She put her hand on the heavy man and frowned. "I'm worried about Frank. He has heart trouble."

"I'm fine." The man was short of breath, but he kept walking. He waved back at Maxwell and the rest of them. "God bless you people . . . There's hundreds more upstairs. Don't worry about me."

A cry came from somewhere above them. "Keep moving, people, please!"

The worried woman and the heavyset man began walking again, and the woman yelled over her shoulder. "How many more floors?"

"Eight." Maxwell moved ahead. "Keep walking."

Jake tried to calculate what they'd find when they reached the sixty-first floor. The building had been burning for about half an hour now. Seconds counted for any critical victims at or above the crash site. And if the stairwells were cut off at the seventy-eighth floor, what did that mean for the people trapped above it?

Again, Jake focused on the matter at hand. Ten floors . . . eleven . . . twelve . . . thirteen. They were making great time, taking three floors a minute. The tanks were heavy on Jake's back, and he was sucking air, feeling the exertion of the climb. *God, get us up there in time to help those people . . . please. And keep us safe too, Lord. We're going to need it.* He remembered the line he and Larry liked to say on the way to a fire. Their motto. *No worries. Put out some flames . . . save a few lives . . . back in time for dinner.*

It had been true every other time they'd taken a call. Jake could only pray it would be true today.

ELEVEN

SEPTEMBER 11, 2001, 9:22 A.M.

Eric Michaels could feel the building trembling.

It had started twenty minutes earlier with the explosion somewhere above him, a blast that had knocked Eric and everyone in the outside hallway to their knees. Immediately, his phone had gone dead, and at the same moment, Allen raced up to him. Together they ran into the main area where dozens of people were screaming at once. What had earlier been merely grave concern and alarm was now full-fledged panic.

"We've been hit! We've been—"

"A plane . . . another plane! A plane went through the—"

"It was coming right at us, then it disappea—"

The voices had shouted simultaneously, and it had been impossible to make sense of any of them. What Eric and Allen had been able to get was the obvious. A second plane had crashed—into their building this time—and they needed to get out fast.

"Elevators are out!" Someone had screamed the news, and a mass of people headed for the stairwells. There were three in the building, and each of them would eventually connect with the lobby. Eric considered joining the group. After all, the battery on his cell phone was dead, and Laura would be waiting for his call. Probably frantic by now. TV news would be reporting that a second plane had crashed into the south tower, and she'd assume he was somehow in the middle of the carnage.

But just as he'd turned toward the stairs, someone grabbed his sleeve. Eric spun around and found himself inches from Allen. The man's brows were lowered almost over his eyelids. "Where are you going?"

Eric glanced at the stairs and then back at Allen. "We need to get out of here."

"There's no hurry, Eric. The stairs will be packed with people." Allen cast a quick look back toward the office of Koppel and Grant. "I have three foreign transactions that have to be made now. Before the morning's up."

Eric turned and stared at Allen. The man was crazy. "Can't you feel it?" His words ran together, and he had to fight to keep from jerking away and running for the stairs. Running for his life. "The place is shaking, Allen. We need to go."

"Look." Anger flashed in Allen's eyes. "Those crazy terrorists have done enough damage—they aren't going to ruin a couple hundred-thousand-dollar purchases on top of it."

Eric's heart raced. He looked from Allen to the crowd at the stairwell and back at his boss again. It would take five minutes, ten even, for the crowd of people to file into the stairwell. Maybe Allen was right. "Okay." He took off toward the office, and Allen fell in step beside him. "But let's make it fast."

They rounded the corner through the door of Koppel and Grant and ran back to Allen's office. Allen worked the keyboard while Eric read from a handful of files. Ten minutes into the transaction, Hank Walden, one of their top financial managers, stuck his head in the office. "Guys, they've ordered an evacuation." The man's eyes were wide, his breathing short and ragged. "Everyone has to go."

Eric was about to say something when Allen held his hand up. "There's no smoke on this floor." He kept his eyes on the screen. "We'll be finished in thirty minutes, forty at the most. We'll lose thousands if I wait on this."

"Sir . . ." Walden exchanged a desperate look with Eric. "We don't have a choice, sir. The building's in trouble."

Allen waved him off without looking up. "This is the World Trade Center. The building's fine." He shot a hurried look at Walden. "Go! We'll be right behind you."

With a final terrified glance at Eric, Walden disappeared, his footsteps echoing down the hallway and out into the main corridor.

Eric stared at Allen. "Can't it wait, sir? No one else in New York City is working right now."

Allen only pointed to the files in Eric's hands and kept typing. Ten more minutes passed and Eric felt something change, something in the way the building trembled. Maybe it was his imagination, but the shaking seemed worse, more noticeable. Eric glanced out the window at the chaos reigning six hundred feet below. Buildings like this one were on rollers, weren't they? That could explain the movement—especially with the inferno blazing above them. But what if that wasn't the reason the building was trembling? Sixty-four floors was an awful long way up.

Eric shuddered.

"Sir . . ." He set the files on the desk and stood. "I'm going. I have a family to think about."

Allen stopped typing and gave him a sad, disappointed frown. "I thought you were committed."

Eric hated the way his boss's comment made him feel weak. He gave a single shake of his head. "I am committed, sir. I think we should both go. The building doesn't feel right."

This time Allen sat back, crossed his arms, and directed his gaze at Eric. "You're not the man I thought you were, Eric." He mumbled something under his breath as he looked back at the screen. Then without making eye contact with Eric again, he waved his hand. "Go . . . join the others. I'll finish it by myself."

Eric didn't waste time giving Allen a response. He turned and raced down the hallway, hurrying through the maze of desks and partition boards as he made for the stairs. Along the way he found a man in his early twenties typing frantically.

"What're you doing? The building's being evacuated."

"No one ordered an evacuation." The man's fingers kept moving. "I'm on a deadline."

"Listen, pal." Eric's tone was frantic. "Yes, they have ordered an evacuation. The fire's headed this way." Eric glanced at the wall, looking for the place where the computer was plugged in. The outlet was hidden by the man's desk, and Eric straightened and shouted at the man. "Get out!"

The man stopped typing and sent a vicious look at Eric. "It's my life. Leave me alone. I get a bonus if I finish this thing today." He pursed his lips. "I'm not letting some fire twenty floors up stop me, you got that?"

Eric huffed and spun around, running once more for the stairs. Fine. If the guy wanted to stay, what was that to Eric? He reached the stairwell a minute later and yanked the door open. The place was empty, and he took the steps at a full trot. At the fifty-third floor he began seeing firemen trudging their way up.

"Anyone else up there?" one firefighter asked him.

"My boss . . . he has a few transactions to finish." Eric huffed, trying to catch his breath. "And a crazy guy on a deadline. Won't leave his desk."

The firefighters nodded and continued up. They were breathing hard, carrying what looked like fifty pounds of equipment each and refusing to slow down in their quest to reach the fire. Eric resumed his pace, and at the forty-third floor, he caught up with the line of people, all moving steadily down the stairs one flight at a time. That's when he noticed something.

The shaking was getting worse; it wasn't his imagination.

He could hear windows rattling beyond the stairwell, feel a subtle sway from above. Eric kept up with the group, wishing they could walk faster. What did the building's movement mean? Were helicopters dropping water on the fire? Or were the flames enough to shake a hundred floors of cement and steel? Whatever the cause, Eric didn't want to think about it. There was nothing he could do, nothing any of them could do but keep taking the stairs.

One step at a time.

The businesspeople making their way down were orderly and calm. Probably in shock, Eric figured. He knew none of them, and the people from Koppel and Grant were probably twenty floors below him by now. Eric tried to draw a deep breath but couldn't. The air in the stairwell was hot and thick and stale, tinged with a sense of barely controlled panic. Every time they cleared a landing, Eric would glance at the number on the door.

Thirty-one . . . thirty . . . twenty-nine . . . twenty-eight . . .

Six more floors and then it happened. Eric tripped on a briefcase left in the stairwell and tumbled face first down five steps. A piercing pain stabbed at his ankle, and he struggled to right himself. At that instant a hand reached out for his. Eric grabbed it, and as he worked to get his feet beneath him, a firefighter's helmet fell against his chest.

People were making their way down the stairs, still inching past Eric as he let the firefighter pull him to a sitting position. The man's helmet was near Eric's feet now, and he took hold of it. But just as he went to hand it back to the firefighter, something caught his attention, something inside the helmet. Eric peered at it and his heart skipped a beat.

It was a photograph of a little girl, four or five years old. And beneath the photo, in a child's printing, was written the name "Sierra." Both were taped firmly to the inside of the helmet. Eric felt a lump in his throat as he leaned up to return it. With people still making their way past him, Eric locked eyes on the firefighter and felt his breath catch in his throat.

The fireman was staring at him too. And now that Eric could see the man clearly, the reason was obvious. The two of them could've been twins. Identical twins, even. Eric blinked hard. Was he seeing things? He'd heard of strangers having an uncanny resemblance. But he'd never seen anyone who looked this much like him. Exactly like him. Not ever. The short dark hair, square jaw, high cheekbones, blue eyes. Even their builds were the same.

Looking at the firefighter was like looking in a mirror.

Eric's mouth hung open, and he couldn't look away. So far the entire incident had taken five seconds—more than either of them had. Eric rose to his feet, his eyes still glued to the firefighter's. "Thank you." He handed the helmet out toward the man.

"That's . . . that's my little girl." The firefighter took his helmet back from Eric and set it on his head. "Better keep walking."

"Thanks . . ." Eric wanted to say more. He wanted to thank the man for helping him up after his fall, for risking his life for all of them, for doing what he was doing, even though it might cost him everything.

Including the chance to see his little Sierra again.

But the moment passed, and the firefighter nodded one last time as he continued his climb up into the building. Eric worked his way back into the stream of people heading down. His ankle hurt, but he could do nothing about it now. They had to get out of the shaking building.

Fifteen . . . fourteen . . . thirteen . . .

Eric moved down the steps, but his mind was back on the twenty-second floor, back with the firefighter and the strange resemblance they shared. Something about the man's expression and the picture of his little girl, Sierra, seemed permanently etched in Eric's mind. It stayed with him, haunted him, made him certain that as long as he lived, he would remember forever the child's face, the way her picture smiled at him from the inside of the firefighter's helmet.

He reached floor number twelve . . . eleven . . . ten . . .

What was it he'd seen in the firefighter's eyes? A raw determination, an intense sort of focus to reach the victims on the upper floors regardless of the danger? Yes, that was it. And more than that, a peace. A peace that Eric knew nothing of.

Nine . . . eight . . . seven . . .

Eric's left ankle was numb now, and his heart raced within him from fear and exertion. But none of that mattered. The only thing he could think about was Sierra and her firefighter father. For a moment he thought about praying for the man. But then, what good would that do? The firefighter was going up, heading straight toward the inferno. And the building was shaking more now than before.

He won't come out, will he, God? He's going to die, and Sierra won't ever see her daddy again. For what? The people upstairs are probably dead by now, anyway. Smoke and heat and fumes. Who could possibly live through the nightmare that had to be happening from the crash site up.

Eric stopped moving for three heartbeats. Maybe he could run up and find the man, grab him, and insist he come down with the other sensible people. That way they could talk about their resemblance and compare notes. Were they related somehow? Was the man a distant cousin who had been born with identical features as Eric? If the firefighter continued making his way upstairs, Eric was almost certain he'd never know, never see the man again.

But there were too many people in the stairwell, and he had no choice but to keep moving down with the others. Six floors left, five . . . The shaking was getting worse now, bending the stairwell as though it were made of rubber.

"Get us out of here!" one man shouted from three floors up. "The whole thing's coming down."

The whole thing? Even with the shaking, that was an idea Eric hadn't considered. Could the World Trade Center actually collapse? An ominous creaking came from somewhere in the core of the building as Eric rounded a corner onto the next floor. *God help me! Just four more sets of stairs and I'll be out!*

He moved as quickly as the crowd in front of him would allow, but even as he did he thought one more time of the firefighter and the little girl who obviously mattered so much to him. Almost at the same time another thought hit him. Why wasn't he worried about his own child, the boy he had never made time for? Josh had to know about this by now. And what about Laura? If the World Trade Center collapsed on top of him, he'd die without having told them the truth—that he *did* love them, even if he never showed it.

Never said it.

Sorrow filled his heart as he moved his feet one agonizingly slow step at a time. What had he done? He'd put success and position and money ahead of the people in his life. Laura, the woman he'd loved from the moment he first saw her. And Josh, the child who looked so much like her. The truth was, he didn't even know the boy.

When had he changed? Had it really been the loss of their tiny daughter? Was that when he began putting all his efforts into work and almost none of them into his life at home? He trudged down another seven steps to the next landing, and suddenly he knew. Of course that was when it had happened. He'd made a decision in the deepest place of his soul never again to depend on God or anyone else. God would let him down and people would die. The only thing he could count on was himself, and that was the way he'd lived every day since.

The air around him grew thicker, more oppressive, and the building was moving so much he could barely keep his balance. He thought about the last conversation he'd had with Laura. For the life of him he couldn't remember whether he'd even told her he loved her.

People all around him were screaming now, pushing more than before and desperate to clear the building. Eric took the stairs as quickly as he could, but still he felt like he was moving in a kind of painful slow motion. One step . . . another . . . another . . .

The building was going to collapse on top of him, and he'd be buried alive . . . everything he'd done to make a success of himself had been for nothing, because now he was about to die, and Laura and Josh would never know how he really felt, how sorry he was for all he'd denied them.

Another step . . . another . . .

The building groaned and lurched, and in that instant Eric had a thought, a notion that seemed to come almost on its own volition. As long as he drew breath he could still pray. A horrific roar sounded from somewhere far above him, but Eric only worked his way down the stairs. And as he did, he begged God for something he never would have asked for prior to the disaster that morning.

A second chance.

* * * *

Jake and Larry and Maxwell jogged up the last thirty floors. They were gasping for breath as they pushed their way onto the sixty-first floor, the site where they'd been told to set up a staging area. There by the elevator bank were twelve other firefighters, each working over victims sprawled out on the floor. Several men—including one Jake had worked with before—were setting up IV bags and giving shots of morphine.

"What can we do?" Maxwell lurched ahead with Jake and Larry behind him.

"They told us the elevators were working." One of the men looked up, his face weary. "We sent two men and five victims down eight minutes ago. So far nothing's come back."

"You mean the car stopped?" Jake came up alongside a woman whose arms and torso were burned nearly to the bone. He felt her neck for a pulse, but it was weak and thready. She was a pretty woman, in her mid-twenties with a wedding ring. Somewhere, her husband was probably crazy with worry about her, the same way Jamie was no doubt feeling about him.

"Hey, buddy." Larry came up beside him. "She's not going to make it."

"I know." Futility welled up inside Jake. The disaster that morning was clearly an MCI—the code firefighters used to define a mass casualty incident. Any MCI meant that resources and energy had to be saved for victims who still had a chance. If a person was mortally wounded, firefighters were supposed to move on to the next victim.

Jake stared at the dying woman, sucked in a quick breath, and held it. He had trained for this type of work, but a disaster like the one they were fighting was so much bigger than anything they could've prepared for. After hiking up sixty-one floors, Jake was exhausted, and now that they'd arrived, there was so little they could do.

Maxwell was still asking about the elevator.

"The building's shaking too much to keep an elevator car moving right," one of the men answered. "My guess is we're waiting for nothing. We'll need to carry these people down."

"What about the crash site?" Maxwell too had positioned himself near one of the victims and was pulling a morphine kit from his pack.

"Seventy-eight has a crew working it right now. They're talking to us on the radio. It's . . . it's worse than anything they've ever seen."

Jake stood and counted the victims. Eighteen, and just fifteen firefighters. "There're more men on the way up. Let's get the ones we can help onto our backs and start down again."

"He's right." Larry straightened and stood next to Jake. "By the time we get everyone loaded up, the others will be here."

A cry came from the burned woman, the one on the floor near Jake. "Please . . . help me."

Jake was on his knees at her side instantly. The building shuddered and lurched, shaking so much that his words vibrated when he spoke. "I'm h–h–here . . . we're getting help as fast as we can."

The woman was quiet a moment, in and out of consciousness. She moaned again. "Pray. Someone . . . pray with me . . . please."

Without looking for approval, Jake took hold of the woman's fingers—the only part of her arms not burned. "Come on, Larry, get down here with me."

Larry dropped to the woman's other side and took hold of her knee. "Go ahead."

Around them firefighters struggled to load victims on their backs, but as they did, the tower groaned and creaked even louder than before. Jake looked up, his eyes darting from the ceiling to the walls and back up again. He understood what the sound meant. The steel supports were melting, giving way more with each passing second.

A shattering sound pierced the room like a gunshot, and everyone jumped. The noise was followed by another, and another. Jake shot a glance toward the noise. Windows were breaking, popping out from the force of the twisting structure.

Jake glanced around the room at the others. The reality of what was about to happen was clear to every one of the firefighters there. The tower was coming down. They were sixty-one floors off the ground and about to be buried beneath tons of cement, steel, and burning jet fuel.

"Larry . . ." Jake locked eyes with his friend. They were still kneeling on the floor on either side of the burned young woman. "We're not gonna make it, buddy. Not this time."

"Nope." Larry's face was pale and he bit his lip. His voice was a choked whisper. "I love you, JB. You've been like a brother."

"You too. I never thought . . ." Jake's voice cracked. "I'm . . . I'm gonna miss my girls."

"We can't think like that. They'll be with us soon enough, right?" Larry's eyes welled up. "Until then I'll still be watching your back."

"Right." Jake tried to sort through his feelings. Fear, anxiety, but most of all a deep sadness. Because he'd never know Jamie's kiss again, never get lost in her eyes. And because he wasn't going to give Sierra her horsey ride that night, after all. He dropped his head, nearly overcome. *What about Your promise, God? What about Jamie's soul?* He let the thought pass. "If I could . . . if I could have one more day with them."

The building lurched. Jake looked at the other firefighters. They were wide-eyed, but still they went about their business, voices calm, loading patients on their backs, and operating on a sort of automatic pilot—the result of training that would have them working the rescue as long as they drew breath.

But none of them were here with their best friend, the way Jake was. Another loud creaking sounded above them.

"Hey." Larry reached across the woman and gripped Jake's shoulder. "I'll meet you on the other side." His hands shook. "Look for me, okay?"

"Okay." Jake's heart raced, and he ordered himself not to run for his life. There was no point now, anyway. And if he was going to die, he wanted to do it here, huddled over a victim, right beside his best friend.

The woman between them on the floor moaned again. "Pray. P–p–pray . . ."

Prayer.

Yes, that's exactly what they needed. The building was swaying harder now. They had seconds, a minute at best. Jake gripped Larry's arm so they were linked together, forming an arc over the burned woman. "God, this is our most desperate hour. We beg You to be kind and merciful, swift and sure. Bring us home safely where we can live with You forever."

"Jake . . ." Maxwell moved closer and hunched near the feet of the woman. He had an unconscious young man over his shoulders. "I . . . I don't know much about Jesus."

Jake opened his eyes and stared at his captain. The man was gruff and seasoned, a weathered veteran with the attitude of a street fighter and the mouth of an angry sailor. Jake had never considered inviting the man to church, never dreamed of talking to him about prayer, let alone Jesus.

But here the need was painfully obvious, and Maxwell wanted answers in a hurry.

"Jesus is the Son of God." Jake's voice was strong, and it filled the area near the elevators. "He died for you. For me. He's alive now in heaven," Jake caught Larry's gaze and held it, "making a place for everyone who believes in Him."

Maxwell was nodding. "I want that. What do I need to do? Tell me quick . . ."

"Pray with me." Jake looked around the room. "Any of you who want Jesus now, pray with me." He closed his eyes and ignored the sadness, ignored the images of Jamie and Sierra and the home they shared together. Instead, he concentrated on the prayer . . . the last prayer he would pray this side of heaven. "Lord, I'm sorry for the things I've done that have kept me from You."

Around the room, hurried voices joined Maxwell's as the prayer was repeated. Jake pushed on, his voice stronger with each word.

"I believe You are the Son of God, and I want Your gift of salvation. I need a Savior."

In unison, both the conscious victims and the firefighters repeated Jake's words. Some were already Christians, men Jake had seen at church or prayer services over the years. But in these, their final moments, there were no other words any of them would rather be saying.

Jake was yelling now, wanting to be heard above the sounds coming from the building. "I believe You're preparing a place for me ..." From not far above them, a roar began to build until it sounded like a thousand freight trains headed straight for them. Jake squeezed Larry's arm and hoped that somehow the next life would offer him a window to the one here. That way he could at least see Jamie and Sierra, pray for them, and watch them live their lives. Even if he could never hold them again. The deafening noise was too loud to be heard over, but Jake continued anyway. "A place in heaven ... where we'll be together even this very d—"

The ceiling collapsed on top of them, and Jake began to tumble, his arm still linked with Larry's. A crushing feeling wrapped itself around Jake and sucked the air from him. He could still feel Larry, still sense his presence beside him as they fell, but the roar was suffocating now, and darkness smothered them.

Then slowly, gradually, the darkness gave way to light. The most brilliant, peaceful light Jake had ever seen. His last thought was not about sadness or terror or loss of any kind. Rather it was a prayer. That one day, Jamie would believe. Because he could already feel the place where he was headed, already see it somehow. It was a land so amazing, so full of love and goodness and beauty that Jamie would want to go tomorrow if only she knew.

Yes, she had to believe. God had assured him of that, hadn't He? And that final knowing was enough to help Jake let go, enough to help him give himself over to the light that lay ahead of him. Enough to believe that one day this long good-bye would be over and they'd be together again. Not just for a day or a year or a lifetime.

But forever.

TWELVE

Jamie had no idea that the country was under attack.

She had taken the nine o'clock step-aerobics class at the Staten Island Fitness Center, and at one minute after ten, she flung a towel around her neck, headed into the hallway and down the stairs toward the lobby. This was all part of Jamie's routine. Work out from nine to ten, head through the lobby to the locker room, take a shower, and pick up Sierra. Then the two of them would go to the park and spend an hour playing before going home for lunch.

But that morning, the moment she stepped foot in the lobby she stopped short. People filled the place, all of them gathered around a single television set anchored to one of the walls adjacent to the snack stand. Jamie couldn't see the picture from where she stood.

A woman with a pair of tennis shoes in her hands broke away from the cluster of people and headed toward the showers. Her eyes were damp.

"Excuse me . . ." Jamie stepped in front of her. A terrible fear filled her throat, and she could barely voice her question. She searched the woman's face. "What's happening?"

The woman stared at her, disbelief etched in the lines on her forehead. "Don't you know?"

"Know what?"

"Terrorists attacked us. It happened an hour ago. The World Trade Center buildings are on fire. The Pentagon too."

Jamie's head began to spin. Why hadn't anyone stopped the aerobics class? And if the World Trade Center was on fire, then Jake—Jamie forced herself to think straight. "Terrorists? Was it a bomb?"

"No." The woman looked almost afraid to give Jamie the details. "They hijacked three planes. Flew two of them into the World Trade Center, one of them into the Pentagon." The woman pointed at the television. "It's all happening live right now." She shook her head. "I have to get home. My husband works on the fifteenth floor of the north tower, and I haven't talked to him since . . ."

121

Jamie was no longer listening. She sprinted across the lobby and found a place near the back of the crowd of exercisers. There it was in all its horrifying reality. Both of the Twin Towers were on fire, the top thirds of each building were engulfed in fire and smoke.

Airplanes had done this? Terrorists had flown them into the buildings on purpose? They'd taken control of the planes and crashed into the buildings? She gripped her waist and felt the room spin. She wanted to sit down before she fainted, but she couldn't make herself move. Her eyes were fixed on the towers, scrutinizing the buildings, as though she might be able to see Jake through one of the tiny windows.

He was there somewhere. She knew it as certainly as she knew his name. Jake's station was practically in the shadow of the World Trade Center. They'd be at the scene for sure. Jake and Larry and all the guys from Engine 57 and Ladder 96. Jamie's chest hurt, and she couldn't draw a deep breath.

The fire was too big, too massive, for them to fight. No number of firefighters could tackle a blaze like that. Jamie clenched her fists and ignored the way her fingernails dug into the palms of her hand. *Get out of there, Jake. Come on, honey, walk away. Help the people on the ground . . .*

A dark-haired journalist came on the television screen, grim-faced and shaken. "We have reports now that fire is tearing through the Pentagon after a third passenger plane, American Airlines Flight 77, crashed into the building sixteen minutes ago. President Bush is declaring the disasters in New York and Washington, D.C. a terrorist attack." The news program cut to live footage of the burning World Trade Center, and the reporter's voice carried on over the images. "To recap here a bit, the airspace over the United States has been closed for the first time in history. Two passenger planes crashed into the World Trade Center at 8:45 and 9:02 Eastern time this morning. Early estimates suggest that hundreds of people may be dead, though that number could be much higher. The Twin Towers hold office space for more than—"

The reporter stopped midsentence.

Suddenly, massive smoke billowed from the flaming section of the south tower. Jamie's mouth dropped open as the roof of the building disappeared and the entire hundred-story structure pancaked into a volcanic cloud of dust and debris.

For a moment no one spoke, no one moved. There were a few quiet gasps from the crowd of people around Jamie, but nothing else. None of them could believe what they'd just witnessed. Finally, in words trembling with disbelief, the reporter voiced what the rest of them didn't dare. "It . . . it appears that the south tower of the World Trade Center has collapsed. I repeat . . . the south tower of the World Trade Center has collapsed. This could mean casualties in the thousands . . . the building was full of business workers and countless firefighters, all working desperately to . . ."

Jamie put her hands over her ears and turned first one direction, then the other. It wasn't possible. There had to be a mistake, a trick somehow. The World Trade Center wouldn't fall; it was too strong, built too well. Still, the images were horrifyingly real. She couldn't stand to see another moment of it, didn't want to hear anyone say anything else about casualties and collapses.

Jake was fine; he had to be.

She took short, frantic steps and made a full circle this time. Where was the locker room? Why was nothing in its place anymore? And how come everyone was standing there watching the television? It was all a lie, a hoax. The World Trade Center wasn't on fire; it was impossible. Now, if only she could get home and talk to Jake.

The TV shouted at her from every corner of the room. Pressing her fists tight against her ears this time, she finally spotted the locker room and made a run for it. Moving as fast as she could, she grabbed her things with both hands and raced to the kids' club. A small television was replaying the collapse of the tower in the corner of the room. Jamie looked at the workers and saw the shadows in their eyes. They knew what was happening.

It's a lie, she wanted to shout. *Everything's fine!*

Instead, Sierra came running up, her blue eyes shining and innocent, completely unaware. "Mommy!" She clung to Jamie's legs and then reached her hands up. "Hold me!"

"Hi, baby." Jamie tried to smile, but the corners of her mouth felt frozen. "Let's go home, okay?"

"What about the park?"

The three day-care workers were avoiding her, looking the other way and sharing quiet whispers between themselves. One of them was crying. Jamie understood instantly. The health club girls knew that Jamie was married to a firefighter; in fact, they knew Jake. He'd been in with her several times over the summer.

Jamie stared at them. "Everything's fine." She stuffed her towel into her bag, swung it onto her right shoulder, and scooped Sierra up onto her opposite hip. "You don't have to worry. Jake wasn't in the building."

Silence hovered between them for several seconds. Finally, one of the workers managed a sad, nervous smile. "That's good." She crossed her arms. "I'm afraid a lot of them were."

"Yeah, well, not Jake." She wanted to tell them the south tower hadn't really come down, but she wasn't up to the conversation. Without saying another word, she spun around and dashed outside to her minivan. She was right, wasn't she? If Jake was fighting the fire, he'd be in the north tower, the one first hit. His station would have been one of the first ones called, right?

She buckled Sierra into her car seat and ran her fingers through her sweaty bangs. What was she doing? The parking lot was full of cars, but not a single person. Everyone was inside watching TV. Then she remembered. She was going home to call Jake. That way she would know for sure that he was okay.

"What's wrong, Mommy?"

Jamie climbed into the front seat, started the engine, and shifted it into reverse. At the same moment, she remembered she'd left her gym bag on the ground outside the van. "Just a minute, honey." Jamie jumped back out, but as she did, the van moved backwards, tripping her and nearly knocking her beneath the front wheel.

The van was backing up without her!

She grabbed the top of her seat and pulled herself back inside. Inches before her car would've hit the one behind it, she slammed on the brakes.

In the backseat, Sierra began to cry. "Mommy ... what's happening? I was driving away by myself."

Jamie gripped the steering wheel with both hands and gasped for breath. "It's okay. Mommy's ... sorry, sweetie. Nothing's going to happen to you." Her heart raced, the sound of it echoing throughout her chest and neck, and a fresh layer of perspiration trickled down the sides of her face. With deliberate motions she put the van in park, stepped back out of the van, grabbed the gym bag, and threw it into the seat beside her.

The club was only five minutes from home, and when she was halfway there, she looked at Sierra in the rearview mirror. "Mommy's not feeling very good today. Let's see if Billy across the street wants to play, okay?"

"Okay." Sierra's voice still held concern. "Is your tummy sick?"

"Yes." Jamie tightened her grip on the steering wheel. It wasn't a lie. "I think if I have a little nap I'll feel better."

They pulled into the driveway and hurried into the house. Sierra hovered near Jamie's leg while she dialed the neighbor. The woman was a stay-at-home mother of three, and she'd offered to baby-sit Sierra anytime. Jamie told the woman that yes, she'd seen the news, and no, she hadn't heard from Jake.

"I need a few hours . . ." Jamie's voice trembled. "To make sure he's okay."

"Oh, Jamie, yes." The neighbor understood immediately. "Bring her right over."

Two minutes later Jamie was back at home. The last thing she wanted was to watch the horrific scenes on television. But the TV was her only source of information, the only place where she might get the details about firefighters and how many were hurt. She was on her way across the house to turn it on when she saw the message light blinking.

Jake must've called! He was fine, somewhere away from the World Trade Center helping from a distance. She darted up to the machine. A red number three was blinking on the front of it. Three messages. Jamie held her breath and pushed the play button.

They were all from Jake's cell phone number. The first two were brief messages saying he would try her again in a few minutes. She gripped the back of the desk chair as the third message began to play.

"Hi . . . it's me again." Jake's tone was upbeat. "Looks like we'll get the call here pretty soon, honey. Everything's going to be okay, Jamie. I love you and I'll be home tonight, I promise. God's with me. Oh yeah, and my angel. Can't forget about him." His voice hesitated, and when the message started up again, his words were thicker than before. "So, I'll see you later, all right? And, sweetheart, tell Sierra I love her."

Jamie stared at the machine, and the room around her began to spin.

She pushed the button and played the message again, searching his words for a hint of worry, some premonition of the danger ahead. There was none. The sound of her heartbeat filled her senses once more, and for a single instant, she thought about tearing through the door and running. Just running as fast and hard as she could until she was sure that none of it was really happening. The World Trade Center hadn't been attacked;

hadn't collapsed to the ground. Jake's unit hadn't responded to the Twin Towers, surely not.

But running would do no good now.

Jamie searched the kitchen, desperately trying to think of who she could call. As she did, her eyes fell on the figurine she'd painted for Jake three days earlier. A firefighter with an angel over his shoulder. But angels weren't real, and there was only one way she could make sure Jake was okay.

She'd have to go to the scene herself.

Jamie grabbed her purse and keys and raced for the van. Eight minutes later she pulled up to a massive traffic jam near the ferry docks. Police officers were waving at the motorists, saying something Jamie couldn't quite make out. She rolled down her window, and suddenly she saw it. One of the Twin Towers was missing. It wasn't a joke or a lie or a hoax. It had really happened. The skyline was grotesquely changed, forever disfigured.

The south tower of the World Trade Center had completely disappeared. In its place was only billowing smoke and ash some twenty stories into the air. The remaining tower was still a blazing inferno.

An officer approached her. "I'm afraid you'll have to clear the area, ma'am."

"I need to find my husband! He's a firefighter in Manhattan."

"I'm sorry." The man's face was taut and pale. "No one's allowed into the city. Port Authority's closed down every entrance. The only ferry service available is leaving Manhattan, not entering it."

"But my husband didn't drive today." She looked away from the officer and back at the single tower still standing, still burning. "With . . . with all the craziness around the World Trade Center, he won't be able to get to the ferry docks and what if—"

"Ma'am . . ." The officer held up his hand and waited until Jamie looked at him. His voice was firm. "No one's allowed into the city. No one." His expression softened. "I'm sorry. Why don't you go home and call his station. Maybe someone there knows something."

Jamie wondered what would happen if she ignored the officer and drove through the closed gates, right onto the ferry. The idea fled her mind as quickly as it came. Breaking the law wouldn't help Jake. Besides, the officer was right. She needed to get home and call the station. Maybe Jake and Larry were still there, still waiting for the call. Maybe somehow they'd been left behind to man the station.

She said nothing. Instead, she took a final glance at the disaster across the harbor and then sped home, her eyes wide and unblinking. The moment she was inside, she dialed the station. A recording came on the line. "All circuits are busy. Please try your call later."

"No!" Jamie screamed at the receiver and slammed it on the hook. Maybe Jake had his cell phone. Firefighters didn't usually carry them out on calls, but maybe this time . . . Jamie picked up the phone again, punched in the numbers, and waited.

"The caller you are trying to reach is not available at this moment." The computer voice sounded oddly happy, as though it belonged to the only person in New York City unaware of what had happened that morning.

And it *had* happened. There was no denying the fact.

Then she remembered Sue. If anyone would've found something out, it would be Larry's wife, Sue. Jamie knew the number by heart, and she punched it in as fast as she could make her fingers work. Sue answered on the first ring. "Hello?" Panic and anticipation filled her voice in equal amounts. "Who is this?"

"Sue, it's me. Jamie." She remembered to breathe. "What've you heard?"

"I called the department public information line. They don't know anything." Sue hesitated and sniffed back a sob. "We're supposed to . . . to stay by the phone and wait for a call. Someone will get in touch with us as soon as they know anything."

Brownie trotted up beside Jamie and licked her fingers.

Jamie absently ran her hand through the dog's soft fur and made her way to the nearest chair. She closed her eyes, terrified about the question she needed to ask. Scared to death that Sue would know the answer. "Sue . . ."

"Oh, Jamie . . . it feels like the end of the world."

"Sue . . ." The room began to spin again. "Did they tell you if our guys went to the scene?"

"Yes." A series of sobs sounded over the phone line. "Engine 57 reported to the . . . to the south tower."

"The south tower?" Jamie hung her head and squeezed her eyes shut. She had to fight to keep her balance even on the sofa. Brownie began to whimper. "Are you sure?"

"Yes, but that . . . that doesn't mean they were caught in the collapse. Lots of them got out, Jamie." Sue took three quick breaths. "We have to believe they're okay."

"What're we supposed to do?" Jamie opened her eyes, but all she could see was the south tower of the World Trade Center disappearing in a giant cloud of debris.

Over and over and over again.

"Get off the phone and wait. Someone will call us as soon as they find them."

Jamie raked her fingers hard through her hair. She had to get a grip. "Okay." Sue was right . . . the guys were fine. They had to be. Her teeth chattered and she struggled to speak. "G–g–good idea." Jamie ended the call and walked halfway to the TV, her steps slow and robotic. The scene was the same one she'd seen from the ferry docks. One tower standing, the other vanished.

A news anchor was on the scene a few blocks from the World Trade Center. His face was dirty, his jacket covered with thick dust. ". . . reports that more than a hundred firefighters may have been trapped in the south tower in the moments before it collapsed." The man was shouting, trying to be heard over the chaos on the street. "Apparently, they had no real warning that the tower was coming down and . . ."

Jamie blinked and the sound from the TV faded. More than a hundred firefighters? A *hundred?* It wasn't possible. And if Jake's station had responded to that building, then as many as eighteen, including Jake and Larry, might have taken the call. Both the night and day shifts. Nausea built within her and she gripped her stomach. A hundred firefighters? It was unthinkable, too massive to comprehend.

She pictured Jake and Larry, hurrying up the stairs to whoever needed their help. If anyone would've stayed in the building, they would've. And that could only mean one thing. Jamie began moving again, crossing the room until she reached the television. He couldn't have been in there . . . he would have found a way out, just as he always did whenever he fought a fire. But if a hundred firefighters had been in the building . . .

She placed her hand on the dusty TV screen, over the hazy image of smoke and dust still billowing from the collapsed area. "Jake!" She screamed his name, and the sound of it bounced around the room. "Jake . . . no! No!"

Then, with her hand still on the cold glass, still gently touching the place where Jake was, she collapsed slowly to the floor.

And for the first time that morning, Jamie hung her head and wept.

* * * *

In Los Angeles Laura Michaels was starting to lose it.

She'd done what Murphy said; she'd waited more than an hour for Eric to call. When the south tower collapsed, just after ten o'clock on the East Coast, she did the math. At one floor per minute, Eric would've barely had time to escape the building. But now it was ten-thirty—seven-thirty her time—and still Eric hadn't called.

As a way of passing time, Laura had focused all her energy into helping Josh get ready for school. The boy wanted to go, and there was nothing he could do by staying home. If the news about Eric wasn't good, Laura would rather tell Josh later after she'd had time to absorb the shock. Besides, school would be good for him; better than a day of watching TV reports and seeing unimaginable images flashed across the screen again and again.

Laura pulled a loaf of wheat bread, a string cheese, and a juice pack from the refrigerator. The feel of it in her hands made her stomach turn, and she glanced at the clock on the microwave. Seven-thirty-three. She opened the twist-tie on the bread, took two slices out, and laid them on a paper towel. *Breathe, Laura . . . keep breathing.* A layer of peanut butter on one slice, blueberry jam over another.

Josh stood nearby, dressed in a blue T-shirt and sweatpants, his hair neatly combed.

He hadn't asked about Eric since he first saw the fires.

"Are you scared, Mom?" He crossed the kitchen, grabbed a bag of cheese crackers, and tossed them on the counter next to his sandwich.

Laura glanced at the clock again. Seven-thirty-five. She turned and looked at Josh. What had he just asked her? Something about being afraid? She slipped the sandwich into a plastic bag. "Yes." Her fingers weren't shaking now, but anxiety gripped her heart and made it feel unsteady, balanced on the edge of an endless abyss of devastation. She leaned back against the counter. "I guess I am afraid."

"Did he call yet?" Josh opened his lunch box and began to pack it.

"No." Laura tried to read her son's emotions as she reached for a napkin and tucked it in beside his lunch. "Not yet." She shifted her gaze. Seven-thirty-seven. *God . . . why hasn't he called? Help him get through to me . . .*

Josh locked his lunch box and stared out the front window. Laura's heart broke for the child. He had to be thinking about the disaster in New York, otherwise he wouldn't be asking questions. But his eyes were strangely flat. Was he denying the possibility that something had happened to Eric? Or was he really not that worried? Or worse, maybe Josh's lack of reaction was the result of one very sad obvious fact. The child felt no connection to his father.

Laura moved from the counter to the other side of the kitchen and put her hands on her son's shoulders. "He'll call. Any minute now."

Josh blinked. "But if he doesn't, does that mean he's dead?"

"Josh!" Laura's voice was louder than she intended it to be. Her hands fell to her side and her jaw dropped. "Don't talk like that! I'm sure he made it out. It'll just take a while before he can call us."

Her son looked at her for a few seconds. Then, with an expression utterly void of emotion, he took his lunch box into the front room, sat down, and stared out the window.

"What're you doing?" Laura trailed behind him.

"Waiting for my ride." There was anger in Josh's tone now, and Laura felt her heart constrict.

Laura sat down a few inches from her son. "Josh, I'm sorry I yelled. It's just . . ." Her voice faded, and for the first time that morning, tears stung at her eyes. "I have to believe he'll call. You understand that, don't you?"

Josh turned around and faced her. "Who cares?" The boy's chin quivered, but his eyes were dry and determined. "He didn't even tell me good-bye."

Her son's words hurt worse than any other news from the day. Worse than Eric's phone call that morning, worse than watching the plane crash into his building. Her suspicions had been right all along. The years of silence and missed opportunities, the list of broken promises and months of absences had severed any hope of a bond between her husband and their son. Whether Eric came home or not, Josh didn't have a father.

And it was all Eric's fault.

Laura let the sorrow spill from her heart. She pulled Josh close and buried her face against the top of his head, her tears mingling with his blonde hair, and leaving them both wet. "Josh . . . I'm sorry. Your dad loves you."

She could feel the anger leave her son's small body, but when he pulled back, his eyes were still dry. "I know, Mom. I want Dad to be okay. And I'm sorry you're scared." He gave her a crooked, wistful smile far older than his years. "He'll call any minute."

A car pulled up outside and Laura sighed. "Your ride's here."

They both stood and Josh kissed her cheek. "I love you, Mom. See ya after school."

"Love you too."

She watched him go, begging God that somehow, when Eric came home—and he would come home—they could talk about their problems and find a way to work them out. Josh needed his father to spend time with him, take an interest in his soccer and schoolwork. Most of all he needed Eric to tell him he loved him.

Laura returned to the kitchen and checked the clock once more. Seven-forty-one. She positioned herself near the phone and stared at it. *Come on, Eric ... call me. God, make him call me. Please ...*

Her silent prayer was pierced by the ringing of the phone. Laura was so surprised she jumped back and stared at it for a moment. It took two rings before she grabbed the receiver. "Hello?" She was breathless, certain Eric's voice would sound any second on the other end.

"Laura ... it's me."

She was unable to speak, overwhelmed with relief. It was Eric; he'd survived, after all. But as soon as the thought raced through her mind, so did the doubts. If it was Eric, why was it so quiet in the background? He still had to be in the middle of downtown Man—

"Laura, it's Clay ... are you there?"

She swallowed back a sob. "I ... I thought you were Eric."

"I just woke up. Laura ... are you watching it?" His voice was tense, frightened. "Eric was there, wasn't he? In the World Trade Center?"

"Yes. He called me right before—" Her composure broke, and three quiet sobs sounded over the phone line. "Right before the second plane hit."

"How about since then? Has anyone heard from him?"

"No." She took a series of quick breaths and saw dark spots dance before her eyes. She had to exhale, had to force herself to stay calm.

"Laura ... are you okay?"

She pinched the bridge of her nose between her thumb and forefinger. "I'm ... waiting for his call."

Clay did a loud breath, and his own fear was tangible. "You shouldn't be alone. I'm on my way."

Clay was right. She needed someone to hold her and tell her everything would be okay, someone who loved Eric as much as she did. "Please, Clay. Come quick. The waiting is killing me."

* * * *

Jamie sat frozen on the floor in front of the TV, convinced that at any moment someone from the fire department would call and tell her everything was okay. Suddenly, the image on the screen changed to a live shot of the blazing north tower. Jamie heard the sound of distant shouts and sirens, then, in a surreal almost slow motion, the outer walls of the building peeled back, and it began to collapse. Like a house of cards, in a matter of seconds, the entire structure disappeared, sending a rush of smoke and ash through the streets of Manhattan and causing the cameraman to run for his life.

Raw terror filled Jamie's heart. If a hundred firefighters had died in the south tower collapse, then . . .

She stood and knew she had only a few seconds. She raced across the room, tore open the bathroom door, and positioned her face over the toilet. With every heave of her stomach, she prayed the same thing. *Please, God . . . not Jake!*

When she was finished she wiped her mouth and stared at her face. It was pale and pinched, stonelike. As if she'd aged ten years that morning. She realized then that her mind-set had changed. The frantic sense she'd had until the collapse of the north tower was gone. There was no fire left to fight, no building left to evacuate. There were two possibilities. Jake had either been in one of the buildings, or he hadn't. If he'd managed to stay outside, Jamie was certain he would have found his way to safety. If he'd been in one of the buildings . . .

Fear placed its cold fingers around her throat and squeezed.

"No," she whispered at her reflection. "Not Jake. Please not Jake."

There was nothing to do now, nothing but sit by the phone and wait. Jamie couldn't inhale fully, couldn't will her heart to slow down. Instead, she shuffled out of the bathroom and took the chair closest to the phone. The TV played on in the background, and Brownie let out an occasional quiet whine. But Jamie didn't really hear any of it. There was only one sound that mattered, one sound that would give her permission to kick fear in the gut and send it on its way. The sound of the phone ringing, and a voice on the other end telling Jamie that Jake was all right.

She stared at the receiver, unable to fathom anything else, unable to blink. It would happen, it had to. Jake was okay. He had found a way to save himself, and Larry too. The phone call would come any minute, and that night they would talk about what could've happened.

They would order take-out Chinese food, and Jake could give Sierra horsey rides for an hour straight if she wanted. They would make love and hold each other, grateful that Jake hadn't been hurt. It was all going to be okay. It had to be; Jake had promised her.

And not once in all her life had Jake Bryan ever broken a promise.

Thirteen

The dust was still thick, but Captain Aaron Hisel didn't care.

He was fifty-two years old, a veteran with mild asthma, but he was going back in if it killed him. There was no telling how many firefighters and civilians were trapped in the rubble. Most of them had to be dead, but as awful as the collapse was, someone might have survived. Every second counted, and he was desperate to make his way to the place where—only an hour earlier—the World Trade Center had stood. The past sixty minutes had been a series of terrifying nightmares, none of which seemed even remotely possible.

After arriving at the scene, Hisel and the men from Ladder 96 had reached the twelfth floor when they'd come across a group of handicapped people waiting alone in an office.

The firefighters had been able to get the disabled workers onto their backs, down the stairs, and outside to a transport bus half a block down from the World Trade Center. They'd been loading the people on the bus when the south tower collapsed.

"Run!" Hisel had shouted, and the entire unit scrambled into a nearby café.

"Our guys are in that building!" one of the men had shouted as they darted under tables. "The whole unit!"

The thunderous roar had echoed to the core of Hisel's being. When it finally stopped, he did a head count. Each of the eight men from Ladder 96 was accounted for. Their rescue of the handicapped workers had saved their lives.

"Okay," Hisel had told the men. "Let's go find our guys."

Lifting his shirt to cover his mouth, he led the others on a charge toward the collapsed south tower. But chaos reigned, and it was impossible to make progress. It took twenty minutes to reach West Street, and by then the warning was being sounded.

The north tower was about to go!

Once more Hisel and the rest of Ladder 96 ran for their lives and this time found shelter in a small flower shop a block away. Minutes later they felt the ground rumble and heard the same awful, unforgettable roar. The force of debris that followed the collapse of the north tower was like nothing Hisel had ever seen. It reminded him of footage he'd seen from Hurricane Andrew. Only this was worse, more like an atomic bomb, hurtling through the air waves of crushed cement, shards of glass, sections of walls, and automobiles. Even inside the store, each of his men had been knocked to the ground from the force of the collapse.

At one point a body had blown past them.

Then slowly, the air had cleared enough to barely see across the street. That's when Hisel had assessed his men one more time and ordered them to pair up.

"It's thick enough to get lost." Hisel wasn't a barker like Maxwell, but he wanted to sound adamant on this point. He coughed twice. "The rubble will be unstable. There'll be pockets, some twenty, thirty feet deep or more. And remember, that jet fuel's still burning."

Hisel didn't have to say the obvious. The death toll among firefighters was bound to be devastating. They headed once more toward West Street, where they'd parked their trucks just an hour ago. Hisel tried not to stare through the smoke at the sickening space in the sky where the towers had stood. Instead, he kept his eyes down, leading his men through a maze of debris and destroyed vehicles. Two inches of gray-white, siltlike ash covered everything, including body parts.

If Maxwell and the men from Engine 57 were still alive, it'd be a miracle.

Finally they reached the foot of a mountain of debris. Though the air was hazy and vehicles lay crushed all around them, Hisel had no doubt: This pile of broken cement and glass and crushed steel was all that remained of the south tower. He directed the men to spread out in pairs.

"Remember what I said." He nodded at them and coughed again. "Be careful. Look out for each other. We need to get in there, find our guys, and get back to the station. I want every man accounted for."

They set out, and Hisel thought about his words. No matter what the evidence before them suggested, he had to believe, had to hope. He nodded to one of the station's probies, Joe Landers, and the two of them took off together, walking along West Street.

"I want to find the rigs." Hisel coughed again. "Just in case any of the men made it back to the engines."

Landers nodded and kept his eyes on the ground.

As they walked, Hisel's cough grew worse. Acrid smoke burned his lungs, and he could taste the ash in his mouth. He stopped and bent at the waist, working to catch his breath. If he didn't find a way to filter the air, he'd have to turn back.

"You okay, Captain?" Landers was using a shirt to cover his mouth.

"Yeah." He coughed again, this time until he could feel his blood rushing to his face. "Just slow."

Why hadn't he covered his mouth earlier? He ripped his shirt open and grabbed the white T-shirt beneath. Shoving it up against his nose and mouth, he finally caught his breath, and they continued down the street.

Through the dense, smoky air they continued. Fire trucks— most of them destroyed—lined their path. But none of them belonged to Engine 57 or Ladder 96. They walked on, and then, up ahead, Hisel could just make out a pair of trucks. One was smashed to half its size, but the other ... the other was still standing. "Those are the station rigs, aren't they?" He picked up his pace.

"Yeah." Landers kept up, his tone excited. "Looks like it."

Hisel was about to yell out, to see if anyone could hear him, when he saw something move beneath one of the trucks, the one that looked less damaged.

"Did you see that?" Landers stopped and stared at the spot where the movement had come from.

They were still thirty yards away, when a man crawled out from beneath the truck on his belly and then struggled to his knees.

Hisel and Landers ran to him, desperate to make out his face. When they were five yards away, Hisel stopped short. "Jake Bryan?" The captain let his head fall back and hooted out loud. "Jake Bryan! Yes! You made it!"

Jake blinked and swayed some. He was covered in ash, his head bleeding, and he had what looked like burns and scrapes over most of his face. In addition, his shoes had been blown off. There was no telling where his uniform was, but Hisel was certain the man was Jake.

"Hey, JB!" Landers reached him first. "Where's everyone else?"

"What ..." Jake's eyes looked funny. He struggled to stand, and Hisel grabbed his arm.

"Steady, JB ... take it slow."

Jake got one foot under him, but as soon as he set his other one down, his knees buckled, and he went limp. Hisel eased him onto the ground and felt the pulse in his wrist. It was weak and racing. "He needs help."

"Head injury." Landers stooped over Jake.

"At least." Hisel pointed Landers to the rig. "Check it out. See if anyone else is under there, or maybe inside the cab. We're still missing eight men."

Landers jogged toward the fire truck while Hisel slid JB's eyelids up and examined them. They were equal, but too dilated, even for the cloud of smoke they were standing in. "Can you hear me, Jake?"

JB didn't move. He was unconscious. And depending on his injuries, if they didn't get him help fast, he might not make it.

Landers returned and met Hisel's eyes. "No one's there, sir. No men at all." He was breathless as he shot a quick look at JB. "How is he?"

"Bad. Help me." Hisel crouched down and scooped Jake into a chair-carry position. Moving as fast as he could, Landers took up his place on the other side of Jake and did the same.

With his free hand, Hisel kept his T-shirt smothered against his face. He only coughed twice as they struggled back down West Street and finally found a waiting ambulance. Two paramedics saw them coming and grabbed a stretcher.

"Where'd you find him?" one of them asked as he helped Hisel and Landers position JB on the stretcher.

"He's a firefighter. Jake Bryan from Engine 57." Hisel's sides heaved, but he hadn't felt better in all his life. If Jake got help right away, he would make it. Hisel was sure.

With expert quickness, the paramedic strapped JB to the stretcher and began an intravenous line. "I know JB. We've worked lots of jobs together." The paramedic looked up and met Hisel's eyes. "Where's his buddy, Larry?"

"We didn't find him. The rest of the men from Engine 57 are ..." Hisel sunk his hands into his pockets and realized something. If the men he'd sent out to handle the search didn't find the missing men, they might all be dead. Eight firefighters from one station. Even more devastating was the fact that every other station in Manhattan had to be facing similar casualties. The enormity of the department's loss was something Hisel refused to consider yet. He cleared his throat but couldn't find his voice.

Landers stepped up and finished the thought. "The rest of the men are missing. We have teams of firefighters looking for them. That's how we found JB."

The paramedics worked to load Jake into the waiting ambulance. One climbed into the back with JB, and the other shut the doors and headed for the driver's seat. "He'll be at Mount Sinai Medical Center," the driver shouted as he climbed in the front seat. "Someone call his wife."

Hisel and Landers watched the ambulance pull away, sirens blaring. When the sound had faded some, Landers drew a deep breath. "You ever meet Jake's wife?"

"Jamie?" Hisel's voice sounded choked. The events of the day were catching up to him, and a cold wind blew across the plains of his heart. He was not a man who cried easily or who expressed his emotions without being prompted. But here, standing in the ashes of the World Trade Center, facing the loss of hundreds of firefighters, Hisel had the strangest longing to find a quiet spot and simply weep. Of course that was impossible; the rescue was nowhere near finished. He exhaled slow and easy, steadying himself. "Sure, I've met her."

"Yeah, well . . ." For a moment it looked like Landers wanted to cry too. Instead, he sucked in hard and gave a shake of his head as he patted the back of the ambulance. "Tonight, when I can't fall asleep because of the people we lost down here, I'm gonna think about Jamie Bryan. We may have to call a lot of wives and tell them their men are missing. But Jamie won't be one of them."

Landers was right. Headquarters needed to be contacted immediately. People were no doubt frantic trying to find out who had survived and who was missing. He grabbed his radio from his back pocket and pushed a series of buttons. "This is Captain Aaron Hisel with Ladder 96. All of our men are accounted for and searching the rubble for survivors." He hesitated. "Their wives need to know they're okay."

There was static at the other end, and Hisel had to put his hand over his other ear to hear the dispatcher. "I'm sorry, I missed that."

"We'll make the calls." This time the words were clearer. "What about Engine 57 from your station? The unit was assigned to the sixty-first floor, south tower, is that right?"

"Right." Hisel felt sick to his stomach at the thought. Eight men, all friends of his, more than sixty floors off the ground when the tower collapsed. It was unimaginable. "Most of the unit's missing, but we just found Jake Bryan near the station's rig on West Street. He was alone, so we're not sure what happened to the others."

"I've got hundreds of people calling. Keep us posted as soon as you hear anything."

"Will do. Hey, in the meantime do me a favor."

"Anything." The dispatcher was quick to answer.

"Look up Jake Bryan's file and add his wife to your list of calls." Hisel thought about that for a minute. "In fact, call her first. She needs to get to the hospital."

"I'll do it right now."

Hisel could hear a smile in the man's voice. There'd been precious few bits of good news that morning. This was one of them. And as they hung up, a single ray of light shone through the shadowy cloud of smoke and ash and devastating loss that darkened most of Manhattan. Because in a few minutes, Jamie Bryan would know the truth.

That though the world had been hit hard that day, her part of it was still intact.

* * * *

The sirens rang out in the deepest area of his brain. He opened his eyes wide and looked around. He was in a vehicle of some kind, traveling very fast, and next to him was a man in a uniform.

"JB, can you hear me? How're you feeling?" The man leaned closer and looked hard at one of his eyes and then the other. "Looks like you got banged up pretty good."

He blinked.

JB? Who's JB? And where am I? He wondered why was he in the fast car and who was the man next to him? He closed his eyes again and tried to remember.

"Jake, we're in an ambulance. We're getting you to the hospital." The man's voice was kind, but urgent. "Hang in there, buddy."

Panic punched him in the gut, and he opened his eyes. Who was Jake, and why did the man beside him think they were friends? He tried to sit up, but a sharp pain sliced through his head and he cried out.

"Take it easy, JB. Relax. Everything's gonna be okay."

He let his head fall back against the stretcher. At almost the same time, the car stopped and the doors flew open. Suddenly, a blur of people surrounded him, carrying him from the vehicle toward what looked like a hospital.

A hundred questions came to mind, but he couldn't make his mouth form a single word. The moment they entered the building, a nurse came up alongside his stretcher and took his hand.

"Jake . . . we're so glad you made it." Her expression changed, but she kept up with the stretcher as the men from the ambulance moved him down a hallway. "What about Larry? Did he leave the building with you?"

What was she talking about? What building? He'd been in a car, not a building. He tried to open his mouth, but his face was in too much pain. Finally he forced his lips to work, ignoring the searing feeling tearing at his cheeks. "Who . . . who's Larry?"

The men carried the stretcher into a large room where more people were waiting, but the nurse stayed at his side. "Larry Henning. He works Engine 57 with you."

"Engine . . . what?" The room was growing blurred, and he had trouble making out the faces around him. The skin on his face hurt so bad he wanted to scream, but he couldn't work his mouth, and nothing made sense. Was he dreaming? Or had he merely woken in a world he knew nothing about? His words were barely audible, and he could feel his strength draining. "I . . . I don't know what . . . I don't know."

Alarm filled the nurse's face, and she gripped his hand tighter than before. "I'll be right back." She left, and almost immediately she returned with a man in a white coat. "This is Dr. Adam Sonney. You've met him before. Do you remember him, Jake?"

He squinted, trying to make out the details of the doctor's face. His head throbbed in a way that coursed through his entire body. All he wanted was sleep. He winced as he opened his mouth again. "N–n–no."

The nurse whispered something to the doctor, and the man muffled an answer. From his place on the stretcher, he caught none of what they said, but he noticed that the nurse had tears in her eyes. A piercing pain tore at him from somewhere near his left foot.

Dr. Sonney approached him and bent over, so his face was inches away. "Jake, do you know where you are?"

Why wouldn't they leave him alone? And why did they keep calling him Jake? "My head . . ."

"You're at the hospital, Jake. We're going to run some tests and get you fixed up, okay? After that we'll call your wife."

The pain was getting worse, and his vision was fading. The doctor's words were breaking up, so he only caught every other word. Something about calling a wife, but that was impossible. He wasn't married. At least not that he knew about. He felt sick to his stomach, and he shut out the doctor's voice. Why was everyone trying to confuse him? "My head . . ."

This time the doctor sounded like he was talking through a megaphone. His words were loud and blurred together. "You've had a head injury, Jake. Let's take a look at it and see what we can do."

"Jake?" The nurse's face appeared again. "I'll call Jamie for you, okay?"

He rolled his head from one side to the other. He wanted to yank it from his shoulders and shake it until the pain went away. On the other side of him, someone jabbed him with a needle, and he winced. Almost immediately warmth began spreading across his body, taking the edge off his pain.

"Can you hear me, Jake?"

He was fading fast, but he had one final question that needed to be asked before another minute went by. His eyelids were heavy, but he blinked them open and searched the faces near him until he found the nurse. "Who . . . who's Jake?"

The woman looked alarmed. "Don't you know who you are?"

The nurse started to say something else, but it was too late. The warm feeling had spread to his brain, and he could do nothing but go with it. He had no idea why people were calling him Jake, but the nurse's last question was the most frightening of all.

If he wasn't Jake, then who was he?

Despite the speed with which he was going under, he was able to concentrate enough to consider the question. And worse, the fact that he had no answer for himself. It was one thing to not know the people at the hospital or the names they were throwing at him. But he didn't know his own name. In fact, he couldn't remember a single thing about who he was or what he did for a living, or why he'd been brought to this hospital with a head injury.

His eyes closed. Next to him he could hear several voices, but they all blended together, and gradually the sound grew quieter. Then, out of the recesses of his mind, a name suddenly came to him. The only name that meant anything at all. He opened his mouth and used all his remaining energy to say it.

"S . . . Sierra . . ."

He heard the word and felt some sense of order return. The vision of a beautiful little girl flashed in his heart, and he was certain this time. Whoever she was, he'd known her before this moment, so he said it again. "Sierra!"

The pain was gone, and he felt himself being sucked into the deepest sleep he'd ever known. He wanted to say her name one more time, but he couldn't make his mouth and brain cooperate.

The last thought that filled his head before he blacked out was this: Somehow a little girl named Sierra would be part of the puzzle whenever he woke up. And maybe she could help him answer the questions.

Who was Larry and what was Engine 57? Who was he married to and for how long, and how come he couldn't remember a thing about her? And, of course, the biggest question of all.

Who in the world was he?

FOURTEEN

For thirty-six minutes, Jamie held the receiver in her hand and stared at it.

During that time she did nothing but remind herself to breathe and will someone to call about Jake. So when the machine finally broke the silence and rang, she dropped the phone and nearly fell out of her chair in her scramble to grab it off the floor and click the talk button.

"Hello? Who is this?"

"Sergeant Riker at the FDNY. Is this Jamie Bryan?"

"Yes." Her face felt cool and clammy against her fingers. She was certain she was floating, because she had no connection whatsoever to the woman sitting in her kitchen waiting to hear news that would change her life forever. She squeezed the phone and ordered herself to sound normal. "This is her."

"Mrs. Bryan, your husband's been found alive. He's—"

"Jake!" Jamie let the receiver fall slowly to her lap as she screamed his name. He was alive! The relief was like a gust of air in a room where she'd been suffocating. Jake hadn't been in the south tower after all, and now he was alive! Just as he'd promised!

Suddenly, she remembered Sergeant Riker, and she jerked the phone back to her ear. "I'm sorry, I . . . I missed that last part."

The man hesitated. "I was saying he's been injured, Mrs. Bryan. He's at Mount Sinai Medical Center being treated. I promised I'd call you."

In a rush, the oxygen left the room once more, and a paralyzing fear returned to Jamie's voice. "How . . . how hurt is he?"

"Actually, the doctors will have to tell you that, Mrs.—"

"I don't want to talk to doctors, Sergeant!" Jamie was shouting now, on her feet and pacing the kitchen. "You must've gotten some kind of report. Please . . ." She forced herself to calm down. "Please tell me what you know."

Again the man paused, and for a brief instant Jamie felt for him. How many of these phone calls had he been asked to make this morning? "Captain Hisel made the report. He said your husband had burns and a head injury. But he thought he'd make it."

The relief offered only enough room to breathe. If Jake had a head injury, anything was possible. She needed to get to the hospital right away, be with him, talk to him. Assure him that everything was being done to get him better.

"Thank you, Sergeant. That means a lot." She was about to hang up when she remembered Sue's request. That Jamie call the moment she heard anything. "What about Larry Henning? Is he with Jake at the hospital?"

"Larry's part of Engine 57, right?"

"Yes. Same as Jake."

"No," the sergeant sighed. "I'm afraid we haven't heard anything from any of the others."

The emotional extremes from the past few minutes were taking their toll on Jamie. She dropped to the chair near the phone and hung her head. "Nothing?"

"Mrs. Bryan, your husband was the only one they've found from Engine 57." He paused, and there was something defeated in his tone as well. "They were headed for the sixty-first floor of the south tower when the building collapsed."

Jamie gripped her stomach and gritted her teeth. The whole day had been nothing but a series of nightmares. The only reason she had survived at all was the hope that Jake was somehow alive. But now that he . . . what would she tell Sue? And how had Jake lived if his entire unit was missing? She found her voice once more. "Th–thank you for calling."

She hung up and stared at the receiver. She should call Sue. The woman was her friend, and she was probably sitting by the phone the same way Jamie had been. But what could she say? That Larry was trapped somewhere in the middle of a hundred floors of a collapsed building? That none of the men from Engine 57 had been found except Jake?

They could still find him, after all. There was no point worrying her if the information the sergeant had was wrong. No, the call to Sue could wait. For now she needed to get to the hospital and find Jake. He was hurt and alone, and he needed her by his side. She made a quick call to the neighbor before she left.

"They found him." Grateful tears spilled from Jamie's eyes, and she sobbed twice before composing herself. "He's . . . he's alive."

"Oh, Jamie, I'm so glad." The woman's voice was shaky. "Sierra's fine. She's watching a movie with the other kids." The woman hesitated. "Should I say anything to her?"

"No." Jamie's answer was quick. "She doesn't know about any of it." Another jolt of nausea shook her. "Listen, Jake's hurt, but he'll be okay. If you can keep Sierra for a while longer, I'll go see him at the hospital."

"Take your time. We'll be here."

Jamie thanked the woman, hung up the phone, and grabbed her keys. Before she left the house, another call came in, this one from the hospital. A nurse confirmed what Sergeant Riker had already said. Jake had a head injury and was unconscious. Jamie should come right down.

"What if the police won't let me on the ferry?"

"They're taking people on a limited basis." The nurse sounded confident. "Explain the situation. They'll let you on."

She was right. This time when Jamie pulled up to the ferry docks she had information that convinced the officer to let her aboard. Her firefighter husband was being treated at Mount Sinai Medical Center, and doctors on staff had asked her to come.

Jamie parked, walked aboard, crossed the ferry to the far side, and found a quiet corner near the railing. In a matter of minutes the ferry pushed off, and Jamie could only stare at the Manhattan skyline. It was like watching the end of the world. The closer she got, the more awful the devastation appeared. The Twin Towers were gone, but the pile of rubble was still sending up clouds of smoke, still glowing red from the flames buried beneath. Other buildings were on fire also, buildings that were part of the World Trade Center. Emergency vehicles were everywhere, and it took Jamie nearly an hour to reach the hospital parking lot by cab. The place was packed, and Jamie wondered how many other hospitals had received victims from the attacks.

She rushed through the doors of the emergency room and made her way through a sea of people. Finally, she found the front desk and gave her name to the woman behind the counter. "I'm here for Jake Bryan. He's my husband."

"Stand over there." The woman had a stack of files on her desk. "Someone will be right with you."

Jamie did as she was told. In less than a minute an older nurse appeared. "Mrs. Bryan?"

Jamie rushed forward. "Yes?"

"This way, please."

"How . . . how is he?" Jamie was out of breath and weak at the knees as she walked alongside the woman.

The nurse's tone was businesslike. "Critical but stable at this point." She led them down a hallway into what looked like a makeshift trauma ward. Partitions had been set up dividing rooms and hall space into treatment areas. The nurse kept walking. "The doctor will give you the full report."

Jamie nodded, and suddenly the nurse stopped and directed Jamie into a room on their right. "Here he is. You can stay as long as you like. Talk quietly to him, watch TV, or touch his hands. But if he starts to stir push the call button. We don't want to agitate him. We have him sedated. Any excessive stimulation could cause his brain to swell."

"Okay." Anxiety made Jamie's legs wobbly. Brain swelling? He must have been hurt worse than she thought. Or maybe it was only a precaution. If Captain Hisel had said he'd be okay, then why were they worried about brain swelling? She entered the room and stopped short, covering her mouth so she wouldn't gasp out loud.

"Jake, honey . . . no." Her voice was a whisper, and behind her, the nurse left to give her privacy.

He looked awful.

With the exception of his eyes, Jake's head was wrapped completely in gauze. There were more bandages on both his arms, and a splint along his lower left leg. The rest of him was covered by sheets, so the only part showing at all was his neck and fingers. The simple gold band he'd worn since their wedding date was still on his left hand. But otherwise, he looked nothing like the strong, vibrant man she'd kissed good-bye that morning. Machines were hooked to his mouth and nose; tubes ran into both arms; monitors beeped and whirred.

But Jake didn't move, didn't make a single sound.

She walked to his side and took hold of the bed rail. Her heart raced within her, fast and hard, and she was afraid her movements would wake him, or worse, that her presence would stimulate him and make his brain swell. She swallowed as quietly as she could. *Calm down, Jamie . . . calm. He's here . . . he's alive. He's not that fragile . . . everything's going to be okay.*

She stared at his bandaged face and willed him to breathe, to survive. *Jake . . . honey. It's me.* Her breath hovered in the back of her throat. *Don't die, baby . . . please.*

Jake lay motionless, and Jamie leaned over the bed rail, studying the subtle rise and fall of his chest. He *was* breathing, wasn't he? He was drawing breath and letting it out again, but she couldn't hear him. The monitors around the bed hummed in a way that seemed louder with every heartbeat. She shot a glance at them and clenched her teeth.

Be quiet!

She wanted to hear Jake . . . was that too much to ask? Ten seconds of silence so she could hear the slow and gentle inhale, the familiar exhale . . . proof that he was really alive beneath all the gauze and bandages. But the machines were constant, relentless. She straightened and studied his chest again.

It was moving. Of course it was moving.

The monitors would scream a warning if he stopped breathing. Jamie took a step backwards and then another, inching toward the chair behind her without ever taking her eyes off Jake. When she reached the chair, she lifted it from its place near the door, brought it silently across the room, and set it next to Jake's bed. When he woke up, she would be there, no matter how long it took. She sat down and took hold of his fingertips. Just the feel of them against the palm of her hand was familiar and intoxicating. Tangible proof that he'd lived, that somehow, someway, he'd been able to escape the building in its final minutes.

Jamie stared at her husband's fingers and realized the hair had been burned off them. They were scraped and lightly burned, but they were warm and alive. And right now they were all she needed to feel connected with him.

She found the television on the wall above the foot of Jake's bed. The coverage of the disaster that day was not something she wanted to watch. But she needed to know about the rest of Jake's unit. Where were they? Had any firefighters been found alive in the rubble?

On the bedside table was a TV remote. Jamie took it, flicked the power button, and immediately turned down the volume. Live pictures from Manhattan came into focus. Carefully, so Jake wouldn't be disturbed, she made the sound loud enough so she could hear it.

A news anchor was giving a recap of the day's events, and Jamie wondered about her sanity. But somehow, with Jake breathing beside her, she felt strong enough to hear the latest details. The reporter droned on. All federal office buildings in Washington had been evacuated; another plane, United Flight 93 from Newark—headed possibly for the White House—had crashed in rural Pennsylvania. In all, some three hundred people were feared dead in what was now a total of four hijacked plane crashes.

"In addition, New York City Mayor Rudy Giuliani has urged all New Yorkers to stay home and any residents south of Canal Street to evacuate to emergency centers set up by local officials."

The list of mind-boggling details continued.

The airports in Los Angeles and San Francisco had been shut down, and experts from the Centers of Disease Control and Prevention were sending an emergency response team to New York City as a precautionary move. Only fifty planes remained flying over U.S. airspace, but none were reporting any problems.

When the station ran out of old news, it switched back to live shots of Manhattan and Washington, D.C. Flames could still be seen in both locations, but there wasn't much to say. The terrorists had made a complete and utterly accurate hit.

"Reports coming in show that very few survivors are being found in the rubble of the collapsed Twin Towers, a place law and fire officials are now calling Ground Zero."

Ground Zero? Jamie tightened the grip she had on Jake's fingers. Wasn't that the term used at atomic bomb sites? Jamie stared at the TV and wondered again if the whole crazy day wasn't some type of bad dream. How could terrorists have taken over four passenger planes on the same morning?

She focused once more on the news pouring from the television. *Come on, people, tell me about the firefighters . . . where are they? Who's getting them out of the rubble? How many are missing?*

A live shot of President George Bush came into view. Speaking from Barksdale Air Force Base, he explained that the country had been attacked by terrorists. Appropriate security measures were being taken to preclude any further attacks, and the U.S. military was on high alert worldwide. He asked for prayers for those killed or wounded, and then he bit his lip. For a moment, Jamie thought the president might actually break down.

Instead, he gritted his teeth and said, "Make no mistake . . . the United States will hunt down and punish those responsible for these cowardly acts."

The camera cut to a different reporter in a studio. Images from the smoldering pile of rubble took up a portion of the right side of the screen. "The news in from fire officials is grim this afternoon. It is feared now that of the hundreds of firefighters who responded to the disaster at the Twin Towers, nearly two hundred are dead. I repeat, nearly two hundred FDNY firefighters are feared dead at this hour. And there is great concern that the actual number of fatalities within the fire department may be much higher."

They cut to a picture of Deputy Chief Bob Atwell, a man Jamie had spoken with at a department softball game last June. Bob was a clown at FDNY functions, routinely dumping watercoolers down the backs of co-workers and running the bases backwards when he'd hit a ball over the fence.

But now Atwell's eyes were grim, deeply set in an ashen face marked with weariness. "Right now, rescue crews are using search dogs to comb the mountain of debris." He ran the back of his hand over his forehead. "We're making every attempt to locate anyone who survived the collapse of the buildings and get them out of there."

A reporter stood up. "Has your department found anyone yet?"

"A few people." Bob sighed and the muscles in his jaw flexed. "Not nearly the numbers we'd like to be finding at this point."

The reporter was persistent. "How many men are missing?"

"Well ..." Bob pursed his lips and let his gaze fall to the ground for a moment before looking up again. "I can't give you a specific number, but we'd estimate more than three hundred are missing."

"Were they all in the buildings at the time of the collapse?"

Bob sucked in a breath, and Jamie wanted to hug him. The man was kind and patient, but these questions had to be the hardest he'd ever had to answer.

"Most of them were in the south tower. It went first and with virtually no warning. The missing men were either in the tower or on the ground. A smaller number were in or near the north tower, as many of our people had time to evacuate that building in anticipation of a collapse."

The image changed, and the screen was filled with a live shot of the burning Pentagon. Jamie lifted the remote and clicked off the TV. She couldn't stand to watch another minute. Bob Atwell's words had said it all, really. They'd only found a few firefighters. A few out of more than three hundred who'd gone into the buildings.

Jamie looked at Jake, and she was hit by a mix of emotions greater than anything she'd ever felt. Her husband was alive, and for that she was filled with a breathless relief and gratitude. But how would he take the news when he came to? If eight men from his company were missing, then there was a good chance they were dead. And what about Larry?

Visions of her husband's best friend flooded Jamie's mind. The times when they'd barbecued together or camped upstate. The jet-skiing trip they'd taken just a few days ago. Larry and Jake were inseparable, like brothers. If Larry was dead, how would Jake handle the fact? Would he blame himself for somehow not watching his friend's back better?

And how about Sue?

Jamie tightened the grip she had on Jake's fingers. What kind of friend was she if she didn't make the call? Without giving herself time to change her mind, Jamie picked up the phone on the table beside her and dialed "9" for an outside line. When she had it, she punched in the number for Sue and Larry.

An older woman answered on the second ring. "Hello?" The woman's voice was thick, as if she'd been crying.

"Hi, this is Jamie Bryan. Is Sue there?"

"Hi, Jamie. This is Larry's mother."

"Oh . . . hi." Jamie let her head fall into her hands. Of course. Larry's mother lived by herself in the Bronx and was constantly at Larry and Sue's house doting on Katy. The woman was probably as desperate about Larry's situation as Sue was. "Have . . . have you heard anything?"

"Someone from the department called." There was a catch in the woman's voice, and she started to cry. "I'm sorry . . . I think I'm still in shock."

"It's okay." Tears stung Jamie's eyes too. "We're all in shock."

The older woman sniffed and finished her statement. "The man who called said Larry was missing. Larry and all the men from Engine 57."

"Not all the men." Jamie almost hated telling the woman. How fair was it that Jake was alive, lying in a hospital bed beside her while Larry and the rest of the company were buried beneath forty floors of cement and steel? "Jake's alive. I'm with him at the hospital."

A cry sounded from Larry's mother. "Oh, Jamie, that's wonderful. I'll let Sue know right away."

"Is . . . is she there? I'd like to tell her myself."

"She's in the bedroom with Katy." The woman hesitated. "I'll see if she'd like to talk."

A full minute passed. Jamie forced herself to think of nothing but the way Jake's fingers felt against her own. Finally, someone picked up the phone, and Sue's voice came over the line.

"Hello? Jamie?"

"Oh, Sue . . . they've got to find him. They've just got to."

Both of them were suddenly crying, the sound of their sobs sounding out in muffled bursts across the phone line. When Jamie could finally speak, her voice was high, pinched by the sorrow that had built in her throat. "I'm sorry, Sue. I'm so sorry."

"They'll find him. I . . . I have to believe it." She took two quick breaths and uttered something that was part laugh, part cry. "Larry's mom says they found Jake."

"Yes." Jamie gripped her temples with her thumb and forefinger. "He was beneath the station rig. He has a head injury and burns. I'm with him at the hospital."

"Is he going to be okay?" There were still tears in Sue's voice, but she'd calmed down considerably.

"I think so. The doctor hasn't been in yet. They're swamped with victims."

"It doesn't make sense, does it?"

Jamie knew instinctively what Sue was talking about. If Jake had been found at ground level, why hadn't Larry been with him? The two of them never left each other's sides on a call. "You mean why they weren't together?"

"Exactly." Sue exhaled hard. "Did they check under the truck? Inside it? Maybe Larry's still down there somewhere."

It was an idea Jamie hadn't thought of. "You should call Captain Hisel. He's the one who found Jake."

"Okay." For the first time there was a whisper of hope in Sue's voice. "I'll do that. If I hear anything, I'll call you."

"I'll be here." It was a moment when most people would offer to pray, but Jamie couldn't bring herself to say the words. They both knew she was more skeptic than believer. And after what had happened today, she was afraid to raise Sue's hopes by offering to do something that couldn't possibly help. "Don't give up hope."

"Okay. And, Jamie, when Jake wakes up, tell him we love him."

FIFTEEN

SEPTEMBER 11, 2001, EVENING

There was nothing Laura could do but wait.

Clay had come over sometime before noon, and together they sat by the phone and watched the television reports come in. Thousands of people were missing and feared dead. Entire staffs from a dozen firms who'd worked in offices on the top floors of the Twin Towers were most likely gone.

She'd called Murphy six times, but now it was getting dark on the West Coast and pushing ten o'clock in New York City. For the past twelve hours, Laura kept telling herself the same thing. Eric was somewhere safe. He had to be. Koppel and Grant was on a floor that would've had time to evacuate. Certainly, he and the others had been among the throng of people who'd managed to escape. But if that was the case, why hadn't he called?

Not only that, but Laura had tried his cell phone at least once every ten minutes since Clay arrived. Each time the message was the same. The caller at that number wasn't available or was out of the service area. Laura curled her legs beneath her and stared at the television, unable to pull her eyes away. In the background she could hear Clay talking with Josh, helping him with his homework.

Laura wasn't sure what she'd have done without Clay. When he wasn't keeping Josh busy, he sat at the other end of the sofa doing nothing but answering her questions.

"He should've gotten out, don't you think?" she'd ask.

"Definitely. People made it out from higher than sixty-four. Everything should be fine, Laura."

"He's just having trouble finding a phone, right?"

"Right."

She'd be quiet for a while, try Murphy again or Eric's cell phone. Then she'd start the questions over again. "He could walk down sixty-four flights of stairs, couldn't he?"

"Yes, Laura. He's in great shape."

"How long do you think that would've taken him?"

Clay would think about the question. "Twenty minutes, maybe thirty depending on how many people were in the stairwell."

"But people were moving down the steps pretty quickly, isn't that what they said?"

"Yes. There was no panic, just an orderly evacuation."

"That's what I thought."

And again she'd focus on the TV. In that manner, she'd passed the entire day. In some strange way, Clay's presence made the day feel more normal, as though Eric was only away on business and Clay was hanging around looking for something to do.

When Josh came home from school, he'd walked up to her and given her a hug. "Did Dad call?"

Laura's heart had felt ice cold, frozen in fear. But somehow she'd managed a smile. "Not yet." Tears had welled up in her eyes. "He will. As soon as he can find a phone."

Clay must have seen it in her face then, realized that she was about to snap. "Your mom needs to rest a little, okay, buddy?" He'd put his arm around Josh.

"Okay." Josh bent over and kissed her cheek. "He'll be all right, Mom. Really."

Laura had only nodded and shifted her gaze once more to the TV. They were interviewing survivors every few minutes, people who had made it out of the Twin Towers. Maybe they'd find Eric and talk to him, ask him about his escape. Laura couldn't afford to miss it if they did. And so she'd watched the screen, barely taking time to blink.

Hours had slipped by while Josh and Clay shot baskets in the backyard. Now Laura could smell something cooking in the kitchen behind her, but she had no interest in eating or even tearing herself from the TV until Clay entered the room and sat down. He set his hand on her knee and waited until he had her full attention. "You need a break."

She shook her head. "I need to find him."

"Thousands of people escaped. There's no reason to think they'll find Eric and interview him. Besides, Eric wouldn't be milling around Manhattan. He'd be looking for a way to find a phone. Don't you think?"

Clay's expression was gentle, and Laura felt her defenses fall. "I need to talk to Murphy."

Clay studied her eyes, and the corners of his lips lifted in a sad smile. "Murphy said he'd call." He nodded toward the kitchen. "I made spaghetti. Come eat."

"I'm not hungry."

"Just sit with us. Have a glass of water." Clay's voice grew even softer. "I'm worried too. But you need a break, Laura. Sitting here isn't going to hurry his phone call."

Laura searched Clay's face. "You think he's okay, though, right?"

"Definitely." The look in his eyes was so certain that it fanned life in the embers of her heart. Her mouth was dry, and she realized she hadn't had any water since breakfast. "Okay."

Laura forced herself to the table. She took three sips from her water glass and nodded. "I'm fine. Just tired." She looked at Clay. "I need him to call."

"He will." Clay's eyes held hers. "I know he will."

They ate in silence, and afterwards, Laura returned to the TV. Clay helped Josh with his shower, and in the distant background, she could hear him reading the boy his favorite book. Laura closed her eyes and listened. Clay's voice was so much like Eric's she could almost pretend her husband was home, safe, sitting next to their son reading to him.

Laura blinked and realized the obvious. Eric never read to Josh, so a scene like that with her husband and her son couldn't be happening upstairs.

Not even in her imagination.

Josh was clean and in his pajamas at eight o'clock when he came down and kissed Laura good-night. Clay was in the kitchen doing the dishes.

"Mom . . . you're still worried, aren't you?"

Laura took her eyes off the TV and looked at him. "Yeah, honey." Her eyes stung from a day of crying and staring at the television. "I'm worried."

"Why hasn't he called?"

"Maybe the phones don't work." Laura hugged Josh and stroked his back. "There's a lot of bad stuff going on in New York City. So that could be it."

Clay came into the room and positioned himself a few feet away. "Ready for bed, buddy?"

"Wait!" Josh drew back and his eyes lit up. "Maybe he's working!" He sounded as though this were the perfect explanation. "Maybe he had some extra things to do. He never calls us when he's on trips."

As soon as Josh said the words, Laura shifted her gaze to Clay. The man had idolized his older brother as long as Laura had known him. Now she watched Clay take the news. The questions in his eyes could only be answered one way, and Laura gave him the slightest nod, confirmation that what Josh had said was true.

Eric never called home when he was out of town.

Laura blinked and focused her attention on Josh again. The look on his face made Laura want to weep. But she couldn't. The boy was serious. All he knew of his father's business trips were that they ranked higher in importance than anything at home, and that when he was gone, there were long stretches of days without any contact. "Yes, sweetie," she patted his knee. "Maybe that's it."

"G'night, Mom." He leaned up and kissed her cheek. "Dad'll be home on Thursday. Then he'll tell us all about the fire."

She hugged him again. "Okay."

Clay held out his hand and led the boy upstairs. Ten minutes later he returned to the sofa where Laura was and sat several feet away from her. "He's asleep."

"Thank you." She held up the remote and flicked off the TV. "I can't watch another minute. Not tonight." She looked at Clay. "There's a lot you didn't know about us."

"He . . . he never calls you when he's gone?"

"Clay . . ." Laura exhaled in a way that seemed to come from the soles of her feet. "He barely talks to us even when he is here."

"I knew there was trouble when I moved here, but nothing like this." Clay's mouth hung open a bit, and he gave a frustrated shake of his head. "Eric's the greatest guy I know, Laura. He . . . he was so in love with you . . ."

Fresh tears poked pins at Laura's eyes. "A lot's happened since then."

"A lot?"

Laura's voice faded some. "More than you know."

"Tell me, Laura." Clay leaned forward and dug his elbows into his thighs. "I've got all night."

And so she did. She took him back to the spring of her twenty-first year when she gave birth to a beautiful baby girl, a baby who would never open her eyes or take a single breath.

"Eric blamed himself." Laura ran her fingers beneath her eyes and sniffed. "He told me I'd never want for good medical care again."

"I'm sorry, Laura." Clay stared at the floor for a minute, and when he looked up, the sorrow in his eyes was deeper than the ocean. "I never knew."

Laura lifted her shoulders and swallowed a sob. "We . . . we never told anyone."

"But then Josh came, right?"

"Right . . ." She looked at the space between her feet. "But things between Eric and me only got worse."

She walked him through the next few years, the birth of Josh and the day when Eric was hired by Koppel and Grant. "You know . . ." She met his gaze again. "He was more excited about the job than the fact that he was a father."

Clay's features were frozen, caught up in disbelief. "I always thought you were the perfect family—money, success, good health, and the kind of love most people never know."

"Hardly." A sad laugh sounded in the back of her throat. "Sometimes it feels like we never loved like that."

Clay opened his mouth to say something, but before either of them could speak again, the phone rang. The receiver was between them, next to Laura on the sofa. She grabbed it, her eyes still fixed on Clay's. "Hello?"

"Laura . . . it's Murphy."

Relief filled her heart. "Thank God, Murphy. When did you hear from him?"

Silence shouted at her from the other end. "I didn't." The man gave a shaky sigh. "I heard from one of the associates in the New York office. Hank Walden."

Clay was watching her, trying to gauge the news. She nodded, impatient for Murphy to get to the point. "Okay, so where's Eric? That's all I need to know."

"Ah, Laura . . . I hate to tell you this."

He hesitated, and Laura wanted to scream at him. "Just say it, Murphy. I've been waiting all day to hear something, now come on!" Laura's hands shook, and she could no longer look at Clay. The sudden fear in his expression only made the moment seem more terrifying. She looked down at her feet. "Tell me!"

"I'm sorry, Laura . . . Eric's missing. Eric and Allen Koppel. Everyone else at Koppel and Grant is accounted for."

The fainting feeling was back.

Laura hunched over her lap and let her head fall near her knees. "That's . . . that's impossible. They must be together somewhere. Eric said they had a meeting today, so maybe . . ." She remembered Josh's idea. "Maybe they're finishing business somewhere before they check in. Maybe—"

"Laura." Murphy cut her off. His voice was filled with regret. "There's more. Hank saw Eric and Allen in one of the offices after everyone else evacuated the floor. They wouldn't come ... they were ... they were working on a few portfolios." Murphy made a soft groan. "The Koppel and Grant group walked down the stairs together and waited near the outside door of the building several minutes—until police cleared them out." He gave a sad huff. "Laura ... Eric and Allen never came. No one saw either of them after that."

Laura could almost feel her world collapsing. She wanted to argue with Murphy, tell him he was wrong and that Eric and Allen were somewhere safe. They had to be. But the information Murphy had told her was hard to dispute. Finally, she sat up some and shook her head. "That's okay, Murphy. Thanks for calling."

Then without waiting for him to speak, she clicked the phone off and dropped it on the floor. A rushing sound filled her ears, and the walls felt like they were closing in. What had Eric done? He and Allen had stayed in an office? Working on portfolios? While the single worst disaster in the country's history unfolded, they could think of nothing more important than financial management and the investment needs of their clients?

She opened her mouth and a cry came out, a cry that was both desperate and quiet at the same time. "No ... Eric ... why?" A wordless moan sounded from someplace deep and desperate, a place in her heart that was only now realizing the horror of her situation. "God ... help me!" Her cry grew louder and she felt Clay move close.

He slid next to her and put his hand on her back. His touch brought her to her senses, and she turned to him, burying herself in his embrace and sobbing from someplace she hadn't known had existed until now. Twenty minutes passed, then thirty. Finally, she pulled herself away from Clay and stood up. The shock and sorrow were wearing off. In its place was a fierce anger like nothing Laura had felt before.

"How dare he!" She moved her stiff legs from one side of the family room to the other. "Even *today* the job was more important to him."

Clay still didn't know what Murphy had said. He wrung his hands, balanced on the edge of the sofa as though he wasn't sure if he should stay seated or come to her. "Did they find him?"

"No." She stopped and blew a stray piece of blonde hair off her forehead. "He and Allen wouldn't go down with the others. They stayed, Clay, and you know why?"

His expression changed, and a knowing look crossed his face. "Not for work?"

"Yes!" She paced again, this time faster than before, with more fury. "They worked while every other person on their floor evacuated." She hesitated and planted her hands on her hips, searching Clay's face for some kind of answer. "Weren't we worth more than that? Didn't he know he'd be leaving us behind, leaving Josh without a father?"

Clay bit his lip, and Laura guessed he was keeping himself from stating the obvious. That apparently Josh had never had a father. Not by any practical sense of the word. Instead, he stood up, crossed the room, and held her the way she needed to be held. In a way that pushed her anger aside and let an incalculable sorrow take its place. "Why, Clay? Why'd he do it?"

"They might still find him, Laura. You can't give up."

"I know." She sniffed and pulled away enough to look at him. Fresh tears trickled down her cheeks. "I'm mad . . . but I keep telling myself he must be alive somewhere. Maybe he and Allen waited a few minutes and then went down. Maybe they took a different stairwell and missed the other people from Koppel and Grant. And maybe they're at some kind of waiting area, trying to get out of the city so they can make a phone call and tell everyone they're okay."

"If we don't hear from him tomorrow, maybe we should go there. Check the hospitals and see if they've found him. He might not have I.D. on him." Clay's voice was soft as he searched her eyes. "If he's lying in a hospital somewhere unconscious, no one would have any way to know who he was or how to reach you."

The muscles in Laura's chest relaxed just a bit, enough for her to catch her breath. "I hadn't thought of that."

"See . . . there's lots of possibilities." He gave her arms a gentle squeeze. "We'll find him, Laura. I'll do whatever I can to help you."

The idea of going to New York seemed outrageous. Especially now. The FAA had said airports could remain closed for days. But if Clay was willing to come with her, it might be their only hope. Then another idea hit her. "We could call first, see if any of the patients are unidentified."

"Right."

"He's gotta be somewhere."

An image came to mind of Eric and Allen talking business on the sixty-fourth floor as the south tower collapsed. If he didn't call by tomorrow, he might be in a hospital or wandering around the city with a head injury, unable to remember his phone number. But the odds were he'd been buried alive. Right next to Allen, devoted to the job until his final moments.

Another series of sobs gathered in her heart. Who were they kidding? If Eric hadn't called her by now, he was dead. It was that simple. He and Allen had made a last-minute attempt at getting an edge in the financial market, and it had cost them their lives.

Her emotions shifted again, and this time defeat settled in and made her legs ache. "Hold me, Clay. I can't bear it . . . I can't."

"Oh, Laura. I'm so sorry." Clay soothed his hand along the back of her head and brought her close again. In his arms she had the slightest sense that maybe . . . just maybe she'd survive. It was a different feeling entirely than the way she'd felt in his arms a few days ago. All questions about whether she'd married the wrong brother were gone now, and only deep friendship and comfort remained. No matter how bad her marriage had been, no matter how differently she'd enjoyed Clay's company a few days ago, in the course of a few hours that morning everything had changed.

Not just for Laura and Clay, but for the entire nation.

Sixteen

September 13, 2001

Whenever Jake might wake up, Jamie wanted to be there.

Now it was Thursday morning, and she'd done nothing but sit by his side, day and night, and try not to think about what was happening across New York and throughout the ranks of the FDNY. Jake's father had driven into the city after the towers collapsed and met with Jamie at the hospital.

"I'll stay with Sierra," he told her as he left that afternoon. "I'll be here as long as you need me, Jamie." He'd cast another look at Jake. "He'll be okay. I can feel it."

Jamie had hugged him then, appreciating the way his presence gave her the hint of hope and strength, something she desperately needed. Every minute Jake lay unconscious only worsened the fog of fear for Jamie, but Jake's father was positive.

"Keep your chin up." Jake's father had kissed her on the forehead as he left. "Jake needs you. He's going to be fine."

Jamie's feelings were all over the board. "The numbers of missing men . . . I can't . . . I can't stop thinking about it."

A shadow fell across Jim Bryan's face. "More than any of us can imagine."

The hours and days that followed had been nothing but a blurry routine. Sit by Jake, catch some sleep, wake up, wash her face at the small sink in Jake's hospital room, call Sierra, talk to Jake's father, and then find her place beside her husband once more.

Wednesday afternoon they'd done another CT scan and found a buildup of fluid near the injured part of Jake's brain. They'd rushed him into surgery and drained the excess fluid. The operation was a success and had kept Jake's brain from being damaged by the pressure. That night she never slept at all, but simply sat in the chair by Jake's bed trying to comprehend what had happened.

The death toll was in by then.

Three hundred and forty-three firefighters were trapped in the collapse of the World Trade Center. Rescue workers were still sifting through the rubble around the clock at a frantic pace, convinced there were people trapped in pockets beneath the surface. But with every passing hour, it seemed less likely that anyone would be found alive in the debris.

It seemed a lifetime ago that Jamie had been troubled by the death of a single firefighter. Ten a year, twenty a year. Each life was a tremendous loss. But those numbers would never compare to what had happened on September 11. Most of the time it was all Jamie could do to concentrate on the matters at hand—talking to doctors and nurses, encouraging Jake to wake up, remembering to eat. Every spare moment her mind was filled with the awful picture of firefighters, hundreds of them, hurrying up the stairs of those towers. Had any of them guessed what would happen? Could they have known that each step brought them closer to their deaths?

She hadn't heard from Sue since Tuesday afternoon, but she was certain the other men from Engine 57 hadn't been found. Captain Hisel had been in to visit twice—once Tuesday night, and again on Wednesday. Both times he gave Jamie the update she'd dreaded. The men were still missing, still buried somewhere amidst the tons of debris.

"If they're alive, we think they'll make it," Hisel had told her. "They're strong men, all of them, in good shape. The rescue workers think there could be areas where people are still waiting for help. Some of the water being sprayed on the smoldering sections might've gotten down to them. It could be keeping them alive."

Jamie had let the man talk, but she wasn't listening. Not really. Who was he kidding? If Engine 57 had been near the sixty-first floor when the south tower collapsed, then the bodies of Larry and the others were smack in the middle of the debris pile. There wasn't the slimmest chance they were alive. But Jamie would nod and look interested. They had nothing if they didn't have hope.

In the hours since Hisel's last visit, Jamie had resisted the occasional urge to catch an update on the attacks. The entire nightmare was too awful, and the more she thought about it, the less able she was to think of anything else. There was only one way she could remove the awful images from her mind, the pictures of firefighters spread throughout the towers in the moments before they collapsed.

By sitting stone still and watching Jake breathe.

She held his fingers, ran her thumb along his bandaged hand, and whispered whatever thoughts crossed her mind. Sometimes she talked about the old days, back when they were kids in the same Staten Island neighborhood. Or about the way their lives had become such a miracle since Sierra joined them. Watching Jake was the only way she could convince herself it was true, that Jake had actually survived the horrendous devastation at the World Trade Center. That though hundreds of firefighter families were grieving even at that moment, she was one of the lucky ones. Her man had lived.

Two doctors had been in to talk to her. Dr. Cleary was her favorite, a kind man with a soothing tone and an easy way of explaining Jake's condition. He had a head injury, of course, that much was obvious. But Dr. Cleary had given her other details, things that helped her better understand the process of recovery once Jake woke up.

The doctor explained that Jake had a concussion, a broken left ankle, and second-degree burns on his face and arms. He had most likely been standing somewhere near the fire truck when the south tower collapsed. Why he was there when the rest of his unit was up near the middle of the building was unclear. Either way, when the tower came down it created a force that must have blown him under the truck.

"He didn't have his uniform on, and that could've been for several reasons," Dr. Cleary had told her. He pulled up a chair and looked her straight in the eye, determined only to help her get through the ordeal at hand. He crossed his arms and continued. "But we know the blast blew his shoes off. That alone tells us we're dealing with a fairly significant head injury. We sedated him heavily when he first arrived—to keep his brain from swelling. That danger is past, in fact . . . the sedation and the surgery probably saved his life."

The doctor bit his lip and hesitated. "Unfortunately, the trauma has left him in a coma."

"But . . . he'll come out of it, right?" Jamie hadn't considered the alternative. That he might not wake up from the coma, or that he could possibly spend the rest of his life being fed through a tube in a hospital bed. She shuddered at the thought and ignored a rush of nausea.

"His brain activity is strong, and the little bit of swelling he had is going down." Dr. Cleary gave her a kind smile. "I expect he'll wake up sometime this week."

The doctor saved the worst news for Wednesday afternoon. He checked Jake's vital signs and then sat down across from her again.

"Mrs. Bryan, we're somewhat concerned about Jake's memory."
He frowned and checked his notes. "The emergency room staff
said your husband didn't know where he was in the minutes before
he lost consciousness."

It was the first time Jamie had heard about this. Her heart sank
to her knees, and she tried to think of what to say. "You mean . . .
all his memory? Like, what's it called . . . ?"

"Amnesia. Yes, that's a concern." The doctor sighed. "Head
injuries can definitely trigger memory loss. The question is how
much loss, and for how long." He looked down at his clipboard
again. "The notes say he couldn't remember his friend Larry . . .
and that Engine 57 meant nothing to him. Would you say that was
significant?"

Significant? Jamie felt the blood drain from her face. She
hugged herself and leaned forward, trying to stop the fear exploding inside her. Jake hadn't remembered Larry? Or his own engine
company? Jamie's voice was weak, as though she'd had the wind
knocked from her. "Are . . . are you sure?"

"I am." Empathy filled the doctor's face. "The notes are very
clear. We're hoping it was only a brief memory loss, and that when
he wakes up he'll remember everything. That's not unusual with
a concussion. But there's chance of a longer amnesia here. I
thought you should be aware." He leaned forward a bit. "So he
should know Larry and Engine 57, is that right?"

Jamie closed her eyes. Her heart was racing again, and she
couldn't breathe. Dr. Cleary was watching her, waiting. "Yes, of
course. He was born a firefighter, Doctor. His father was one, and
now he's one. It's all he's ever known." She tried to fill her lungs,
but the effort only made her feel more anxious. "Larry is his . . . his
best friend. They work together on Engine 57. Jake should've . . .
he should've known that in his sleep."

Dr. Cleary shifted his gaze to Jake and stared at him for a
moment. "There was one thing he said that might be a good sign,
something that might mean his memory loss won't be complete
or even long-term."

Jamie's hands began to tremble. She waited while the doctor
flipped through several sheets of paper. "What did he say?"

"Here it is." He read straight from his notes. "The patient
called out the name 'Sierra' several times before he slipped under."

Tears flooded Jamie's eyes and her heart sang. Jake had remembered Sierra! The doctor was looking at her, waiting for a response,

but she could barely make out his features. He might not have remembered Larry or his engine company, but he'd remembered his precious daughter. "Sierra is ... she's our little girl."

"Good." A smile broke out on the doctor's face. "That's wonderful." He angled his head and looked at Jake again. "In fact, it's possible with the swelling going down that he won't have any memory loss once he wakes up. We'll have to wait and see. He took a pretty serious blow to the head. Anything's possible."

It was Thursday morning now, and Jamie had been awake for half an hour, long enough to know there were no changes in Jake. She crossed the room and stared out the window. The view was obscured by another building, and it was impossible to tell anything other than the fact that night had come and gone. Jamie turned back to Jake and gripped the bars on his hospital bed. *Wake up, baby ... please ...*

She waited, studying him. But there was no change, nothing to indicate he was ever going to come out of the coma.

Her eyes caught the clock on the wall, and she moved around the bed toward the phone. Sierra would be awake now, and Jamie missed her badly. She sat on the chair by Jake's bed and dialed the number.

Sierra answered on the second ring. "Hello?"

Jamie closed her eyes and felt the corners of her mouth inch upward. "Hi, honey, how's it going with Papa?"

"Good." She sounded small and worried. "When are you and Daddy coming home?"

"Very soon, baby. As soon as Daddy wakes up, we'll come home, okay?"

"I'm praying, Mommy. All the time. Papa says God's working on Daddy, making him a little bit better every day."

Jamie ignored the comment. If Jake walked out of that hospital, it wasn't because God had allowed it. After all, what about Larry? Larry loved God, didn't he? Why hadn't God kept him out of the south tower that day? There had to be countless others in similar situations, many of them devoted to God, praying to Him faithfully. And for what? For the random chance to live or die, depending on where you stood at nine o'clock Tuesday morning?

"Mommy?"

"Yes, sweetie, I'm here." She concentrated on her daughter's voice. "Are you being good for Papa?"

"Mmmhmm. Papa said he's gonna take me for ice cream tonight, okay? The 'nilla kind."

"Yes, silly girl. You go have your ice cream with Papa. Me and Daddy will be home real soon."

Jake's father came on, and they talked about Sierra for a while. When they were finished, Jamie fell silent. There were details about what had happened to Jake that didn't make sense. "Okay." She sucked in a slow breath. "I have two questions."

"Sure." The man must've been sitting near Sierra, because Jamie could hear her giggling. "Ask me anything."

"Why would Jake have left the group and gone back downstairs to the truck?" A frustrated huff slipped from between her lips. "That doesn't sound like Jake at all."

"What's your second question?"

"Why wasn't he in his turnouts? I mean they were fighting the worst fire of their lives, and Jake wasn't in uniform? It doesn't make sense."

Jamie heard Jake's father leave whatever room he'd been in and move to a quieter place.

"I've thought about that. I know Jake as well as I've ever known any firefighter in my life. I spent a few years on the job with him, remember, and you get a feel for these things. But with Jake, of course, it's even more because he's my son. He's a part of me. Not just his technique and skill, but the way he thinks, the way he moves on a call."

"So tell me." Jamie's entire being was focused on Jim Bryan's words. No matter how many ways she'd looked at the situation, it didn't add up.

"Okay, first . . . we know Jake went up into the tower on the main stairwell, Stairwell B. That's the only one of the three sets of stairs in the building that goes straight from the top to the bottom."

"Right. Captain Hisel told me about that." Clearly, Jake's father had thought this through. He didn't hesitate as he continued.

"The way I see it, the men from Engine 57 were probably halfway up to the sixty-first floor when someone going down the stairs got into trouble. Heart pains maybe, exhaustion, panic. Whatever it was, the person couldn't keep walking."

"Jake would've been the first to help." Jamie was beginning to understand. She'd never actually thought it through like this, because she couldn't get past the idea of Jake leaving Larry. It was something he'd never done before.

"Right. And immediately, Larry would've done the same. But at that point Jake wouldn't have known the building was in trouble, so what would he have done? He would've told Larry to go on without him."

"But why? The two of them always stayed together."

"Because, Jake would've intended to take the victim downstairs, and then catch up with the other men. There was no point putting Larry through the extra climb when they only had one victim to carry down the stairs."

A dawning burst in Jamie's soul.

The explanation was perfect! Jake's father was right—the way Jake would've figured it was obvious. They hadn't been at the fire yet. They'd only been on their way up. If they'd been at the fire, Jake would never have left Larry. But if only one of them needed to carry a victim down, Jake would've been the first to volunteer, and he never would've asked Larry to come with him. What reason would there have been? Only one man would've been needed to carry a victim down. Jamie swallowed and tightened her grip on the receiver. "But what . . . what about his uniform? He'd completely lost his turnouts when they found him."

"That got me at first, too." Jim Bryan gave a soft chuckle. "Then I remembered something that happened back in 1993. Jake and I were two of the last firefighters who responded to the bombing at the World Trade Center. The fire was out, but as a precaution, we walked up the stairs, making sure people were handling the evacuation okay. We walked up fifty floors that day checking each stairwell, looking for stranded office workers who'd given up or collapsed. Jake said something on the way back down that I just remembered yesterday morning."

Jamie waited, anxious for the rest of the story. She glanced at Jake. He was unmoved, unchanged. His chest fell in a gentle rhythm, but he showed no signs of waking up.

Jim Bryan chuckled again. "On the way back down, Jake kept wanting to take off his turnouts."

"Why?" Jamie still didn't understand.

"Because once you've walked fifty flights in a suit that heavy, you're pretty well exhausted. On the way back down, we knew we were out of danger. All Jake wanted to do was take off the turnouts and bound down the stairs two at a time. In the uniform, we had to pace ourselves."

"So you think . . ."

"I think Jake had a victim on his back, and after a few flights, he realized there was a better way to go about it. He probably slipped out of the stairwell at one of the floors, set the victim down, and took off his turnouts. Then he would've put the victim over his back again and continued down the rest of the way."

The notion made perfect sense. "He could've found the turnouts again on the way back up so he'd be ready to fight the fire."

"Exactly." Jim's tone changed. "Only he never got the chance. He was probably out near the truck helping the victim when the building collapsed."

"So . . . if that's the explanation, I wonder what happened to the person he saved."

"Maybe he was taken away by ambulance." Jim Bryan paused. "Or maybe he was buried in the rubble. I'm guessing that if Jake hadn't gone over to the truck, he might've been buried too. Jake's the only one who'll be able to tell us."

"If he remembers." Jamie had already shared the doctor's concerns with Jake's father.

"Yes . . . I guess we won't know until he wakes up."

They ended the conversation and Jamie stared at Jake. It had been an hour since anyone had entered the room, and she was sleepy. Still, she kept her eyes on Jake, whispering to him, coaxing him to surface from the deep place where he was sleeping. She clutched tightly to the fingers on his right hand.

"Guess what? I just talked to Sierra. She wants you to come home. Your dad's with her right now, but the doctor says it won't be long. You're doing a lot better." She studied him. His face was still bandaged because of the burns. Only now, what with the surgery, his short dark hair had been shaved, and his head was wrapped even bigger than before. She ran her tongue along her lower lip. "We're all pulling for you, Jake."

She no sooner had his name out of her mouth when she felt his fingers move. "Jake?" This time she didn't whisper. The danger that too much stimulation might make his brain swell had long since passed, so she didn't need to keep her voice down. "Jake, honey, can you hear me?"

A moan came from deep in his chest, and then it stopped. *False alarm*, Jamie told herself. But what if it wasn't? "Jake . . . wake up! It's Jamie, honey. I'm right here waiting for you."

Again he made a moaning sound, only this time his head moved an inch or two in each direction. Jamie jumped to her feet. It was happening, Jake was waking up! She rushed into the hallway and waved at a nearby nurse. "Quick . . . get Dr. Cleary. My husband's coming to!"

Jamie felt so wonderful she darted back into the room and barely felt her feet touch the ground. If Jake woke up now, if he had his memory and his health, the doctor would have to peel her off the ceiling. The idea was more than she could hope for.

She came up to Jake's side and took his hand again. He was still moaning, still moving about. First his head and shoulders, then his feet and legs. His injured left ankle was in a cast now, one that would stay on for six weeks. But otherwise, Jake's body was fairly healthy. The burns would heal quickly. Dr. Cleary had said so.

The only questions were about Jake's brain.

"Jake . . . can you hear me?"

He blinked, opening his eyes only the slightest bit. He looked like someone peering into the sun for the first time after spending a week underground. "Mmmmmm." The moan was louder now, more distinct, and Jamie's heart soared. He was trying to talk!

"I'm here, Jake." She was still standing, grasping his knee with her right hand and squeezing his fingers with the left. "You're doing great. Can you hear me, honey?"

He blinked wider this time and squinted, looking around the room until he found her. And the most terrifying realization hit Jamie. He was looking at her without even the slightest bit of recognition.

They were Jake's eyes, for sure. Same shade of blue, same eyelashes. But since Jake was a boy, his eyes had lit up when they found her, every single time they saw each other.

Until now.

Now, as Jamie stared at Jake, there was no love, no sparkle, no pool of shared memories. Nothing at all. What had the head injury done to him? What if he was different now, changed. She banished the thought as quickly as it came. He wasn't changed. He was dazed and hurt, and he needed to heal. He'd suffered a head injury, after all. What did she expect? "Jake? Honey, can you hear me?"

Footsteps echoed in the hallway, and Dr. Cleary's voice sounded above a handful of others. The doctors were coming. They needed to see him, of course, but not yet. She wanted to know for herself first just exactly what Jake remembered. And what he'd forgotten when the south tower slammed him beneath the fire truck.

He was still looking at her, the blank stare giving her a pain in her stomach. She tried one more time. "Jake . . . can you hear me?"

Her husband's lips parted and came together again. Then in a burst of determination he opened his mouth a fraction wider and said the thing that must have been troubling him since he woke up. The thing that brought her world down around her and made her wonder if life between them would ever be the same again.

"Who . . ." he said, his words slow and parched. "Who is Jake?"

SEVENTEEN

SEPTEMBER 13, 2001

Almost nothing made sense anymore.

Jake, if that was his name, had figured out he was in a hospital. But for the past few hours, the only thing he'd been able to hear was the unfamiliar voice of a woman. A pleasant voice he'd never heard before in his life.

She talked to him constantly, even though his eyes were closed and he couldn't move. There was no question the woman was worried about him, but then that was understandable. He was worried about himself. The thing that seemed strange was that she kept calling him Jake, and talking about their house, and his father, and their little girl.

Out of everything she'd said that day, only one name brought to mind a face. The name Sierra. He could picture her as clearly as ... well, as anything.

And it was with that understanding that he knew something was very wrong. Now that he was finally able to make his mouth work, he'd voiced his single most frightening question to the pretty dark-haired woman standing beside him. Who was Jake? Her face went from hopeful to horrified. But that didn't help answer his question, so he tried again. "Who's Jake?"

A pair of doctors walked into the room, and the woman turned to them. Jake couldn't make out what she was saying, but whatever it was, she was upset. He wanted to shout at them. *Hey ... what about me?* He had no idea who he was, and *they* were upset? He felt like a crazy person, as if he'd woken up on a planet he didn't recognize.

He had a terrible headache, but otherwise everything seemed to move all right. His left ankle was in a cast, and there were bandages on his arms. He lifted both hands over his head and used his uncovered fingers to feel his face and scalp. They were covered too. He must've been in an accident, a car accident maybe. That must be it. But why couldn't he remember his name? And why wouldn't anyone answer him about this Jake person? Was that supposed to be him? A name that wasn't in the least bit familiar?

The trio was still whispering halfway across the room. He raised his voice and spoke so they could hear him. "Will someone . . . answer me? Who's Jake?" His words were coming more easily now, but they were still painfully slow and raspy. "This . . . is a hospital?"

One of the doctors looked past the woman and smiled at him. The man nodded at his partner, and both of them made their way over to his bedside. The woman stepped aside and leaned against a wall. Her face was pale and her eyes looked red and watery.

"Yes, this is a hospital." The younger doctor had taken the closest position. "I'm Dr. Cleary, and this is my partner, Dr. Hammond. You've been—"

"What happened?" His voice was suddenly loud and rude, but he didn't care. At first it felt like some kind of dream, as if maybe he was merely having trouble waking up. But now things were starting to feel weird. Really weird. He didn't know his name, didn't know Jake, and he'd never seen the woman at the back of the room. But clearly the woman knew him. It was the most unsettling feeling he'd ever had.

Dr. Cleary hesitated. "You were in an accident."

"Yeah . . . I got that." He rubbed his head and winced. His body felt like it had been trampled by wild horses. The throbbing in his head made it hard for him to think straight. Talking was an all-out effort. "Did I . . . did you operate?"

"We did. You're healing up very nicely."

"How long?" He looked around the room, and met the woman's gaze. As quickly as he could, he tore his eyes from her. "How long . . . have I been here?" The doctor shared a glance with his partner, and Jake had the distinct feeling they weren't telling him everything.

"Three days. They found you beneath your fire truck, Jake. Your head was hurt, and your face and arms were burned."

"Burned?" He was too stunned to say anything else, though a hundred questions fought for position in his mind.

"You were lucky. Nothing worse than second-degree. In six months or so it'll be hard to see your scars."

The information was coming too fast. Jake narrowed his eyes, and nausea hit him like a sledgehammer. What had the doctor said? "I have a fire truck?"

Dr. Cleary smiled. "Not you, exactly. It's the one you and the men from your unit travel in when you take calls."

The doctor was crazy, that had to be it. "You mean I'm a firefighter?"

"Yes, Jake."

This time the doctor's smile faded, and the room was perfectly silent. From her place against the wall, the woman was no longer watching him. She hung her head and seemed to study something on the floor near her feet. For a moment, the doctor checked back at the woman, and Jake guessed that she had provided this information. The doctor shifted his position, and his eyes found Jake's again.

"You've always been a firefighter. It's all you've ever done."

Jake's mouth hung open. "I'm not a fireman, and I . . . my name's not Jake." He covered his eyes for a minute, each word deliberate. His voice was so hoarse it took everything to make himself heard. The tension in his head was getting worse. Why couldn't he remember anything? The entire scene was like something from a pyschotic ward. "I'm not Jake."

The woman covered her mouth and stifled a cry, then she ran from the room. Dr. Cleary watched her go and made a move in her direction, then changed his mind. He turned back to Jake, but this time Dr. Hammond cut in first. "Okay, if you're not Jake, then who are you? Give us your name, and we'll do what we can to help you."

He thought about the question, but for the first time since he'd woken up, he had no answer. He knew he wasn't Jake, and he'd certainly never fought fires. But then who was he? "I . . . I'm not sure."

Dr. Hammond gave a slow nod of his head. "Are you a businessman? Do you work in Manhattan?"

"Manhattan?" The word felt familiar on his tongue, but he wasn't a businessman. The notion felt completely foreign to him. "Where's Manhattan?"

The doctors exchanged a quick look, and Dr. Cleary took over again. "In New York City. It's the business district."

"No." He shook his head. "That's not right . . . I don't work there."

Dr. Cleary nudged his partner and motioned for him to leave. He dropped his voice to a whisper, but Jake could hear him anyway.

"Make sure she's okay, will you?"

The other doctor nodded and left the room. When he was gone, Dr. Cleary turned back to Jake and gave him an understanding look. "I know this is hard for you, Jake. The memory can take a pretty tough blow when a person has trauma to the brain. Let's try a few more questions, okay?"

"No." He wanted to put the pillow over his head and go back to sleep. Maybe that would give his brain time to work right again. "I just want . . . to be normal."

"I realize that. We're doing everything we can to help you." He hesitated. "Just a few more questions."

He clenched the muscles in his jaw, and his face stung. "Fine." He gave a frustrated huff. "Ask."

"Are you married?"

It wasn't meant to be a trick question, but his mind went completely blank. He glanced at his left hand and held it up. "I have a wedding ring."

"Okay, good. But do you remember anything about your wife or your marriage?"

"So I *am* married?" Jake started to feel cold. A shiver passed over him and his teeth chattered. "Was . . . was that woman in here . . . is she my wife?"

Dr. Cleary nodded. "She's ready to help you, Jake. She loves you very much."

The conversation might as well have taken place between two strangers. The skin on Jake's face felt like it was on fire, and his head hurt no matter how much pain medicine they gave him. But he had to figure out who he was. Even if it took every bit of the energy he had left. It was unthinkable that the questions coming from his mouth were his own. His name was Jake . . . he was a firefighter, happily married to a woman he didn't even recognize. He had no choice but to work through the pain until at least something made sense.

Jake licked his lips and realized they were swollen and cracked. "Were . . . were we happy?"

"Your wife says you were very happy. You spent every free moment together."

"Doing what?" His teeth clicked against each other and he shook.

"Would you like a blanket, Jake?"

"Yes, sir."

The doctor disappeared out the door and returned in less than a minute with a blanket. He spread it over Jake, and a warmth made its way through his body. The doctor looked at him. "Do you know where you live?" The man's voice had a serious tone, as though the question was a difficult one, and he didn't really expect an answer.

Jake's heart ricocheted around beneath his rib cage. Where did he live, anyway? Was it New York? Or Florida? Maybe Michigan or San Francisco. His face stung deep to the core of his being, and his head throbbed. How was he supposed to answer questions when he could barely draw the next breath?

"I'm sorry . . ." The doctor was waiting. "Maybe this is too much for now. We can try again—"

"Could . . ." Jake interrupted him. He winced at the effort each word cost him. "Could you give me . . . choices?"

"Cities, you mean?"

Jake gave a slight nod. "Maybe . . ." His tone was impatient again. If only the pain in his head would let up. "Maybe something . . . will sound familiar."

"Okay." Dr. Cleary had a clipboard, and he held it to his chest, his head cocked. "New York?"

He shook his head, barely moving it an inch in either direction. "Not New York."

"Los Angeles?"

"No."

"Tell you what, I'll give you a list, and when you hear something that sounds familiar, let me know."

He hated this. What was wrong with his brain that he couldn't even remember where he lived or who he was? And worse, what if he never found out? Panic bubbled up in him, and for a moment he had a strong desire to flee, run as fast as he could and find a bench somewhere. Then he could sit down and wait until everything made sense.

But he was hooked up to a dozen monitors and tubes, and his ankle was in a cast, so running wasn't an option. Besides, it wouldn't help. "Fine." His voice was gruff and laced with frustration. He was thirsty, and tired, and his mouth was pasty dry. "Please . . . give me the list."

"Boston . . . Detroit . . . Santa Fe . . . Colorado Springs . . . Phoenix . . ." Dr. Cleary paused and raised his eyebrows. "Anything?"

"No . . . nothing." Sweat broke out along his brow as he waited for more possibilities.

"Staten Island . . . Seattle . . . Portland . . . Oklahoma City . . ." The doctor hesitated. "Did anything come to mind when I said Staten Island?"

"Water." He moaned and his eyes closed.

The doctor blinked. "Water?"

"Please."

Dr. Cleary took the plastic pitcher from beside Jake's bed and held the straw up to his lips. He drew in a steady stream of water and winced at the way it hurt to form his mouth around the straw. Two more sips and the doctor set the pitcher back on the table. Jake settled back against his pillows.

"Staten Island, Jake. Did that make you remember anything?"

"No . . . nothing. I have no idea where I came from." He sucked in a slow breath. "Or who I am." He closed his eyes and willed himself to remain calm. When he opened them, he gazed out the window. "This is scary stuff, Doc." His words were coming a bit easier. "Isn't there something you can give me? A pill . . . something that would help me remember? I feel like I'm crazy."

"There's no pill for this, Jake. Just time." The doctor gave him a concerned look. "Is there anything . . . anything you remember about your life before today?"

He closed his eyes and thought as hard as he could. The action was like looking through a dense cloud of fog. He could make out nothing, absolutely nothing. He concentrated again until . . .

Something began to take shape in the vast emptiness, but at first he couldn't tell if it was a person or a flower. It was something, and in a few seconds he could see the face of a little girl with long curly hair. A name came to mind with the picture, a name he could practically see scribbled on the inside of his eyelids.

"Yes." He opened his eyes and stared at the doctor. "When I think hard enough, I can see a little girl, long curly hair." He bit the inside of his lip and willed away the burning around the outside of his mouth. "I . . . I can't quite make out her eyes. She isn't old . . . maybe four or five."

The doctor seemed happy with this latest bit of information. But his enthusiasm did nothing for Jake, because he had no idea who the child was. Just that she was familiar to him. "I'm not sure if it's her name." He motioned to the water, and the doctor gave him another sip. The sweaty feeling was going away, but his world was still upside down. "I keep seeing the word 'Sierra.' I see it whenever I see her picture in my head."

"Very good. Your memory isn't completely gone."

"Am I supposed to know her?"

"Yes." The doctor gave him a half smile. "She's your daughter."

Jake blinked twice. His daughter? He had a daughter? Whenever had he become a father? And who was the child's mother? Why couldn't he remember anything about the little girl except her face and her name? The anger was back. "This is crazy." Tears stung at his eyes, and he pursed his lips, ignoring the pain the action brought. "I have to know who I am."

"Let's see if this helps." The doctor's voice was slow and deliberate without a trace of humor. "Your name is Jake Bryan, and you're married to Jamie. The two of you have known each other since middle school, back when you lived in the same Staten Island neighborhood." He glanced at his clipboard and appeared to be reading some notes. "Your father was a firefighter, a chaplain, and all you've ever wanted to do is fight fires. You joined the FDNY, New York's Fire Department, when you were just out of school, and you married Jamie the year after that. You live in a house given to you by Jamie's parents, who died in a car accident when you were much younger. Four years ago you and Jamie became the parents of Sierra Jane." The doctor paused, the corners of his mouth lifted just a little more. "The two of you are very close. At least that's what Jamie says."

Jake's head was spinning.

He was drowning in an ocean of pain and fear, and now he felt like a secret agent. One who'd just been handed a new identity, and for whom only Sierra's name and face were familiar. Nothing else about what the doctor had just told him struck even the simplest chord in his memory. But then, maybe he had no memory. Just an empty shell of a brain, somehow able to function and talk, but without the ability to remember anything worthwhile.

But it wasn't the doctor's fault. And nothing the man could say was going to make the truth any easier to grasp. He looked up at Dr. Cleary. "Thanks, Doc. I . . . I need some time to myself, if that's okay. In about ten minutes you can send in that wom—" He stopped for three full seconds and cleared his throat. The effort did no good—his voice was still little more than a raspy whisper. "My . . . my wife. Send her to me later, okay?" His anger was fading now. There was no point being mad at the doctors or the pretty brunette. They were only trying to help him.

"Very well." The doctor nodded and left his room.

When he was gone, Jake clenched his fists and pressed them over his eyes. Tears tried to build there, but he wouldn't let them. Something like this needed time, not tears. Lots of time all by himself so he could figure out who he was. He'd been robbed of his very self, and he needed hours, days maybe, to sift through his losses and grieve; time to make an inventory of all the empty places in his brain. Something terrible had happened to him, and now every memory, every recognition that had been a thread in the tapestry of his persona, had been stolen from him. Every single memory.

Just to be sure, he did another inventory. For nearly five minutes, he thought as hard as he could about his childhood, his school days, his firefighting history, his life with this . . . this Jamie woman. His experience as a father. But no matter where he parked his brain, the results were the same.

His house of memories had been robbed blind.

He still had questions, like what were the chances his memories would magically return to him? And how was he supposed to work a job he no longer knew anything about? But those questions could wait. For now there was a bigger question looming among all the others, one that he had asked early in his discussion with the doctor, but had never gotten an answer to.

What had caused this?

Maybe the woman—his wife—would tell him. Whatever it was, the trauma of it must have been very bad, too bad to talk about. The doctors had obviously avoided telling him the details. What if he'd been driving the fire truck and killed someone? The possibilities were too frightening to imagine.

There was a noise at the door, and Jake let his hands relax and fall back to his side. It was the woman. She wasn't tall, but she had long legs and she looked fantastic in her worn-out jeans and red T-shirt. Her face was a creamy white, and her brown eyes took up almost half of it. What was he supposed to say to her? Until this week they'd been friends or lovers since they were in middle school. Wasn't that what the doctor had said?

She crossed the room slowly and set her shaking hands on the rail of his bed. "Jake . . . I know you don't remember me."

He swallowed and tried to maintain eye contact with her. There was a depth in her eyes that couldn't be measured, and that's what made the moment so difficult. He couldn't look at her the same way she looked at him; it was impossible. Not without the memories they apparently shared. Jake waited for her to continue.

"Anyway . . ."

Her voice was thick, and he guessed she was doing everything she could to keep from breaking down. The sight of her made his heart soften. If only he could dredge up one single memory about her. Maybe then the others would come rushing back, and he could take this woman in his arms and love away her sadness. But no matter what they'd told him, for now this Jamie person was nothing more than a stranger.

She shook her head as if she was trying hard to keep her composure. "What I'm trying to say is, I'm here for you, Jake." She smiled, even as her chin trembled. "As long as it takes, I'll help you remember who you are, what we have together. I promised you that a long time ago at our wedding, and the promise is still true today." She took hold of his hand, lifted it to her lips, and kissed it. "I love you, Jake. I always will."

The kiss stirred something in him, but it wasn't a memory. His fingers stiffened some. He pulled his hand gently from her and let it fall back onto the hospital bedsheet. "Thank you."

"Would . . . would you like me to bring Sierra up tonight?" Jamie looked suddenly awkward, and she took a step backwards. "She's dying to see you."

Something about the little girl's name brought relief and recognition to him in a way that was priceless. "Please."

He softened his tone some and managed a partial smile. This woman, this Jamie who was supposed to be his wife, deserved his kindness. Her touch might confuse him, but her heart was easy to read, and it represented no threat. Besides, in a few days he would no doubt go home with her, back to a house he couldn't picture, one that was full of a history that no longer existed for him.

If he was ever going to find his memory, she would have to lead the search. "Jamie . . ." Her name felt completely foreign on his lips. "Thank you."

Her eyes welled up with tears as she started to back away. "Dr. Cleary says you need some sleep."

He nodded. His head hurt worse than when he first woke up, and he was too tired to move. "Yes."

"Okay, then . . ." Jamie lifted one hand and gave him a sad little wave. "See you in a few hours."

When she left the room, he realized something. She must have been sitting beside him, waiting for him to wake up for most of the past three days. Whatever had happened to him, she was probably glad he was alive, anxious to talk to him. And now he didn't even remember her.

No wonder she was crying.

He felt himself being sucked into a deep sleep again, and as he drifted he realized he hadn't asked Jamie about the accident. Where was it and who was involved? Was anyone else hurt? Darkness clouded in around his eyes, and they fell shut, too heavy to keep open. Whatever it was, he could ask her about it that night.

Then at least he'd have answers . . . answers and something else. A person he could see and hold and hug. A person whose name and face he actually remembered.

His little Sierra.

EIGHTEEN

SEPTEMBER 13, 2001

Clay Michaels wasn't sure how much more he could take.

It was Thursday evening, and he and Laura were helping Josh with his homework. Clay had spent every moment with Laura and Josh since Eric disappeared. That's what they were calling it now, a disappearance. Rescue workers hadn't given up hope, and Laura wasn't going to either, but Clay had long since stopped thinking his brother had simply vanished.

The man he'd looked up to since he was a small boy, the brother he admired and loved like a best friend was dead. And not only that, but Eric's marriage had been in trouble, and Clay hadn't done a thing to help. He hadn't even acknowledged how bad things had gotten. The truth about Eric's life was something Clay was desperate to talk about, but other than the conversation they'd shared that first night after the attack, Laura had said nothing. She was too busy believing Eric would call at any minute. And pretending she was right was wearing on Clay almost as much as it was wearing on Laura. But there was nothing he could do about it, no way he could let his guard down and grieve. Because if he gave up hope, Laura would have no choice but to do the same. And right now she was counting on him to not only be there and to be strong for her as well as for Josh, but to be hopeful.

He'd arranged for vacation time the afternoon of the attacks. He had explained the situation, and his police chief had told him to take as much as he needed.

"If we can do anything, let us know," the man had told Clay the day before. "The whole country's reeling."

"Yes, sir. My brother . . ." His voice broke, and it took a moment before he could continue. "We were very close."

Josh had gone to school both days since the terrorists' attack, but Laura was barely holding herself together. They'd been visited by the pastor and several others from church. Each person prayed with them and promised to do what they could to help. The church secretary brought a casserole Wednesday night, and a couple from the mission committee had picked up a pizza for them that afternoon.

By Thursday night Clay had called every hospital, Red Cross center, and rescue mission in the New York and New Jersey areas. "I'm calling from Los Angeles," he'd say. "My brother worked in the World Trade Center south tower, and he's missing. I just wondered if you have any victims not yet identified."

At that point Clay would launch into a description of Eric: six-foot-three, two hundred pounds, short dark hair, a nice-looking face. Blue eyes. But each time the answer was the same. "I'm sorry, all our patients have been identified."

Clay reported his lack of findings to Laura after every call. Most of the time she sat in the same chair looking out the window at a world gone mad, nodding her head as though he were giving her a weather report. But there were times when her shock faded some, and usually when it did, she gave way to fury.

"What was he trying to prove?" she'd yelled earlier that day when Josh was at school. "That he was as dedicated as Allen? That he cared more about their clients than about a national disaster?"

Clay had watched her pace the room. There was nothing he could say, no way he could defend his brother's actions if he had, indeed, stayed in the building working while thousands of others had the common sense to flee. And all for the sake of closing one last deal?

No, there was nothing Clay could say to ease Laura's anger.

But that afternoon her bout of temper had ended in tears. "Why didn't I shake him, Clay? I should've told him a long time ago how I felt. He cared more about work than us. I tried to stop him, tried to tell him he was destroying everything we had." Her eyes held a type of sorrow that was painful to look at. "I keep thinking maybe I could've done something more, something to keep him home."

Her shoulders trembled, and Clay wanted to go to her, soothe away her sadness. "You didn't know."

"But maybe he wouldn't have gone ... maybe he would've done everything in his power to stay home with us."

When Laura would exhaust the angles of guilt and sorrow, she'd become strangely normal. She'd make her way through the house visiting with her housekeeper, checking her e-mail, and listening to CeCe Winans on the CD player. Whenever she stepped outside even for a moment—to check the mail or water a plant, she would run back in through the door and find Clay. "Did he call?"

But Clay had noticed how that mood never lasted more than an hour. It must've been too much work, and when the façade had cracked at about three that afternoon, Laura spent the next hour crying quietly in the living room chair, staring out the window, as though somehow Eric might pull up any minute.

"He was supposed to come home today, you know . . ." She must have repeated the line a dozen times that afternoon. Her denial was so strong that at times Clay was actually afraid for her, not sure if he should take her in for emergency counseling or let her work her way through everything that had happened in the past few days.

Clay watched her now, her face tense as she helped Josh with a math problem at the kitchen table. *She's still waiting for the phone to ring, God . . . how long will this last?* He'd been praying for her constantly, as easily as he breathed, but she was acting nothing like herself.

Clay thought he understood why. Losing Eric would just about kill her. He remembered a few things about her past, details she'd shared with him back when they were high school kids together. One memory particularly stood out, a time back then when Laura had given Clay a glimpse of her heart, a glimpse he'd never forgotten.

"All my life, ever since I was taken from my parents, I've felt lucky to have a home." They had been walking in the hallway after lunch that day, talking about their families. "My adoptive parents are wonderful, but still, I became theirs so late in life that I guess I feel like they're doing me a favor. Like I'm a permanent guest."

"Come on, Laura." He kicked at her feet, hoping she would laugh and tell him she was only kidding. "Your family loves you."

But Laura didn't even smile. "I know that. I love them too. It's not their fault I feel this way. You know what?" She stopped and faced him. "I can't wait to grow up."

"Why?"

A dreamy look had come over Laura's eyes. "I'll get married and have my own family. My very own." The corners of her lips had lifted just a bit. "And I'll never feel like a guest again."

The memory lifted, and Clay leaned back in the kitchen chair, his eyes fixed on Laura. All she'd wanted was a place where she could belong. But she'd gone and fallen in love with Clay's big brother, a man who hadn't had it all together after all. Not if he could choose success and power over being the family man Laura and Josh needed. Before his move to Southern California, he hadn't had any idea that Eric and Laura were having trouble. But after the move the evidence had been hard to miss. The incident at the pizza parlor ... the comments from Josh ... the pain in Laura's eyes. No doubt Eric had let the most important things in his life fall away. And in the process, Laura had wound up in the very position she'd tried to avoid. Living in a home where she couldn't possibly have felt needed or desired, a marriage where she must have realized she would never be anything but second place to Eric's job. Clay could've kicked himself for not saying something back then. While there had still been time.

Eric's money bought her maid service and luxury, but the life they shared wasn't the one Clay had thought they were living. And it was obviously not the dream Laura had hoped for back in high school. In fact, when Clay listened to Laura spill her heart the other night after Josh had gone to bed, he'd had only one very sad thought.

Married to Eric, she was living in the very role she'd wanted to escape as a teenager. The role of a glorified houseguest.

Clay let his gaze wander, and he took in the lavish surroundings that made up his brother's home. The finest natural stone floors, professionally decorated walls and windows, state-of-the-art lighting. None of it could replace love and companionship. Clay shook his head, but not enough to catch Laura's attention. His brother must've been crazy. All those days and hours and weeks at work when Laura and Josh were right here. What could possibly have been important enough to keep him away?

His eyes fell on a framed photo of Laura and Eric. *I thought you ruled the world, big brother. And all the while you thought happiness rested at the top of some ladder. But it didn't. It never did.* His eyes found Laura again, her face still angled close to Josh's, still caught up in the job of helping him with his homework. Clay worked the muscles in his jaw, his emotions suddenly exposed and raw. *What you were looking for was right here, Eric ... right here with them all the time.*

Laura looked up and gave him a small, grateful smile. "Maybe Uncle Clay can help with that last problem." She tousled Josh's hair. "It's got me beat."

"Sure, buddy." Clay coughed, clearing the lump in his throat. "Bring it over here."

Josh jumped up from the table and squeezed into the seat between Laura and Clay. "Mom says it's kinda hard for third grade." Josh shrugged.

"Well ..." Clay looked up and met Laura's eyes. "Moms are usually right." He pulled the book closer. "Let's see what we can do."

Clay helped Josh figure out the problem, and just as they got the answer, the doorbell rang. For the whisper of a second, Laura's eyes grew wide, and she stood up a little too quickly. Then almost as fast, she slipped into the practiced calm persona and waltzed across the kitchen toward the front door. Clay and Josh exchanged a look, and Josh shrugged. "Is it my dad?"

The child's words were like a series of knives in Clay's heart. "No, buddy. I think . . . I think he'd use a key."

"Oh . . ." Josh's expression fell some. "Yeah."

They followed Laura through the living room toward the foyer.

Laura opened the double doors, her expression, her posture, her pace all that of a woman without a care in the world. In fact, watching Laura now, it was impossible to tell that she'd been personally touched in any way by the events of September 11.

"Can Josh come out?" A redhead about the size of Josh stood on the porch. "We're playing catch."

Josh's sad face lifted immediately. "Can I, Mom, please?"

"Sure." She kissed the boy on the top of his head. "Stay out front."

Clay waited three feet from Laura and watched as she closed both double doors and turned to him. Sadness stirred his soul as their eyes locked. He wanted to go to her, take her in his arms and release her from the pretense, tell her it was all right to cry, that they should be crying, in fact, because maybe, just maybe Eric wasn't coming home. Tell her that it was all right to grieve the fact and believe that somehow, someday she'd be okay again. They both would be.

She must've read his thoughts because her smile faded and fear filled her eyes, as though finally the denial was lifting, and suddenly she was face-to-face with the most frightening possibilities in all her life. Her body seemed to shrink as she fell lightly against one of the closed front doors. "I can read your mind, Clay."

He took a step closer and let his shoulder lean against the wall a few feet from her. "What's it saying?"

Laura let her head fall forward. There was silence for a moment as the late summer breeze sifted through the open windows in the vast living room and into the place where they stood. The smell of some kind of flower hung in the air and mixed with the distant sounds of Josh and his friends playing catch in the front yard.

When she looked up there were tears in her eyes. "You don't think he's coming back."

Clay felt her pain, felt it wrap around his heart and take his breath away. He said nothing, not just because his throat was too thick to speak, but because anything honest he might utter now would only hurt her more.

Her gaze was direct, unwavering; this time she wanted an answer. "You think he's dead, right?"

"Well . . ." His mouth opened, but nothing came out. *Give me the words, Lord . . . help me get her through this.* "What do *you* think, Laura?" He kept his voice low, gentler than the breeze. "Do you really think he's coming home?"

It was the first time he'd tried to reason with her, tried to get her to see the impossibility of her unfounded hope. The question seemed to hit her in stages, and Clay took in each of them as they played across her face. Shock . . . anger . . . frustration . . . and finally a sense of cavernous sorrow and futility. A knowing that all the pretending in the world wasn't going to change the facts.

"No . . ."

She took a step back and slid slowly down toward the floor, her shoulder still pressing into the wall. As she hit the floor, a sorrowful sound came from her. It was raw and gut-wrenching, and it became a series of sobs unlike anything Clay had ever heard. As a police officer he'd often been the bearer of bad news, the one who'd rung a family's doorbell in a way that would interrupt their lives forever. He'd held countless devastated friends and family members at the scenes of fatal accidents.

But grief does not follow a pattern, and the weeping coming from Laura was more than a dawning reality that Eric might be dead. It was that, but it was something more, as though she wasn't only grieving the loss of Eric, but the loss of her own life as well. The loss of their marriage, their family, and all that she and Eric had failed to be.

He went to her, slipped his hands under her arms, and lifted her until she fell into his embrace. "Laura . . . I'm sorry."

She buried her head in his chest and held on to his shirtsleeves. Twenty minutes passed while she stayed that way, letting the sobs empty from a place that must have carried them around for far too long. Finally, when he could no longer feel her sobs shuddering against him, she spoke, her voice so broken she could hardly speak. "He . . . he isn't coming home, is he?" she said as she tightened her grip on his arms.

He pulled her close again and spoke softly against her hair. "I don't think so."

She pulled back and wiped her fingertips beneath her eyes. They were swollen and bloodshot, and she looked faint, as though she might collapse again. "I kept thinking today was the day. Somehow . . . somehow he hadn't been able to get through, but he'd find a way to get home when he was supposed to. On a bus or a train . . . something." She drew in a slow, shaky breath. "But if he and Allen were on the sixty-fourth floor . . . They're still looking for people, right?"

Clay studied her, but the face he saw wasn't that of a weary, frightened woman facing the death of her husband. It was the face of a girl he'd known since his freshman year in high school. "They haven't found anyone alive in the rubble since yesterday afternoon."

"I know. I guess I just thought . . ." She sniffed. "I thought God might give me a miracle. That somehow despite all the evidence, Eric had actually survived."

He smoothed his hands down the lengths of her arms. "I want to believe that too." Clay thought about the news report he'd heard that morning when Laura was in the shower. Apparently, cell phones were ringing deep in the rubble. He hadn't told her. None of the reports said anything about anyone actually answering the calls.

Laura took a few steps back and glanced out the window toward Josh and his friends. "He missed so much over the years."

Clay worked the muscles in his jaw. "He should've told me." He hesitated. "You should've told me, Laura. I could've talked some sense into him."

"No, Clay." Laura hugged her arms against her chest and whispered a sad laugh. "If he wouldn't listen to me, he wouldn't have listened to you, either."

"You tried, though . . . the two of you?" This new image of Eric still didn't ring true. As though they were talking about someone else, and not the brother he'd looked up to all his life.

"Yes." Laura turned back toward him. "After we lost the baby, nothing was ever the same. Over the years, we tried three times since then. Tension would build, I'd force the issue, and we'd have counseling six, maybe eight weeks. For a while things would seem better, but it always came back to his first love."

The phrase caught Clay off guard. Back when they were young, when their own parents had divorced, Eric would find his mother in the den and reason with her. "Mom . . . if God's your first love, then you have to at least try. You and Dad owe it to each other."

The words echoed in Clay's mind. *If God's your first love* ... He blinked the memory back and searched Laura's eyes. "His first love?"

She exhaled through her nose and gave a small shrug. "Koppel and Grant, Clay. Always Koppel and Grant." Laura touched his arm and nodded toward the boys outside. "Go play with him, will you? I need a few minutes by myself."

"Okay." He met her eyes once more. "You sure you're all right?"

She nodded. "I just need a few minutes with God."

"To pray for Eric?"

"No." She gave him a smile that stopped short of her eyes. "To ask Him why He took him from me. Before we found a way to work things out."

Clay reached out, gave her hand a tender squeeze, and left through the front door. He jogged toward the boys playing outside near the street.

"Hey, Josh ... you got room for another rookie?"

"Uncle Clay!" The child's face lit up. He ran to Clay and jumped into his arms before falling back to the ground and racing over to the other boys. "My uncle's gonna play with us. He's so good, you guys won't believe it!"

* * * *

Inside the house Laura heard her son's excitement, saw the look on his face as he hugged Clay and led him into an impromptu game of baseball. The tears were gone for now, her eyes and her heart dry as she thought about the possibility. Was it true? Could Eric really be gone, buried in the ruins of the World Trade Center? Without ever finding a way back to the love they'd once shared?

Laura swallowed, and her heartbeat pounded in her temples. Her headache would only be worse after so much crying. She hung her head and closed her eyes. The façade had been for her benefit, hers and Josh's. She'd convinced herself that Eric would call or grab a train or find his way home, but now even that was too much effort. The truth was as clear as air. Unless they found him soon, she wouldn't ever see him again.

If Eric wasn't in one of the hospitals or rescue missions, if he hadn't called her or found a way to get a message sent home, then there was only one other answer. He was somewhere in the pile. Laura hadn't watched TV reports since Tuesday, but she wasn't completely ignorant. She'd watched the tower come down, after all, the force so great it looked like a bomb had gone off. And not just any bomb. But a nuclear bomb, like the one they'd dropped on Hiroshima at the end of World War II.

The truth was, no one could've survived that force. Especially not sandwiched somewhere in the middle of it.

Laura found her favorite chair, the one that faced the front windows and allowed her to stare at the sky and wonder. She sat down, leaned her head back, and let her eyes get lost in the deep cloudless blue. What could she say to God now? If Eric was dead, then it was too late to ask for help or strength or a miracle. Besides, why would God answer her now. He hadn't answered her prayers that Tuesday morning. She blinked and thought about that. It would've been nothing to a mighty God to alter the course of those planes or cause Eric to leave the building with the others. Eric could've taken his business trip a week before or a week after. God could've foiled the hijackers' plans somehow, or held the buildings up with His bare hands to keep them from falling. But He didn't.

She watched a hawk circle over the chaparral-covered hill that bordered their neighborhood, and she felt the hint of a smile play at the corners of her lips. Eric used to love eagles. *God . . . is he dead? Have you taken him home?* She blinked, her eyes dry.

Nothing about prayer seemed natural these days, so she sighed and lowered her gaze to Clay and the boys playing in the street. She clenched her teeth and leaned back into the chair. Forget counseling and stale cures for the things that ailed their marriage. She should've screamed at him, shaken him, demanded that he love her and Josh the way they needed to be loved.

Begged him to stay home from New York.

She glanced up once more. The hawk overhead soared in another circle, this one closer to her hillside home.

God, I'd do anything for another chance with him. Anything.

Often, in days past, Laura would feel some sort of response to her prayers, a Scripture that might come to mind, or a whispered word of encouragement echoing deep in her soul. But this time there was nothing. No bits of direction or sense that somehow God had heard her prayer. Only the awful certainty that now, after all her missed opportunities to make a difference with Eric, she'd run out of time. He wasn't going to call or walk through the front door, not now or ever again. Laura felt the familiar sting of tears, and she wasn't sure which hurt worse. The tragedy of what had obviously happened to Eric, or the loss of all they could've shared in the future.

If only she'd had one more chance.

NINETEEN

SEPTEMBER 13, 2001

Bringing Sierra to the hospital that night to see Jake took every bit of Jamie's strength. In the end she begged Jake's father to come with her. He'd planned to save his visit for the next day so Jamie and Sierra could have time alone with Jake.

But Jamie was terrified to see him again.

"He didn't know me, Dad. Not at all." Jamie's hands shook, and she could barely think. Anxiety gnawed at her insides. "Come with me, please. I can't go alone. Besides, maybe he'll remember you."

Jim Bryan had agreed, and now he was getting ready. Sierra had dressed herself in the new pink church dress, the one Jake had made such a fuss over just last Sunday. The child was sitting sweetly in the TV room playing with her dolls. Jamie watched her from the kitchen and wanted to join her, sit beside her and tell her everything was going to be okay with her daddy. But she couldn't stop shaking long enough to string a sentence together. Obviously Jake had a brain injury, something terribly wrong. The two of them had known each other forever, it seemed. FDNY shifts were twelve on, twelve off. Jake had gotten day shifts almost from the beginning, and they were never apart for more than a single night.

How could he not know her?

Her mouth was dry and her mind raced. She poured herself a glass of water and emptied it in three gulps. What if his memory never came back? How was she supposed to teach him to love her the way he always had, as far back as she could remember? She bit the inside of her lip and gripped the kitchen counter, looking out over their small backyard. Jake's love was something she had absolutely counted on. He might die, yes, but as long as he drew breath, Jake Bryan would love her. Never in all her hours of worrying had she considered he might get hurt, that a head injury could rob him of a lifetime of memories they'd built together.

Sierra popped up from the sofa and skipped toward her, the pink dress fluffing softly behind her. "Let's go." She tilted her head and smiled. "I wanna see Daddy."

"As soon as Papa's ready." Jamie exhaled and felt herself grow just a bit calmer. At least Jake's father would be with them. She ran her fingers over Sierra's brow and realized something. She needed to prepare her daughter for what she was about to see. "Honey . . . Daddy's at the hospital because he got hurt. You know that, right?"

"Papa said he's at the hos'apul, and his head has an owie."

"Right." Jamie nodded and studied Sierra's eyes. The child had no idea. "But the doctors put lots of bandages on Daddy's head and face. He won't look . . ." Her voice caught and she swallowed a sob. "He won't look like he used to."

"You mean because he got a hurt face, too?"

"Yes, sweetie." Jamie pulled Sierra close and hugged her. "But the doctors are making him better." She drew back and locked eyes with her daughter again. "Okay?"

"Okay." Sierra's eyes grew wide and she did a little gulp. "Can he come home with us?"

"Not for a few days."

Footsteps sounded from the other room, and Jim Bryan walked up to them, his eyes narrow, braced in anticipation. It was a look Jake got when he talked about working a tough call, the look he and his father probably both had at any fire. He reached out and gave Jamie's arm a gentle squeeze. "Let's go."

She was grateful beyond words for his presence. It allowed her to think through the situation, to imagine how they were going to survive it. They left the house together, and forty minutes later all three of them walked into Jake's hospital room. He lay flat on the bed, his head still fully bandaged. They filed inside, and Jamie couldn't tell if he was awake.

"Daddy?" Sierra stopped short, her eyes wide.

"Jake . . ." Jamie took Sierra's hand and stepped closer to her husband's bed. "Sierra's here."

At the sound of her name, his eyes blinked open. With small, strained movements, he turned his head and peered at her. All that showed of his mouth was a small opening in the gauze, so it was impossible to tell if he was smiling, if seeing his daughter was enough to jolt some sort of awakening in him. He kept his eyes locked on the girl, and finally he was able to make his lips work enough to speak. "Sierra . . ."

Sierra squeezed Jamie's hand and hid partially behind her. She tilted her face up, and Jamie was struck by what she saw there.

The child was scared to death. She'd never seen Jake as anything other than the muscled, active, healthy man he'd been before Tuesday morning.

This man—lying on a hospital bed wrapped in bandages—was someone she not only didn't recognize. But someone who scared her.

"Mommy . . ." Sierra's voice was a whisper. "What's wrong with him?"

Jim Bryan took a few steps backwards and let them have this moment, the three of them. Jamie tried to find the right words. "Daddy got hurt at work, baby."

Her little girl eyes became almost perfect circles. "In a fire?"

"Yes, sweetie." Jamie looked at Jim for help, but he was staring at Jake. Probably as stunned as Sierra at the sight he made there in the hospital bed. "He got hurt in a fire."

"Then . . ." Sierra shifted her gaze to Jake and swallowed hard. "I'll pray for him. So he'll get better."

"Yes, let's do that in a few minutes, okay?" Jamie stepped closer and looked down at her husband. "How're you feeling?"

His eyes met hers, but it was impossible to make out his expression. "My face stings."

"I'm sorry." Seconds of silence felt like hours, and Jamie searched for something to say. Finally, she reached back and motioned for Jake's father to come alongside her. He was hesitant, but finally he took his place on the other side of Sierra.

Jamie looked back at Jake. "I brought your dad."

Jake blinked and moved his head enough to see Jim Bryan. "You're . . . my dad?"

"Hello, son." Jim took Jake's hand, his eyes glistening. "Everything's going to be fine."

"I'm your son?" Jake stared up at Jim.

Jake looked as fearful as Sierra, and Jamie wanted to jolt herself, make herself wake up from the nightmare they were suddenly thrust into. It wasn't happening . . . it couldn't be. Jake would never not know her . . . or his father. It was impossible.

"Yes, Jake." Jim Bryan nodded as a single tear made its way down his weathered cheek. "I'm your dad."

"Oh." Jake stared at him for another few seconds and then let his gaze fall back to Sierra.

When she realized that Jake was looking at her, she must've decided to be brave. She peeked out from behind Jamie and touched her small fingers to Jake's hand. "Hi, Daddy."

"Hi." Jake's eyes were flat.

"Is Jesus going to make you better?"

He gave a quick glance at Jamie and his father. "I hope so."

Jamie's knees felt weak. How must it feel to Jake, lying there unable to recognize any of them except Sierra? And why Sierra? Why not her, when he'd loved her forever? How could he remember one of the girls in his life but not the other? The entire scene felt disjointed and uncomfortable, like a poorly scripted play.

Jake's father cleared his throat and was about to say something when Jamie heard footsteps behind her. She turned and saw Captain Hisel from the station. He was in his work pants and shirt, and his face looked haggard, as though he hadn't slept in weeks. Jamie could only imagine the heartache he was dealing with at the station and throughout the city.

The station's losses made Jamie think about Sue, and how she still hadn't spoken to the woman. Not since Tuesday when they'd first learned Larry was missing.

The captain nodded at Jake's father and took slow steps into the room. "I had to check on him." His eyes met Jamie's, and he managed a weary smile. "Everyone at the station's pulling for him, praying for him to remember who he is."

Everyone still alive, Jamie wanted to add. But she didn't dare. Jake had no idea how he'd been hurt. He couldn't even remember the fact that he was a fireman, let alone the names of friends he'd had. Now that they were gone, the truth, the gravity and immensity of the situation, would have no bearing on Jake. It would only frighten him more.

Jake's father stepped back so Captain Hisel could find a place up against Jake's bed. "JB ... how're you feeling?"

"My head hurts." There wasn't a flicker of recognition in his eyes.

The captain looked down and patted Sierra on the head. "I see your best girls came to visit you."

Jake looked at their daughter. "I ... I remember Sierra."

"Well, that has to be a good sign." Captain Hisel hesitated, not knowing what to say.

As Jamie watched the captain's awkwardness, she sympathized. What did you say to a person who no longer remembered any of your shared experiences?

"I need ... to know something." Jake's voice was still hoarse and raspy, and it was an effort for him to talk. He strained to look from the captain to Jamie and over toward the wall at his father.

"What happened to me?" He winced as though he was in awful pain. "Tell me about the accident."

Jamie took the initiative. Jake's doctors had said it would be better to wait and let him find out what happened in a few weeks—when some of his memories might be returning. "You were fighting a fire." Jamie sent a quick look to the others, silently begging them to refrain from adding details. "You hit your head when part of the building collapsed."

"Was anyone else hurt?" Jake lifted his hand slowly toward his face and then changed his mind and let it fall again.

"That isn't important, Jake." Jamie's tone put an end to the line of questions. "Let's focus on getting you better."

Captain Hisel cleared his throat. "We miss you down at the station."

Jake blinked. "What station?"

Captain Hisel looked at the others around the room and finally back at Jake. "The fire station." The man's eyebrows formed a deep-set V. "Don't you remember?"

"Look . . ." Jake gave a pained shake of his head and released a heavy sigh. "I don't know if this is . . . some wacky dream or . . . or if I've lost my mind." Jake met Captain Hisel's eyes again. Discouragement tinged his voice. "But I don't remember the station . . . or you." He shifted his gaze to Jamie and his father. His words were slow and machinelike, dimmed by his raspy voice. "Or either of you . . . or anything about being a fireman." He looked at Sierra, and his eyes softened some. "The only thing I remember is Sierra."

Jamie's head spun, and she had to grip the bed's guardrails to keep from falling. She flashed the captain a look and motioned toward the hallway. He nodded and turned as she leaned in closer to her husband. "We'll be out in the hall for a bit. Go ahead and rest, Jake."

Taking Sierra by the hand, Jamie followed the captain and Jake's father into the hallway. The moment they were out of earshot from Jake, Captain Hisel stared at Jamie, his mouth open. This was the first time the captain had seen Jake since he'd regained consciousness. "He really doesn't remember."

"No." Jamie bit her lip to keep from crying. Her head was spinning harder now, and the black spots were back, dancing before her eyes and making it hard to hear. "Not . . . not even me."

The men must've known she was about to fall, that she couldn't possibly stand up another minute under the weight of all that had happened. Jake's father came up along one side, Captain Hisel along the other, with Sierra in the middle. Together they formed a circle, arms linked, heads bowed, silenced by the tragedy of it all.

And for a long while no one spoke.

Jake's words had said it all.

* * * *

Questions had been weighing on Jake since he came to, and now he wanted answers. Here and there he'd caught snippets of conversations in the hallways—sometimes when he was in and out of sleep. Something major had happened in New York City, a disaster that involved more than him.

If he really was a firefighter, then Jake had the feeling he wasn't the only man injured in the incident—whatever it was.

He reached for the television remote and clicked the On button. Strange, that his brain could remember how to talk and operate a remote control. He could even picture New York City. But if his life depended on it, he couldn't remember his name or the woman who apparently was his wife.

A picture began to take shape on the TV screen, and a logo at the corner said CNN. The all-news channel—another thing he remembered. A man was standing behind a podium talking, and Jake glanced at the doorway, hoping the people he was supposed to know wouldn't come back. Not yet. If they weren't going to tell him what had happened, he had to find out for himself.

Jake focused, and someone offscreen asked the man a question— something about football games that weekend.

"The NFL will take this weekend off in honor of the victims of September 11," the man said. "We believe this is the least we can do to show our respect."

NFL? That was the National Football League. So why were they taking a week off? And what had happened September 11 that would cause them to cancel all their games? They wanted to honor victims that had been hurt how? What was the man talking about? A realization hit him like a fist in the stomach. What day had he been injured, anyway? He wasn't sure, but he thought he'd been in the hospital just two days. Maybe he was one of the people hurt on September 11.

The image changed, and a somber-looking man announced that the station was going to do a recap of the events from the past two days. A picture flashed of two towering buildings. Fireballs and thick black smoke poured from the top of one of them, and before Jake could remember where he'd seen the buildings, an airplane came into view and flew smack into the other tower.

His mouth went dry. The reporter was saying something about terrorists and suicide missions, but none of it made sense. Terrorists? Flying planes into buildings? Had this happened while he was unconscious, or had he been in one of the buildings, even fighting the fire in one of them?

His hands shook, and the remote control fell to his lap.

Over the next few seconds, the recap showed the collapse of first one building, then the other. One image showed a different flaming structure—wider and nowhere near as tall. And finally, the picture changed to a rural-looking field, with what looked like a charred crater.

A chart appeared on the screen with a banner across the top that read, "Attacks on America." The information detailed the apparent loss of four airplanes, multiple buildings in New York City, and Washington, D.C., and the deaths of some three thousand people, more than four hundred of which were firefighters or emergency personnel.

Three thousand people dead? And hundreds of firefighters?

Jake clicked off the TV, and suddenly a memory filled his mind, clear and detailed. The tall buildings were part of the World Trade Center—the famous Twin Towers in downtown Manhattan—situated in the heart of New York City.

The memory of the buildings was so clear it was striking, and Jake settled back against his pillow. There was only one reason why he would remember the buildings this well. He must've spent time there, and that meant the people outside were telling the truth. He was a firefighter, probably stationed somewhere near the towers. He and the other guys at his station had probably been in the buildings hundreds of times.

If that was true, then he must've been injured in the terrorist attacks. And not only that, but he was probably lucky to be alive. The numbers flashed through his head again. Thousands dead . . . hundreds of emergency personnel. How had he survived? And which close friends and colleagues had been killed when those buildings tumbled to the ground?

He tried to remember the captain's name. Hiser or Hisen. . . . Whoever he was, no wonder he looked so shaken. The station hadn't responded to a fire. They'd responded to a national disaster, a tragedy worse than anything America had ever seen. And he'd been right there in the middle of it.

Reality took a moment to introduce itself.

So, his name was Jake, after all, and he really was a firefighter. He had to be; he'd been found beneath his fire truck, and the captain recognized him. Jake worked the sore muscles in his jaw and tried to imagine fighting fires, wearing the heavy uniform and holding the high-pressure hoses while flames raged around him. He could conjure up such scenes in his head, but not one of them felt familiar. And nothing came to mind when he tried to picture the station, the one the captain had asked him about.

Jake closed his eyes and concentrated so hard his face hurt beneath the bandages. He had obviously worked at the station dozens of hours every month for who knew how many years, so why couldn't he remember any of it? If he could picture the World Trade Center buildings, why couldn't he picture the fire station?

And what about the woman? At first the idea of not remembering her had seemed so strange he merely dismissed the thought altogether. He couldn't be married to her, otherwise he'd know at least something about her. Instead, he'd assumed that somehow she must've been confused about him, and by believing that, he was able to convince himself the whole situation was some kind of enormous mistake.

But clearly he'd been wrong. Everything the people in the hall outside his room had been telling him was true. He was a firefighter, married to Jamie, and he worked at a station in New York City that had most likely been decimated by the terrorist attacks on September 11. Somehow he'd fought the biggest fire in the country's history and walked out of it alive. Sure, he'd lost his memory, but his doctors could do something about that. The important thing was, he'd survived.

Another understanding dawned in the dark corridors of his confused brain. If he was ever going to find his way back to the person he used to be, he'd need the support of the people outside in the hallway.

Especially Jamie and Sierra.

Recent memories came to mind, the terrified look on the woman's face each time she entered his room, the anxiety in the eyes of the other men, the man who was obviously his father, and the captain. No, Jake didn't recognize them. But he hadn't so much as smiled at them, either. However hard this ordeal was on him, they were going through something equally awful. Until a few days ago they'd shared intimate relationships and friendships with him, and now he was so disoriented he hadn't found it in himself even to be kind.

He was alive, after all. He had a family and friends who loved him. Jake pictured them again, Jamie and his father, the captain. Combined, he had not a single memory of any of them, and the reality of that would have left him utterly despondent if not for one thing—he remembered Sierra. His little daughter gave him a starting place, a single rock to cling to as he set out on the climb of his life. The hike back to reality as it had been before September 11.

But if he was going to begin the journey, if he was going to do it with a smile, he needed to get started. And that meant he couldn't go another moment without having Sierra by his side and telling her something he should've said the moment he first saw her. Even if he didn't remember ever having said it before.

"Sierra . . ." His voice was quiet and scratchy, lost in the hum of hospital machines around him. It fell far short of the door. He tightened the muscles in his stomach and tried again, the raspy words much louder this time. "Sierra . . . come here."

The little girl popped her face just inside the room, and Jake felt a surge of emotion for the child, a wave of feeling that fell just short of recognition. Her hair fell in a cascade of curls, and her pink dress flounced below her knees as she moved into the room, still latched tightly to her mother's hand. "Daddy . . . ?"

"Yes . . ." Jake swallowed hard. His throat hurt and his words sounded unnatural. Or maybe this was his normal voice, and he simply didn't recognize it. Jake tried not to think about the possibility. "Come here, Sierra."

A smile lifted the corners of her little mouth, and she lowered her chin, her eyes wide and tentative. The woman lowered her face to Sierra's. "Stay here for a minute, baby. I'm going to talk to Daddy first."

Sierra did as she was told and waited by the door. The men stayed in the hall, and that was fine with Jake. They were probably talking about how terrible it was that he couldn't remember them. Or maybe they figured he needed these moments alone with his family. Jamie made her way to his bed. The fear was still in her eyes, but this time Jake forced his bandaged face into what he hoped was a smile.

"Jake . . ." She bit her lower lip to keep it from quivering. Her voice was barely loud enough for him to hear. "I know you don't remember me. I'm not sure how much you remember Sierra." She paused and gripped the guardrails on his bed once more. "But please . . . if you don't remember, at least pretend. For Sierra's sake." She opened her mouth, and a quiet laugh tangled up with a cry. She put the back of her hand against her mouth for a moment. "Last week you were curling her hair and taking her to church. At least act like you know her. Okay?"

Jake held her eyes for a long while. "Okay." His voice was so hoarse he could barely speak. "I'm sorry, Jamie. I'd give anything to . . . to remember you."

Her eyes glistened. She sniffed and straightened, as though she was desperate to keep her composure, and she nodded her thanks and then returned to Sierra.

"All right, honey. Daddy wants to talk to you."

Sierra looked past Jamie to Jake, and this time he managed to wave his fingers at her. She followed Jamie back to his bed and found the courage to step up, her face inches from his. "Hi, Daddy."

A lump grew in Jake's throat, and he considered his feelings. Each time he looked at the girl or thought about her, he was swallowed up in emotions. "Hi, Sierra." He cast a quick look at Jamie, then back to his daughter. "Thanks for coming."

Sierra cocked her head, her eyes wide. "Did you lose your voice, Daddy?"

"Yes, honey." This time his smile wasn't forced. "I think I hurt it in the fire."

"Oh." She nodded.

The moment felt awkward again, and Jake's mind raced. He would have to find familiar ground—even if none existed. He reached his bandaged arms through the holes in his bedrails and took hold of Sierra's fingers. The lump was back, and speaking was still more difficult. "Daddy's gonna need your help to get better, okay, honey?"

"Okay." She beamed at the notion. "I'll bring you water and toast and ice cream in bed when you come home."

"Perfect." Out of the corner of his eye, Jake saw Jamie wipe at a tear. He kept his focus on Sierra.

"I'm glad you're okay, Daddy." She lowered her face to his hand and planted a gentle kiss on each of his fingers. "You can't do butterfly kisses yet, but I can. Okay?"

"Okay." Jake used what was left of his energy to extend his fingers a bit farther and stroke the child's feathery soft cheek. Then he said the only thing he could say, the single truth he hoped, would somehow bridge his past and his present. Though he couldn't remember saying it before, though he wasn't sure it reflected his feelings perfectly, it was the only thing he had to hang onto.

"I love you, Sierra. I'll always love you."

TWENTY

SEPTEMBER 17, 2001

The doctor's information was more than Jamie could process at once.

But somehow, after a weekend of emotions too jumbled to sort through, Jamie was sure of one thing. This meeting with Dr. Cleary was the only way any of them could move forward.

By now they all knew that Jake was aware of how he'd been injured. So in addition to the pain of his injuries and the frustration of not remembering his past, he had to deal with the awful enormity of what had happened to him and his friends on September 11.

Jamie sat by Jake's bed, her hands folded on her lap. She didn't have the nerve to hold his hand, not since he woke up. A few times over the weekend, Jake had made an effort to cast her a kind look or even the hint of a smile. But it was obvious by the things he said—and the things he didn't say—that he still saw her as a stranger. Dr. Cleary had already explained what type of head injury Jake must have suffered in order to lose his memory. Now the doctor was getting specific.

"Let's talk about amnesia." He looked from Jake to Jamie. "You've had a few days to see where Jake's at, what he remembers." The man hesitated. "I'm sure you have questions."

Jake was partially sitting up in bed, and he gave a nod of his bandaged head. "Lots." Doctors had removed most of the bandages on his arms and replaced them with smaller, patchlike sections of gauze. His voice was still raspy. "It's so random, what I remember and what I don't."

"Exactly." Dr. Cleary leaned forward, and his expression grew serious. "The brain compartmentalizes information, and memory is no exception. A part of your brain contains the memory of learned behavior—sitting, standing, walking, eating, even vocabulary. Another part contains functional memory—language, the meaning of various terms and expressions, memories of places and routines."

"Jake remembers those things." Jamie glanced over her shoulder at him. "At least I think you do. Right?"

"Yes." Jake nodded. "And I can remember everything that's happened since I woke up."

"Exactly. A third of the brain's memory bank is devoted to that type of remembering. Short-term memory, it's called." He pursed his lips and studied Jake. "The problem we're dealing with is long-term memory—an area of loss that's most common with head injuries like yours."

"I don't get it." Jamie closed her eyes and pinched the bridge of her nose. Her stomach was in knots as she dropped her hands into her lap and looked at the doctor again. "If his long-term memory is gone, how come he can remember how to eat or the fact that he worked in New York City?"

Dr. Cleary shifted his position and nodded as though he'd expected her questions. "Again, the brain sees those memories as more learned behavior or functional information. Occasionally, a person with a head injury will lose that part of his memory as well. But long-term memory loss is something different." He paused and took a slow breath. "Picture a storage unit filled with information about specific people and experiences shared with those people. That's a picture of a person's long-term memory."

"That's what I'm missing?" Jake adjusted himself so he was partially on his side, facing the doctor.

Jamie caught the way he still winced when he moved.

"Definitely not. Every memory you've ever made is still in that storage unit." The doctor managed a sad smile. "But right now the door's locked, and none of us can find the key."

Jamie folded her arms tight and pushed her fists into her stomach. The information was interesting, but it didn't tell her what she wanted to know, what she was desperate to know. When would Jake recognize her? She did a little cough and tried to find a way to voice her feelings. "Are you saying . . . that someday he'll get his memory back?"

"Almost always." This time the doctor's smile was fuller. "Long-term memory loss generally lasts no more than six months. The exact timing is different for every patient, but most of the people suffering from this type of amnesia get flashbacks as early as two or three months into their recovery."

"Flashbacks?" Jake ran his fingers over his right forearm. Though the bandages had been removed, the burns on that arm were the worst of all.

Jamie's heart went out to him. She moved to put her hand on his shoulder, to comfort him and let him know she was sorry he was hurting. But she stopped herself. Any small shows of affection would only make Jake nervous.

Dr. Cleary stood and walked closer to Jake's bed, looking from him to Jamie. "Flashbacks are definitely part of the healing process. They're the brain's way of letting an amnesiac see through the window of the hidden storage unit I was talking about earlier." He leveled his gaze at Jake. "They're a little scary sometimes."

Scary? Jamie felt her heart skip a beat. How could anything be more frightening than looking into her husband's eyes and seeing not a bit of recognition? "In what way?"

"The first memories that return are usually those closest to the point of memory loss." Dr. Cleary gripped the railing along the side of Jake's bed. "That means memories of the accident."

Whatever he'd been through in those final moments, it had to have been horrific. Dr. Cleary looked at Jamie. "At first the flashbacks tend to come just before or after sleeping. He might sit up suddenly in bed or yell out in the middle of the night." He hesitated. "You'll have to help him through that."

She nodded. "Okay."

Dr. Cleary moved to the end of the bed and lifted Jake's chart. "That about covers the amnesia." He shot a brief look at Jamie. "I'll talk about that a little more with you later. For now, let's go over his burns."

Jamie had been so caught up with her husband's memory loss, she'd barely considered the fact that he had burns to deal with. Yes, they were painful, but beyond that Jamie hadn't given it much thought. She narrowed her eyes, grateful for the diversion.

"How's the skin on your face feeling, Jake?" The doctor kept his eyes on the chart as he returned to the side of the bed.

Jake lifted his left hand and gave a light touch to his bandaged cheeks and forehead. "It stings."

"By the looks of it, you were headed back into the building when it collapsed." The doctor bent over and carefully lifted the corner of one of the bandages on Jake's right arm. "A burst of searing hot air must've knocked you back, pushed you under the fire truck. In the process it burned your arms and face." He lifted the corner of another bandage and looked at the burn beneath. "Your arms are healing nicely. Second-degree burns, which means you'll have some scarring, a deep redness for the first six months or so, but much of it will disappear in the first year."

This time the doctor peered beneath the top section of the bandages still covering Jake's face. "You were very lucky with your face. The skin on your cheeks and forehead took the brunt of the heat and came close to being third-degree burns." He straightened and glanced at the clipboard again. "The wrap we're using is helping a lot. I think we'll be able to avoid skin grafts."

"What about scars?" Jamie didn't want to ask, but she had to. Jake's face had been the first thing that made her fall in love with him when they were kids. Not that it mattered; she would love Jake no matter how he looked. But still, she had to know.

"He'll have some." The doctor lowered the clipboard and held it against his side. "But nothing drastic. In a year or so you'll have to look close to even see them. Of course, his throat and lungs have been damaged too. Burned by the same hot blast."

"That's why I sound like this?" Jake held a hand to his throat. "And why I can't breathe right?"

"Yes. But you'll heal up." Dr. Cleary nodded. "We've been giving you moist air breathing treatments, and that'll continue for the next week or so, and after that you'll be much better. We won't be sure until then if you have permanent damage to your voice, but that won't affect your release date." He took a step back and looked at Jamie. "The head incisions are healing nicely. His brain size is back to normal." He slipped his hands in the pockets of his white jacket. "If nothing else changes, you can go home next Monday or Tuesday."

Panic slammed into Jamie's heart, and she crossed her arms more tightly around her waist. How was she supposed to bring Jake home when he didn't remember her? "That ... that soon?" She caught Jake's eyes and saw he shared her concern.

"Yes." Dr. Cleary gave Jake a pointed look. "The sooner you get situated in a familiar environment—even one you can't remember now—the sooner your memory will return." He smiled and set the chart on a nearby table. "Why don't you get some sleep, Jake. I'll talk to your wife out in the hall."

Jamie followed the doctor out of the room, but she felt dizzy and detached. As though she still couldn't believe this was her life. Jake? Jake her lifelong love didn't remember her? It was like some kind of crazy joke.

They walked a few feet away from Jake's room, and Dr. Cleary turned and faced her. "I have to be honest with you, Mrs. Bryan. A lot about Jake's recovery will be up to you."

"Me?" Her voice was the slightest whisper.

"Yes. You need to be patient, let him come along at his own pace. The flashbacks will happen more quickly if he feels comfortable."

Jamie's head was swimming, and she raked both her hands through her bangs. "I . . . I'm not sure I understand."

"He has no memory of being married to you." The doctor met her eyes and held them. "For the next few months, treat him like a good friend—be kind to him, considerate, answer his questions, help him with his bandages. But don't expect anything more."

"Meaning . . ." Jamie's hands fell to her sides, and her knees felt weak. "Don't talk to him like we're married?"

"Don't *act* like you are." The doctor angled his head, and his eyes filled with sympathy. "Do you have a guest room, Mrs. Bryan?"

"A guest room?" He was talking about sleeping arrangements. Something Jamie hadn't considered once since she'd known about Jake's memory loss. She felt the blood rush to her cheeks. "Yes . . . Jake's dad is sleeping there."

"Have him go home. Jake needs to relax and heal. The fewer people around him the better. His memory will return more quickly that way."

"And . . ." Jamie couldn't fathom the direction the conversation was headed. "Have Jake sleep in the guest room?"

"For now." The doctor put his hand on Jamie's shoulder. "Remember, he doesn't know you, Mrs. Bryan. He won't expect physical contact between the two of you, and I have to ask you not to initiate it. Not even something simple like a hug or kiss. These actions must come from him."

The heat became a full-fledged blush, one that worked its way down her neck and onto her chest. She felt like a schoolgirl getting a lecture from her father. "Wouldn't . . . wouldn't that *help* him remember?"

"It'll mess with his mind and confuse him." The doctor stuffed both his hands in the pockets of his white jacket. "You'll know his memory is starting to return when those actions come from him, when he initiates them."

Jamie's shoulders slumped forward some, and a heaviness settled across her shoulders. Pretend she wasn't married to Jake Bryan? The idea was insane. She would have to take Jake home and make him comfortable, but never be anything more to him than a friend? All in the hopes that somehow, someday his memory would return? "Okay . . ." She exhaled and lifted her eyes to the doctor's once more. "You've told me what I can't do. But what can I do . . . how do I help him remember?"

"Think back to when you and Jake first fell in love, back before you were dating. If you can interact with him like that, it'll put him at ease and speed his recovery."

Jamie blinked back tears and leaned against the wall for support. "I was twelve when I fell in love with Jake Bryan, Doctor. Twelve years old." Her voice was strained, aching from the ocean of tears she was holding in. "How could acting like I did back then help him remember the love we shared last month? What healing could that possibly bring about?"

"The best part of all, Mrs. Bryan." The doctor spoke straight to her heart. "When a person loses memory of his learned behavior, he has to be taught basic skills again. Yes, eventually he'll remember. But in the meantime he has to be taught. How to sit and stand and feed himself. How to walk."

Jamie listened, desperate to understand, hanging on every word. "But you're asking me to be Jake's friend and nothing more. What would that possibly teach him?"

"Very simple, Mrs. Bryan." The doctor narrowed his eyes. "It would teach him to love you."

That last line was almost more than Jamie could bear. She wanted to break down, collapse in the doctor's arms, and weep for the mountain that lay ahead of them. Jake had always been her support, the one who loved her as easily as he moved. Now, instead of lying in his arms at night, making love to him, or getting lost in his embrace, she would have to be his friend. And, in the process, hope that somehow they'd find the same connection they'd found a lifetime ago, back when they were just kids. And that connection would have to carry them up over the mountain, at least until Jake's memory started to return.

Jamie steeled herself against the hard times still ahead and thanked the doctor. Then she turned and with slow steps made her way back to Jake's room. Sierra was at home with Jake's father. Jim Bryan had continued to be wonderful, but now—if she wanted to follow the doctor's orders—she would need to send the man away. The idea of bringing Jake home and handling his recovery by herself was daunting, but at least she had another week before it would happen.

She sucked in a slow breath and straightened herself. Act as if she were twelve again? How could she when Jake had shown not even a modicum of interest in her since he'd woken from his coma? Jamie tucked her fears into the back pocket of her heart and entered the room. She didn't have to have all the answers today.

The room whirred with the sound of hospital machines, and the closer Jamie drew to Jake, the stronger the smell of antiseptic got. Jake was asleep, lying on his side facing the window, his face and body utterly still beneath the bandages and sheets.

Jamie sat down and exhaled hard.

As she did she glanced at the table a few feet away and saw Jake's chart. Maybe there was something in it the doctor hadn't told her. She reached for it and let her eyes drift past her husband's name and address, down to the place where Dr. Cleary had written notations about Jake's prognosis. Amnesia . . . second-degree burns . . . broken ankle.

Suddenly, Jamie's eyes fell on a place in the notes where the doctor had written something about a blood transfusion not being necessary. Next to that he had jotted down Jake's blood type.

O-negative.

Warning bells screamed their alarm through the hallways of Jamie's soul. O-negative wasn't Jake's blood type. He was AB-positive—one of the rarest blood types of all, the type most in need at blood drives. The clipboard in her hands might as well have been coiled and hissing. She dropped it and took four careful steps backwards. Jake's voice—the one he'd had before he was hurt—played in her mind.

"Of course I have rare blood." He'd told her that a hundred times. He'd lift his chin high, make a fist, and pound it gently against his heart. "When God made me He broke the mold."

The subject came up often throughout the year, whenever Jake dropped by the Red Cross and donated blood. "What can I say," he'd tell her when he got home. "I'm a precious commodity."

It was true. The Red Cross sent him requests often, reminding him that AB-positive was a rare type of blood and virtually begging him to come back in and donate. But now . . .

Jamie was grabbing short, quick breaths, and she felt herself fainting. She grabbed the nearest chair and fell into it, dropping her head between her knees to stave off a complete collapse. What could it possibly mean? If the man sleeping in the bed a few feet away had O-negative blood, then he wasn't Jake. And that would explain why he didn't recognize her, why his eyes didn't flash with love the way they always had, as far back as she could remember.

A thin layer of sweat broke out across her forehead, and her mind raced with the possibilities. Maybe Captain Hisel or one of the other guys had said something about Sierra to the man . . . maybe that's why he remembered her name.

Or maybe the strain of all that had happened since Tuesday was making her delusional. Maybe she hadn't seen O-negative on the chart, after all. She wanted to stand up, grab the clipboard, and prove herself wrong. Let her eyes find that place on his chart and see once and for all that it actually held the truth. That his blood type was AB-positive.

But she was suddenly paralyzed by a single thought.

If the man in the hospital bed wasn't Jake, if he was someone else with O-negative blood, who by some strange mix-up knew Sierra's name, then that could only mean one thing.

Jake was dead.

And that was a possibility Jamie simply couldn't fathom. So instead of reaching for the clipboard, she stood and staggered out the door to the nurse's station. Somehow—regardless of what she would find out—she had to know the truth. And since she didn't want to go near the chart, this time she would have a nurse read it.

The moment she walked up to the counter, a nurse stared at her. "Ma'am, are you okay?"

Jamie opened her mouth, but at first nothing came out. Her heart was lodged so high in her throat she couldn't speak. But finally, slowly, the words tumbled from her, words that in all her life were the hardest ones she'd ever spoken.

"I think . . ." She leaned on the counter for support. "I think the man in that room might not be my husband."

TWENTY-ONE

SEPTEMBER 17, 2001

The nurse gave Jamie a strange look, one that quickly became a confused smile.

"I'm not sure I understand."

"Look . . ." Every word was a struggle. "I feel like I'm losing my mind." Jamie could feel her heart racing, and she pointed across the hall toward the bedroom where the man lay. "I need . . . I need you to check his chart. Please . . ." The last word was more of a cry, and in that instant compassion cracked the woman's expression.

"First . . . are you sure you're okay?"

"No!" Jamie's voice was louder now. "I'm not okay. I need you to tell me that the man in that room is my husband!" Her voice softened, and she gripped the counter to keep from falling. "Please."

This time the nurse didn't hesitate. She came out from behind the nurse's station and led the way back to the hospital room. "What gave you the idea he might not be your husband?"

"His blood type. It's written on his chart." That was all Jamie could manage. She followed the nurse back to the room, her body shaking with the fear of what might lie ahead.

The nurse picked up the clipboard while Jamie's eyes found him in the hospital bed. The woman's eyebrows knit together as she held it up and looked at the information it contained. What if all this time he'd been merely a confused stranger . . . and what if Jake had been halfway up the building with Larry and the others? She held her breath while the nurse scanned the information on the chart.

What the woman was about to say would change Jamie's life forever.

She looked up, the confusion gone from her expression, and pointed to a spot halfway down the first page. "You mean here? Where it says O-negative?"

Jamie couldn't speak. She could barely breathe. Instead, she leaned against the chair and nodded.

A pleasant look filled the woman's face. "In the wake of a big accident, someone from the emergency room staff does a blood check and writes down the type that person should get if a transfusion is needed. O-negative works for every blood type."

"But . . ." Jamie's teeth rattled, and she hugged herself to ward off the sudden chill. "But my husband's blood is AB-positive."

"Well, then"—this time the nurse smiled—"that would explain it."

Jamie was baffled, but she felt better. If only there was an explanation for the error, then everything was okay. "I'm not sure I understand."

"AB-positive is a very rare blood type."

"Yes." Hope lit a candle in the pitch-black part of her soul.

"Most likely they drew his blood in the emergency room and realized his type was rare. With a disaster like what happened Tuesday, they would've written down simply O-negative, meaning if he needs blood, give him the universal donor type because his is so rare."

Jamie stared at the woman, and her heart skittered back into a normal rhythm. "So you don't think there's been a mix-up?"

"No, of course not. I've never heard of such a thing." The woman looked over her shoulder at Jake and then back at Jamie. "But you would know better than any of us."

Jamie nodded, and the nurse gave her one more smile before returning Jake's clipboard back to the hook at the end of his bed. When she was gone, Jamie sat motionless and straight, watching Jake with an uncertainty that hadn't been there before. Was there no end to the wild emotions she'd suffered since the terrorist attacks? First thinking Jake was dead, and then getting the call that he was in the hospital. The race to be by his side, only to have him wake up not knowing her or anything about his life. Never in the midst of the whirlwind of tragedy and sorrow did she ever consider there might've been a mix-up.

That the man lying there beneath the hospital sheets was anyone other than her husband.

She studied him and tried to remember the strapping, jovial man who'd walked out of their bedroom early Tuesday morning. The man in the hospital bed had Jake's size, the right length and body structure, from what she could see. The muscled arms and shoulders were his, the narrow feet. Certainly his eyes were the right color, though without the benefit of memories there was nothing familiar about them.

The nurse's words ran in Jamie's mind again. *No, of course there hadn't been a mix-up . . . something like that had never happened before.*

But it could, couldn't it? Wasn't it possible?

Suddenly, Jamie remembered something she'd seen on television that morning while she was getting ready to come to the hospital. Grieving family members were flocking to the V.A. Hospital on First Avenue, taping photos and flyers of their loved ones to the hospital's red brick wall. Hundreds were being added each day as desperate people held out a fraction of hope that maybe ... just maybe ... their son or daughter or husband or wife was not among the thousands feared dead.

"Missing ..." the flyers read. As though perhaps one of those who went to work at the World Trade Center Tuesday morning might have found his or her way out alive only to lie unidentified in a hospital or to wander the streets, the victim of a traumatic head injury.

Or mistaken identify.

A shudder worked its way down Jamie's spine. There was only one way to know for sure, to be certain there wasn't some desperate soul roaming Manhattan looking for a man who had Jake's build and appearance. She left without saying good-bye and took a cab to the area near the hospital where the flyers were posted. If she'd been a praying woman, this would have been her direst hour, the moment when she would've begged God to let this be the craziest thing she'd ever done, to assure her that not one missing person pictured on the wall looked even remotely like Jake.

But she wasn't someone who prayed, and she was hardly going to start now. Especially in light of all that had happened.

Jamie paid the driver and stumbled from the cab, her feet and head moving at frantic but different paces. She'd once watched a scene from a movie where the main character's child was missing. The actress darted first in one direction, then another and another, her eyes shining with raw fear.

That was how Jamie felt now.

She wore brown loafers, tailored jeans, a turtleneck, and a navy pullover sweater, the type of tailored outfit Staten Island mothers wore to do their grocery shopping. But there was nothing conservative about how she worked her way through the crowd, darting and weaving herself closer to the place where the flyers were posted.

Finally, she found a spot near the beginning of the wall, and she stopped, stunned. Only then did she realize how desperate the situation truly was. Smiling at her from the wall were hundreds of faces, one after the other. Pretty young women in the arms of their lovers, proud men with babies cradled against their chests, happy-faced gray-haired folks captured at a recent vacation spot or sitting with family at a barbecue.

Everyday people who'd done nothing more crazy than show up for work one day. And now they were gone. Clearly most of them were dead. Yet somewhere in the city someone had loved them enough to print up the flyer and post it, missed them enough to hope against all reason that somehow the person they loved might somehow still be found.

Jamie was barely breathing. She worked her way down the wall, taking in face after face after face. Most of the flyers listed the person's name, their height and weight, and the company and floor they worked for at the World Trade Center. Every few steps Jamie took, she'd have another two dozen flyers to look at. Finally, after an hour she'd looked at every single flyer, let her eyes wash over the faces of more missing people than she could possibly fathom.

And not one of them looked anything like Jake.

Jamie turned to summon a cab, but she could manage only to fall onto a nearby bench. For all the times she'd run a race or played a basketball game or ran a jet ski all afternoon without a break, Jamie had never felt more exhausted. Her arms and legs shook, and her temples pounded. As bad as she felt, as awful as the wall had been to look at, one bit of truth sustained her.

Jake was alive.

He had to be. Captain Hisel had found him under the fire truck and recognized him immediately. No doubts whatsoever, and that was before they'd bandaged Jake's face. Clearly the man must've been Jake—his hair and build and eyes, his way of carrying himself. Otherwise, the captain wouldn't have known him.

And of course there was the other bit of irrefutable information—the fact that Jake knew Sierra—both her face and her name.

Jamie focused on the people milling about. Nothing about Manhattan looked like it had before the terrorist attacks. Ash and smoke still hung in the air, and groups of people stood in clusters along the wall and adjacent sidewalk. Many of them were weeping.

Jamie watched them until she couldn't stand to look any longer. She covered her face with her hands and closed her eyes, her breath jagged and shaky. Was she crazy, coming all the way down here to check a wall of missing people flyers? Of course the man lying in the hospital bed was Jake. All the proof was there. And the nurse had explained the situation with the blood type. Everything made perfect sense.

She lifted her head and peered through the spaces between her fingers. A woman about her age stood near one of the flyers, her head hung as quiet sobs racked her body. One of her hands was tucked deep in the pocket of a long jacket. But the other covered the face of the person on the flyer, as though by keeping her hand there this woman could somehow connect with the person she was missing.

Jamie wanted to go to the woman, put an arm around her and comfort her, promise her everything was going to turn out okay. But it wasn't—not for any of the people standing near missing persons' flyers or tacking them along the brick wall. Jamie inhaled, and pungent air filled her lungs. She stood, turned her back to the grieving stranger, and waved for a cab.

She had nothing to say to the woman, no words of comfort. After all, no matter how badly Jamie hurt for her, the two of them had nothing in common. Jamie was one of the lucky ones, and though she and Jake would face losses, none of them would be permanent. No, she need not spend any more time swimming in this sea of sorrow, fighting the tide of death. Not when her husband was alive in a hospital room a few miles away.

It was time to get back there and do whatever it took not only to teach Jake Bryan how to live with her again.

But how to love her.

That night when she was back at home, when Jim and Sierra were asleep, Jamie climbed into her sweats and T-shirt and crawled into bed. And there she began a strange sort of rehearsal, imagining how the coming weeks would go once Jake came home. How would she help him remember who he was, help him find the place where his laugh and smile came easily, the place where giving Sierra horsey rides was as natural as his name?

She thought of something then, something that hadn't come to mind since Jake had been hurt. Jamie leaned over, flipped on the bedside light, and sat up. Every morning as far back as she could remember, Jake had spent the early morning hours reading his Bible and jotting things down in his journal.

A time or two, Jamie had been tempted to take a look, tempted to see exactly what thoughts stirred in the heart of the man she loved more than life. But the idea of looking at Jake's private thoughts had never sat well with Jamie's conscience, and the occasional notion had never been more than that—a simple, wayward idea that she quickly dismissed.

But now . . . now things were different.

If she was going to teach Jake how to be himself again, she

would need all the help she could get. And what could be more helpful than having access to his deepest thoughts and writings, words that might indeed trigger the return of Jake's complete memory?

She slid off the bed and ran with light steps around to Jake's side. Then she stooped down and pulled two books from underneath the box springs, books that Jake had left there that Tuesday morning before he went to work.

One was black leather with Jake's name engraved in gold at the bottom right corner. It was the Bible he'd gotten from his father his first day with the FDNY. Part of the lettering was worn off, so that all Jamie could clearly see were the capital *J* and *B*.

Appropriate, she thought. Since that's what the guys at the station called him. *JB.* She opened the front cover, and there inside, scribbled on paper that was transparently thin, was this inscription: *To Jake . . . No matter what else happens, the words in this book will keep you safe. I love you, Dad.*

Did Jim Bryan know that Jake still had this old book, that he still read it every morning before work? And how come she'd never taken an interest before, never wanted to look at it or read the inscription written inside? It was one thing to stay away from his journal . . . but his Bible? That would've been okay, except for one thing.

She'd never wanted anything to do with it.

Jim Bryan's words caught her attention again, and then she knew the reason why she'd never touched it. Because as nice as it all seemed, there wasn't any truth to the sentiment Jake's father had written. The words in the Bible wouldn't keep a firefighter or anyone else safe. They were just words, after all, no matter how nice they sounded. Larry believed in God, didn't he? And where had Bible verses gotten him? Buried beneath the rubble of a hundred-story building, that's where.

Nothing safe about that.

A sigh slipped from Jamie's lips, and she thumbed through the thin, worn pages. Toward the back of the book, there were whole sections of text Jake had underlined or highlighted in yellow. Notations were written in the sidelines, and as she flipped, one page caught her attention. She stopped and held the Bible up a few inches closer to her face so she could see it clearly.

The heading at the top of the page read "Matthew."

Jamie felt awkward, ignorant looking at the text now. Other than the time when she'd attended youth camp with Jake, she'd never opened a Bible, never taken the time to know the names of the various chapters or what they represented. Now—seeing Jake's notes and highlighted areas—she chided herself about the fact. Clearly, her husband's heart was very taken with the importance of this material. Couldn't she have at least shown some kind of interest? Even if she and Jake didn't agree about the significance it held?

Her eyes narrowed and she read the verse. It was from a section marked Eleven.

Come to me, all you who are weary and burdened, and I will give you rest. Take my yoke upon you and learn from me, for I am gentle and humble in heart, and you will find rest for your souls.

A strange feeling worked its way into Jamie's heart, a faint but different kind of peace, a peace she'd never known before. For a moment Jamie almost wished the text were true. Perfectly true the way Jake thought it to be. Strange, really. Because Jamie had never believed the Bible to be more than a series of nice letters about a nice man. Some details true in a historical sense, some not true. But definitely nothing more than that.

She scanned the text a few verses up until she was clear that the person talking in that section of text was Jesus. Everything about the words seemed warm and wonderful—especially the part about getting rest for her soul. But that wasn't what Jake had underlined. The part that had apparently touched him the most were these three words:

Learn from me . . .

And there in the margins next to the verse, Jake had written, *My goal: learn everything I can from Jesus.*

Jamie's gaze shifted to the underlined text once more. *Learn from me* . . . *learn everything I can from Jesus* . . .

That was what had motivated Jake all these years, wasn't it? He kept no secrets from her. Some nights after they'd been intimate, in the quiet waning moments before sleep found them both, she'd whisper into his ear.

"I'm the luckiest woman in the world, Jake. You know that?"

But he'd only put his arm around her and hold her close, his starlit smile illuminating the depths of her heart. "God brought us together. All I want now is to be a man that makes Him proud. You know, a little more like Jesus every day."

Jamie sat straighter on the edge of the bed. Those were the same words he'd said every time she complimented his skills as a father. "As long as I can be like Jesus, I'll be okay."

Now it was all coming together in a way that made goose bumps rise along Jamie's arms. All his life Jake had studied Jesus Christ, and in the process—though Jamie didn't hold to her husband's beliefs—Jake had taken on some of the mannerisms and actions of Jesus. It was part of who he was as a man, a husband, and a father. And now ... now that he'd forgotten who he was, what better way for him to learn than to read the highlighted sections of text in his old Bible—memorize it, soak it in, go over once more the notations in the margins? The information nestled between the leather covers of his Bible might actually be a road map of sorts, a guide to help him remember who he was and help him become that person once more.

Carefully, as though the book was worth more now, Jamie shut the Bible and opened the other book, Jake's journal. Again she was poked by pushpins of guilt, but nothing strong enough to stop her. The pages, after all, contained Jake's deepest stirrings, the thoughts and feelings at the center of his heart. Combined with the information in the Bible, there wasn't anything Jamie could say or do that would better serve to help Jake remember who he was.

She flipped through dozens of entries until she found the one he'd written that last morning, the morning of the terrorist attacks. The other entries, the ones she'd passed on the way to this one, were for the most part merely solid blocks of wording. But the one dated September 11, 2001, was a letter.

A letter written to her.

Tears stung Jamie's eyes and blurred her vision. She blinked them back, and when she could see clearly again she began to read.

Dear sweet Jamie,

I have this feeling, deep in my heart, that something's about to change for me and you. Maybe it's your questions about church or the way you seem to hang on to Sierra's Bible stories a little bit longer these days. Whatever it is, I've prayed for God to touch your heart, baby. He means everything to me, and I know that one day He'll mean everything to you too. On that day, you'll no longer have to be afraid because you'll have God Almighty to lean on. I want you to know, honey, that when you find that precious faith, I'll be smiling bigger than you've ever seen me smile. Because the thing I want even more than your love is the knowledge that we'll have eternity together.

I simply cannot bear the idea of being in heaven without you. I love you too much to lose you.

The letter went on, but Jamie's tears made it impossible for her to see. She shut the journal, stacked it on top of Jake's Bible, and slipped the books back under the bed where Jake had last left them.

Sweet, wonderful Jake. Always thinking about her.

He had always been so good about keeping his faith to himself, careful not to badger her or preach at her. Here, though . . . here was his heart. Not that she take up some ritualistic form of faith to appease him. But that she believe—so that by his understanding of life and death and eternity, they would never, ever be apart. In his own crazy mixed-up way, he loved her that deeply. God, Sierra, and her. Those were his life, and together they made up the core of who he was. After reading his words, Jamie understood that better than she ever had before.

Now she would simply have to help him understand it too.

TWENTY-TWO

The trip was Clay's idea.

A week after the terrorist attacks, Laura had nearly given up all hope. Yes, firefighters and police officers in New York City were still calling their efforts at Ground Zero a rescue, still desperately lifting one bulldozer scoop of debris after another off the pile of rubble that had once been the World Trade Center in hopes of finding someone buried alive.

But Laura couldn't believe there were many people who actually believed that would happen. How could anyone still be living in the smoldering heap of tons of cement and steel? Still, the rescue continued, and somehow Laura and thousands of others like her were supposed to stay close to the phone, praying for a miracle.

Something had snapped inside Laura after that Thursday night, the evening when Eric would've come home if he were still alive. Her conversation with Clay had been both painful and eye-opening. Since then there had been fewer moments when she would catch herself wondering about Eric and how his business trip was going, or when she would find herself looking out the window calculating his time of return. She still held out hope, but the reality of what she feared most was setting in. And with it a hole in her heart the size of the Grand Canyon. Somehow the details of their sorry marriage and the current state of their relationship were not in the forefront of her mind. Instead, her memories were of the two of them back in their early married days, back when they used to sit in the backyard near their garage apartment and sing together. Fond memories of the days when she was pregnant with their daughter, back when Eric would cuddle up against her and play songs he'd written on the guitar.

"So my baby will know my voice." He'd grin and gently place his hand on her abdomen.

Laura could still feel his fingers pressing against her.

Another memory haunted her that week. The memory of Eric's panicked voice, his stricken face when the doctor told them that their little girl was stillborn. A chaplain had found them in the delivery room an hour later and offered to pray with them.

"No." Eric's answer had been quick, and he tightened the grip he had on her hand. "We need time."

A month later the pastor at Westlake Community Church had held a baby dedication, and he invited Laura and Eric. "We all feel your loss," he told them. "This way your friends here can pray with you about what happened."

But Eric wouldn't consider it. "I'm not going." His eyes had flashed with an anger that had never been there before. "Besides, it's a little late for prayer." The fire in his expression faded quickly, but Eric's determination to stay away from church never did.

They rarely talked about the loss of their daughter, and to her great disappointment, they never named her. But years later, at a counseling session, Eric said something that would stay with Laura forever. The counselor had asked Eric to talk about his greatest disappointment in life.

His answer was quick and pointed. "I never knew my little girl."

Laura couldn't remember her answer that day, but she knew what it would be now.

That Eric had never known his little boy, either.

The memories were all that kept Laura from losing her mind as the days dragged on. Since Thursday, Clay had been there constantly. He played catch with Josh and helped him with his math homework; he made pasta or ordered pizza at dinnertime. He listened anytime Laura wanted to talk. Last night he'd brought her a glass of water and sat at the opposite end of the sofa. For a long while he'd said nothing.

Then he turned his body so he could see her better. "You still think there's a chance, don't you?"

Laura squirmed and fought off the wetness that gathered in her eyes. "Sometimes." She took a sip of water before finishing her thought. "Not that he's alive in the rubble. But ... somewhere maybe. Walking around in a daze, disoriented. Lying in a hospital bed." She blinked back the tiresome tears. "That's possible, don't you think?"

"Sure." Clay had let silence fill in the gaps of their conversation. Laura understood. What could he say? If Eric was wandering the streets of New York City or somehow holed up somewhere unconscious, how would they ever know?

It wasn't until that morning—a week after the attacks—that Clay arrived with an idea. He waited until Josh was off to school, then he poured coffee for the two of them and sat across from

Laura at the dining room table. After a long moment, he met her eyes and said simply, "We need to go to New York."

Laura stared at him, and almost in slow motion, she set her coffee cup back on the table. "Why?"

"To look for him."

A pit formed in her stomach. She stood and made her way to the window. Their backyard was one of her favorite places. The manicured grass and sparkling pool always relaxed her. But nothing could relax her now, not in light of Clay's statement. "We've called the hospitals every day." She glanced at Clay over her shoulder. "He isn't there."

"No . . . but he could be somewhere else. Maybe at someone's house or at a homeless shelter. Something."

Clay folded his hands on the table, and Laura gazed back out the window. She heard Clay's chair slide across the floor and felt him come up alongside her a few minutes later.

"I hate seeing you like this, Laura." His right shoulder barely brushed against her left one, and his voice was a whisper. "Not knowing whether you should grieve Eric's death or wait for him to come home."

Laura let her chin fall to her chest. The sorrow was back, a sorrow that blocked her throat and made speaking impossible.

"We have to go."

From the corner of her eye Laura saw him clench his teeth. When he spoke again, his voice was thick. "He's my brother, Laura."

Laura kept her gaze straight ahead, seeing visions of Josh and his friends playing in the pool. No matter how hard she tried, she couldn't picture one poolside memory that included Eric. He didn't swim with Josh or his friends or even with her. He never had. She thought about what Clay had said. It was something they could've talked about in counseling, if only they could somehow find him. "What . . ." She turned and faced him. "What would we do once we got there?"

He raised his left arm and leaned it against the window. "Make flyers and post them near the hospital—same thing everyone else is doing."

Laura felt a hundred years old. She was dying to believe something good might come from Clay's plan, but the idea seemed virtually hopeless. She crossed her arms and leaned against her husband's brother, letting her head fall on his shoulder. She pictured herself boarding a plane with Clay, flying to New York City, and posting flyers of Eric on empty walls and park benches. What would it prove? She turned and leaned her back against the window so she was facing Clay. "Then what?"

Clay studied her, and a layer of tears sprang up across his eyes. "We check the missions, the homeless shelters. Talk to police and fire officials, show his picture to everyone. Then we come home and wait."

The longer they talked about the idea, the more sense it made to her. Nothing good could come from sitting at home in Los Angeles wondering about Eric. If he was—by some strange miracle—still alive, there was only one way to find out, and that was to follow Clay's plan and go to New York City.

Clay still had vacation time, and by two that afternoon, Laura had booked them a flight out for the next morning. Someone at church had been more than willing to take care of Josh, and that night she explained the trip to her son.

"Uncle Clay and I are going to go to New York for a few days."

Josh was lying in bed, his face pale against his dark hair. "To find Daddy?"

"To try." Laura soothed the boy's bangs off his forehead. "If he's hurt or sick, he might not know who he is. The only way to find out is to look for him."

For a long while Josh lay there, unmoving, his eyes dry. Then he reached up and placed his fingers over hers. "Mom . . . can I ask you something?"

"Of course, honey." Being alone like this with Josh made Laura realize how different life had been since the terrorist attacks. Normally, she and Josh spent lots of time together, reading or talking about his day. Sometimes playing Scrabble or crazy eights. But in the past week they'd barely spoken.

Josh winced. "Promise you won't be mad?"

"Mad? Honey, nothing you could ask would make me angry with you. Just say it . . . whatever's on your heart, I want to know."

"If Daddy's not in New York City somewhere, that means he's dead, right?"

The question was so blunt it nearly took Laura's breath away. But now—a week after the collapse of the World Trade Center—the idea that Eric might be dead was less shocking than it had been at first. Laura swallowed and kept her eyes on Josh's. "Yes. That's right, honey. If he isn't in New York somewhere, he's probably dead."

"Okay, then . . ." The child drew in an exaggerated breath and sat up, meeting her gaze straight on. He was more nervous than Laura had ever seen him. He worked his mouth for a moment, swallowing until he found his voice. "If you don't find him, can Uncle Clay be my dad?"

Her son's words hit her full force and knocked her into a riptide of pain until she thought she would drown from the lack of air. Finally, slowly, a stream of oxygen found its way in through her nostrils, and she put her arms around Josh and held him close. How had Eric not seen what his long hours at work were doing to their son? The boy neither knew nor loved his father. In fact, Eric hadn't lost just a daughter when their baby died all those years ago.

He'd lost a son too.

She didn't want to cry, didn't want the boy to think he'd done something wrong by voicing his heart. But she couldn't speak, either.

"Mom?" Josh's voice was muffled against her shoulder, and he pulled back, searching her eyes. "Are you mad at me?"

"No, son. It . . . it was a fair question." In the hidden places of Laura's soul, she was still gasping for breath. It was all she could do to appear normal for Josh.

"So . . ." The child angled his head and picked at a ball of fuzz on his bedspread. "Can he?"

"Well . . ." *God, calm me down . . . give me the words.* "Uncle Clay will always be your uncle, Josh . . . not your father. That's how God made it."

"Oh." Her son's face fell, and his chin dropped closer to his pajama top. "Okay." His head stayed down, but his eyes lifted just enough to see her. "Can I pretend he's my dad, then? I mean, if you don't find Daddy in New York?"

What could she say? She clasped Josh's hands in hers and nodded. "Uncle Clay loves you very much, buddy. You can pretend whatever you'd like."

"God won't be mad at me?"

"No. Not at all."

"And you, either?"

Her heart was breaking, but she managed a smile. She leaned forward and kissed Josh on his nose, hugging him once more before drawing back. "The fact that you love your uncle will never make me mad, honey. Even if you pretend he's your dad."

* * * *

Clay picked Laura up at her house the next morning and drove the two of them to the Burbank Airport. He'd stayed up late the night before and used a photo of Eric from the previous summer to make a flyer. The picture showed Eric standing behind a podium at a business dinner. Eric had given a speech that night, and someone from Koppel and Grant had snapped the picture. Eric had found it in his box at work a few weeks later and brought it home.

The flyer was simple, Eric's name and description, the fact that he'd been working on the sixty-fourth floor of the south tower at the time of the attacks, and three phone numbers for people to call if they knew anything of his whereabouts. Laura had a hundred copies in her carry-on bag.

Air travel had resumed in limited amounts, and the two of them had to pass through additional security stations before boarding the plane, but still they were early. They stored their bags in the overhead compartments and took their seats, Clay against the window and Laura on the aisle.

"I'm glad we're going." Laura adjusted her seat belt and glanced out the window. "I'd always wonder otherwise."

"Yeah." Clay couldn't bring himself to smile. "Me too."

They fell silent, and Clay turned to the window. Were they really on their way to New York? To look for Eric? A week had passed, and the idea that Eric was gone was no more real today than it had been when the attacks first happened. It wasn't just for Laura that he was going to Manhattan. It was for himself. Whenever Clay needed to talk, all he had to do was find Eric. Because as far back as he could remember, he and Eric had been honest with each other.

Until the problems in Eric's marriage had started.

By going to New York, there was a chance that just maybe he might find his big brother once more. And then he could look in his eyes and ask him why? Why hadn't he said anything about his troubles at home, and how could he have put his work ahead of Laura and Josh for all those years? Laura, who had wanted only to love him. Maybe if he found Eric the two of them could talk about everything Eric hadn't said and done, and maybe . . . just maybe everything would go back to how it was before.

For all of them.

Clay sat back in his seat and willed his nerves to settle down. He was a police officer who'd faced volatile situations with armed drug dealers or crazed gang members. But as the plane began to taxi down the runway, the fear that sliced through him was unlike anything he'd ever experienced. Not because he was afraid to fly. But because he was afraid of what they would find when they touched down in New York City. Afraid that Eric wouldn't be at a homeless shelter or lying in some makeshift evacuation center near Ground Zero. But that he'd be buried in the midst of it.

Clay blinked and exhaled slowly. *Calm . . . be calm for Laura.* The baggage handlers were heaving luggage into the belly of the plane, and Clay closed his eyes and thought about the magnet on his refrigerator door. *Lean not on your own understanding; in all your ways acknowledge him, and he will make your paths straight.* The Scripture trickled across his soul like a stream in the desert, and Clay's heart breathed with gratefulness. The Lord hadn't abandoned him, despite his fears.

"Clay?" Laura touched his hand, and he twisted in his seat so he could see her. "Are you okay?"

"Sorry. I . . ." He gripped his knees and met her gaze. "I was thinking."

"Let's pray, okay?" Her eyes were liquid green, filled with a kind of hope and anticipation that were illogical and maybe even downright crazy.

Still, there was a chance.

One they definitely wouldn't find without God's help. He took her hand and bowed his head near hers. "Lord, give us safety as we travel, safety and peace. Calm the fears in both our hearts and guide us every step of the way in New York City." He paused just as the plane lifted off. "And please, help us find my brother."

* * * *

The next few days passed in a blur of taping posters to various walls and talking with officials at hospitals and homeless shelters. By Monday morning Laura was exhausted and ready to go home. The sights and sounds of a crippled Manhattan were more than she could bear. She and Clay had taken adjoining rooms at the Marriott, but at night when they returned from a day of walking the streets of the city, Clay would spread out on the bed adjacent to Laura's and let her talk. For the most part their conversations involved strategy. Where to put the posters, who to talk to, where else to check. In the end, no matter how much they planned, the results had been the same each day.

"I'm sorry, we haven't seen him."

"No, he isn't here—every one of our patients is accounted for."

"Nope, he's not familiar."

At one point they'd even walked the halls of Mount Sinai Medical Center in the hopes of finding Eric lying somewhere, forgotten and unidentified. But every patient had a name, and at least one visitor. None were waiting for a family member to show up and identify them.

Now—with the weekend behind them, Laura had convinced Clay they needed to get as close to Ground Zero as possible. They were allowed past a few checkpoints, simply because they flashed a copy of their flyer and asked for permission to post it closer to the rubble pile.

They were a block away from the collapsed towers when a police officer stopped them, came up to the back of the cab, and moved his hand in a turning motion. "No one's allowed past this point . . . only official personnel in this area, you'll have to turn around."

Laura rolled down the window and felt her heart skip a beat. "My husband was in the south tower." Laura peered at the officer from the back of the cab and showed him the flyer with Eric's picture. "We're here from Los Angeles. Please . . . can we get a little closer?"

"No one goes past this point." The man anchored his hands on his hips and looked at Laura. His eyes were a dark, haunting reflection of all he must've seen since September 11. "No one but official personnel."

Clay leaned over Laura's legs and looked at the man. "I'm a police officer from Los Angeles." He pointed to the flyer. "The missing guy's my brother. Are you sure we can't get closer?"

The officer's face softened some, but he shook his head. "Look . . . it's been nearly two weeks since those buildings fell." He pointed down the street to a line of dump trucks slowly heading up a hill of debris. Loud machinery sounded in the background, and the officer's voice could barely be heard over the noise. "If your brother's in there, believe me—you don't want to find him."

"We won't stay." Clay was persistent. "If we could post a few flyers, at least we'd feel like we did our best."

For a moment the officer only looked at them, his eyes moving from Clay to Laura, and back to Clay again. His mouth hung open just enough to show his astonishment. "Can I be straight with you?"

"Definitely." Clay's answer was quick.

For a split moment Laura considered covering her ears. She didn't want straight talk this close to Ground Zero; she wanted Eric.

"I don't care what they're calling this in the newspapers, but it's not a rescue effort." He pressed his lips together, and though his eyes stayed dry, his chin quivered some. "What's going on in there is a recovery. And they'll be darn lucky if they recover even a few hundred bodies." He shook his head. "It's that bad."

The cab driver shot them a look over his shoulder. "Meter's running."

Laura ignored the driver and locked eyes with the officer. "So we're wasting our time?" Clay was still stretched out over her knees, peering out the window. "Is that what you mean?"

"Yes." He sniffed hard and stared in the direction of Ground Zero. "Everyone wants to believe that their person is missing, but I'll tell you something, lady. There just aren't any missing persons. The patients at every hospital have been identified, and the homeless shelters have no victims." He tossed his hands in the air and met her eyes once more. "It's too late for any of that. Your husband ain't missing, lady. He's dead. Go back to LA and have a service for him. Then find a way like the rest of us to get on with life." The officer glanced at Clay and back at her. "I'm sorry."

He stepped away, turned around, and yelled something to an officer across the street. Then he walked beyond Laura and Clay and headed for the driver of the cab behind them. "No one's allowed past this point," he yelled. "Only official personnel beyond this . . ."

Clay sat up and stared straight ahead. Then he dug his elbows into his knees and rested his head in his hands. Laura watched him, and something inside her began to die, something she couldn't quite peg. Through every day, every hour, since September 11, Clay had been strong for her, positive, encouraging. Even when they'd considered the worst possible scenario—that Eric might never come home—he'd been cautiously optimistic.

But not now.

Laura closed her eyes for a moment and remembered the officer's words. *Your husband ain't missing, lady. He's dead . . .*

If it was true, she couldn't break down here, not parked in lower Manhattan with an anxious cab driver casting glances at her from the front seat. She sucked in a quick breath and put her hand on Clay's knee. "Clay . . ."

After a few seconds he looked at her. His watery eyes told her they were thinking the same thing. It was over . . . the search, the second chance, the hope that Eric would ever come home. All of it was over. She leaned forward and tapped the driver on the shoulder. "To the Marriott, please."

Their efforts in New York City were finished. The police officer's blunt words had told them all they needed to know. It was time to go home, have a service for Eric, and get on with living.

Twenty-Three

September 25, 2001

The day of reckoning arrived on Tuesday, September 25, two weeks after the terrorist attacks. That morning Jamie was in Jake's hospital room, sitting by his side, when Dr. Cleary walked in and gave them a crooked smile.

"Today's the day." He planted himself near the doorway and studied Jake. "How're you feeling?"

"Ready." Jake sat up straighter in bed and stretched his arms forward. "I was ready yesterday."

Much of the bandaging had been removed from Jake's cheeks and head, and the shock of seeing his burned face was wearing off. Beneath the red and blistered skin, he was still Jake Bryan, the only man she'd ever loved. And he'd heal eventually. There'd be a few light scars, but otherwise it was only a matter of time before he looked more like her husband and less like an accident victim.

With the bandages off, Jake could talk easier than before. His voice was still a bit raspy, but from everything he'd told Jamie, he was feeling well enough to go home.

"Yesterday your white count was still a little high." The doctor crossed the room and found Jake's chart at the end of his bed. "Today's numbers are better."

An hour passed while Dr. Cleary handled Jake's release papers, and sometime around ten o'clock that morning, Jake fell asleep. Jamie watched, awed at how quickly he was making a comeback.

A physical comeback, anyway.

He still didn't remember anything more than Sierra, but if his body was healing, Jamie could only hope that very soon his mind would, also.

Infection in Jake's arm had set in a week ago, and at one point Jake's fever had spiked to nearly 104 degrees. Dr. Cleary explained that infection was common where second-degree burns and lacerations were concerned, and rather than send Jake home on antibiotics, he'd kept him in the hospital and administered them through an IV. Jake had finished the treatment a full twenty-four hours ago, so there was nothing more to keep Jake in the hospital.

Jamie was actually glad.

For one thing, she no longer had any doubts that the man in the bed beside her was her husband, Jake. Even with his painful-looking burns, the face was definitely Jake's. The blue eyes and rugged lines that had been his trademark since he was a teenager. Regardless of his memory loss, this was the man she had married. In some ways Jamie wished the bandages had come off earlier—back when she'd been crazy with fear that somehow there'd been a mistake, a mix-up. At first she'd dreaded Jake's homecoming, especially the idea of setting him up in a guest room when he belonged in bed beside her. Now that she was sure the man was Jake, she was beyond anxious to get him home and help him regain his memory.

Over the past ten days—while Jake's father stayed at the house with Sierra—Jamie had spent every day and several nights at the hospital, cozying up in a chair next to his bed and covering herself with whatever blankets the nurses could find for her. In the process something was happening.

She and Jake were becoming friends.

The connection between them had come gradually, in small bits of conversation and shy glances, but it was happening. That much was obvious. They'd be watching a rerun of the *Cosby Show* on his hospital TV, and they'd laugh at the same funny line. Then he would shoot a quick look in her direction, and she'd see something familiar. The hint of a sparkle in his eyes, the seeds of a smile.

She had asked Jake if he wanted to play cards or read or work on a puzzle while he was in the hospital, and he'd tried all three. He couldn't remember any card games, but one day last weekend he stared out the window for a moment until suddenly his eyes lit up. "Backgammon. I think I know how to play backgammon."

"Okay." The statement had taken Jamie by surprise. The two of them had played backgammon back when they were first married, but only for one summer. They were too active to spend much time indoors, and both of them quickly tired of the game.

But still, if Jake remembered it, that had to be a good sign. Jamie had dug through their basement storage area, found the old backgammon set she'd bought years earlier, and brought it to the hospital. Since then they'd played it several times each day, and more often lately, Jake would make a move and follow it with a friendly comment or competitive gibe. Something like "Try beating that" or "Nice move."

Constantly, Jamie would catch herself wanting to share some memory with him, something about Sierra or some time in their past, but always she caught herself. Dr. Cleary had been adamant that at first all communication had to be kept in the present. As though they were starting all over again.

One afternoon, when they'd had enough backgammon, Jamie found an old puzzle in the hospital waiting room and set it out at the end of Jake's bed. His ankle was still in the cast, but he slid it over to create a surface for the puzzle. For three hours straight, they worked the pieces into first a frame, and then a complete picture. Every few minutes their fingers would brush against each other while they worked, and sometimes Jamie would lift her eyes to find him watching her.

She'd been tempted to bring Jake's journal and his Bible into the hospital, but in the end she decided to wait. It'd be better for him to read those while sitting on their bed—sometime when Jamie wasn't around. He might remember better that way, encouraged by the combination of a familiar setting and deeply precious words that not so long ago had meant the world to him.

Instead, she'd brought him John Grisham novels—his favorite before getting hurt. She had laid three of them out on his bedside and watched while he picked them up, one at a time, and looked them over.

"Interesting." He'd lifted his eyes to hers.

"You remember them?" Jamie had been breathless, having walked up the stairs to his floor. She wasn't working out, wasn't playing racquetball or jet-skiing. If it wasn't for the stairs, she'd go stir crazy with how sedentary her life had become.

"No." He looked at the books again. "But I'll try to read them."

Jake's reading skills were fine, but his headaches weren't. Whenever he tried to read more than a few paragraphs, he'd close his eyes and rub them, grimacing from the pain. At that point she'd take over, reading the text out loud, stopping now and then when he'd have a question.

"So, wait a minute. Is the book about that guy or the other one?"

"Which one?"

"The one in the first chapter."

Once in a while Jamie's mind would go blank, and Jake would raise an eyebrow at her. "Hey, I'm the one with amnesia, okay?"

They would both giggle, and the sound of their combined laughter would ring so clear and true in Jamie's heart she would be convinced beyond a doubt that Jake was returning to her. That he was making his way back through the mire of forgotten moments to a place where they could live and love and laugh again, a place where they could resume life where they'd left off.

There'd been hard times that week too. Times when she'd be staring at Jake, watching him sleep, and he would wake up and see her. Instead of the smile she was used to, he'd jerk back, his eyes filled with confusion and fear. "Where am I?" he'd ask. Other times he'd sit straight up in bed glancing around the room, caught in some nightmare.

Jamie was handling those moments better now, because all of Dr. Cleary's predictions were coming true. She was becoming her husband's friend, and once they were able to go home—in just a few hours now—that friendship would grow until finally the flashbacks began. After that it would only be a matter of weeks before he would remember everything about his past and they could get on with the business of living.

Jake was still sleeping, so Jamie kept her voice to barely a whisper as she called Jim Bryan and told him the news.

"He's coming home." She was excited, but she could hear the fear and doubts in her voice all the same. They had miles of ground to claim back before she could truly celebrate. "His burns look good and the infection's gone."

"What time should I be there?"

"One o'clock." Jamie soaked in the sight of Jake. Even with his burns he was handsome, and if he never looked the same again, that didn't matter. His memory was worth more than anything else.

"I'll get Sierra ready."

They'd made the plan days ago. When it was time for Jake to come home, his father would bring Sierra and leave her with Jamie and Jake. Then the older Bryan would head back home straight from the hospital, just as Dr. Cleary had ordered. Jamie had left her car at the ferry parking lot back in Staten Island. She and Jake and Sierra would take a cab to the ferry, make their way across the harbor, and then drive their car home.

Jake's father had decided that once he went home, he'd take a driving trip across the country to visit his brother-in-law in Arizona. He'd spend a few months there until Jake was better and could handle visits.

Jamie sat back to wait. All the hours and days of living at the hospital and wondering when Jake would be well enough to go home were finally coming to an end. The first part of the nightmare was almost over. The tips of her fingers trembled as she folded her hands and counted the minutes.

Just before noon someone brought in two meal trays and Jake's release papers. An hour later a familiar nurse showed up with crutches and a wheelchair. "Your chariot, Mr. Bryan."

Jamie carried the crutches and a bag full of cards and gifts from her and Sierra and the guys at the station.

"You two need a cab?" The nurse glanced at Jamie as she wheeled Jake down the hallway, into the elevator, and out to the front of the hospital.

"Not yet. We're waiting for my father-in-law."

The woman helped Jake from the wheelchair to his feet, and Jamie handed him the crutches, working to fit them under his arms. Jake was thinner than before, ten, maybe fifteen pounds, and the size in his shoulders had atrophied some. But the doctor had said that was normal after an extended hospital stay.

Jamie's fingers brushed along the length of Jake's arms as she helped him tighten his grip on the hand rests of each crutch. The feel of her fingers against his muscled arm was more familiar than anything she'd experienced since he'd been hurt. He'd lost some weight, but his arms were still lean and defined, the way they'd always been. Suddenly, his nearness made her heartbeat double, and she chided herself. *Come on, Jamie. Platonic . . . remember?*

The nurse took a step back and smiled at them through teary eyes. Then she patted Jake on the shoulder. "Listen now . . ." She uttered a cough and tried to regain her composure. "You stay away from here, okay? We need you heroes back on the streets."

"Okay." Jake leaned into the crutches and tried to smile.

Jamie saw the now familiar confusion in his eyes. When the woman was gone, Jake's father pulled up in his Lincoln sedan, with Sierra buckled into the backseat. He stopped the car and helped her out.

The moment she was free, her face lit up, and she darted across the sidewalk to Jake. "Daddy!" She grinned at Jamie for a brief moment and then threw her arms around her father's legs. "You're coming home!"

Jamie studied Jake's face. She could see the awkwardness he was struggling with, and for a second, she feared what he might say. But then he smiled, and she sighed with relief.

"Hi, Sierra." He cast a hurried look at Jamie, and then back at Sierra. "I missed you, honey."

Jake's father nodded at Jamie. "We'll be talking, okay?"

She went to him and hugged him. "Thanks for everything."

She pulled back and searched his eyes. "I couldn't have done it without you."

"Let me know when he starts to remember." Jake's father cast a casual look at Jake. "Take care of yourself. I'll be praying for you."

Jake nodded but said nothing. He let his gaze fall to his hands.

Without drawing out the moment any further, Jim Bryan waved once more at Jamie and kissed Sierra on the cheek. Then he climbed in his car and pulled away. After he was gone, Sierra grabbed hold of Jamie's fingers, and with the other hand, she clasped the lower part of Jake's left crutch. Jamie flagged down a cab, and when it pulled up, they climbed in—Jake on one side of Sierra, Jamie on the other.

"Ferry docks, please." Jamie turned her attention to Sierra. She couldn't remember when she'd seen the child so happy, and the best part was this—Sierra had no idea about Jake's memory loss. Dr. Cleary had said it was better that way, and that her assumption that all things were normal with Jake might help Jake's memory return sooner.

"Okay, Daddy." Sierra bounced up and down on the seat. "Let's sing."

Jake shifted so that his back was partially against the car door. "Sing?"

"Come on, Daddy." Sierra giggled. "The song we always sing when we're in the car."

Jake lifted his eyes above their daughter and sent Jamie a desperate look. "Help!" He mouthed the word so that Sierra would miss the exchange.

Jamie cleared her throat and cut in on the moment. "Honey, Daddy's voice is still a little scratchy. How 'bout you and me start it."

Sierra's eyes clouded some. "Okay. It's the song me and Daddy sing when we go to church."

Again Jake met Jamie's eyes. This time he whispered just one word. "Church?"

Jamie nodded and had to resist the urge to laugh out loud. As hard as the next few months would be, she would survive it better by looking for the humor. And the idea that Jake Bryan didn't know he attended church was so strange it was almost comical.

Jamie cleared her throat. "I think I can give it a try."

"But, Mommy . . ." Sierra's expression was part frown, part pout. "You don't know it."

Jamie raised her eyebrows at her daughter. "I think I can pull it off." She paused a beat and began to sing. "Jesus loves me," Jamie let her eyes move from Sierra to Jake, "this I know . . ."

Sierra sat a little straighter and chimed in. "For the Bible tells me so. . . ."

The song continued, and Jamie studied Jake's face, looking for any sign of recognition. Now and then something familiar lit up his eyes, and by the time Sierra began the second round, Jake joined in, his raspy voice joining theirs. As he did, Jamie gradually stopped and fell silent. In that moment she couldn't have sung if she'd wanted to. The lump in her throat as she watched Jake and Sierra singing together would've made it impossible. Halfway through the song, with Sierra still bouncing to the beat, Jake reached out and took their daughter's hand. When Jamie's eyes met his in the space above Sierra's head, the corners of Jake's mouth lifted just enough to notice.

Sierra chattered and sang the entire way home—during the drive to the docks, throughout the ferry ride across the harbor, and all along the final few minutes as they drove down their street. When they finally pulled into their driveway, Jamie caught a quick look at Jake. He was tiring fast. Dr. Cleary had warned about that too. The combination of head injury and burns meant Jake should get set up in the guest room and lie low for a few weeks. Until his energy returned.

They headed inside, and Jake made small circles in the foyer, casting quick looks in ten different directions as he soaked in the surroundings. *It's as though he's never seen it before*, Jamie thought. The truth of the matter made her heart ache, but there was nothing she could do about it. He would remember it one day, just not yet.

Sierra watched Jake, his strange circles and baffled expression, and her little face became a mask of sudden confusion. "What're you doing, Daddy?"

Her question snapped him back to the moment, and he turned with a jolt toward their daughter. "Uh . . ."

"Come on." Sierra didn't let him finish. "It's time for my horsey ride."

Jamie stepped in and patted Sierra on the head. "Sweetheart, Daddy's tired. Why don't you go up to your room and play with Sarabelle."

"Ahh, Mommy, do I have to?" She clung to Jake's crutch and leaned her head against his side. "I want Daddy to give me a horsey ride."

The singing in the car, the horsey rides . . . there were dozens of routines they'd known as a family, routines Jamie could've shared with Jake while he was in the hospital. But the doctor had advised against it.

"Let those things happen naturally, in the setting where they're the most familiar to Jake," he'd told her. "That way he's more likely to remember them."

At the mention of the horsey rides, Jake blinked and gave Sierra a light shrug of his shoulders. Once more he shot Jamie a desperate look. She gave him a slight nod, dropped to her knees, and hugged Sierra for a moment. "Daddy wants to play horsie too, honey. But right now he has a hurt leg and he needs a nap. You can talk to him later, okay?"

"Okay." Sierra made a sweet frown, one that immediately turned into a smile as she looked up at Jake. "I'm glad you're home, Daddy. I missed you bunches and bunches."

When Sierra had trudged upstairs and disappeared into her bedroom, Jake turned to Jamie and blinked. "I have *two* daughters?"

"Two daughters?" A ripple of concern stirred the already troubled waters of Jamie's soul. Was Jake suffering delusions on top of his memory loss? "What makes you think that?"

He looked up the stairs in the direction of Sierra's room. "Who's Sarabelle?"

A burst of laughter started low in Jamie's throat, and she tried to stifle it. Nothing good could come from her laughing at Jake, no matter how crazy his questions. But something about standing in the foyer of the home they'd lived in all their lives, discussing whether Sierra's baby doll might actually be a second daughter, was so ludicrously funny, Jamie couldn't stop herself.

Her laughter came swift and full, and knocked her back against the wall. Jake watched her, and when Jamie stopped laughing long enough to catch her breath, he leaned forward, his eyebrows slightly raised. "Either Sarabelle's even more adorable than Sierra, or I said something funny."

Jamie was breathing hard, and she reveled in the feeling. How long had it been since she'd laughed? She dabbed at the corners of her eyes. "Sarabelle's . . . a doll. Sierra's had her since she was two."

Jake gave a single shake of his head and looked relieved. "That's good. Between horsey rides and Jesus songs, I have enough to handle without some surprise second daughter waiting in the bedroom upstairs."

The laughter faded, and Jamie straightened herself. She didn't want to ask; she wasn't supposed to, really. But she had to know the answer to at least some of what Jake was feeling. "Do . . . do you remember it? Any of it?"

Jake gave her a sad smile and shook his head. "It's like I've never been here a day in my life."

Her gaze fell to the floor for a moment, and she sucked in a quick breath. When their eyes met once more she worked her mouth into a smile. "Time . . . everything in time." Then she walked past him and motioned for him to follow. "The guest room's this way."

He took two steps in that direction, but then stopped. "Wait a minute."

"Yes?" Jamie turned around, and for the first time since they'd left the hospital, she took in the full-length sight of him. There were still bandages on both his arms, though less now than a few days ago. What showed was blotchy and red, but Jamie had to agree with the doctor. It didn't look like it would scar. As for his face, there were gauze pads on both cheeks and beneath his chin, but otherwise it was covered only with a fine layer of ointment—something Jamie would have to spread over his burns every four hours.

It was easy to look past the injuries and see Jake the way he'd looked just two weeks earlier. Tall and handsome, the man she'd woken up beside every morning for years.

She snapped herself from the distraction. Jake was still stopped, still studying her, his eyes full of concern.

"What's wrong?" She was careful not to use terms of endearment with him. Nothing that would make him feel uncomfortable.

Jake bit his lower lip and his eyes searched hers. "The guest room?"

Jamie was sure her cheeks must've turned an instant shade of red, because a wave of heat flashed from her scalp to her collarbone. Her eyes fell to her shoes for a beat and then met his once more. "That's . . . that's where you'll be staying until . . ."

He finished her sentence, his scratchy voice softer than before. "Until I remember?"

"Yes." She nodded. "Until then."

"Is that okay with you?"

Compassion filled his partially bandaged face, and she was touched. "Yes . . ." They were treading unsteady ground, and she faced him full on, her arms crossed. "It was Dr. Cleary's suggestion."

"Okay . . . good."

And in that instant Jamie had a sudden understanding of just how far they still had to go. Because in the past, Jake would have been sorely disappointed to be confined to a bed other than the one he'd shared with Jamie. But the look on Jake's face now was far from disappointment.

It was relief.

Twenty-Four

September 27, 2001

He was attracted to her, and that had to be a good sign.

But still the dark-haired woman who was supposed to be his wife stirred in him no real feelings, no memories of intimacy. Not that it was his top priority. He had to figure out himself before he could work on restoring his relationship with Jamie. Because no matter how many waking hours he'd spent trying to remember, he still had no memory of who he was.

It was just before eight in the morning on Thursday, the beginning of his second full day in what was apparently his home. He had mixed feelings about staying in the guest room. It certainly wouldn't evoke any reminders of his past, but there was no question it took the pressure off him. Sharing a bed with the pretty brunette he was married to would've had its benefits, but physical intimacy didn't seem right or even natural. Not when his mind told him he'd only known Jamie a few weeks.

Jake looked around the room. It was small with high ceilings and beautifully ornate moldings. The walls were pale yellow trimmed in white and accented in deep blue around the windows. Jake guessed the house was at least sixty years old, and it held a sort of charm that helped him feel at ease. Someone had hung a set of shelves along one wall, and Jake studied them for a moment. Had *he* put them there, held the brackets in place and driven the screws into the wall for those very shelves?

If so, he couldn't remember doing it.

His eyes worked their way around the room, past the photos of Sierra and a series of older people, including the man who'd visited him in the hospital. His father. Jake stared hard at the picture, at the man's kind eyes and the proud way he stood in his uniform outside what Jake guessed was a New York fire station. But when he tried to remember anything about the man, about growing up with him or living life as his son, not a single thought came to mind.

Jake closed his eyes. How could he not recognize either his wife or his father? The idea was only barely believable, but true all the same. He simply had no recollection about any of what had brought him to this place in life, this charming guest room.

He blinked and looked around the room once more, hoping for anything that might make him remember. Sliding forward a few inches, he twisted around and checked the walls adjacent to his bed. As he did, his breath caught in his throat. A mirror hung on the wall adjacent to where he'd been sleeping. A mirror! Why hadn't he thought of that before? He'd spent so much time trying to remember what lay inside himself, he'd forgotten entirely about the outside. What did he look like, anyway? He was tall obviously, fairly well built because he could see the muscles in his arms and legs. But what was his face like, his eyes and nose?

Maybe by looking at himself in the mirror, he'd have a sudden awakening, a memory jolt that would break up the logjam of details about his past. He glanced at the clock next to the bed. Jamie would come any minute to help him up, help him into a white robe he didn't recognize, and hand him his crutches. Then she'd lead him into the kitchen where she'd have breakfast ready.

But with an intensity stronger than his desire to breathe, Jake was suddenly desperate to see himself in the mirror. So far he hadn't gotten up without her help—the two times he'd tried, dizziness or nausea would wash over him, and he'd fall back on the bed. But this morning he felt stronger than before. He drew in a slow, deep breath and sat up, easing his legs out from beneath the covers and over the other side of the mattress, the side that had only a narrow pathway between the bed and the wall with the window.

Normally, Jamie helped him get out of the other side of the bed, the one closer to the door. No wonder he'd missed the mirror until now. A thought occurred to him as he caught his breath. Were Jamie and the doctor trying to keep him from a mirror? If so, why?

Jake held his hands out in front of him and examined his skin. The bandaged burns took up a four-inch area on both his upper and lower arms, and what wasn't covered was red and tender. He ran his fingers along the tops of his thighs. His legs seemed to have handled the blast better than any other part of his body. Obviously because they'd been covered. The broken ankle still ached, and it would be another week before he could put weight on it. Eventually, though, his arms and legs would heal.

But what about his face?

He sucked in another huge breath and steeled himself to what he was about to see. Then he stood on his good leg, hopped to turn himself toward the mirror, and stared at the image that met him there. For a few beats he merely looked at the strange face, unblinking, his heart pounding within him.

No wonder Jamie and the doctor hadn't rushed him to a mirror sooner than this.

Every bit of exposed skin was dark red, as though he'd been the victim of a terrible sunburn. His lips were cracked and swollen, and gauze strips remained across most of his forehead and cheeks. If he'd been handsome at one time, it was hard to tell now.

Jake steadied himself against the wall and looked more closely at his reflection, this time at his eyes. They were clear and blue, but that was all. Beyond that there was nothing striking about them. No depth marked the center of them, no flicker of anything familiar. Almost as though the person who once lived inside him had packed his things and taken a permanent leave of absence.

He worked his jaw first one way, then the other, and brought his fingertips up to the bandaged areas. Dr. Cleary had said he wouldn't scar, that sometime in the next year it would be nearly impossible to tell he'd ever been burned. Jake doubted that very much. Not that he was terribly troubled by the fact. If he could remember who he was, he would've gladly settled for a few unsightly scars on his face.

He believed them, of course, Jamie and the fire captain and the man they called his father. Everything they said seemed to line up. His name was Jake Bryan, and he was a firefighter with an apparent deep love for God and his family. That was respectable enough. At least he wasn't a criminal or a heathen, a maniac obsessed with greed or a Casanova carrying on with two women at once. But having the information about his identity on paper wasn't enough. He didn't want a resumé about his background. He needed to feel the facts in his heart, breathe them and speak them and own them in the core of his being. He'd only been home for two days, and so far he'd spent much of his time sleeping, hoping he might wake up and look out the window and everything about his past would suddenly and miraculously come rushing back. Instead, his only true peace came from the moments he spent with Sierra.

The child loved him unconditionally, unaware of even the slightest change in him since September 11. Jake still had no memories of the times he'd shared with his daughter, though her face remained familiar and so did her name. But in the past two days he had remembered something.

He had a daughter.

That much resonated deep in his soul and convinced him that he was where he was supposed to be, that somehow he'd become Jake Bryan again one of these days, and when it happened, everything would fall into place. He was sure with everything inside him, and not because of a doctor's diagnosis.

But because of his little girl.

In fact, the more he thought about her, the more familiar her name became. Sierra wasn't just a word he recognized, it was his daughter's name . . . a name he'd known for years. Whatever he'd once shared with the little girl, the experience—at least in part—had left an indelible impression written on his heart.

And for now that would have to be enough.

If only he could remember that much about Jamie. She'd been wonderful, making sure his every need was met and careful not to expect anything of him. She'd greeted visitors from his church or fire station at the front door and graciously accepted meals or balloons or flower bouquets.

"Yes . . . he's doing much better," Jake would hear her say. "No . . . not right now. He can't see anyone for a while. Not until he has his strength back."

Then her voice would drop some, and she'd talk in hushed tones. Jake guessed those conversations were about the missing men, the people who must've been like family to him before the terrorist attacks. Hundreds of firefighter family members had to be devastated over the news, and though Jake had only recently had the strength to read the headlines, he knew enough to understand the enormity of the loss.

When Jake would ask her about the visitors, she'd give him a simple smile and say it wasn't important, just people reaching out to let him know they cared. She tossed no names at him, gave him no memory tests. Nothing that would lead to the disappointing realization that he remembered none of them.

In addition to protecting his privacy, Jamie brought him water and sliced fruit and sandwiches, and tended to his burns with an outpouring of love and patience that awed him. Every now and then they'd be talking about functional things—how his head felt, whether he wanted coffee or lunch—when he'd say something that made her laugh. At first he hadn't known what to make of that, but as the days passed, he found himself laughing along with her. Once when a funny moment had passed, she looked at him, her head cocked.

"Do you remember that?" She'd been sitting on the edge of the guest bed, careful to keep space between them.

"Remember what?" Her eyes had grown soft and thoughtful, and he'd been struck again by how difficult his memory loss had to be for her.

"Laughing. We used to laugh a lot, you and me."

With everything in his limited understanding, Jake wanted to tell her yes, he remembered laughing with her and sharing happy moments. If he'd spent a lifetime with Jamie, much of it sharing humorous happy times, it only made sense that laughter would trigger his memories. But he could only give a sad shake of his head and tell her the truth. That laughing didn't feel even a little bit familiar.

The recent memory lifted, and Jake's head spun. The dizziness was back, and he dropped to the bed once more. He could hear Jamie working in the kitchen, and he didn't want to be exhausted before breakfast. He stretched out on the bed and remembered his first breakfast with her, just twenty-four hours earlier. Midway through the meal he'd thrown her a handful of tough questions, ones that had been working their way to the surface since he'd come out of his coma. Clearly, she'd been taken aback by the blunt manner in which he'd suddenly voiced his curiosity, but she'd been wonderful, answering him without breaking down, without letting her emotions get too close to the surface.

Sierra had been across the street at a neighbor's house, and he and Jamie had sat at a modest dining room table eating scrambled eggs and wheat toast. For the first five minutes their conversation had been the polite banter of two total strangers.

"Pass the salt, please." The idea that he'd known how he liked his food was another mystery. Why would his brain remember something like salt, yet shut out memories of his wife?

Jamie had done as he asked, careful not to make eye contact with him for more than a few seconds at a time. "I cooked the eggs too long."

"No." Jake took a bite and shook his head. "They're great. Perfect."

"Thanks."

Silence.

"The blisters on your forehead are down some."

"That's good." Another bite. "The ointment must be working."

They were five minutes into the meal when Jake set his fork down, pushed his plate aside, and studied her. She took two more bites and then lifted her eyes to his. "You okay?"

That's when the questions came, one after another in no particular order. What mattered was that he held only a few pieces to the jigsaw puzzle of his past, while the tired-looking woman across from him held most of the rest. He couldn't wait another moment for at least some of the answers.

"How did we meet?" Jamie had blinked, and her fork froze in the air. From what he could read in her eyes, she loved him very much, maybe too much. He wasn't sure why he felt that way. A subtle desperation that she was careful not to voice. She set the fork on her plate, and her eyes fell.

Finally, after several seconds, she raised them once more to his. "We were kids, twelve years old." She moved her plate aside and leaned forward. "Our families lived down the street from each other."

"Here? On Staten Island?"

"On this street." Her voice was quiet, tinged with something Jake guessed was sadness. "I grew up in this house."

"When did I become a fireman?"

"Your dad was a fireman." Jamie caught his gaze and held it. "You really don't remember that?"

Jake had looked down at the leftover eggs on his plate and shrugged. "I saw a picture of him in the guest room. He was in uniform, so I figured it was some kind of family thing."

Jamie's mouth had opened a bit, but she said nothing.

"Who's my best friend?" His eyes met hers again and waited.

"At work?"

"Okay, yeah. At work."

"Larry Henning."

"He works at the same station, the place where I work?"

Jake had seen deep pain in Jamie's expression then. But she only sat a little straighter and gave a soft exhale. "Larry's missing, Jake. He was with you that Tuesday at the World Trade Center."

The news had hit Jake hard, not because he felt a connection to the missing man, but because at some point—whenever he began to remember again—he had so much pain yet to work through. After that his questions had stopped. The dialogue had tired him out, and the dark reality of the terrorist attacks and the changes they'd wrought in every aspect of their lives had been a wet blanket on his curiosity.

Jake yawned and let the memory go. He heard footsteps just outside the bedroom door, and Jamie opened it.

"Good morning." Her smile didn't quite reach her eyes. "How long have you been awake?"

"Awhile." He sat up, glad for the unfamiliar pajamas she'd given him. They gave him a sense of modesty, something he desperately wanted.

She entered the room and sat at the foot of his bed. "How're you feeling today?"

"Better. More energy." He pointed to the mirror over his left shoulder. "I got my first look a few minutes ago."

Alarm flickered in Jamie's eyes, but then it passed. "You're . . . you're okay?"

"I'm burned pretty bad." He worked his mouth open and closed a few times and gently touched his burns. "I can't believe the scars will ever go away."

"Did you, you know, feel anything when you looked? Remember anything?"

"About myself? No . . ." He uttered a sad sound that was more cry than laugh. "It was like looking at a magazine or television screen. Like the person staring back at me wasn't me at all."

Jamie nodded. Resignation filled in the tiny lines near her eyes. "Breakfast's ready."

"Thanks."

"I made oatmeal."

"Okay . . . do I like oatmeal?" For some reason, Jake didn't think so.

"Yes." A smile flickered on the corners of Jamie's mouth. "It's your favorite."

"Oh." Jake nodded a few quick times. "Right."

This dry, factual interchange felt safer to Jake, more enjoyable and familiar than anything else Jamie might've chosen to talk about, and again he was grateful. Not once had she tried to pressure him in any way. She was doing everything in her power to make him feel comfortable. She helped him to his feet and eased his crutches along the sides of his body, under his arms. "Do you want me to help?"

She'd been walking alongside him, acting as a support so he wouldn't lose his balance. But this time he shook his head. "I think I can handle it."

Jamie took the lead, and as Jake hobbled out of the room, he stopped short, his eyes glued to something he'd missed every other time he'd walked through this door. Down the hall a few feet, hanging on the wall, was a wedding portrait, a beautiful full-size photograph of a younger Jamie. But it wasn't her picture that made a layer of sweat bead up on his forehead.

It was his.

Because even with his burns there was no question that the man looking back at him from the portrait was the same one who'd looked back at him from the mirror that morning. Jake leaned hard on his crutches and took a few shaky steps toward the picture.

Jamie had caught the fact that he was no longer behind her, and she turned around. "What're you doing?"

Jake glanced at her for a moment, then nodded back at the portrait. "That's . . . that's me."

"Yes." Jamie's eyes shone a little brighter as her gaze followed his. "Our wedding picture."

"It looks familiar . . . it's the first time anything has."

Jamie uttered a quiet cry but quickly covered her mouth. She had to be thinking the same thing he was—that it was a start. At the very least it was a start. Jake only hoped that the reason his photo looked familiar was because his memory was returning, and not because he'd seen himself in the mirror for the first time a few minutes earlier.

They made their way to the table and ate breakfast, the air between them somehow more relaxed than before. When they were done eating, Jamie turned to him and drew a slow breath. "I think you're ready, Jake."

"For what?"

"Ever since we were married, you've kept a journal." She crossed her arms, her words breathy and nervous. "Not every day, but often enough." Her eyes found the ceiling, and for a moment, she wondered if she should change the conversation and make it wait for another time. Instead, she looked at him again, more resolutely this time. "Every morning you'd read your Bible, and most of the time you'd add something to your journal." She hesitated. "I . . . looked at both books the other day, after we first knew about your memory. There's so much there, Jake. Notes and highlighted sections in your Bible . . . and the journal . . . Jake, it's your life story. If you want to remember how to be Jake Bryan, everything you need is right there."

Jake simply stared at her. A journal? And a Bible with notes and highlighted sections? It was exactly the type of information he needed. He struggled to his feet and reached for the crutches leaning against the table near his seat. A wild hope surged through him, hope greater than anything he'd felt since he woke up from the accident. "Where are they?"

"Upstairs." She crossed her arms more tightly around herself. "I'll be busy down here all day and, well, I thought it'd be better if you read them upstairs on our . . . on the bed up there. A place that was more familiar." She angled her head. "Can you handle the climb?"

"Definitely." Jake nodded and took a few wobbly steps toward her. "Lead the way."

Jamie did, and as he followed her upstairs, Jake had the sense he wasn't only finding his way back to a bedroom where he'd slept all those thousands of nights. He was finding his way back to yesterday, and every wonderful thing about it.

They entered the room, and Jake stopped at the doorway. A candle burned on an antique dresser, and the hint of vanilla mixed with the pungent smell of eucalyptus and dried flowers that hung on a wreath over the bed. A thick comforter with a delicate blue design was spread across the mattress, and the dark mahogany wood that made up the four-poster frame matched the dresser and four other pieces.

Everything about the room was warm and welcoming, a perfect haven for two people who loved each other. But as inviting as it was, Jake had to admit there was nothing familiar about it. Nothing at all.

"The books are over here." Jamie pointed as she walked toward the bed.

Her words were hurried, and Jake could sense that being in their bedroom together made her feel uncomfortable again. She stooped down and reached under the bed. As she did, her sweatshirt rose up, exposing the skin on her back. She was pretty; no question about it. Jake looked out the window so she wouldn't catch him staring. Something about seeing her bare back made him feel awkward. Jamie stood up, and he glanced back in her direction.

"Here." She had the books in her hand, and she crossed the room and handed them to him. "I'll be downstairs. Take as long as you want."

"Thanks, Jamie." He held her eyes a bit longer than usual. His words felt clumsy, especially with his raspy voice, but he had to try anyway. "About . . ." He used his chin to gesture toward the bed. "About that. I'm sorry . . . I . . . I'm just not ready."

"That's okay." Her face turned a deep red, but she didn't look away. "We'll find our way back." She tapped the books in his hands. "That's the best place I can think of to start."

When she was gone, Jake set his crutches down against the dresser and hopped around the edge. Then he climbed up and stretched out along the side of the bed where she'd found the books. He sat up against two oversized pillows and pulled the books onto his lap. Holy Bible, the first one read. The cover was made from worn leather, and at the bottom—nearly rubbed off from use—was his name: Jake Bryan.

He opened it and read the inscription inside. Then he made a quick glance at the pages. Jamie had been right on. There were highlighted sections of text nearly every few pages, and just as many scribbled notations in the margins. He stopped at one in the book of Hebrews.

The highlighted section read, *Therefore, since we are surrounded by such a great cloud of witnesses, let us run with perseverance the race marked out for us. Let us keep our eyes on Jesus, the author and perfecter of our faith.* . . . Jake's eyes scanned the page and found the tiny, handwritten words beside the verses. *I must always keep my eyes on God . . . there's no other way to run the race of life, no other way to win.*

Twice more he read the words until the truth began to sink in. He was not just a religious guy, a guy who went to church and paid his taxes on time. He was in love with God, ruled by the Lord's truth, guided by His principles.

Jake could feel sections of the missing puzzle falling into place all at once.

His father—also clearly a man of God—had given Jake the Bible as a means of passing on his faith, and clearly Jake had caught the baton. Whatever else might not have felt tangible at the moment, the part that involved God was as real as his heartbeat. Tears gathered as he closed the cover of the Bible and held it to his chest. The crying surprised him, and he closed his eyes to keep the moment private between him and God.

Help me, God . . . how do I do this?

He wanted to pray; in fact, the thoughts he had for God swelled within his heart. But something about praying didn't feel completely natural. Jake understood that. The amnesia stood like a fortress wall in the way of his remembering exactly how to voice the words. But the thing that brought tears to his eyes was this: At least he remembered how. And that meant in addition to his memories of Sierra, he also had memories of God. Since that was true, it would only be a matter of time before he would remember Jamie and his father and everything about being a New York City firefighter.

A slow sigh eased between his lips. The words he wanted to say to God grew and built within him until speaking them in the silent places of his soul was the most natural thing he could ever remember doing.

Lord, it feels so good to find You again, to read the notes in my Bible and know that here, with You, is the place where I've always found my strength. He paused, and a tear squeezed its way from the corner of his eye. He let it go. *I'm a firefighter, God, so I know I've been in some tough places before. I was in a tough place that Tuesday morning at the World Trade Center. But this . . . this not knowing the people I love . . . this is the hardest thing I can imagine.* He sniffed. *So I need Your strength again, God . . . I need to spend time with You and Your words and pray that You'll hold me up, like You've obviously done all my life.* He rubbed his thumb over the leather of his Bible. Strength unlike any he'd felt since he'd been injured washed over him, and he tightened his grip on the old book. *Thank You for letting me live . . . thank You for Jamie and Sierra and for bringing me safely to this place. Now . . . please, God . . . if You could just help me find my way home.*

Jake spent the rest of that day and most of the next two weeks praying and poring over the highlighted sections of his Bible and the hundreds of entries in his journal. Jamie had been right about that too. The things he'd written gave him an intimate understanding of his passion for God and Jamie and Sierra. The entries spoke of his fear that Jamie might never share his faith and her fears that something might happen to him on the job. They told of happy times and family vacations, and they detailed his hopes for Sierra's future. They talked of the tougher calls he'd taken as a firefighter and the fun times he and Larry Henning had shared.

Never mind that his head still hurt when he read, the material was both fascinating and gripping, filling in the missing pieces of his past until at the end of those two weeks he didn't merely know everything there was to know about Jake Bryan. No, it was more than that, a feeling that ran much deeper.

Because of the two books, he was actually becoming him.

TWENTY-FIVE

OCTOBER 13, 2001

Bit by precious bit, Jamie could feel her husband returning.

The day after she'd led him to his Bible and journal, Jake had taken them down to the guest room, and from that point he'd been lost in the information. All of which was a wonderful thing, because when the two of them were together with Sierra over dinner or breakfast, his conversations and quiet reflections sounded more like Jake Bryan all the time.

It was late Saturday afternoon, nearly three weeks after he'd come home from the hospital, and she was tired of staying away from him. Even if he was busy reading, she wanted to be near him, talk to him. See if his memory was bursting through the fog in his brain. She walked from the kitchen to the guest room and gave the door a quiet push open. He was reading the Bible, too caught up even to notice her, and so she leaned against the doorframe and studied him. This reading was all he'd done, really, the thing that had taken up most of his time since she'd showed him the books on his second day at home.

Jamie had been in touch with Dr. Cleary and explained Jake's fascination with the material. "Should I be worried about him? I mean he'd rather read all day than get on with life outside the guest room."

"That's perfect. No alarm for concern, Jamie. It's just the kind of thing that'll help him remember. He'll let you know when he's ready to start living again."

And so for two weeks, Jamie had done nothing but tend to his burns and prepare his meals while he buried himself in the books. The church friends and firefighter visitors had continued to stop by, wanting to wish Jake well and offer whatever help they could in his recovery. By now the surviving men he'd worked with knew about his memory loss.

But so far, Jamie hadn't allowed them in. She'd greet them at the door, hug them, talk with them, tell them the latest about Jake. But she intended to stick as closely as possible to Dr. Cleary's orders, and he'd made it clear that visitors would only slow the healing process of Jake's brain. Jake needed a simple life, as close as possible to the one he'd had before he was hurt.

Once that felt familiar to him, he could see the guys from the station. Besides, Jamie felt terrible around Jake's buddies, because none of them wanted to talk with her about Larry Henning or the others who'd been lost the morning of the attacks. Surely they talked among themselves about the emptiness, the enormous losses of so many great men who had risked their lives to try to save others. But around her they said very little.

She didn't want to talk about the missing men either; in fact, she still hadn't talked with Sue since September 11. The few times Jamie had called, Sue had been sleeping or talking with family. Certainly, the depth of the tragedy was setting in throughout the department, and Jamie was content to be shielded from most of it.

The efforts at Ground Zero were no longer being called a rescue. They were a recovery operation, and that could only mean one thing. Larry was dead. At some point Jamie and especially Jake would have to deal with the loss, but not yet. Not until her husband could figure out who he was. And until then, Jamie was more than willing to focus all her energy on Jake and, in the process, delay her own grieving, as well.

She studied him from the doorway, and he still didn't see her. He was too caught up in a world he was desperate to find again. His burns were healing. Only a few spots still required bandaging—an area on his forehead and his left cheek, and spots on both his forearms. His skin was red and blotchy, and his voice was still not back to normal, but he was looking more like himself all the time. He was finished with the crutches too, and though the boot cast remained, he could get around without assistance. She'd talked to Dr. Cleary about some of the subtle differences that remained, especially the way he walked and carried himself. The man was Jake, for sure, but there was something subtly different about him. Even Brownie, their old lab, had noticed. More than once when Jake had limped into the room, she would bare her teeth at him. Not until Jamie would assure the dog that everything was okay would she lie back down. But even then she seemed to keep a close eye on Jake.

"That's part of the amnesia," Dr. Cleary had explained. His tone had been reassuring and Jamie was grateful. She still remembered that terrible day when she'd read Jake's chart, and how it had felt to doubt whether he was indeed her husband. The doctor went on, explaining the situation in a way that eased her vague concerns completely.

"When a person loses his long-term memory, he sometimes loses the ability to act like himself. In this case, Jake remembers how to talk and walk, just not how to talk and walk like himself. This could affect his word choices, his mannerisms, even the way he carries himself. It's only natural that your dog might not truly recognize him."

The news was helpful, and it made Jamie feel better. But still, it was strange to have him walk past without working his arm around her waist and pulling her close for a slow kiss, odd to see him talk to Sierra without stooping down and giving her the horsey rides she missed so much.

Jamie drew in a sharp breath, and the sound of it caught his attention. Of the two books, this time he was reading his journal, and he peered at her over the top of it. The moment he did, his eyes lit up and he set the book down beside him. "We need to go to the beach."

She stared at him. What was this? Was he actually starting to remember? "The . . . the beach?"

"Yes." Enthusiasm filled his scratchy voice, and a smile flashed on his face. "So we can jet ski."

"You mean you . . ." Jamie's jaw dropped, and her mouth was suddenly dry. "You remember that?"

The corners of Jake's mouth fell back into place. "No." He pointed to the journal on the bed beside him. "But I know I used to love it. We both did."

Disappointment cast a momentary shadow over the moment. When it was gone, Jamie nodded, willing away the tears that stung at her eyes. "So you're ready to get out again?"

"Yes." He sat up a little straighter in bed and grinned. "I want to play tennis and jet ski with you—even if I'm no good at it now. And I want to have picnics with Sierra."

"Jake . . ." She angled her head, and a single happy cry came from deep inside her. "I want that too."

"And that's not all." He ran his fingers through his stubby dark hair. It had grown nearly half an inch since the surgery, and it needed to be styled. But he would have to wait and go to a barber later, once he was getting out more. He was so anxious his words ran together. "I want to see the guys from the station, talk to them, and hear about the men we lost." His eyes held hers, and his smile faded again. "I want to see Sue and Katy. Hug them and cry with them and grieve the death of my best friend the way I should've done weeks ago."

Jamie's mind raced. The doctor had said this moment would come, but she hadn't expected it to come all at once. Listening to Jake now, it was as though he'd never lost his memory at all. She blinked and took a few steps closer. "Did ... did you get all that from those books?"

"Yes." He narrowed his eyes some. "It's funny, because at first everything I read was fascinating, but I had no memory of any of it." He glanced out the window and then back at her. "I've read the journal four times through now, the highlighted parts of the Bible, three times. And God is so good to me, Jamie. There's no question that at this point, the information, the thoughts and memories written there are starting to feel familiar. I'm not sure if that's because I've read it so often or because I'm starting to remember." He gave her a sad grin. "But either way it feels wonderful."

She crossed her arms, and a hundred questions demanded expression. What about her? Was he starting to remember how they'd been together, how much he'd loved her, or how beautiful their physical love had been before his injuries?

He seemed to sense her thoughts, and he patted the place on the bed beside him. "Come here, Jamie."

Her heart skipped a beat, but she did as he said. Her gaze never left his as she took small steps and made her way beside his bed. She hesitated there, but he tapped the spot next to him once more. This time she sat down on the edge of the mattress, unable to breathe for her nervousness.

"Jamie, I'm sorry." He brought his hand up and framed her face with it, his eyes searching hers. "I know that I love you. I know it in my head." He touched the journal with his other hand. "I study my words, and I'm breathless with how much I love you. But I haven't been able to tell you, because when I do ... I want it to come from my heart, from the way it'll be when my memory returns. Not because it's a fact, but because it's really how I feel."

The tears came, and there was nothing she could do to stop them. She blinked so she could see him clearly. "I ... I understand, Jake."

"The thing is ..." He let his voice trail off and gazed at the ceiling for a moment. Frustration etched itself into his expression as he caught her eyes once more. "The thing is I *do* love you. I see the way you care for me, the steps you've taken to keep things simple for me these past few weeks. Then I read about my feelings for you in the journal, even in my notes in the Bible. And I can't feel anything but love for you."

She nodded, not sure what to say. How could she be last on his list? How could he remember Sierra and God, but not her? It didn't make sense . . . in fact it made her doubt whether he'd ever remember her fully again.

When she didn't say anything, he gently pulled her close and kissed her cheek. She stayed there, her face near his, breathing in the smell of him, the combination of his aftershave and deodorant, the faint scent of familiar detergent woven into his clothes. "Jake . . ." Her heart pounded and she hung her head. "I miss you."

"Me too." His voice was a whisper, a gentle breath against her cheek. "What we shared before . . . before this nightmare." He paused and nuzzled the healed part of his cheek ever so lightly against hers. "What we shared is something I can't wait to have again." He pulled back and locked eyes with her. "I miss it, Jamie. I wish I could remember everything right now so we could start right here where we left off."

The nearness of him was more than she could bear. She wanted to beg him to take her in his arms, lie down with her there on the guest room bed, and love her the way he'd loved her so many times before. She trembled with a desire that threw common sense out the window and made even thinking all but impossible.

"Jamie . . ." Again he seemed to sense her feelings, and he slipped his arms around her, drawing her up against his chest, allowing her to be lost in the warmth of his embrace the way she'd been dying to do ever since he came home. His breathing became faster, and this time there was no question—he too was caught by the passion of the moment.

He brought his lips to her neck and made a trail of tender kisses from her collarbone to her ear. "You're so beautiful, Jamie . . . I lie here thinking about you, wondering how long it'll be until . . ."

His kisses were driving her crazy with desire, and she could feel herself angling her face toward his lips, drawing closer to him so they could kiss the way she wanted to. But she had to ask him something first, had to know what he was feeling inside. Not just physically, but emotionally. "Do . . . do you remember this?" Her words were breathy and almost desperate as she arched her back and pressed in against him. "Do you, Jake? Do you remember how it was?"

"Oh, Jamie . . ." A moan sounded from deep inside his chest, and he drew back slowly. His eyes were clouded in a desire that was as familiar to Jamie as her own heartbeat. Jake placed his hands on either side of her face and looked to a place inside her that she'd kept from him since he'd come home. "Jamie, I want this, I want all of it. Right here . . . right now." He blinked and the desire faded some, but it was difficult for him to go on. "But I can't lie to you. I still don't remember it. Not the way I should."

His words cut her deep and made her draw back a few inches. She wanted to cry or shout or scream that it wasn't fair, that she couldn't survive another day without knowing his love the way it had been before September 11. But she couldn't. It wasn't Jake's fault, and nothing good could come from upsetting him now. Lovemaking for the two of them had always been a sweetly subtle dance, but now Jake no longer remembered the steps or the music.

She sucked in a steadying breath and waited until she had the upper hand over her unbridled emotions. "Okay . . . then let's wait."

He pursed his lips and let the air ease from his lungs. His hands fell to his sides once more, and pain filled his eyes. "I'm sorry."

"Don't, Jake." She gave a few quick shakes of her head and stood, turning to face him, her back to the wall. The wanting she'd felt only a moment ago faded completely, and in its place was a different kind of desire. The desire only to see Jake return to the person he'd once been. She made her best attempt at a smile. "One of these days you'll remember."

He swung his legs over the edge of the bed and looked up at her. Something about his expression reminded Jamie of Sierra. There was no question Jake was her father. He stretched his hands over his head.

"My body remembers, Jamie. Believe me on that, okay?"

She thought about how his breathing had quickened as he kissed her neck. "I know." A sad chuckle sounded on her lips, and she waited, letting the moment pass. "So when do you want to start?"

"Start?" He blinked, his face blank.

This time she laughed out loud and tapped his foot with her tennis shoe. "Start living. You know, jet-skiing and picnics and talking with the guys at work. All that stuff you mentioned."

He grinned. "That stuff. Yes . . ."

A moment passed, and she enjoyed the struggle on his face, how difficult it was for him to switch gears. If her nearness had made that kind of impact on him, then his days of remembering couldn't be far away.

He raised his eyebrows and grabbed a short breath. "How 'bout tomorrow?"

"Okay." Jamie leaned against the wall and lowered her chin. "What should we do?"

"Hmmm." Jake studied her, his eyes thoughtful. "Something the three of us can do together."

"Right." She was starting to like the idea. It seemed like years since they'd been out as a family.

"And something where I won't overdo it. Not on my first time out."

"Okay."

"I've got it ..." He gave her a pointed look tinged with innocence. Suddenly, she knew that this was the thing he'd wanted to suggest to her all along.

"Let's go to church together. Then we can take a drive down to the beach and maybe walk along the shore."

The word "No" was almost out of Jamie's mouth when she stopped it. She searched Jake's eyes, trying to see if there was any guile there, any devious plan or ulterior motive. There was none. His journal entries obviously stated his concerns about her lack of faith and the fact that she didn't go to church. But his desire to have her beside him tomorrow for a Sunday service was only his attempt to join the living again in a way that involved Jamie and Sierra.

She bit her lip for a moment and then nodded. "Okay. We can do that."

As soon as she said the words, panic tapped her on the shoulder and sneered at her. If she went to church tomorrow, he'd expect her to go every week. And church simply wasn't something Jamie did. Not when the whole idea of God was still so senseless and unbelievable.

Jake reached out to her then and took her hand. "Thanks, Jamie." He glanced at the journal and then back at her. "I know it won't be easy for you. In fact, I kind of thought you'd say no. But I think it'll be good for me. It'll ... it'll mean the world to have you and Sierra there."

Throughout the evening, Jamie had her doubts. But in the end, as she fell asleep that night alone in their bed, craving the feel of Jake beside her, and drowning in the memory of their nearness earlier that day, she knew she had no choice. She would gladly give up a part of herself, her convictions, her determinations, her right arm, if it meant she could in any way help Jake's memory return.

Going to church wouldn't hurt her. But living without Jake beside her, missing his touch and his kiss for much longer, might do worse than that.

It might kill her.

TWENTY-SIX

OCTOBER 14, 2001

The moment they climbed out of her van and headed across the church parking lot, Jamie wondered if she'd made a mistake. Jake's presence at church that Sunday was bound to cause more than a little stir among the congregation. None of them knew about his amnesia, and the attention wasn't something Jamie had considered.

It took just seconds before a family pulled up in a sedan two parking spots away, climbed out of their car, and stared at Jake. The man pulled himself from the group and took three long strides toward them. "Jake ... we've missed you." He looked at Jamie. "I'm Tom. You must be Jake's wife."

"Yes." She gave him a polite smile but kept her distance.

"Jake ..." Tom reached his hand out, and Jake shook it. The stranger's eyes welled up. "I'm ... I'm sorry about your buddies. About all of it. We've been praying." He shrugged. "The whole country's praying."

Jamie could feel Jake's uneasiness.

He shifted his weight some and nodded. "Thanks."

There was a sad hesitation, then the man gave Jake a half grin. "You look great."

Sierra worked her way to the other side of Jake and took his hand. A smile lit up her face, and it was obvious she agreed with the man. "Daddy's getting better!"

"It must feel good to get out." The sun was bright that morning, and a cool breeze played through the trees that lined the parking lot.

"Yep." Jake squinted and cast a look toward the church entrance.

There was nothing left to say, and Jamie could feel the moment grow awkward. "Excuse us ..." She nestled against Jake's side and took two small steps forward. "We don't want to be late."

"Right." The man dropped Jake's hand and shot one more smile at him. "We're here for you." He looked at Jamie. "All of you. Anything you need."

"Thanks." Jamie's answer was quick, and the man got the hint. He nodded once more and returned to his family. When he was out of earshot, Jamie leaned close to Jake and whispered, "They don't know about the amnesia, right?"

"Not unless you've told them."

"No." She fell in step beside him. "I only told the guys at the station. I haven't said a word to anyone else." Jamie thought about that as they headed for the church's front door. Of course she hadn't said anything. She didn't know these people, not one of them, because Jake had kept this part of his life separate from her, not wanting to pressure or force her to believe as he did. Not wanting to burden her with talk about faith or religion or even God. Unless it was something she wanted. And even though they'd been very kind, bringing meals by and making promises of prayer for their family, Jamie wasn't about to share private details with them.

Fifteen yards separated them from the church doors, and along the way three other people waved or approached Jake with hugs and statements that they'd been praying for him. Jamie cast an occasional glance at Jake, and she felt him press in closer to her. He seemed to sense the way the attention of these strangers made her feel uncomfortable. He might not remember his past, but his journal had taught him lots about her. He had to know that attending church with him was not easy for her.

He brought his head close to hers and spoke in a voice only she could hear. "You okay?"

She licked her lower lip and shrugged. "Nervous."

Sierra was skipping along on the other side of him, her hand tucked in his. But now, for the first time since the terrorist attacks, Jamie felt Jake reach for her hand and weave his fingers between hers. The sensation made her knees weak. In a rush of familiarity, she felt instantly at ease. She was with Jake and Sierra, together as a family for the first time in more than a month. And not even a sermon could touch the joy of that.

They went inside, Jake limping and leading the way. With every person who approached them, Jake pretended he remembered.

"God is always faithful," he'd say. Or, "I felt your prayers every hour."

These were things Jake would've said, without a doubt, things he believed. But Jamie knew they weren't statements he ever remembered saying. In fact, in a ten-minute period Jake pulled off a performance that was worthy of an Academy Award, one that would've been impossible without the time he'd invested in reading his Bible and his journal.

People continued to approach Jake, and the attention he was getting gave Jamie the chance to glance around the inside of the church. It was actually fairly nice looking. A few banners with Bible words written on them, but none of the statues and stained glass she'd found so intimidating back when she was a child.

The people continued to come, thrilled for a chance to connect once more with Jake and to pass on their thanks. He was among the city's most famous heroes now. Not that he hadn't been before. But the status awarded firefighters in the weeks since September 11 went way beyond ordinary hero and skyrocketed up into the realms of celebrity. Normally this much attention might have shaken Jamie, but as long as Jake had hold of her hand, as long as he stood tall and strong by her side, she felt perfectly content.

They checked Sierra into Sunday school and then made their way to a pew toward the back of the church. As soon as they sat down, a dozen people came up and offered still more kind words and assurances of continued prayer. Jamie watched them, struck by the light in their eyes. It was then that she finally noticed something about these people. Their love wasn't only for Jake.

It was for her too.

Though Jamie had never come with him, though these people had never seen her even once at church, they hugged her and offered whatever help she might need. Several of them had tears in their eyes. The realization brought back Jamie's feelings from before September 11. Sierra had been asking her to come to church with them, and Jamie's interest had been roused.

Here, now, she was curious once more. She might not believe, but she didn't have to hold something against these people. Clearly, they loved her family and even her. The least she could do was give them a chance.

An older woman approached and patted Jamie's hand. "Well, hello, dear. It's so good to finally meet you."

A man behind her smiled big at Jamie. "We're family, remember. If there's anything we can do to help, please let us know."

By the time the service started, Jamie's head was spinning. She'd gone from curious to baffled. Was this what she'd been afraid of? A warmly lit building filled with kind people, a place where she felt surrounded by comforting words? She stared at her lap for a moment and tried to collect her thoughts. It didn't matter how nice the place felt. What mattered was the fact that by sitting here she was making a mockery of herself. She didn't believe in God.

Especially since September 11. It was wrong for her to be here, and as soon as Jake's memory returned, she wouldn't be back.

She wouldn't be a hypocrite.

The pastor took the pulpit, and Jamie steeled herself. This was the part where he'd do one of two things. He'd either shout at them about hell—making them feel guilty for every careless thought and pressuring them to believe. Or he'd give a sugarcoated message about how everything always worked out for those who believed.

Jamie huffed quietly to herself. *Tell that to the people buried in the rubble of the World Trade Center.* She dismissed her thoughts and worked her fingers more tightly between Jake's. The preacher could talk all day as long as she had Jake's hand in hers, his warm body beside her.

Someone had handed Jamie a bulletin when she came in. Now she opened it and scanned the list of pastors until she found the name of the man about to speak. Pastor Jason Ritchie. Jamie closed the pamphlet and set it on the seat next to her.

"Good morning and welcome to First Community Church." He smiled, and something about the man reminded her of Jake's father. "If you're visiting with us today, we're glad you came." He looked around the congregation until his eyes fell on Jake and Jamie. "We have someone very special with us today. Many of you know that Jake Bryan is part of the church family here. He's a firefighter with FDNY, and back on September 11, he nearly lost his life in the World Trade Center." The man paused. "Jake's here today, well enough to join us this morning." The man's voice sounded strained, and for a moment he seemed to fight tears. "Let's give Jake a welcome back."

People all around began to clap, and after a few seconds, a row of people stood and then another and another until the entire congregation was on its feet, clapping and looking at Jake. Tears streamed down the faces of several of them. Jamie leaned in closer to Jake, her heart touched by this outpouring. Was this what she'd been missing? People young and old who saw Jake as part of their family?

In a way it reminded her of the love at the fire station. But this was different. These people didn't love Jake because he was a firefighter; they loved him because they shared the same faith, the same God. Whole or broken, flawed or not—their common bond was one Jamie had only that morning begun to understand.

When the people returned to their seats, Pastor Ritchie began telling them a story about Jesus and a few of his friends. Mary,

Martha, and Lazarus—siblings who shared a home together. The story went that Jesus cared about these three in a special way. So it was when Lazarus took sick and died, Jesus was deeply moved.

"See," the pastor's voice rang clear and true, and Jamie found herself listening, so caught up in the story that she forgot to be leery of it. "Death was not a part of Christ's plan. It never had been." He hesitated. "Certainly as he listened to Mary and Martha cry for their dead brother, Jesus was reminded that life was never supposed to hold that type of pain and loss." His voice dropped a notch. "What did Mary and Martha say to Jesus, anyway?" He paused. "They said, 'Lord . . . if you'd been here this wouldn't have happened.'"

Pastor Ritchie sauntered across the stage and made eye contact with people on the far side of the church. "Since the terrorist attacks, we're tempted to say the same thing, aren't we?" He gave them a sad smile before turning and making his way toward the other side of the congregation. "We rail and shout and shake our fists at God, yelling at Him through our tears. 'If only You'd been here, God . . . in the buildings where You were supposed to be . . . none of this would've happened.'" The pastor stopped and squared himself toward the middle of the room. "But is that really the way it is?"

He returned to the story of Mary, Martha, and Lazarus. As he did, Jamie waited anxiously for each word. Why hadn't she heard this story before? And when was he going to start yelling at them? She glanced at Jake beside her, but his attention belonged completely to Pastor Ritchie—almost as though this were a part of his life he remembered perfectly. Jamie wondered if he really did, or if spending all those hours in the Bible had created a new belief as strong as the one he'd forgotten.

Finally, the pastor reached the part in the story where Jesus went to the tomb, the place where Lazarus was buried. The congregation was silent as Pastor Ritchie searched their faces. "Jesus was surrounded by weeping people, folks He knew and loved, and He was staring at the tomb of a man who had been like a brother to Him." The pastor narrowed his eyes. "What did Jesus do? Did He look at them and tell them everything would be okay?"

Jamie wanted the end of the story so badly she could barely sit still. She squirmed and leaned forward a bit.

"No." The pastor gave them a half smile. "Did He shout at them, yell at them, ask them where their faith was? Berate them for grieving when He'd promised them it would all work out in the end?" Pastor Ritchie shook his head. "No, Jesus did none of those things. Do you know what He did?"

Jamie had no idea.

"He cried." The pastor's voice dropped a notch. "He wept right alongside them." Pastor Ritchie held up a Bible, and the man had tears in his eyes. "Sometimes I think John 11:35 is my favorite verse in the whole book. Because it tells us Jesus cares. If we cry, He cries. No question about it."

The pastor began to pace again and wrapped up his sermon. "The truth was, Jesus had it all figured out that day. He shouted at the tomb and ordered his dead friend to come out, and that's exactly what Lazarus did." Pastor Ritchie smiled bigger than before. "And everything worked out just as it was supposed to." He cast a look in Jake's direction. "But that didn't mean death would stop dancing on our earthly days. Since the snake entered the garden, it has done that, and it always will." He gave a shake of his head. "Rather ... the story of Jesus and Lazarus is a prototype, an illustration that with Christ, death will not have the last dance. Not ever."

He took a few more steps, stopped, and faced them again. "Those of us in Staten Island lost seventy-eight firefighters on September 11. Some of you here today worked with or lived among those fallen heroes. Others of you lost family and friends who worked in the World Trade Center."

He paused, and across the church, Jamie could hear the muffled sound of several people sniffing or reaching for tissues. Tears filled her own eyes as the pastor continued.

"God's message for you this morning isn't that everything will be okay here on earth, because it won't. The rotten, sorrowful smell of death is still too strong among us for me to tell you anything but the truth." He held up a single finger. "But death will not have the last say. For those who believe in Jesus—in a God who would cry alongside you—death will never have the last word. And that, dear friends, is the hope we can take home with us. Hope that comes packaged in that very special story about Mary, Martha, and Lazarus."

He was finished speaking, and he asked them to close their eyes, bow their heads, and pray. "Every Sunday I do my best to give you a glimpse of Jesus, a picture of the man that He was, the God that He is. And each week I give you the same chance I give you today. The most important decision you'll ever make is what to do with

Jesus Christ. Today, right here, you can decide to have a friendship with Jesus, a relationship with the One who weeps alongside you in all your pain, the One who knows that if only you'd take His hand, everything really will work out in the end."

Jamie's heartbeat doubled, and her defenses dropped like so many autumn leaves. She'd never thought about God that way, never imagined Him as a friend who cried with her and cared for her. It was all she could do to remember that she wasn't a believer, that this information was fine for people like Jake, but not for her. Not when God had taken her parents so swiftly and surely; not when He'd robbed Jake of his best friend and allowed the deaths of so many innocent people. She blinked and tried to focus.

"Others of you have been believers for a long time, but you need a chance to recommit, a chance to tell God yes all over again. Yes you believe, yes, you want Him to lead your life from this point on. Yes, you want to know your eternity is safe with Him." Pastor Ritchie's voice was filled with concern. "If you fit into either of these categories this morning, please—right now while everyone has their eyes closed—raise your hand." He waited for a minute. "Okay, I see you over there. And you near the side."

Jamie felt a subtle movement beside her, and she opened her eyes just a crack. Jake's hand was high in the air, and watery streams made their way down either side of his face. The image of her husband weeping, his hand high in the air, seized Jamie's heart and shot it into her throat. She had the sudden urge to join him, to raise her hand and say yes to a God who would stand by her and cry with her.

If only she could believe.

Instead, she tucked her free hand beneath her leg and gritted her teeth. A God like that wouldn't want her, anyway. Not after she'd spent so many years rejecting Him, dismissing Him, and refusing to believe He even existed.

Pastor Ritchie's voice interrupted her thoughts. "If you're one who has your hand raised, why don't you come down here to the front. We have people who want to pray with you, help you nail down what a relationship with God actually looks like."

Jake stood, and Jamie could feel his good leg shaking. He tapped her on the shoulder and motioned for her to come with him, but this time she shook her head. She couldn't go, couldn't venture into a place where people were doing the one thing that had terrified her all her life—putting their stock in a God who allowed bad things to happen.

An older man with a name tag pinned to his shirt appeared at the end of their pew. He held out his hand, and Jake went to him. He turned back just once and gave her a final sad look. Then he met up with the man, and together they moved slowly down the aisle until Jake disappeared through a door to the right of the stage.

After the service Jake found her back at the pew, and the moment Jamie's eyes met his, she began to shake. He no longer had that vacant, uncertain look she'd come to expect. Instead, his eyes glowed with a love and depth that Jamie hadn't realized was missing until now. It was a look that had always set Jake apart, a look that gave people a glimpse of his soul. The peace and joy Jamie saw there now made her wonder if a miracle had happened in the room, if maybe now that Jake had his faith in God back, he might've remembered everything else too.

It wasn't until after they'd picked up Sierra and made their way out to the beach that Jake shared his thoughts about what had happened back at church. They'd brought folding chairs and they set them up on the sand. Sierra took a shovel and pail and set about building a castle closer to the shore.

"Why didn't you come with me?" He gazed out at the harbor, his voice more curious than hurt. The breeze had picked up, but the afternoon was still warmer than usual for October.

"I couldn't." She exhaled hard and watched Sierra, the simple joy written across her face. "It wouldn't be right. Not when I don't believe." She cast him a quick glance. "Surely you know that much, at least, Jake. Doesn't your journal tell you how I feel about God and church?" He reached over and took her hand in his, and Jamie silently celebrated. The familiar gesture was becoming natural again. For a long time he was silent, rubbing his thumb over the back of her hand.

"You believe, Jamie. I could feel you there beside me, believing every word the pastor said."

Jamie's mind raced. No . . . he couldn't say that, couldn't make her admit to something she wasn't ready to admit to herself. "I've . . . I've never believed."

This time he looked at her. "Yes, you did. At camp that year, back when you gave your life to Christ and told me you'd never felt better in all your life."

"Jake . . ." Time seemed to stand still, and Jamie could feel the color drain from her face. "You remember that?"

His eyes met hers, and he searched her heart. "Yes." The uncertainty in his eyes matched what he must've seen in hers. "I mean,

I've read it five times in my journal. But yes . . . I remember it." He looked away. "At least I think I do." A few minutes passed while they both watched Sierra. Jake slipped the shoe off his good foot and wriggled his toes in the sand. "It feels so good to be out here. To be with you and Sierra . . . after being together at church with you. Like it's the most right way we could've spent our Sunday."

Jamie crossed her arms. Her heartbeat was fast and jittery. She was still trying to catch her breath from the idea that Jake might be remembering, that he could—at least in part—recall their time at summer camp that year. "Can I tell you something?"

"Sure?" Jake's expression was bathed in peace.

"I'm afraid about God." There . . . she'd said it. She'd voiced a thought that even she hadn't been sure of until that very moment.

"Why?" Jake brought her hand to his lips and kissed it. "What about God scares you?"

"He . . ." She leaned back in her chair and clenched her jaw. Angry tears forged their way down her cheeks, leaking from a place in her soul that had been boarded up for too many years. "He took my parents." She made a fist with her free hand and placed it over her heart. "I was just a girl, Jake. But my parents both died and . . . and neither of them believed in God."

Jake listened, giving her the space she needed to finish.

She sniffed hard and wiped at her tears, but they only came harder. "What am I supposed to think? That a loving God would allow my parents to die and go to hell? All because they made the fatal mistake of not believing?"

Jake waited a moment, and when he finally spoke, his raspy voice was filled with a tenderness that felt achingly familiar. "Did you ever think . . . that maybe as they lay in that car that night they might've changed their minds? The Bible says God doesn't care when people come to Him—He just cares *that* they come. I read that the other day. Maybe your mom and dad cried out to God in those last moments . . . maybe they're in heaven even now, Jamie. Did you ever think of that?"

Maybe they were in heaven?

The idea made Jamie dizzy, but it struck a note inside her heart that had never been played. What if Jake was right? What if just maybe her parents had given their lives to God there on the highway, amidst their dying moments? And even if they hadn't, a God who could stand beside His friends and weep with them wasn't one that would make a mistake with her parents. "Okay, but why did they have to die? Can you tell me that?"

Jake looked at her again, his eyes tender. "People die, Jamie. There're no promises here on earth. God didn't make your parents die that night; and He didn't bring the World Trade Center down. The devil did that." Jake hesitated. "One of my favorite verses in the Bible—at least lately—is a reminder that the thief comes only to kill, steal, and destroy. But God ... God comes to give us life— life to the fullest."

A sob worked its way up from Jamie's breaking heart, and she let her head fall into her free hand. "God wouldn't want me any-way, Jake. I'm ... I'm not good like you."

"Good?" He slid his chair closer to hers. "Sweet Jamie, God isn't looking for us to be good or perfect. He's just looking for us to be His. That much I remember." Jake paused and released the hold he had on her hand. Instead, he ran his fingers lightly over her back, comforting her in ways he couldn't even know. "That's why I raised my hand in church today. I couldn't go another minute without telling God that even though I can't remember my past, I want Him to be with me. Today and tomorrow. For-ever." He exhaled, and the sound of it breathed peace into her. "I have to tell you, Jamie, the feeling of knowing I'm safe with God was better than anything I could imagine."

Jamie sniffed and peered at him through the spaces in her fingers. "Can I go with you again next week?"

"Of course." He grinned and helped her to her feet. "But right now we have a little girl to play with."

Jake led her to the place where Sierra was struggling with the outside frame of her sandcastle. Jake plopped down next to her, sticking his boot cast out to one side so it wouldn't get too sandy. Then he twirled his finger into one of Sierra's ringlets and kissed the child on the head. "Next week I get to curl your hair, okay?"

Sierra's eyes lit up. "Really, Daddy?"

Jamie watched the exchange, her mind numb once more. Jake wanted to curl Sierra's hair? Was there a detail Jake missed in that journal of his? And at what point would the details of his past come from his memory, and not the pages of a book?

They finished the sandcastle and then walked along the shore, the three of them, hand in hand. Halfway back to their chairs, Jake stooped down and patted his backside. "Is the princess ready for her horsey ride?"

Sierra clapped her hands and squealed. Then she ran toward Jake and easily propelled herself onto his back.

"Jake—" Jamie felt a rush of concern. He wasn't strong enough to carry Sierra yet. "Be careful."

But even before she finished the warning, Jake was off, hobbling down the beach with Sierra bounding along on his back, occasionally digging her heels into his side, her little-girl giggle mingling with the sound of the surf. "Faster, horsey! Faster!"

* * * *

That night as Jamie fell asleep she realized that the day was a breakthrough in more ways than one. Not only had Jake begun living again, but her time at church and their discussion afterwards had left her vulnerable to the reality of God in a way she'd never guessed would be possible.

The changes from that day ushered in a period of two weeks in which Jake wanted to do everything they'd once done together, everything he'd mentioned that afternoon in the guest room. The temperatures had dipped some, but it was still unusually warm, and together they picnicked and played games and continued to go to church.

Early one cool sunny afternoon they left Sierra with the neighbor and brought the jet ski out to their favorite spot. Jake slipped a plastic bag over his boot cast, and Jamie gave him a gentle ride across the cool harbor, reminding him the whole time of how the machine operated and how they'd once used it. On the way back to shore, he gently squeezed her waist. "Faster, Jamie. Like we used to ride."

"Are you sure?"

"Absolutely."

Jamie opened the throttle until they were flying across the water. She even cut across a few mild wakes.

"No wonder I loved this!" A cold windy mist brushed across them, and Jake nuzzled his face next to hers, his words filled with exhilaration. "As soon as my cast's off, I get to drive, okay?"

Jamie laughed. "You got it."

And taking the jet ski out became something they did twice more that week, even once when temperatures hovered in the sixties and a light drizzle fell. Jamie didn't care and neither did Jake. The relationship they were rebuilding between them was warmth enough. Jake's memory wasn't exactly returning, but his place in their family was almost what it had once been. At least outside their bedroom.

Jamie credited the Bible and Jake's journal, of course. But each week Pastor Ritchie made her realize that his slow return had to be more than that. It had to be an act of God Himself. And finally, on Jamie's third Sunday, when the pastor asked if any of them wanted a friendship with God, Jamie's hand was one of the first ones up. After a lifetime of running from her husband's God, she'd finally come full circle. And that morning her running led her right into His holy arms, to a place where she and Jake and Sierra could love and serve Him forever. A place she would never have known if Jake hadn't been hurt.

Because of that, Jamie could see a truth playing out in their lives, the one Jake had talked about at the beach after her first Sunday service. God had indeed come to give them life—all of them. And not just any life, but life so full that she was nearly bursting with joy. After all, she had Jake and Sierra and a friendship with God that was only just beginning. One day soon Jake would have his memory. And even though he was falling in love with her all over again, she could hardly wait for the day when everything about his past would come rushing back. And it would . . . because God was making good on His promise—giving them life to the fullest possible measure. And as wonderful as things were now, Jamie knew her life was about to get even more full. It would happen the moment she and Jake could get back to sharing not only their days.

But their nights as well.

TWENTY-SEVEN

NOVEMBER 3, 2001

Laura hadn't planned to do anything more than clean Eric's closet.

Clay had taken Josh to play basketball, and Laura had made the decision days ago that Eric's things needed to be gathered and packed away. It wasn't something she wanted to do with Josh around. The first hour passed without anything too emotional. She'd come to grips with the reality of the loss of Eric, and still her greatest grief was that they'd never figured out what had driven them apart. The deep ache that went along with that was something she would hold forever.

But still, his closet needed to be cleaned.

She worked her way through his dirty clothes basket and his dress slacks and ties. Next she began packing a stack of sweaters from his top shelf. Eric didn't get rid of things easily, and Laura uttered a sad laugh as she lifted the dusty clothes from the shelf and placed them in the box. He hadn't worn the sweaters since before Josh was born, but he'd saved them anyway.

Now she would pack them up and give them to the local rescue mission.

She was pulling off the last sweater when something white slipped from the shelf and drifted to the floor. Her eyes followed it, and as she leaned over, she saw that it was a white envelope with nothing written on the outside. Laura dropped the sweater in the box, picked up the envelope, and lifted the flap.

Inside was a greeting card she'd never seen before. Her heartbeat quickened as she pulled it out. Why would Eric keep it here, beneath his sweaters? Was it from some secret lover, someone Laura had never known about? Were her fears in the months before September 11 justified, after all? A part of her screamed to put the card back in the envelope and throw it away, never look at what her husband had kept hidden here in his closet.

But she had to know, and she turned it over so she could see the front. A blue and white sky was punctuated by a single word printed across the background. *Forever* . . .

Laura clenched her teeth and stared at the card. Then without waiting another second, she opened it. The rest of the printed message read simply, "Forever I'll remember you."

Beneath that was something Eric had written. It was dated, and suddenly Laura's breath caught in her throat. She stared at the date, not believing what it said. October 15, 1989. It was the birth date of their daughter. The birth date and date of death. Her eyes fell to the words Eric had written, and through eyes clouded by tears, she began to read.

Hello, darling daughter . . . this card is from your daddy. . . .

A sob escaped Laura's throat, and she dropped in slow motion to the floor of Eric's closet. He'd written their stillborn daughter a card? How had he cared that much about the child without ever saying so? She covered her eyes with her free hand and waited until she could see again. Then she pressed her fingers against her eyes and blinked back the tears. *God . . . how come he never showed me this?*

No answer flashed in her mind. She brought the card closer to her face and continued reading.

Your mommy misses you so much, and I know it would only hurt her if I talked about this. But you were my daughter, sweetheart, and I have to write to you now. I want to give you a name, honey. The name your mom and I had talked about before you were born. That way I'll always know that you were real . . . and that you were part of my life. Laura closed her eyes for a moment and held back the sobs. Tears would only make it harder to read. She found her place again and continued.

And so I want to name you Sarah. Sarah Anne. And one day when we meet again in heaven, I'll see you and know you . . . and call you by name. I can't wait until then, to finally get to hold you for the first time. I love you, Sarah. Like the card says, I'll remember you forever. Love, Daddy.

Laura read Eric's words again, and slowly she closed the card and clutched it to her heart, and in the silence of the closet, she could almost hear God crying. The sobs came then, waves of them. He had cared, after all. But he'd hidden his feelings for more than a decade, buried them beneath a stack of dusty old sweaters.

Why hadn't Eric told her how he'd grieved the loss of their daughter? He'd been upset the first day, but after that he'd never talked about her again. How could she have known that he'd named the child Sarah? The name they'd agreed on weeks before her birth.

Years had passed before Laura got pregnant again, and even then Eric never brought up the daughter they'd lost. But here ... now ... there was no doubting the fact that Eric had grieved her loss. Grieved it from a place he hadn't let anyone see even one time since then.

The truth created a loss Laura had never known. If only she'd found the card before Eric died, they could've used it to walk their way back to the love they'd known before. They could've talked about the real issues at the counseling sessions, how the loss of Sarah Anne had made Eric doubt God and family and love and everything good about life. Somewhere deep inside him, Eric had cared. He'd cared more than he'd ever let on ... more than even he remembered.

But now ... now it was too late, and that fact was almost more than Laura could bear.

The minutes passed, and suddenly something dawned on her, something that made her smile despite her tears, despite the cavernous loss she felt deep in her heart. Today ... somewhere on the streets of heaven ... Eric was doing the thing he'd wanted so badly to do.

He was holding Sarah Anne.

TWENTY-EIGHT

NOVEMBER 4, 2001

The first flashback hit a week later.

It was three o'clock in the morning the day that Jake and Jamie and Sierra had planned to attend a spaghetti dinner at the fire station. One minute Jake had been sound asleep, and the next he was thrust in the middle of a moment so chaotic and terrifying, it took his breath away.

He was scrambling down an endless stairwell in some high-rise building, when suddenly he began to tumble. The fall happened in slow motion, and as soon as he hit the steps, a hand reached out to help him. He took it, and when he looked up, he was suddenly staring into his own face, the image of himself in a firefighter's uniform.

"Help!" He shouted long and hard, and the sound of his own voice woke him up.

Then just as quickly, the image disappeared.

Jake sat straight up in bed, his heart racing. *God ... what just happened to me? What was that, and where does it fit into my past?* He licked his lips and stared at his hands. His fingers were shaking, but before he could beg God to settle his heart, the door flew open and Jamie raced into the room.

"Jake ... what is it?" Her face was pale as she made her way to the side of his bed and sat down. Her breaths came fast and anxious as she searched his eyes. "You screamed."

Calm me, God ... help me make sense of whatever that was. He took Jamie in his arms and held her. She was terrified. He could feel her heartbeat pounding hard against his chest. "It's okay ... it was just a dream."

She went utterly still and pulled back far enough to see him. "A dream ... or a flashback?"

He knew the answer immediately, but he didn't want to frighten her. Especially when the image still didn't make sense to him. He locked eyes with hers and exhaled as he caught his breath. "It was a flashback, I think."

"Dr. Cleary said they might come in the early morning. Before you woke up."

Jake nodded. "It was very, very real."

"Well . . ." Jamie studied his face. "What was it? What'd you remember?"

"I was in a building . . . with a stairwell that seemed to go on forever."

"The World Trade Center." Jamie's voice was quietly urgent.

They'd both waited so long for this moment that he knew better than to keep her guessing. He took a slow breath and finished detailing what he'd seen. "The strange thing was that I wasn't the fireman, Jamie. I mean, I was the fireman, but I was someone else too. Someone who had fallen on the stairs. When the firefighter helped me up, I looked at him and it was me."

Jamie's shoulders fell a bit, and the panic faded from her face. "Maybe it wasn't a flashback. Maybe it was a dream."

"Maybe." Jake ran his fingers lightly down Jamie's bare arms. In a handful of seconds, the idea of whether he'd had a flashback or a dream seemed irrelevant. Instead, all that mattered was her nearness, the way she looked sitting beside him on the bed in an oversized T-shirt, the moonlight glistening in her hair. "I'm sorry I woke you."

"It's okay." She swallowed, and the space between them began to disappear. "Jake . . . ?"

"Yes." His voice was healing, and here in the darkness it sounded almost normal. Like Jake assumed normal would sound if he could remember his past.

"Hold me, Jake. Will you please?" She hung her head, clearly embarrassed by the raw desire in her voice.

Without a bit of hesitation, Jake took her in his arms and stroked her back, soothing away the weeks of separation. Though they'd gotten closer those past few weeks, they'd never had the near occasion to kiss the way they had that one time. But here, in the quiet dark of the night, Jake didn't care if he couldn't remember being married to her. She was beautiful and loving, and they'd obviously spent a lifetime together. He whispered against her neck. "Jamie, you're beautiful. Do you know that?"

"Mmmmm." She pressed herself against him, and his desire for her doubled. Her voice was thick with passion as she whispered near his ear. "I miss you more each day. This part of you."

She drew back and their eyes locked. Before he could ask himself whether it was right or wrong, before he could consider the fact that he'd promised to keep his distance until he remembered her, Jake brought his face to hers. Slowly . . . in a way that seemed as natural as the feel of her in his arms, their lips met, and Jake kissed her the way he'd been dying to do for weeks. "Jamie . . ." He was breathless when he came up for air. "What you do to me."

He studied her and realized there were tears in her eyes. Her mouth opened as though she wanted to ask him something, but instead she worked her fingers up along the tender places on his burned face and through his hair. The sensation felt unbelievable, and it lit a fire deep within him, a fire that could only be quenched one way.

"I love you, Jake." She drew him to her, kissing him again and letting her tears brush against his face. "I love you."

An impatience began to build, and suddenly he wanted her more than he wanted his next breath. He gently pulled her closer, drawing her down onto the bed beside him. "I love you . . . Jamie."

She kissed him, balancing over him, not quite letting herself be swept away on this wonderful wave of passion. When she drew back she studied his face, knowing that he saw a fear in her eyes that hadn't been there before. Her voice was only a pinched whisper. "Do you love me . . . because you remember?"

His eyes closed, and he could feel her pulling away from him, straightening. *No, God . . . don't let her ask this. We belong together . . .*

In all yours ways acknowledge Me, and I will direct your paths, My son.

The words sounded on the front porch of his heart and echoed through his being. Jake had no doubts. The still small voice was from God. And if this wasn't the time for Jamie and him, then one day soon their time would come. He sat up and tried to still the flames within him. "Jamie . . . is it that important?" He opened his eyes and found her watching him, studying him. "I love you. I loved you before, and I love you now. Isn't that all that matters?"

She sat back up, her body close to his, and clasped her hands. Then she stared at the wedding ring on her finger. "No." Her eyes raised to his. "I don't want to reinvent what we used to have." She tilted her head, her tone laced with a raw pain that cut at Jake's heart. "I want the real thing, Jake. As badly as I want you right now, I want all of it." She ran her fingertips beneath her eyes. "All of you."

He leaned close and with slow, tender movements he kissed her once more. When he pulled back he wanted her so badly, he could barely stop himself from lying to her, from telling her that yes, he did remember. But instead he took her hands in his and bowed his head so their faces came together in a different way. "Pray with me, will you, Jamie?"

Slowly, his passion was replaced with something richer, something etching itself in the walls of his soul. "Pray that whatever woke me up was a flashback, and that it's only the beginning. Because I do want you. But you're right. I want to remember everything else first."

There in the dark of the guest room they prayed for God's mercy and blessing. Jamie finished the prayer in words that were both simple and sweet. "Bring him home, Lord . . . all the way home. Please."

At just after four o'clock that afternoon, they took the ferry across the harbor and went by cab to his fire station. Eight men and their families had gathered there, all waiting for him when he walked in.

Jake wondered if he'd ever been more nervous in all his life.

Because of the strange dream or flashback that had happened earlier, he sort of hoped that seeing the station would jar another series of memories. The same way reading his Bible and journal had seemed to restore his soul. Instead, nothing about it looked the least bit familiar, and when they went inside, he felt like he was back at church all over again.

Men he didn't know began to hug him and shake his hand; women who must have been their wives had tears in their eyes, and they hung on to him as though they were afraid to let go. "Jake, we're so glad you made it!" And "We've missed you, man. When're you coming back?"

Captain Hisel was there, and Jake was grateful. At least he looked familiar, even if it was only because of their visit in the hospital. "Hey, Jake . . . you're healing up."

"Yep." Jake shook the captain's hand and managed a smile. He glanced about the room looking for Jamie. Out of the crowd of people at the station, she and Sierra were his only friends, and he hated being apart from them.

"How's it going with your memory?"

"Slow." Jake leveled his gaze at the captain. "I picked up a lot from my journal and the notes in my Bible. But I can't really say I've started remembering again."

Captain Hisel waved his hand around. "Any of this look familiar."

"No." Jake frowned and shook his head. "Not a bit." He stuck his hands in the pocket of his jeans. They were loose on him, maybe a quarter inch too long, but that wasn't surprising. Jamie said he'd probably lost fifteen pounds since the accident. He glanced at the wall behind Captain Hisel and saw a series of photos. Men, all of them firefighters, with two dates listed beneath.

The second date for every man was September 11, 2001. Jake took a step closer and scrutinized the faces. "Those our guys?"

The captain worked the muscles in his jaw. "Every one."

Jake hadn't kept up with the news. It meant nothing to him, since he had no memory of fighting fires or even working in New York City. Besides, he'd been too busy reading his Bible and journal to care what the papers said. But here, now, he was touched beyond words at the enormous tragedy that had happened to the New York Fire Department that awful Tuesday morning. He dropped his tone a notch and stared at the captain. "How's everyone handling it?"

"It's crazy, JB." Captain Hisel's voice cracked, and he stared at the floor for a moment. When he found his voice, he lifted his chin and met Jake's eyes. "The department had to create its own Funeral Desk." He ran his hand over his balding head. "Three hundred and forty-three men. Funerals every day, sometimes three and four a day. One Saturday there were two dozen. Two dozen funerals, JB. Can you believe it?"

Jake wasn't sure what to say or how to react, but he was struck by the pain he saw in the captain's eyes. The anxiety within him made him better understand Dr. Cleary's orders to keep his life as simple as possible until he remembered. Should he hug the captain? Maybe utter something about the losses being too bad? He didn't know, and so he merely put his hand on the captain's shoulder and said nothing.

Captain Hisel sniffed and raised his chin some. "Not just that, but ever since the attacks we've become famous." He shrugged. "I mean we couldn't shut our doors the first few weeks after September 11. Everybody and their brother was coming by, bringing us cookies or meals or flowers. Telling us how wonderful we were, sometimes even getting our autographs."

The captain huffed. "You know how that made us feel?" He didn't wait for a response. "Like garbage, that's how. Because we should've died up there in those buildings right beside the men we lost. Heck, we weren't the heroes, JB. We were lucky. The guys who died in the buildings—they're the heroes, you know?"

Jake nodded, again not sure what to say. Clearly the captain needed to talk to him, to catch him up on all that had happened. But without a past to anchor it to, it was almost like hearing a news report. Jake was saddened, horrified even. But he wasn't personally touched, not the way Captain Hisel would've expected him to be.

The captain studied him again. "You look different, JB. Something about your face."

A few people at church had said that as well, and Jake gave the captain the same answer he'd given them. "Must be the burns."

"You're thinner."

"Yeah ..." Jake gave the captain a crooked smile. "I guess that's not the worst thing."

"You talked to Sue since you've been up and about?"

"Sue?"

"Sue Henning." The captain looked baffled for an instant, then a knowing look filled his face. "I keep forgetting about your memory." He gave a sad chuckle. "Sue was married to Larry. Your best friend."

Suddenly, Jake remembered the journal entries, the times when he'd written about Larry and Sue and Katy, how close he'd felt to Larry and how deeply he'd cared for the man's family. His eyes darted to the wall of photos once more until he found the one that read *Larry Henning, August, 23, 1968—September 11, 2001.* The man was stockier than Jake imagined him, his full face taken up almost entirely by his smile.

He remembered something from his journal, something he'd written about Larry. *The two of us will always be best friends, looking out for each other at the station and in our marriages. Even in our love for God. Larry Henning is the closest God ever came to giving me a brother.*

Jake searched the man's eyes. *Why, God ... why isn't Larry even a little familiar. And how come I can't remember the good times we shared.* A deep sorrow welled up inside Jake, not the type of sorrow that came with missing someone you've loved and lost. But the sorrow of a distant, incalculable loss. Because seeing the smiling eyes of the dead stranger, Jake believed that somehow if Larry were there in the room at that moment, the two of them would have found a way to hit it off.

Even if his memory never returned.

Jake let the thought pass as he took a step back and faced Captain Hisel again. "How's she handling it?"

"She's a mess. I asked her if she'd talked to Jamie, and she said not since September 11, that the three of you needed your space. Because of the memory thing."

Jake nodded. "Can you do me a favor?"

"Anything, JB ... you know that."

"Give me Sue's address ... directions to her house. Jamie and I want to drop by with Sierra and let her know we care."

Captain Hisel narrowed his eyes and stared hard into Jake's, almost as though he were looking for the man who lived somewhere within him, the one who would remember all that the guys on Engine 57 and Ladder 96 had been through together over the years. "That's you, right, JB? Even though you can't remember?"

The question jolted Jake's confidence and made him want to run from the firehouse. What did the captain mean? Of course he was Jake Bryan ... who else would he be? He managed a weak chuckle. "Don't say things like that, Captain. You scare me."

The captain waved a hand over his head as though he were chasing away an errant fly. "I'm sorry. It's just ... it's too weird talking to you about Larry and seeing in your eyes that you don't remember him." The captain paused and gave him that same look, the one where his eyes bunched up and narrowed to mere slits. "You really don't remember, do you, JB?"

"No." He caught a half breath and backed up a step. He needed to find Jamie and Sierra. Now. "I really don't." Voices sounded in the next room, and Jake recognized one of them as Jamie's. "Hey, good talking to you. I've got to find Jamie."

Jake made his way into the next room. Sierra saw him first, and her eyes lit up as she broke away from Jamie and ran to him. Though he still had the cast on his foot, Jake had learned how to brace himself on one leg and capture his daughter as she jumped into his arms. He wished Captain Hisel could see him now. Of course he was Jake Bryan—there was no way his daughter would've loved him like that if he weren't.

The rest of the evening he stayed by Jamie's side, keeping his conversation to one- and two-word answers. He avoided any discussion about his memory. When it was time to go, Jake took from the captain a slip of paper with directions to Sue and Larry's house. In the cab on the way back to the ferry, Jake pulled them from his pocket and showed them to Jamie.

"I think we should stop by and see Sue."

Jamie stared at the slip of paper and gave him a sad sigh. "I know how to get there, Jake. We were close friends before September 11."

Jake thought about that for a moment. It was only seven o'clock, but Sierra had fallen asleep between them, and her tiny body lay nestled against his side. "If we were so close, why haven't we been over to see her yet?"

"You weren't ready."

Jamie's answer was a bit too quick, and Jake picked up on the fact. "There's more to it, isn't there?"

Pain filled Jamie's eyes. "I've called her a few times, but she's never able to talk." She looked at Jake. "Last time I talked to Sue, we were hoping that Larry was only missing. That somehow they'd find him in the rubble." Jamie lifted a single shoulder. "Now . . . now we know the truth. He's dead, and, Jake . . ." her voice broke, "I'm not sure if I can handle seeing her. Because . . ." She sniffed twice, and Jake slipped his arm around her.

"It's okay, honey. Tell me . . . I'm here." She rubbed her thumb and forefinger into her brow and shook her head. Then her eyes met his again, and for the first time he could see the type of terrifying fear that he'd written about in his journals.

"Jake . . . that could've been you. But since it wasn't, I didn't know if Sue would even want to see me. I mean . . ." She tossed her hands up. "I know God was there with Larry. He was there with you. I believe that. But still . . . I *have* my husband, and she doesn't. Looking at each other and admitting that, well, it'll be the saddest thing I've ever done."

Jake waited a moment until Jamie had control of her emotions again. Then he kissed her gently on her temple and spoke in a voice that sounded almost healed. "I'll help you through it."

"Okay." She gave a single nod, her face brushing against his burned face.

The gesture caused a slice of pain across his tender cheek, but he didn't care. Especially not now, when all he wanted was to see Jamie through the next few hours. And pay his respects to the wife of his best friend.

They were quiet on the ferry ride back to Staten Island, and Jamie left to find a restroom. Jake pulled Sierra onto his lap and smiled at her. "You look sleepy."

"Mmmhmm." She yawned and rested her forehead against his. "Butterfly kisses?"

Jake refused the faint sense of panic that tried to seize him. He kissed Sierra's nose and winked at her. "Okay, silly girl."

"Well, Daddy . . ." Sierra angled her face expectantly. "Do it then."

He hesitated, his heart pounding twice as hard as before. "You start."

With that he fooled her, and her eyes sparkled. "Okay." She brought her nose to his and rubbed it back and forth a few times. Then she turned her face a few inches and blinked her eyelashes several times against his cheek. He caught on within a few seconds and did the same thing, blinking his lashes against hers.

"You know what, Daddy?"

"What?"

"That's a favorite thing for me and you."

"Yes, Sierra." He pulled her head to his chest and clung to her, grateful that he'd lived, grateful that he still had a chance to love this darling child. "I'm glad too."

"Are we going to Katy's house tonight?"

For an instant Jake had to search his mind before he remembered. Katy was Sue and Larry's little girl. "Yes ... just for a little while."

Sierra sat up so she could see his eyes. "Did Katy's daddy get hurt in that big fire? The one with the airplanes in the building?"

Jake felt his heart sink. The child didn't know, and he had to tell her. They could hardly stop by Sue's house and have Sierra asking Katy where her daddy was. "Honey, I have to tell you something very sad about Katy's daddy."

Jamie returned then and took a seat beside Jake. "What's the conversation?"

Jake gave her a knowing look. "Sierra was asking about Katy's daddy. Whether he got hurt in the bad fire, the one with the airplanes in the building."

"Oh." Jamie inhaled sharply through her nose and looked at the dark fall sky for a moment. Then she shifted her gaze to Jake, and her eyes pleaded with him. "You tell her, okay?"

Jake turned back to Sierra. "Katy's daddy died, honey. He went into that bad fire to save people, but he never made it back out."

Sierra's expression filled with fear, and then as though she'd suddenly sprung a leak, her innocent eyes filled with tears. "You mean ... he's never coming home again?"

"No." Jake placed his hands on his daughter's shoulders and searched her face. "But we know where Katy's daddy is, don't we?"

"Yes." A huge tear rolled down Sierra's nose and plopped on Jake's jeans. "He's with Jesus."

"And that isn't so bad, is it?"

"No." Sierra sniffed. "But Katy doesn't have a daddy anymore."

"Aw, sweetheart, yes she does. It's just that her daddy lives in heaven."

Sierra thought about that for a minute. "I don't ever want you to live in heaven, okay, Daddy. Not until I go there too."

"I won't." Jake chose his words carefully. If September 11 had taught him one thing, it was that life held no guarantees. He exchanged a meaningful look with Jamie and continued. "But if Jesus has a job for me to do—like saving some people in a fire— and in the middle of it He tells me to come home to heaven. I'll have to go. You know that, right? Just like Katy's daddy."

Sierra tilted her head, and her golden curls fell gently across her pink sweater. "You mean Jesus told Katy's daddy to come home while he was helping people?"

"Yes." Jake gave a firm nod of his head. "That's exactly what happened."

"Oh." She wiped her nose. "I still hope Jesus doesn't do that to you, Daddy. Because I want you with me forever."

Jake kissed his daughter's nose and reached next to him for Jamie's hand. "I want that, too, honey. Forever and ever."

The ferry pulled up at the dock, and the three of them made their way to the car. Ten minutes later they were standing on the front porch of another house Jake didn't recognize. A pretty blonde opened the door, and when she saw them, her hand flew to her mouth. The tears were instant for both her and Jamie.

"Jake . . . Jamie . . ." She opened her arms, and Jake, Jamie, and Sierra met her in a group hug. There, for nearly a minute, the three of them embraced, weeping for the loss of a man Jake was desperate to remember.

Sierra squirmed her way free of the circle, and Jake looked up to see her tug on Sue's sleeve. "Mrs. Henning . . ."

Sue sniffed hard, and through her tears she smiled at Sierra. "Yes, honey."

"Can I go play with Katy?"

"Yes, doll. Katy's upstairs."

The group of them watched Sierra scamper inside, and then Jamie turned to the blonde woman. "I'm so sorry, Sue . . . I've tried to call." Jamie's voice was muffled in Sue's T-shirt.

"No . . . it's my fault. I didn't think I could look at Jake without . . ." She pulled back and stared at Jake as a series of sobs overtook her. "W—w—without seeing Larry too."

They went inside and spent an hour listening to Sue, letting her cry and at the end praying with her. The only time Sue smiled was when she was remembering Jake and Larry together, and again when she found out that Jamie had become a Christian. "God is still so good . . ." Sue dabbed at her tears. "He's been with me even more since Larry's been gone. I can feel Him, every day, every minute."

* * * *

Sometime after one in the morning, Jake was struck by the same series of vivid images he'd seen the other night. He shot to a sitting position, his breathing hard and fast, but he didn't scream or cry out in fear. He had no doubt this time—the vision was a flashback, and not a crazy dream.

He was rushing down an endless stairwell—maybe helping someone who needed assistance, as Jamie had guessed. But then he'd fallen down the steps, and someone had reached a hand out to help him. It was only natural that another firefighter would be the one to pull him to his feet, but he would've expected the man to be Larry or one of the other guys from the station.

That was the part of the flashback that simply didn't make sense. The part that kept Jake up an extra hour that night trying to figure it out. Because the face of the firefighter belonged to someone Jake definitely recognized, but it wasn't Larry or anyone else, for that matter.

It belonged to him.

TWENTY-NINE

NOVEMBER 6, 2001

The phone call from Captain Hisel came two days later.

By then, Jamie could practically watch the flashbacks happen. Jake had been having the same ones—not only at night but in the daytime as well. He would be reading his journal or playing on the floor with Sierra, when suddenly his expression would change and he'd go perfectly still. Seconds later, his body would start to shake from the images in his head. In less than a minute the moment would pass, and Jake would search the room until his eyes locked on hers. For a moment his mouth would hang open, his eyes filled with confusion.

Then he'd tell her what he'd seen.

"Why would I see *myself?*" Always Jake's question was the same. "The flashbacks are supposed to be *real* memories, right?"

Jamie had to agree that what Jake was seeing was strange. More to ease Jake's concerns than her own, she had called Dr. Cleary and gotten the response she expected.

"Head injuries are a tricky thing. The recovery of a person's memory isn't a perfect science. Strange things—seeing yourself as someone else, for instance—are not unheard of. I would expect the memory to get clearer, more correct as time goes on."

The doctor was right—every time Jake experienced the flashback it was more vivid. But instead of eventually *becoming* the firefighter, Jake still seemed to be someone else, someone who saw the firefighter very clearly—helping him up off the stairs.

It was just after four in the afternoon, two days after their visit to the fire station, when the phone rang. Jake was in the living room reading a book to Sierra, and Jamie was getting dinner ready. She dried her hands on a nearby dishtowel and answered the phone. "Hello?"

"Jamie, hi . . . it's Captain Hisel."

"Hi." She went back to measuring rice into the pot of water on the stove. "It was nice seeing you the other day. I think maybe it helped." She stirred the pot and set the spoon down. "Jake's been having flashbacks. Seeing a firefighter in the stairwell of what must be the south tower."

"A firefighter?"

"Yeah. The doctor said sometimes it takes a while before the flashbacks make sense."

"What direction was the firefighter headed?"

"Ummm." Jamie wasn't sure why, but for some reason the captain's question caused a hesitation in her heartbeat. "I don't know. I'm not sure he can tell yet."

Captain Hisel sighed in a way that made him sound tired and old. "Jamie, after you left a bunch of us had a talk about Jake." He hesitated. "I know I'm going to sound crazy . . . and I'm not trying to upset you, really I'm not."

"Whatever it is, just tell me." Jamie heard herself utter a single, forced laugh. "What?"

"Jamie . . . are you sure he's Jake?"

The question made her knees weak and sent her across the kitchen to the dining room table. She sat down and leaned her elbows on the worn-out oak top. When she finally had her bearings, there was anger in her tone. "What in the world are you talking about?"

"Jamie, the guy just didn't seem like Jake." The captain released a frustrated huff. "I mean, he looks like Jake and he's about the same size. But something about his face, the shape of his jaw. I don't know, but the other guys agreed with me." He paused. "I just wondered if you were sure."

Suddenly, the doubts Jamie had suffered when Jake was in the hospital came rushing back. She pictured the words "O-negative" written on his medical chart and the fact that he neither talked nor walked like Jake. And what about Brownie? Even their old dog had doubted whether the man in their house was Jake.

Those thoughts—all of them—came in as much time as it took for her to draw a single breath. Then just as quickly she let them go, banished them from her mind, and clenched the phone more tightly in her hands. "Listen, Captain . . ." Her voice was a study in controlled fury. "Tell the guys at the station to have a little compassion, okay? Jake's doctor said that people with amnesia don't completely act like themselves until their memory returns. His face looks a little different because he's lost weight. And Jake's memory is only just starting to come back."

"I know, Jamie . . . I wasn't going to call. I just thought that maybe you were too close to the situation to see what the rest of us saw as soon as—"

"Please, Captain Hisel, stop." Jamie stood and headed back to the kitchen. "I've got dinner to make. Thank you for calling." Then without waiting for a response from the man, she clicked the off button and returned the phone to its base. Adrenaline surged through her veins and made her heart race. A fine layer of perspiration broke out on the palms of her hands and across her face.

Of all the nerve, calling to say something so completely absurd. Did he think a call like that would help her feel better? Make her more relaxed while she waited for Jake's memory to return? Or was he merely so self-centered that he couldn't see past the amnesia to the man who was trying so hard to become the person he'd left behind? Either way, Jamie couldn't believe he'd called.

It was the meanest thing she'd ever heard.

A few minutes later Jake and Sierra came into the kitchen, holding hands. Sierra was smiling, skipping along beside Jake, but Jake's eyes were troubled, more confused than she'd seen them in weeks. "I had another one."

Sierra broke away and headed into the backyard toward the swing set.

Jamie stared at Jake and barely noticed the child leave the house. "Another flashback?"

Jake nodded and leaned against the wall, his eyes locked on hers. "It's getting more vivid, longer than before."

The roof of Jamie's mouth was dry as dirt. "What . . . what do you see?"

"The same thing." Jake shrugged. "I'm running down the stairs and I fall, a fireman stops to help me, but when I look at him, it's like looking in a mirror."

Doubts ricocheted across her mind like so many pinballs. Jamie closed her eyes and thought about God. *Lord . . . I hate feeling like this . . . Please take away the awful thoughts Captain Hisel's put in my mind. Please.* She blinked and opened her mouth, but it took several seconds before she could form the question. "Which way was the firefighter headed, you know, the one who looked like you?"

Jake lowered his brow and angled his head. "What do you mean?"

"I mean," Jamie ran her tongue along her lower lip, "I mean was he going up the stairs or down?"

For a moment Jake stared out the window, then his eyebrows relaxed as the answer came to him. "Up." He gave a firm nod of his head and slipped his hands in the pockets of his sweats. "The fireman was going up."

* * * *

The flashback grew even longer the following day, and Jake shared the details with her. Now, after the firefighter—who seemed to be Jake—helped him to his feet, Jake noticed a helmet on the ground, a helmet with something taped to the inside.

Jamie was terrified about what the flashbacks meant and how they lined up with Captain Hisel's concerns. She started scrutinizing Jake more closely, watching the way he brushed his teeth and combed his hair, calculating in her mind the dozens of little ways that the captain was right. The man living in her house did *not* act exactly like Jake Bryan. Once when Jake had turned and found her staring at him, she jumped—as though she'd been caught looking at a stranger.

After that incident she prayed for nearly an hour, and God helped her relax. It was amazing, after doubting His existence for so long, how quickly she'd adapted to calling on Him. Not because she was supposed to, but because she knew no other way to find solid ground in the midst of all that was happening. And always when she prayed, she felt her doubts dim, at least a little.

So what if Jake could see himself in the flashback. At least he was a part of the memory; that had to be a good sign, right? Jamie begged God to eliminate her fears altogether, but by nightfall the tension grew again. What if Captain Hisel was right? What if by some freak mix-up Jake wasn't really Jake? She kept her fears to herself, but they made it impossible for her to eat or sleep.

By Friday night she felt like she was losing her mind.

That evening after dinner, Jake and Sierra headed into the family room and popped the *Cinderella* video into the VCR. Jamie bundled up in a sweater and grabbed the phone off its base just as Jake looked back into the room. His smile was easy and warm. "What're you doing?"

Jamie felt like a convict. She swallowed hard and held up the phone. "I'm going outside to call Sue."

"Okay." He winked at her and pulled Sierra up onto his lap. "We'll be waiting for you."

The picture he made sitting in his favorite chair, cuddling Sierra close and watching *Cinderella*, was so familiar Jamie almost hung up the phone and joined them. Jake's face was still red, still thinner than it had been. His voice wasn't quite back to normal, and neither were his mannerisms. But the man was Jake; he had to be. What was the alternative? Someone else who looked just like Jake had been in the stairwell at the same exact instant . . . someone who knew the look and name of Sierra.

It was impossible.

Still . . . the few times she'd talked to Sue since their visit the other night, they hadn't discussed Jake, other than to agree that he was doing well—all things considered. Instead, they'd focused their conversations on the search for Larry's body and the hard time Katy was having handling her daddy's death. Not once had Jamie wanted to voice her irrational fears or the comments that Captain Hisel had made.

Until that moment.

Now she needed to share every doubt that plagued her, needed her friend to listen and assure her that these crazy concerns were completely unfounded. Most of all Jamie needed perspective, and as she headed outside to the picnic table with the phone, that's exactly what she intended to get.

Sue was home, and they spent the first few minutes talking about two more firefighter bodies that had been found in the rubble. When there was a lull, Jamie cleared her throat and stared at the stars overhead. A cold wind found its way down the back of her jacket, and she pulled it tighter to her body.

"I want to tell you something . . . something about Jake."

"Okay." The anxiety in Jamie's tone was enough to make Sue sound suddenly serious. "What about him?"

"Captain Hisel called the other day." Jamie held her breath. She wouldn't cry, not when she wanted so badly to tell Sue what the captain said. "He . . . he and the guys honestly wonder if Jake's really Jake." She paused. "Can you believe that?"

"That's . . . crazy." Sue hesitated just a bit too long. "Don't you think so?"

"Of course I do. That's why I'm telling you."

Sue waited a beat. "Jake isn't acting strange, is he?"

Jamie wanted to stand up and throw the phone over the fence. She worked to keep the frustration from her tone. "What's that supposed to mean?"

"I don't know . . . I mean, *you* think he's really Jake, don't you?"

"Yes." Jamie stood and paced across the yard to her dying flower garden. She'd planned on telling Sue about Jake's strange flashbacks, but then, she'd also planned on Sue acting more shocked about

Captain Hisel's phone call. Somehow, instead, her friend seemed almost ambivalent, as though maybe a mix-up really were possible. "Look, Sue, I feel like I'm losing it here." She raked her fingers through her hair and turned around, her back to the garden. "Tell me I'm having a couple of bad days. Tell me doubts are normal. Tell me that Jake is who I think he is. But don't let me just sway here in the wind."

"All right." Empathy filled Sue's voice, and her tone was softer than before. "You're having a couple of bad days, and your doubts are normal. Is that better?"

"No." Jamie's mouth hung open, and she let herself fall back against the wooden fence. "Not if you don't mean it. I mean tell me the truth, Sue, did he seem like Jake to you?"

"You want the truth?" Sue's voice caught.

"Yes . . . I want it desperately." Jamie's teeth chattered, but not because of the cool night air.

"Okay." A shaky sigh made its way across the phone lines. "When you left that night, Katy found me in the kitchen. She asked me a question that has bothered me ever since."

Jamie held her breath. "What?"

"She asked me who the man was with you and Sierra."

The phone slipped from Jamie's hands and fell to the dirt below. Ignoring the damp ground, she dropped to her knees and stared at the place where the receiver lay. *Breathe*, she ordered herself. *This is all just a dream, a nightmare, and any moment you'll wake up and everyone will know the truth. That Jake Bryan really was who everyone thought him to be.*

Jamie could hear a small tinny voice coming from the phone. "Jamie . . . Jamie, talk to me. Jamie, are you there?"

God . . . help me. I haven't been praying long enough to know what to say, but help me. I can't stand up underneath this.

Words that Jake had highlighted in his Bible filtered through her mind. *Come to me, all you who are weary and burdened, and I will give you rest. Take my yoke upon you and learn from me, for I am gentle and humble in heart, and you will find rest for your souls.*

Jamie's head was spinning. She closed her eyes and forced herself to blow the air from her lungs with slow breaths. The voice was still calling out to her. "Jamie . . . pick up the phone. Please."

Finally, her fingers worked their way across the damp soil and found the receiver. She brought it to her ear and tried to think of what to say. Control, that's what she needed. God would give her rest, but she needed to give herself a little control. She gave two short coughs. "Sue ... I'm ... I'm sorry. I'm back."

"Jamie, are you okay? I can come over if you need me."

"No." *Control ... control ... control ...* "Everything's fine." She opened her mouth, and a quiet, strange-sounding laugh came out. "The doctor said Jake wouldn't act like himself until his memory returned. Really, Sue ... tell Katy the man was Sierra's daddy. And that everything's okay."

"Of course." Sue's answer came fast. "I mean the guy is Jake. Obviously. I'm just saying that Katy didn't recognize him right off, but that's to be expected what with his broken ankle and his burns, the way he walks and talks a little different. I never meant to ..."

Jamie stopped listening. Sue was rambling, her words running together in an attempt to make up for scaring Jamie. When she was finished, Jamie worked the muscles in her jaw and looked up at the sky once more. "Thanks for listening, Sue. I need to get back inside. Don't worry about me. Everything's fine. We're watching *Cinderella* tonight."

THIRTY

NOVEMBER 12, 2001

There was no question Jamie was acting different around him.

Maybe it was the flashbacks, or something else Jake wasn't aware of. But she seemed distant and distracted, and several times he'd caught her staring at him. Her attitude didn't help ease his concerns—especially in light of the latest flashbacks.

The newest imagery started appearing over the weekend while Jake was taking a nap after church. His head had been hurting, so he sprawled out on the guest room bed. Almost as soon as he fell asleep, the flashback came. He was standing in an office talking to an older man, a man with white hair. They were in the World Trade Center surrounded by hundreds of office workers and looking out a window. There, in vivid colors, he could see balls of fire and billowing black smoke so close he could nearly touch them.

Then the memory had stopped, and Jake sat straight up in bed, out of breath as he stared at the closed bedroom door. What office had he been in, and who was the white-haired man? Why weren't firefighters in the picture, and how come he'd been able to see so clearly out the windows at the fire in the other building?

Nothing about the memory gelled with the idea that he'd been called to the scene with his Engine company and had headed up the stairs to help rescue survivors. Because if that had been the case, he wouldn't have been in an office, looking out a window. He would've been in a stairwell headed up until something—or someone—caused him to head back down.

Wouldn't he?

The flashbacks were supposed to help life make more sense, not less. And that night after Sierra was in bed, he found Jamie alone in the living room, sitting in a chair and facing out the front window. He came up behind her and worked his fingers into the base of her neck. "You okay?"

"Mmmm." Jamie reached up and covered his hands with hers. "Just thinking."

"About what?"

"Nothing." The chair was a swivel rocker, and Jamie turned it so she was facing him. The whole time, she never let go of his hand, but the smile on her face looked unnatural. "Nothing in particular."

Jake didn't believe her, but he wasn't about to force the discussion. Not when it might mean she'd get that strange look on her face again, the one that made him think something was wrong. And even though he'd have to tell her about his latest flashback at some point, now simply didn't seem the time. "I'm going to bed." He bent down and kissed the top of her head. "Good night."

She searched his eyes and continued to hold his hand. "Any memories, Jake? You know . . . of the two of us?"

"No." He gave her a sad, knowing look. They both wanted him to remember. It would be impossible to move forward until he did. "But things are happening in my brain. I can feel them. One of these days it'll all come rushing back, and we can be the way we were again."

"Right. I know." She nodded once.

Something about her face touched his heart. She was nothing more than a frightened little girl. He squeezed her hand and released it. "I'm begging God every night to help me remember. The moment I have anything for sure, you'll be the first to know."

"Okay." She worked the corners of her mouth up a notch. "Good night, Jake."

He'd been asleep three hours when a different flashback hit. He was running down the stairwell as fast as he could, and the building was shaking. The sound of breaking windows and creaking walls filled his senses, and he doubled his pace, racing as fast as the crowd in front of him would let him. All of a sudden he could actually remember what he'd been thinking as he ran down the stairs.

He'd been praying. Asking God to let him have one more chance about something. He rolled over in bed, and in an instant another image flashed in his mind. A blonde woman and a little boy, maybe seven or eight years old. He was still tearing down the steps, one flight at a time, and now he knew why he wanted one more chance. It was something about the blonde woman and the little boy.

Then a horrible sound rang out all around him, and he screamed out loud. Not the kind of shout he'd let out after his first flashback. But a bone-chilling scream that had Jamie at his door in six seconds flat.

Again her face was pale. "Jake . . . what is it?" She tore into the room and stood next to the bed, staring at him. "Is it a flashback?"

Jake opened his eyes and felt them grow wide. "Yes . . ." His voice was breathy and filled with fear.

Jamie sat on the edge of his bed with several feet between them. "What did you remember?"

Jake's heart raced, and he felt as if he were falling off a cliff. Falling, falling as fast and far as he could to a place where certain death awaited him only moments away. Why weren't his memories headed in the direction he'd expected them to go? He'd studied everything in his journal, every notation in his Bible. All of it told him that when his past returned, it'd be of a terrifying moment trying to rescue someone from the south tower, and other than that they'd be of Jamie and Sierra, of fighting fires and hanging out with Larry. But the flashbacks he was having now contained none of that.

Who was the blonde woman and the little boy? Why had he been thinking about them as he tore down the stairs of the World Trade Center? Had he been unfaithful to Jamie? Or . . .

He blinked and searched Jamie's face. She was still waiting, still staring at him, practically willing him to say that he remembered her, that everything about his past as Jake Bryan, firefighter and devoted father, was coming back to him.

But it wasn't. And because of that, he needed to tell Jamie the truth about his flashbacks. She'd know what to do, how to help him relax and make sense of the things he was remembering. Maybe he had a sister with blonde hair or a mother. Who could tell what his brain might do as it struggled to clear the fog from his memory?

They had both caught their breath now, and Jamie crossed her arms, her hands clenched. "Tell me what you remembered, Jake."

And then, without waiting another moment, Jake did just that. He started with the memory of himself talking with a white-haired man on one of the upper floors of the World Trade Center. "We rushed together through a series of offices to a bank of windows." He paused, his throat dry with fear. "That's when we saw the fire. It was huge—worse than anything I've seen on television about the attacks, Jamie." He placed his hand inches from his face. "It was right here. I could practically feel the heat."

"Is that what you remembered just now? When you screamed?"

He shook his head, and this time his mouth was dry. "It was something else." How could he tell her about the other flashback without terrifying her, without shaking her certainty that they'd ever find their way back to what they'd shared before? Or worse, without making her doubt that he really was the man he'd thought himself to be these past two months?

"What, Jake? Tell me." Her voice was a strained whisper, her face ashen. "I have to know."

"You're right." He reached for her hands and told her about the memory, how he had been running down the stairs as fast as he could go, taking one flight at a time and desperate to get out of the building. "That's when I begged God for one more chance with my family . . . one more chance to make things right again."

"Right again?" Jamie shook her head and dug her fingernails into the palms of his hand. "You were always right, Jake. Everything about you."

He stared at her, his mouth open, heart frozen.

Jamie exhaled through pursed lips and hung her head between her knees for a moment. When she looked up she had just one question for him. "Did . . . did you picture us? Me and Sierra? The people you wanted another chance with?"

He turned his head but kept his eyes on her. "I pictured two people . . . but . . ." Jake would've given anything to not finish the sentence. But it was too late now. The only way he could make sense of the strange memory was to share it with Jamie. No matter where that took them afterwards. "The people weren't you and Sierra."

Jamie let her head drop as she slid her hands over her ears and then down the tops of her thighs. She looked as though she might spring up at any moment and run from the room, but instead she found his eyes once more. "I . . . I don't understand. Who were they?"

"I don't know." As frightened as the memories had made him feel, he was more concerned with Jamie's reaction. He put his hand on her shoulder and bit the inside of his lip. "The woman was taller than you . . . with straight blonde hair. And the child . . . was a boy. Maybe seven years old."

"Who . . . who are they?" Jamie sucked in a sharp breath through her nose and shook her head several times.

"I thought you might know." He shrugged. "Like maybe she was a sister or a friend, someone married to one of the guys at the station." He hesitated, his eyes pleading with her. "Tell me you know who she is, please."

Jamie stood up then and backed away from him. Without saying another word, she turned and ran from the room. He could hear her bare feet patter across the entryway and tear out the front door into the yard. She sprinted away from the house as fast as she could and after a few seconds the sound faded to silence. Jake thought about going after her, but whatever process she was working through, she needed to do so without his help.

He sat stone still, waiting to hear her footsteps again. When she didn't come back after a few minutes, he climbed out of bed and paced the room. His boot cast had been removed two days earlier, and his ankle was still tender. But in that moment, he didn't care about the pain. He walked over to the dresser and scanned the photographs.

All he wanted were answers.

Somewhere there had to be a blonde woman. Why else would he have remembered her? And what about the little boy? One of the pictures must've contained the image of him—maybe sitting on the lap of a favorite uncle or long-lost friend.

Without thinking Jake pulled open the top drawer.

What he saw there surprised him. All this time living in the guest room and he'd never looked in any of the dresser drawers. This one was filled almost to the brim with dusty old, framed photographs. Jake was ready to race through the lot of them, when his eyes fell on a simple five-by-seven near the top of the stack. It was a picture of a man in a firefighter's uniform. But that wasn't what caught Jake's eyes.

It was the man's helmet.

With almost trancelike precision, Jake lifted the photo from the drawer and stared at the firefighter. Clearly the man was supposed to be him, but something about the helmet set off a flashback that until that moment had been incomplete. Once more he could see himself falling in the stairwell, feel himself being helped to his feet by a man who turned out to be a firefighter. Again, the uniformed man looked identical to himself, but this time the firefighter's helmet fell off, and Jake picked it up. The scene was so real in his mind, it made his head hurt. As he handed the helmet back to the firefighter, Jake saw Sierra's photo taped to the inside. Beneath the picture was her name, scribbled in big block letters.

Jake could see the little girl's image as clearly as he must've seen it that awful Tuesday morning. The flashback continued, and he remembered looking up, catching the firefighter's eyes, and thinking something very strange, something that hadn't been a part of the flashback until just that instant.

The thought was this: Never in his life had he seen someone who looked so much like himself.

Footsteps sounded near the door, and Jake looked up. It was Jamie. Her eyes were red and swollen, but she was more in control than she'd been fifteen minutes ago. She walked toward him, never taking her gaze from his face. When she was just a few feet away, she narrowed her eyes and whispered the same question that was suddenly shouting at him.

"Who . . . who are you?"

His heart pounded in his chest, but he could do nothing to save her, nothing to erase the doubts for either of them. Instead, he merely set the photograph down and gave a slow shake of his head. "I don't know, Jamie. I really don't know."

* * * *

The answer was simple.

The next morning Jamie called Dr. Cleary, and in sentences broken with tears, she explained about Jake's flashbacks. "What if it's not him? How could we find out?"

The doctor had answered with the obvious. "Didn't you say he had a rare blood type?"

"Yes." Jamie massaged her temples and tried to ease her aching head. "AB-positive."

Dr. Cleary sighed. "I really don't think you have anything to worry about. But since you're both having doubts, go down to University Hospital and have his blood drawn. I'll call in the order, and they should have the results in about thirty minutes."

"Right now?" Jamie closed her eyes and steadied herself against the kitchen counter.

"Right now."

When she hung up the phone, she took Sierra across the street to the neighbor's. "Jake has to do some testing at the hospital."

Her neighbor was more than agreeable. "Take your time. I'm home the rest of the day."

Five minutes later she and Jake were on their way. Jamie drove and kept her thoughts to herself. The idea that the family in his mind was a blonde woman and a young boy was terrifying. It made her want to turn around and drive the other direction, as fast and far away from the hospital and the blood test as possible. To a place where the man beside her would be Jake Bryan, no questions asked ever again. But running wouldn't make the problem go away.

Jake slipped his hand in hers and squeezed once. "You okay?"

She nodded and blinked. Her throat was too thick to speak, and Jake seemed to understand. She could barely breathe for the tears fighting their way from her eyes. But she wouldn't cry; not now. Maybe this was just a crazy thing they were doing. Maybe the flashbacks would make sense in time. She ran her thumb along the side of Jake's hand.

But if not ...

The hospital was just around the corner, and still neither she nor Jake had said a word to each other. They pulled into the hospital's front lot and found a place to park. Only then did Jake turn toward her and touch her cheek. "Jamie ..."

She found his damp eyes and allowed herself to get lost in them. His gaze went to the deepest place of her heart.

"Whatever happens in there, I'm here for you. You have to believe that."

Jamie studied him and willed away the tears that blurred her own eyes. He had to be Jake, didn't he? Those were Jake's words, Jake's tenderness. His way of caring for her above himself, especially when she was afraid. She leaned closer, and they came together in an embrace that seemed to last an hour and an instant all at once. As though neither of them wanted to climb out of the car and take the chance that somehow—in the span of half an hour—everything they had believed about their future together would suddenly and swiftly vanish.

She was the one who pulled back first. "Let's go." Her eyes met his, soaking in the face she still believed was her husband's. "We have to find out."

The test took only twenty minutes. Jamie and Jake were holding hands in the lobby when a nurse approached them. She had a white piece of paper in her hands. "Mr. Bryan?"

Jake stood up and Jamie joined him, leaning against him for support. The nurse's face was calm and pleasant looking. *She has no idea,* Jamie thought. *One way or another, the information she's about to give us will change our lives forever.*

The woman handed the piece of paper to Jake, and Jamie craned her neck to read the details. *Come on, where is it?* Her eyes darted across the page. *His name ... his birth date ... his age ...*

lines and lines of information, but not the part they needed. Jamie wanted to scream.

Where was the blood type?

After only a few seconds, Jake looked at the nurse and shook his head. "I can't read it." His voice was urgent, almost impatient. "We're trying to find out my blood type."

Jamie closed her eyes. *AB-positive ... his blood type is AB-positive, God ... let her tell us that, please.*

"Let's see ..." The nurse took the paper back again and glanced at it for just a moment. "Well, you're one of the lucky ones." She handed the paper to Jake once more and smiled. "You're O-negative. The most common blood type of all."

THIRTY-ONE

NOVEMBER 12, 2001

They collapsed together on a bench outside the hospital.

Jamie had no memory of how they'd gotten there, just that they were. The realization of the blood results hit her in waves. The first nearly knocked her to her knees. The man she'd been living with since the end of September was not Jake Bryan, but someone else, someone who merely looked like him.

The second realization took a minute to sink in, but by the time they reached the bench and sat down, it hit her full force.

If that man beside her wasn't her husband, then . . .

She buried her face in her hands, her body shaking so badly she could barely stay seated. "No, Jake . . . No! God, please . . . not Jake." Her words were drenched in grief and the quiet, desperate sound of a person in shock. But this time the person wasn't someone on television or someone pasting flyers on a wall in New York City. It wasn't one of the other firefighter wives—it was her.

Jamie Bryan.

The thing she had feared all of her life had actually happened, and she hadn't known it until now. Next to her, the man who looked so much like her husband placed his hand on her back and brought his head close to hers. "I'm sorry, Jamie . . . I'm so sorry."

Part of her wanted to fall into his arms, take the slip of white paper he still held in his other hand, rip it into a hundred pieces, and dump it in the nearest trash can—where it belonged. But somewhere in the soil of her conscious, the truth had taken root and there was nothing she could do but watch it grow.

Of course the man next to her wasn't her husband. He hadn't had a firefighter's uniform on, not even his helmet. Why hadn't that sounded crazy to her before? Jake might've taken his uniform off so he could run faster, but he would've at least kept his helmet. After all, the sky was raining debris from the Twin Towers—bodies, steel beams, broken glass.

At first—back when they were in the hospital—Captain Hisel had said that Jake's helmet must have fallen off his head in the blast. But if that was true, why hadn't they found it? All of it made sense now.

Sobs broke free and shook Jamie until she was almost certain she was going to throw up. Of course they hadn't found Jake's helmet. It was still on his head, still buried with him somewhere in the pile of debris. No doubt next to the body of Larry. The irony was as painful as it was sweet. She'd ignored that sign too. The fact that Jake would've been with Larry. The two never would've separated, even if it meant they both had to walk a single victim down the stairs before joining the rest of their men.

"Jake . . ." The word was a moan, a cry that came from the depths of her soul. "Why, God . . . why?"

In all her recent days of doubting the truth about the identity of the man she'd been living with, she'd never allowed herself to take the possibility this far, never acknowledged the fact that if the man wasn't really Jake, then Jake was dead. She'd never see him again, never kiss him or hold him.

Hadn't she noticed the same things Captain Hisel had seen? The subtly different shape of the man's face, the differences in his mannerisms? Had it been merely wishful thinking to believe that somehow when the man in the guest room regained his memory he would magically turn into the Jake Bryan she'd loved since sixth grade?

Jamie cried until she couldn't breathe, mourning the loss of the strapping man who'd been everything to her—her mentor and protector, her lover and friend. The most amazing father a little girl could ever hope to have.

Thoughts of Sierra made the sobs come twice as fast. What would happen now? And how would she break the news to the carefree child, especially when the little girl had no doubts that the man who came home from the hospital with them was anyone less than her wonderful daddy?

The entire mess was more complicated than Jamie could begin to work through. And there was something else too. What would happen to the man beside her? Suddenly, it hit her that he had nowhere to go, no one to turn to. For nearly three months he'd been training himself to be Jake Bryan, and even though the blood test told him he was someone else, neither of them had any idea who that person was.

The tears slowed, and after what felt like a lifetime, Jamie strained back to a sitting position. It was impossible to sit straight, her shoulders bowed as though a mountain had grown across the back of them. After a moment she looked up and found the eyes of the man next to her. His face was wet, his eyes red. Sorrow and confusion, guilt and grief were among the emotions swimming there.

"I'm sorry . . . about Jake," he said, his voice strained and more than a little terrified.

They came together in a hug then, an embrace that was different from the one they'd shared in the car. This time it was the embrace of two people lost in a world gone mad, a world in which they suddenly had only each other to understand the pain life had dealt them.

"We still . . ." She sniffed and pulled back, taking his hand in hers. The touch of his skin felt comfortable, but not sensual, as though even her senses finally realized the truth about his real identity. "We still don't know who you are."

"No."

"And somewhere you probably have a . . . a blonde wife and a little boy. Don't you think?"

He nodded, and fresh tears welled in his eyes. "My memory tells me that, but right now . . . I still feel like I'm married to you." His gaze drifted to a distant row of trees and then back to her. "Like I'm still Sierra's daddy."

"What are we supposed to do?" Jamie sounded like a child herself as she searched the man's face. "Where would you go?"

For a long while he said nothing, just looked at her. Then he angled his head, his eyes pleading with her. "Can I stay with you, Jamie? Until I remember."

Tears blurred her vision once more, and she stared straight up at the sky. A cry came from her, and she shook her head. *God . . . how can You ask this of me? To share my life with someone who looks so much like Jake he takes my breath away?*

A line from the sermon that past week flashed in her mind. *Love one another . . . as I have loved you, so you must love one another.*

Love?

Jamie closed her eyes and tried to make sense of the notion. Her heart was utterly broken, her life forever changed. In what way would Christ's love help her find the strength to love a stranger? One who looked exactly like her dead husband? And what would be the point?

Then ... as though God was speaking the words directly to her soul ... the answer came. Jesus had loved her with His entire being. He had laid down His life so that she might live. And now that's what God wanted her to do for the man beside her. Love him ... in a way that meant laying down her own feelings, giving up her own pain. She must ignore the canyon of grief within her and help him find his way home. Even if it killed her.

All so that someday he might find life again.

She opened her eyes and found his face once more, studied his eyes, the fear and anticipation there as she considered her answer. Then she took his hands in hers and felt the corners of her mouth inch their way up her swollen cheeks. "Yes ... you can stay with me until you remember." She drew a breath and felt a supernatural presence within her, holding her up and sustaining her, preparing her for the painful times ahead. "I know you're not Jake ... and I know our time together will be short." She grabbed two quick breaths. "You're not my husband and ... and you're not Sierra's daddy." She paused, breathing in the sight of him, doing everything in her power to convince herself that he really wasn't Jake. "I have just one request."

"Okay." The kind man's eyes swam with tears as their eyes held. "Anything."

"Please ... as long as you're living with us ... don't tell Sierra the truth."

* * * *

With each passing hour, the shock echoed more loudly across the arid plains of Jamie's heart. By the end of the first night she knew she was still breathing because of God's strength alone. The nurse's words sounded in her mind at least every minute or so.

You're one of the lucky ones.... O-negative ... the most common blood type of all. You're one of the lucky ones ... lucky ones ...

How was it possible?

Jake had died, and she hadn't even mourned his death, hadn't even known that his body was one of the thousands crushed in the collapse of the towers. Would she have gone to Ground Zero, or maybe stayed at the station waiting for word? She would've been crazy with fear, desperate for news. But eventually she would've known, and then she would've grieved with the other firefighter wives. She and Sue would've sat together at the memorial services, each of them holding the other up when standing was no longer an option.

But Jamie had missed all of it.

The next day, morning had the nerve to come, having no respect for her feelings, and bringing with it all the awful reality of her life. That the man in the downstairs guest room, the one who looked and talked and smelled like her husband, the one who even thought like him, wasn't him at all, but a perfect stranger.

Jamie imagined that in firefighter households across the city a proper time of grieving was taking place. But not here, not now. Absent were the phone calls from friends, the comfort of family. Her public grieving would have to wait until the man downstairs— whoever he was—found his way home. Only then could she admit to Jake's buddies, to Captain Hisel and Jake's father, that the man they'd prayed for and held bedside vigil for was not the man they knew and loved.

She'd spent the past two months living with another woman's husband. Meanwhile, Jake was gone . . . he was gone. Lost forever. A part of her wanted to get dressed and head for Ground Zero, the place firefighters were calling "the pile." Maybe they'd found something—his body or his helmet. His wedding ring.

The morning sun streamed through the window, and she rolled over onto Jake's side of the bed. His pillowcase didn't smell like him anymore, but she buried her face in it anyway. If she'd known he wasn't coming home, she never would've washed it. She moaned his name into the fibers of the pillow and felt another wave of sobs come over her.

I'm sorry, Jake . . . God, let him know I'm sorry . . . I didn't know. I would've been there looking for him myself, waiting for him. Willing him to live. Oh, God . . . I'm sorry. I can't do this . . .

Daughter, I'm with you always . . . even now.

The thought was the faintest breeze in the still, dark place where her heart once lived. They were Jake's words . . . words she'd seen in his journal. Or maybe the words were from God. Yes . . . that had to be it. They were highlighted in Jake's Bible. God was with her, and that was at least some comfort.

But that didn't ease the pain.

She still clung to Jake's pillowcase. She wanted to stay buried there, but she had to breathe. The pillow was soggy from her tears, and she stared at their wedding photo, the one on Jake's bedside nightstand. "Jake, why . . ." She ached all over, and her words were muffled and blurred. "You told me God wasn't finished with you . . . that nothing . . . nothing would happen to you."

A sound made its way up the stairs, and she held her breath for a moment and wiped at her tears. Sierra! She was awake and moving around downstairs in the kitchen. Probably about to find the man in the guest room and wake him up, beg another horsey ride. The man she thought was her daddy.

It was time to dry her tears and begin pretending.

"Daddy . . . where are you? Time to get up." Her daughter's voice filtered up the stairs, each word a dart to the centermost part of Jamie's soul.

God . . . help me . . .

She moved like someone who'd aged a hundred years overnight, but she managed to climb out of bed. The covers couldn't hide the truth about her life. Just when she thought it might all go back to normal, now it was unraveling before her eyes. And besides, the man who looked like Jake needed her. Thirty minutes later she had showered and dressed and applied enough makeup to hide her swollen eyes.

As ready as she'd ever be to face the day, her first day as a widow. Her first day without Jake.

They had a few things to work out, and Jamie wanted a plan sooner than later.

After breakfast they agreed she would continue to call him Jake so Sierra wouldn't be confused. In addition, they had to consider the guys at the fire station and people at church.

"The newspapers will have a field day with this story if we let the truth out now." Jamie shared that with him over breakfast. She dragged her hand over the air above her head. "'Mistaken Identity Leaves Man Without a Home.' We can't do that."

"So what's the answer?"

The only solution that would work for everyone was an obvious one. They would simply have to pretend. Until he remembered enough details to find his way home, they would act as if he were Jake. He would spend every waking moment trying to recall his name, his address . . . his place of employment. Anything that might help. And in the meantime, he would be Jake Bryan to everyone who knew him.

Everyone but Jamie.

Then, when the time finally came for him to go home, he would do so quietly without fanfare. And only then would Jamie tell Sierra that her father had died helping people in a fire. That Jesus had asked him to come home, after all.

The days that passed were painfully slow. The gentle man living in her home still carried with him dozens of Jake's attitudes and attributes. He still gave Sierra horsey rides and curled her hair before church on Sundays. The three of them shared a quiet Thanksgiving, but several times during the meal his eyes met hers, and the two of them knew.

It was only a matter of time.

On Jamie's worst days, when she and Sierra and the man living with them still felt like a family, when her heart simply couldn't be convinced that Jake wasn't alive and well and living among them, Jamie would have the most awful thought. She would wish that maybe—just maybe—the man would never find his way home and she and Sierra could keep him forever.

But that wasn't right, and it wasn't really what she wanted. She wanted Jake, and since she couldn't have him, she could hardly force a stranger to take his place. Even if the man's memory never returned. Always when those thoughts hit her, Jamie would find a quiet place and read Jake's Bible. She'd read over and over again the verses about the strength of God and the plans He had for His people. Plans to give her a hope and a future.

After an hour with the Lord, Jamie could usually think straight again, straight enough to know that the thing she really wanted was to love the stranger in the guest room enough to help him find his way home. And whatever pain would come after that, she had to believe that somehow God would see them through it.

Gradually, the flashbacks became more regular, the details within them more fine-tuned. He hated the way they confirmed the truth— that he wasn't Jake Bryan after all. He remembered looking at the helmet of the firefighter, seeing Sierra's picture and name taped inside. The river of people heading down the stairs, and the firefighters going up. When he thought they might help, that they might lend some type of healing to the pain Jamie was going through, he'd share the details of his flashbacks with her.

They spent nearly every evening at the computer working their way through news articles from September 11, and a photolisting of the thousands of people killed in the World Trade Center, searching for a face that might look like Jake's. The photos were organized in alphabetical order, and by Thursday they were making their way through the Ts. One in ten victims names had no photo attached—so there were no guarantees the exercise would turn up anything.

Still they had to try.

Jamie pointed to an image that was blurred. "Can you tell what color his hair is?"

"Too red."

Jamie gave a hard sigh. "You're right." She moved to the next image.

Suddenly, the flashback returned. Him walking down the stair-well and tripping, Jake helping him up, and then . . . something else. He turned so his chair faced hers. "Jamie . . ."

"Definitely not." She was looking at the picture of a balding man ten years his senior. "Way too old."

"Not the picture, Jamie . . ." He waited for her to look at him. "I remembered something."

She blinked, her hands frozen over the keyboard. "What?"

"Something Jake said." Tension filled the space between them. "He told me Sierra was his little girl."

Jamie's eyes widened. "You remember that?"

He nodded. "I do."

"What . . ." Tears filled her eyes, and her face grew a shade paler. "What else did he say?"

"Jamie . . ." This was the hard part. His memories were giving her a window to Jake's final minutes.

"Tell me." She swallowed hard. "I want to know."

There was a pause. "He said he'd better get moving. His bud-dies were going up without him."

She stared at him a moment longer, and her voice was the qui-etest whisper. "The building was already shaking, right? Isn't that what you said?"

He nodded. "Yes."

"Then why?" Her shoulders slumped, and she leaned toward him, letting her head rest on his shoulder. "Why didn't he get out of there?"

"Ah, Jamie . . ." He took gentle hold of her arms and kissed the top of her head. "Don't. You know he couldn't do that . . ." He kept his voice low and soothing. She wasn't crying, but she was obviously drained, and she leaned forward as his arms came around her. The familiarity between them had changed since they'd gotten the news about his identity.

But it definitely hadn't disappeared.

"Listen . . ." He wanted to say something before the moment passed. "I didn't know Jake when he was alive . . . but I know him now, Jamie. I do. I know his thoughts, and believe me, he would never have gone back down those stairs."

She sat up, her movements slow and deliberate. Their eyes met and held, and he could see a hint of acceptance, one that hadn't been there before. She shrugged and managed a sad smile. "I know." For a second it looked like she might say something else, but then she shook her head and gave a soft huff. "I know."

The days wore on, and Jamie reminded herself every hour that the man living with them wasn't Jake. But some moments it was just about impossible to convince herself.

Once they were at the breakfast table, and Sierra finished her cereal and came up behind him, wrapping her arms around his neck and kissing him on his cheek. "Let's go to the library today, Daddy." Her eyes danced with possibility. "We need more books."

"More books? What about that bookcase upstairs?" He tapped his finger on the end of her nose and grinned at her. "Let's get through those first."

"Oh, Daddy. Please . . ."

Then he tousled her hair and winked at her. "No's a no, sweetheart."

And Jamie closed her eyes and thought somehow there had to be a mistake. The words, the tone, the expression, as he talked to Sierra. All of it was Jake. It had to be . . .

Another time she found him in the guest room sitting up in the bed, poring over Jake's Bible. He was so lost in whatever he was reading that once again he didn't hear her enter the room. Jamie had been crying that day and her eyes stung, but she refused to blink, refused to do anything but stare at the image the man made and pretend, just for a heartbeat, that Jake was alive.

She was still looking at him when he glanced up and smiled at her. "Have you read the book of James?" He pointed to the worn pages on his lap. "It's amazing, Jamie. Come look."

She hesitated, forcing herself to stay calm. Jake did that, didn't he? Asked her to sit beside him while he read James or Ephesians or Romans. Whichever book he was studying that week.

And that was something else she did. When they weren't working to find out his identity, or taking Sierra to the park or cleaning or cooking or shopping—she read Scripture. The pastor at church had given her a Bible, and she would take Jake's journal or his scribbled margin notes and find verses he'd once loved. The exercise made her feel as close to him as anything she could do. Almost as though he were sitting beside her as she worked.

In those times she was more at peace than at any other. Jamie understood why, of course. God was helping her, drawing her close and preparing her for the pain that lay ahead. Because it was coming, no question about it. But not now, not yet. Not as long as the man who looked like Jake still lived with her.

And her imagination was sometimes fierce.

All she had to do was look at him and watch him, talk to him and hug him for the questions to start coming. Could the blood test have been wrong? Were flashbacks sometimes seen in reverse, somehow? The more doubts that came, the more she would wish they'd never find the man's identity. As the days drifted by, there were times when she would've sworn in a court of law that the man living with her was no longer some businessman, a stranger with a blonde wife and a little boy waiting at home for him.

He was Jake Bryan once more, the one she'd fallen in love with back when she was twelve years old.

THIRTY-TWO

DECEMBER 4, 2001

By the end of the second week, Jake had no doubt that he'd been a businessman working in the south tower when the building collapsed. Somehow halfway down the stairwell he'd met up with a man who must've been Jake Bryan.

There, he must've fallen and been helped up by him, and in the process Jake must've lost his helmet. That's when Jake would've seen Sierra's picture and her name. The rest of the way down, he would've known that the firefighter who'd looked so much like him wasn't going to get out of the building alive. And that the little girl, Sierra, wasn't going to have a daddy after that awful morning.

The moment must've been so powerful that it was the only one not erased from his long-term memory when the south tower collapsed and shot him beneath the fire truck.

That much of the story—as wild and crazy as it was—finally made sense both to him and to Jamie. But other details were slow in coming. The blonde woman had appeared in many flashbacks since that first one two weeks earlier. She was his wife; he had no doubt about that.

Some of the scenes he remembered now were so vivid they made him cry. Times when he and his pretty wife had first met, and the two of them would sit outside some small outbuilding, her singing while he played the guitar. The love he felt for her in those moments was overwhelmingly real. But it clashed strongly with memories that felt more recent, memories of him rushing out the door to spend another weekend at the office—wherever he worked.

He had enough pieces of the puzzle now to know that he'd been nothing like Jake Bryan.

Though his memories told him he'd loved the blonde woman at first, though he'd celebrated the birth of the son they apparently shared, he had let everything about their love grow cold. All so that he could get ahead in whatever business he'd been involved in.

And something else hit him. Somehow he remembered having a daughter, but never actually holding her. Nothing about her face or voice flashed in his mind, but her presence was real all the same. He wondered if he was only thinking of Sierra, wishing her to be his, or whether there really had been a little girl in his life, maybe a child he and his wife had lost.

He hoped that someday the memory of her would make sense.

In his quiet moments, when Jamie was playing outside with Sierra and he was able to spend time remembering, he found it sadly ironic that a job might've become more important than his family. A job he couldn't even remember now.

And then there was the matter of his faith. He was fairly sure he'd been a believer before the terrorist attacks, but his faith must've grown cold in recent years. All of that had changed, of course. God had allowed him to become the husband and father he'd never really been, by living in the shoes of a man who no longer was.

The idea was almost more than he could grasp.

Many nights since he'd taken the blood test, Jamie would sit up with him after Sierra was in bed and go over a list of the companies that had once been located in the south tower of the World Trade Center. They were both fairly positive that he'd worked in that building, because that was the one Jake would've been in. And his brief meeting with Jake was something they both agreed must've happened.

They'd go down the list of names one at a time. Seabury & Smith. . . . Harris Beach & Wilcox . . . Frenkel & Company . . . Morgan Stanley. Jamie would say the name of the company out loud and then show it to him. He'd ponder it for a moment, repeating it over and over again. When no memory was stirred, they'd go down the list until finally he couldn't take another moment of it. By now they'd been through the various companies two times, and still nothing sounded familiar.

Eventually, he would remember who he was, but how would he ever let go of them? Sierra had claimed a piece of his heart he'd never regain. And what about Jamie? Up until the blood test, he'd been sure he was falling in love with her. But his memories made it clear that somewhere out there—probably only a dozen miles away—a woman was grieving his loss, believing him dead. A woman and a boy he had treated badly for who knew how many years.

A woman and a boy he wanted a second chance with, the second chance he'd prayed for in the moments before the building collapsed.

It was Monday night, and Jamie had just finished giving Sierra a bath. "Daddy . . . come kiss me good night." Her little voice sang out through the old house and tugged at Jake's heart.

"Okay, baby. I'll be right there."

He stood up and headed toward the stairs. They were familiar to him now, and he took them two at a time. The truth was, he had two families. One he knew, but didn't belong to. And one he belonged to, but didn't know. The entire situation was too strange to fathom completely. He reached the last step. *God . . . make it all work out somehow. Please . . .*

He walked through the door and met Jamie's stare in the shadows of Sierra's pink bedroom. Their eyes held for a moment, and then he let his gaze fall to Sierra. She held her arms out. "Daddy . . ."

"Good night, princess." He moved to the edge of her bed and ran his fingers through the wispy blonde curls that surrounded her forehead. "Let's pray."

This was their routine, the one they'd established since Jake had come home from the hospital. It was nothing new to Sierra, because Jake Bryan had been the kind of man who made a point of being home when his daughter went to bed each night. The kind of man who prayed with her and played with her, giggled with her and gave her horsey rides on demand.

And now, because of Jake—because of all that the man had written in his journal and in his Bible—he had become that kind of man too.

Jamie put her hand on his shoulder as the three of them closed their eyes and bowed their heads. "Dear Jesus." Sierra's voice soothed the anxious places in his heart. "Thank You for a good day, and thank You for my mommy and daddy." She paused and added the line she'd added ever since finding out about Larry. "Please tell Katy's daddy in heaven hi for us, and when Katy's sad because she misses him, give her a little hug, Jesus. Amen."

Jake felt the gentle squeeze of Jamie's hand on his shoulder. "Lord, thank You for giving us strength each day, and for the joy to know that Your mercies are new every morning. Please protect us as we sleep. Amen."

It was his turn. He cleared his throat and began. "Lord, You are faithful and true, and Mommy is right. Your mercies are new every morning. Help us hang on to that all the days of our lives, no matter what tomorrow might bring." He paused. "And help Sierra know how very much we love her."

He bent to kiss Sierra, usually a simple kiss on her cheek. But this time she framed his face with her little-girl hands and searched his eyes. "Butterfly kisses, Daddy. Okay?"

Jake knew the routine by now, and he rubbed his nose against hers three times. Next without hesitating, he turned his face just enough so that they could brush their eyelashes against each other's cheeks. When they were done, a smile lit up her face. "You're the best daddy in the whole world."

As Jake and Jamie held hands and left the room, he thought of the blonde woman and the lonely little boy. The one he hadn't seen nearly enough in the past few years. And that moment he uttered a silent prayer, one that he'd been praying more often lately.

That one day, the words Sierra had just said would be true.

* * * *

The breakthrough happened an hour later.

Jamie was upstairs brushing her teeth when a commercial came on television. It showed a man walking across the floor of an office building, and then stopping to look at the camera. "Koppel and Grant took a big hit on September 11. We lost two employees and our entire New York City office." The man leaned against a nearby desk. "While we grieve with all of Manhattan over the losses wrought upon us by the terrorist attacks, we are here today to say that we survived. This month we will open a new office in Manhattan." The man gazed out a window at the altered skyline of the city. "Koppel and Grant wants the evil people who sought to destroy us to know one thing very clearly. We're still here. And with the help of people here in New York and all across America, we'll be here for many years to come."

The image faded, and an insignia flashed on the screen while the man's voice repeated. "Koppel and Grant. In Los Angeles and now . . . again . . . in New York City. An investment name you could trust then. An investment name you can trust now."

Jake stood up, his knees trembling. "Jamie!" He hissed her name, careful not to wake Sierra.

He could hear her padded feet running from her room and down the stairs. In the time it took her to reach his side, he was certain beyond any shadow of a doubt.

"I remember something."

For a single moment, he saw grief and regret mingle in the depth of Jamie's heart, and he understood. They'd talked about it before;

how there were times when they wished he would never remember. But just as quickly, the sorrow passed and Jamie swallowed.

"What . . . tell me?"

He pointed at the television. "I used to work for Koppel and Grant."

* * * *

Jamie made the call the next morning.

They'd decided to start with the new office in Manhattan. After all, Jake must've worked in New York, since he was in the building when the terrorist attacks took place. It took Jamie only a few seconds to locate the phone number for the new Koppel and Grant headquarters, and then for a long moment she and the kind man across from her merely stared at each other.

They both knew the score.

If the phone calls Jamie was about to make led them to the man's actual identity . . . to his family . . . then their days together would be over. Maybe as soon as the following day. Once more Jamie entertained the wild idea of tossing out the number and begging this man who looked and acted so much like Jake to stay with her and Sierra. But he belonged to someone else, and again the moment passed. Instead, Jamie took his hands in hers, bowed her head and prayed, begging God that this detail about Koppel and Grant might be the answer they'd been looking for.

"We pray that even in the next few minutes You would help—" Jamie had been about to say Jake's name, but she caught herself. "Help my friend find his family."

Through teary eyes, Jamie leveled a sad smile at the man. "Okay, then . . ." She drew a deep breath and picked up the receiver. "This is it."

Sierra was across the street once more, so they had privacy to take as long as they needed to make phone calls. She punched in the numbers, and over the next ten minutes, she was passed from a secretary to a division manager to the department head and finally to the director of personnel.

Each time Jamie explained the situation, how she was trying to help a victim from September 11 find his family, and how the man now thought he'd once worked for Koppel and Grant. But always the person on the other end would fall silent for a moment, and then explain how he or she was new or how they didn't handle those types of matters. Then Jamie would be connected to someone else, someone who might *really* be able to help her. By the time the director of personnel answered the line, Jamie's patience and anxiety were both at the breaking point. Next to her, the stranger she'd come to love sat barely breathing, his eyes locked on hers.

"Can I help you?"

The woman on the other end sounded pleasant, but Jamie had to close her eyes for three seconds before she felt calm enough to speak. "Yes . . . I have a friend here with me who was hurt in the World Trade Center on September 11. He . . . he's had amnesia." Jamie met the man's eyes and felt the familiar bond they'd built in the days since the attacks. She looked away so she could concentrate. "The thing is, this man now thinks that maybe he once worked for Koppel and Grant. What I need to have is a list of the people from your company who were killed when the south tower collapsed."

"Well," the woman hesitated. "It's a short list. Koppel and Grant lost just two employees."

That's the information the commercial had provided the night before, but Jamie wanted to make sure. Her heartbeat quickened. If there really were only two names on the dead or missing list, then it should be easy to figure out whether the man sitting across from her was one of them. Jamie rested her forehead in her hand and closed her eyes. *Give me strength, God . . . help me desire what You desire.* "Can . . . can you give me their names, maybe tell me a little bit about them."

"Ummm." The woman considered the request, and for a few painful seconds silence filled the line. Then the woman lowered her voice some. "Oh, why not. The guys are dead, anyway." She drew a slow breath. "Everyone knew them—they were the top people in the company."

Jamie shot a look at the man beside her. The top men in the company? The man who'd shared her home these past months acted nothing like a business mogul. He smiled and covered her free hand with his. Jamie blinked at the thought. An executive? It wasn't possible. She focused on the matter at hand. "What were their names?"

"One was R. Allen Koppel, and the other was Eric Michaels."

Jamie held her breath. "That's all?" She forced herself to exhale. "Can you tell me something else about them?"

"Sure." The woman took her time. "Allen was a nice man in his fifties, married a few times with no kids. He never loved anyone like he loved Koppel and Grant." The woman hesitated. "Eric ... he was a young guy. Good-looking. Stationed at the LA office. He was here on business that Tuesday morning."

Jamie felt her heart sink to the floor. *Eric Michaels?* Was that who she was sitting next to? The man who had shared her home, her life, her very soul, these past few months? She squeezed her eyes shut. "What ... what did he look like?"

"I told you ..." A phone was ringing in the background, and the woman was losing interest. "The guy was nice-looking. Tall, maybe six-two, dark trim-cut hair. Sort of an athletic build."

Jamie had heard enough. The woman might as well have been staring at the man across from her as she described him. She was going on, repeating the details about the Los Angeles office, and Jamie tried to listen.

"Eric worked too hard. He never spent a minute at home from what I understand. In fact," her tone filled with regret, "it was the job that killed him. Both of them, really."

"What do you mean?"

"When the plane hit the south tower, everyone else in the office left down the stairwell. They were on the sixty-fourth floor, so they had just enough time to get out." She paused. "But not Allen and Eric. The last anyone saw of them, they were crunching numbers, trying to finish one last transaction before heading down."

"So everyone at Koppel and Grant's pretty sure both men are dead?" Again Jamie hated herself for hoping.

"That's the thought. Of course anything's possible." The woman clucked her tongue. "After all, there's still a thousand people unaccounted for. They never found either of their bodies."

Jamie thanked the woman and hung up. Then she looked at the man across from her, and in the depths of her being, she knew their time together was almost up. Her tone was soft, kind, as though she knew the answer to her question before she asked it. "If I say the name Eric, what comes to mind?"

He blinked, and a dawning came over his expression, a knowing that was undeniable. His mouth opened, and what he said made her feel like both weeping and shouting for joy all at the same time.

"When I hear the name Eric, I can think of only one thing." He swallowed and tightened his grip on her hand. "The name Michaels. Eric Michaels." He searched her eyes. "Is that ... is that me?"

The tears came regardless of her desire to stop them. "Yes ..." She uttered a happy cry and hugged him, held him as she would only get to do a handful of times again in her life. "Your name is Eric Michaels."

THIRTY-THREE

DECEMBER 4, 2001

It was December, and the shock had finally begun to wear off.

Laura had come to terms with the fact that the problems in her marriage were both Eric's fault and hers. There was no one to shake a fist at, no point hanging on to either guilt or anger. She had never realized how badly hurt he'd been by the loss of their daughter. After that, they had simply let their love die, and Eric had replaced her with his position at Koppel and Grant.

A position that had demanded everything from him. His time, his devotion, his heart and soul. Eventually his life.

She and Josh were getting on with living. The hotel where Eric had been staying had finally shipped his suitcase back to Laura. His belongings held nothing of interest, no postcards or souvenirs. A month later they'd accepted an urn of Ground Zero ashes from officials in New York City as a way of remembering Eric, but they'd turned down an invitation to attend a memorial service in Manhattan. The two of them didn't need a memorial service to remember Eric.

They needed a miracle.

Because in a practical sense, adjusting to life without Eric had been relatively simple. Once Laura got over her anger and self-recrimination, once she stopped running the list of what-ifs and should-have-dones and might-have-beens through her head and came to grips with the reality of the situation, there really wasn't much else to mourn.

Eric had disappeared from their lives long before he left for New York City.

And in his place—or maybe as a way of feeling loved again—Laura had taken to spending much of her free time with Clay. It was Tuesday morning, and Laura, Clay, and Josh had shared a pleasant dinner the night before. Now Josh was outside playing football with his friends, and Clay was on his way over. The three of them were going to do some early Christmas shopping at the Thousand Oaks Mall.

The doorbell rang, and Laura ran her fingers through her hair. Every day she enjoyed Clay's presence a little more, but she wasn't sure what

God thought of their relationship. Not much, she guessed. The fence that stood between friendship and love for the two of them was chain link and razor wire. Neither of them had any intention of crossing it.

Not yet, anyway.

Still, Laura had to admit that over the past few weeks, she'd found herself attracted to Clay more than once, feeling the hint of interest she'd felt for him back in her junior year of high school.

Laura let the thought pass, and for a fleeting moment, she was angry at Eric again. This confusion, the wayward thoughts of her heart, they were all his fault. If only he'd told her years ago that he'd named their daughter and grieved her still. If only he'd opened his heart to her, maybe he would've never gotten so involved at work.

Maybe he would've been home that terrible September morning.

The thought passed as she opened the door. Clay stood there, a bouquet of roses in his hand. "Here." He handed them to her. "For dinner yesterday." A grin climbed his face.

Laura took the flowers and tilted her head. Clay had always been like this, hadn't he? Caring for her, placing her on a pedestal despite the fact that her heart belonged to Eric. Something in his crooked smile made her go to him willingly. She held the flowers in one hand and hugged him with the other. When she pulled away, his arm stayed around her waist.

"You know something?"

"What?" Laura lowered her chin and smiled at him. She kept her voice playful and upbeat so the moment wouldn't become something she wasn't ready for.

"I love to see you smile."

"Thanks." A dying piece of her heart gasped for breath and began beating again. "It feels good."

Before either of them could move away, he brought his face to hers and gave her a tentative kiss on the lips. It was over almost as soon as it began, but it left them looking at each other, frightened and curious and lost in each other's eyes all at the same time. In some ways, being here in Clay's arms was as natural as the California sun. They'd known each other forever, after all, and they'd always cared about each other.

But not like this.

Laura was about to say something when the phone rang. She blinked, took a few steps backwards, and held up the flowers. "I'll . . . I'll put these in water."

With light steps and a heart that felt freer than it had in years, Laura returned to the kitchen and picked up the phone. "Hello?" She walked to a cupboard near the sink and pulled out a dusty flower vase.

"Laura . . . this is Murphy." The man paused. "Are you sitting down?"

The blood began to drain from Laura's face, and she uttered a forced laugh. Only one thought planted itself in her mind. They must've found Eric's body. "Murphy . . . what're you talking about."

"I'm serious, Laura. Get a chair."

Murphy had always been gruff and to the point, short on words and shorter still on personality. Not once in all the years Laura had known him had he ever tried to be funny. She set the flowers down on the counter, made her way into the living room, and sat on the nearest sofa.

From the corner of her eye, she saw Clay make his way inside and take a seat near her. She shot him a look and whispered the word, "Murphy." She sucked in a jagged breath. "What's going on, Murph? You sound funny."

Murphy muttered something. Then he inhaled sharply. "Laura . . . I got a call today. A lady from New York City." He did a short huff. "You aren't going to believe this. I know it because I still don't believe it myself."

Laura's throat was thick, and her heart had slipped into an unrecognizable rhythm. "Just say it, Murphy. What was the call about?"

"The woman told me she has Eric. He's alive, Laura. He got amnesia when the building collapsed, but he's alive. He's been living in Staten Island."

Laura would've dropped the phone, except her hands were suddenly frozen. "What!" She stood up and walked a few hurried steps in one direction, then the other, then back. "Murphy, don't do this to me if you're not serious. You're telling me Eric's alive?"

She looked at Clay and saw a series of emotions pass across his face. Shock, disbelief, and confusion. Followed quickly by the proper look of hope and anticipation. He was at her side in an instant, and he slipped his arm around her shoulders as she learned the details of what had happened.

"I guess Eric looked just like this other lady's husband. A fire-fighter from New York City." Murphy hesitated. "They found out yesterday it wasn't her husband, after all. It was Eric."

Laura couldn't begin to identify her emotions. Eric was alive? How was it possible, and were they sure it was him? She squeezed her eyes shut. "What if it's not him?"

"His memory's coming back, Laura. He remembers who he is now."

So, it was true! Eric was alive, and the reality of that fought to make its way into her consciousness. Ever since September 11, Laura had found most comfort by reliving the good times, the days back when they were first married, before they'd lost their baby daughter. Sarah. But now, in light of the fact that he was living, more recent memories barged their way in. So he was alive? Did that mean he'd come home ready to take on life at Koppel and Grant again? Would he even want to come home? And what place did he have there after being gone so long? There were details that suddenly needed figuring out, and Laura didn't know what to begin to feel.

She barely listened as Murphy rattled on about his conversation with the New York woman. Only one thing was absolutely sure in her mind. She was grateful she had never let herself fall in love with Clay Michaels. She cared about him, yes, but she would never love him. Not the way she knew he loved her. Because her entire heart and soul were still given to the only man who had ever laid ownership to them.

Yes, their marriage was a mess, and they had issues they needed to talk about. Maybe it would be months or years before things would be right again. But he definitely had a place in her life. Of course. He was alive again—and that could only mean that she'd been given the second chance she'd prayed about. A chance to love a man who wasn't dead, after all, and who—whatever he'd been through—might come home soon. A man who one day might be willing to break down and mourn the loss of their baby daughter, a man who in time might even choose to make changes in their marriage that could give her the family she'd always dreamed about.

A man named Eric Michaels.

THIRTY-FOUR

DECEMBER 4, 2001

The arrangements came together quickly.

Now that Eric's wife knew the truth, Jamie had no choice but to make the call. A call that would send the man who looked like Jake home where he belonged, one that would leave Jamie's heart as empty as her house.

Eric had asked her to do the talking, because after being gone so long, after changing so much, he didn't want to speak to his wife until they were face-to-face.

Jamie understood.

And so she called the woman, and as simply as possible, she filled in the details about what had happened to her husband. "He . . . he could've been my husband's twin." Jamie sat next to Eric, holding his hand as she explained the situation to Laura Michaels. "It wasn't until he started getting flashbacks that we realized he might not be the man I married."

The woman listened, and the few times she had questions, her voice was filled with empathy. Only once did the woman ask about the friendship Eric had obviously developed with Jamie. "Is . . . does my husband love you?"

A lump formed in Jamie's throat, and she squeezed Eric's hand. "We've become very good friends." She sniffed, forcing herself to stay composed. She glanced at Eric and held his eyes. "But he's married to you, Mrs. Michaels. He wants to come home as quickly as possible."

An hour later Laura called back with flight plans. She would fly into La Guardia the following morning just before noon and escort Eric home. And for Jamie, that would be the end of it, the end of believing for two months that her husband was alive. The end of hoping that a few memories were all that stood between her and the life she'd once shared with Jake.

When Jamie hung up the phone, she hugged Eric and whispered near his ear. "Pray for Sierra . . . it's going to be so hard on her."

"Oh, Jamie, honey, I'm sorry . . . I never meant for any of this to happen." He stroked her back as a single sob worked its way through her chest. "If only my memory would've come back sooner, maybe none of this—"

She drew back and placed a finger on his lips. "No, Eric ... God wanted you here." She sniffed and smiled at him through her tears. "As hard as this is for all of us ... you being in my life these past months was part of His plan." A happy cry came from her, and she wiped her cheeks. "Think about it. Without you I wouldn't have learned to believe in God. And you ..." She brushed away another series of tears. "You would still be some business executive who didn't know how to love." She shook her head and held his face gently in her hands. "And now ... as long as you live, you'll take a little bit of Jake Bryan with you."

"But how ..." Eric's voice was barely more than a whisper, and tears choked every word. "How I am ever going to say good-bye?"

* * * *

The two of them spent their last night together with Sierra.

They shared Hawaiian pizza, and Eric dutifully collected his pineapple pieces and gave them to Sierra, who had declared herself a pineapple princess some weeks ago. After dinner, Eric and Jamie took turns reading to her, and finally they cozied up on the sofa on either side of her and watched *Little Mermaid*. At the end when the mermaid decides to return to land and has to bid her father good-bye, Eric could do nothing about the steady stream of tears on his cheeks. He didn't dare look at Jamie; he already knew she was crying.

Their nighttime ritual was no different than usual, except that this time Eric kissed Sierra good-night and walked out of her room for the last time. After he shut her door and took two steps, he turned and fell into Jamie's arms. "She deserves a daddy, Jamie." He let out a quiet, desperate sound. "It kills me to think she won't have one after tomorrow."

Jamie cried too, but she had a strength that surprised him. Clearly she'd been praying about this good-bye, asking God to prepare her heart and see her through it. Eric only hoped God would do the same for him. A piece of him couldn't wait to be back with Laura, to show her how he'd changed and beg her forgiveness about how he'd treated her in the past. He was remembering more with each passing hour, and he knew that he'd all but abandoned both his wife and his young son.

He prayed they'd forgive him.

But though he looked forward to being with them, he was torn apart at the thought of leaving Jamie and Sierra. That night as he and Jamie parted at the foot of the stairs and said good-night, Eric was tempted beyond reason to follow her. Just this one time. To lie beside her and hold her, love her and cry with her and wish that somehow they could keep the sun from rising in the morning.

The thought left as soon as it had come, and he merely hugged her once more and kissed her on the cheek. He was asleep almost as soon as his head hit the pillow, and he spent the entire night dreaming of Laura and Josh. What if they didn't want him back? Maybe the damage he'd done wasn't something he could fix? Questions and strange bits of imagined conversations played in his mind all night.

In what felt like five minutes, he woke to the sounds of Jamie and Sierra in the kitchen. She had told him he could wear one of Jake's outfits home. Other than that, he had nothing to pack. Everything he'd thought was his really belonged to Jake.

Eric showered and shaved—surprised at how the scars on his face had faded. He still had to be careful with the new skin, but it appeared that the doctor had been right. Eventually, it would be almost impossible to tell what Eric had been through.

Except in the private places of his heart.

He made his way to the kitchen, and Sierra ran to him, the way she had done every day since he came home from the hospital. Jamie smiled at him from her place near the stove, and he gave her a quick wink before turning his attention to Sierra.

"Daddy! Guess what?"

Eric had to swallow hard to keep from crying. "What?"

"Mommy's making blueberry pancakes! Isn't that great? It's my bestest kind of all!"

He swept her into his arms and nuzzled his face against hers. *God . . . watch over this child . . . and one day give her the father she needs. Please, God.* "You're sure pretty today, princess."

"Yeah, but my hair's too straight, and Mommy says I get to play with Katy." She pulled back, her chin lowered in a way that tugged hard at Eric's heart. "Can you curl it, Daddy, even though it isn't Sunday?"

Eric blinked back the beginnings of tears. "Of course, honey. I'd love to." He slid Sierra back to the floor and watched her scamper to her spot at the table. Then he went up alongside Jamie and leaned his head close to hers. "I don't know if I can do this."

She sniffed and raised her eyes up for a minute. "I've been up since four . . . talking to God." The pancakes sizzled and she flipped them. Then she looked at him and smiled. Her eyes were dry, but he could see she'd been crying. "You can do it, Eric. We both can. And one day everything will all be okay again. God promised me."

They took their places at the table, and Sierra chattered happily about being in kindergarten the following fall and Christmas coming up and the fact that pineapple was her favorite fruit. Next to blueberries.

When the meal was over, Eric cast a glance at Jamie. "Want help with the dishes?"

"No, thanks." She shook her head, her eyes glistening. "I think you have some hair to curl."

Eric followed Sierra up to Jamie's bedroom and plugged in the curling iron. It was a routine he'd learned weeks ago, and one that had given Sierra and him many special times to talk. Sierra bopped about along the bathroom counter, looking at Jamie's makeup and perfume bottles, completely unaware of the way her life was about to change.

The curling iron was ready, and Eric clicked it a few times. His signal that Sierra needed to come to him and stand still while he worked. She did, turning her back to him and letting her long blonde hair cascade down her little back. Eric opened the iron and pinched it around one section of Sierra's hair. Then he rolled it halfway up her back.

"So ... you're going to Katy's today, huh?"

"Yep." Sierra held her chin high, careful not to move. "Katy's never seen my hair with curlies in it."

One by one Eric worked his way around her head until gorgeous curls surrounded her like a halo. Eric unplugged the iron and set it back on the counter where it could cool.

At that moment, they heard Jamie calling to her. "Sierra ... I have to run you over to Katy's house. Come on ... it's time."

Sierra wriggled her nose at Eric. "Thanks, Daddy. No one does curlies like you."

Eric caught the child's chin between his thumb and forefinger and looked straight into her eyes. "You know something?"

"What?" Her little-girl eyes danced, the way they always did whenever she was with him.

"I think Mommy would do an even better job at curlies." Eric lowered his voice and glanced at the door. "Actually, she's the best curler in the whole world. She just doesn't want everyone to know."

Sierra's eyes grew wide. "Really?"

"Really." Eric could feel his heart breaking. "So this Sunday before church . . . I think Mommy should get a chance to curl your hair." He forced a smile. "Okay?"

"Okay! Can I tell her?"

Eric gave a quick shake of his head. "Not yet. Not until Sunday, all right?"

"All right." Sierra took his hand then and led him toward the door. "We gotta go now. Katy's waiting."

Jamie was in the foyer, watching them as they walked hand in hand down the stairs. She spoke to Sierra but kept her eyes completely on Eric. "It's time to go. Say good-bye to Daddy, and we'll head over to Katy's, okay?" She took a few steps back, her eyes still locked on Eric's. He understood. She was giving him this time, this space to say one last good-bye.

Eric worked the muscles in his jaw and sat back on his heels. He met Sierra's eyes for what would be the last time and whispered, "Come here, baby."

She wrapped her arms around his neck. "Bye, Daddy. Have a good day."

A sob lodged itself in Eric's throat, and for a full minute he couldn't say anything. Instead, he simply held her, stroking her back and begging God to be the father she wouldn't have after that morning. When he could finally speak, he pulled away some and smiled at her. "I love you, Sierra. You know that, right?"

She giggled. "Silly, Daddy. A'course I know that. You love me better than pumpkin pie."

"That's right, honey. Much better than that." Eric could barely breathe for the pain in his soul. He raised his eyebrows. "Butterfly kisses?"

She clapped her hands and gave a quick nod of her pretty head. Then their noses met and brushed against each other three times. Next his eyelashes brushed against her cheek, and hers brushed against his. When they were finished, he took hold of her shoulders. "Bye, Sierra." And in that instant he remembered something from Jake's journal, something he had always told Sierra whenever he'd left for a shift at the fire station. "Be good, honey. And don't forget to pray to Jesus."

"Okay." She kissed him one more time and then spun around and skipped over to Jamie. With one final wave over her shoulder, she grabbed hold of Jamie's hand, and the two of them disappeared around the corner.

Eric pulled himself up and sat on the third stair, his head in his hands. He listened as Sierra and Jamie made their way into the garage, Sierra chattering and giggling about the day she'd be spending with Katy. He heard the garage door open and the car back out and slowly drive away.

Only then did the tears come, tears he'd been holding back since he'd learned his real name. He cried for Sierra who would find out that afternoon that her daddy had died in a fire, and for Jamie who would have to raise her by herself. But he also cried for himself, and for the piece of his heart that had just driven off with one very special four-year-old little girl.

A girl he would never give butterfly kisses to again.

* * * *

Jamie had known for the past few days that the pain wouldn't really come until she told Eric good-bye. She'd been honest about her time with God, and the promise He'd made her that morning. She'd been lost in prayer and Scripture, reading Jake's highlighted verses, when very clearly she'd heard a whisper in the center of her soul.

I will neither leave you nor forsake you, My daughter ... I know the plans I have for you ... plans to give you a hope and a future, and not to harm you.

All her life Jamie had stayed away from pat answers, from preachy people who seemed to have a Bible verse for every situation in life. But the words she'd heard that morning from God were nothing short of divine. They breathed life into her at a time when she surely would've suffocated from the heartache otherwise.

After she dropped Sierra off at Sue's house, Jamie and Eric drove together to La Guardia. She knew it might be awkward, but she wanted to see Laura, wanted to watch Eric and her together so she could have closure on this time in her life. Two minutes into the drive, Eric reached for her hand and wove his fingers between hers.

"You've been wonderful, Jamie." He studied her, his eyes still red from the tears he must've cried after saying good-bye to Sierra.

"Thanks." She smiled and shifted her gaze back to the road ahead of her.

The morning traffic was light, so the drive took less time than usual. They found a spot in the parking garage and made their way to the security checkpoint, where the airport had created a waiting area for guests, who since September 11 could no longer go all the way to the gate without a boarding pass.

Jamie looked at her watch and led Eric to a quiet place near a wall of windows at the back of the waiting area. Laura Michaels' United Airlines flight was supposed to land in three minutes.

They faced each other, leaning against the windows with less than a foot separating them. Jamie reached into her bag and pulled out a wrapped package. The ache in her heart had spread to her arms, and the gift felt like it was made of lead. "Here." She handed it to Eric. "It's an early Christmas present."

Eric took the bag and for a long time he looked at her, lost in her eyes. Jamie wanted to cry, but she couldn't. Not yet. She nodded to the package in Eric's hands, and finally he glanced down. He peeled back the paper and tossed it in a nearby trash can. Inside the package was a bound set of pages. Blue letters across the top page read only this: "In case you ever forget . . ."

He opened the cover page, and Jamie heard his breath catch in his throat. She had copied dozens of pages from Jake's journal— key entries about the importance of fatherhood and the joys of being married to his best friend. At the back were another twenty or so pages, copies from Jake's Bible, complete with the shaded highlighting and scribbled notes in the margin.

His eyes met hers again, and he needed no words. He clutched the bound document to his chest and pulled her close. "Jamie . . . I'll never forget you. Not you or Jake."

She lifted her head, desperate to keep from breaking down in this, their final moment. "You're so much like him, Eric." Her smile was genuine, growing from someplace that, despite her sorrow, could understand the value all their time together had wrought. "One day in heaven the two of you will have to have a long talk."

A rush of people began to make their way past the security gate, and Eric turned. Jamie watched him, wondering if he could see his wife yet. Then he pointed, his voice thick. "There she is. Near the back."

He faced Jamie once more and their eyes held. This was it . . . in a few minutes he'd be gone from her life forever. "I love you, Jamie. I'm a different man because of you. Because of Jake."

She listened, still stunned by how easily he could've *been* Jake. She could feel the tears building within her, but she only nodded at him. "Go, Eric." Jamie cast a glance toward the blonde woman, getting closer to the waiting area. "She's looking for you."

Eric nodded. "Do you want to meet her?"

"No." Jamie struggled to find her voice. "I'll leave quietly. Besides . . . the two of you have a plane to catch."

"Okay." He worked the muscles in his jaw, his eyes still searching hers. "Kiss Sierra for me, will you?"

Jamie gave a quick nod, and the moment faded. Eric hugged her once more, a long hug, the last they would ever share. Then, without saying another word, he turned to leave. Jamie watched him work his way through the crowd of waiting people, until finally his wife spotted him. The blonde woman hurried her pace, her mouth open in a kind of unbelieving shock. The two of them came together, and Eric swung her in his arms.

Jamie felt something pierce her heart, and the tears came then.

She blinked so she could see clearly, and she watched the woman kiss him square on the mouth. For a moment they spoke to each other, their faces inches apart, lost in the moment despite the milling passengers making their way around them.

Then the woman linked her arm through his, and without looking back, Eric led her toward the security line where they would pass through before boarding their plane.

"Good-bye, Eric . . . take care of her." Jamie whispered the words and then slowly, her soul aching, she turned her back on the man she'd thought was her husband, the man who—because of Jake—had taught her to love God, and live without fear. The man who—because of Jake—had learned how to love again.

She passed a hundred people and saw none of them. Every step took her farther from the delusion that somehow she could keep Jake alive, that by living with Eric she still somehow had a piece of Jake.

Six minutes later she walked out of the airport and into her new life—the one where she would only have Jake's words to remind her of a man whose love would stay in her heart a lifetime. A love that no terrorist attack could ever take away. One that had continued to live within her, growing her and changing her. And not just her, but Eric Michaels, as well. A love that would live on long after the rubble from September 11 was cleared and hauled away.

A love so great it lived even now.

Jamie drove with the window open, and the breeze mingled with her tears and stung at her cheeks. She allowed herself to grieve the loss of not just Jake, but Eric and the tangible presence of her husband's love—even as it had played out in the life of a stranger.

She had to find Sierra now, had to tell her that her daddy was dead. The words she was about to say would be the most difficult in all her life, words she knew would've killed her if not for the time she'd spent with God that day, those past months, hanging on to Him for dear life. Her strength came from Him alone, from the truth she'd gained by reading Jake's Bible.

A truth she could hear Jake whispering in her heart even now.

She pulled up in front of the Hennings house, parked the car, and forced herself up the sidewalk. In the end it had been the right decision, keeping the truth from Sue and everyone else. Accepting it had been hard enough for her and Eric. And telling anyone would've opened up potential situations neither of them wanted to deal with. Not that Sue would've called the newspapers. But word would've gotten out, and then what? That wasn't what they'd wanted. And by keeping the news to themselves, they'd been able to focus on what was important—helping Eric find his way home.

Jamie ordered her feet to climb the Hennings' porch steps. In some ways she couldn't truly grieve Jake's death until now, when she could share it with everyone else who made up her world.

She knocked on Sue's door and took a slow breath. *Give me the strength, God . . . please.*

The door opened and Sue appeared. Her smile faded as soon as the two of them made eye contact. "Jamie . . . what is it?" Sue's voice was breathless, her eyes filled with fear.

Jamie only held up her hand and swallowed back another sob. "Give me . . . let me talk to Sierra first. Okay?"

Sue hesitated for only a moment. Then she hurried back into the house and returned with Sierra. The child stopped, her eyes wide when she saw that her mother was crying. "Mommy, what's wrong?"

Jamie held out her hands and picked Sierra up the way Jake had always done. The way Eric had done. One day, when she was old enough to understand, Jamie would explain about the man who had lived with them after the attacks on New York City. But for now, the simple delayed truth was all the child would understand.

"Baby . . . Mommy has some sad news to tell you . . ."

Thirty-Five

December 5, 2001

Eric hadn't stopped talking since Laura met him at the airport. The whole way back to Los Angeles, he caught her up on all that happened to him since he woke up in the New York hospital.

Laura was dumbfounded by the story. "So you really thought you were this . . . this Jake Bryan?"

"I didn't know any different." Eric took hold of her hand, and she tried not to look shocked. How long had it been since he'd held her hand? Laura couldn't even remember, but she dared to hope that maybe . . . just maybe he'd had a change of heart living with this Jamie woman.

He launched into another chapter of the story, the part where he'd found the dead man's journal and Bible. "For two weeks all I did was read that thing. I memorized everything about what it meant to love my family and care for the people around me."

Laura wasn't sure what to say. "Jake was a great guy, huh?"

"Better than great." Eric looked around as though he were searching for the words. "He loved God so much, Laura. So much. And everything about his life and his family was a reflection of that love."

Constantly throughout the conversation, Laura had to remind herself she wasn't dreaming. It was one thing to have the shock of finding out Eric was alive. And another altogether to dare to dream he'd become the man of her dreams while living the life of a man she'd never met.

They were crossing Arizona by the time Eric finished the story. "So what I want to say, Laura, is . . . I'm sorry." He drew close to her and kissed her slowly on the lips.

Again she had to convince herself that the moment was real. Eric never kissed her like that, not in years. He pulled back some and studied her eyes.

"I remember now, and I know how awful I've been." His eyes narrowed, and the pain there was something he'd never let her see before. "And I remember Sarah."

Tears filled her eyes as soon as he spoke her name. "I never knew . . ." She shook her head. "I found the card you'd written for her. I . . . I thought I'd never get to talk about her with you."

"I should've told you sooner, worked it out with you." He pulled her close again and held her, unaware of the flight attendants or passengers or turbulence as they headed over California. "Can you ever forgive me?"

Laura leaned back and wiped at her eyes. "We have so much to work through. Of course I forgive you, Eric." She sniffed and held her breath, refusing the sobs that gathered in her throat. "You never gave me a chance."

They talked more after that, and Eric told her everything he remembered about losing little Sarah and turning his back on God. For Laura it was like having her first drink of water after a decade in the desert. The feeling was more miraculous than anything she could've imagined.

Nothing about it wore off that first day. When Eric walked through the door of their home, Clay was there, and he hugged Eric long and hard while Josh stood quietly in the background. "Clay . . ."

"We thought . . ." Clay squeezed his eyes shut and tightened his grip on Eric. "We thought you were dead, big brother."

Laura watched the brothers hug through teary eyes. Clay's feelings had to be mixed. Of course he was thrilled that Eric was alive. The two had miles of ground to make up. But there was something painful about the entire situation as well, something Clay hadn't voiced to her, and probably never would.

But whatever he was feeling, he was careful to hide it now that Eric was home.

When the two men pulled apart, Laura watched Eric take a step toward Josh. The child looked frightened, as though he were seeing a ghost. Or maybe he was simply scared by the change in Eric. Laura had tried to warn him the night before.

"Daddy's coming home," she'd told him. "He's got a hurt face, and he might look a little different."

Josh hadn't said much. Clearly Josh wasn't altogether sure he wanted his father back. After all, the man had done little over the past years but hurt his son with broken promises and a lack of affection.

Now Eric's voice was thick as he stooped down to the boy's level. "Come here, Josh."

Laura watched their son and did what she could to remember to exhale. *God . . . let things be different between them . . . please.*

Josh blinked and stared at the floor for a moment. Then with short tentative steps he made his way to Eric. Laura willed him to keep moving toward his father. As he did, Eric smiled in a way that once again made Laura think she was dreaming. The old Eric would never have taken time to single out their son, not unless he was in trouble.

Josh stopped a few feet from Eric. "Yes, sir?"

Eric held out his arms, and as he did, a confused look fell over Josh's face. Eric closed the gap between them and pulled him into a hug that lasted half a minute. Afterwards, he drew back and kissed his son on the cheek. "I love you, Josh. I haven't told you nearly enough, but I love you."

Josh looked at Laura and raised his eyebrows. Laura didn't know whether to laugh or cry. The poor child had no idea what to make of the change that had come over his father.

He shrugged and met Eric's eyes again. "Thanks."

Eric was undaunted by Josh's ambiguity. He grinned and gave Josh another quick hug. "How 'bout a bike ride tonight? Me and you and Mom . . ." Eric shot a smile at Clay. "And Uncle Clay if he wants."

Clay cleared his throat and stepped forward. "Actually, I was just leaving." He smiled at Eric and patted his shoulder. "You and Laura need time alone together."

"Okay . . . but come back tomorrow. I want to have a barbecue for all of us." He looked at Laura and held her gaze. "And let's call my dad. I want him to know things are different now. Time's too short to waste."

He looked back at Josh. "And guess what? I learned how to jet ski, buddy. I can't wait to teach you. But first we have our bike ride tonight . . ."

Through it all, Josh only stared at him, his mouth open. Laura could see in his eyes something that hadn't been there before, not as far back as she could remember.

Something that looked an awful lot like hope.

Eric made good on his promises that evening, and for enough days in a row that finally Laura actually believed it. A miracle had taken place, a miracle only God Almighty could've brought about. And all because the words of one very special man had taught her husband everything he needed to know about love and faithfulness.

Laura wondered about Jake Bryan.

Because the story of her life wouldn't be complete until some far-off day when she would find him on the streets of heaven and thank him for the footprints he'd left behind.

Footprints she was starting to believe Eric would follow until the day he died.

Thirty-Six

September 11, 2002

A year had passed since the terrorist attacks, and summer had blended quickly into fall. Somehow Jamie had survived it, survived telling the truth to the guys at the station and breaking the news to Jake's father when he returned from his cross-country trip. She had kept her promise to Eric and refused to tell his identity to anyone who asked, even the few reporters who had managed to call her after news of Jake's death was reported in the paper.

They'd found his body—his and Larry's, side by side—on a spring day when the remains of more than a dozen firefighters were found. The department had given both of them a proper funeral—the type Jamie no longer had any reason to dread. Jake's helmet sat on Sierra's dresser now, a constant reminder that her daddy was up in heaven, waiting for the far-off day when they'd be together again.

In some ways Jake's presence lived on in their home, brought to life again and again each time Jamie read the words in his journal. She was still learning the depth of how he'd loved them, how he'd cherished his time with God and his family.

Every now and then Jamie could hear her father's warning, the one he'd spoken to her as he peered over his newspaper so long ago, back when she first fell in love with Jake. *It's a tough job, fighting fires in New York City. The danger's always there, Jamie, as close as the next call.*

In the end her father had been right about that. But he'd been wrong about the rest, the part where he'd told her that a man didn't need anyone but himself, that religion was a sign of weakness. Jake Bryan would always be the strongest man she knew ... so strong that even now his words, his faith, his love were sometimes all that held her up—even from as far away as heaven.

And God had given her other help too. Over the months Jamie and Sue had become closer than sisters, helping each other through the missed birthdays and lonely holidays. As the anniversary of the terrorist attacks neared, Sue had agreed with Jamie. They didn't want to spend the day gathering with a group of mourners or honored in some sort of ceremony.

They wanted to spend it alone. Lost in the memory of all September 11 had cost them.

Now that the one-year date was finally there, Jamie and Sierra packed a picnic and bought a single white helium balloon. They headed to the place that Jake would've wanted to go, a place that was bound to be virtually empty that morning.

Sierra was quiet as they held hands and made their way across the sandy beach to the spot where they had come as a family so often before. It was windy as they set their things down and carried the balloon close to the shore. A seagull sounded in the distance, and Sierra looked up. She was taller now, a kindergartner whose eyes were a little less quick to sparkle and dance the way they once had. She gazed into the sky. "Mommy . . . do you think Daddy can see us?"

Jamie hadn't cried as much lately. God was sustaining her, just as He'd promised. For the most part, she did her grieving in private. Jamie looked at the sky overhead and smiled. Yes, that was something else Jake was still teaching her. That it was okay to cry, okay to love deeply enough to hurt. And here, now, she felt the sting of tears as she considered her daughter's question.

"Yes, honey. I think Daddy can see us." Jamie pulled a pink marker from her jacket, pulled off the cap, and handed it to Sierra. "Go ahead, honey."

They'd planned this weeks ago, and now her daughter didn't hesitate. Jamie held the balloon for her, and Sierra hovered over it, carefully printing out each letter until she'd written a simple message across the white. "I love you, Daddy. From, Sierra."

She finished the final "a" in her name and then handed the marker back to Jamie. "Mommy, I just thought of something."

"What?" The beach was empty, just as Jamie had pictured it. They were the only two people near the water as she looked at Sierra.

"Do you think if I give the balloon a butterfly kiss, it'll make it all the way up to Daddy in heaven?"

Jamie bit her lip and swallowed back the lump in her throat. "Yes, baby. I think Daddy would get it that way."

Sierra nodded and held the balloon near her face. She was about to kiss it when she stopped and looked at Jamie. Her eyes glistened with tears. "I miss him, Mommy."

"I miss him too."

Then—the same way she'd always done with Jake—Sierra rubbed her nose against the white surface of the balloon and held her cheek against it the way she might if her daddy was brushing his eyelashes against her. Then she turned it slightly and finally blinked her own silky eyelashes against the smooth rubber.

"Okay." Sierra looked at Jamie. "I'm ready."

Jamie nodded, and Sierra held the balloon string high over her head. "Jesus . . . please let my daddy get this. Okay?" She waited for a single moment, then she opened her fingers and watched the balloon shoot into the sky. At first it seemed to drift in the air currents, but in only a few seconds it began moving quickly toward the heavens, and in no time at all it disappeared.

They walked back to the shore, and Jamie could almost picture the scene in Paradise. Jake standing there with Jesus, capturing the balloon as it went by and sending back butterfly kisses and enough love to last them a lifetime. Not just for Sierra, but for her.

Always for her.

Only then, with the balloon safely on its way to heaven, did Jamie pull out the piece of paper from her pocket. A copy of the last letter Jake had ever written to her.

Dear Sweet Jamie . . .

A teardrop fell onto it, and Jamie brushed it off. Beside her, Sierra dropped to the sand and stared at the spot in the sky where the balloon had disappeared. Jamie blinked so she could see the words once more.

I have this feeling, deep in my heart, that something's about to change for me and you. Maybe it's your questions about church or the way you seem to hang on to Sierra's Bible stories a little bit longer these days. Whatever it is, I've prayed for God to touch your heart, baby. He means everything to me, and I know that one day He'll mean everything to you too. On that day, you'll no longer have to be afraid, because you'll have God Almighty to lean on. I want you to know, honey, that when you find that precious faith, I'll be smiling bigger than you've ever seen me smile.

Jamie stifled a sob as she looked up toward heaven again. She sniffed and ran her fingers through Sierra's golden hair. The truth was unbelievable, really. That in her search to teach a stranger how to be Jake, she'd discovered the one thing that had been her husband's single source of strength, the faith that mattered so dearly to him.

She swallowed and finished reading the letter.

Because the thing I want even more than your love is the knowledge that we'll have eternity together. I simply can't bear the idea of being in heaven without you. I love you too much to lose you, and sometimes, Jamie, honestly it seems like you're running. Like you're too afraid to live and love and laugh the way you could. I want you to know it's okay, sweetheart. It's okay to love and it's okay to lose. Once you figure that out you can stop running . . . and start truly living. The way God wants you to live. Wherever you are when you read this, honey, know that I love you. And I'm praying for you. Always and forever . . . Jake.

She folded the piece of paper and tucked it back in her pocket. Beside her Sierra stirred, and Jamie knew it was almost time to eat their picnic lunch. They'd had their moment of remembering, of marking September 11, and all they'd lost on one single Tuesday morning.

But there was one more thing she wanted to do.

Leaving Sierra there by the picnic basket, Jamie walked a little closer to the shore, closer to the water where she and Jake had played together. When she was a few feet from the surf, she slipped off her shoes and took a few more steps until her toes were wet. Wet with the same water that had splashed against her and Jake as they tore across the bay all those summer days a lifetime ago.

Then she lifted her face toward heaven and narrowed her eyes, willing herself to see him as he was now, watching her, praying for her. The words she wanted to say to him, she would say in her heart . . . where the echo of them was bound to reach him even as far away as heaven. *Hello, Jake . . . it's me.* She paused, searching the sky. *I believe now . . . and I've stopped running. Isn't it amazing? How God answered your prayer?* A wind gust brushed over Jamie, and she closed her eyes. *I miss you, baby. Every day, every minute.* Her tears felt cool on her cheek, but she smiled despite them. *Save me a place, will you, Jake? Because one of these days we'll be together again.*

She opened her eyes, and in that moment, she didn't have to wonder what Jake was doing, how he would look if she could see him now on the streets of heaven. She could see him as surely as she could see the clear blue sky. As easily as if he were standing in front of her.

The moment passed and Jamie returned to Sierra. They shared their picnic, and after an hour they packed up and left. Before they piled into the van, Sierra stopped and stared up at the sky. "Mommy . . ."

"Yes, honey."

"You know when you went and stuck your feet in the water before lunch?" She shifted her gaze to Jamie.

"Yes, baby." Jamie set the picnic basket on the backseat and came up alongside her daughter. "I remember."

"Well, for a minute I thought I could see Daddy in the sky."

Jamie sucked in a quick breath. "Really?"

"Mmhmm." Sierra looked back at the expanse of blue overhead. Her eyes were serious, but less sad than before.

"What was he doing?" Jamie hugged Sierra's shoulders as the child turned and met her eyes.

"The most wonderful thing, Mommy." Sierra's eyes sparkled. "He was smiling."

AUTHOR'S NOTE

Dear Reader,

On the morning of September 11, I was getting my children ready for school, when the phone rang.

"Karen … are you watching it?" It was my sister, Sue. Her voice was frantic.

"Watching what?" I slipped on a sweatshirt and headed downstairs with Austin in tow.

"The TV … America's under attack."

Her words ran together after that, and all I could do was move quickly toward the television. There I witnessed—along with most of you—the collapse of the World Trade Center south tower. By then we had my mother on the line, and for a moment none of us spoke. Finally, my mom's voice broke the silence. "What just happened?"

It's a question we're still asking ourselves, isn't it?

What crazy madness and hatred was unleashed on our world that day? And how was it possible that the evil men who planned the attack were so accurate, their aim so deadly? For a while that morning I turned the TV off and helped the kids prepare for school. We ate breakfast and packed backpacks and had our devotions the same way we would've on any other morning.

But when they were gone, I turned the television back on and watched in horror as the events of the day unfolded. By noon, the story of Jake and Jamie Bryan, Laura and Eric Michaels began to grow in my heart. It wasn't something I asked for, rather it was simply something God gave me. A story born in the ashes of the collapsed Twin Towers.

I felt about the story the same way then as I do now … that it could've happened. That with all the wild madness and destruction that day, a story like the one that happened to these people truly could've taken place.

But that wasn't the point—not then and not now.

The point was much deeper.

We were all changed by what happened on September 11. In the days and months that followed, we grieved and got angry and came together in a way that had never happened before. We loved more easily. Some of you who are faithful readers wrote me letters saying that you'd made amends with a family member or learned to express your feelings for someone you cared about.

"I tell my father that I love him every time we talk now," one of you wrote to me. "Life is too short ... I know that better today."

We all do.

The lessons Eric Michaels learned while living in the shoes of Jake Bryan are lessons we would all do well to take notice of. The essential need for God in our lives, the value of faith and family and special times together. The importance of daily Bible reading. And most of all, the fact that a job will never be more important than knowing God or treasuring the smiles of our little ones before they're grown.

No promotion or job title is more important than our relationships.

There were other lessons of course, the ones Jamie Bryan learned. That we cannot run from death. Eventually, it will catch each of us, and often at an hour when we are unaware. For that reason we need to love without limit and be ready to face our Maker as long as we draw breath.

I am grateful that you journeyed the pages of *One Tuesday Morning* with me. It was a difficult story to write—especially the scenes in the south tower—and I am certain it was difficult to read. For those of you who were touched personally by the attacks on America, please know that my heart grieves with you. I have prayed that this book might be sensitive and compassionate, and that it might help you grieve, also.

Perhaps in a way you haven't done until now.

I've been asked many times—even by my own father—whether it's too soon for a story like *One Tuesday Morning*. But always I say the thing that is in my heart. As a nation we have shared our shock and our anger.

Now it is time to share our grief. And often that is best done through story. *One Tuesday Morning* was my way of grieving, and maybe ... just maybe it'll be your way too.

For those of you who've read all my novels, let me tell you that my family is doing well. My husband is enjoying his time away from coaching, a time to be with our children and lead our family into a closer walk of faith. Kelsey is a young teenager now, and our relationship with her is sweeter than ever. Tyler still gravitates toward storytelling and drama, and the four younger boys are most easily found on a sports field. As always, we cherish your prayers ... especially for my family and my ministry of writing.

I leave you with the words of Jake Bryan—*"I've prayed for God to touch your heart ... He means everything to me, and I know that one day He'll mean everything to you too. On that day, you'll no longer have to be afraid, because you'll have God Almighty to lean on."*

For those of you whose faith is as strong as Jake Bryan's ... I celebrate with you the joy of knowing the peace that passes understanding. But if the tragedy of September 11 has you confused or depressed, if your questions about that day still stand in the way of your relationship with the Creator, please, find a Bible-believing church and voice your concerns. I am convinced that only then will you find out the truth about the love of God.

Though death will one day find us all, we are not without hope. For God has won the victory over death.

Remember that.

In Christ's light and love ... until next time,
Karen Kingsbury

PS ... I'd love to hear from you at my website:
www.KarenKingsbury.com
or by emailing me at *rtnbykk@aol.com*

BEYOND
TUESDAY
MORNING

Beyond Tuesday Morning

(A song)

By Karen Kingsbury

(Chorus)
Let's not move too far beyond Tuesday morning
Let's not forget all the lives that were lost
Let's not move too far beyond Tuesday morning
Remember the heroes remember the cost.

Time has moved on as time always will do
Healing has come both to me and to you.
The towers that stood now stand only at times
A memory that's fading from all of our minds.

The flag on your bumper is yellowed and frayed
It's only on Sundays we take time to pray
For families of folks who did nothing but go
To work Tuesday morning and never came home.

(Bridge)
Still they are crying and still they are trying
To understand all that America lost
Take time to remember, there is no denying
That one Tuesday morning and all that it cost.

Smile at a stranger or do a good deed
Help out a neighbor, love someone in need
Do it to honor the women and men
Who died Tuesday morning and ever since then.

Let's not move too far beyond Tuesday morning
Let's not forget all the lives that were lost
Let's not move too far beyond Tuesday morning
Remember the heroes, remember the cost.

DEDICATED TO

Donald, my prince charming, who is forever praying for me, encouraging me, and giving me reasons to laugh. The wings are from God, but you are the wind. Every letter I receive, every life changed by the words God gives me to write, all of it is as much your ministry as mine. That's how much I rely on your love and prayers. You told me when we married that you'd always love God more than me. Ever since then I've been thanking the Lord for that truth, because the love and light you bring to me and our children could only come from heaven above. I love you, Donald. With you, life is always a dance.

Kelsey, my precious daughter, so grown-up. Sometimes I look at you and do a double take. When did that kindergartner with the poofy bangs become the beautiful fifteen-year-old with model good looks? Back then I would say, "Who made you so pretty, Kelsey?" You'd giggle and answer, "Jesus!" It's still so true today, only now, as you grow closer to Him, I see an even greater beauty. The beauty of Christ within you. I'm in awe of your choices, your high standards, your determination to keep God first in your life. High school already, Kelsey? Can you believe it? Your life is everything you dreamed about and the ride gets faster all the time. But in the quiet places of my heart you will always be my little Norm. I love you.

Tyler, my Broadway boy. Once upon a yesterday you would find whoever was home, stop what we were doing, and gather us together. Audience in place, you would sing. Song after song after song. Not regular kid songs, but songs from *Annie*, *Oklahoma*, *Les Misérables*, and *Phantom of the Opera*. We always knew you had a gift, but now we gather together in one room *hoping* you'll sing. More people are listening, Tyler, and many more will in years to come. You are only twelve, but the gift God has given you in song and drama and writing leaves me speechless. The mother heart in me is trying to find balance between my excitement for your future and my trepidation, because one day I won't have you and Kelsey singing and dancing in the background of our lives. You are the music of our home, dear Son, and even after you grow up, I will hear your song in my memory forever. I love you, Tyler.

Sean, my sunbeam. You are ten already and I can't believe it's been almost four years since you came from Haiti to live with us. You were the first one to open up about your past, to tell us of the hard times, days when you had to fend for yourself, eating dirt to survive. But today you are the first one with a hug and a smile, looking out for other people as easily as you breathe. You are a talented reader, a devoted son, and a respectful young man. I couldn't be more proud of you. You are gifted in sports, yes, but that's not why you're the first boy picked when they form teams at recess. It's because of who you are on the inside—the kind, loving person God made you to be. I'm forever glad God led you to our family; you belonged here from the beginning. I love you, Sean.

Josh, my rough-and-tumble sweetheart. Since I met you, I've known you had an amazing gift of persuasion. There I was at the Haitian orphanage, meeting Sean and EJ for the first time, but the first one to talk was you. "I love you, Mommy," you told me, using beautiful English. Do you know that the room went silent, Josh? Forty-two children clamoring and laughing and yelling in that tiny orphanage courtyard, and all I could hear was you, a child I'd never met until that day. No question, God wanted you in our home, because you arrived on September 8, 2001. Three days later political tensions might have meant you would never come home. Isn't God amazing? At ten years old, your talents are too numerous to mention, but above all God will use that wonderful charisma to bring people to Him. Save me a seat in the front row, okay, honey? I love you, Josh.

EJ, my wide-eyed overcomer. Like a precious, beautiful flower, you continue to unfold a little more each day, proving to everyone in your world that you are capable of great things, even at eight years old. I'm so proud of the way you hold your head high, the picture of kindness and character you present to the world. In the garden of life, you are becoming a leader, one forged by hanging onto Christ and letting Him pull you to the top. I know God has plans for all of His children, but yours gets a little clearer every day. I cherish our quiet times, when you sit beside me during devotions. Your smile makes our home so much brighter. I love you, EJ.

Austin, my six-year-old Green Beret. When God brought you safely back from infant heart surgery, I knew He had a special reason for letting you live. Now I can only dream of what He has in store. "I don't need to learn piano, Mommy. I told you . . . I'm going to be a Green Beret!" That and a Green Bay Packer. Oh, and the next (blond) Michael Jordan. Or maybe a champion bull rider. All that rough, tough men's town stuff, and you still cry when you think of Jesus on a cross. Talk about a heartbreaking cutie! But for now, the only broken heart is mine, because already our special babyhood days together are over. You are out of kindergarten, into full-day school like the others. But don't be surprised, little first-grader, if one morning you look up and I'm there to take you out for a special date. One more time to share lunch and give-and-go and cuddle time. Whoever said it was harder letting go of your youngest was right. Keep holding onto Jesus, Austin. I love you.

And to God Almighty, the Author of Life, who has — for now — blessed me with these.

ACKNOWLEDGMENTS

As always, when I bring my heart's thoughts and dreams to the computer keyboard, it's not without the help of a host of people.

In the writing of *Beyond Tuesday Morning*, I must first thank the people of St. Paul's Chapel. It is every bit the mighty mission I tried to make it in the fictional story that plays out on the following pages. The volunteers at St. Paul's continue to play a role in a healing that is far from complete. I learned much from my time at St. Paul's, talking to volunteers and studying the mementos and memorabilia there.

While the rest of us watched in horror that terrible Tuesday morning as the Twin Towers collapsed, we eventually got on with our lives. Not so for many of the people in Manhattan—especially for hundreds of firefighters and their families. Because of that, I am grateful to each of you who still devotes his or her time to the healing process at Ground Zero.

Thanks also to the information office of the fire department of New York. With the cooperation of this office, we were able to send a thousand copies of *One Tuesday Morning*, the first book in this set, to the FDNY—four books per station. The letters I've received from New York City firefighters have often left me in tears.

They tell me they are desperate for light and hope, that the pain lives on every day. And that, in many cases, reading *One Tuesday Morning* gave them a reason to believe again, a reason to turn back to God and their families after being consumed by pain, grief—and even hatred.

I thank each one of you who wrote those letters, because it was your story that I had to complete in this book. Not literally, of course. *Beyond Tuesday Morning* is fictional, and any similarity to real-life people or situations is purely coincidental. But I pray that the hurting people in New York find hope the way Jamie Bryan does in this sequel.

The fact is, with God, the story need not end in grief and despair but with *life*. I pray you'll find that message in this book.

Also thanks to my brilliant editor, Karen Ball, and to marketing expert Sue Brower, and to all my friends at Zondervan Publishing. Thank you for taking my idea about a story of life springing from the ashes of September 11 and helping it become what it is today. Also, a thanks to Cheryl Orefice who listened while I brainstormed the possibilities of *Beyond Tuesday Morning*.

A special thanks to my mother, Anne Kingsbury, who is also my assistant. You have a mind like mine and a heart for the ministry these books have become. Your presence in my life is heaven sent. I love you, Mom. I couldn't do my job without you. And to my father, Ted, who continues to be my greatest cheerleader. Dad, remember when I was writing poetry as a teenager, and you told me I could do anything with God's help? Even becoming an author? Well, I believed you—and look what God has done! I love you more every day.

Thanks also to my agent, Rick Christian. Rick, you pray for me and push me and protect me in ways that go beyond my highest expectations, proving I'm the most blessed writer of all. I stand amazed at your talents—and grateful that beyond anything in the publishing world, you desire God's will for my life, that I serve Him, that I have time for my beloved husband and children, and that I listen to His call. How amazing it is to have found you!

When it comes to crunch time, and I find myself pouring out my heart on deadline, lots of people come together to fill in the gaps. With six kids, it would be impossible otherwise. And so a warm and heartfelt thanks to my husband Donald, my kids—who don't mind having tuna sandwiches for a week on end, my sister Tricia, my parents again, and my good friends Cindy Weil, the Schmidt family, the Chapmans, Thayne Guymon, and Aaron Hisel, all of whom have on occasion caught frogs with Austin in my place.

Thanks also to my special prayer warriors, Ann Hudson, Sylvia Wallgren, Sonya Fitzpatrick, Marcia Bender, Christine Wessel, Teresa Thacker, and so many others who have written to me with promises of prayer. I feel you lifting my ministry up to Jesus time and time again. Sometimes with every breath. I couldn't do this work without your support. Please, please, please keep praying.

And a thanks to my extended family, and to my friends Randy and Vicky and Lila Graves, Bobbi and Tika Terret, John and Melinda Chapman, Mark and Marilyn Atteberry, Kathy Santschi, and my many friends at New Heights Church, Christian Youth Theater, and at the local schools. Your encouragement, love, and support are a constant source of strength.

Also thanks to my retail family across the U.S. and Canada. I've met so many of you—store owners, managers, and frontliners—these past few years, and I still mean what I said back then. You are the other half of what I do. I'm so grateful for the way you've partnered with me. Please know that I continue to send people your way, and that I will always pray for your ministry in books.

Finally, thanks to God Almighty. He is the reason any of this is possible. The words are His, the ideas are His, the gift is His. I pray I might remain obedient to all He is asking of me in this season of writing. Thank You, God . . . thank You.

ONE

She was surviving; the commute proved that much.

Jamie Bryan took her position at the far end of the Staten Island Ferry, pressed her body against the railing, eyes on the place where the Twin Towers once stood. She could face it now, every day if she had to. The terrorist attacks had happened, the World Trade Center had collapsed, and the only man she'd ever loved had gone down with them.

Late fall was warmer than usual, and the breeze across the water washed over Jamie's face. If she could do this—if she could make this journey three times a week while seven-year-old Sierra was at school—then she could get through another long, dark night. She could face the empty place in the bed beside her, face the longing for the man who had been her best friend, the one she'd fallen for when she was only a girl.

If she could do this, she could do anything.

Jamie looked at her watch. Nine-fifteen, right on schedule.

Three times a week the routine was the same. From Staten Island across the harbor on the ferry, up through the park, past the brick walls that after September 11 were plastered with pictures of missing people, into the heart of lower Manhattan's financial district, past the cavernous crater where the Twin Towers had stood, to St. Paul's. The little church was a strangely out-of-place stone chapel with a century-old cemetery just thirty yards from the pit. A chapel that, for months after the attacks, had been a café, a hospital, a meeting place, a counseling office, a refuge, a haven to firefighters and police officers and rescue workers and volunteers, a place to pray and be prayed for. A place that pointed people to God.

All the things a church should be.

Never mind the plans for a new World Trade Center, or the city's designs for an official memorial. Never mind the tourists gathered at the ten-foot chain-link fence around the pit or the throngs gawking at the pictorial timeline pinned along the top of the fence—photos of the Twin Towers' inception and creation and place in history. Souvenir picture books might be sold around the perimeter of the pit, but only one place gave people a true taste of what had happened that awful day.

St. Paul's.

The ferry docked, and Jamie was one of the first off. When it was raining or snowing she took a cab, but today she walked. Streets in lower Manhattan teemed as they always had, but there was something different about the people. It didn't matter how many years passed, how many anniversaries of the attacks came and went.

The people of New York City would never be the same.

Yes, they were busy, still driven to climb the ladders or make a name for themselves in New York City. But for the most part they were more likely to make eye contact, and when they did, they were more likely to smile or nod or give some sort of sign that the bond was still there, that a city couldn't go through something like New Yorkers went through September 11 and not be changed forever.

Jamie breathed in hard through her nose and savored the sweet mix of seawater and city air. Jake would've liked this, the way she was facing the situation, allowing her pain to work for good in the lives of others. She had lived in paralyzing fear for so long, but now—now that she'd lost Jake—she could face anything. Not in her own strength, but because Jake's faith lived deep within her.

Funny how she'd come to be a volunteer at St. Paul's.

It was Captain Hisel's idea. He'd been Jake's boss, his mentor. He'd found Jake—or the man he *thought* was Jake—in the aftermath of the collapse of the towers. Of course the man hadn't been Jake at all but Eric Michaels, a Los Angeles businessman who came into Jamie's life by mistake. A man she believed was her husband for three agonizing months.

A man who'd gone home to his family three years ago without looking back. And rightfully so. Jamie had told only a few people the details of that tender, tragic time. Captain Hisel was one of them.

The captain became a special friend in the months and years since the terrorist attacks. At first they shared an occasional Sunday dinner, but since shortly after the first anniversary of the attacks they were together at least twice a week, volunteering at St. Paul's and sharing lunch or dinner. He was *Aaron* to her now, and the two of them had everything in common.

Or at least it seemed that way.

Jamie turned a corner and saw the old cemetery. It was clean now, free of the ash and debris that had gathered around the tombstones and remained there for months after the attacks. The island of Manhattan was a different place since that terrible Tuesday morning, more vulnerable, less cocksure. But warmer too. Stronger. For most of America, time might've dimmed the horror of what happened to New York City when the Twin Towers fell. But those who were there would always remember. The connection it gave Manhattan residents was undeniable.

A few feet in front of her, a street vendor nodded. "Nice day."

"Yes, it is." Jamie smiled and kept walking.

See. There it was again. Before September 11, a vendor wouldn't have made eye contact unless he wanted to push a hot dog or a bag of caramelized almonds. Now? Now the man was familiar. She saw him every time she volunteered at St. Paul's; he probably knew where she was headed, what she was doing.

Everyone in lower Manhattan knew about St. Paul's.

Jamie crossed the street, stopped, and turned—same as she did every day. Before she could enter St. Paul's Chapel, before she could open her heart to the picture-taking tourists and the quietly grieving regulars who couldn't stay away, she had to see for herself that the towers were really gone. It was part of the ritual. She had to look across the street at the grotesque gargantuan hole where the buildings once stood, had to remind herself why she was here and what she was doing, that terrorists really had flown airplanes into the World Trade Center and obliterated the buildings—and two thousand lives.

Because Jake had been one of those people, coming to St. Paul's kept him alive in some ways. Being at Ground Zero, helping out . . .

that was something Jake would've done. It was the very thing he'd been doing when he died.

Jamie let her gaze wander up into the empty sky, searching unseen floors and windows. Had he been on the way up—he and his best schoolboy buddy, Larry—trying to reach victims at the top? Or had he been partway down? She narrowed her eyes. If only God would give her a sign, so she would know exactly where to look.

She blinked and the invisible towers faded. Tears welled in her heart, and she closed her eyes. *Breathe, Jamie. You can do this. God, help me do this.*

A deep breath in through her nose. Exhale . . . slow and steady. *God . . . help me.*

My strength is sufficient for you, daughter.

She often prayed at this stage of the routine, and almost as often she felt God whispering to her, coaxing her, helping her along as a father might help his little girl. The way Jake had helped Sierra.

The quiet murmurs in the most hurting part of her soul were enough. Enough to give her strength and desire and determination to move ahead, to go through the doors of St. Paul's and do her part to keep the vigil for all she lost more than three years ago.

She turned her back to the pit and took determined steps beside the black wrought iron fence bordering the cemetery, around the corner to the small courtyard at the front of the chapel. The hallowed feeling always hit her here, on the cobbled steps of the little church. How many firefighters had entered here in the months after the attacks, firemen looking for food or comfort or a shoulder to cry on? How many had passed through it since the building had reopened, looking for hope or answers or a reason to grieve the tragedy even if it had never touched them personally?

Just inside the doors, Jamie turned to the left and stopped. There, scattered over a corner table, was a ragtag display of hundreds of items: yellowed photos, keepsakes, and letters written to victims of the attacks. She scanned the table, saving his picture for last. Beneath the photo of a balding man holding a newborn baby, the grin on his face ear to ear: *Joe, we're still waiting for you to come home* . . . Scribbled atop a wedding photo: *You were everything to me, Cecile; you still are* . . . Tacked to the side of a wallet-sized picture of a young FDNY guy:

Your ladder boys still take the field every now and then but it's not the same without you. Yesterday Saul hit a homer and every one of us looked up. Are you there?

Every time Jamie did this, her eyes found different letters, different snippets of pain and aching loss scattered across the display. But always she ended in the same place. At Jake's picture and the letter written by their daughter, Sierra.

Jake was so handsome, his eyes brilliant blue even in the poorly lit corner. *Jake . . . I'm here, Jake.* When there weren't too many people working their way into the building, she could stand there longer than usual. This was one of those days. Her eyes locked on her husband's, and for a moment he was there again, standing before her, smiling at her, holding his arms out to her.

Her fingers moved toward the picture, brushing the feathery photo paper as if it were Jake's face, his skin.

"Jake . . ."

For the briefest moment she was sure she could hear him. *Jamie, I'm not gone, I'm here. Come see for yourself.*

She drew her hand back and wrapped her arms around her waist. People had caught her touching his picture before; it made the volunteer coordinators nervous. As if maybe she wasn't ready to comfort others when she was still so far from healed herself.

She didn't mean to touch the photo; it just happened. Something about his eyes in the picture made him seem larger than life, the way he'd been before . . .

Before.

That was it, wasn't it? Life before September 11, and life after it. Two completely different lives. There were times when she thought she could hear Jake. His voice still rang in the corridors of her heart, the way it always would. Tears blurred her eyes and she gritted her teeth. She wouldn't break down here, not now. On his birthday or their anniversary, maybe. On the anniversary of September 11, of course. But if she was going to keep Jake's memory alive, she couldn't break down every time she volunteered.

She glanced at the letter, the one Sierra had written a few weeks ago on the third anniversary of the attack. Her daughter's other letters were safe in a scrapbook, a keepsake for Sierra so she wouldn't forget the closeness she'd shared with Jake. Every few months Sierra wrote a new note, and that one would replace the old one on the display table. The letter showed that Sierra still didn't know how her father had died. As far as she knew, her daddy didn't die on September 11 but three months later. In a fire, trying to save people trapped inside. It was a half-truth; the best Jamie could do under the circumstances.

She just hadn't known how to tell Sierra that the man who'd been living with them for three months wasn't really her father but a stranger. In the three years since Eric Michaels left them, Jamie had yet to figure out a way to talk about the subject. For that matter, Sierra still had a picture of herself standing next to Eric. Once, a little more than a year ago, Jamie had tried to take it down. She could still see the look on her daughter's face when she came running down the stairs into the kitchen, her eyes red with tears.

"My picture of me and Daddy is gone!"

Jamie felt awful about that one. She'd gone up with Sierra and pretended to look for it. That night while her daughter slept, Jamie took it from the closet where she'd hidden it and placed it on Sierra's dresser again. Right next to Jake's fire helmet.

Two other times she'd tried to replace it with other photos, pictures that actually were of Sierra and Jake.

"The one after Daddy got hurt is too sad," she'd tell Sierra. "Let's put it away, okay?"

But Sierra would move the other photos to her bookshelves, keeping the one of her and Eric on her dresser. "That's the last picture of me and Daddy. I want it there forever. Please, Mommy, don't make me move it."

The memory lifted.

Sierra had never even been to St. Paul's; she didn't know that's where her mother volunteered her time. The whole story about Eric and his time with them was getting harder to stand by. Deception wasn't Jamie's style, and lately she'd been feeling that one day soon she'd have to tell Sierra the truth. Her daughter deserved that much.

Jamie worked her gaze along her daughter's neat handwriting and read the letter for the hundredth time.

Dear Daddy, how are you doing up in heven? I'm doing good down here; I'm in second grade, and Mommy says I'm smartst in my class. But I'm not that smart cuz I have some things I don't know. Like how come you had to go to heven when I need you so much rite here? How come you had to help those peple in that fire? Why culdnt they wok out by themselfs. Somtimes I clos my eys and I remember how you lookd. Somtimes I remember budrfly kisses. But somtimes I forget. I love you. Sierra.

Sometimes she forgets.

That was the hardest part of all lately. The chapel entrance was empty, and Jamie closed her eyes. *God, don't let either of us forget Jake. He's with You, still alive somewhere in Paradise with You. But until we can all be together again, help Sierra remember him, God. Please. Help her—*

Someone tapped her shoulder, and she spun around, her breath in her throat. "Aaron!" She stepped back from the display table and forced a smile. "Hi."

"Hey." He backed up toward the wooden pews that filled the center of the chapel. "Someone wants to—"

Aaron looked past her at the picture of Jake, as if he'd only just realized the reason why she was standing there. For a long while he said nothing, then he looked at her, his eyes filled with a familiar depth. "I'm sorry. I didn't realize you were—"

"No, it's okay." She slipped her hands in the pockets of her sweater. "I was reading Sierra's letter. It's been three years; she's forgetting Jake."

Aaron bit his lip and let his gaze fall to the floor.

"It was bound to happen." She gave a slight shrug. The corners of her mouth lifted some, but the smile stopped there. "She was only four when he died."

"I know." A respectful quiet fell between them. "Still hard to believe he's gone."

"Yes." Once more she glanced at Jake's picture. "Still hard to believe."

She felt strangely awkward, the way she had back in high school when some boy other than Jake smiled at her or flirted with her. But

Aaron wasn't flirting with her, and she wasn't in high school . . . and Jake was dead.

But not really; not when he lived in her memory as fully as he'd once lived in her home.

No wonder the strange feeling, the hint of guilt at being caught looking at the picture of her husband. She'd felt this way before on occasion, though only when she was with Aaron. Even so, she refused to make too much of her emotions. They were bound to be all over the board, even if she and Aaron were only friends.

He nodded his head toward the center of the chapel. "There's a lady in the front pew; she could use your help. Husband was a cop, died in the collapse." His eyes met hers and held. Concern shone through, and the awkward feeling disappeared. "You ready?"

"Ready." Jamie fell in beside him and headed down one of the pews toward the other side of the chapel. She wanted to glance once more at Jake's picture, but she didn't.

He pointed to a blonde woman in the front row. "You got it?"

Jamie nodded. "What about you?"

"Over there." He glanced toward the back of the chapel. The memorial tables framed the perimeter of the room. A couple in their seventies stood near the back wall. "Tourists. Lots of questions."

They shared a knowing look—this was what they did at St. Paul's: being there for the people who came through the doors, whatever their reason—then they turned and went their separate ways.

With slow, hushed steps, Jamie came alongside the blonde woman. Many of the widows who visited St. Paul's had been there before, but this one wasn't familiar. Jamie sat down and waited until the woman looked at her.

"Hi, I'm Jamie Bryan; I'm a volunteer."

The woman's eyes were red and swollen, and though she opened her mouth, no words came. She lowered her head into her hands, and a few quiet sobs worked their way through her body.

Jamie put her hand on the woman's back. The woman was in her late forties, Jamie guessed, heavyset with an ocean of pain welling within her. When the woman's tears subsided, she sniffed and found Jamie's eyes. "Does . . . the pain ever go away?"

This was the hard part. Jamie was here at St. Paul's for one reason: to offer hope to those devastated by the losses of September 11. The problem was just what Martha White, the volunteer coordinator, had warned her from the beginning. She couldn't work through her own pain by giving advice to people about theirs.

"I'm fine," she'd told Martha. "I'm working through it, but I'm fine at St. Paul's."

Martha looked doubtful. "You tell me if it's too much." She wagged a motherly finger at Jamie. "You're a victim same as everyone else."

The coordinator's words came back to Jamie now, and she swallowed hard. What had the weeping woman just asked her? Did the pain ever go away?

Jamie looked from the woman to the front of the church, the place where the old ornate cross stood like an anchor. Without taking her eyes from it, Jamie gave a slow shake of her head. "No. The pain doesn't go away." She turned back to the woman. "But God helps us learn how to live with it."

Another wave of tears hit the woman. Her face contorted, and she pinched the bridge of her nose. "It still . . . feels like September 12. Sometimes I think it always will."

A strength rose from within Jamie. Every time she'd been needed in a situation like this one, God had delivered. Every time. She turned so she could see the woman better. "Tell me about your husband."

"He was a cop." She lifted one shoulder and ran the back of her hands beneath her eyes. "Everyone's always talking about the firemen, but the cops took a hit too."

Jamie had heard this before from the wives of other police officers. "Have you been around the chapel yet?"

"I just started when . . ." She held her breath, probably stifling another wave of sobs.

"It's okay to cry."

"Thank you." The woman's shoulders shook again. "This chapel . . . That's why I'm crying." She searched Jamie's eyes. "I didn't think anyone cared until I came here, and now . . ."

"Now you know the truth."

"Yes." The woman grabbed a quick breath and stared at a poster on a wall overhead. *Oklahoma Cares.* Beneath the banner title were hundreds of handprints from children who had experienced the bombing of the Murrah Building in Oklahoma City. One line read, *We love our police!* "I didn't come before because I didn't want to be angry at anyone. But this is where I need to be; I should've come a hundred times by now."

"I'm Jamie." She held out her hand, and the woman across from her took it. "What's your name?"

"Cindy Grammar." The woman allowed the hint of a smile. "Is it just me, or do you feel something here?"

"I feel it. Everyone who comes inside feels it."

"It's the only place where the memory of all those people still lives. You know, as a group."

"Exactly." Jamie folded her hands in her lap and looked around the chapel at the banners, then at the memorabilia lining the walls— items collected from the edge of the pit or left near the chapel steps. One day the city would have an official memorial to the victims of September 11. But for now, those two thousand people were remembered with grace and love at St. Paul's.

"This city loved my Bill. I could sense that the minute I walked in here."

"You're right." Jamie gave Cindy's hand a gentle squeeze. "And no one will forget what he did that day. He was a hero, Cindy. Same as the firefighters."

The conversation continued for nearly an hour before the woman felt ready to finish making her way around the inside of the building. By then her eyes were dry and she had shared the story of how she'd met her husband, how much they'd loved each other. Jamie knew the names of the woman's two sons, and the fact that they both played high school football.

"Thanks, Jamie." The woman's expression was still filled with sorrow, but now it was also tinged with gratitude and peace. "I haven't felt this good in months."

Jamie's heart soared. Her job was to bring hope to the hopeless, and to do it in Jake's name. Again and again and again. She took Cindy's hands again. "Let's pray, okay?"

The woman squirmed. "I'm . . . I'm not sure about God, Jamie."

"That's okay." Jamie's smile came from her heart, from the place that understood God the way Jake had always wanted her to understand. "God's sure about you."

"Really?" Doubt colored Cindy's eyes.

"Really. We don't have to pray; just let me know." Jamie bit her lip, waiting.

"I want to." The woman knit her brow together. "I don't know what to say."

Jamie gave the woman's hand a gentle squeeze. "I'll say it." She bowed her head and began, the way she had dozens of times over the past two years. "God, we come to You because You know all things. You are sovereign and mighty and You care about us deeply. Help Cindy believe in You, Lord. Help her to understand that You hold a flashlight as we walk through the valley of the shadow of death. And let her find new life in You. In Jesus' name, amen."

Jamie opened her eyes.

A fresh sort of peace filled Cindy's face. She leaned closer and hugged Jamie. "I'll be back."

Jamie smiled. "I know."

The woman stood and headed for the outer rim of the chapel with a promise to return some day so that maybe the two could talk—and even pray again.

When she was finally alone, Jamie's hands trembled. Her legs were stiff from sitting for so long. Meetings like that were emotionally draining, and Jamie wanted water before she talked to anyone else.

But before she could reach the stairs, another woman approached her, four young teenage girls in tow, each holding a notebook. "Hi, maybe you could help us."

"Of course." Jamie gave the group her full attention. "What would you like to know?"

"We're a homeschool group and—" she looked at the girls— "each of the students has a list of questions for you. They want to know how St. Paul's was instrumental in serving the people who cleaned up the pile of debris after the towers collapsed."

"Okay." Jamie smiled, but something grated against her heart. The pile of debris? Jake had been in that pile. It was okay for *her* to call it that, but these people were ... they were on a quest for details, like so many reporters. She ignored her irritation and directed the group to the nearest pew. "Let's sit here and we can talk."

School groups were common, and always needed help from volunteers. They wanted to know how many hundreds of gallons of water were given out—more than four thousand; how many different types of services were offered free to the work crew—podiatry, massage therapy, counseling, chiropractic care, nursing care, and optometry among others; and what sort of impact did St. Paul's and its volunteers have on the work crew—a dramatic one.

The questions continued, but they weren't out of line. By the time Jamie was finished talking with the group, she regretted her first impression. The girls were well-mannered, the parent sensitive to the information Jamie shared. It was nearly noon when the group went on their way. Jamie scanned the pews first, and then the perimeter of the chapel. She was thirsty, but the visitors came first. The week she trained as a volunteer Martha had made that clear.

"Look for fires to put out." A tiny woman with a big mouth and a heart as vast as the Grand Canyon, Martha was particularly serious about this detail. "Look for the people breaking down and weeping, the ones sitting by themselves in a pew. Those are the ones you should approach. Just so they know you're there."

No fires at the moment.

Aaron was across the room, talking to another pair of tourists. At least his conversations looked less intense than the one she'd had with Cindy. She trudged up the stairs to the volunteers' break room. An open case of water bottles sat on the table; she took one and twisted off the lid. Chairs lined the area, but she was tired of sitting. She leaned against the stone wall and looked up at the aged stained glass.

Funny, the way Martha had said it. *Fires to put out.* It was one more way Jamie was keeping Jake's memory alive. No, she didn't deal with flames and fire hoses. But she was putting out fires all the same. He would've been proud of her.

In fact, if he'd survived, he'd be right here at St. Paul's with her. All the more reason to volunteer as long as the chapel was open. It gave her purpose, and in that sense it wasn't only a way to keep Jake's memory, his sacrifice, alive.

It was a way to keep herself alive too.

TWO

From the moment Clay Michaels started his shift, he felt strange about the day, as if God was trying to tell him something—to warn him. The unsettling sensation churned in his gut and worked through his spine and neck and brain. A knowing, almost, that things weren't right. Or maybe worse. Maybe something awful was about to happen.

Clay wasn't sure exactly what the feeling was, but it bothered him.

All day, while he hunted down the usual speeders on the Ventura Freeway corridor between the San Fernando Valley and the beach exits, the feeling weighed on him. Each time he approached a car his senses went on heightened alert. A college kid late for his classes at Pepperdine; a business guy making time to his office in Camarillo; a carload of tourists unaware of the speed limits. The stops had been routine, nothing more.

Still the feeling stayed with him.

At lunchtime he picked up a McDonald's salad, drove to one of his lookout spots near the westbound Las Virgenes exit, and settled back into his seat.

Maybe the feeling meant it was time to move on.

He'd been to Eric and Laura's house the night before, and the scene had been the same as always. Or the same as it had been since Eric returned home from New York City. Eric and Laura holding hands; Eric and Laura stealing a kiss or two in the kitchen; Eric and Laura sharing a private glance or a joke or an embrace when they thought no one was looking.

Clay tried not to notice. He was happy for them, grateful that the horrific events of September 11 had wrought only good for two people he loved so dearly. Still, he couldn't help but wonder . . .

He took a bite of his salad and watched a car speed past. *Lucky day, buddy.* Only something dangerous would pull Clay away during a break. Especially when the strange feeling was still gnawing at him. It must've stemmed from his regrets about Laura, about the fact that their closeness had dissolved—as it had to—the minute Eric walked back through the door. The thing was, too often Clay caught himself watching Laura, remembering the way things were when Eric was gone, when they thought he was dead.

Clay had gone to college in the Midwest and he'd only been back in Los Angeles a few months when the terrorist attacks occurred. After September 11, while they grieved Eric's loss, he and Laura grew closer every day. They even traveled to New York City together to search for him.

When it was finally obvious that he had died in the collapsed towers, they went home, and the bond they shared grew even stronger. Clay had been convinced that he and Laura would wind up together. After all, they'd known each other since high school. Laura had been his first crush.

Josh—Eric and Laura's son—connected with Clay immediately, barely missing his father. And Laura had relied on him for everything. But that was not a surprise. Back then, Eric was a sorry excuse for a husband and father. He'd been obsessed with climbing the corporate ladder, making another deal, traveling to Manhattan as often as the company's president demanded. All at Laura and Josh's expense.

Clay took another bite of his salad and rolled down his window. The air smelled of late summer and fresh-cut grass.

Yes, he'd been shocked to discover Eric was a lousy husband and father. While he was away at school, he assumed things were great between Eric and Laura. Laura was golden, a beautiful woman with a tenderness and compassion that worked its way through everything she said or did. She was worth more than any job, and Clay intended to tell Eric so.

He never got the chance.

Instead his brother headed for New York City and disappeared from their lives for three months. When he returned, he was a changed man, the victim of amnesia and mistaken identity.

Clay stared at the rolling hills in the distance and watched a hawk land on a lone oak tree. God was here; he could feel it. Never mind the strange certainty that something bad was about to happen, God was here. That was all that mattered.

God . . . what You did with Eric . . . it was all part of Your plan, wasn't it?

Even now, after three years, he could hardly believe what had happened to his big brother. The story was as strange as it was miraculous. Mistaken for an FDNY guy, a man who apparently loved God and his family in a way that should have earned him honors, Eric was taken to the man's home and family. For weeks he'd done nothing but read the man's Bible, his journal, his notes on loving his wife and their daughter.

When Eric finally remembered who he really was, the other man's wife helped Eric find his way home. He didn't talk about the woman much, but she must have been something, first surviving the shock that Eric wasn't her husband, and then helping him return to Laura and Josh. And though Eric never spoke about his time with the woman, one thing was certain: he was a changed man. Because of that, Laura was the happiest woman in the world, and Josh the happiest eleven-year-old boy.

And Clay?

He dated now and then, but no one ever worked their way into his heart the way Laura had. Though his feelings for her weren't right, they were there. And that made it hard to find someone else, someone he could fall in love with and marry and start a family with. The way he dreamed every day of doing.

Clay exhaled hard and tossed the empty plastic salad container into the backseat. He was about to take a swig from his iced tea when his radio crackled to life.

"Urgent! Calling all cars!" The code that followed told Clay the unthinkable had happened. A carjacking and fatal shooting at the gas station at Las Virgenes exit and Ventura Freeway. Suspect a twenty-five-year-old Hispanic male, five-ten, muscular, driving the victim's blue 2002 Chevy Tahoe. "Suspect is headed west on 101. Suspect is armed and highly dangerous. Repeat, suspect is armed and dangerous."

Clay straightened as a rush of adrenaline shot through him. He started his car as he grabbed the radio receiver. He identified himself and confirmed that he was at the location and headed toward the suspect.

Other officers gave their location and stated their intent to begin pursuit immediately and provide backup. But none of them were within ten minutes of Clay's location. He would be first on the scene.

"God, go with me."

He whispered that prayer every time he took a call, but this time there was urgency in his voice. He'd known, hadn't he? That something would go down today? He flipped his siren on, spun his car around, and darted across the overpass and down the on-ramp onto the westbound lanes of the freeway. The dispatcher's words screamed at him again. *Armed and highly dangerous.* He leaned toward the windshield, both hands on the steering wheel.

Chases were fairly common on California freeways. Chases involving a crazy man who'd already killed one person were not. It took three minutes for Clay to spot the blue Chevy tearing down the freeway, weaving in and out of traffic. This was their guy. But without backup . . .

He spoke into the receiver again. "This is Officer Michaels; I've got the suspect in sight. How close is backup?"

Another series of crackling noises filled the car. "We've got CHP officers fifteen minutes away. LAPD detectives ten minutes behind you and catching up. Wait if you can."

If he could?

Too late. The suspect must have seen the red lights and heard the siren. He was picking up speed, darting in and out of all three lanes, jeopardizing everyone on the road. That meant Clay had two choices. Pursue him a few feet from his bumper to help warn drivers he was approaching, or back off until he had assistance. But backing off didn't guarantee the man would slow down or drive more responsibly. He'd just killed a person; he wouldn't mind if someone else died.

Clay decided to pursue. It was his job, and he wouldn't back off just because he was alone.

He maneuvered his patrol car through the traffic until he was a few yards from the suspect's bumper. He could see the man looking over his shoulder, but he couldn't make out his face. Then the man waved his weapon out the window. It wasn't any ordinary handgun; it was an AK-47. The man aimed it at the sky and fired—clear warning that he intended to kill whoever tried to stop him. Clay tightened his grip on the steering wheel, his palms sweaty. Still no backup in sight.

Come on, guys . . . hurry.

His foot pushed harder at the gas pedal, moving his patrol car even closer to the suspect. He was in firing range, for sure. If the man were able to fire the machine gun at him while still maintaining his high speeds, Clay would already be dead.

Cars were pulling over now, the way he'd wanted them to do. Amazing what the sound of a siren or the sight of a flashing light could accomplish. Clay glanced at his speedometer. Nearly a hundred miles per hour.

At that instant, the suspect darted across all three lanes of traffic, sped up the hill at the Kanan Road off-ramp, and made a sharp, squealing left turn. He bumped two cars traveling in the right lane, but kept going.

Clay pressed the button on his radio receiver. "Suspect has exited the freeway at Kanan Road, heading west."

"Copy. Backup is closing in, a few minutes away."

Clay gritted his teeth. *Please, God . . . I need help. Hurry them up.* He heard no holy whispers or answers. But the strange feeling grew stronger. Whatever was up ahead, he had to be ready. *God, be with me, whatever happens.*

They sped past a series of condos and buildings as other cars pulled to the side or darted out of their way. Again the suspect waved his gun out the window, and Clay checked his rearview mirror. Nothing.

They neared the twisting turns of the canyon, turns that would force Clay to slow down or risk flying over the edge. Suddenly the suspect jerked his car onto the gravelly shoulder, kicking up a cloud of rocks and dust. Clay was still close behind him, and for a moment he couldn't see anything. He heard the debris hit his windshield as he slammed on his brakes.

The cloud settled, and he saw the man was out of his car, the assault weapon trained on Clay's vehicle. He was going to fire before Clay had a chance to get out of his car, let alone grab his revolver. The cloud of dust and rocks had been the suspect's cover, and now Clay was trapped.

Here he sat, the barrel of an AK-47 pointed straight at him, and he could only think of one thing: *I knew this was coming.*

He ducked just as the man braced himself and fired.

A spray of bullets peppered Clay's windshield, shattering the glass and piercing where he'd been sitting just seconds ago. Clay cocked his revolver, glanced over the dash and fired. He dropped back down as the suspect sprayed another round of bullets. This time they came at closer range, louder, more fierce. The man's footsteps were closing in. Clay gritted his teeth. What could he do? At this close range, he couldn't fire without making himself a target. He raised his hand above the dash and fired blindly. Again the man let loose a burst of gunfire. He was closer now. It was only a matter of time.

How could God let it end this way? Death before he'd ever really found life—the sort of life he'd wanted, with a wife and a family. Senseless death because of a crazy man with an assault weapon. Clay's breathing came in short bursts. *God . . . no! Help me, please!*

At that instant he heard two things: sirens and footsteps, both coming closer. Backup was almost here. A few more seconds and everything would be okay. The man shouted something in Spanish, something about having a bad life.

Anger welled up in Clay. He wasn't going to sit there and wait to be shot at; if he was going down, he'd go down fighting. *God . . . be with me.* He peered over the dash and spotted the man, ten yards away and closing. The suspect saw Clay too. The man pulled the trigger just as Clay fired once—straight at the man's chest—then ducked to the floorboard area.

Even as another spray of bullets ripped through his car, Clay heard the sirens getting louder. His heart pounded. He listened, but he couldn't hear the man coming closer. Had he shot him? Had he actually killed a man? The sirens were right behind him now, and he heard two cars pull onto the shoulder, then the sound of doors slamming. A voice yelled, "Police, don't move!"

Someone was running up from behind, along the passenger side of Clay's car. It could be the suspect, but not likely. Still, Clay aimed his revolver at the opposite door just as Detective Joe Reynolds flung it open and looked inside. "Michaels, you okay?"

"The suspect?"

"He's dead." The officer was a black man, a former attorney who'd grown tired of the corporate world and took up police work. He was a detective now, one of the best. He worked the west end and had an office down the hall from the lunchroom. Clay considered him his closest friend in the department.

"I . . . I killed him?"

"You did everyone a favor."

Clay's body shook as relief worked its way through him. "A few more seconds and . . ."

"What'd he do, pull over and come after you?"

"Yeah." Clay set his gun on the seat and pushed himself up. "The guy . . . he was crazy."

"Must've been flying over a hundred."

"He was."

Reynolds was still out of breath. "We got here fast as we could. He was dying on the ground, still reaching for his weapon when we pulled up." He ran his fingers over the bullet holes scattered across the front seat. "Someone must be looking out for you, Michaels. AK-47s don't usually miss."

It was true. Even though he'd ducked into the floorboard, he should've been hit. Weapons like the assault rifle spray their bullets, and one easily could have ripped through the dash and killed him. "I was praying the whole time."

Reynolds cocked his head. "I'd say the Big Guy heard you."

Clay glanced around and saw another officer, one he didn't know as well, in his patrol car on the radio. Probably calling for someone to come get the body.

Clay looked at the covered figure lying a few yards from his car. Nausea rushed up in his belly. "First time I ever shot a suspect."

"They'll want you to take some time, a paid leave." Reynolds studied him. "Part of the investigation."

"Right." He'd had no choice, of course. The man would have killed him if he hadn't shot. In a situation like that—with a crazed suspect running at you, firing a gun—Clay had been taught there was just one way to do it: shoot to kill.

"You okay?" Reynolds brushed the glass off the passenger seat and sat down beside Clay, his feet hanging out of the car.

"Yeah, I guess." He couldn't take his eyes off the covered body. "I don't like how I feel."

"Look, Michaels—" Reynolds stared straight ahead, as though remembering something far away—"I've been on the other side of this game." He looked at Clay. "Let's say you miss. Let's say ol' crazy man takes you down instead of the other way around. He could be out on the streets shooting again in twenty, fifteen if the circumstances were right."

"Fifteen years?"

"I saw it all the time when I wore a suit and tie. All the time." Reynolds glared at the place where the body lay. "No cop likes to shoot his gun. But in this case it was your life or his and, well, let's just say things worked out right today. You handled him better than the courts could've." He gave Clay a halfhearted shove in the shoulder. "Of course, you didn't hear me say that."

Reynolds climbed out of the car and shut the door. Clay wasn't shaking anymore, but the ache in his stomach hadn't gone away. A man was dead because he'd fired his gun. The thought sank in. He'd killed a man on the job; the possibility that always exists for an officer had actually happened.

Clay looked down. He still had shattered glass on his pants. He climbed out of the car, dusted off the crumbly pieces, and leaned against his door. Reynolds was right. It was his life or the suspect's. And if he was honest with himself, in a small way it felt good to fire the gun at a man who'd already killed someone, who'd put every driver they'd passed on the freeway at risk. Yes, things had worked out for the best, and if he were faced with the situation again, he'd respond the same way.

But a man lay dead on the ground because of him. No matter how good and right his actions were, he still felt sick.

It took an hour for investigators to arrive and collect data, and for the body to be removed and taken to the morgue where an autopsy would be performed. During that time, Clay learned more information about the man. He'd crossed the border south of San Diego two days earlier, killing two border patrolmen in the process. Witnesses said they saw him heading south, and when police dogs lost his trail, the search was called off.

No one knew how he'd gotten from San Diego to the San Fernando Valley, but he stayed beneath police radar until the carjacking.

An investigating officer took a statement from Clay and assured him the process was routine. "Your car's shattered with bullets, Michaels. Don't sweat this for a minute."

When Clay got back to the office, Reynolds spotted him and nodded. "They want to see you in the office." He paused, his eyes full of concern. "After that, come see me. I have an idea."

The meeting with the brass was what Clay expected. He was being placed on paid leave until an investigation could be completed. Probably two to three weeks. He was already heading out of the office when his boss stopped him.

"Michaels."

"Yes, sir." Clay felt better than before, but he still didn't have an appetite.

The man tapped a pencil on his desk. "We all hate when this type of thing happens."

"Yes, sir."

"But in this case, I'm glad your aim was on." He leaned forward, eyes intense. "It would've killed me to lose you, Michaels. You're one of the best. Take the break and when you get back, if I have anything to do with it, you'll get a promotion."

A promotion? He'd wanted that since he started with the department. He should be celebrating with a victory fist or a shout. Something. But in light of the day's events, Clay managed only a sad smile. "Thanks, sir. I appreciate that."

The man's eyes clouded. "Don't beat yourself up, Michaels. You did the right thing."

"Okay." Clay held the man's gaze a few seconds more and then turned and headed through the door to Reynolds's office. He shut the door behind him.

"Paid leave?"

"Two or three weeks." Clay shrugged. "When I get back my office might be across from yours."

A grin played out across his friend's face. "I *knew* it. They asked me last week who I thought was ready."

"You told 'em me?" Clay sat down and planted his elbows on his knees.

"Nope, I told 'em Hardy down the hall." Reynolds chuckled. "Of course I told 'em you."

Clay stared out the window behind Reynolds and wondered. On a day like today, what would it be like to have someone to go home to? Someone to share the details of the chase and the gun battle, someone to hug him and hold him and spend three weeks' paid leave with. Someone to congratulate him for getting promoted.

Someone to comfort him for what he'd had to do.

"Michaels, you daydreaming again?" His friend raised one eyebrow and slid back from his desk. He kicked his feet up. "I asked you a question, and you just stare out the window like you're daffy or something."

"Sorry." Clay understood. Reynolds was trying to keep things light, helping take the focus off the shooting. "Ask again."

"I was saying I think I know where we can go for a vacation."

"Vacation?"

Reynolds pushed a file across the desk. "Take a look."

Clay opened it and read the flyer inside: *Detective Training Offered by New York's Finest.* Starting in late November and running through the second week of December, the NYPD was offering a series of workshops and on-the-job training for officers from anywhere in the United States.

"You can't take three weeks, can you?"

Reynolds smiled. "I can when it's part of my ongoing training."

"Hmmm." There was no one waiting at home for Reynolds, same as Clay. It wasn't something the man ever talked about, and Clay didn't ask. But on the man's desk was a small photograph of a pretty brown-skinned woman and a little boy with eyes like Reynolds's. Clay had the feeling the man had some hidden pain, a story he shared with no one.

"I already talked to the chief. He says he could count three weeks for your leave. Three weeks in the Big Apple, Michaels. Whaddaya say?"

The idea sounded better with every passing second. He'd wanted to get back to New York ever since the terrorist attacks—same as every police officer and firefighter he knew. But he hadn't had time. Besides, he knew it would be hard—looking at the crater, imagining the lives lost in a single morning. When he had time off, he usually went hunting with guys from the department or boating up at one of the northern California lakes. A trip to New York hadn't figured into his plans.

"Well?" Reynolds crossed his arms, looking proud of himself. "Can I call and sign us up?"

Clay stared at the flyer again. The department had a block of rooms in a hotel on Staten Island. An effort at saving money, no doubt. If the department picked up his bill, it would be a fantastic opportunity. He would come back ready to step into his new role, the sickening memories from earlier that day at least a little dimmer.

He looked at Reynolds. "The two of us, huh?"

"That's right." Reynolds dropped his feet to the floor. "Showing the New York boys how to get it done."

Clay closed the folder and tossed it back on the desk. "Let's do it."

That night when he was back home Clay didn't turn on the television, didn't take a swim in the community pool down the street, didn't do anything except run a mental tape of what happened that day. Every time guilt tried to say something, he stopped it with the truths others spoke to him all day long.

Reynolds telling him he'd done everyone a favor; his captain assuring him he was glad the outcome hadn't been different. The news that the suspect had killed two border patrol officers.

It was his life or the suspect's. Plain and simple.

By the time he turned in for the night, God had replaced his nausea with a certainty that he'd done the right thing. The only thing he could've done. He should be at peace with the situation and how it had played out.

But he wasn't.

Three weeks away would do him good—less because of his gun battle than because he needed a change of scenery. His last thoughts before he fell asleep were proof of that because they were even more wrong than the earlier ones involving the shooting. They were thoughts of his brother's wife. Wrong thoughts. Thoughts that had him wondering what would've happened if Eric had never come home, if he'd never found his way back.

And whether Laura ever wondered the same thing.

THREE

Jamie was back at St. Paul's, her second time that week.

Aaron worked the night shift, and on the days she was at the chapel, he wound up there too. It was just a few blocks from the station, so he would go home and catch some sleep when their shift ended after lunch.

It was still early. Aaron hadn't arrived yet, but a young woman sat in the center of the pews, crying. Jamie drew a deep breath. *God . . . give me the strength.* She kept her eyes on the woman and took soft, respectful steps toward her.

"Hello, I'm Jamie Bryan, a volunteer here." The woman was actually a teenage girl. In her hands was a picture of a middle-aged man in a suit and tie. The girl's father, no doubt. "Would you like to talk?"

The girl looked up, her eyes swollen and bloodshot. "It's his birthday." She held up the photo. "My father."

A pang of guilt stabbed at Jamie. At least this girl had somewhere to go, a place where her father's memory was honored. Sierra had the right to come here too. If the timing was right, if God gave her the words, she would tell her daughter soon. Maybe before Christmas.

Jamie sat beside the girl. She'd been trained to keep her questions minimal. That way the visitor would steer the conversation the direction they wanted to go. Her heart ached for the girl, who looked a little like Sierra might look in ten years. Long blonde hair, pretty face—and a hole in her heart where her daddy had been.

The girl sniffed and looked at the picture. "He wasn't supposed to go in that day. He was on vacation, but someone called and said they needed him." Her eyes lifted to Jamie's. "I told him I needed him more, but he . . ." She hung her head. "He thought I was teasing him. 'You have school,' he told me. He kissed . . . me on the forehead and said he'd see me that afternoon. After I got home from school. Our family was supposed to go away the next morning for a family reunion." She shook her head. "But it never ..."

Jamie slipped her arm around the girl. "I'm sorry." So much pain, so many wounded and battered hearts still wandering the streets of New York, searching for hope. Sometimes she wasn't sure she could take another day at St. Paul's, and yet moments like this, she knew. She was exactly where she was supposed to be, no matter how much it hurt. If she came to St. Paul's, she would never forget what Jake had done that awful Tuesday.

He might have been helping this girl's father, for all she knew.

Jamie gave the girl a light squeeze, a half hug that told her she wasn't alone, that anyone who stayed long at St. Paul's could understand the hurt she was feeling. Then she took her arm from the girl's shoulders and faced her. "Are you ... I guess I didn't get your name."

The girl looked at Jamie again. "Sami. Sami Taylor."

"Hi, Sami." Jamie's tone was soft. "Do you believe in Jesus, Sami?"

"I used to."

Jamie could almost hear herself telling Jake the same thing, back when he'd wanted nothing more than to share a Sunday morning church service with her. If she could have anything in the world it would be to tell him yes, just once. To go with him to church and sit beside him and pray to the God he'd always believed in. Her only comfort was that somehow, up in heaven, he had to know the truth, had to see that his prayers for her had been answered. She held her breath for a moment. *God ... she's just like I used to be. Give me the words.*

The girl spoke before Jamie had a chance. "When my dad was alive, we'd go to church every Sunday. My mom too. He was a rock, I guess. Sort of the anchor for our family."

She could've been describing Jake. "My husband was that way too."

"Your husband?"

"Yes." Jamie swallowed back the lump in her throat. "He was a firefighter." The past tense still got to her. Her eyes felt the sting of tears, but she blinked them away. "He was in the South Tower helping people when it collapsed."

"That's awful!" The girl's mouth hung open. "Were you ... were you married for very long?"

"Not long enough." Jamie tried to smile, tried to keep the conversation from going to the deep places where she would break down and cry. Not that it hadn't happened before, but it couldn't happen every day. And she didn't want it to happen now. "We have a daughter. She's seven now—in second grade."

"How can you ... how can you be here?" Sami waved her hand toward the memorabilia lining the walls. "I would never stop crying."

This time Jamie's smile was sad but easy. "I come because God gives me the strength."

"God let the towers fall." Her answer was quick, sharp.

"No, Sami." Jamie took the girl's hands in her own. "God is good. He has nothing to do with evil."

Fresh tears filled the girl's eyes and spilled onto her cheeks. She looked at the picture of her father again. "But He could've stopped it."

"There are some things we won't ever fully understand this side of heaven." Jamie squeezed the girl's hands. "What happened September 11 is one of them. But I know this ..." Jamie's voice lowered. She waited until Sami was looking at her. "I couldn't have survived it without faith in God. Faith that I found after my husband died, even though he prayed for me to find it every day while he was alive."

Sami's eyes widened. "So you didn't always believe?"

"No." Jamie released the girl's hands and leaned her shoulder against the hard back of the pew. "My parents died in a car accident when I was about your age. I stopped believing in God that day and didn't talk to Him again until three years ago."

The girl shifted and set the photo on her knee. She ran her fingers beneath her eyes. "We were very close." She looked at Jamie and stifled another sob. "My mom's a wonderful person, but my daddy knew me best." Her gaze fell to the picture again. "I miss him so much."

"Tell me something, Sami."

She looked up. "What?"

"Would your dad want you angry at God?" It was more than she would usually say, but that didn't matter. It was what Jake would've said. And since she did this in his honor, she would gently prod and push people back toward God as often as she had a chance.

The girl picked up the photo and held it tight against her chest. She hung her head and uttered a gut-wrenching whisper. "No."

"If your father loved God, then he's in heaven now. Probably grateful that you wound up here today."

Sami nodded. "I think I've missed God almost as much as I missed my dad. I had to . . . had to work at being mad at Him."

"I know." And she did. Jamie remembered a conversation she'd had with Jake not long before he died. He'd found out that she'd been asking Sierra about Sunday school. He wanted to know if maybe she'd changed her mind, if maybe she wanted to come one Sunday just to see what it was like. Just to find out if she still wanted to hold a grudge against God.

At the time she'd had to work to tell him no. It was her pride, really. The fact that she didn't want to need God, didn't want to love Him. But it wasn't that she didn't believe. No matter what she told herself about God not existing and about the Bible being made up of fine-sounding fairy tales, she always knew the truth. God was alive and waiting for her. Hounding her relentlessly until finally He used Jake's Bible and journal to catch her, to break down the walls and allow her the chance to run to His arms.

"It's just . . ." Sami lowered the photo so she could see it again. "I want to be with him on his birthday. And when I get married one day, I want him to walk down the aisle with me. I want it so bad."

"But you can't blame God that you won't have it, okay, Sami? God loves you very much. He loves your dad too." Jamie took the girl's hands again. "Let's pray, okay?"

"Okay."

They bowed their heads and Jamie prayed. "Suffering is a part of life, God. You showed us that on September 11. We almost never understand why." She hesitated, trying to keep her composure. "But we know this: You love us. You loved us so much You gave us Jesus. And no matter how much Sami's suffering right now, You're here holding her, speaking peace into her heart and soul." A Scripture came to mind. "Jeremiah 29:11 tells us that You know the plans You have for us. Help Sami remember that, God. Give her Your hope as she leaves this place, Your certainty that You haven't forgotten her, and that one day she'll see her father again."

There was a silence while Jamie waited. She was about to finish up when Sami cleared her throat. "I'm sorry, God. I hate trying to get through this without You. Plus . . ." She sniffed once more. "Plus You've got my dad with You. So please, Lord, tell him happy birthday for me. Please."

When they finished praying, Jamie hugged the girl and promised to keep praying for her. Before she left, Sami gave Jamie a lopsided grin. "I came here because it was something I could do for my father. But instead . . . my heavenly Father did something for me." She stood and touched Jamie's shoulder. "I wasn't expecting that."

After Sami left, Jamie looked across the chapel at Jake's picture. She could make it out from any spot in the building—maybe not the details of his handsome face, the strength in his jaw, or the sparkle in his eyes, but she could find it all the same.

Sami was right. St. Paul's was a place where the unexpected happened. It had been that way for three years, ever since the towers collapsed, leaving the old church completely unharmed. It was an unexpected rescue mission back then and, because of conversations like the one she'd just had, it was an unexpected rescue mission now.

She noticed Aaron talking with another volunteer near the television at the back of the chapel. But before she had a chance to tell him hello, two women approached her. They were FDNY widows, women who had been in before.

"Hi, Jamie." The first one smiled.

She couldn't remember their names, but she didn't want to say so. Instead she exhaled and rose to greet them. "Back again?"

The women looked tentatively at each other. Then the first one crossed her arms. "We want to see about becoming volunteers."

"Like you," the other woman said.

"Like me?"

Jamie could hear Martha's words of warning. "Most FDNY widows won't ever be ready to take on a job like volunteering at St. Paul's. Discourage women who want to be like you as much as possible, for their sakes."

Jamie had bristled at the coordinator's comment. "It's good for me; why wouldn't it be good for them?"

"You're the exception, Jamie. Trust me. For most people volunteering at St. Paul's wouldn't work them through the stages of grief, it would stall them."

"What if someone asks about it and I'm not sure?"

Martha had given her a wry sort of smile. "You'll know. Ask them a few questions. If they break down, they're not ready."

Jamie blinked at the women, hating what she was about to do. The questions she had to ask were like poking a pin at an open wound to see if it was healing. But if Martha was right, it was the only way to make sure the women were able to move past their own grief long enough to help strangers with theirs.

"Why don't you come this way and we'll talk about it." Jamie led the women back to the pews, to the same place where she'd been sitting with Sami a few moments earlier. She started with the more outspoken of the two. "I'm on your side, ladies, but sometimes people only think they're ready for volunteer work here." Her voice was low, discreet. "Can you each tell me what you've done to work through your losses?"

The first woman nodded. "I've been in counseling at my church for a year. Sometimes I take my children with me—so they can talk about their feelings."

"Do they remember their father?"

"Yes." The woman's eyes flooded. She folded her hand and stared at her lap for a moment. "The youngest doesn't, but the other three remember him."

"If someone sat across from you and told you they'd stopped believing in God because of what happened September 11, would you feel comfortable helping them find their faith again?"

This time the woman looked up, and a strength filled her eyes. "Absolutely. That's why I'm here. I believe God wants me to share His truth with people who come here hurting." She looked at her friend, and then back at Jamie. "The way you shared it with us the first time we came in."

Jamie patted the woman's shoulders. She was passing with flying colors. Usually by now widows who weren't ready would be breaking down, asking questions of their own. Questions they had a right to ask, but that proved they weren't ready to work at St. Paul's. Not this woman.

"I understand there's an application we have to fill out?" The strength in the woman's eyes was softened by a compassion that only came from knowing pain personally.

"Yes." Jamie hesitated. "I'm sorry. I remember you, of course, but I've forgotten your names. A lot of people come through here."

"I'm Janice." She nodded to her friend. "This is Beth."

"And Beth, what about you? Tell me about your husband."

She lifted a dainty shoulder. "I don't know; he was my hero, I guess."

"You were married a long time?" Just because Jamie was ready for work at the chapel didn't mean Beth was.

"We'd only been married three years. I was—" Her voice broke. She looked up at the cross and bit her lip. "I was expecting our first baby, our son, when he died."

"I'm sorry." Jamie leaned forward. "Would you feel comfortable talking about that with strangers?"

For a moment Beth said nothing, only kept her eyes glued to the cross. Then, as tears streamed down her cheeks, she gave a slow shake of her head. "No, his memory is too precious for that."

Jamie waited.

Beth looked at Janice and then at Jamie. "I guess I'm not ready for this. I'm sorry. I thought I was. I wanted to be ready."

"There are lots of things you can do, Beth, even if this isn't one of them." Jamie's heart ached for the woman. Next to her, Janice gave her friend a hug.

After a moment, Jamie handed Beth a tissue. When she was more composed she looked at Jamie. "What can I do? Everywhere I go, people have forgotten about September 11. It's as if it bothers them to remember that it ever happened at all. But I want to do something."

"You can go home and love that little boy. He's three years old, Beth. He needs you. And you can keep alive every single memory you ever shared with your husband. You can write them in a journal so that when your son is old enough he'll feel as if he knew his daddy personally."

Beth's eyes filled with another layer of tears, but there was something else there. A light, a ray of hope the woman hadn't had before. "I never thought of that."

Jamie kept her tone compassionate. "If you don't do that for your son, who will?"

When the women left late that morning, Janice had an application, and Beth had a plan, a purpose. Proof again that Jamie's work at St. Paul's was important, that it did indeed carry on Jake's legacy—offering people hope in the name of Jesus Christ.

And that morning, the results were so strong, so eternally important, Jamie could almost feel Jake working beside her.

FOUR

Some volunteers stayed on at St. Paul's indefinitely—people like Jamie and Aaron Hisel. But most worked for a season and then moved on. Which meant the little chapel always needed new volunteers.

As Jamie headed for the stairs that morning, she thought about Janice. From what she could tell, the woman would be a wonderful addition to the staff. Close enough to share the pain of visitors who needed comforting; strong enough to offer them the spiritual hope they needed.

But as wonderful as the morning's outcome had been, Jamie was exhausted, emotionally drained. More so than usual. She headed for the break room and grabbed a blueberry muffin from the table. People were always bringing in cases of water or trays of baked goods for the volunteers. A way of encouraging them to continue the work they did at St. Paul's.

Jamie peeled back the wrapper and took a bite. The issue with Sierra was weighing on her. How was she supposed to tell her daughter the truth? Should it happen in stages? Maybe start by telling her that her father was killed in the Twin Towers with hundreds of other firefighters, and then see if she remembered having someone who looked and acted like her daddy living with them after that?

Footsteps sounded on the stairs and Jamie looked up to see Aaron step into the break area. "How'd it go?" He took a bottle of water and dropped to the nearest seat. "That first one looked tough."

"It was."

"A couple of volunteers from the weekend showed up." He crossed his arms and gave a slight tilt of his head. "Let's leave early. We can grab a bite to eat and take it to the park."

"Battery Park?"

"Right." He grinned, something she couldn't remember seeing him do until well after the second anniversary of the attacks. "Central Park might make you late for Sierra."

"True." She pulled herself to her feet, finished her water, and waited for him. There was something different in his eyes, something she couldn't quite make out. She didn't say anything. She'd ask him later, on the way to the park.

He finished his drink, stood, and led the way down the stairs. They bid the other volunteers good-bye and left. The sun was overhead now, warming the early October afternoon. Jamie pulled a pair of sunglasses from her small bag and slipped them on. She and Aaron were comfortable together. Every moment between them didn't need to be filled with conversation, and they stayed silent as they passed the crater where the towers had stood.

Jamie waited a few more blocks, then she shaded her eyes and looked at him. "What's on your mind?"

"Hmmm?" Aaron raised his eyebrows. "Nothing, why?"

"Yes, something." She looked straight ahead again. "I saw it in your eyes back at the chapel."

The captain shoved his hands into his FDNY windbreaker and kept his tone even. "What'd you see?"

"I don't know." Their conversation had a casual pace. "Something I haven't seen before. I'm not sure."

"Hmmm." The corners of Aaron's lips raised just a notch. He turned into a café and looked at her over his shoulder. "Let's get lunch."

They ordered turkey sandwiches, chips, and two cans of pop, which the deli man packed in one bag. Aaron carried it, and ten minutes later they reached Battery Park and found a bench with a view of the harbor.

Aaron pulled out her lunch first, and then his. He was about to take a bite, when she bowed her head and started praying. "Thank You, God, for our food. Thank You that we can find meaning and purpose helping the people at St. Paul's. You're a good God, Lord, and You know the plans You have for us. Amen."

A chuckle came from Aaron. "You insist on doing that, don't you? Praying for me?"

Jamie smiled. "If I don't do it, who will?"

She and the captain didn't exactly see eye to eye on matters of faith, but she would never preach at him or force him to see things her way. It hadn't worked for her when she was the one on Aaron's side of the fence. It wouldn't work for him, either.

"No one, and I'm fine with that." He took a bite of his sandwich.

"I know, Aaron." Her tone was mixed humor and mock boredom. "God doesn't exist. Same drivel I used to drive Jake crazy with."

He opened his mouth to say something, then changed his mind. Instead he took another bite. "Good sandwich."

"Okay, fine." She held up her turkey roll. "Good sandwich."

"Brat." He gave her a light nudge in the ribs with his elbow. "I'm not that stubborn. You could try a little harder."

She felt her eyes dance in light of the easy banter. "Would it work?"

"No." He set his sandwich down and laughed again. "But you could at least try."

They finished their sandwiches, their arms occasionally brushing against each other. Two people had stepped up and become her support system since Jake died. Sue, who'd been married to Jake's friend, Larry—another FDNY man lost on September 11—and Aaron.

She appreciated Aaron most at times like this, when she couldn't rattle off another statistic about the terrorist attacks, couldn't give another hug without running to the picture of Jake and falling in a heap on the floor. Times when the chance to smile or laugh gave her one more piece of tangible proof that yes, she would survive. Somehow she would keep waking up, keep breathing, keep raising Sierra the best she knew how, and the world wouldn't come to an end.

Aaron finished his sandwich, tossed the wrapper in the bag, and set it on the ground. He turned to her and the look was back, the one she'd seen earlier in St. Paul's break room.

"There it is again." She had her sandwich in her hands, but she let them fall to her lap. "That look, the one I was telling you about earlier."

"You don't let up, do you?"

"No. You can't hide anything from me." Jamie stuffed what was left of her sandwich into the bag and pushed the wrapper in after it. "You shouldn't even try."

"Is that right?"

"Yes." She crossed her ankles and stared out at the harbor. Aaron would tell her what was on his mind. He always did. He was a man of few words, the type who communicated more through glances and nuances. And because of that, he was nothing like Jake. Certainly he lacked Jake's way of lighting up a room, the charisma that came so naturally for Jake. No, Aaron's appeal was subtler, but after sharing her grief with him over the past years, they were close enough that she was right.

Jamie could read him perfectly.

They were quiet again, watching a triple-decker boat of tourists sail past on their way to the Statue of Liberty.

Finally he cleared his throat and looked at her. "Can I throw something out there?"

"Of course."

His eyes grew deeper than before. "How long, Jamie?"

"How long?" For the first time in a long while, Aaron had her stumped. "How long what?"

Aaron squinted at the sun's reflection on the water. "How long before you're ready to move on with life?"

"Move on?" Fear kicked Jamie in the gut and left her breathless. "I am moving on. Working at St. Paul's is moving on."

"Not that way." He leaned over and dug his elbows into his knees. His eyes found hers. "Jamie, I have feelings for you." His tone was heavy and certain. A long sigh sifted between his lips, and he looked out at the water again. "I've wanted to tell you for a long time."

Jamie felt her eyes grow wide, frightened. She wasn't sure what to do next. Had she read Aaron wrong from the beginning? He'd wanted friendship, right? So where had this . . . this change of heart come from? Or had it been there all along and she just hadn't wanted to see it? Part of her wanted to back up slowly, turn around, and run for her life. But still another part needed to hear him out. Not because she was ready for what he was saying, or because she could even manage the thought of Aaron being anything more than her friend. But because deep in her soul she'd known he was going to say this.

She'd known it and been so afraid she hadn't been able to admit it even to herself.

Her fingers shook. She laced them together to keep them from catching Aaron's attention.

He looked at her again. "Don't leave me hanging here, Jamie." He forced a laugh. "I cough up the hardest words I've ever said and you're speechless."

"I don't . . ." She raked her fingers through her hair and leaned hard against the back of the bench. "You're one of my best friends, Aaron. I haven't . . . I can't . . ."

Aaron shifted his position so he faced her squarely. Then, while his eyes never left hers, he took her hands. His voice fell and mixed with the breeze coming off the water. "You can, Jamie. We're together all the time, anyway. We've been through more than most people ever go through before having a first date."

First date?

The words hit her like fingernails on a chalkboard. She could feel the blood draining from her face. What if Jake could somehow see her from heaven? What if he could see her sitting on a bench beside Aaron Hisel talking about a first date? The idea made her shudder.

"Look, Jamie." Aaron straightened and his expression eased. "I know it's going to take time, but I've been thinking about it." He stood and pulled her to her feet. "We belong together. I'll take it as slow as you want to go. Just give it some thought, okay?"

Everything in her wanted to scream at him. No, it wasn't okay. No, she wouldn't think, even for a split second, about dating or loving or mar—

She couldn't bring herself to finish the thought. She wanted to turn around and see Jake standing there laughing, wanted to hear him telling her it was all a bad joke, that Captain Hisel certainly wasn't suggesting they find their way into a relationship when Jake Bryan was the only man she'd ever love.

But she couldn't do any of those things, because Jake was gone. He'd been gone three years and he wasn't coming back. And the truth was, if she didn't want to be alone for the rest of her life, it was only logical that she might wind up with someone like Aaron, someone who shared September 11 with her, who could relate to the losses she'd suffered because in some ways they were his losses too.

Aaron wasn't quite six feet tall, but he had her beat by a few inches. He looked down at her, his eyes a sea of patience. "Just think about it, Jamie. Okay?"

"Okay." She felt all disconnected, as if her mouth was operating separate from her heart and mind and soul. "I'll think about it."

A smile played in Aaron's eyes. "Good." He pulled her close and gave her an easy hug, then walked with her toward the ferry. It was earlier than she usually left, but she needed some alone time, time to process what he'd just told her.

All afternoon while she was waiting for Sierra to come home from school, and even while she helped her daughter with home-work, Jamie tried to consider the idea of dating Aaron Hisel.

By the time she tucked Sierra in for the night and gave her but-terfly kisses the way Jake used to do, she had willed herself to con-sider the idea without feeling sick with betrayal. He was handsome, a great guy who knew her pain better than any other man except Eric Michaels—and she'd never see him again.

She and Aaron shared an event that would forever color their pasts, forever shape their futures. Maybe he was right; maybe it was a logical idea, a way to ensure that she and Sierra wouldn't be alone.

It wasn't until she was falling asleep that she remembered some-thing from earlier that day. They'd been eating lunch and Aaron's arm had brushed up against hers. She'd made a note of it, but only in the most comfortable sense. Because Aaron was her friend.

But when her arm had brushed up against Jake's arm—even the last week of his life, when they were jet skiing together—she felt the sensation throughout her body. Jake's touch was electrifying; it had always been that way. But Aaron? Aaron's was comfortable, nothing more.

So maybe that wasn't a bad thing. Maybe there'd never be any-one who electrified her heart and soul the way Jake did, but maybe that was okay. It was still possible she and Aaron could build a rela-tionship. After all, Jake was gone, and she was more lonely than she wanted to admit.

There was one problem.

She'd always been honest with Aaron. She could tell him she'd think about the possibility of the two of them; she could promise he would always be her friend no matter what, even if that meant a comfortable friendly out-together-sometimes relationship. That would be the truth. But if she told him she was open to the possibility of finding their way together, to the chance of falling in love with him, she'd be doing something she'd never done to him before.

She'd be lying.

The place in her heart for electricity and sparks and fireworks, the place that still went weak at the knees at his memory, would always belong to one man and one alone: Jake Bryan.

Even if she had to wait a lifetime to see him again.

FIVE

Sue Henning was walking past a picture of Larry, hurrying from one room to another trying to clean the house for Jamie's visit, when it hit her. Larry had been dead for three years. Three long years.

The anniversary of September 11 didn't allow her time for private reflection, but sometimes—without warning—she would hear Larry's hearty laugh, or smell a faint whiff of his cologne from the bathroom where it stood to this day, untouched. Something would trigger his memory, the image of his sweet freckled face—and the enormity of his loss would hit her all over again.

It happened less often these days, and that, in and of itself, was painful. How dare her mind and heart and soul move on without him, without the life they'd known and loved? They had two children, and once in a while something seven-year-old Katy said or the way little Larry—not quite four—waved at her with one finger, the same way her Larry had always waved at her, triggered the loss.

This time it was the photograph.

The look in Larry's eyes reached out and stopped her in her tracks, demanded that here, now, she remember all he was and all she'd lost. Sue sucked in a fast breath and grabbed the edge of the countertop where the photo stood.

Larry . . . I haven't forgotten.

She looked at the edges of his face, the way his eyes twinkled, and she tried to remember those same lines in motion, smiling and talking and loving her late at night. The memory of them was dimmer now, and there was nothing she could do about it. Time stole a little more of it every day.

The doorbell rang, and just as quickly the moment passed.

Jamie hadn't been by in a week, and Sue missed her terribly. The two were closer than sisters since September 11. They talked about their kids—Katy and Sierra were still best friends—and the ways they spent their time. But mostly they talked about the past, about happy moments and memories that had no chance of surviving if they weren't unfolded and held up for display every now and then.

Her friendship with Jamie was God's gift, no doubt. A safe harbor, a place where they could each be completely vulnerable, no matter if the world thought it was time they moved on. And in the midst of that harbor, Sue had found in Jamie the best girlfriend she'd spent a lifetime wishing for.

She gave a last look at Larry's picture and called out over her shoulder. "Just a minute . . ."

It was four o'clock in the afternoon, so Sierra would be with Jamie. The girls could hardly wait to play together and days like this—when the sun was still shining and winter seemed a month away—they could go out back and play the way they'd played since they were toddlers.

Her house was on Staten Island, same as Jamie's. It gave them more room to spread out than they'd have had with a house in the city, and a way to feel disconnected from the hustle of Manhattan. She opened the door and grinned at Jamie. "I miss you, girl. You have to come more than once a week!"

Jamie hugged her. "I know. I was having withdrawals."

Sierra stepped in, her blonde hair falling like a silk curtain over her shoulders. "Hi, Mrs. Henning. Is Katy upstairs?"

"Yes, honey." Sue hugged Sierra. "She's waiting for you."

"Thanks." Sierra ran off and stopped only a moment to brush her fingers through little Larry's hair. "Hi, buddy. Whatcha doing?"

The boy was wearing a miniature Nets jersey, and he had a basketball under one arm. "Shooting hoops."

Larry's small plastic basketball hoop stood on one side of the living room, surrounded by a sofa and a loveseat. Sue didn't mind the boy shooting baskets in the house. The child was practically fanatical about the sport; as long as he had a ball in his hands he was happy. And if he was happy, she and Jamie could hold a conversation without interruption.

Sierra ran off, and Sue motioned to a quieter alcove, a place where they could sit and still see little Larry, but not be hit by loose balls. Sue had made iced tea, and two tall glasses stood on a table surrounded on two sides by comfy chairs.

Jamie was quieter than usual. She dropped into one of the over-stuffed chairs, planted her elbows on the arms, and covered her face. After a moment she let her hands fall to her lap and she looked at Sue. "I wanted to come earlier, but Sierra begged me to wait until she was out of school." Jamie's tone was serious, the corners of her eyes tight with the small lines of worry. She pursed her lips, her eyes locked on Sue's. "You aren't going to believe this."

Sue took the seat closest to her friend and tried to seem interested. "Something at St. Paul's?" Jamie almost always started their conversations with a story from St. Paul's. There was a time when Sue wanted nothing more than to be at the quaint little chapel. For months she would've gladly gotten up every day and gone to St. Paul's, walked the walls of memories and mementos, and pretended even for an hour that the souls lost that day were still vibrant and alive.

But never once had she considered volunteering there.

She was worried about Jamie. It was one thing to help out for a while. But Jamie had been working three days a week, sometimes four, ever since the first anniversary, the day they reopened the chapel to the public.

Jamie shook her head; her face was tight and pale. "Not St. Paul's. Captain Hisel."

"Captain Hisel?" Sue wrinkled her nose. Jamie and the captain were friends; everyone knew that. Now Sue felt her heart skip a beat as she waited for the news. "He's okay, isn't he?"

"Yes." She gave a quick nod. "Nothing like that."

Sue felt her heart skitter back into a normal rhythm. That was one thing about September 11. Before that day, Sue was vaguely aware of tragedy; now in some morbid sort of way, she expected it. As if by expecting it, the eventual blows life dealt would somehow be easier to take. "Okay. Then what am I not going to believe?"

"I wanted to call you yesterday, but I had to work through it."

Sue was even more confused. "Work through something with the captain?"

"Aaron."

"Okay, Aaron." Sue took a sip of her tea. "It's still weird to think of him that way, I guess."

"Yeah." Jamie sat back in her chair and gripped the arms. "Wait till you hear this."

Sue waited. The quieter she was, the better chance Jamie would get to the point. At that moment the girls came barreling down the stairs.

Katy skipped into the room, breathless and happy. Sierra was close on her heels. "Can we go outside and play?"

Sue looked at Jamie and caught her look of approval. She smiled at Katy and pointed to the closet. "Get your coat. It's almost dark and the nights are getting colder now."

"Yes, Mommy."

Sierra raised her eyebrows at Jamie. "Me too?"

"Yes, silly. You too." Jamie was clearly trying to keep her tone light.

When the girls were gone, Sue looked at Jamie. "So . . . ?"

"Okay." She breathed in slow through her nose. "Here's what happened." Jamie's fingers came together. The tips of her knuckles were white. "Yesterday after working at St. Paul's, Aaron and I went to Battery Park with our lunch. I didn't think anything of it, I mean, at the time I didn't, anyway. We eat out together all the time, especially after working at the chapel."

Sue nodded. "All the time."

"But yesterday there was something different in his eyes. I couldn't put my finger on it while we were at St. Paul's, but when we were sitting on a bench at the park, watching the tourist boats in the harbor, I asked him about it." Jamie paused. Her shoulders sank a notch, and the lines on her forehead grew more pronounced. "He told me he has feelings for me, Sue. That he could picture the two of us together some day, and that . . . that I should at least think about it."

Relief flooded Sue's veins. Relief and sorrow all at the same time. Her question to her friend was both kind and pointed. "Can you blame him, Jamie?"

Jamie leaned forward. Her eyes held an angst Sue had never seen there before. "Can I blame him?" She uttered a sound that fell short of a laugh. "I wasn't sure whether to kick him or run for my life."

Sue tried to picture her feisty friend having that reaction to Captain Hisel's admission. "Jamie, you didn't kick him!"

"No." She bit the inside of her lip. "But I didn't run, either."

"Because . . ."

"Because maybe I didn't want to run." Her voice cracked. "And maybe that's worse."

Sue set her tea down. Her heart hurt for her friend. Moving on was going to be painful for both of them, but it was bound to come. Time would see to that. She reached out and took hold of Jamie's knee. Her voice was just loud enough to hear. "Because maybe deep down you've considered the possibility yourself? Is that it?"

"I don't know." Jamie's lower lip and chin quivered. "I don't know, Sue. I only know that I feel this terrible guilt, as if I'm betraying Jake by even talking about this."

For a long while, Sue said nothing. There were no rule books or guidelines about how to start living again. Some FDNY widows had already remarried, some not much more than a year after the attacks. Neither Sue nor Jamie could imagine moving on so quickly, but everyone handled grief differently.

And not everyone had a husband like Larry or Jake.

Sue tucked her feet beneath her up onto the chair and stared out the window. The girls were swinging, pushing their toes toward the sky and giggling all the while. She looked back at Jamie. "I've wondered about this, about whether I could ever even find another man attractive after Larry."

Jamie massaged her temples. "You never told me."

"It's like you said, just mentioning the idea feels like a crime."

"But when you do . . ." Jamie looked at the floor for a moment, and then back up at Sue. "When you do think about it, how do you usually end up feeling?"

Peace hugged Sue's shoulders and settled in beside her. She spread her hands out before her and nodded toward little Larry and the girls in the backyard. "Like this is enough. My children, my memories. They're all I need. At least for now, until God shows me something different."

"What if that's what He's showing me?"

"Well . . ." Sue took hold of her tea again. She ran her fingers along the dewy moisture that had built up on the glass. "Do you, you know, do you feel anything when you're with Capt—" She caught herself. "When you're with Aaron?"

Jamie closed her eyes and scrunched her face. When she opened them she looked more bewildered than before. "Not really." She lifted her hands from her lap and dropped them again. "But the idea of being more than friends isn't altogether horrible, either."

"Hmmm."

"Yeah, I know." She stood and paced across the room. For a few moments she watched little Larry make three baskets in a row. Then she came back and sat in her chair again. "No one ever teaches you how to do this."

"No."

"I've been thinking what would Jake want, and even there I'm not sure." Jamie ran her finger around the rim of her iced tea glass, her eyes distant. "He wouldn't want me alone, not for the rest of my life." She looked up. "But how could he want me with another man?"

"I've thought about that too." Sue's stomach turned. The conversation was as difficult for her as it was for Jamie. They hadn't wanted their marriages to end; they'd simply been cut short. And in their place was a void that even the best memories couldn't fill completely. "Of course Jake wouldn't want you to fall in love with someone else, not if he were here. But he isn't. He's gone, and so is Larry."

"But it feels so wrong, like they aren't really dead unless . . . until we move on with life, find someone new." Jamie's voice was thick with emotion. "You know?"

"Yes." Sue thought of something. "There is something else."

"What?"

"What's Aaron think of your faith?"

Jamie hesitated, but only for a minute. "He . . . he teases me about it, especially when I say I'm praying for him. He tells me there's no point."

"Hmmm. I didn't know that."

"Some of the guys at the department struggle with faith, at least that's what Aaron tells me. I hadn't thought much about that." She took a sip from her glass and looked at Sue over the rim. "Too busy trying to sort through my feelings, I guess."

Quiet came over them again. Sue wasn't sure what to say. She was certain a relationship with Aaron should never materialize as long as he didn't share Jamie's faith. But it was probably too soon to say anything. Still, she couldn't stay silent; her faith wouldn't allow it. She bit her tongue and tried to pick the right words.

After another minute, Jamie said, "I know what you're thinking."

"What?" Sue crossed her legs.

"You're thinking Aaron isn't a believer. Right?"

Sue pursed her lips. "Was it written on my forehead?"

"No." Jamie sank back into her chair. She sounded defeated. "In your eyes."

"I'm not saying I'm right, Jamie, but if I were you I'd keep his friendship and consider anything more a closed subject."

"Except for one thing."

"What?"

"Jake didn't do that to me. He loved me despite my lack of faith . . . and look what happened."

"You were kids when you met, that's different." Sue could've said more, but she didn't want to push, not now. "God will make it all clear to you—however things work out."

"Yes." The lines on Jamie's forehead eased completely and her eyes looked more peaceful. "I'll keep you posted. I guess the whole discussion has made me wonder if it's time to move on, to think of myself as single, not widowed."

Sue smiled, the first time either of them had done so since they sat down. "Since you brought it up . . ."

"Brought what up?"

"Moving on." Sue uncrossed her legs and slid to the edge of her chair. "Jamie, maybe it's time you stopped working at St. Paul's."

Jamie's eyes grew wide and her mouth hung open. "Quit St. Paul's?" Jamie uttered a hard exhale and raked her fingers through her dark hair. "St. Paul's and Sierra—that's all that drives me, Sue. God's given me those two as a reason to get up every morning, to keep existing even when I feel like I'm already dead."

Sue put her hand on Jamie's knee again. "But maybe that feeling is because of St. Paul's, because you're reminded of September 11 over and over again."

"No." Jamie gave a hard shake of her head. "It's not because of St. Paul's. That chapel gives me a way to keep Jake's legacy alive, a way to help other people have faith and hope, the way Jake would've helped them if he were still alive. Every day I go there I feel a little better about myself, my purpose in life. Even when I leave there exhausted."

Sue didn't say anything; she didn't have to. If Jamie was leaving St. Paul's feeling emotionally drained, then maybe she would see it was time for a break. She'd said as much before, but Jamie was determined to stay at St. Paul's. The place made her feel closer to Jake. Only Jamie could make the decision about leaving. "Okay." Sue looked at the girls again. "I'll ask you the same thing Aaron did." She caught Jamie's eyes again. "Just think about it."

They were too close to argue, and even now Jamie didn't seem frustrated by Sue's request. Just certain. "The day it doesn't feel like Jake's up there smiling at me, I'll turn in my notice, deal?"

"Deal."

The conversation shifted to the girls, and Jamie admitted she was thinking of telling Sierra the truth about Jake's death, and the fact that the man who had lived with them after September 11 hadn't been Jake at all.

Before their conversation ended, they joined hands and prayed that God might give Jamie wisdom about how and what and when to tell Sierra. After dinner and a game of Uno with the kids, Jamie and Sierra headed home.

Sue tucked in Larry and then Katy. They had their own rooms, but most nights Katy liked sleeping on Larry's top bunk.

"He likes company, Mommy," Katy had told her. But the truth was something different. Since losing her father, Katy hated being alone. It was one more reminder that nothing would ever be the same again.

This time when Sue passed the photo of Larry, she didn't feel any sharp reminders or rushes of sorrow. Instead she smiled back, and as she did she remembered something Jamie had said earlier that evening. The day it didn't feel like Jake was up there smiling was the day she'd turn in her notice.

Jake was always smiling. He and Larry could've been brothers that way, even if they looked nothing alike. Sue could picture Jake smiling at Jamie out on the water, flying over the harbor on her jet ski, or while taking Sierra to dance classes, even helping out at church.

But talking about what happened that Tuesday morning, over and over and over again?

No matter how hard she tried, Sue couldn't picture Jake Bryan smiling about that.

Sierra was trying to get to sleep, but she couldn't. Something Katy said while they were swinging made her stomach feel bouncy. Like the curls on Cinda May in her second-grade class. She did a big breath and rolled onto her side. "C'mere, Wrinkles. Where are you, boy?"

Wrinkles was her big gray cat. Sierra named him *Wrinkles* because when he was a little baby he had a wrinkly face. He slept in Sierra's room, but not always on her bed. Mommy said that was 'cause Wrinkles had an attitude. Most cats had attitudes, actually.

"Wrinkles . . ." Sierra made her voice a loud whisper. Mommy thought she was sleeping, so she couldn't be loud. But she needed to talk to someone. Wrinkles was the only other person in the room.

Sierra heard a little meowing sound, and Wrinkles jumped onto the bed. He padded over with his soft cat feet and looked straight at her.

"Hi, Wrinkles." Sierra patted the cat's back. "Lay down."

Wrinkles pushed at the covers three times and then curled his legs beneath him. As soon as he was down, he started purring. Purring was when cats were happy; that was something else Mommy had told her.

"I'm glad you're happy, Wrinkles." Sierra rubbed her nose against the cat's tiny pink one. It was cold and wet like the morning grass. "Wrinkles, I'm feeling a little sick." She studied the cat. "You know, in my tummy. That kind."

Wrinkles leaned his head back and yawned. He yawned so big she could see the little prickly things on his tongue. When people yawned it meant they were bored, but not Wrinkles. When he yawned it meant he wanted her to keep talking. That's what he always did when she talked to him at night.

"I'm gonna talk to Jesus about it before I go to sleep, but I thought I'd tell you first." Sierra sat up and folded her legs crisscross applesauce. "Wanna know what Katy said?" She waited. "She said it was weird that Daddy died in a building fire saving people because he was with her daddy in the Twin Towers and they never stayed apart." Her nose itched. She gave it a little scratch. "Doesn't that make you feel kind of sick, Wrinkles? Because if my daddy and Katy's daddy were together in the Twin Towers, how come they didn't die at the same time, actually? How come my daddy came home for a little while and then he died, huh?"

Wrinkles looked at her, but only for a few seconds. Then he began licking his skinny legs. Sierra liked when he did that. The way his tongue was all bristly, licking his fur was kind of like combing it. But the trouble with Wrinkles was, he didn't have a lot to say. He didn't have anything to say, really.

And this was the sort of problem that needed words on the other side. Words from someone who could help her understand. Otherwise Katy was right; it was weird.

Sierra did a yawn, almost as big as the one Wrinkles did. She lay back down, careful not to wake up her cat. Then she pulled the covers up to her chin, closed her eyes, and thought about it again. If her daddy and Katy's daddy were together, why didn't they die together? She squeezed her eyes shut very hard and tried to remember.

Daddy was hurt, because she remembered him in the hospital. Then he came home and he slept downstairs. Sierra remembered that too. At first he didn't know things—like where he was or who people were, actually. But then he started 'membering and doing all the things Daddy always did. Like curl her hair and make her blueberry pancakes and watch *Little Mermaid* with her.

Then one day he was gone.

Mommy said he was helping people in a fire when Jesus called him home to heaven. And that made pretty much sense, except for now Katy thought it was weird.

Sleep was coming to get her; she could feel it. She did another yawn and thought about Jesus. She liked talking to Him out loud, because you talked to real people that way. And Jesus was very real.

"Hi, Jesus, it's me, Sierra."

Wrinkles snuggled a little closer to her.

"I'm up late tonight because my tummy hurts. Well—" she opened her eyes and saw the room was shadowy dark—"it doesn't really hurt, it just feels bouncy, actually. And it's all because of what Katy said. First it was weird that my daddy didn't die at the same time as her daddy because they were both in the Twin Towers together." She scratched the tip of her nose again. "But something else, too. She said they found our two daddies' helmets at the same time. At the very same time, Jesus. Isn't that weird?"

Sierra's tummy started to feel a little less bouncy. That always happened when she talked to Jesus. One time Katy asked her if she was mad at Jesus for taking their daddies home too soon. Sierra had to think about that for a long time, but she decided no. She wasn't mad. Sometimes people die—that's what Mommy said. She couldn't be mad at Jesus for that because guess what? Jesus was taking care of Daddy right now. So how could she be mad?

She closed her eyes again. "Jesus, I think I'll talk to Mommy about it, okay? She'll know what to tell Katy, plus she can tell me about the helmets. If it's even true." Sleep was coming faster now. "Good night, Jesus. Tell my daddy I love him."

SIX

Clay was at the wheel of his Ford pickup, heading for Eric and Laura's house. They wanted to have him over for dinner before he left. He stopped at a light and leaned back, adjusting his sunglasses. Now that he'd made up his mind to go, he couldn't wait to get out of Los Angeles.

Eric teased him that he'd freeze to death. Southern California winters rarely dipped below seventy degrees, whereas Manhattan would most likely be buried in snow by mid-December. Clay didn't care. In three days, he and Reynolds would be on the flight bound for LaGuardia and a three-week stay in New York City. Three weeks. It felt like an eternity, and that was a good thing.

New scenery, new people, new challenges. All of it would take his mind off the bucket of things that had been bothering him. The light turned green, and he took a quick lead away from the pack of cars. He was five minutes late and he didn't want to hold up dinner.

But he didn't exactly want to go, either.

The whole thing with Laura was ridiculous, really. She'd never been more than a friend, and the fact that she was happily married to his brother was nothing but good. At least, that's how he wanted to feel. If only he could meet the right person, someone who would fill that yearning in his heart for love and companionship. Someone to laugh with and pray with, someone to walk alongside in faith, one who he could play tennis with and watch ESPN with late at night.

Did people pity him when they saw him out by himself? Eating out alone, shopping alone, seeing a movie by himself. He hated the looks from strangers. Often they came from women—attractive women, even—who let their look linger awhile. The questions were written on their faces. What was a guy like him doing alone, first of all, and was he interested in company?

Another red light. Clay came to a hurried stop and gritted his teeth. He wasn't interested. Not at all. He'd tried that route and nothing but awkward meetings had come from it. Guys from the station tried to set him up more times than he could remember, either with a sister or a friend of their own wife or girlfriend.

"You're a good-looking guy, Michaels," Reynolds told him once. "But you'd think you had three eyes and horns growing out of your head the way you can't keep a girl."

Clay had laughed. "Thanks, buddy. I needed that."

The trouble wasn't with him or the girls. They were generally young and beautiful and fun to be with. Los Angeles had no shortage of pretty women. The shortage was in women of faith. Women who believed the way he did, who saw faith in Christ not as a religion but as a relationship with the Creator.

He'd be out on a blind date, or at a barbecue where one of the guys was trying to set him up, and he'd say something about his job being a blessing or how he was sure God had a plan for people, and the girl would go slack-faced.

"Do you . . . go to church anywhere?"

Blank stare. "Church? You mean, like religion." The girl would offer a polite smile. "I'm not very religious."

Of course not. After three years of such exchanges, Clay wondered if there was even one single woman in Los Angeles who cared about the things he did. They were out there, of course. But he worked so many nights and weekends, he had a hard time connecting with a church group. When he could, he attended Sunday services at a growing church not far from his home—West Valley Christian. But he hadn't had time for any of the weekly groups, and so far he hadn't met single women his age.

The light turned green. He worked his way into the right lane and turned at the first street. Eric and Laura lived in a beautiful subdivision a few minutes up the hill and past a gated entry. He used to love seeing them, visiting with Eric and Laura, and spending time with Josh. But lately when he visited he couldn't wait to leave.

That's why the trip to New York would be so good for him.

He pulled into the driveway, made his way up the sidewalk, and knocked once before letting himself in. Josh saw him first, through the foyer from the kitchen table where he was sitting, working over a textbook.

"Uncle Clay, hey, guess what?" The boy was tall like his father, sandy hair, with the same blue eyes. He had Laura's fine bone structure, but little else.

"Hey, buddy." Clay set his keys on a table near the door and headed toward him. "What's up?"

Josh pushed back from the table and grinned. "I made the A team!"

"Your first year at middle school?" Clay gave the boy a high five. "You'll be playing at UCLA before you know it!"

"You think so?" His eyes grew wider, excitement sparkling. "The Bruins are the best."

"Just wait till they've got you on the team. Then they'll really be something."

Clay took a few steps closer and looked at the textbook. The page was a smattering of geometrical shapes. "Math, huh?"

Josh's tone fell. "Yeah, the worst."

"Need some help?"

"No." Josh nodded his head toward the back door. "Dad helped me when I got home from school. I get it." He gave Clay a crooked grin. "I just hate it, that's all."

There it was again. The reminder that this family was perfectly fine without him. Josh no longer needed him for homework or playing catch or an hour of jump shots outside. Eric took care of all that now.

And Laura . . . obviously she didn't need him. He was her friend, but they spent no time alone together, nor did they have any reason to do so. This was the new way of things. After three years, it wasn't even all that new anymore.

Eric worked from home. He maintained the same type of job, the same income, the same membership to the country club, while spending ten times as many hours with Laura and Josh. It was the type of miracle setup only God could've worked out.

The sliding door opened, and Clay turned to see Eric walk in with an empty platter. "Barbecue's on." He smiled first at Clay, then at Josh. "How's it coming?"

"Okay." Josh made a face. "I wish I was done."

"Why don't you take a break?" Eric set the platter on the vast granite island at the center of the kitchen. "You can help me cook the steaks."

"You mean turn 'em and everything?"

"Yep." Eric chuckled. "Mom's out there finding zucchini. You can help her till I get back out."

Josh didn't hesitate. He pushed his chair away from the table and ran out the door, gangly legs flying beneath him. Clay leaned against the counter and watched, amazed. How much happier and at peace with the world Josh was now that things were different at home. Further proof of what he already knew—the unequaled power of a good father in a boy's life.

Their own father had checked out long before Clay and Eric were teenagers. The man didn't divorce their mother until they were in high school, but by then they barely knew him. Neither he nor his brother had been in touch with him in the years since.

Clay shifted his lower jaw. *That's why I want to be a dad, God . . . so I can be the kind of father a child wants. The way Eric is with Josh.* He gritted his teeth. *Why's it taking so long?*

Eric popped open a Sprite and slid it across the counter to Clay. "You okay?"

"Huh?" Clay straightened himself. "Yeah. Fine."

"You look a little pensive."

"Nah, I'm fine." He wasn't, but Eric didn't need to know that. His older brother wasn't to blame for any of the feelings that had been poking at him lately. "Need help with dinner?"

"No, it's under control." Eric took a pop for himself and came up alongside Clay. "So . . ." He put the can down and crossed his arms. "How did it feel?"

How did it feel? Then it hit him. Of course . . . Eric was talking about the shooting. That's why all the questions. Clay shrugged. "Like target practice, I guess."

"Really?" Eric narrowed his eyes. "No difference?"

"Of course it was different." Clay uttered a sharp laugh and gave a sideways shake of his head. "The guy was spraying an AK-47 at me, and I was shooting from the floor of my patrol car. And instead of ripping some paper target, I killed a guy."

Eric's tone grew softer. "It was self-defense, Clay. Obviously."

"I know." He downed half of his pop and set the can back on the counter. "I was sick about it at first, but the truth was, I had no choice. It was me or him."

"How'd you fire at him without getting hit?"

Clay shrugged. "Same way you found your way home after September 11?" Clay loved this, the easy banter with his brother. For all the ways he was tempted to be jealous of him, he couldn't do anything but enjoy their time together.

Eric nodded, but he didn't answer the question; he didn't have to. They both knew the reason they were standing there that October afternoon. God alone got the credit.

"Josh says he made the A team."

"Yeah." Eric chuckled. "He has me playing better hoops than I did when I was a college boy." He shot an invisible ball toward the patio door. "The kid can't get enough."

"I'll have to catch a few games when I get back."

Eric's smile faded. "So what's this I hear about you spending three weeks in New York?"

"The idea came from Reynolds, one of the detectives at the station. I have three weeks paid while they investigate the shooting. I can also count it as training."

"Training?" Eric gave him a knowing look. "You mean you finally got your promotion?"

"Yeah." Clay gripped the countertop behind him. "Funny timing, huh? Kill a suspect in a shootout, come back to the office, and find out they've made you detective."

"Hey!" Eric slapped him on the back. "Way to go, little brother. You've had that coming for a few years at least." He hesitated. "But why New York? Couldn't you get training here?"

"Sure." Clay pulled away from the counter and stretched first to one side, then the other. He'd pulled a few muscles in his back when he jerked his body to the floorboard during the gunfight. He was still sore. "Reynolds wanted New York, for one thing. Not sure why. But I figure, why not? I've wanted to get back there since the terrorist attacks. After all the firefighters and police officers lost, it's sort of a trek, I guess. Something all of us want to do at one time or another."

Eric finished his pop and headed around the counter toward the sink. He ran the platter under water and sprayed it with a squirt of soap. "I don't miss it."

"Don't miss what?" Clay turned around and faced him. "Working there ... or living there?"

Eric didn't look up. "Actually, I didn't live there. I lived in New Jersey."

Clay waited, but as usual, Eric didn't go into details.

"To answer your question, I don't miss working in Manhattan every month or so. I can't believe that was my life before September 11."

"And the other? Staten Island?"

Eric's eyes met his. "I think about it once in a while."

"You never talk about it."

"Nope." Eric turned off the water and grabbed a dish towel. "My time with her gave me a life I never would've had otherwise. But we promised each other we'd never talk about it. Not to anyone."

"Not even Laura?"

"Once in a while she'll say something about the firefighter, about how she's glad he kept a journal, glad he wrote notes in his Bible."

"That's what changed you, right? Believing you were this great family guy, a man with an unshakable faith?"

"That—" he ran the towel over the platter—"and her."

"The woman?"

Eric nodded. "She was very special. It killed me to leave her."

This was more than Eric had ever shared about that time in his life. Clay wasn't sure what to make of his brother's statement. "Did you ... were you in love with her?"

"I thought she was my wife; I was *supposed* to love her. And the girl ... I remembered her name when I woke up. It wasn't until the end that we figured out that part."

"The helmet?" It was one detail Clay did know.

"Yep. I tripped, as close as I can guess." He set the dry platter on the counter. "The fireman bent over to help me up and his helmet fell off. I picked it up, I remember that. Inside was a picture of the little girl and her name." He knit his brow together. "When I woke up, her name was the only thing I remembered."

"She got to you too, didn't she?" Clay cocked his head. "The little girl?"

"They both did." Eric gave a slight shake of his head. "But not like you think. When I left them it was no regrets. I was a different man." He took the platter and headed toward the patio door.

"You said it killed you."

Eric opened the slider and looked at Clay over his shoulder. "It did." He exhaled through pursed lips. "When I realized I wasn't her husband, things changed between us. I was a married man, so loving her went from being the thing I was trying to remember to something I could never do." He leaned against the door frame. "Yes, it killed me to leave her. Not because I was in love with her or her daughter, but because I knew how alone they would be."

"Hmmm." They stepped outside. Smoke curled up from the sides of the barbecue. A hundred feet away Josh was bent over the garden next to Laura. Clay didn't look for too long. "What was her name?"

"Doesn't matter. I don't like talking about her."

"Sorry. I guess I always wondered."

"It's okay. I was kind of mysterious about her when I came home. I figured no one needed to know."

Clay let that sit for a minute. "You ever call her, to see how she's doing?"

"Nope, can't do that either. God had a very clear reason why I wound up in her house. But when I left, both of us knew we wouldn't see each other again. It was how we wanted it." He lifted the barbecue lid. "I have a new life, one I wouldn't trade for the world. I could never love anyone but Laura, so you see, there's no room for looking back." He poked at the steaks. "The good-bye we said that last day at the airport was final."

Clay stared at the steaks, sizzling and deep brown at the edges. Two minutes passed, maybe three. "But you think about her, right? Once in a while?"

"Once in a while." Eric sprinkled salt on the meat. "She was incredible, Clay. More strength than any woman I've ever known. She loved me unconditionally. We helped each other find a friendship with God. Pretty heady stuff."

"Was she pretty?"

"Very." Eric smiled, his eyes distant. "I'm never sure which was the bigger miracle. That I came home completely in love with my wife, anxious to spend time with Josh, a changed man, really." He looked at Clay. "Or that I was able to walk away from Staten Island."

Laura and Josh were approaching them, carrying a big bowl of zucchini and strawberries. Laura smiled first at Eric, then at Clay. "Josh says he gets the strawberries." She stopped and hugged Clay. Her eyes were serious, concerned. Probably because of the gunfight. "How are you?"

"Fine." He cleared his throat. The conversation about Staten Island was over, and he could sense from his brother's body language that Eric was glad. Clay doubted they'd ever talk about it again.

Josh moved in beside Eric and, under Eric's guidance, the boy began turning the steaks. Laura was persistent. "I was so worried about you, Clay."

Of course she was. She still cared about him, the same as always. The fact that they'd crossed a line or two back in the months after the terrorist attacks probably never figured into her thinking.

She took a nearby chair, her brow knit together. "We watched it on TV and they showed your car." Laura put her fingers over her mouth. "Clay, it was awful. I can't believe you didn't get hit."

"I was praying big time." Clay took the chair opposite Laura. The smell of the steaks filled the air. Dinner would be nice, and then he'd be on his way. Until then, this was good; keeping his thoughts on the current day, the matters at hand. "I was on the floorboard and I could hear him coming closer. He'd already fired at me, so I knew he wanted to take me down."

Josh's eyes got wide. "That's crazy."

"It was." Clay worked his fingers into the muscles at the back of his neck. "I was asking God for a way out, and all of a sudden I knew. If I didn't look over the dash and at least try to stop the guy, I'd be dead in a few seconds."

Laura shuddered. "I haven't stopped thanking God ever since I heard."

"Dad says you're a good shot." Josh grinned at him. "All the kids at school thought it was way cool that you are my uncle."

Clay felt himself relax. How could he need a break from this? His family loved him, cared about him. "Thanks, Josh."

"Well—" Eric turned and looked at them—"Josh is doing wonders with the steak. We'll be ready in about five minutes."

Laura popped up and headed for the patio door. "I'll have everything ready inside." She looked at Clay. "Come help me."

He could hardly say no. He followed her into the kitchen as a memory came screaming back at him. After the Twin Towers collapsed, Laura had been frozen with shock. For five days she did little more than stare at the television and wait for Eric's call. From the first day on, the kitchen—this same kitchen—had been his territory. He made all meals, fed Josh, and helped the boy with his homework.

"You're quiet today." Laura led the way and handed him the bowl of zucchini. "Wash and slice. The pan's on the stove." She took up her position beside him and began rinsing the strawberries. "You sure everything's okay?"

Her chatter interrupted his thoughts, pulling him back to the here and now. Where he wanted to stay, no matter how much his heart refused to cooperate with him. The whole thing was ridiculous. He grabbed a zucchini from the bowl. "I'm fine. Just thinking about New York, I guess. I'm anxious to go."

"Eric was saying something about that." She set into a routine, rinsing a berry, pulling the stem from the top, and tossing it into a china bowl next to the sink. "I think it'll be good for you, Clay." Her eyes met his. "You need something different."

Clay held her gaze. Was she talking about having time away from them, time to find a life of his own? He wanted to ask, but he was afraid of where the conversation would go. "Yeah." He looked back at the vegetables. "The change'll do me good." He finished washing and sliced them into a pan already seasoned with oil. "They're making me a detective when I get back. That's the good news."

"Really?" Laura grinned at him over her shoulder. "Congratulations!"

"The time in New York will get me ready." He put the lid on the zucchini. "Funny how things work out."

Laura put the bowl of berries on the table and cleared away Josh's homework. "Could you hand me four plates?"

"Sure."

"They're in the—" Her eyes caught his. "I guess you know where they are." This time something in her expression told him he'd been right earlier. He must've been.

Again the motions were familiar. Reaching for the right cupboard, finding the plates as easily as if they were his own. He decided to take a chance. "It feels funny, working in here again. Brings back a lot of memories."

He felt Laura come a few steps closer, felt her wait until he was looking at her. "I couldn't have gotten through it without you." She tilted her head. "But sometimes I worry about you, Clay."

"Why?" He forced a laugh. He took the stack of plates and passed them to her. He tried not to notice the way their fingers brushed against each other in the transition. "The police work, you mean. The danger?"

"No." Her eyes were softer than before. "I've been praying for you, do you know that?"

"Since the shooting?"

"No." Her voice was clear and quiet and her eyes reached all the way to his soul. "Since Eric came home." She set the plates in a stack on the table. "I want you to find someone, Clay. If . . ."

He took a step closer. "Go ahead. Say it, Laura."

She let out a small sigh and looked at the floor. When she looked up he knew for certain that she understood how he felt—that he had no intention of coming between her and Eric, but somehow that wasn't enough to stop him from caring about her. Sometimes too much.

She took his hand and gave it a gentle squeeze, then released it. "If Eric hadn't come home, I'd be your wife by now. I believe that, Clay. You're a wonderful man, and I was falling hard for you when Eric came home. We both know that."

"Does Eric?"

"Yes." She stared at the ceiling and drew in a slow breath. "My marriage to Eric was a formality, it was all but over when he left for New York that September day. He knew that." She looked at him again. "You know what he told me?"

Clay wasn't sure he wanted to know. "What?"

"He told me if he hadn't survived, he would've wanted you and me together."

Clay had no idea how to react. He searched Laura's eyes for a minute and then walked past her. He grabbed a handful of forks and knives and carried them to the table. Then he turned to her again. "So that's why you think I need a change of scenery?" He wasn't mad. He simply wanted to know her feelings.

"I have Eric. Things are different for me." She took a stack of napkins from the counter and placed them one per setting. When she was finished she found his eyes again. "But if I didn't, if I were in your place, I'd still be in love with you, Clay. That's how strongly I felt for you." She gave him an understanding smile. "Sometimes I catch you looking and I wonder . . . if maybe you still feel that way about me."

"I don't. I—" Clay stopped himself. Her eyes told him instantly that she didn't believe him. "Laura, I wouldn't do anything to come between you and Eric."

"I know that."

"I hate that I think about you at all."

"Thanks."

He sat on the arm of the closest chair. "You know what I mean. I want to forget those three months ever happened."

"Really?" Laura gave him a small grin.

"Come on, Laura, quit kidding." He chuckled. "It isn't good for me to remember it. I'm happy for you and Eric, but sometimes . . . yeah, sometimes I wonder. And when I do, I beat myself up trying to forget you were ever more than my brother's girl."

She lowered her chin. "That's why I'm praying for you. New York's a vibrant place, from what I hear. Why don't you go there and do something crazy? Meet a perfect stranger and ask her for a walk in Central Park. I don't know." Laura ran her hand over her straight blonde hair. "God has a plan for you, Clay. Maybe New York is part of it."

The patio slider opened, and Josh led the way with the platter of steaks. "Dad says I'm ready for Beverly Hills."

"The boy has the touch." Eric breathed on his knuckles and rubbed them on his shoulder. "Chip off the old block."

Clay caught Laura's eyes one more time before they sat down, and that was it. Another conversation that wasn't bound to come up again.

That night, as Clay drove home, he thought about the evening. How was it he'd had such strange talks with both Eric and Laura? Must've been the fact that he'd almost been killed. Or that he was leaving for New York in a few days.

Something had triggered it.

Whatever it had been, it felt good that Laura knew his feelings. Better still, that she understood. Laura was right about New York City. He should talk to strangers, make friends with the guys in the program, find someone to take in a Broadway play. Why not? He'd only be there three weeks. After that he could come home and start life as a detective. When he did, he promised himself something.

He would get more connected at church, if not his church, another one in the Valley. He would look into the church's singles group or join a Bible study. After all, the people there had everything in common with him. Only by walking through the doors of a church would he ever find someone to fall in love with.

Because maybe Laura was right about that too. She'd been praying for him to find someone, and he'd been praying the same thing. And if this was the time in his life when he might meet someone and fall in love, he knew one thing for certain.

It wouldn't be in New York City.

SEVEN

Jamie still had her hair in a towel when the doorbell rang.

She darted down the hall and leaned into Sierra's room. "I've got it, honey. Keep getting ready." Then she took the stairs as fast as she could. "Coming."

It was Aaron, of course. He was meeting them at her house, taking them to lunch, and then to Chelsea Piers. Sierra had been wanting to visit the indoor pool there, and that Saturday morning was the perfect opportunity.

There was just one problem.

Jamie opened the door and glanced back up toward Sierra's room. She hadn't told her daughter that Aaron was coming. She meant to, but time had gotten away from her and now it was too late.

"Oh." She smiled at Aaron. "Sorry, come on in."

"Hi." He was dressed in a denim button-down shirt and jeans a shade lighter. His look took her by surprise. She was used to seeing him in his FDNY uniform—that was what he wore to work at St. Paul's, and what he had on just about every time they'd ever gone out for a meal. "I'm early."

"That's okay." She nodded toward the living room. "Do you mind waiting?"

"Not at all." He smiled at her, but it wasn't the easy smile they'd shared for the past few years. Jamie's skin crawled, and she chided herself. He'd been to her house before. Why couldn't she see this as just another visit, another chance to spend an afternoon with a friend who'd come to mean a great deal to her?

She gave Aaron a quick smile and hurried back up the stairs. She knew the answer. Nothing would ever be light between them again. Not until she either agreed that it was time to think of being more than friends, or until she put the idea to rest.

Even if she did that, she was pretty sure things wouldn't be the same. She would always know his intentions, and that was bound to make things awkward. The towel fell off her head as she rounded the corner into her bedroom. *Their* bedroom. Hers and Jake's. She hated when she slipped and thought of it as only hers. It had been theirs; it would always be theirs.

She tossed the towel in a laundry basket and set about drying her hair. If only he hadn't come early. She needed to finish getting ready and find Sierra. Before Sierra found him.

Five minutes later, she was dressed and on her way to find Sierra when her daughter stepped out of her room and stared down through the entryway toward Aaron. She made a face and looked at Jamie. "What's he doing here?"

"Sierra!" Jamie held a finger to her lips and closed the distance between them. "He's coming with us."

"To Chelsea Piers?" Her voice was loud and whiny; Aaron was bound to hear her. "I thought it was just me and you, Mommy."

"Look." Jamie took her daughter by the hand and led her back into her bedroom. "I'm sorry; I should've told you he was coming. But don't be rude, Sierra. That isn't like you."

She knit her blonde eyebrows together. "But why's he have to come? I wanted it to be just us. You and me."

"Mr. Hisel wants to be our friend; sometimes Mommy needs a friend, okay?" Jamie straightened herself and made an attempt to fix her hair. "Try to understand, okay, honey?"

Sierra's shoulders drooped a notch. "Okay."

They headed down the stairs together. Jamie had to remind herself to smile so Aaron wouldn't think anything was wrong. The plan was for a round of miniature golf followed by an hour in the pool. Jamie had hinted that she might swim too. But with Aaron along, she had no intention of getting into a bathing suit.

Aaron smiled at her, a smile that told her he was in no hurry. Not that morning for their outing, and not when it came to his interest in her. Jamie felt herself relax. There was no need to feel strange and awkward. This was Aaron Hisel, the man she'd counted on and shared her deepest sorrows with. Certainly they could share a day at Chelsea Piers together without her feeling all tied up in knots.

He crossed the old wooden floor and came up to Sierra. "Looks like we've got us a fun day ahead, huh?"

"Yes, sir." Sierra shot Jamie a look, but at least she remembered to keep both her expression and her tone pleasant.

They headed for Jamie's van, and when Aaron climbed into the front seat, Sierra hesitated and looked at Jamie. No words were needed; Jamie could read her daughter's thoughts perfectly.

Small talk filled the ride, and Sierra remained silent. It wasn't until they were finished golfing and Sierra was in the pool that Aaron finally turned to Jamie and frowned. "She doesn't like me, does she?"

Jamie tried to look surprised. "Who? Sierra?" She forced a chuckle. "She's a seven-year-old, Aaron. She imagined our trip one way, and when it wasn't how she pictured it, she got an attitude. It has nothing to do with you."

Aaron put his hand on her knee. "Come on, Jamie, it's okay. I'm not Jake and I never will be. I won't ever try to take his place. I can understand if Sierra feels funny having me around."

Having him around? Jamie felt her head start to spin. He was talking like they'd already made a commitment to each other. She was probably supposed to be reassured by the fact that he didn't want to replace Jake, but what exactly did that mean? That if by some turn of events they wound up together, he wouldn't try to be a father to Sierra? That he'd treat her with kindness and civility but never the passionate love of a daddy?

It was too much for Jamie. She glanced at her knee and felt her breath catch in her throat. It was one thing for them to be together when they worked at St. Paul's or when they ate together at Battery Park. But here? With Sierra swimming nearby?

She stood up and collected her purse. "Want something to drink?"

Aaron lowered his brow. "Weren't we talking?"

"Yes, but . . ." She massaged her throat. "The chlorine in here. I'm dying of thirst."

"Okay." He made a sound that was almost a chuckle. "Get me a Coke, if you don't mind."

Jamie felt anger bubble its way through her veins as she walked away. She *did* mind, in fact. She minded that she wasn't in the pool with her daughter, and that Aaron wanted a relationship with her.

And most of all she minded that Jake had died in the first place. He should be here now, splashing and swimming with Sierra, picking the little girl up and tossing her into the water until she couldn't breathe from laughing so hard.

She minded all of it.

After she paid for the drinks, she stepped into an alcove, where she could see Sierra through a long window. *God . . . what am I doing here with Aaron? I'm not ready for this, I'm not.*

Daughter, be still.

The holy whispers skimmed across the rough waters of her soul, calming the wind and whitecaps, giving her a moment of peace. *Thank You, God . . . even now You're here.* She leaned against the glass. *I'm so confused.*

I'm here. Be still and wait for Me.

Be still and wait? Jamie took a step back. Where had she heard that before? It was a Scripture, wasn't it? Something Jake had written about in his journal. The journal she'd read a hundred times. *Be still and wait on the Lord.* Yes, that was it. Be still and wait. Being still was something Jamie was never good at. Oh, she'd gotten better. Losing Jake had done that for her.

But times like this, she was glad for God's reminders.

Ever since the fateful lunch with Aaron, she'd been going a hundred miles an hour, running from the future the same way she used to run from God. Be still and wait? It was exactly what she needed to hear, what she needed to do.

She folded her arms against her waist and stared at her shoes. Her heart was still racing, still screaming at her to run or tell Aaron the truth—that she simply couldn't make herself feel something that wasn't there yet.

Calm, Jamie . . . be calm. God knows what you need. Bit by bit she felt the waves grow still, felt order restored to her soul. Her heartbeat slowed and she breathed in long and steady. Everything was going to be okay. Somehow the pieces of her future would come together, and the process would be easier if she didn't fight it. If she was still and waited on God.

She'd been gone almost ten minutes, and Aaron was bound to wonder about her. Holding tight to the direction God had given her, she rounded the corner and found a smile. Aaron was watching for her as she walked up.

"Long line?"

Lying would be the easy way out. She shook her head. "Not really." One of the drinks in her hands was his, and she handed it to him. Then she took the spot beside him on the bleachers and looked for Sierra.

"She's over there." Aaron pointed to the shallow end where a group of girls Sierra's age were playing a game.

"Thanks." She glanced at Sierra and saw her stand on the side of the pool, her legs long and skinny. One of the girls in the pool motioned for her to jump, but she looked for Jamie first. Their eyes met, and Jamie waved, just as Sierra did a cannonball into the water and came up laughing.

Jamie set her drink down. "Aaron . . ."

"Uh-oh." His smile didn't hide the regret in his voice. "Here it comes. The part where you tell me you've thought it over and you only want to be friends, right?"

She was about to explain herself but he kept on.

"Look, Jamie." As a fire captain for the FDNY, Aaron had to be one of the toughest leaders in the department. And, from everything Jake had ever said about him, he was. But now his eyes were kinder than she'd ever seen them. "I never meant to pressure you. It's just . . ." He lifted his hands and let them fall again. "I guess I never would've known if I hadn't said something."

The awkwardness from earlier that morning seemed ridiculous now. Her sudden fear of him was a slip back to the old Jamie—who was so often motivated by a paralyzing fear. The new Jamie, who believed in God's plan for her life, hadn't had to deal with fear in nearly three years.

Until Aaron told her he had feelings for her.

"You're not saying anything." Aaron cocked his head. "I can take a lot, Jamie. But I can't take losing your friendship." He reached for her hand, squeezed it once, and let go. "Okay, say something."

"I will." Her heart swelled with feelings—care or concern or friendship. Or something more, Jamie wasn't sure. "You're right, I have thought it over. But I'm not sure I want only a friendship, Aaron."

I don't know *what* I want. I feel crazy saying it's too soon." She allowed a sad laugh. "Three years is a long time, I know that. But in here—" her hand rested on the place above her heart—"I'm not ready to love someone else. At least, I don't think I am."

Aaron sucked in his cheek and narrowed his eyes. He watched Sierra for a minute, splashing near one of the pool's smaller slides. "So . . . you haven't completely written off the idea?"

"No." This time Jamie gave him a sideways hug. The sensation wasn't strange or awkward. In fact, it felt nice. Safe and warm, if not quite electric. She kept her fingers cupped around his shoulder and waited until he looked at her before letting go. "I care a lot about you, Aaron. I love having you there, talking with you—" she gestured toward the pool—"being together on days like this. It feels right, it feels like it could be more serious one day."

Aaron slid closer to her so that their arms were touching. "That's more than enough for me." He looked at Sierra again, and the hint of a smile played in his voice.

Now that the awkward feeling was gone, Jamie realized something. She wasn't only enjoying his company, she was enjoying the feel of his body against her arm.

A handful of emotions raced around in Jamie's heart. How terrible she was to enjoy the physical contact of a man who had been Jake's boss, his mentor; how awful that she could ever find another man's company, his presence, enjoyable. And the most dominant emotion—how good she felt, now that they'd talked things out, with him at her side.

She ignored the pangs of guilt and leaned into him for a few seconds. "Thanks for understanding."

"I know you, Jamie." He glanced at her and pressed a gentle kiss to her forehead. Then, just as quickly, he straightened and shot another look at Sierra. "I knew you'd need time. I just wanted you to know how I felt."

She remembered Sue's warning, that Aaron could never be right for her as long as he didn't share her faith. Never mind his age or the fact that he'd been Jake's boss. If he didn't believe in Christ the way she did, what depth could they ever share together?

This would be the time to say something about it, to ask if he would ever be interested in learning more about God, maybe going to church with her. But somehow the subject didn't seem to fit. Besides, Jake had never pushed her toward God. He'd lived out his faith every day of his life. Maybe it was her turn to do that where Aaron was concerned.

She remembered the holy whispers in her heart a few minutes earlier. God wanted her to be still and wait. Didn't that mean waiting before making faith an issue with Aaron? Besides, she didn't want to upset him, didn't want him to slide back down the bench from her.

"I like this. Sitting with you like this."

"Me too." He gave her an understanding smile. "As long as we don't think about getting serious just yet, right?"

"Right."

In the distance, Sierra climbed out of the pool and grabbed her towel. It was clear by her actions she was about to run toward them—probably needing something to eat or drink. Panic shot through Jamie. It was one thing to sit this way when Sierra wasn't looking, when she was too far away to make out exactly how close Jamie was sitting next to Aaron. But to have her daughter run up and see them . . . that was more than Jamie was ready for.

She nodded in Sierra's direction. "I think I'll get her a drink. Want anything else?"

"I'm fine." The look in Aaron's eyes told her he understood, and better still, he was at peace with her actions.

Before she turned and went to meet Sierra, she smiled once more at him. "Thanks, Aaron. I . . . I feel so much better about things."

"Me too."

The awkwardness and angst and even the guilt lifted as Jamie walked away. Her steps were lighter than they'd been in a long time. And throughout lunch, only one thought about Aaron remained.

How kind and understanding he'd been through this new phase in their friendship, and how maybe—one day not too far off—his kindness might open doors to a place she would never before have considered.

EIGHT

The angry butterflies were back. Sierra was dressed for bed and heading to the bathroom to brush her teeth, but all she could think about was the talk. This was the night she was going to talk to Mommy about the thing Katy said, the thing about their daddies and the helmets.

"Sierra, are you in your nightgown?" Mommy was in her room folding some towels.

"Yes." Sierra did a gulp.

"Did you brush your teeth?"

"That's what I'm doing right now."

"Okay, sweetie, I'll be there in a minute to pray with you." Mommy's voice was happy, the way it sounded ever since the swimming at Chelsea Piers.

Why was she so happy? Was it because of a fun day out with Sierra? Or was it Captain Hisel? Captain Hisel was nice, but Sierra wasn't sure. He wasn't like her daddy at all, and that's another reason why the angry butterflies were in her tummy.

A boy named James in her class at school lost his firefighter daddy. And last summer his mommy got married again, so now James had a new daddy. No, not a new daddy, but a second daddy.

Sierra walked into the bathroom and made a face at the mirror. She didn't want a new daddy. But sometimes she looked at James and thought how lucky he was because now he had a second daddy. And that wouldn't be so bad, but not Captain Hisel. He was old and he didn't talk to her or play with her the way a second daddy should.

"Ready, honey?" More happy voice.

Sierra jumped. "Almost." She took the cap off the toothpaste and set it careful on the counter. Sometimes if she wasn't careful the cap rolled onto the floor and once when that happened she couldn't find it again. Then she squeezed out a pea-sized spot on her pink Barbie toothbrush, because before she used to put a whole caterpillar size on but then it would grow inside her mouth and come out the sides. When that happened it usually got on her nightgown, so Mommy said use a pea size.

Thinking about her teeth made her tummy feel a little better. Her toothbrush was the best kind. It had a little motor on it. She put the bristly end in her mouth and pushed the white button. The toothbrush wiggled and jiggled and cleaned every tooth sparkly clean. Sierra spit out the old toothpaste and rinsed out her brush.

She was just looking for one of her dinosaur flossers when Mommy walked in and leaned by the door. "Hi."

"Hi." Sierra didn't look up. She found a new flosser, opened it up, and pushed it between her teeth. That way she didn't have to start having the talk with Mommy just yet.

When she was finished, she put everything away, and dried the wet spots off her face. "Okay. I'm ready."

"Well." Her mommy lifted her eyebrows high and looked at the sink area. "That's the neatest teeth-brushing job I've ever seen."

"Thank you." Sierra stood perfectly still, feet together, and waited. "Can we go to my room now?"

"Sure." A strange look was in her mommy's eyes. "Everything okay, honey?"

"Yes." Her tummy did a drop. This was the moment she'd been waiting for. She followed her mommy across the hall and into her own pink bedroom. Then she flopped up on her ruffly bed and let her feet hang over the edge. "Can I ask you something?"

"Sure." Her mommy still sounded happy, even though she looked curious. She sat on the bed too, up near the pillows. She pulled her feet up and hugged her legs. "What's up?"

Sierra turned so she could see her mommy better. "Katy said something weird when we were at her house."

Right away Mommy got a funny look on her face. "Something weird?"

"Mmhmm." She nodded. "She told me how come my daddy didn't die in the Twin Towers if he was with her daddy."

Her mommy's mouth opened, but no words came out. Also her face looked a little whitish. Finally she said, "Well, Sierra, that's a good question."

Good question was what Mommy said when she didn't want to give an answer. At least not a quick answer. Sierra made sure her tone was nice. "So what's the answer?"

"That was a very hard time for everyone, honey. Nothing that happened was easy to understand." Her mommy leaned her head back for a minute. When she looked at Sierra again, her eyes were wet. "God knows exactly when each person will come home to heaven. I guess that's my best answer."

Sierra tapped her fingers on her leg. Her mommy's words still didn't feel like an answer, really. "So that's why he didn't die when Katy's daddy died?"

"Sierra, why did Katy start talking about that? What brought it up?"

"The helmets."

This time Mommy looked sickish around her eyes. Her voice got quiet and shocked. "The helmets?"

Her daddy's fire helmet sat on her dresser. It was cleaned off because it got dirty in the fire where Daddy died. It sat right next to the picture of her and Daddy from one of the days after he came home from the hospital. He had bandages on his head, and crutches. The picture was special, just like every picture Sierra had of her daddy. But the helmet was the most specialest thing Sierra owned. Katy had one too.

"That." Sierra pointed to the helmet. "Katy has one on her dresser too."

"Yes." Her mommy made a coughing sound. "That's because Katy's mommy felt the same way I do. That you girls should have the helmets that belonged to your daddies."

"That's not what I mean." Sierra shook her head. Her stomach still hurt a little but she was getting frustration inside her. "Katy says they found their helmets at the same time. When they were cleaning up the Twin Towers."

Her mother looked at her and blinked. Then she leaned close and hugged her for a very long time. When she pulled back, her eyes said very certain that their talk was over. "Sierra, it's too late for this tonight." She kissed her and gave her butterfly kisses, the way Daddy used to do it. "Let's talk about it tomorrow."

"Tomorrow's Halloween. And it's Sunday. I'll see Katy at Sunday school and then what if she says that thing again? What am I supposed to say?"

Her mommy looked down and said the quiet words, "Help me, God," which Sierra did not understand. Why did her mother need God's help to answer one easy question? Next her mommy looked up and said, "Let's have church at the beach tomorrow, Sierra."

"At the beach?"

"Yes." Her mommy's chin was shaking a little bit. "You and me by ourselves. We'll go to the same beach where Daddy and I used to take you jet skiing, okay?"

"Won't it be too cold?"

"Probably." Mommy did a sort-of smile. "We'll wear our sweaters and bring chairs to sit in. Then we can read from the Bible and pray and have a little talk."

"About the helmets?" Sierra wasn't sure she could wait that long, plus she wanted to tell Katy she was wrong. It wasn't weird at all. But the part about the helmets still didn't make sense.

"Yes, about the helmets."

"And then go to Katy's dress-up party for dinner?"

"Yes, that too."

A good feeling came into Sierra's tummy, then. Because even though she had to wait, at least she would know the answer. She wouldn't have any more questions about her daddy or why he didn't die in the Twin Towers or how come Katy said they found his helmet next to her daddy's helmet.

After tomorrow, everything would make sense.

Jamie barely closed the door and made it to her bed before she collapsed to her knees. "God!" The sound was a whisper soaked with anguish and fear and desperation. "I'm not ready for this."

This time there were no holy messages, no still, small voice assuring her that God was there, standing ready.

Always she had known it would come to this, that someday she would have to explain to Sierra how her father had actually been killed in the terrorist attacks. But now it seemed impossible to say the words, impossible to explain that the man she'd brought orange juice to, the man she'd sat with and sang with and read stories with for three months while he got better, hadn't been her father but a stranger.

In the years since then, Jamie had always figured she'd know when the time was right. But that wasn't really what she'd counted on. The truth was, she hoped she wouldn't have to tell Sierra until she was a teenager, eighteen maybe. That way her daughter wouldn't remember anything but a blur of hazy images from the time in her life when Eric Michaels lived with them.

But now? When she still had the picture of the man on her dresser?

She'd probably looked at it a thousand times in the last three years, and now, tomorrow on the beach, she would have to tell Sierra that the man in the picture wasn't her daddy.

I don't want to tell her, God . . . She hung her head. *What's wrong with me? I should've said something a long time ago.*

Her knees hurt. She struggled to her feet and fell onto her bed. Her own questions echoed in her heart until an answer started to form. She didn't want to tell Sierra because a part of her still wanted to believe it herself. That was the problem, wasn't it? Those were the three most difficult months of her life, and having Eric Michaels, believing he was Jake, was the only reason she'd survived.

God knew she would've crumbled much like the towers if she'd learned that week that Jake was one of the dead. So instead he brought her a substitute. A Jake look-alike.

Once she knew he wasn't Jake, she had helped him to figure out his identity. After that he'd gone home to his wife and son, but a part of her still held on to the comfort of knowing that she'd had Jake three months longer than Sue had Larry, than any of the other FDNY widows had had their husbands.

Telling Sierra the truth would change that time, alter the memories so that none of them brought comfort. How could they if the man in the memory wasn't Jake but a stranger? If she was forced to paint the situation with truth, those memories would be shocking, abrasive. How could she have mixed them up? What was *wrong* with her that she could sit and talk and eat and laugh with a stranger and all the while think him Jake?

No matter that a part of her wanted to tell Sierra the truth. It was easier the way she'd chosen to deal with it.

For three months she'd had Jake back, almost the way she'd always had him. And then, overnight, he turned into someone else, someone with a family in Los Angeles. Before he found his wife and son, she wished he never would, that somehow she could keep him. Even after she helped him find his family, even at the airport with his wife about to get off a plane and take him home, Jamie wanted to grab his hand and run away with him.

But that would've been wrong. First, because the man belonged with his family; second, because he wasn't Jake.

Even now, it felt like Jake had been with them. Eric had done such a good job of studying Jake's Bible, his journal, that as the weeks passed he actually sounded like Jake and acted like him. He even learned to curl Sierra's hair the same way Jake would've curled it.

He was *like* Jake in every way. But he wasn't Jake.

When Eric Michaels said good-bye, Jamie felt God's peace like never before. She watched him walk away, kept her eyes on him while he went to his wife and hugged her, then Jamie turned around without ever looking back. She had kept her promise and told only Sue and Aaron. The media called often back then, but she shared the story with no one.

Jamie stared at the ceiling. What had she done? Were her efforts to close the door on Eric Michaels so good, she'd forgotten to work through her emotions? She'd broken down when they had his blood tested, the day they realized he wasn't Jake. But her grieving had been over losing Jake, not about believing a stranger was her husband.

She looked at the clock. Nine-forty-five; Sue would still be up. The cordless phone was a few feet away, off the charging unit as usual. Jamie grabbed it and punched in Sue's number.

Her friend answered on the first ring. "Hello?"

"Sue . . ." Jamie's throat was thick.

"Jamie?"

"Yes, I . . . Sue, could you pray for me?"

"What's wrong?" Concern flooded Sue's voice. "You sound upset."

Jamie's lungs hurt, and she realized she was holding her breath. She exhaled and pushed her fingers into the roots of her hair. "It's been a long day."

"Weren't you out with Aaron and Sierra?"

"Yes." Jamie closed her eyes. "That's not the problem."

Sue waited. "What then?"

"I guess the girls were talking, and Katy told Sierra that rescue workers found both their daddies' helmets at the same time, in the rubble of the Twin Towers."

"What?" Shock rang in Sue's tone. "Where on earth would she have heard that?"

"I don't know. Maybe she overheard us talking one day, or maybe someone else told her. Anyway, that's not the point. Katy's right; I don't blame her for telling Sierra the truth."

"Did Sierra ask about it?"

"Yes." Jamie opened her eyes, sat up, and slipped out of bed. She had nowhere to go so she stood there, unmoving. "She wanted to know why Katy's daddy died in the Twin Towers and her daddy didn't. And then she wanted to know about the helmets."

"Great." Sue sighed. "I'm so sorry, Jamie. You don't need this right now."

"It's okay. I need it sometime and apparently God wants it to be now."

"What are you going to do?"

"Tell her the truth." Jamie took slow steps toward the tall dresser, the one that had been Jake's. His Bible and journal sat on top, where she could easily find them when she needed to get lost in his heart, his mind, his faith.

"Oh, Jamie, no wonder you want me to pray."

Tears stung at Jamie's eyes, but she resisted them. She put one hand on Jake's Bible. Beside her, within her, she could feel the Lord watching, standing guard, even though she hadn't heard Him speak to her that night. He was there and He would see her through the next day. "Yes, that's why."

"I'll be praying the whole day. Call me when you're ready to talk about it, okay?"

"Okay." Jamie ran her fingers over the Bible's worn leather cover. "Thanks. And who knows. Maybe it'll be the best thing for both of us."

They said their good-byes and Jamie clicked the off button. She tossed the phone back onto the bed and took Jake's Bible from the dresser. With her eyes on the cover, on the smudged place where his engraved name had all but worn off, she backed up until she hit the rocking chair that had always been in their room.

She sat down and opened the old book to a section of Scripture she'd read before. Philippians, the fourth chapter, thirteenth verse. Carefully she turned the pages, savoring the yellow highlighted sections and the precious notations Jake had written in the margins until she reached the right spot.

Her eyes found the Scripture immediately.

I can do all things through Christ who gives me strength.

She looked out the window at the old elm tree outside. It was hidden in the shadows, but she could see its leaves rustling in the evening breeze. She'd been sitting outside watching Sierra play the first time she found that verse. Her mind savored the words again. *I can do all things through Christ who gives me strength.*

Once more she looked at the page, wanting to soak in the truth long enough to lean on it come morning. But instead of seeing the Scripture about strength, her eyes landed on verse four. Jake had highlighted the next few lines in blue, and Jamie couldn't remember ever reading them.

She squinted so she could see the words more clearly in the dim light of the room.

Rejoice in the Lord always. I will say it again: Rejoice! Let your gentleness be evident to all. The Lord is near. Do not be anxious about anything, but in everything, by prayer and petition, with thanksgiving, present your requests to God. And the peace of God, which transcends all understanding, will guard your hearts and your minds in Christ Jesus.

It wasn't one verse but four. Four wonderful, hope-filled lines of truth that breathed new life into her. The best part was that the Lord was near. Wasn't that exactly how she'd been feeling while she was talking to Sue? That the Lord was truly near?

And what were His words of advice for troubled hearts? Rejoice! Find a reason to be glad, and then don't get anxious. Instead pray, and God, because He's so good, will provide a peace the world knows nothing about.

A thin dark line was drawn from that section of Scripture to a scribbled notation near the top of the page. This was her favorite part of reading Jake's Bible. The words he'd added gave her an insight she hadn't had when he was alive.

She shifted so the light was better.

God wants everyone to be gentle, even us tough FDNY guys. The reason? He is closer than we think.

Jake was an amazing man, strong and gutsy and gentle in every way. But times like this she wished she could see him one more time, see him face-to-face and tell him how much it meant to her that he'd left a road map for her and Sierra to follow. Yes, Jake was right; God was closer than they thought.

She closed the book and held it to her heart. *Jake . . . if only you knew how much I miss you.* Tears came and this time she didn't stop them. *I know you so much better now.*

For a while she sat there, pretending Jake was beside her, lying in bed sleeping, ready for an early-morning shift. If only she could crawl into the covers and find him there one more time, his sweet breath warm against her face. Nights like this, if she thought hard enough, she could almost feel him stirring in his sleep, putting his arm around her and making her feel like the safest, most loved woman in the world.

She opened her eyes and looked out the window again.

God had pulled her through every day since September 11; He would get her through the talk with Sierra. She set Jake's Bible back on the dresser, brushed her teeth, and climbed into bed. Lying there, she did a quick inventory of the day: the trip to Chelsea Piers, how she had enjoyed sitting by Aaron.

But as she fell asleep it was something else that made her smile.

After tomorrow, Sierra would know the truth about Jake's death; there would be nothing left to hide. She would simply tell their daughter what really happened and be there for her, whatever she needed.

And best of all, God would be with her. Strength would come not only from the truth in the Scriptures but from the truth Jake himself had written. And that was almost like having him there too.

NINE

The beach was cold, just like Sierra thought. But it wasn't rainy, and that was a good thing. Rainy days were better for inside, cuddled up near the fire with Mommy and Wrinkles. She didn't care about the weather; just that Mommy would finally tell her about the weird thing Katy said about her daddy and his helmet. She was dying to make sense of it all.

Mommy was driving. She turned the car into the parking lot, and Sierra sat a little straighter so she could see. Yep, it was their favorite beach. The one they came to last summer with Katy and her mommy. But it looked different with winter on it, not as blue and happy. The water was ice gray and the sand looked wet. "You sure it won't be too cold?"

"If it is, we won't stay long, okay?" Mommy smiled at her. She reached out and took Sierra's hand. "I've always wanted to come out here in the winter, before the snow comes, all by ourselves."

Sierra peered down the beach a ways. "There's two people in chairs there, Mommy. And three over by the water."

Her mommy did a little laugh. "I don't mean all by ourselves, exactly. I mean without the summer crowds."

"Oh." Sierra wiggled her nose. She could already smell the seawater.

The car stopped and Mommy squeezed her hand. "Okay, let's go." Mommy took the picnic basket and the big Bible, the one that belonged to her daddy before he died in the fire. She also took two chairs from the back of the van and a big, bushy blanket, the warmest kind they had.

Sierra grabbed her pink Bible and pulled her coat tight around her middle. Out on the sand it wasn't as cold as she thought. A medium sort of cold, but that's all. Plus the sky was the bluest blue. The seagulls looked like white kites against that sky.

She pushed her feet over the sand and kept up with Mommy. They already had a plan. Sierra would read something favorite from her Bible, and then Mommy would read something favorite from hers. Well, not really hers, but sort of hers. She always read the Bible that *used* to be Daddy's.

The more they got close to the water, the more Sierra started to remember. This was the place they came a year after Daddy died. They brought a balloon that day. Sierra squinted at the water. She gave butterfly kisses to the balloon and wrote something on it. A message for Daddy. Yep, that was it.

This was the same exact place.

She stopped, and after a few steps, her mommy stopped too.

"Sierra?" Her eyes had sun in them so she made a shade with her hands. "What's wrong, honey? You need a rest?"

It was a long way from the car to their spot near the water. But she wasn't tired. "No."

"Okay, then . . ." Mommy sounded curious and maybe a little confused. "Come on. Let's set up."

"I'm sad."

Her mommy's face got melty. "Sad? Why, honey?"

"Because this is where we sent the balloon to Daddy when I was in kindergarten."

A lonely breath came from her mommy. "Yes. You remember that?"

"Mmhmm." She started walking again. Her mommy did too. "I was just a little kid, but I remember a lot. Even now that I'm grown-up."

"Yes." Her mommy bit her lip. "I remember too. And you're right, honey. It is sad."

A few more steps and her mommy set down the chairs and basket. But not the Bible. Sierra helped her open the chairs. They sat down and Mommy spread the blanket over their legs. With their coats and the blankets, it was actually sort of snuggly warm.

Sierra looked out at the water. "It's kind of happy too."

"What?"

"Being here." She gave her mommy her best smile she could. "I think Daddy can see us in this place, all the way from heaven."

"Yes." Her mommy's eyes got small. She looked out at the water. "Yes, Sierra, I think there must be windows in heaven. And I'll bet you're right; I'll bet Daddy is up there smiling at us right now."

Heaven was a long ways away, but Sierra liked to try to see it. She made a shade over her eyes and stared straight into the blue. For a long time she just looked and didn't say anything. The seagulls and the waves did all the talking.

"Sierra?" Her mommy scooched her chair over closer. Now their arms were touching. "Ready to read your favorite verse?"

"Yes." She pulled her children's storybook Bible out from beneath the snuggly blanket and turned to the story about Peter and his friends in the boat one stormy night. She was an excellent reader. That's what everyone said. She looked at the first words and did a cough so her voice could say them.

"'One day Peter and his friends were in a boat in the middle of the night.'" She used her finger to follow along, but it wasn't hard. This story was one she read to Wrinkles all the time. "'A storm came up and Peter saw a man out on the water. "Who is it?" Peter asked. The man on the water said, "It is me, Peter." Peter was very amazed. The man on the water was Jesus. "If it is you, Lord, tell me to walk on the water . . ."'"

Sierra made a tired sound. She needed a little rest. A seagull landed close by because he wanted to listen to the story. She laughed out loud at the bird.

"What's so funny?" Mommy did a little laugh too.

"That seagull." Sierra pointed at him. "He wants to listen to the story."

"Hmmm." Her mommy raised her eyebrows at her. Raised eyebrows meant Come on sillypants, get back to reading. "I'd like to listen to the story too."

Sierra looked out at the ocean and took a big breath. "I'm doing good, huh, Mommy?"

"Very good. I can't wait to hear the rest."

A big smile came on Sierra's face, because Mommy was funny. "Okay, here it is." She found her place on the page. "'Jesus said,

"Peter, come to me." So, Peter went out of the boat and came to Jesus on top of the water. But when he saw the wind and big waves he began to sink. He held his hand out to Jesus. "Help," he cried. Then Jesus helped Peter out of the water. He said, "Peter, you need to have more faith."'" She closed her pink Bible. "The end."

"Nice job, honey. I like it." Mommy was quiet for a little bit. "What's your favorite part?"

"The part about Jesus helping Peter out of the water."

"Why that part?"

"Because sometimes . . ." Sierra closed her eyes and listened to the waves. She kept them closed, even when she started talking again. "I hate not having a daddy. No one to swing me around or give me horseback rides or curl my hair or anything." She opened her eyes and looked at Mommy. "I hate it so much." She leaned her head back so she could see the sky again. "Sometimes I miss my daddy so much I feel like I'm drowning. Just like Peter. But then I reach for Jesus, and He helps me be okay."

"I'm sorry, Sierra." Her mommy's voice was full of sad.

"About what?" It wasn't Mommy's fault.

"I'm sorry you don't have a daddy. I can only tell you I miss him as much as you do."

"Probably more, 'cause you knew him longer."

"Yes." Her mommy's smile was still very sad. "Probably more." The sound in her voice was like when sometimes she was going to cry. But her eyes were dry when she opened the big Bible and turned some pages. "This is a Scripture your daddy gave me, long before I even knew Jesus."

"You mean when me and Daddy used to go to church by just ourselves?"

"Right." Mommy made a frown. "Back then." She looked at the pages and started to read. "It's from Jeremiah 29:11. It says, '"For I know the plans I have for you," says the Lord, "plans to prosper you and not to harm you, plans to give you hope and a future."'"

Sierra nodded. "I've heard that before. I like it."

Her mommy closed the Bible but kept it on her lap. Then she put the blanket back over them. "I wanted to read that because you and I need to have a little talk, Sierra. I want to answer your questions from last night, okay?"

"Okay." Sierra's stomach did a somersault. 'Cause this was the big answer, actually. Mommy's voice was serious, only that didn't make sense. Because Katy didn't know that every person has a time when they die. At least that's what Mommy said. So that meant Katy's daddy had September 11, and her own daddy had another day. That's all. She squiggled her toes in her shoes and waited.

"Whatever we talk about here, I want you to remember that Bible verse, Sierra. God has a plan for you and He has a plan for me. Sometimes strange things happen and God can make them into something good, all right?"

"Yes." Sierra held tight to the arms of her chair. "Can you tell me now?"

Her mommy nodded. "Let's pray first. That way we can end our Bible study."

"Okay."

She took hold of Sierra's hand and looked out where heaven was. "God, we are so glad You're always there for us, that when we fall, You pick us up. Even when it feels like we're drowning." Her voice sounded sad again. "Right now I ask You to be with Sierra, so she can understand what I'm about to tell her. Give me the right words. Be with both of us, Lord. We need You. In Jesus' name, amen."

When she was finished she looked at Sierra. Her eyes were the same as they were last summer when Sierra woke up one morning and Mommy told her some sad news. That their old dog Brownie died in her sleep. Yes, her eyes were the same now. Sierra liked the way her mommy's hand felt around her smaller one. "I'm ready now."

"Okay." Her mother took in a long breath. "Sierra, Katy is right about Daddy. He did die in the Twin Towers, just like her daddy."

Sierra frowned. She stared at her mommy. Why would she say that? The pieces of her heart felt all mixed up.

Mommy looked a long time at her. "After the towers fell down, Captain Hisel was walking around and he saw a man who looked like your daddy." She stopped and looked up. Then she whispered, "God ... help me. This is harder than I thought."

That was a problem. Whenever Mommy prayed in the middle of talking it was a problem. She swallowed. "It's okay, Mommy. I want to know."

"Anyway, they took that man to the hospital, and told me it was your daddy. He was hurt and he had bandages on his face, but he looked . . . he looked exactly like your daddy, Sierra. Exactly. But he wasn't Daddy. He was a man named Eric Michaels. A man who—"

"That's not true!" Sierra pulled her hand away from her mommy and crossed her arms tight. "He was *so* my daddy! He gave me horse-back rides and curled my hair and made me blueberry pancakes." Her tummy hurt very bad now. "He *was* my daddy, Mommy. Maybe you got your story wrong."

"Sierra . . ." She had a strange sound this time, like she was scared. "I *promise* I'm telling you the truth. You *thought* he was Daddy, and I thought he was Daddy. I was shocked when I found out he wasn't Daddy. But, Sierra, Daddy died in the Twin Towers. That man—Eric Michaels—was from California. He only *looked* like Daddy." Tears broke into her voice and made it scratchy. She did a few sobs and covered her face for a long time. When she looked up she was more sad than Sierra had ever seen her. "Can you believe me, honey? Please?"

She had to think about this, actually. Before she could answer her mommy's question, she needed a little time for her brain to work. "I want to walk for a minute, okay?"

"Okay." Her mommy sat back in her chair. New tears were in her eyes, but she didn't sound as sad.

Sierra pushed the blanket off, set her Bible down, and walked down the little hill to the water. It was colder there, but she didn't care. How could it be true? How could Daddy have been someone else for all that time? She scrunched down the way they did in gym class sometimes, sort of sitting but not touching the sand with her bottom. Her head felt all swishy inside, but Sierra knew one thing.

Mommy never lied to her. She might wait a long time to tell the truth, but she never lied.

Never.

So if Mommy wasn't lying then it had to be true. The daddy who came home from the hospital wasn't her daddy. Sierra felt sick, the way she felt when they served tuna casserole for hot lunch. Even if it was true, her head was still all mixed up.

She stood and walked up the hill, careful not to get sand in her tennis shoes. When she got there she put her hands on her hips, because this was very serious business. "The man who lived with us in the downstairs bedroom? He wasn't Daddy?"

Mommy's eyes were still wet and a few tears spilt onto her coat. "No, honey. Your daddy died in the towers right next to Katy's daddy."

"That's why they found the helmets together?"

"Yes, that's why."

"So he gave me horsie rides and curled my hair, but he wasn't my daddy?"

"No, sweetheart. He really wasn't."

Sierra sat back down in her chair, picked up her Bible, and pulled the blanket up around her. All of a sudden she thought of something, something that took away some of the sick feeling in her stomach. She looked at her mommy. "Then that daddy who lived with us is still alive, right?"

"Yes, but he—"

"I know! Let's find him and he can be my second daddy! James in my class—remember James?"

"Sierra, you don't understa—"

"His daddy was a firefighter and he died in the Twin Towers, but now his mommy got married again and he has a second daddy. Isn't that nice for James, Mommy?"

"No, Sierra, it's not like that. The man who—"

"So maybe that man who looked like my daddy could be my second daddy." She made a sad face. "He would never be my special first daddy, because no one could ever be him." Her smile came back, just a little. "But that man was very nice, Mommy. I liked him a lot, even if he wasn't my real daddy. He looked like Daddy and he seemed like Daddy. So now you can go find him and marry him and we can be a family like when he was here." Sierra was out of air so she breathed in real fast. "Could you do that, Mommy? I really like him and plus, he's alive."

Mommy pulled her arms out from under the blanket and put them on her knees. Then she put her head down on them, like maybe she was tired. She stayed that way a long time, and also her shoulders did a little shaking.

"Mommy?"

Her fingers covered her face, and she sat up straight. Then she wiped her tears and let her hands fall back to the blanket. Her cheeks were almost as red as her eyes. "No, Sierra." She looked at her really close. "It can't be like that. It can *never* be like that. The man who lived with us—Mr. Michaels—didn't have his memory because his head got hurt in the towers. Everyone told him he was our daddy, and even he thought so. But then he got better and he found out he wasn't our daddy. That's when he left to find his real family."

Sierra didn't want to hear those words. "His real family?"

"Yes. His real family."

Sierra stared at her lap. Maybe that was why he left, and that was when—

She looked at her mommy. "When he went away . . . that's when you told me about Daddy dying in the fire, right?"

"Right." Her mommy's eyes still had wet in them. "I'm sorry, Sierra. I should've told you a long time ago, but I didn't know how or when." She sniffed and wiped her eyes again. "I'm so sorry, baby. I just didn't know how to say it."

Sierra looked at the sand and made her brain think very fast. When she looked up she had an idea. "Are you sure that other daddy has a different family?"

"Yes, honey. They live in California."

"Oh." Sierra stretched her feet out and thought some more. "Can I see him sometime?"

Her mother's breath came out long and she looked very tired. She shook her head. "No, Sierra. We can't see him."

Sierra didn't like that very much—but she did like that at least she had a second daddy for a little bit of time. That was more than Katy had. She stared out at the water. The daddy she really wanted was her own daddy. She looked to heaven, and little tears came into her eyes. At least Daddy was with Jesus. Plus, one day they'd be together again.

"Are you okay, honey?" Her mommy reached for her hand, and Sierra let her take it.

"I think so." Two seagulls danced around a piece of bread a little bit away from them. She yawned and held tight to her mommy's fingers. "Can I keep his picture in my room?"

"Honey, why?" Mommy's mouth dropped open. A wave came up and smashed onto the sand at the bottom of the hill. Mommy made a huffy sound. "I told you, he wasn't your daddy. Not even for a little while."

"Yes, Mommy. He was my *second* daddy. For that little bit of days he was my second daddy." Sierra rubbed her thumb over her mommy's hand. "So, can I keep the picture?"

Her mommy waited. "I don't know, Sierra . . . "

"Please, Mommy."

"Oh—" her shoulders dropped a little bit—"Okay. I guess so."

"Thank you, Mommy. I can remember him better with the picture." One hand was still in hers. With the other one, she tapped on her Bible. She wasn't sick anymore, but she was still a little bit sad. "Guess what, Mommy?"

"What?"

"I like it better that Daddy died in the Twin Towers. Know why?"

"Why?" Her mommy snuggled close to her and their two heads came together like best friends.

"Because Teacher said the firefighters who died on September 11 were heroes. And Daddy was a hero, that's why."

"Sierra . . ." Her mother made a funny sound. Not really a laugh or a cry. "All people who die in the line of duty—firefighters, police officers, soldiers, missionaries—all of them are heroes."

"But you know what, Mommy?"

"What?"

"Our daddy was a superhero." She stretched her hands out as wide as she could. "The biggest superhero of all. Right?"

She could hear a smile in her mommy's voice. "Yes, honey, he was." She gave Sierra another little hug. "He was the best superhero of all."

TEN

The plane couldn't go fast enough for Clay.

It was Halloween—not that a wasted holiday like that meant much—but it was the last Sunday in October, and Joe Reynolds was beside him. The adventure was underway. On the following afternoon they'd be in orientation for the course. Now that he'd said his good-byes to Eric and Laura and Josh, now that he'd made his mind up that somehow God was doing something in his life, Clay couldn't wait to get to New York.

Reynolds felt the same way. The first hour of the flight they guessed at what the training might include, talked about a kidnapping case from a year ago that Reynolds had worked, and speculated about the outcome of a robbery case that was still open.

Small talk, really.

Clay looked out the window. Funny how a person could go years thinking someone was his friend and never really know him. Reynolds was in the middle, sandwiched between Clay and a big man on the aisle. When they ran out of things to talk about, Reynolds nodded off. He'd been sleeping ever since.

The main thing Clay wanted to ask was, why New York? There were twenty cities where they could've gone for training. San Diego, for instance, where the weather was at least warm, or Phoenix, which would be heaven this time of year. The man didn't make impulsive decisions, as far as Clay could tell, so why New York? And what about the picture on his desk, the one of the pretty woman and the little boy? The one he never talked about?

The flight attendants came through with lunch, and Clay elbowed Reynolds. "Time to eat."

His friend opened one eye and then the other. He stretched as much as he could and pulled his tray down. "Gourmet, no doubt." He grinned at the young woman serving them. "Are you single?"

The woman was a redhead with striking caramel eyes. Clay looked at her left ring finger; it was bare. He could've gladly strangled Reynolds for what he figured he was about to say.

The flight attendant returned the smile, but her cheeks turned red as she gave Reynolds his meal. "Who wants to know?"

Reynolds punched Clay in the shoulder. "My single friend here, that's who." Reynolds looked from the flight attendant to Clay, then back again. "He's handsome, wouldn't you say? The flight won't last forever—it's late and getting later."

Clay held up his hands and gave a shake of his head, as if to tell her he was definitely not the instigator.

"Yes." The woman was still blushing. She made eye contact with Clay, but only for a few seconds. Clay couldn't blame her; he was thirty-five and she looked ten years younger.

Clay gave Reynolds a kick. He caught the flight attendant's attention and gave her a weak smile. "Don't mind my friend. He's delusional when he first wakes up."

The flight attendant laughed and pushed the food cart down a few aisles. Twice she looked back and caught Clay's eyes. When she was busy helping another passenger, Clay turned and stared at his friend. "Reynolds, remind me not to go out in public with you when we're in Manhattan."

Reynolds held up his hands in mock surrender. "Just trying to help. My friend can't seem to connect with the ladies . . . I figured I could make something happen."

"Yeah, well, figure not." Clay looked at his meal. It had the look of lasagna, but it smelled suspiciously of fish. He caught his friend's eyes again. "I'll meet someone soon enough."

Reynolds chuckled. "I'm not sure."

They poked at their meals and took a few bites. "You taste any fish in that stuff?"

"No." Reynolds sniffed close to his plate. "But I smell it." He pointed to a small dish of something white. "Could be the warm cottage cheese."

"Mmmm." Clay put his fork down and wiped his mouth. "I think we were lucky to get a meal at all."

Reynolds pointed to a few passengers across the aisle with Subway sandwich bags. "Those are the lucky people, man, let me tell you."

They ate what they could, and after the flight attendant filed back to clear their trays, they shared a comfortable silence. Clay looked out the window again. It was another hour before they arrived in New York, and night was trying to fall on the East Coast. Several thousand feet below was a layer of puffy white clouds, but otherwise the sky was starting to turn colors—deep blues with streaks of lavender and pink.

God's artwork.

"Beautiful." Reynolds was leaning forward, watching the sunset.

"Yep. Only God can paint a sky."

Reynolds settled back in his seat. "You a believer?"

"Longtime believer." Clay sat back too. Funny, but the two had never talked about God before. "What about you?"

"Pretty much." Reynolds stroked his chin and his eyes grew soft. "Not like I used to be."

Clay let that sit. After a few seconds he leaned against the window and looked at Reynolds. "I got a question for you."

"Shoot."

"Why New York?"

The shadows that fell over his friend's eyes told him he'd hit a nerve. Reynolds looked past Clay to the sunset. Lines appeared at the corners of his eyes. "You wouldn't believe it if I told you."

So there *was* a reason. Clay kept his voice low. "Try me." He thought about his brother, Eric. "I've seen some pretty strange things."

At first it didn't look like Reynolds would talk, but maybe because they were suspended between two cities, thirty thousand feet above the ground, he gave in. Reynolds made his lips into a tight straight line and began to tell his story.

"Her name's Wanda. She's the girl in the picture on my desk." He sucked in a breath and held it before letting it ease through his nose. "I was crazy in love with her from the moment I met her— our senior year of high school."

Clay knew Reynolds tended to spit out details in starts and fits, so he waited.

"After high school, I joined the service so I'd have a way through college." He stroked his chin again. "Wanda went with me, lived with me on the base. A year later she had Jimmy and everything, well—" He let out a little laugh, one that lacked humor. "Everything was great until the Gulf War."

"You fought?" Another surprise.

"Yeah, I fought. I was in the first wave, the ground attack." The muscles in his jaw flexed. "It was crazy." His tone was soft, but intense. "That sissy guy you shot the other day? That was nothing to the Gulf War, man. Nothing."

"How long?"

"I was there the better part of three years." He made a sharp sniff. "Came home and found Wanda and Jimmy having dinner at the cafeteria with one of the commanders." He looked out the window again. "I came unglued. Stormed out of there, straight to our apartment."

"Did she see you?" Clay had no trouble picturing Reynolds angry; that's how he worked. Angry and focused.

"Yeah, she saw me. Flew after me with Jimmy running behind her. I heard her, heard both of 'em. Wanda calling my name, Jimmy shouting for his daddy." Reynolds shook his head. "I was so mad, I wouldn't stop, wouldn't turn around for nothing. Not even my little boy."

Clay felt the tension in his friend's voice. Whatever was coming, it wasn't good.

"A road ran through the base, and I crossed it no trouble. Wanda ... she was twenty yards behind me, running like crazy. She got to the road just as some crazy drunk came flying up the hill." He looked up at the airplane's vents and shook his head.

"Hey, it's okay, man." Clay's stomach tightened. He never would've asked about New York if he'd thought it would lead to this.

"No." Reynolds looked at him again. "I'll finish." He searched Clay's eyes. "Wanda saw the car and stopped in time, but Jimmy—" His voice broke, and he pinched the bridge of his nose. His words were barely audible over the sound of the jet engines. "He called my name one more time, and that's when I heard the thud." Reynolds dropped his hand back to his lap. Gone was the invincible look that made him a hero at the police department. His eyes were red and full of pain. "He was dead before he hit the ground."

Clay's stomach sank. No wonder there were no updated pictures of the boy on Reynolds's desk.

"Watching that boy hit the ground . . . seeing Wanda kneel next to him, screaming for him to be okay . . . seeing that drunk stumble out of the car . . ." He bit his lip. "I still have nightmares about it."

Clay wanted the rest of the story. What happened to Wanda? And how come they weren't together any more? But he wasn't going to push. He looked at his hands for a minute and then back at Reynolds. "I'm sorry."

"It was an accident, I know that." He crossed his arms. "But it was my fault. And you know what?"

"What?"

"Turns out the commander wasn't seeing Wanda at all. He was asking her if we wanted an upgrade in our living quarters."

Clay dug his elbow into his thigh and let his forehead rest on his knuckles. Reynolds was right; he never would've believed a story like that one, never would've thought a man as bulletproof as Joe Reynolds would've suffered such a loss.

"Guess we all have a story."

The captain's voice came over the speakers then, advising them of weather conditions in LaGuardia. Cold with a storm moving in.

Clay lowered his hands and looked at his friend again. He had to ask. "What happened to Wanda?"

"She couldn't look at me, couldn't talk to me." He hesitated. "I mean, Michaels, she was crazy with grief. Absolutely crazy. Her baby was dead and it was my fault." A sad smile hung on the corners of his mouth. "We had a strong faith back then; everyone at church tried to help us. After the service we got counseling, and the army gave me a paid leave." He knit his mouth together and shook his head. "Wanda wanted none of it. A week later we found out the guy who hit Jimmy, he was a child molester out early for good behavior. Got himself drunk and crashed through the gate at the base." Reynolds fired the words like bullets. "Never shoulda been out of prison in the first place."

"I hate that."

"Yeah." He made a sarcastic sound that wasn't even close to a laugh. "Talk about having an incentive to get to work."

Now Clay understood something else. When Reynolds showed up on the scene, a minute after Clay had shot the carjacker the other day, his words had been something of a surprise. *You did us all a favor.* Wasn't that it? Yes, that was what he'd said. *You did us all a favor.* Reynolds worked by the books, arresting criminals, forming cases against them, testifying in court. But when a killer made a fatal move in a gun battle with a cop, Reynolds wasn't going to lose any sleep over it.

"For three months we kept trying, me and Wanda. She was hurting so bad, and there was—" he gave a sharp shake of his head— "there was nothing I could do to help her. Finally one day I asked her if she wanted me to leave."

Clay already knew what Reynolds was going to say and it made him sick. Two people who loved each other so much, who shared a faith in God, torn apart when they were both hurting the most.

"She said yes. Seeing me every day, remembering what happened, it was too hard for her." Reynolds's eyes were distant again. "I told her I felt the same way; if she wasn't going to let me help her, I wanted out too." He shrugged. "So I finished my service in California and she moved to Queens. Soon as I had the chance I started college classes and I didn't look back until I had my law degree. Figured I'd fight the bad guys in courtrooms, where I could lock 'em up longer than the jerk who killed my boy."

"Didn't work out that way, huh?"

Reynolds chuckled, and the hurt in his eyes dimmed. "Not for a minute. The whole thing was a game, Michaels. Just one big stinking game." He straightened himself and buckled his seat belt. "I like it better in uniform. At least we get 'em off the streets for a while."

A flight attendant came on this time, telling them to prepare for landing. Clay let the details of his friend's story play again in his mind. "You and Wanda? You've kept in touch?"

"For a little while." He looked at Clay. "She married a firefighter, FDNY. Guy wasn't around much, at least that's what Wanda's mother said. She told me Wanda never stopped loving me; she just didn't know how to show me after Jimmy died."

Clay frowned. "Her husband was FDNY?"

"Yeah." Something more serious crossed his expression. "After the terrorist attacks, I had to know if the guy was one of 'em." He paused. "He was. Lost right up there in the South Tower. Every day since then I've wanted to call Wanda, just to tell her I'm sorry. Sorry about doubting her, sorry about running that day when I came home, sorry about Jimmy. Sorry about her husband." His voice was shakier than before, broken. "Sorry about all of it. But I never made the call."

"Instead you're going to see her in person, is that it?"

The plane was coming in for a landing. Reynolds glanced out the window at the skyline of Manhattan. "I'm not sure." He looked at Clay again. "You're a praying man, is that right?"

"I am."

"Then pray for me. So I'll know if I should look her up, or if seeing me again would only make things harder for her."

They didn't say anything else until they touched down and the pilot welcomed them to New York City. That's when the idea hit him. He turned to Reynolds as he pulled his travel bag from the floor beneath the seat in front of him.

"Hey, we're off tomorrow morning, right?"

"Right. Orientation begins at four o'clock. I guess a few of our shifts will be with the night crew."

"Right, so I have an idea for the morning."

"Okay." Reynolds looked like he was back to himself again, with one small change for the better. His guard was down. "What's your idea?"

"Ground Zero."

Reynolds hesitated. "Hmmm." He gave a slow, thoughtful nod. "Might be a good place to pray."

"That's what I was thinking. We could take the ferry over early."

"Hey, I just remembered. One of the guys from the downtown precinct was telling me there's this little chapel there, right across the street from where the towers stood. St. Peter's, something like that. All sorts of letters and pictures from the attacks."

"Now that—" Clay patted his friend's back as they stood to make their way off the plane—"would be a good place to pray."

ELEVEN

Jamie was looking forward to seeing Aaron on Monday.

She boarded the ferry at nine o'clock and took a seat inside. A storm had kicked up the night before and it was still sprinkling. The forecast included snow later in the week, and Jamie thought they might be wrong. With the weather outside, it might snow before lunchtime.

The inside of the ferry had two levels. Jamie took the first, which was practically empty; few tourists were willing to brave a day like this. Jamie settled into a corner seat and held her bag to her waist. Whitecaps covered the harbor, evidence the ride would be rougher than usual.

For the tourists' sake—if there were any—the captain was saying something about the sights, the part about the Statue of Liberty welcoming the masses, and Liberty Island being a symbol of freedom. Funny how she'd never really listened to the spiel before Jake died. When the two of them crossed the harbor, they were too caught up in their own conversation to notice much else.

Now she knew it by heart.

The ferry rocked and rolled, but Jamie wasn't worried. She'd crossed over in far worse conditions.

She looked around at the other people on the first level. Across the way were two guys—one blond, one black. They were good-looking, tall and well built. Jamie wondered if they were coaches, maybe, or tourists meeting up with their wives.

Not far from her, three guys in their early twenties sat in a circle. They might've been college kids, but they looked a little shady. Probably actors. Lots of Broadway dreamers lived in Staten Island and commuted to Manhattan for a shot at a role. Now that she'd noticed them, though, she saw something else. Every now and then, one of them would smile at her or do something to catch her attention, and then whisper to his buddies.

Strange... Did she spill something? Was her zipper undone? She glanced down at her white turtleneck sweater and dark jeans. No, everything looked fine. Just as she was about to look up she felt someone standing near her table.

"Excuse me." The guy couldn't have been even twenty-one. He had a baby face with freckles and a crew cut—but there was something hard about his eyes. "Are you on vacation?"

"Me?" Jamie looked around to make sure he was talking to her. Maybe it was some sort of practical joke.

"Yeah." He glanced back at his buddies. Both of them were smiling at him, egging him on. "We're here with our history class, headed for the Statue of Liberty." He grinned, and two dimples cut into his face. "We, well, we wondered if you were a tourist. You know, by yourself. Maybe you might want to join us."

Jamie resisted the urge to laugh out loud. It wasn't a practical joke at all. This college kid was hitting on her! Her face grow hot. "You're serious?"

"Sure." The guy looked toward the bathrooms. "You're by yourself, right?"

"Yes." Jamie wasn't offended. If anything, it made her feel good.

But before she could say anything else, the guy pushed into the spot beside her and put his arm around her. "Don't say a word, got it?"

At his low, hissed words, Jamie's heart slammed into double time. How could she have been so stupid? She never should have said she was alone. She should've gotten up as soon as he started talking to her.

"I'm armed, but I don't want to hurt you, see?" He kept smiling, but his fingers jabbed into her shoulder.

She winced and tried to jerk free, but the guy's friends stood and came over. One of them took the seat on her other side.

"Hey there, baby doll." This one had dark hair. His eyes were bloodshot, and Jamie's fear increased. *God, help me ... they've got to be on something.* His sweatshirt said OSU Football.

"Leave me alone." She hissed the words at the newest member of the group. "Go back to your seats or I'll scream."

"Do it, witch, and I'll shoot you straight through the heart." The freckle-faced kid laughed, and the rough sound made Jamie's skin crawl. "We killed two people earlier this morning. We'll kill you if you don't do what we say."

Jamie doubted he was telling the truth, but just then she felt something jab into her ribs.

"We're serious, lady." It was the third guy, the one with the baseball cap. "You're ours for the day, whatever we want to do with you. Got it?"

"Yeah, and don't make a scene, or we'll shoot everyone on board."

"God . . ." Jamie closed her eyes and tried to be still. It wasn't possible. Her mind was racing too fast to make a plan. "Get me out of here, God."

The crew cut laughed hard at that. "Oh yeah, God'll show up here. Sure thing."

His buddies joined in the laughter, and Jamie looked around the first level. Couldn't someone see she was in trouble? Or was the laughter from the three men convincing the other passengers that she was part of their group, a bunch of friends having a great time together?

"Wait till you see what we've got planned for you, baby." The football sweatshirt sneered the words up against her ear.

His breath smelled like marijuana, and she jerked away, repulsed. *God . . . help me out of this.* Her heart raced so fast she couldn't catch her breath. The most logical way out was to scream or make a run for it. But what about the gun?

It was one thing to take her chances on her own. So what if they shot her? Seconds later she'd be in heaven with Jesus, being welcomed home by the husband she missed so badly. But she didn't have only herself to think about.

She had Sierra.

And because of that, she couldn't scream, couldn't make a run for it. Instead she had to think. The only passengers in sight were the two men across the way. If only they'd look at her, she could send some sort of signal with her eyes. Her captors wouldn't notice—two of them were slurring their words; none of them were paying her that much attention now that they had her trapped.

Come on, God. Make one of them look at me. Please . . .

At that moment, the blond man stood and headed toward them. He looked back at his black friend and pointed to the restrooms. This was it, the chance Jamie needed. He had to walk right past her! If only he'd look at her. He was tall with a square chin, and he looked strong enough to handle all three of the punks circled around her.

Jamie stared at him, blinking as hard as she could, willing him to look.

"So whatcha going to do to her when it's your turn?" The crew cut rattled off a string of expletives. He was so loud, he didn't see the blond man coming up along the aisle to his left. "My turn might not leave much. I better go last."

Suddenly the blond man stopped, pulled out a gun, and pointed it at the four of them. "Police, everyone freeze!"

Jamie couldn't believe her eyes. She had to be dreaming, but she wasn't. A second later the black man pulled out another gun and jogged over.

"You punks better get your hands up!" He glared at them. "Which one of you has the gun?"

All three of the young guys instantly put their hands in the air. "Hey, man," the crew cut kid forced a laugh. "We're just havin' a little fun. Come on, nothin' to get riled over."

"Sure." The blond officer pointed the gun straight at the guy and looked at Jamie. "Do you know these men?"

"*No!*" The word was more a cry than an answer. Jamie jerked away and hurried up next to the blond officer. She pointed at the dark-haired kid. "Be careful! He's got a gun!"

"We saw it." Her protector took her hand with his free one and guided her behind him. "Stay there; I'll cover you."

With the blond still aiming his gun at the young men, the black officer moved in and grabbed the gunman. "Give me your weapon. Now!"

"Hey—" He managed a nervous chuckle, his hands still in the air. "It's like my man Jason said, we're just havin' a little—"

"Give me the gun!" The officer's voice left no room for negotiation.

Jamie could barely see the drama unfolding. Was it really happening? Had three guys tried to abduct her in broad daylight? And who were the police officers? Angels?

Her heart was still racing, but she felt safe behind the blond man. He was much bigger than she, and with his body covering hers, she knew she was safe. *Calm, Jamie . . . be calm. God's with you; it's okay.* She pictured Sierra and felt tears sting her eyes. If things had been different . . .

Jamie squeezed her eyes shut until the bad thoughts went away. She opened them and stared at the officer a few feet away. The situation was under control; the kid was going to give up his gun. God had given her a miracle, one that was still playing out in front of her.

"I said, give me the gun!" The black officer was angry now. His voice told all of them he was sick of the charade.

"Whatever." It was the dark-haired kid. He snarled at his friends. "Look, I'm not going down for this." He lowered one of his hands to his pocket.

"Slow!" The blond barked. He still held Jamie's hand.

"Okay, man, okay." The kid pulled the gun from his pocket and reached it out, slowly. His hand shook. "Take it, already."

"Shut up!" The blond officer barked at him and turned to the others. "Any other weapons before we search you?"

A round of muted "No, sirs" came from the trio. All three of them had their hands in the air; none of them were laughing.

"Hold the cover." The black officer glanced at his partner. Then he slipped his own gun back in his pocket, spun the dark-haired kid around and slammed him against the ferry wall. With rough, sharp movements he ran his hands along the kid's sides. "You have the right to remain silent." He jerked his hands up and down the guy's chest. "Anything you say or do can and will be used against you in a court of law . . ."

Jamie's hands and knees were shaking now, probably from the adrenaline. What were the odds that the only two other people on this level of the ferry were police officers? *Thank You, God . . . thank You.* Her heart rate was barely slower, though.

The blond officer leaned his head back, keeping his eyes on the other two kids. "Did they threaten you?"

"Yes." Jamie tried to swallow but her throat was too dry. "They . . . they said they'd kill me if I screamed. They were going to rape me."

The officer turned to his partner. "Did you hear that?"

"Loud and clear." He finished frisking the kid and shoved him onto the bench. "Keep your hands in the air."

He repeated the process with the other two, and found no weapons on either of them. Even so he took his gun out and kept it aimed at the trio. With a glance over his shoulder, he grinned at his partner. "Go tell the captain we've made us some friends down here."

The blond officer laughed. He was still holding her hand, and now he motioned for her to follow him. They were halfway up the steps when he looked back at her. "I'm Officer Clay—"

The horn on the ferry blared, and Jamie strained to hear him. ". . . from Los Angeles."

"Clay Miles?" The wind was whipping on the upper deck and she had to shout to be heard.

"Yes," he stopped at the top of the stairs and faced her. Even then it was hard to hear. "What's your name?"

"Jamie Bryan." She was safe now, and the fact that he still had her hand in his felt . . . actually, Jamie couldn't figure what she felt. The man was tall, obviously strong, and rugged looking. All that and he'd just saved her life. "I don't know what to say."

Officer Miles let go of her hand and pointed to the captain's office. "Let's talk in there."

She nodded and followed him into the glassed-in area at the top of the ferry. He explained that he was a Los Angeles police officer and then told the man what had happened. They were almost at the Manhattan shoreline, but the captain called dispatch and found out the guys were wanted. They'd held up a convenience store at gunpoint before boarding the ferry. Police lost track of them and were about to contact the captain—in case they were aboard.

The captain held out his hand to Officer Miles. "Nice work." He shook his head. "You're on vacation from LA, is that it?"

"No. We're here for detective training in Manhattan. NYPD." He leaned against the glass wall and looked at Jamie. "We saw the suspects approach this woman, and my partner saw the gun."

Jamie wanted to run over and hug him. Instead she steadied her knees and gripped the back of the captain's chair. "They . . ." She looked straight into the officer's eyes. "You saved my life."

He grinned and shrugged one shoulder. "I guess the training started sooner than we expected."

The captain was on the phone, making arrangements to have an NYPD officer at the docks when the boat pulled up. He was saying something about stalling until the unit was on location.

"So, Jamie Bryan—" Officer Miles gazed out at the choppy water—"why're you going into Manhattan by yourself on a day like this?"

"I'm a volunteer. At St. Paul's." She met his eyes again. What was it about him? She'd never seen him before. At least, she didn't think she had. But something in his eyes made her feel as if she'd known him all her life.

The officer raised his eyebrows. "St. Paul's? You won't believe this. That's exactly where we were headed."

"Really?"

"Yep." He angled his head and studied her. His eyes were beyond kind, the perfect compliment to the tough guy she'd seen a few minutes earlier. "We have the morning off. Orientation's this afternoon."

Jamie smiled. "I think you just had it."

"True." He laughed, much more relaxed than he'd been with the bad guys downstairs. A sober look filled his eyes. "The chapel, it's across the street from the pit, right?"

"Right." Their conversation was easy, and Jamie realized she was drawn to him. "You aren't an angel, are you?"

"I'm afraid not." He grinned. "Just a regular guy, warts and all."

Jamie didn't see any warts. "I prayed for help, and a minute later you had your gun out."

"Hmmm." He kept his gaze on hers, unblinking. "I prayed God would use me in New York however He saw fit."

The captain was still on the phone, but he'd put the ferry back into gear. They weren't far from the dock now, and Jamie saw three squad cars, lights flashing. She shuddered; how different things might have been if the officers hadn't been there.

"So . . . you believe in prayer, is that right, Officer—"

"Call me Clay." He slipped his hands in his jeans pockets. His leather jacket looked sharp against his beige oxford. "And yes. To tell you the truth, God's just about everything to me."

Her voice dropped a notch. "Me too."

"Is that why you volunteer at St. Paul's?"

"Sort of." It didn't seem right to talk about Jake. She would probably never see the guy after today. Why trouble him with her personal heartache? "How 'bout you?"

"My partner's got some stuff going on. It's a long story."

A gentle bump told them the ferry had reached the dock. The captain picked up his radio and made an announcement to the passengers: "We are requesting all passengers stay seated; I repeat, all passengers please stay seated. A police matter has arisen and officers will need a few minutes to take care of the situation. Again, please stay seated."

During the captain's announcement, Jamie thought she saw Clay glance at her left hand. But it happened so fast, she wasn't sure. What with the scene downstairs—and the inexplicable connection she felt to a total stranger—she had no doubt her imagination was working overtime.

The captain thanked Clay again and bid them good-bye. "I need to be downstairs when they take the suspects."

"Fine, sir. Glad we could help."

The captain left and they were alone.

"Do you need to go?" She looked again at the police officers scrambling out of their cars and heading for the ferry ramp.

"Nope. This isn't our jurisdiction. We can stop a crime in progress, but after that it belongs to the locals."

"I see." Jamie should've thanked Clay for saving her life and proceeded to make small talk. But the feeling that she'd known him—known him well—wouldn't go away. She studied her hands. "I'm still shaking."

He closed the distance between them and, as naturally as if they'd been friends all their lives, pulled her into a hug. "I didn't want to say anything." He drew back and smiled at her. "You were flushed at first, but now . . . you're white as a ghost."

"I am?" She didn't know why, but she didn't want anything to interrupt the moment. "Even now? I'm still pale?"

"Mmhmm." He put his hands on her shoulders. "Blow out a few times, long and slow, that should help."

She did as she was told, and he studied her. "Do you feel light-headed?"

"Maybe that's it. I have this feeling I can't explain."

He still had his hands on her shoulders, watching her, making sure she was okay. "You're looking a little better now." His tone was polite, the public servant caught in a time of need.

But his eyes held more. Jamie wasn't sure she'd ever get her color back under that blue gaze.

Another announcement came over the loudspeakers: "Thank you for being patient. It's now safe to debark."

Clay pulled back and nodded toward the door. "Can a couple of LA cops escort you to St. Paul's?"

Jamie smiled. "Please."

Clay grinned. "It's late and getting later. Let's go."

They made their way back to Clay's partner, Officer Joe Reynolds, and the three of them grabbed a cab and headed for St. Paul's. They were halfway there when Jamie finally identified what she'd been feeling, the strange sensation that came over her when Clay held her behind his back, sheltering her from the suspects, then again when he pulled her into his arms. It wasn't fear or shock or even light-headedness.

It was electricity.

TWELVE

She was gorgeous, no doubt about that.

Clay wouldn't have noticed she was in trouble if it wasn't for the fact that from the moment he boarded the ferry, he hadn't been able to take his eyes off her. Reynolds had even teased him about it. "Take a picture, pal. She'll think you're a tourist."

Things happened so fast since then. He'd managed to come off as a professional, but taking her in his arms was totally out of character for him. Out of line, really. He could justify it because she looked faint, but he'd seen far worse cases. More than her health, he was concerned about her feelings. She looked scared and shocked and vulnerable; he simply wanted to hold her.

But who was she? And where was she going alone? He was almost certain she was married, why wouldn't she be?

He'd tried to get a look at her left hand, to see if she wore a ring, but he hadn't gotten a clear view.

Now they were in the cab, with Clay in the middle. Reynolds raised an eyebrow at him, but Clay silenced him with a look. This was no time for the flight attendant act he'd pulled earlier. Reynolds seemed to get the point. He gave Clay a halfhearted scowl and made light conversation about the buildings in the area and plans for rebuilding the Twin Towers.

With Jamie talking to Reynolds, Clay tried again to steal a look at her ring finger. This time she had her hands beneath her, probably trying to keep them warm. Clay looked straight ahead out the windshield of the cab. Was he losing his mind? What did it matter if she had a ring or not? He'd known the woman less than an hour.

Reynolds waxed on; the man was brilliant at carrying on empty conversations. Clay didn't pay much attention. Crazy or not, his focus was on the woman beside him. From time to time, he glanced at her and found her looking at him. And he got the sense she'd felt a connection with him, same way he had with her.

The cab pulled up in front of the chapel, and Clay paid the driver. The three of them climbed out, and Reynolds nodded toward the gaping hole, the place where the towers had stood.

"So that's the place."

"Yes." Jamie looked up and squinted, as if picturing the buildings the way they had been. "No matter how many times I look up, it's still hard to believe they're gone."

Reynolds stuffed his hands in his pockets and looked at the others. "Wanna walk over?"

Clay looked at Jamie. "You probably have to get inside, right?"

"It's okay, I'll come with you." She glanced back at the chapel. "There'll be other volunteers on by now."

The three of them crossed the street and moved as close to the chain-link fence as possible. Maybe thirty or forty people stood along the length of the fence, some in small clusters, some alone.

"Most people expect to see flowers or notes stuck in the fence." Jamie kept her voice low, respectful. She stood between the two men and folded her arms. "The city cleans it up every night; some of the stuff gets tossed—flowers, mostly. Teddy bears get donated to the children's hospital, and photos, letters—" she sighed—"they come to us."

"At St. Paul's?" Clay figured he was nearly a foot taller than her. He turned to hear her better.

"Yes." She met his eyes, and again the connection was there, a familiar current, a sense that he knew what she was going to say before she said it. "Wait till you see it."

Reynolds headed up the sidewalk, eyes on the cavernous hole. Clay and Jamie followed, silent. Along the fence, city personnel had posted oversized mounted photos of the history of the Twin Towers. Together the three of them worked their way west, reading the captions, taking in the enormity of both the force it had taken to bring those buildings down and the rebuilding project.

They reached the last photo, and something caught Clay's attention. It was a subway entrance, the stair rail and steps that led down to what at one time must've been one of the busiest subway stations of all. He leaned against the railing and looked down. From the eighth or ninth stair down, the entrance was still filled with debris— jagged cement blocks and twisted steel.

Jamie came up beside him and looked down. Instantly she stiffened and backed away.

"Jamie?"

Her face was pale again. She shook her head. "I . . . I hadn't seen that before."

"It's still full of debris." Clay fell in step beside her, and they moved beyond the stairwell.

"Yes. They should clean it because . . ."

She didn't have to finish her sentence; Clay could see where she was headed with it. The bodies of countless people had never been found. Wasn't it possible a body was trapped in that tunnel?

Of course it was.

She pulled herself away and fell in beside Clay again. Their steps were slow, waiting for Reynolds to catch up. Clay allowed his arm to brush against Jamie's as they walked.

"Are you okay?"

"Yes." Jamie shuddered. She stopped and turned, her back to the chapel. "It was three years ago, after all." She looked up at the bleak gray sky and crossed her arms tight against her chest. "It's freezing out here."

He wanted to put his arm around her and keep her warm; to shelter her from not only the cold weather but whatever had caused her to react so strongly to the damaged subway entrance. Instead he took off his coat and handed it to her. "I'm too warm. Why don't you wear it?"

Though Jamie's teeth chattered, she hesitated—then let him slip it over her shoulders. She reached up to tug it in place.

That's when Clay saw the ring.

On her left hand. No question it was a wedding band. Clay's heart dropped to his knees. So that was that. She was married, probably a bored housewife volunteering at St. Paul's to find purpose in her life—maybe as part of a calling from God.

Either way, she was taken.

Clay jammed his emotional gears. He'd saved her life. She was bound to be friendly, welcoming. Whatever he'd imagined seeing in her eyes was only wishful thinking on his part. He made a subtle move to the side, allowing a gap between them. "You didn't leave your coat on the ferry, did you?"

"No." She gave a slight roll of her eyes. "I'm so scatterbrained. I left it at the chapel last week. Coldest day of the season so far, and I don't have a coat." She wrinkled her nose. "I thought a turtleneck would keep me warm until I got inside."

"Yeah." Clay made a face and grinned. "Then you had to go and meet a couple of tourists, right?"

His jacket was huge on her. She slid her arms in the sleeves and buried her hands in the pockets. Her eyes met his and held. It was as though she looked far beyond the surface, deep into his soul. "You saved my life, Clay. After what you did, I can brave a little cold weather to show you around."

Reynolds met up with them, and they crossed the street again. They were silent as they headed up the sidewalk, along the fenced-in cemetery, and around the corner into the chapel. Jamie turned to the left, toward a display of memorabilia. She hesitated, then turned back to them.

Without moving, Clay let his eyes wander the inside perimeter of the chapel. There must've been thousands of photos and letters and pictures, buttons from firefighter uniforms and badges with NYPD embroidered on them. It was too much to take in without doing what the few other people in the chapel were doing: making their way, with slow steps, around the wall to the other side.

Jamie spread out her hand and gave them a sad smile. "This is St. Paul's."

There was a reverence to the place, a sense that merely by walking through the doors a person was on hallowed ground. No wonder. Clay looked around again, this time noticing the banners that lined the walls, banners from other cities and states offering hope and love and prayers for the people in Manhattan. Between the walls of mementos and the old wooden pews in the center, the place was truly a memorial.

He looked at Jamie. "I can feel God's Spirit here."

"Yes." She smiled. "It's that way every day."

Reynolds was already absorbed in the details, reading notes and inching his way along the displays that lined the first wall. Praying would come later. For now, Clay had a thought: What if Reynolds's wife had been to St. Paul's? Reynolds hadn't been sure where to find her or if she still lived in the area. At breakfast that morning, Reynolds told Clay that Wanda's mother died in 2000, which left him no way to find his wife but to come to New York and look for her.

Did St. Paul's keep a record of visitors? If so, maybe they could figure out if she'd been there, get a name and a city. It was worth asking.

Jamie removed Clay's jacket, gave it back to him, and took a name badge from her purse. She pinned it to her sweater and smiled at him. "Thanks." Her eyes held his. "Are you going to walk around?"

"Well . . ." Clay chewed on his lip. "Could we talk first?" He shot a look at Reynolds. "My friend is looking for someone very special to him. She might've come here."

Jamie was about to answer when an older woman with a volunteer pin like Jamie's came up to them. "Jamie, thanks for coming. The weather's awful."

"No problem." She met Clay's eyes. "I wasn't sure I was going to make it in."

"We're slow." She held up a finger. "That reminds me. Captain Hisel said to tell you he couldn't come today. He's got a meeting at the department."

"Okay." She touched the woman's hand. "Thanks."

The older woman nodded and wandered off, heading for a middle-aged woman in the back pew. It looked like the woman was crying. Clay and Jamie watched the older volunteer make contact, speak quiet words for a moment, and then sit down. Their conversation looked deep from the get-go.

"So this is what you do?" Clay's voice was barely a whisper. He leaned in toward Jamie, but only so she could hear him. "Talk with people who come here?"

"Exactly. Talk, pray, counsel. Listen." The tenderness in her eyes caught at him. "We do a lot of listening." She turned toward a pew in the middle of the chapel and motioned with her head for him to follow.

They sat down, but not too close. Clay made sure their knees didn't touch. Even so, the subtle fragrance of her perfume stirred his senses.

"What's your friend's story?" No pretense, no guarded layers to work through. Jamie simply opened her heart to whatever Clay might have to say, ready to help—just as she must've done countless times here.

"I just found out myself yesterday, on our flight here." Clay looked toward the front of the church. *She's another man's wife.* But the reminder didn't help as much as he'd hoped.

Clay told the story Reynolds had shared with him the day before. When he got to the part about Jimmy getting hit by the paroled felon, Jamie's quiet gasp drew his gaze to her.

"That's awful."

"Yes." He wanted to pull her close, hug away the pain in her eyes, the hurt that surrounded them. A young couple entered the chapel and began moving along the wall, a few yards behind Reynolds. "It gets worse."

Clay shared how Reynolds and his wife tried to make their marriage work, but neither of them could see past their grief. "They were strong believers, but they were blinded by what happened. They divorced a few months later."

Jamie brought her lips together and looked at her lap. She gave a small shake of her head. When she looked up, her eyes were damp. "He hasn't seen her since?"

"Actually, his wife married an FDNY officer stationed somewhere in Manhattan. They lived in Queens, and he commuted in. Like a lot of firefighters, I guess."

She squirmed. "Was her husband killed in the attacks?" A flicker ignited in her eyes.

"Yes. Joe meant to call and see how she was, how she was handling her husband's death, but he couldn't do it; wasn't sure how she'd react after so many years." Clay crossed one leg over the other and braced his arm along the back of the pew. "He heard about the training course out here." Clay spotted Reynolds nearing the end of the first wall. "I think he wants to find her."

Jamie knit her brow together and leaned forward, resting on the pew in front of her. "Something about the story sounds familiar. What was his wife's name?"

"Wanda." Clay thought for a minute. "I can't remember her last name."

"I know a Wanda, at least I've met her. We prayed together here a few months ago. If I remember right, she said something about losing a little boy ten years ago." Jamie sat a little straighter. "What did she look like?"

"Not sure what she looks like now." Reynolds was partway along the back of the wall, still looking at the items collected in the past three years. "Joe has a picture of her on his desk, the last picture taken with her and Jimmy. She was beautiful, a black woman with brown skin and straightened hair. Big, childlike eyes."

Jamie's eyes widened. "That's got to be her." Sadness replaced her excitement. "She's . . . a very troubled woman, Clay. Too many losses."

"Wait—" disbelief worked its way through him—"so you *know* her? You've prayed with her?" He hadn't been in New York twenty-four hours and already amazing things were happening. He didn't wait for Jamie's answer. "Do you have any idea how we could find her?" A realization hit him. "Or if she'd want to be found?"

Jamie put her hand on her forehead. "This is so weird."

"What?"

"I just remembered something we prayed for, Wanda and I." Jamie looked straight at him. "We prayed she might find her first husband. So she could make peace with him."

A chill ran down Clay's spine. He wanted to fall to his knees and look around, in case angels were hovering overhead. "Do you know how to reach her?"

"I think so." She stood, motioning for him to follow her.

They went to the opposite side of the chapel, to a set of stairs that led to a break room. Off to one side was a small office, and inside that, a file cabinet. Clay waited in the doorway while Jamie searched, and after only a few seconds, she pulled out a single sheet of paper. "Here it is!"

"What?" Clay took a step closer and squinted at the paper.

"Wanda thought she might want to volunteer here. She filled out an application, but decided it was too soon. We kept the information on file, in case she changed her mind." Jamie scanned the sheet. "It has everything. Her name's Wanda Johnston, and she lives in Queens. Her phone, her cell phone, it's all here."

Clay couldn't speak. The day was already so full of miracles, he couldn't find the words to sum it up. Finally he managed a question. "What should we do?"

Jamie shrugged. "I'll call and ask her. I can't give the information out unless she agrees."

"Okay." Clay nodded. *God . . . be with Wanda, let her want this meeting. For Joe's sake.*

The phone on the desk was an older model, with a short cord. Jamie sat down, picked up the receiver and began to dial. After a minute she hung up and looked at the application again. "I'll try her cell."

Please, God . . . An answer this soon would ignite Reynolds's faith and bring him the healing he needed.

Jamie dialed again and waited. Her eyes lit up after a few seconds. "Wanda? Hi, this is Jamie Bryan over at St. Paul's. How are you?" Silence. "Well, you won't believe this. Remember how we prayed when you were here, that you would find your first husband so you could make peace with him?" She grinned at Clay, her eyes dancing. "Well, he and a friend just walked into the chapel this morning." Pause. "No, I'm serious. Joe wants your phone number; I told his friend I'd call you to see if it was okay to give it out. Sure. We'll work it out." Jamie hesitated, then laughed out loud. "I know. We serve a mighty God." She gave Clay a pointed look. "That seems to be the message of the day."

The conversation ended, and Jamie held the application in the air. "Yes!" She scribbled some numbers on a piece of paper and ripped it from the pad. "She wants to see him!"

It was the second time in as many hours that Clay wanted to hug her, but he resisted. They walked back downstairs, Clay reminding himself with every step to keep calm. The mood in the chapel was as hushed and somber as before. Reynolds was at the right side of the back wall, still lost in the items on display.

Clay led the way. When he reached his friend, he tapped him on the shoulder.

"Huh?" Joe turned around. His eyes were watery. "Oh, sorry." He looked at his watch. "Guess I got a little carried away. Like you always say, it's late and getting later."

"I'm not worried about the time." The sense of awe still had a grip on Clay. He gave a single shake of his head. "C'mere, buddy. You won't believe this." He took Joe's arm and led him back to the center pew. Jamie followed along, and she and Clay sat with Joe in the middle.

"Joe, listen." Clay gave Jamie a quick look and couldn't keep from grinning. "I told Jamie your story." He hesitated, studying his friend. "She knows Wanda; she had a volunteer application on file."

"What?" Joe's mouth hung open as he looked at Jamie. His chin quivered and he swallowed hard. "You *what?*"

"I know her, Joe. I called her a few minutes ago." Jamie smiled. "She wants to see you." She handed him the piece of paper with Wanda's numbers on it. "I told her you'd be calling."

Joe took the piece of paper and stared at it, as if it might disappear if he looked away. He clenched his jaw, stood, and looked first at Jamie, then at Clay. "If you'll excuse me." His voice was raspy, filled with a decade of fear, regret, and grief—but layered with a joy that rang out. He smiled despite the wetness in his eyes. "I have a phone call to make."

They watched him go, and Jamie looked to the front of the chapel, at the towering white cross. She took in a long, slow breath and turned to Clay. "What a day, huh?"

He leaned back against the hard wood. It was his turn to walk the perimeter, to look at the remembrances and pay homage to the people who had lost their lives in the attacks. But he couldn't pull away, couldn't cut the conversation with this woman short. So she was married. No harm in talking to her, especially after what they'd been through that morning.

"What's your story, Clay?" She had an easy way about her, gentle words and eyes that hit him at his deepest level. "Married? Kids?"

The question wasn't suggestive, just curious. Clay rested his elbow on the back of the pew. "Never married. I've got a brother not far from me in California, so I spend time with his family." He gave a light-hearted laugh. "Lots of girlfriends, but never the right one."

"Hmmm." She smiled, teasing. "A California playboy, huh?"

"Hardly." Clay chuckled. "Work keeps me busy; I don't get out much. When the time's right, I want to get married, have a family. I guess God'll let me know." He crossed his arms. "What about you? What's your husband do?"

The humor faded from her eyes. A stricken look froze her features, and she looked at her hands for a long while.

Clay studied her, wanting to help. What had he said? Was her marriage in trouble? He hadn't meant to hit a nerve. "Jamie? I'm sorry."

She looked up. "It's okay."

"It's just that—" he looked at her left hand—"you're wearing a ring, and I thought . . ."

"Don't be sorry. I haven't taken it off." Her eyes were dry, but somewhere inside it was clear that she was weeping. "Jake was a fire-fighter. He . . . he died in the attacks."

Of course. Clay hung his head against his forearm and exhaled hard. Why hadn't he figured that out? She was alone on the ferry, trekking in from Staten Island to volunteer at what was basically a memorial site for the Twin Towers. He pulled his head up slowly and looked at her. "I'm sorry, Jamie."

"The department lost more than four hundred men that day. Dozens more from the NYPD." She sniffed and a smile tried to break through the clouds in her eyes. "I'm hardly alone in my loss."

It was a line she must've repeated over and over a hundred times a month, but Clay was struck with how hard it was for her to say it, even after three years. He wanted to know more, but the timing didn't feel right. "Do you have children?"

"A daughter. Sierra." At the mention of the girl, Jamie's eyes came back to life. She sniffed. "The two of us are very close. She's seven now, in second grade."

Reynolds came through the front door, a grin on his face that warmed the whole chapel. As he got closer, he held his cell phone up in the air and beamed at them. "I'm meeting her for lunch."

"Really?" Clay sat straighter. "You ready for that?" The reunion was bound to be emotional, especially if Joe told her all the things he planned to say.

A sober look flashed in his face. "I was ready years ago." He sat down next to Clay. "Talk to the Big Man for me, will you? It's been awhile." He checked his watch again. "It's noon. I told her I'd take a cab to the restaurant." He looked at Clay. "I'll meet you at orientation."

"Oh, sure." Clay grinned at him. "Ditch me in downtown Manhattan our first day."

"I'm off at 12:30." Jamie looked at Clay. "I'll buy lunch." Jamie stood and ran her fingers through her dark hair.

"You don't have to do that." Clay's heart still ached for her. They hadn't gotten to finish their conversation. "I can find something to do."

"Clay—" The sorrow faded a little more from her eyes. "You rescued me. I think I can cough up lunch."

Before Clay could reply, Joe chuckled. "Yeah, that's right. Try to look upset that I'm ditching you, man." Joe winked at him and raised an eyebrow at Jamie. "I think the two of y'all will be just fine without me."

THIRTEEN

Rain was falling hard again, gusting in torrents and pounding on the roof as Joe left St. Paul's.

Jamie looked up at the old ornate ceiling. "Hope it isn't hailing."

"Could be; it's in the forecast." Clay met her eyes. "He's gonna get soaked."

"Somehow—" Jamie smiled—"I don't think he'll mind." Jamie spotted an older man come through the entrance. She stood up. "Well, back to work."

"I'll look around." He pulled his legs beneath the bench so she could get by. Then he stood and headed toward the closest display, the one near the exit. "Maybe I'll start at the end and go against the crowd."

"Suit yourself." She met his eyes once more before she turned around. It wasn't until she was a few steps away that she felt a sense of relief. By starting at the opposite side, he'd miss seeing Jake, and that was just as well. She wasn't ready to talk about him with Clay, not when her heart was whirling around inside her.

A draft whistled through the old building, but Jamie didn't feel the cold. Not with her mind racing out of control. In three years she'd never met anyone like Clay. What was it about him? His strength, or the way he'd so easily protected her on the ferry? Or was it his eyes? The way she felt she'd known him all her life?

Whatever it was, he made her feel something she hadn't felt since Jake.

And that's why her head was spinning. How dare she allow herself to compare a stranger with the man she'd loved since she was twelve years old? She clenched her hands and chided herself. *Get a grip, Jamie . . .*

She could shout it at herself, but there was no denying what was happening inside her. She felt wonderful.

The man looked up as she approached him. He was well dressed, with the air of an executive at one of the financial firms in lower Manhattan. He was still standing near the entrance—not far from Jake's picture and Sierra's letter. His blank expression told her he wanted assistance.

"Hello." She held out her hand, and he took it. "I'm Jamie Bryan, a volunteer here. Can I help you with anything?"

The man took his hat off and tucked it beneath his arm. "I'm Wilbur George." He stared at the collection along the first wall. "My son worked for Cantor-Fitzgerald."

That was all he needed to say.

Cantor-Fitzgerald had been located near the top of the South Tower; the death toll for that firm was the largest for any company hurt by the terrorist attacks. Jamie lowered her voice. "He didn't make it out?"

"No." His mouth made a straight line. "He . . . he had a wife and two children. A boy and a girl. The wife . . . she's getting married again in March."

The idea of people remarrying was coming up more often lately. Not that all of those widowed by the attacks waited this long. Some would wait much longer. But three years seemed a benchmark, of sorts. Jamie let the man set the pace of the conversation.

"I've met the young man; he's very nice. Our daughter-in-law will be happy with him, and so will the kids." He stared at his shoes for a minute and gave a sad shake of his head. When he looked back up, his stoic veneer was cracked down the middle. "I'm here because of my wife." He blinked three times fast. "She's not handling it well."

"I'm sorry." Jamie motioned to the nearest pew. "Can you sit and talk for a minute?"

The man nodded and followed her. He took his overcoat off and laid it across the pew's wooden back. His hat remained clutched in his hands. "We aren't really praying people, you see." His sad laugh floated around her. "My son was. Good Christian boy, his wife too. But my wife and I never really . . . we never believed much in God."

"I see." Jamie studied the man. *Lord, let this be the day he changes his mind.*

The man worked his fingers into the rim of his gray flannel hat. "Lately I've started wondering." He glanced around the chapel. "Look at all the good that's come from people since that terrible day. Look at the beauty of life itself." He looked at her. "One of my partners at work lost a niece in the Twin Towers. His family pulled together and prayed that her death wouldn't be in vain."

Jamie listened, praying.

"That man's a new person today." Wilbur George worked his mouth sideways, the way men sometimes did when they didn't want to cry. "All he talks about is God this and God that, and whether the Lord would be happy with his dealings at work and how he can live some way that would please his Creator." He hesitated. "At first I thought he was wacky. But now . . ."

"It's starting to make sense?"

"Yes." His eyes widened at Jamie's answer. "That's it exactly." His shoulders drooped a notch. "At least for me. For my wife, she says if there was a God, He'd be her enemy after what happened to our boy."

A heaviness weighed on Jamie. It was the same story again and again and again. Different faces, different names, different floors of the Twin Towers, but so often when the walking wounded found their way here it was with one question. How could God let it happen?

"I guess the question, Mr. George, is whether *you* believe." She studied him. *Father, open his heart. Please.* "Do you believe in God and His Son, Jesus?"

"I do." His eyes shone for the first time since he'd walked into the chapel. "I really do."

She wanted to tread lightly, but if she didn't get to the crux of faith she was wasting her time. The real hope was found in the rest of the story. "Do you want Jesus as your Savior?"

The man frowned. "That's where I'm a little confused. I thought . . ." He looked around the chapel. "I thought someone here might be able to help me. That way I could help my wife."

He looked at the wall of artifacts and letters again. "I've done some reading, talked to a few people including my partner at work. All good things are from God—" his eyes found hers again—"right?"

For the next ten minutes Jamie talked with the man about the basics of faith in Christ. All the things she'd learned from Jake's Bible and his journal, from a hundred or so church services since the terrorist attacks and from her training at St. Paul's. At the end of their conversation, the man was nodding, practically desperate to have Jesus as his Savior.

They prayed together, and when they were finished, Jamie gave him ideas that might help his wife find faith in God. When they were done talking, he looked like a mountain had been lifted from his shoulders.

"Thank you, Jamie. I want to take a look around." He patted her hand. "I haven't been here before." He stood and slipped his coat on. Then he stopped and looked at her. "All good things are from God, right?"

"Right. That's what the Bible says."

"Then God didn't make those towers fall. Something evil did, because evil exists in our world."

Jamie gave him a sad smile. "Yes, Mr. George. That's right."

As he walked away, she looked at her watch. Her shift was over; she and Clay could head out for lunch. She stood, grateful for her time with the man. Without that, she would have been consumed by one thought.

Counting down the minutes until she could go someplace and talk to Clay without interrupting the grieving going on all around her.

She found him not quite finished with the exit wall. "Clay?"

He stepped back, his focus still on a child's letter posted near a photo of a police officer. "It's so sad, Jamie. The pictures and letters, even from people who weren't touched by the attacks, at least not personally." He looked at her, his eyes glistening. "The loss was so enormous."

"I know." She resisted the urge to glance across the room at the first display table, the one where Jake's picture was. "Even after working here all this time, it's bigger than I can really grasp."

"I didn't get halfway through." He drew back from the wall and came up alongside her. "Maybe I can finish it another day."

Jamie thought about Jake. "You could." She cast him a sad smile. "It's really just more of the same."

"I guess." He drew in a sharp breath and peered through the closest stained-glass window. "You have an umbrella?"

"You mean you don't?" She was teasing him and it felt better than she could've dreamed. "What, it doesn't rain in California?"

He tossed her a sheepish look. "Not much."

"Don't worry." She held up her finger. "Wait here, I'll get my coat and be right back. And yes—" she started up the stairs toward the break room—"I have an umbrella."

They caught a cab and found a quiet café fifteen blocks north on Broadway. It was busy, but Clay spotted a table near the front window, overlooking the bustling sidewalk. "Good?"

Jamie nodded. "I like people watching."

"Me too." He stared at the parade passing by, businesspeople mostly, some obvious tourists, a random group of kids decked out in black T-shirts and dog collars. Together they carried enough umbrellas to form an overhang along the sidewalk. Clay rested his forearms on the table. "Doesn't it ever slow down?"

"Not much." She smiled. "I can only take Manhattan in small doses."

He looked at the crowds outside. "I can see why." His heart was racing, even faster than it had that morning on the ferry. What was he doing here? He'd been in town a few hours and he was having lunch with a beautiful widow? Clay Michaels, the guy who didn't rush anything?

The whole scene couldn't have been more out of character for him than if he spiked his hair and dyed it pink. At his soft laugh, Jamie looked at him.

"What's so funny?" She lowered her chin.

"Me." He drew invisible circles on the table with his finger. "Joe told me New York would be exciting, but I wasn't sure."

"And then I enter the picture." She eased off her coat and slid it over the back of the chair.

"That's for sure." He laughed out loud this time, a laugh that was brief and full of amazement. "I had no idea anyplace, not even New York, could be that exciting."

The waiter brought them ice water and took their order, chicken sandwiches with tea for her and black coffee for him. When he was gone, Jamie put her elbows on the table, linked her fingers, and rested her chin. "Do you think he would've shot me?"

Clay wanted to drown in her eyes. She was making his head spin and he barely knew her. "I've asked myself that a dozen times today. Usually punky kids like that won't shoot someone in broad daylight. A move like that could wind them up on death row." He brought his knuckles together and took a drink of his water. "But you believed them, otherwise you would've screamed."

"I tried to catch your attention, but I didn't think you saw me."

He felt his eyebrows lift a notch. "Oh, I saw you."

Her shy smile as she pulled her glass closer was pure sweetness. "Is that a good thing?"

"Yes. Very good." He studied her. The conversation was easy, comfortable. The same way it had been in the ferry captain's office and at St. Paul's. It wasn't the rush of the moment with the criminals or the emotion of the chapel. It was Jamie. She was as transparent as a summer breeze.

"So you really think they would've killed me if I got off the ferry with them?"

A chill ran down his spine, and he felt his smile fade. "I don't want to think about what would've happened if you'd done that."

She looked out the window. "At first I was going to scream anyway. I figured, let them shoot me. Someone would save me or I'd wind up in heaven. I'd win either way."

"Why didn't you?"

"Because of Sierra."

"Your little girl." Clay leaned against the window and watched her. Emotions played out on her face. "You just started telling me about her when Joe came back. She's seven?"

"Yes." She looked at him again. "Long golden hair and a heart as big as the ocean. She's very special."

She must be, if she's anything like you. "What does she like to do?"

"She likes cats and horses and movie nights with me. Right now her favorite is *The Lion King,* but for at least two years it was *The Little Mermaid.*" Jamie laughed and poked her straw at the ice in her water. "I enjoy her so much."

"I can see that." Clay hesitated. "What was your husband like?" Clay already knew the answer; he must've been a great guy. The haunting look in her eyes at the chapel earlier told him that the loss had all but killed her. Still, he wanted to hear it from her, wanted to give her a chance to talk about him if she wanted to.

For the first time that day, a wall went up in Jamie's eyes. "We were very close." She bit the inside of her lip. "I fell in love with him when I was twelve. We ... we grew up down the street from each other. His dad was a firefighter." She pressed the corners of her lips up, but it was hardly a smile. "That's all Jake ever wanted to be."

Clay didn't want to push, but he needed to know her, to find out what made her cry when she was alone at night, what memories kept her going when she didn't want to take another step. "Did he share your faith?"

A knowing look crossed her face, as if the answer wasn't an easy one. But she only nodded and took a sip of her water. "Yes. He loved the Lord very much."

He must've loved Jamie very much too. After all, she still wore his ring. The feeling was clearly mutual.

"Jake and I shared something rare. There's never been anyone else." Jamie hugged herself and looked straight at him. "It hasn't been easy."

The sense that he should go to her, pull her into his arms, and soothe away the hurt, was so strong this time he almost gave in. Instead, he willed himself to stay seated. "Is that why you help out at St. Paul's?"

"I think so. It's complicated, really. I go for a lot of reasons, but yes." She looked out the window again. "It's what Jake would've done; I guess I do it as a way of remembering him."

Clay studied the woman across from him. The connection he felt to her was something he couldn't explain. The fact that she was still in love with her dead husband didn't bother him. This woman was loyal to the core, and after loving someone since she was twelve? Of course she still had feelings for him. She always would.

The waiter came with their sandwiches and hot drinks. When he left, Clay met her eyes. "Pray?"

She nodded and bowed her head.

"Lord, we thank You for this food, but more than that, we thank You for bringing us together this morning. You answered both our prayers. Mine that I would make a difference, and Jamie's. It's all You, Father, and for that we thank You. Amen."

"Amen." She was smiling when she looked up, and he sensed she didn't want to talk about her dead husband anymore; not now, anyway. She used her knife to cut her sandwich into smaller pieces. "Okay, Clay. What about you? Isn't three weeks a long time to be away from work?"

"Actually it's four." He took the top slices of bread off his sandwich and shook salt over the meat inside. His body was a priority, one he took care of, but salt was one of his few vices. He used it liberally.

"You're here four weeks?" She looked surprised. "I thought Joe said it was three weeks of training."

"It is." He put the top pieces of bread back on his sandwich, then looked at her for a few seconds. If he told her the reason, would she think differently of him? He took a slow breath. It didn't matter; he couldn't be anything less than honest with her. "I had one week off before I left."

"Vacation?" She held her sandwich, but she held it in midair waiting for his answer.

"I was in a gunfight. A man was coming at me, firing an AK-47." Clay searched her eyes looking for her reaction. "I had to kill him."

Jamie's eyes widened. "So they fired you?"

"No." He smiled. She wasn't repulsed at the shooting so much as worried that he'd lost his job. "No, it's standard procedure when a suspect is shot and killed by an officer during a crime. It's a paid leave; they hold an investigation and make a report. As long as everything was on the level, the officer reports back in three or four weeks."

"Oh. I didn't know that." She took a bite of her sandwich.

"My captain told me not to worry about it. There was nothing else I could do." He thought about telling her how close he'd come to getting killed himself, but it didn't seem like the right time. "When I get back they're promoting me to detective." He grinned. "That's the long answer to your question. I'm here because I need the training, and Joe picked New York City."

"Oh." Understanding filled her eyes. She put her hands around her cup of tea and held it to her lips. "Because of Wanda."

"Right."

The conversation moved to what the training would include and how long he'd been an officer, then went back to the men on the ferry.

"Did you really see a gun?" She tilted her head, her eyes doubtful. "You were all the way across the deck."

He grinned. She was very perceptive. "I saw the guy move in on you, and I could tell by your face that you didn't know him. I told Joe, and we both kept an eye on you. When the second guy came over and pressed in against you, the look on your face was clear even from where we were sitting."

"I was scared to death."

"Yes." His hand itched to hold hers, but the idea was ludicrous. He clenched his fingers. "That's what I saw. Then the second guy jerked something near your ribs, and you jumped. I asked Joe if he saw a gun, and he said, 'Why, yes, I did.' So I said, 'Well then, I better go get it from him.' And Joe said, 'Me too.'"

Jamie giggled and took a long sip of her tea. "But you never actually saw one?"

"Well, see, the thing was, it *felt* like we did."

"And as it turned out—" Jamie was smiling, playing along with him—"your feeling was right."

He waited a beat, breathing her in. "It's been right a lot lately."

Her eyes told him she understood what he was saying. Her cheeks grew a shade darker. "Clay?"

"Yes, Jamie." *God . . . let me see her again. Don't let this be the last time we're together.*

"Can I see you again? While you're here?" Her fingers were shaking, though she tried to still them on her teacup.

Clay wasn't sure whether to laugh or look for angels again. The answers were pouring down as fast as the rain. He wouldn't tell her about his prayer. That could come later. Besides, he didn't want her to think he took her question lightly. In light of what she'd just told him about her husband, it couldn't have been easy to ask it. He nodded. "I'd like that."

"You're staying on Staten Island, right?"

"Yes. Cheap hotels, or so I'm told."

"Much cheaper." The nervousness—or whatever it was—lifted. She smiled the comfortable way she'd smiled at him on the ferry and at St. Paul's. "Could I make dinner for you and Joe?"

Clay felt his heart soar. He never took his eyes from hers as he nodded. "That would be perfect."

Jamie had to catch the ferry back to Staten Island to pick up her daughter, so they finished their lunches and took cabs in different directions—him to the NYPD station staging the training orientation, her to Battery Park. He resisted the urge to hug her. She was no longer a victim needing to be held. She was a woman who, in an instant's time, had captured his thoughts and imagination.

Maybe even his heart.

Was it her vulnerability or the way she looked straight to his soul? *Cool it, Michaels. Slow down.* He turned his thoughts to Joe. How had his friend done with Wanda? Had Joe been able to apologize the way he planned, or was Wanda still upset with him?

He tried to imagine their encounter, but instead saw Jamie's face, the way she'd looked on the ferry when she walked past, her terrified eyes when the thugs accosted her, the way she'd let him hold her in the captain's office . . .

All of it played again and again in his mind. As the cab let him off at the police department, two very strong thoughts stayed with him. First, this new friendship would have to develop slowly.

And second, how many hours he had until he saw her again.

FOURTEEN

By the time Jamie put the casserole into the oven, she was so nervous her throat was dry.

She stared at the dial above the glass door. Was she supposed to set it at three-hundred-fifty degrees? Or was it four-fifty? She gritted her teeth. *Focus, Jamie . . . come on.* She turned back to the counter and the recipe still lying there. Her enchilada casserole was something she could make in her sleep. So why couldn't she remember how high to heat the oven? She scanned through the list of ingredients and finally found it on the back side. Three-fifty. Of course.

Four times that day she'd picked up the phone to cancel the dinner.

There were a hundred reasons why she shouldn't have Clay and Joe over. It was too soon. Her entire house was a shrine to Jake. The buffet table in the dining room still had the same six photos— pictures of him and Sierra, him and Jamie, the three of them at the beach, him in his uniform the day he was hired by the FDNY.

And then there was the bigger framed photo taken on their wedding day.

She would keep those pictures forever, but she didn't want Clay and Joe looking at them. Didn't want their pity. Poor firefighter's widow, still stuck in the past. The fact was, until the past two weeks the thought of other men hadn't crossed her mind. Sure, several FDNY widows had remarried, and she knew others who had started dating.

But her? Jamie Bryan?

The idea was laughable. No one could fill the place in her heart but Jake. No one. She felt scared and sick and guilty just thinking about starting over with someone new. But then, Aaron brought up the question, opened the door to possibilities she hadn't wanted to consider before.

And now . . .

There was no denying the way she felt with Clay. She'd relived the moment on the ferryboat at least once an hour in the past twenty-four. How he'd taken charge of the scene and kept her safe, his body shielding hers. Things she hadn't been conscious of at the time were now vivid in her memory. The pungent fragrance of his leather jacket, his fresh-showered soap smell mixed with a subtle cologne. How she had inched closer to him, wanting his protection, his closeness.

It was crazy.

She hadn't asked for these feelings or looked for them or ever even imagined them. She'd only felt them for one other man in all her life. And now, in just a day's time, she was willing to serve Clay dinner in the house where she and Jake had built their life together?

It was all wrong.

Still . . . every time she picked up the phone to make the call, she stopped herself. She couldn't go back on her offer. It wasn't polite, for one thing, and the men *did* save her life, after all. Clay picked up the lunch tab. The least she could do was make dinner for them—a home-cooked meal, something they wouldn't be getting much of in the next three weeks. She would make good on her invitation because it was a nice thing to do, a Christian thing.

Unfortunately, as soon as she told herself that, the truth screamed at her so loud she couldn't think: her dinner offer had nothing to do with Christian goodwill.

She wanted to see Clay again.

It was that simple. He was all she'd thought of since their first meeting, no matter how wrong that might've been. That truth ran wild through her heart for a few hours until she walked across the house and picked up the phone, determined to cancel.

Then the whole goodwill thing came back around again.

The cycle was driving her crazy. Finally she stopped fighting herself. Yes, she was attracted to him. So what? Jake was dead; it wasn't a crime to have a nice-looking man over for dinner. He would be gone in three weeks, back to California. What harm could come from a single dinner together?

She looked at the clock on the kitchen wall.

They'd be there in half an hour.

"Sierra?" She wiped her hands on her jeans and ran lightly to the base of the stairs. "Did you finish your homework?"

"Yes, Mommy. I was just playing with Wrinkles." Jamie heard her daughter's small feet padding toward the top of the stairs. "Can you play too? We're playing house and we need a mommy."

Jamie smiled. Sierra always put everything into perspective. "Okay, baby. I'll be up there in a few minutes."

"Good! I'll go tell Wrinkles."

"Okay." Jamie turned and gave the house a critical glance. What needed last minute touch-ups? She took quick steps into the dining room. The table was set, Sierra had put the vase of silk roses in the middle, and—

Jamie looked at the buffet table. She hadn't done anything with the pictures of Jake. They would stay, of course. But tonight? Both men would pity her for sure, pity her and think her delusional, trapped in a life lived more back in yesterday than today. She moved to the buffet.

The pictures were dusty, and that shot another arrow of guilt through her. How long had it been since she dusted them, since she'd come this close and actually looked at them? She picked up the one of Jake in his uniform and went to dust it with her shirt, but stopped herself.

She had on a new sweater—a ribbed pale blue pullover. Dust would show on it for sure.

The buffet had extra linens, didn't it? She opened the top drawer and pulled out an old cloth napkin, wrinkled from lack of use. Jake's pictures shouldn't get dusty. She ran the napkin over the glass until she could see his smile, the pride in his eyes, as easily as if she was taking the picture all over again.

The dust fell to the floor. She started to shove the napkin back in the drawer when an idea hit her. It wasn't that she wanted to hide his pictures. Rather she wanted to protect them from the curious looks and silent questions that were bound to come if she left them up. The drawer was deep enough for all of them. She swallowed back a tidal wave of guilt and one at a time she dusted the pictures and layered them in the drawer with more cloth napkins.

There. She shut the drawer and dusted off her hands. As she did a picture came to mind. Pontius Pilot, rubbing his hands together, convincing himself he wasn't guilty when he clearly was.

Just like her.

Here she was, hiding Jake's pictures, burying her past in a buffet drawer and then dusting off her hands, as if that could make her innocent.

She stared hard at the closed buffet drawer, willing herself to see through the wood at the pictures laying there, put away like so many outdated knickknacks.

"Jamie," she whispered out loud, "you're losin' it."

If only Jake had stayed home that day, gone with her and Sierra to the zoo. If he hadn't gone in that Tuesday morning they would have other, newer pictures on the buffet, and dinner would be for Jake and Sierra. Not two strangers she'd met just the day before.

Jake . . . it's so hard. I don't want to live without you, but . . . I keep waking up. Life keeps coming whether I like it or not. She gripped the edge of the buffet and closed her eyes. *God . . . am I bad? Should I keep the photos up? Help me . . .*

No holy words came to her, no Scripture verse. But after a few seconds, a calm settled over her. She could put the photos away for a night if she wanted to. If it helped her take one step toward tomorrow then it was the most right thing she could do. She opened her eyes.

She wouldn't be able to think straight if she had to get through the night with Jake's eyes on her the whole time. With hers on him.

"Mommy?" Her daughter's voice came from the upstairs bedroom. She sounded frustrated.

Jamie gave one last look and then turned her back on the buffet. "Coming."

What was the big deal, anyway? It was one dinner, one simple dinner for two police officers far from home. She could do this one thing, show them some East Coast hospitality and be done with it. She darted up the stairs and stopped at the top.

She'd forgotten perfume.

"One sec, Sierra." More quick steps, through her bedroom, to the bureau near the end of her bed. She grabbed the amber bottle and gave first her neck, then both wrists a quick spray.

When she walked into Sierra's bedroom, her daughter sat up straight and studied her. "How come you're dressed up?"

"I'm not." Jamie dropped cross-legged on the floor across from Sierra and Wrinkles. The cat had a pink scarf tied around his head and white lace socks on his front paws. His look was one of attempted dignity and mild disgust. "Wrinkles is the one who's dressed up."

Sierra grinned at the cat. "She's my big sister."

"I see." Jamie loved her daughter's imagination. That she could dress up a tomcat and convince herself he was her sister was testimony to the delightful reaches of her creativity. For the occasion, Sierra wore a blue velvet hat and long white gloves.

"You be the mommy, okay?" Sierra bounced up and grabbed an old straw hat with loud purple plastic flowers glued to the sides. It was her favorite dress-up hat for Jamie. "Here, this is for you."

The hat was big and obnoxious; it flopped over Jamie's ears, but she didn't mind. The game was a welcome distraction. "Well?" She held her arms straight out. "How do I look?"

"Fabulous." Sierra giggled. "Isn't she fabulous, Wrinkles?"

Jamie petted the cat. "Wrinkles is speechless, I think."

The cat started to get up, but Sierra stopped him. She cooed near the cat's face. "It's okay, Wrinkles, he isn't the only pretty girl in the family, actually." She looked at Jamie. "Wrinkles is jealous because he doesn't have a pretty dress."

"Tell Wrinkles it's okay. I don't have a pretty dress either."

Sierra blinked and her eyes grew serious. "Wait, Mommy. Who's coming for dinner again?"

"Two police officers. I met them on the ferry yesterday, going to my volunteer work."

"Oh." She kept one hand on the cat's back. "Were they hungry?"

"The police officers?"

"Yes. You invited them for dinner so they musta been hungry."

"No." She hid her smile behind her fingers. "I mean, not at the time, they weren't hungry. I hope they're hungry tonight, though."

Jamie studied her daughter. "Actually, they saved me from some bad men."

Sierra opened her eyes wide. "Bad men? Like with guns?"

"Yes." Jamie adjusted her hat. "Three bad men tried to scare me." She wanted to keep the story simple. "And before they could make me too scared, the officers came and took them away."

"Wow." Sierra adjusted Wrinkles's scarf so that it came down closer to his eyes. "He looks more like a girl now."

Jamie studied the cat. "Yes, you're right."

"So they took the bad guys away and then you asked them to dinner?" Sierra kept one hand on the cat's head. In case he had any ideas about ending the game prematurely, Jamie guessed.

"Well, no. I talked to them for a while. They're both very nice."

"What's their names?"

"One man is Clay . . ." Jamie felt her heart skip a beat. What if Sierra could see through her? What if she could tell the minute the men arrived that Jamie had feelings for Clay? "The other man is Joe. They're from California."

"Oh." One of the socks was slipping off Wrinkles's paw. She pulled it back on. "So they didn't know Daddy?"

It took Jamie a moment to catch her breath. "No, sweetie. Why would they know Daddy?"

"You said they're policemen. Sometimes policemen and fire-fighters know each other." She patted Wrinkles's head. "Didn't you know that, Mommy?"

"Yes, I guess I did." She never stopped being amazed by the things Sierra said. "But these two men don't know Daddy, okay?" Jamie pointed at Wrinkles. "Now listen, daughter. Where have you been, out so late and dressed like that?"

Sierra giggled. "Mommy, don't be mad at us. We had dancing lessons with our boyfriends."

"Boyfriends?" Jamie used her best mock mean mother tone. "No boyfriends for you! Besides, where are the boyfriends?"

The wheels in Sierra's head must've been turning. She looked around the room and in a rush she pointed at the closet. "There. We keep our boyfriends in the closet."

Again Jamie had to stifle a laugh. She sat a bit straighter, more authoritative. "There will be no more boyfriends in closets anymore."

The cat tried to pull away, but Sierra stopped him again. He settled back down and meowed.

Jamie pointed a finger at him. "No talking back, sister. And don't try to run away, either."

The doorbell rang. They were here! Certain moments since yesterday Jamie was sure she'd dreamed the whole thing up. Men couldn't have tried to accost her on the ferry in broad daylight, and certainly two police officers didn't happen to be watching. She hadn't spent the morning with a man who had mesmerized her from the first few seconds, and she didn't have lunch with him, talking with him like they were old friends. And she certainly didn't invite them for dinner.

But she really did. The whole day really happened, and now Joe and Clay were downstairs waiting to be let in.

She jumped into action. "Come on, Sierra, let's go meet them."

Sierra swept the cat into her arms and the two of them bounded down the stairs to the front door. Jamie shot Sierra a look. "Best manners, okay?"

"Okay." Sierra held the cat to her chest. "Best manners."

Jamie opened the door and found Clay on her porch. He held something behind his back. "Hi." Warmth stirred inside her at the sight of him, and she felt her cheeks get hot. Sierra came up beside her, still holding the cat, and suddenly Jamie remembered what she was doing. She put her arm around her daughter. "Come in."

"I don't know." Laughter danced in Clay's eyes. He looked himself up and down. "Looks like I'm underdressed."

Jamie gasped and grabbed the hat from her head. "We were playing—"

The laughter came all at once, and after a day of worrying and overthinking, it felt too good to stop it. Dress-up games were normal fare for Jamie and Sierra. But how must they have looked? Sierra with her old-lady blue velvet hat and white gloves; her with the cheap plastic flowers? And what about Wrinkles?

She was laughing too hard to say anything. Instead she backed into the house, gesturing for him to join them.

Sierra apparently didn't see anything funny. She gave Jamie a strange look and then turned to Clay. "Mommy's silly sometimes."

Jamie let out another burst of laughter.

"Yes." Clay stooped down to Sierra's level. "I see that." He petted the cat's chin. "I'm Clay."

"I'm Sierra." She smiled at him, not quite smitten, but close.

Clay winked at her. "You have nice taste in outfits, Sierra."

"Thank you." She was still in character, assuming it perfectly normal for a cat to have a scarf and lace socks. But she did a little giggle and spoke in a loud whisper, as if she were sharing secret information. "We're playing pretend."

Jamie had tears in her eyes. Still laughing, she leaned against the foyer wall so she could catch her breath.

Clay's eyes widened. "Oh, I see." He gave Jamie a quick smile. "She must be the crazy neighbor lady?"

Sierra giggled. "No, she's the mom."

"Are you the princess?"

"No, I'm the little sister." She held Wrinkles up and one of the socks slid off his paw onto the floor. "Wrinkles is the big sister."

"I see."

Jamie sucked in two quick breaths and dabbed the corners of her eyes. Sierra held Clay's attention, so she took the moment to study him. He wore a tan sweater, khaki dress pants, and the leather jacket. His hair was short, cut conservatively in a way that complimented his face.

He looked at her. "I don't know, Jamie. I kind of liked the hat."

Another giggle worked its way up, but she held back. She was on the verge of being rude as it was. She exhaled hard. "Whew! I'm sorry." She lifted her shoulders and gave him a grin. "What a bad hostess I am." Jamie drew another breath and fanned her face. "Welcome to our home. We're a little loony, but we have fun."

"I like it." His eyes were full of teasing. "But under the circumstances, I think I need a hat."

Sierra's eyes lit up. "I'll get you one!" She started to run off, and the motion frightened the cat. He jumped from her arms, losing the other sock and causing the scarf to slide down around his neck.

"Wrinkles!"

The cat was off and around the corner before Sierra could stop him. She watched him for a minute and then she shrugged. "I'll be right back."

"Wait, Sierra." Clay straightened. He was still hiding something.

Sierra pulled her gloves up a little higher and turned around. "I can get you one, really. I have a whole box."

"Okay." He gave her a kind smile. "First I have something for you."

Jamie watched from her place against the wall. Her heart swelled as she took in the scene. In all the time they'd known Aaron, he'd never brought Sierra a present.

Sierra came and stood in front of Clay. "Really?"

"Yep." He pulled a pink bag out from behind his back. "Here. This is for letting me come over for dinner."

"Wow!" She took the tissue paper from the top and gasped. "It's Nala!"

Nala? Jamie blinked, stunned. Nala was the girlfriend of Simba in *The Lion King*. Jamie met Clay's eyes and caught his knowing look. The gift wasn't an accident. He had remembered their conversation at lunch, remembered that Sierra's favorite movie was *The Lion King*.

With great care Sierra pulled a honey-colored stuffed lion from the bag. She turned to Jamie and held it up. "Look, Mom! She's perfect! Next time, *she* can be the big sister!"

"I'm sure Wrinkles will be glad to share the scarf."

"Yeah, I'm sure too." She stared at Clay, awed. "Thanks very much." She gave him a quick hug and then ran to Jamie. "She's super soft, Mommy, look!"

Sierra gushed about Nala for another few minutes before running off to find a beat-up hat for Clay. The conversation shifted to their orientation and Clay's expectations for the three weeks of training.

"I'll go home a better detective." They moved into the kitchen. "Joe'll see to that."

"Isn't he coming?" The silliness at the front door made her forget about his partner. She grabbed an old pair of pot holders, opened the oven door, and pulled the casserole out. The cheese on top was barely golden brown.

Clay looked over her shoulder at the dinner. "Whatever that is, I'll take two." He helped clear a spot on the counter. "Smells delicious."

"It's a family favorite." A memory flashed in Jamie's mind—the first time she'd made the casserole for Jake in the days after they were married. She'd burned the cheese and mixed the sauce wrong. They couldn't eat it, but it gave them something to laugh about for days afterwards. She blinked and the images were gone. "So what about Joe?"

"Wanda invited him to her place." He leaned against the counter and crossed his arms, watching her.

Jamie took the milk from the refrigerator and poured Sierra a glass. "Things must've gone well."

"I guess." Clay made a slight frown. "Joe felt awkward; he couldn't find the right time to tell her he was sorry." He unfolded his arms and rested the palms of his hands on the counter behind him. "I guess she sent her kids to the neighbor's house for the night yesterday. Joe thought it was sort of strange."

"They both have a lot to work through." Jamie took the casserole to the table.

Clay followed behind with the salad and milk. "Definitely."

They heard Sierra before they saw her. She raced around the corner, a jester hat in one hand, the oversized hat with the purple plastic flowers in the other. On her head, the older velvet hat had been replaced with a sailor's cap. Sierra collected hats for her dress-up box, and these were three of her favorites. "Hi, guys!" Her cheerful voice struck Jamie. Sierra was a happy child. More subdued, maybe, than before the terrorist attacks. But happy all the same. But now—for whatever reason—she was practically bubbling over with enthusiasm, her eyes dancing with a joy that Jamie hadn't seen in years.

"Here, Clay." She handed him the jester hat. "I think you're right. Let's wear hats for dinner."

Jamie was about to tell her no, but Clay took the hat and adjusted it on his head. "Whaddaya think, Jamie. Would I scare off the bad guys with this?"

She had to bite her lip to stop another wave of laughter. She looked at Sierra and angled her head. "Honey, I'm not sure our guest wants to spend dinner wearing a jester hat."

"Actually—" Clay lifted his chin with mock dignity—"I'm quite fond of jester hats."

Sierra clapped her hands. "Yeah, Mommy. This'll be the funnest dinner in forever." She put the sailor's hat on her own head and handed the one with the plastic flowers to Jamie. "Please, Mommy. Wear it, please."

"She'll wear it." Clay stooped down some, so he was more on Sierra's level. "Hats are required at this dinner."

"Fine." Jamie rolled her eyes. "Give me the hat."

Clay took it from Sierra, stood up, and placed it on Jamie's head. "You look pretty in purple."

"Thank you." Jamie's knees felt shaky, her stomach warm from the effects of her melting heart. Not since Jake had anyone told her she looked pretty. She gathered herself and looked at Sierra. "All washed up?"

"Yep." Sierra sat down at the table and folded her hands.

Jamie sat beside her and Clay across from them. His jester hat flopped to one side as he held his hands out. "Can I pray?"

"Yes." The warmth moved up to her cheeks, and she smiled. He looked silly, but his voice, his eyes, were as deep, as vulnerable as they'd been the day before. She took Clay's hand and watched Sierra take the other.

They bowed their heads and Clay began. "God, thank You for this food—" he gave Jamie's fingers a gentle squeeze—"and the hands that prepared it. And thank You for new friends. In Jesus' name, amen."

Throughout the meal, Jamie expected to be nervous, unsure of how to carry on a conversation with a man she'd only just met. She was sure she'd be distracted, guilty at having moved Jake's picture. Instead, the meal flew by, and all she could think about was how wonderful she felt. Having Clay there, his hand in hers during the prayer, his presence at their table. All of it felt impossibly good, right in a way she couldn't begin to understand.

During the meal, Jamie caught him looking at her, glancing away from Sierra and finding her eyes, almost as if he wanted to see for himself that the attraction or chemistry or whatever they shared was still there.

It was. Jamie used her eyes to tell him so. He'd been dropped into her life and nothing had been the same. She hadn't had time to analyze how or why God had brought them together, just that He had. Only one thought threatened to mar the night. It wasn't of Jake or his picture or how she would get on with life without him.

Rather it was what would happen to her in three weeks—when Clay went home.

Sierra felt it in her heart the minute she pulled Nala from the gift bag. Clay liked her. Because how else did he know about Nala? Nala was the coolest present ever, and it wasn't even her birthday. All her friends had Lion King, but not Nala. Plus Nala was a girl, which meant she could wear hats and scarves and fancy socks and bows in her hair and play the big sister.

Without getting mad, the way Wrinkles sometimes did.

Clay wasn't a regular kind of grown-up like Captain Hisel. Captain Hisel would smile at her and pat her head, and sometimes he'd talk to her for as long as a TV commercial. But he didn't really like her because he never asked her questions.

Sierra was counting. While they ate dinner Clay asked her eight questions, like who was her teacher and how many kids were in her class and who were her bestest friends and what did she want for Christmas?

By the end of dinner, Sierra was having a secret thought. Secret thought was when she had an idea in her head but she didn't share it with anyone else. Not even Mommy. Her secret thought was this: Since the other second daddy had to go back to his real family, maybe Clay would make a good second daddy.

She spied on him when he wasn't watching, and her heart had a sense about him. A sense that he acted sort of like a daddy, actually. He smiled big and wore his jester hat all night. Also, after dinner he played Uno with her and her mommy. The three of them laughed a lot, and Sierra didn't even care who won.

When Clay left, he stooped down and told her to have fun with Nala. Then he gave Mommy a short hug, sort of like when Captain Hisel came over.

Before he left, Clay looked at her one last time and winked. And Sierra did a little gasp because that's something she'd seen before. Maybe it was her daddy who used to do that, or her second daddy— the one who lived with her after the Twin Towers fell down. But instead of feeling confused, her heart felt happy. Because maybe the wink was a sign that God knew how lonely she was without her daddy.

And maybe God would take away the lonely forever.

FIFTEEN

Jamie reported to St. Paul's the next day, but for the first time she didn't stop and look at the gaping hole where the towers had stood. Her head was still spinning from the night before, from the new feelings stirring up her heart and soul. How could she care so much about a man she'd only known a few days? Was she using the situation to avoid Aaron Hisel? Or was Clay Miles really as wonderful as he seemed?

Allen, a young man in college, was the first person she talked with that morning. His father, an investment broker, was trapped near the top of the North Tower when it collapsed. Allen had a small photo of his father, one that he wanted to leave as part of the memorial. Jamie helped him find a spot for the picture, and then asked him if he wanted to talk.

"Not really." He shrugged. "I don't talk about it much. It happened, Dad's gone, end of story."

Jamie leaned against one of the thick white pillars that separated the memorial along the perimeter from the sanctuary area of the chapel. Memories of Clay and her dinner the night before came to mind and she willed them away. "Allen, would it be okay if I prayed for you?"

The surprise in the young man's eyes changed to anger, then vulnerability. "The last time I prayed was the morning of September 11." He clenched his jaw and gave a shake of his head. "Apparently God didn't hear me, so I stopped talking."

"But you're here." Her eyes found the pew where she'd sat with Clay the other day. Was he in training now? Would he call her again the way he'd promised? Was she crazy? She blinked hard and focused on the young man.

Allen looked over his shoulder at the tables of memorabilia. His eyes were damp when he found Jamie's eyes again. His chin quivered. "I don't know how to move on."

So many visitors to St. Paul's faced the same thing.

Their loss was so great, they practically limped through the doors. Anger, hurt, and grief kept the calendar at a standstill. Regardless of time's incessant marching, every day was September 12—and without God's divine intervention it always would be. She led the young man to the closest pew and sat down with him.

Her mind drifted back to the night before, to something funny Clay had said about his jester hat. She tightened her hands into fists. *Focus, Jamie . . . focus.*

"I understand." She looked at the stained-glass window across from them. "My husband was a firefighter; he died in the South Tower."

The young man looked at his knees. "I'm sorry."

"It's okay. He's in heaven; I'm sure about that." She told him about Jake, about finding the faith her husband had always held to, how she wouldn't have survived without that faith.

Sometimes even while she was counseling at St. Paul's her mind wandered. But always she would rein in her thoughts and focus on the matter at hand. Usually the distractions came because of Jake. His picture across the room, or the thought of him kissing her goodbye that brilliant sunny Tuesday morning, hearing his voice telling her he loved her that last time.

But not today.

Today she had to remind herself to stop thinking about Clay Miles and the way her spine tingled when she was with him. Distractions about Jake were a normal thing, especially working at St. Paul's. They were constant reminders that she was in the right place, working alongside people most touched by the tragedy of the terrorist attacks.

But thoughts of Clay?

Every time she had a spare moment that morning she saw Clay's face, the way his eyes met hers over dinner the night before, felt her body protected against his as he handled the men on the ferry.

She dismissed the thoughts. The young man across from her deserved her complete attention. He was going on about his relationship with his father, and Jamie had to listen to him as if there'd be a test later.

She struggled through two meetings that way before she sensed someone behind her.

"Hey." Aaron's tone held a layer of hurt. "You haven't fallen off the planet after all."

The sound of his voice shot darts at her conscience. She turned around and smiled at him. "Hi." She was suddenly short on words, not sure what to say. "Did you just get here?"

"A few minutes ago." He searched her eyes. "I called you twice last night."

"I know." She forced a light laugh. "Sorry I didn't call back. Sierra and I were crazy busy." It wasn't a lie, not really. But with her feelings so jumbled it was the most she was willing to say.

"Whatever." Aaron tried to look nonchalant, but he didn't pull it off. He lifted his shoulders. "I was just worried. You always call back."

"I'm sorry." Jamie didn't know what else to say. Another visitor walked through the doors and turned to look at the memorial set up on the first table. "It's been busy."

"That reminds me—" Aaron pointed at the displays along the back wall—"let's talk to the others about redoing that area. We have stacks of kids' drawings in the back, letters from children sending wishes to the New York survivors, that sort of thing. It's okay the way it is, but if we built it up some, maybe added an additional shelf along the wall, we could bulk up the display."

Odd. The idea left Jamie flat. A week ago she would've made plans for someone else to pick up Sierra so she could go through boxes of letters, looking for a way to make the makeshift memorial more emotional, more meaningful for the people who passed through.

But today . . .

"Jamie?" Aaron crossed his arms, his feet spread just enough to give him the look of a New York City fire captain. "Did you hear me?"

"Yes." Her answer was quick this time. She cleared her throat. "Yes, that'd be great." The words sounded forced, even to her.

He took a step back and studied her. "Are you okay?"

More darts. She let her gaze fall to her shoes. His friendship meant a lot to her; she had to tell him at least something of what she was going through if she was going to stay close to him. She looked up. "Can we have lunch today?"

"Sure." Hope replaced some of the uneasiness in his eyes. "Casey's Corner?"

"Perfect." She wanted to tell him it wouldn't be the type of lunch he was looking forward to, that she had some difficult things to discuss with him. But a visitor was approaching them, a woman in her thirties with red, swollen eyes.

Aaron nudged her. "You get this one; I'll be in the back if you need me."

Jamie struggled through the next two hours.

Not only with thoughts of Clay, but with the work at hand. Instead of the usual meaning and emotion that came with her job, she felt trapped. At one point she breathed in through her nose and looked around, alarmed. Was there a gas leak or a ventilation problem? There had to be, because the oxygen was gone. As hard as she tried she couldn't draw a relaxing breath. Finally, she had to go outside to grab a few mouthfuls of fresh air. Back inside it was more of the same. Just the old, musty smell of the building, and too little air.

She glanced about. Unless she was imagining things, the walls looked closer together, as if the whole place was shrinking, trying to swallow her up whole.

Of course all of it was a delusion. It was her confusion with Aaron and Clay and her memories of Jake, that's what was sucking the air from her. The building wasn't running out of oxygen any more than the walls were closing in, but that didn't change the tightness in her lungs or the way she longed for her shift to be over. It was the first time she'd ever felt this way. Trapped, anxious to leave.

She pondered the idea until finally it made sense. Of course. September 11 was everywhere around her—in the voices and conversations and pictures and artwork. In the streaming video that ran on the TV against the back wall and the displays set up along the exit wall, the ones honoring the massage therapists and cooks and counselors who volunteered their time during the cleanup.

It was all so suddenly overwhelming. Jamie couldn't quite catch her breath until she and Aaron were in a cab headed for Casey's Corner—a bright and cheerful café where they'd shared dozens of lunches. She was glad they were going there. The day was gray and cold, threatening snow. Combined with the strange mix of thoughts in her head and the things she wanted to tell Aaron, she would need an upbeat atmosphere to get through the lunch.

They were almost at the café when he leaned against the cab door and watched her. "You're quiet."

"Yes." She looked over her left shoulder at the city, the buildings and people, all of it passing before her eyes like a familiar river. Thoughts from earlier came rushing back. "Today was hard."

He didn't push her until they were seated at a booth in a quiet part of Casey's Corner, sipping coffee and waiting for their sandwiches. Aaron leaned back against the padded seat. "Why was today hard?"

"I don't know." Her hands were cold. She cupped them around her coffee mug and watched the traffic outside. "I didn't want to talk about September 11 with anyone."

Aaron leaned forward. "Maybe you need a break."

"Maybe." The idea sounded good, but she wasn't sure. "I know I'm supposed to be there; it's the least I can do for Jake."

He didn't add anything. Casey Cummins, the owner of the café, brought their sandwiches over. It was part of the charm of the place—that the owner took a personal interest in his customers. "Coldest day of the season." He smiled at them as he set the food down. "Let me know if you want a cup of minestrone." He brought his thumb and forefinger together in the shape of an *o*. "It's perfect today."

They both thanked him but turned down the soup. When he was gone, Aaron took the toothpick from his sandwich and poked it at his water glass. "You want to talk about something?" The look of hope was gone from his eyes. Clearly he could sense some of what she felt.

"I do." She gripped the bench she was sitting on and sucked in a quick breath through her teeth. Whatever happened, she didn't want to lose his friendship, didn't want to hurt him after all he'd done for her. She wasn't entirely sure she wanted to shut the door on the future. Still, something needed to be said.

"Well?" He uttered a small laugh. "You gonna tell me or make me sit here guessing?"

"Aaron." Jamie closed her eyes. When she opened them, she was looking straight at him. "I need space."

His brow lowered into a subtle *v*. "Am I crowding you?"

They hadn't even seen each other in the past few days. Jamie folded her hands and rested them on the table. *Please, God . . . give me a way to make him understand.* She ran her tongue over her lower lip and tried again. "I told you I could see things getting more serious, that maybe all I needed was time."

"Right."

"Well—" she held her breath—"things have changed." She couldn't tell him about Clay. The entire story sounded ridiculous. She raked her fingers through her hair and cupped her coffee mug again. "I need time away from you, Aaron. So I can sort through my feelings."

He rested his forearms on the table and looked out the window. He shifted his jaw from side to side, the way he did when he had a lot on his mind. Finally he looked at her again and let out a quiet breath. "We barely see each other."

"I know. But I need time from that too."

"Everywhere? Even St. Paul's?"

"Yes. Even there." She wanted to disappear under the table. He was her friend, after all, the person she'd leaned on and turned to more times than she could count. But as much as she appreciated his friendship, she couldn't let him believe there'd be more between them. Not now. Not when she was almost certain there wouldn't be.

Aaron sat a little straighter. "Is it something I did?"

"No." She reached out and touched his hand, but only for the briefest moment. "None of this is your fault. I think it's something I'm going through. I need to close the last chapter in my life before I can start a new one. Does that make sense?"

His expression told him it didn't, but after a few seconds he swallowed hard and looked at her. "Whatever you need, Jamie. I care that much." He was clearly shocked at the change in her, especially after the nice time they had at Chelsea Piers. "I'll talk to the coordinator and tell them I'm only available in the afternoon." Since he worked nights, afternoons were bound to be more difficult. More hours awake without a break.

"I'm sorry, Aaron. When I have things figured out I'll tell you. It just . . ." A lump filled her throat; she waited until it was gone. "It isn't fair to keep you guessing. And unless I take some time, maybe I'll never know what I want. What God wants for me."

At that last part, his eyes hardened. "I understand." He pointed to their sandwiches and the regret in his small laugh tore at her. "We better eat."

Jamie tried, but she barely forced down three bites. She wasn't hungry, not as long as her heart was in a tailspin. The rest of the lunch was awkward, and Jamie wondered if she was losing her mind. Why cut Aaron out now just because she'd met Clay? Just because she had a bad day at St. Paul's?

Not until she was on the ferry, two minutes from Staten Island, did she have an answer for herself. She didn't need time away from Aaron because of her feelings for Clay, but because of her feelings for Aaron—feelings that seemed more and more like friendship with every passing hour. She needed her distance to be sure this thing with Clay wasn't some sort of desperate ploy to avoid getting serious with Aaron. With the captain out of the picture for a while, she could think clearly.

And maybe, when a few weeks had passed, she would know without a doubt that she belonged with Aaron Hisel.

The thought simmered in her mind until she reached her car where she found an envelope in a plastic bag tucked beneath her windshield wipers. She wrinkled her nose. Funny. The ferryboat people didn't usually allow canvassers through their parking lots. She pulled the envelope from the bag and saw her name written across the front.

It was from him; it had to be. She knew it before she opened it, and her fingers trembled as she slipped them beneath the envelope flap and pulled out the note.

Jamie, Thanks again for the great dinner and dress-up party, even though I was disappointed I didn't get to keep the jester hat. I thought it would be a nice touch for the ferry ride.

He'd jotted down his room number at the hotel. She laughed out loud and turned so she could lean against her car. Her eyes moved further down the page.

> *Anyway, Joe's going to see Wanda again tonight. I'll be at the Holiday Inn if you want to talk. Thinking about you, Clay.*

She read that last part three times in a row. *Thinking about you, Clay . . .*

He was going to be at a lonely hotel room. She folded the note, put it back in the envelope, and slid into her car. The least she could do was invite him over. They could order pizzas and maybe watch a movie after Sierra went to bed.

Her heart rate picked up at the thought. Yes, that would be a great idea.

She glanced around the lot. What type of car was Clay driving? Some sort of rental, but she wasn't sure what. Then she remembered the note. He was staying at the Holiday Inn. She checked the clock on her dashboard. Forty minutes until Sierra was home. With a heart half a ton lighter than it had been at lunchtime, she headed for the Holiday Inn, parked, and grabbed a piece of paper from a notebook she kept in her van.

> *Clay, I can't let you stay here alone all night. Especially without your jester hat. After you catch your breath, come over. We'll get pizza and watch a movie if you want. Hats are optional.*

She stared at the rest of the page, the blank part. If she told him she was thinking about him, it would be the truth. But was that more than she should say? After all, she hadn't known him for a week. Still . . .

Her pen was poised over the page, ready to tell him he wasn't the only one, that she hadn't been able to stop thinking about him all day. But at the last second she just signed her name, folded the paper, and ran in to the front desk. She wrote his room number on the front, handed the note to the clerk, and asked her to see that Clay Miles got it.

When she picked Sierra up at school, her daughter looked at her longer than usual. "Something's different about you, Mommy."

Jamie waited until Sierra was buckled into the backseat. She gave a small, nervous laugh. "You're silly, Sierra. I'm same as always."

"Nuh-uh." Sierra set her backpack on the seat beside her. "Didn't you have your volunteer work today?"

"Yes." Jamie focused on the road, but in her mind all she could see was Clay, coming off the ferryboat, tired, not sure if she'd gotten his note or what her response would be, then getting back to the hotel and reading her letter.

Sierra was saying something. "Most times when you do your volunteer work you look sad, Mommy. But not today, a'cause you know why?"

"Why?" Jamie turned right, onto their street.

"Because today you look happy, so it's a nice change. Don't you think so?"

Suddenly her distracted thoughts settled down long enough to understand the thing her daughter was saying. Most of the time when she worked at St. Paul's she came home looking sad? Was that really how Sierra saw her? If so, what sort of life was that for her daughter? No father, and a mother who was sad more days than not?

Sierra chattered on, something about school and music class and the girl next to her singing too loud. Jamie tightened her grip on the steering wheel and turned into the driveway. She looked different today.

What a profound observation. One more bit of proof that God was bringing about some sort of change in her life—if only she understood exactly what it was. As they walked into the house, Jamie wondered which was more telling: how working at St. Paul's left her downcast, or how today—for a change—she looked happy. Because after working the hardest shift since becoming a volunteer, and then telling the captain she didn't want to see him for a while, there could be only one reason why she'd look happy.

His name was Clay Miles.

Sixteen

Clay was in his room changing when he noticed the light blinking on his motel phone. Probably the front desk asking if he wanted fresh towels. He ignored it and searched through his closet.

The day had been a long one, full of drills and workshops on technique. The group of officers in training would spend the first part of the three weeks learning the most up-to-date detective skills—crime scene forensics, blood-spatter evidence, ballistics testing. The last eight days would send them into the streets of New York, working alongside some of the city's top detectives.

One of the captains briefed them that morning about the realities of the job.

"Some of our crime scenes are, well—" sarcasm filled his tone and his smile—"let's just say they're not in the penthouse district. And some of our investigations take place at night." The grin faded. "You'll wear flak jackets and carry weapons. The streets of New York City aren't for the faint of heart."

Clay received approval to carry a weapon during training from his captain in Los Angeles. Some of the paperwork had to be fast-tracked, but during his first week off the department was able to clear him of any guilt in the shooting of the carjacking suspect.

Good thing. Clay couldn't have made the trip without clearance to carry a weapon. It was why he'd been armed on the ferryboat, and why he'd met Jamie Bryan. Jamie, who'd made it difficult to concentrate these past few days. He was drawn to her in a way that consumed him, left him breathless. Even now he wondered if she'd gotten his note, if she'd considered leaving one on his car, as well. He slipped on a pullover and glanced at the phone again.

What if the message was from Jamie?

He took light running steps to the phone, dialed 0, and sat down on the bed.

"Front desk."

"Yes, hi." Clay kicked his feet up and leaned back against the headboard. "My message light was flashing."

"Okay, sir, let me check that for you. Just a moment." She was gone for a few seconds. "Yes, a woman came in and gave us a note. It has your first name and room number on it."

The smile took hold of his face and didn't let go. It had to be Jamie. "Could you send it up?"

"Certainly, Mr. Michaels."

A minute later there was a knock at his door. "Bellman."

Clay opened it, took the note, and tipped the man. He unfolded the note and read it.

She'd gotten the note, after all. He felt giddy as a schoolboy with a first-time crush, and no wonder. After three years of bad setups and superficial dates, he'd finally met a woman like he'd always hoped. One with goals and values and a faith that colored everything about her.

But this relationship wouldn't be easy.

He folded the note, tossed it on the nightstand, and grabbed his keys. On the way across the island he thought about how there had been no pictures of her dead husband anywhere. Not that he was looking, but it seemed strange. She was still single, after all. It would make sense to have pictures up.

Of course, maybe it was part of her healing process. Keeping his image out of sight so she could move on with life. Clay wasn't sure. Just that the look in her eyes when she'd talked about him said very clearly she'd never loved anyone the way she'd loved him.

Sadness settled over him, weighing his heart down like a sodden wool cloak.

How smart was it to fall for a woman with that sort of devotion to someone else? Even dead, the man might always hold the first place in her heart, and what sort of life would that be? Second place?

He dismissed the thought.

All of it was insane, anyway. He'd only met her two days before. They'd be friends for the three weeks he was in New York, and maybe write once in a while. What more could ever come of it with him living so far away?

Not until she opened the door did he admit he was fooling himself. Big time.

Through their pizza dinner, he could hardly take his eyes off her. During the ice cream sandwich dessert and a story, compliments of Sierra who was learning to read, he could hardly tear his gaze from her.

Jamie Bryan had captured his imagination from the moment he saw her. There was no logical reason, no explanation, but he was falling. Hard.

And nothing in his power could make him stop.

The story was finished and Jamie moved to the edge of Sierra's bed. She looked back at Clay. "Wanna pray with us?"

"Sure." His heart thudded against the wall of his chest. This was the picture, wasn't it? The family scene he'd been longing for all his adult years? He took his place between them and bowed his head, not sure of their routine.

Sierra reached out and took one hand while Jamie took the other, giving his fingers a light squeeze. She spoke the prayer in hushed tones.

"Dear Jesus, please be with Sierra as she sleeps and please watch over her. Help her to have peaceful dreams and wake up happy about a new day. We know You have great plans for Sierra, God. Please help her to look for those every day of her life. We love You, Lord. Amen."

Clay held onto Jamie's hand a few seconds after the prayer ended, then let go. When they left her room, he stopped outside Sierra's door. "I love that."

Jamie smiled. "What?"

"The way you are with her, projecting God's blessings onto her."

"Oh." Jamie started down the stairs. She looked over her shoulder as she walked. "You mean the part about God's plans for her?"

"Right." He stayed close behind her. "Jeremiah 29:11. Kids need to hear that so badly."

"They do." She turned around at the foot of the stairs and her smile eased some. "It'd be easy for her to grow up mad at God, because of what happened to Jake." Her eyes shone with a strength that Clay knew only came from walking in faith. "But God has plans for us no matter what bad thing has happened. Even losing Jake."

They went into the family room, and Jamie pointed to a shelf of videos. "Feel like a movie?"

"Hmmm." He sat down at one end of the sofa, glanced around the room, and spotted a backgammon board. "Hey, you play?"

She followed his gaze. "Backgammon? Sure." She grabbed it and brought it back to the sofa. "Just a minute." She slipped a CD in the player and before she was sitting down, Kenny Chesney started playing in the background.

"Country, huh?"

"There's something about a good country song." She took the spot at the opposite end of the sofa so there was enough room to open the game between them. She held his eyes for a few beats. "Country songs tell a story; I like that."

"Me too." Clay set up the backgammon pieces and tried to sort through his feelings. They had everything in common, and a chemistry that couldn't be denied. But in less than three weeks he'd be back in LA. He didn't want to think about it.

They played five games and several times his fingers brushed against hers. Each time he could feel the sensation throughout his body. Once in a while he would look at her, almost certain she was feeling the same thing.

"I believe I'm the winner." Jamie lifted her chin and closed the board. It was almost ten o'clock, and they both had to go into the city in the morning. She set the game on the floor and leaned against the sofa arm. Her eyes were soft again, shining with the vulnerability that had caught his attention the first time they'd spoken. "I had fun tonight."

"Me too."

They were silent for a moment, studying each other. Clay had so many questions. What was happening between them? How was she feeling, and why were they playing with each other's hearts when he had to go home in a few weeks? Did she and her husband play backgammon together?

Instead of voicing his thoughts, he put his arm up on the sofa back and tried not to dwell on the fact that he had no answers.

"How's Joe doing?"

"He was glad Wanda invited him back; after last night he wasn't sure he'd get to see her again."

"Maybe tonight's the night."

"The apology?" Clay leaned sideways and rested his head in his hand. "I hope so." He shook his head. "Crazy guy. If someone's got something to say to a person they care about, they should come out and say it."

Not until the words were out did he realize what he'd said. She raised her brow and gave a subtle sideways nod. "Good idea." Her eyes found a deeper place in his heart. "But it's not always easy . . . or wise."

"No, it isn't." Clay watched her. Was she talking about herself or him? He wanted to ask, but she was right. It wasn't easy or wise to talk about what was happening between them. It was simply too soon. Besides, what if he was imagining the chemistry between them? Maybe Jamie was merely a lonely widow hungry for company. Since Clay was a police officer, and he'd rescued her on the boat, and he was only in town for a few weeks, he was a pretty safe bet.

He checked his watch, stood, and stretched. "I guess I better go." His neck still hurt from the shooting, but it was getting better. "Thanks again for dinner."

"It was fun." Jamie stood and led the way toward the foyer. "Let's do it again."

"Sure."

They reached the door and Jamie turned to face him. The entryway was dark and shadowy, the only light coming from two rooms away. Somehow the mood of the moment became more intimate. She leaned against the door. "Can I tell you something?"

"Okay." He rested his shoulder against the wall, careful to keep several feet between them.

"I haven't . . ." She bit her lip, her eyes locked on his. "I haven't done this since . . . since Jake died."

Though her eyes were vulnerable, transparent, she hadn't said anything that dipped below the surface all night. Until now.

"Jamie." His heart melted. It must have been so difficult to have him over, give him dinner, and share a night of backgammon with him in the place where she and her husband had loved and laughed and started their family.

She hung her head and in the shimmer of distant light a single tear fell to the floor. "I thought you should know."

The hug was inevitable. Everything about the moment cried out for him to take her in his arms and soothe away the pain.

He reached out to her. "C'mere."

"I'm sorry." She sniffed and took two slow steps toward him. "I'm really not sad." Her eyes lifted to his. Though they were wet, they shone with something more than sorrow. "I like you being here, Clay."

Their faces were inches apart, but Clay wouldn't kiss her. Not even when everything in him wanted to. Instead he folded his arms around her and held her close. He stroked her hair and let her rest her head against his chest. "Guess what?" He leaned down some and whispered near the side of her face.

"What?" She uttered a sound that was more laugh than cry. "You think I'm crazy?"

"Nope." He pulled back and spoke into her eyes. "I like being here too." He let go of her and smiled. "Maybe you and Sierra can join me in the city tomorrow night . . . find something fun to do."

Her smile in the shadows warmed him in a way nothing else had. "I think we'd like that."

He stepped closer to the door and opened it. "Good night, Jamie."

"Good night." A cool breeze shot its way into the house and she crossed her arms tight. "Thanks for understanding."

He nodded, and then he was outside and the door was closing. The air was freezing cold, but the sky was crystal clear. It was amazing, this close to Manhattan, that he could see any stars. But that night the sky was full of them. He stopped and stared up. *God . . . it's too soon, but it feels like something's happening.* He pulled the edges of his coat tighter around him. This time he spoke out loud. "Lead me, God . . . don't let me get ahead of You."

Halfway to the car he was going over the evening in his mind— especially the last few minutes, the way Jamie leaned on him, the way she held him—when something occurred to him. One of the main questions he had about Jamie and whatever it was they'd found together had just been answered.

The chemistry between them definitely was *not* a figment of his imagination.

SEVENTEEN

Jamie stood with her face against the door until she heard Clay drive away. What had she done? Opening up to him in the dark foyer, practically begging him for a hug? How could she be so shameless? Here in her own house, the place she'd shared with Jake? And what did Clay think, now that she'd practically thrown herself at him?

She rubbed her hands along her arms. Dirty, that's what she felt. Dirty and cheap and completely disloyal to Jake. It was one thing to invite Clay over, to give him dinner and play backgammon with him. But the hug at the end was over the top.

Even if she didn't have Jake's memory to protect, she'd acted too quickly. Still ... that was the strange thing about Clay. He seemed so familiar, already so much a part of her life.

She drew a long breath, then made her way through the house turning off lights and locking doors—what used to be Jake's nighttime ritual. Finally she pushed herself up the stairs to the bedroom. No matter if Clay felt familiar or not, she'd acted inappropriately. Guilt and embarrassment mixed in her gut and shot through her heart, leaving her cheeks hot.

While she brushed her teeth, she could only stare at her reflection. What was *wrong* with her? How could she have changed so quickly, let go of the past in a forty-eight-hour window? And what about Aaron? No one would ever understand her loss the way Aaron did. Because it was his loss too, they forever shared a connection. But Clay? He was sympathetic, of course, but he'd never known Jake, could never understand the relationship she'd shared with him.

It was all so confusing.

She rinsed her toothbrush and set it back on the charger. The best idea was to forget about both of them, Aaron *and* Clay. All she needed was God and Sierra and memories of Jake. That was more than enough to get her through life until she could be with her husband again. She would work at St. Paul's, and when the new Twin Towers were built, she would apply for a position at the official memorial.

If she spent her life helping the victims of September 11, she would be honoring Jake's memory and never—not ever again— would she suffer the horrible pangs of regret that jabbed her now. She gripped the bathroom counter and hung her head. *God . . . I'm sorry. I acted on my feelings, but it was wrong. I know it was wrong. Help me to live a life that would please You and Jake and Sierra. And help me keep my distance from Clay Miles.*

She looked up and her eyes fell on a small wooden plaque, one that had hung in her bathroom since her first birthday after Jake died. It had been a gift from her friend, Sue Henning.

"I bought us each one," she told Jamie at the time, "because there'll be days when we can't leave home without remembering the message written there."

Jamie looked at it now, studied it, and a chill ran down her neck and arms. The words were from the Bible. They read, *Trust in the Lord with all your heart and lean not on your own understanding; in all your ways acknowledge him, and he will make your paths straight.* Beneath that it said, *Proverbs 3:5–6.*

Her path felt crooked, for sure, after the evening with Clay, after their hug. If she was honest with herself, she wanted to kiss him. But how *could* she, when in her heart she was still married to Jake?

The Bible words gave her a different perspective, a peace. Never mind about Clay or Aaron or any of the emotions churning up her soul. Don't try to figure it out. Rather trust God. He'd take care of making her paths straight; that was His promise. That's what He was telling her, wasn't it?

She straightened and headed into the bedroom.

Tonight she needed more than a single Bible verse. She wanted to get lost in Scripture, to swim through the verses and chapters until she found the safe harbor she desperately needed.

Jake's Bible was on the dresser—where it always was. She picked it up, dropped into the nearest chair, and flipped it open. Some nights she used a study guide and read specific parts of Scripture. Other times, like tonight, she flipped through until something caught her eye. Jake had read this Bible thoroughly, and nearly every book was replete with highlighted sections, underlined verses, and notes written in the margins.

Jamie started at the beginning and thumbed through the books of Genesis, Exodus, Leviticus, and Numbers, passing various highlighted areas. But as she passed over Deuteronomy, something caught her attention.

It was her name; she was sure of it. Her name in a part of the Bible she'd never read before. She flipped back, turning the pages until she saw it again, scrawled in Jake's printing above Deuteronomy, chapter 30. Jake had drawn a line from her name to a section of Scripture that read, "I have set before you life and death, blessings and curses. Now choose life, so that you and your children may live."

Next to the text Jake had written this:

Jamie, this is for you. If I could get anything into your head, your heart, it would be that one point. Choose life, Jamie. Whenever you have the chance, choose life.

Choose life?

She read his words again and again and one more time before her tears blurred the letters. Sweet Jake, still lending her his wisdom and understanding. But what did it mean? She sniffed and wiped at her eyes. Then she started at the beginning of the thirtieth chapter of Deuteronomy and began to read.

Clearly the story was about God's people on their journey to the Promised Land. Jamie remembered hearing a sermon series on the topic at church the year after Jake's death. Chapter 30 told the people that God was giving them a choice. Choose His ways, His truth, His leading, and they would be choosing blessings and prosperity. Choose their own ignorant, prideful ways, the ways of idols or false gods, and they would be choosing destruction and curses.

Jamie stored the words in her heart as she finished the chapter. Yes, that's what it meant. Life or death—the choice belonged to God's people back then much as it belonged to every person born on earth. Choose God, choose life. Choose an alternate way, choose death.

Jamie, this is for you. If I could get anything into your head, your heart, it would be that one point. Choose life, Jamie. Whenever you have the chance, choose life.

Jake's words had been aimed straight at her lack of faith.

An ache started in her chest and consumed her heart and soul. She hugged the Bible's open pages close.

Jake had loved her with a love so great it could only have come from God. A love that left her to make her own decision. But not until she had a chance to read his Bible did she understand the angst she'd caused him. He prayed daily for her eyes to be opened, for his faith to become real to her.

That's why it hurt so much now.

Jake died longing for one thing—the chance to share his faith with her. Yes, God answered his prayers. Through his journal, his Bible, through the confusion of trying to teach a stranger to be her husband, God answered Jake's prayers. She found God and she would hold on to Him until her dying day.

But she never got to share Him with Jake.

The enormity of all she had cost the two of them had never been more clear. She'd missed the intimacy of praying with her husband, missed holding his hands and coming before their God with a single heart, single purpose. She'd missed looking into Jake's eyes and seeing the love of Christ reflected there. Sure, she'd seen love in his eyes. Every time he looked at her, she saw love. But not God's love, because she wasn't aware of that sort of love. A deeper love, a bond that could only come through shared faith.

She'd missed all of it because of her stubborn pride.

Faith in Christ was the most important thing to Jake Bryan, and she'd missed the chance to understand that, to connect with him on that eternal level. She'd missed it and there wasn't a thing she could do about it.

A canyon of sorrow cut through her heart. If only she could have one day to hold him again, look into his eyes, his soul, and tell him that she had done what he'd asked of her. She had chosen God's life. One time to share the intimate bond of faith, an intimacy that would've made them even closer, more connected.

But it was a closeness she'd never know with Jake, and the truth of that pushed the canyon deeper until she could feel her heart breaking. For a long time she let the tears come, sadness that hadn't taken the form of weeping for months.

Eventually her sobs subsided, and she blinked so she could see clearly. Then she lowered the Bible and read the underlined part once more.

I set before you life or death . . . choose life.

Choose life . . .

Bit by bit, realization formed. She'd made the choice for life when it came to Jesus. But what about the way she *lived* her life?

Images flashed at her, the days and months she'd spent at St. Paul's, the conversations with Aaron about keeping the memory of September 11 fresh in the minds of people, helping the country to never forget. Then she heard Sierra's innocent voice telling her she looked happy today, but not usually. Usually after her volunteer work she looked sad.

How could she have been so blind? She'd surrounded herself with death and destruction ever since Jake died. Talking about the dead, remembering the dead, commemorating the dead, honoring the dead. Reliving the destruction, imagining the destruction, putting herself next to Jake amid the destruction, staring at the place where the destruction happened.

It consumed her.

Not that working at St. Paul's was a bad thing. They needed volunteers, and her time there had been a necessary part of her healing.

She closed her eyes. What was the prayer she'd said in the bathroom a few minutes ago? *Help me live a life that would please You and Jake and Sierra?* Wasn't that it? Then she walks in, flips open Jake's Bible, and reads a verse about choosing life?

Another chill worked its way down her spine.

Was it an answer from God? Was He telling her she'd spent enough time living in a cemetery, existing in a memorial? Was God giving her permission to move on, to choose life?

She read her husband's words again and for a moment she could see him standing before her, smiling at her, running his thumb beneath her eyes to dry her tears. "Jake . . ."

His name hung in the air and the image of him faded.

All this time she'd volunteered at St. Paul's so she could feel closer to him, closer to his memory. She'd done it to honor him and make him proud, because it was the sort of thing he would've done.

But not for two years straight.

The truth was suddenly clearer than air. Jake embraced life, lived it to the full without fear or doubt. He woke up each morning praising God and loving his family, and headed to work with a full heart. Always he had known he might die on the job, but the fact had never stopped him. The windy possibility of death had never so much as dimmed the brilliant candle that was Jake Bryan's life.

Maybe she'd acted too quickly that night by hugging Clay; maybe it would be years before she was ready to fall in love with someone new. But if Jake were standing here now he would tell her it was time to step out of the darkness, time to turn away from death and destruction.

Time to choose life.

Now Jamie had only one question for God. How? She dug her elbows into her knees. Should she leave St. Paul's? Invest her time somewhere other than memorializing the victims of September 11?

Find someone new to share her life?

The options were overwhelming.

She stood and set the Bible back on the dresser. Maybe she should call Sue, ask her what she thought of the verse. It was late, but Sue was a night owl. She'd still be up. Jamie was about to pick up the phone when it rang. The unexpected sound of it made her jump back.

Caller ID told her it was from a cell phone. Clay Miles. It couldn't be anyone else.

She picked up the receiver. "Hello?"

"Hi." The smile in his voice sounded over the phone lines. "I know it's late, but I had two things."

"Okay." She felt herself smile, felt her eyes lighten and the burden lift from her shoulders. "Tell me."

"First, I got a call from one of the guys on the department. He had a bunch of Broadway tickets donated to the police force; they had three left for *The Lion King*, and I snagged 'em. It's Friday night. I thought you and Sierra might want to join me."

"*Lion King?* At the Amsterdam Theater?" Four different times Jamie had looked into tickets for Sierra, but the show was sold out months in advance. "Are you kidding?"

"Serious. They're orchestra level, ten rows from the stage."

"Clay!" She did a light scream. "Sierra will flip!"

He laughed. "I had a feeling. How about we head into the city about five o'clock. That way we can get some pizza before the show. Sound like a plan?"

Jake's words came flying at her. *Choose life, Jamie . . . whenever you have the chance, choose life.* "Yes, Clay." Happy tears stung at her eyes and she swallowed against the thickness in her throat. "A wonderful plan."

They made a decision to have lunch the next day, then hung up. Jamie stared out the bedroom window at the shadowy bare trees, swaying in the early winter night. The timing of Clay's call was unbelievable. There she'd been, overwhelmed with the idea of choosing life, of moving on. What did it look like and where should she start? She smiled, the tide of sorrow waning. Most of her questions were still unanswered, but at least she knew what she was going to do first.

She would take in *The Lion King* on Broadway with Clay and Sierra.

God would show her what to do after that.

Eighteen

Sierra had barely enough time to talk to God when she got home from school.

Clay was taking them to *Lion King!* The real live *Lion King!* She bounced into her bedroom and found Wrinkles on her bed.

"Wrinkles, guess what?"

The cat yawned and stretched out his skinny arms. He didn't look that interested. Sierra dropped down on the edge and rubbed the soft fur between his ears. "Clay's taking us to *Lion King*, can you believe it?"

Wrinkles looked at her and blinked. Sierra did a big breath because maybe that cat was jealous. Or maybe he didn't understand. But God would, so she closed her eyes super-duper tight and tried to be serious. Only instead a squeally sort of laugh came from her mouth, so she jumped up and danced around the room until she bumped into the wall.

Then she settled down. *Settle down* is what Mommy said when she had a little too much energy. "God ... Clay's taking us to *Lion King!* Isn't that the bestest news in the whole wide world?"

Of course God didn't talk to her like her friend, Katy, or like her mommy would. But she could feel Him listening all the same. She licked her dry lips and did a smaller, shorter dance. "I think I like that Clay, God. Thanks for letting him meet Mommy on the boat when he saved her life from the bad guys."

She opened her eyes and gasped. She didn't have a nice dress picked out yet, and Mommy said to hurry. The closet had six nice dresses in it, so she picked out the frilliest and prettiest one, the one with blue and white and ruffles and a big bow in the back. Then her white socks with the lacy tops, the ones Wrinkles wore the other day.

Speedy fast she was ready and running down the stairs. That's when she stopped, because Clay was already there and he and Mommy were smiling at each other. Real quick she added a P.S. for God, because she had something else to say. But this time she said it in her head so Mommy and Clay wouldn't hear her. *God . . . I know Clay lives in California, but maybe he could change his mind and live here. Because he would make a nice second daddy, don't You think? A second daddy like James has? Please think about it, God. Thanks.*

Clay looked up at her. "Don't you look pretty."

"Thank you." She did a curtsy, the kind she and her mommy did when they played princess. "And you look like Prince Charming." He really did. He was tall and he had blond hair and his eyes looked like Prince Charming in the movie.

Clay did a prince-type bow and smiled at her. "That's very nice of you, Sierra."

Her mommy covered her mouth and laughed. Then she made smiling eyes at Sierra and said it was time to go. The trip into the city was the longest in the world. It felt like the week before Christmas because it lasted forever. But finally they ate their pizza and took a cab to the theater and went inside. The theater was the prettiest place in the world, with fancy decorations on the walls and ceilings and even the floor and seats.

They walked down toward the front until Mommy said, "This is it."

Sierra went down the row first, then Mommy, then Clay. She wanted to stand up and dance around a little because this was the real *Lion King!* Instead her stomach did the dance by itself, twisting and jumping and proving how much excitement she had inside her. Plus also her head and shoulders did some moving and turning and looking at the other people and then her knees got involved.

Mommy leaned close to her. "Sit still, Sierra. Young ladies sit still at the theater."

Sierra already knew that because Mommy took her here to see *Annie* once. But because of *Lion King* getting ready to start, she forgot. "Okay, Mommy. Sorry."

"It's okay." Her mommy smiled. "You're excited."

"I'm *so* excited, Mommy. My tummy and head and shoulders and even my knees are excited."

Clay leaned over Mommy's legs. "That's exactly how I feel." He gave a nice nod, then he looked at Mommy. "I might need a reminder about sitting still too."

Sierra giggled, and just then the lights went out. A squeal started to come from her mouth, but she smacked her hand over her lips and looked at her mother with a quick look that said she wouldn't squeal again. Promise.

But she definitely did a lot of gasps.

The giraffes came up the aisles around them, and the lions covered the stage, and painted people were singing in the trees, and more of them from someplace near the ceiling, and it was all so amazing she could hardly stand it. A dancing person started singing "Circle of Life," and that's when the most amazing thing of all happened.

In the corner of her eyeball she saw Clay holding Mommy's hand. And that's when she was sure she would remember this night all the way until forever.

The moment Clay arrived at her house, Jamie knew the truth. No matter what she'd told herself the night before about jumping in too quickly or being ashamed of herself for her attraction to him, seeing him in person told the real story.

There was no turning back.

If she was going to choose life, if she was going to embrace it, then she couldn't berate herself for hugging a man whose company she enjoyed. Never mind whether they ever saw each other again after these three weeks, for now all she wanted was to be with him. When he walked through the door, their eyes met. They stood there, looking at each other. Then—almost in slow motion—they came together in another hug. Not the sorrowful hug of the night before, but a hug of friendship and promise and something that defied time and reason.

A hug she neither regretted nor wanted to end.

Conversation had been light and upbeat since then, with Sierra providing the main source of dialogue. From her perspective, everything about the city was super bright and super busy and super big. She talked about all of it right until they took their seats.

It was when the music started, when the fullness of it surrounded them and swept them away on the story, that Clay reached out and took her hand. At first she expected him to squeeze her fingers or pat them, his way of telling her he was glad they were getting a chance to see the show, glad they were together.

But then he eased his fingers between hers, and the sensation sent a tingling feeling all the way to her knees. She was afraid to look at him, afraid the emotions tossing her soul around would be too transparent. Instead she focused on the way her fingers felt against his, the warmth of his large hand covering her smaller one.

The play was amazing.

She'd heard people say that *The Lion King* was in its own category theatrically, that nothing compared to it, and they were right. The costumes, the singing, the sets, it was more than Jamie could've imagined. Once in a while she looked at Sierra, and always her daughter's eyes were wide and dancing, her mouth slightly open. She neither talked nor fidgeted, mesmerized by the experience.

And through it all, Clay held her hand.

At the part where Simba, the young lion king, meets up with his old childhood girlfriend, Nala, and the two sing about feeling the love in the air that night, Clay ran his thumb over hers. Tears stung at Jamie's eyes, though she wasn't sure why. Whether it was because she and Jake had been childhood friends ... or because that very night love, or something like it, was indeed in the air. And it had nothing to do with Jake.

Then when Mufasa's memory spoke to Simba, Jamie felt tears again. The message was the same as what she'd read in Deuteronomy. What Jake had written to her in the margins of his Bible. Loss was part of the package of living, but the fighter remains. He fights the good fight, he gets back in the ring, he never gives up.

He chooses life.

Jamie's heart almost broke when the play ended. Not because the story was so moving, so brilliantly performed. But because when the lights went up, Clay released her hand. Probably for Sierra's benefit. The two of them hadn't had time to talk about what was happening between them, let alone involve Sierra.

On the way home she was more aware of him, the way he walked beside her, his arm brushing against hers, how he sat next to her in the cab, their legs touching. Once in a while she'd catch him watching her. Their eyes would meet and hold, and she'd feel the tingling again, a floating sensation that made her look down to see if her feet were still on the ground.

Back at the house, they went through the nighttime ritual with Sierra, and this time Clay took her hand and Sierra's and offered to pray.

"God, thank You for a wonderful night. Thanks for singing and music and drama." He paused. "And stories that touch our hearts."

Jamie was supposed to have her eyes closed, but she couldn't. She kept them open just enough so she could watch Clay, the way he bowed his head and prayed so easily, with a heart for God alone. She'd missed this with Jake, the praying. The thought shot a quick burst of pain into her heart, but it faded as Clay continued.

"You have a plan for each of us. A good plan. Help us keep our eyes open so we won't miss it. Thank You, Lord. Amen."

Her heart skipped a beat. *Help us keep our eyes open so we won't miss it?* Was he talking about her, the two of them? She didn't ask, and a few minutes later they were downstairs fixing snacks.

The atmosphere remained easy, uncomplicated throughout the evening. They watched country music videos and played backgammon—with Clay winning five out of seven. Jamie told him that Wanda had called her the night before. Joe finally had a chance to meet her children, and when he saw her little boy he broke down.

"I guess he looks exactly like the boy they lost." Jamie bit her lip. "The kids went upstairs, and Joe wept. The thing was, Wanda didn't know what to do with him. She hadn't drawn comfort from him when their son was killed, and now she didn't know how to give him comfort."

Clay frowned. "Tough for both of them."

"But get this." Jamie dropped the dice she'd been fiddling with, her eyes locked on his. "Joe apologized. He sat her down and even through his tears he told her he was sorry for walking out, for not being there for her when she needed him most."

"Wow." Clay crossed his arms. "God's doing something between those two."

"Definitely." She looked at the game board. "But I guess he left with things still awkward. Wanda asked me to pray for something to happen, something that will help them break the bonds of the past so they can find a new way to relate to each other."

The conversation switched to the carjacker Clay had to shoot, and a handful of other calls—gang fights and domestic violence and drug busts—runs that had taken all of his training to pull off.

It was the first time Jamie considered the danger of his job. Just as dangerous as Jake's had been—more so, in some ways.

Her reaction was proof she was different now; she wasn't afraid for him. Whether he remained her friend or something more, she would never again live in fear for the safety of someone she cared about. Besides, like Jake, Clay loved God. And that was enough. Every day when he hit the streets he put on two kinds of armor. His bulletproof vest, and the armor of God.

Fear couldn't add anything to that.

He closed the game board and dug his shoulder into the back of the sofa. "So tell me about you, Jamie. Other than St. Paul's and playing dress-up, what do you do? Hobbies? Sports? Jester training?"

She giggled. "Definitely jester training." Her smile eased. The question was harder than it seemed. What did she do with her time, after all? "I like to jet ski." An image of Jake and her flying across the water filled her mind. She willed it to disappear. "And I used to take a ceramics class. You know, pottery, painting little statues, that kind of thing."

"Not anymore?" Clay angled his head, his expression mildly curious.

"No." She made a slight lift of her shoulders. "I haven't gotten back into it, I guess."

"What about the jet skiing?"

She looked at her hands. He wasn't probing, really. Just learning more about her, maybe learning more about how far she'd come since losing Jake. Her eyes met his again. "Not as much as before."

A knowing filled his eyes. "It was something you did with Jake?"

"Yes."

He winced a bit. "Sorry ... I wasn't ... I didn't mean to bring up something that ..."

"Something about Jake?" Her heart hit another level of respect for the man across from her. On top of everything else, he was compassionate.

"I guess." He exhaled through pursed lips. "Sorry."

"Don't be." She hesitated. "For the rest of my life Jake's name will come up. It has to; I shared twenty years with him." Her voice softened. She was letting Clay see a part of her that few people saw. "At first, after September 11, I couldn't talk about him without breaking down." She tucked her feet beneath her. "What happened to Jake will always be sad, but I can talk about him now." She lifted the corners of her mouth. "Time does that to you."

"You loved him very much, didn't you?" He set the game board on the floor and slid closer.

"Yes." She shifted her gaze to the chair across the room, the one that had been Jake's. "His memory is always with me." A Shania Twain song came on the television, a love song that lent an intimacy to the moment. She looked at him again. "And you, Clay? What hearts have you broken?"

"Not many." He chuckled and shifted so his back was against the sofa. Only a few inches separated them. "The LA girls I've met don't have hearts; just brains and beauty."

"New Yorkers can be that way too."

"I'm sure." His laugh was slow and easy. "Actually, there was one girl, someone I met in high school."

She studied him, the way his eyes didn't change when he talked about the girl. Whoever she was, Jamie guessed she no longer had a hold on Clay Miles. "Did you date her?"

"No. We were friends. In fact—" his light chuckle made her smile—"she married my brother."

Jamie raised her eyebrows. "Really?"

"Yep." He sounded comfortable, as if whatever pain had been involved no longer hurt him.

"Did it make things hard between you and your brother?"

"No." Clay looked straight ahead at the wall. "My brother's a nice guy. They're happy together; she belongs with him. Besides . . ."

She waited, but when he didn't finish his thought she had to know. "Besides what?"

He turned to her and searched her eyes. "She never made me feel like this."

And there it was.

The admission they knew was coming. The special something that had been between them from the moment they met was now out in the open. Her pulse picked up speed. What was she supposed to do? How could she respond when she was blind as a bat in the ways of new love?

She looked down; her hands were trembling. "I . . . I've felt it since the ferryboat." Her eyes met his again. "I thought it was just me."

"It's not." He took her hand, and worked his fingers between hers. "It's crazy; I haven't known you a week." She understood the bafflement in his tone, felt it herself. "But I feel something with you I've never felt before."

They were quiet for a while. Tim McGraw was singing something slow and pretty, and Jamie felt no need to talk. What would they say? Regardless of their feelings, he would go back to California in two weeks.

He spoke first. "I lay awake at night in the Holiday Inn wondering what I'm doing, what could come of this after only three weeks." He gave her a crooked grin. "I guess that's why I brought it up."

"Mmmm." She gave the back of his hand a gentle squeeze. Her heart still tore along, but no longer at breakneck speed. She was nervous, not sure where the conversation was going or whether she could bare her heart enough to tell him her true thoughts—that she struggled with feeling guilty because of Jake, that he would've wanted her to move on. "I've done my share of wondering."

Clay released her hand and put his arm around her, positioning her so she could rest her head on his shoulder. "When I pray about it, I feel God's hand on this—" he gestured to her and then back at himself—"whatever this is between us." He held his breath for a moment. "I guess we need to let Him answer the other questions."

"Exactly." His statement was the perfect wrap-up for the night, a way to stop herself from overthinking the situation and let the night come to an end. She smiled at him, savoring the feel of her head on his shoulder. "Thanks for a great night."

"Well . . ." He raised his brow in mock sarcasm. "We didn't get to wear the hats, but still . . ." His eyes danced. "It was a pretty good night."

He stood, helped her to her feet, and walked with her to the front door. His hug didn't linger, didn't suggest anything more than the closeness he'd already admitted to. When he was gone, she stared out the window and watched his car pull away. She explored her feelings. No guilt. No shame.

Something was changing inside her.

Talking about their feelings had been a good thing. Neither of them was willing to rush ahead, to assume they should start a relationship simply because they shared a chemistry. In the meantime, they would enjoy the next two weeks and believe God had a plan for them. Whether that plan found them together.

Or apart.

NINETEEN

The next week passed in a blur, in which Jamie Bryan was Clay's single focus.

They met at St. Paul's every day Jamie worked and walked through Battery Park, stopping for a few silent moments at the giant globe that was once the courtyard between the Twin Towers. It had been damaged in the terrorist attacks but not destroyed, and now it was on display to commemorate the city's fighting spirit, its will to survive. They took a tour boat to Liberty Island and held hands as they walked along the base of the Statue of Liberty.

There were lunch dates, and dinners with Sierra, and once Clay wore the jester hat when they went bowling.

Now it was Sunday night, and Clay wanted to stop time.

He and Jamie had spent the day in Central Park with Sierra. The temperatures were in the thirties, so they bundled up in coats and hats and scarves, and Sierra convinced them to consider coming back later in the week for an hour of ice skating.

The city was taking on the look of Christmas. Lights were strung across much of the park's perimeter and preparations were being made for the Macy's Thanksgiving Day Parade, coming up a week from Thursday. Clay's flight was set for Saturday; five days later he'd be sitting around the Thanksgiving table with Laura and Eric and Josh, wondering if his time in New York was all some sort of marvelous dream.

Wondering how soon he could find his way back.

Time had flown by. In six days his training would be over, and he and Joe would be on a plane back to Los Angeles, ready to start his department training for his new position as detective. He should be excited, focused on the future, the fascinating cases he'd be working on and getting involved in his local church—as he'd planned before he left for New York.

Funny, the last thing he'd told himself was that he'd meet a girl at church. Who knew it would be a church in the heart of New York City?

He stretched out on his hotel bed and stared at a blank spot on the wall. It was just after nine o'clock; Sierra and Jamie had homework to focus on, so he'd made an early night of it. But the day had been amazing, full of the sweet glances and joined hands that had come to mark their time together.

He wanted to get back in his car and drive to Jamie's house so they wouldn't miss a minute of the time they had left. But this was good, this time apart. Even for a single evening. He needed time to think of a plan, a way to connect her world with his. The holidays were coming up, so maybe that was the answer.

Pictures played in his mind: Jamie and Sierra sitting around the table with Eric and Laura and Josh. Jamie would love all of them, but then what? Would she consider relocating if things between them continued? She had nothing concrete holding her in Staten Island—nothing except a lifetime of memories and her work at St. Paul's.

There was the possibility he could find a job in Manhattan with the NYPD, but that wasn't what he wanted. The weather was already near freezing, when back home it was still in the midseventies. Then there was the obvious—it would be close to impossible to start a life with Jamie in the place where she and her husband had shared a million memories, the place where he worked and died.

He exhaled and glanced at the nightstand. His cell phone was finished charging. Maybe he could call Eric and ask for advice, suggest the Thanksgiving idea and see what he thought. He picked up the phone, dialed the number, and waited.

Eric answered on the second ring, his voice upbeat. "Hey, it's my little brother! We thought you fell off the face of the earth."

"Sort of." Clay laughed. "I haven't had a free minute."

"They have you working twenty-fours, huh? I thought for sure they'd give you a few hours off here and there to call home." Eric was enjoying the moment. "Laura and I were trying to guess what had happened to you, so I told her you probably met someone, fell in love, and decided to get a police job in New York."

"Well . . ." Clay formed a stack of pillows behind his back and leaned into them. "I'm not getting a job in New York."

Eric was silent for a moment. Then he uttered a single chuckle. "You telling me the other part's true?"

"I don't know." He tried to picture his brother, face expectant, certain Clay was messing with him. "I think so."

"*Really?*" This time Eric sounded excited. "You met someone? Hey, that's great! Where'd you meet her?"

"It was the strangest thing." Clay laughed again and told Eric the story. "They had a gun in her ribs by the time we pulled our weapons on them."

"Serious? That's amazing!" Eric paused. "So basically, you saved her life?"

"Pretty much." He smiled. The room was cold, but he didn't mind. Any time he thought about Jamie he felt warm inside. "I've seen her every day since."

"Every day?" Concern tinged Eric's tone. "What happens when you come back home?"

"We haven't talked about it really. Jamie's told me she has feelings for me, and I've told her the same thing. But that's as far as we've gone." He let his head fall back against the headboard. "I'm thinking about inviting her for Thanksgiving dinner. She and her daughter could fly out and join us at your house." He paused. "What do you think?"

The line was silent.

"Eric?" Clay checked his cell phone; he hadn't lost the call. "Hey, Eric, you there?"

"I'm here." His voice held none of his previous excitement. "Her name's Jamie?"

"Yeah." Clay forced a chuckle. What did his brother care about her name? "Anyway, I've spent a lot of time with her and her daughter. Even their cat. I'd love to invite them for Thanksgiving."

"Definitely." Eric's answer was quicker than before but his tone was still distracted. "Invite her; if she's got your attention we'd love to meet her."

The conversation stalled after that. Clay promised to call again toward the end of the week—to let them know if Jamie and her daughter would be coming. Then he hung up and stared at the phone. What was Eric's deal? Was he hesitant about Jamie because Clay had only known her for a few weeks? Or because something at home had his attention?

It didn't matter.

What did matter was how he was going to convince Jamie to fly to LA for Thanksgiving. The plan was crazy because who did that? Who invited a woman across the country for dinner when they'd only known each other a few weeks? But it wasn't impossible. People found love at first sight all the time, didn't they? Besides, they weren't fresh out of college. They were adults; they knew enough about love to recognize it when it hit them square in the face.

Not that what they shared was love. Not yet. They still hadn't kissed, hadn't allowed their conversations to get deeper than that one night over backgammon. But they held hands, and he could read her eyes well enough to know she cared.

Would she come for Thanksgiving? Clay didn't know, but he was sure of one thing. If she and Sierra came for Thanksgiving, they would hit it off great with Eric and Laura and Josh. His brother was bound to make Jamie feel comfortable, a part of the family.

Clay would have to be patient. He would simply tell Jamie she was invited and let her make the decision about whether to come. He set the phone back down on the nightstand. She would come; he was sure of it.

He could hardly wait to tell Jamie about the idea.

Eric set the receiver on the base and stared at the phone. Jamie and her daughter? From Staten Island? Adrenaline had shot through his veins at the mention of the name, and now—now he wasn't sure what to do next.

"Who was on the phone?" Laura padded into the bedroom. She wore jeans and thick fuzzy slippers. She had a small pink gift bag in her hands.

"Clay." He couldn't change his distant tone. Eric caught his wife's attention. "He met someone."

"Is that so?" Laura's eyebrows lifted and she gave him a sly smile. "Good for him." She watched him for a moment and her mouth relaxed. "What's wrong?"

"What's wrong?" He blinked and tried to focus on what she was saying.

"Yes, you look like someone died." She took a few steps toward him. "Didn't you say Clay met someone?"

Eric stared at her, wondering if he should put his fears into words. Finally he did a quiet gulp. "Her name's Jamie." He slowed his words down, so each one would have an impact. "She has a daughter and she lives on Staten Island."

"So, she—" Laura stopped and the color drained from her cheeks. "What's her last name?"

"I didn't ask."

"What about her daughter?"

"Didn't ask that either."

She groaned and her shoulders slumped some. "Why not?"

"Because." He shook his head. "I didn't want to know."

"Eric . . ." Laura dropped to the edge of the bed. "Staten Island is a big place. Ten million people live in the New York City area. You don't think it's the same woman."

He turned so he was facing her. "What if it is?"

"It isn't."

"No, seriously, Laura. What if it's her?"

"I'm telling you, it's not." She brought her voice back to an even level. "There must be a thousand women named Jamie living on Staten Island. Half of them probably have daughters." Her eyes told him that she was flustered, but she smiled. "Forget about it. Clay would've told you if it was the same Jamie."

Eric gripped his kneecaps and studied the wall for a moment. Then he found her eyes again. "Clay doesn't know her name; I only talked about her with you." He shrugged. "It was too weird, the whole thing was something most people wouldn't believe in the first place." His voice fell a notch. "God used my time with Jamie to save my life, Laura. I'm the man I am because of her husband. But that sort of thing doesn't exactly come up over lunch. Even with my brother."

Laura stood and came around in front of him. This time she kept the pink gift bag in front of her. "You're worrying about nothing." She stopped near his knees and smiled. "She lives on Staten Island, right?"

"Right." Eric pictured her, working in the kitchen, making blueberry pancakes for Sierra, sitting across from him sharing coffee each morning.

"Did she work?"

"No." Eric tried to focus on his wife, but the memories were strong. Jamie had plenty of money—an accident settlement she'd inherited when her parents died in a car accident when she was barely twenty years old. She'd shared that with him when he was recovering, one of many facts meant to trigger his memory. He shook his head. "She had money in the bank; she didn't need to work."

Laura's smile faded. "She didn't?"

"No. Her husband didn't need to work either. Fighting fires in New York City was a family thing, something in his blood."

"You never told me that." She shifted her weight to one foot. Her voice was higher than before, threatened. "So Jamie had a lot of money."

"Yes." He hadn't talked much about his actual time with Jamie as much as he'd shared the ways of life and faith he'd learned from her husband's journal, from the pages of his Bible. What was he supposed to do if she'd made a connection with Clay? He smiled and tried to hide the pounding of his heart. "Where's this going?"

Laura hesitated. The doubts lifted and cleared from her expression. "What I'm saying is, if she didn't work, then why on earth would she head into the city on a weekday morning?"

Eric hadn't thought about that. He looked at the ground for a minute and stroked his chin. "You're right." He found his wife's eyes again. "She would never have had to work, not with the money she had put away and the insurance settlement she would've gotten from her husband's death." His heart rate slowed. This was good. Thinking things through helped. His shoulders relaxed and he drew a calming breath. "If she decided to get a job—you know—just for fun, she never would've worked in the city; she hated that her husband worked there."

"Okay." Laura's tone was pleasant again. She was still standing in front of him, and she moved closer. "See? There's nothing to worry about."

Eric looped his arms around her waist and smiled. "I guess I overreacted a little. Like you said, there are millions of people in and around the city."

"Exactly." She bent down and kissed the tip of his nose. "Enough talk about that, all right?" Her eyes danced as she straightened. She held the pink bag out to him. "I've got my own news."

News? Wrapped up in a small pink gift bag? Eric felt his heart flip-flop as he took the package. "News?" His voice was a hoarse whisper.

"Go ahead." Her eyes were suddenly damp. She sat down beside him and motioned to the bag. "Open it, Eric."

He gulped. Was it what he thought it was? They'd tried to have another child ever since he came back home, after the terrorist attacks. Laura's doctor wasn't sure why she hadn't gotten pregnant, but in the next few months they were planning to look into some options that might help speed the process along. He met her eyes, looked deep into her heart, and he knew. Before he lifted the tissue and found the tiny pink pair of booties, he knew. "Are you . . . ?"

She nodded. "Six weeks already." Her eyes welled up and she massaged her throat, looking for the words. "I bought pink because I just know, Eric. I know she's a girl."

Eric memorized her face, her expression, the look in her eyes. It was all worth it—the horrible injuries he'd received on September 11, the time with Jamie, his three months of recovery and learning to be a man of God. All of it led to this. "Laura . . ." In a slow rush they came together, holding each other, and Eric couldn't describe the feeling inside him. Warm and full and grateful beyond words. He whispered against her hair. "You think it's a girl?"

"I do." She let out a happy cry. "God is so good. He had a plan all along."

Indeed.

Eric held his wife and thought about the little girl they'd lost, the one Laura miscarried before Josh's birth. He'd known he had a daughter, even in the throes of amnesia. It was why he felt right fathering Jamie's daughter, Sierra, for three months. And it was one of the hardest things about realizing his real identity. He had a loving wife, a wonderful son.

But no daughter.

He nuzzled Laura's cheek, her ear. "I'll be happy with a baby—boy or girl."

"I know." She pressed her face against his and sighed. "It's just that God has already worked so many miracles in our lives."

And in that moment, the way everything was going—even things for Clay—Eric could do nothing but take Laura's face between his hands and kiss her, long and slow, with the kind of love he'd never felt for anyone but her. Because she was right. God *had* already worked so many miracles in their lives. Why wouldn't He be pulling together one more? A baby girl? A daughter? The thought was more than he could imagine.

Eric couldn't think of a better miracle.

TWENTY

Jamie had a new favorite spot on the ferry from Staten Island. If it was sunny—and that Monday morning the sky was brilliant—she stood against the ferry's back railing. It wasn't a place she would've considered before—not on the trip to Manhattan. Because she couldn't see the empty place in the skyline from there.

But now ... Every hour the message from Jake's Bible, the words he'd written in the margins, became more clear. *Choose life.* That meant she didn't have to stare at the empty skyline every day. She could stand at the back of the ferry, protected from the wind by the indoor seating area. She could stare back at Staten Island, the place where she was trying to learn how to live again, and she could think about things relevant to her new life.

The one without Jake.

She lifted her chin and let the sun hit her face square on. Something in her heart told her to savor the ferry ride, because she might not be making the trip much longer. Not to St. Paul's anyway.

Father ... She breathed in the feel of God around her, the sensation of His Spirit inside her. The brisk air, the brilliant spray of shine from the early morning sun on the water. Being out here always made her feel closer to God. *I'm trying, Lord, trying to choose life. But what about Clay? Where does he fit into my—*

There was a tap on her shoulder. She turned around and gasped. "Clay!"

"Hi." He looked deep into her eyes, straight to her heart. "Fancy meeting you here."

Her breath caught in her throat. She'd wondered if he might be on her ferry since he had training that morning, but she hadn't seen him during the boarding process. She turned back toward the water and he took the spot beside her. Without the headwinds, it was easy to hear each other. "I was just praying about you."

"Hmmm." He edged closer, his arm full against hers. "Sounds interesting."

"It was." She stared at the rough water behind the boat. Her tone was light, teasing even—not giving away the electricity coursing through her veins, the way her mouth was dry because of his nearness.

He leaned his head back, taking the sun on his face the way she had earlier. "Let me guess. Praying that I'd find a new hat? Or that just once I might make dinner for you?"

She giggled and angled sideways to see him. Something about the winter air and the crisp blue sky made it feel as if they were the only two people on the boat. Her silliness faded and she looked at him, searching his eyes. "Wanna know what I was praying?"

"Wanna tell me?" His tone was measured, asking her questions his words did not. Questions like whether she was ready to share the heart behind her faith, whether she was ready to give even a glimpse of what she'd been feeling those past two weeks.

"Yeah." Her eyes stayed locked on his. For days Jamie had wanted this moment, a reason to go beyond the obvious—that she enjoyed his company. And now—even as she was praying for wisdom—God had provided it. "I do want to tell you, Clay." She hesitated. "I was asking God where you fit into my life."

He had no clever volley, no thoughtful comeback. Instead his eyes grew more narrow, his gaze deeper than before. "Tell me, Jamie."

She lifted one shoulder. "I don't know, except . . ." She glanced at the water, then back at him. "Except I don't want you to leave in a week."

"Me neither." He turned so they were both leaning against the boat's railing, facing each other. "I worry about you, Jamie. That maybe you're not ready for this." He angled his head. "Any of this. Have you thought about it?"

She did a small laugh, but it was lost on the sound of the ferry engines. "That's like asking me if I'm breathing." Her smile faded. "Yes, I think about it." She reached out and took hold of both his hands. The sensation took her breath away, his fingers intertwined with hers. "I read something in Jake's Bible the other day; it's helped."

"What did it say?" He rubbed his thumbs along the sides of her hands.

The sudden thickness in her throat made it hard to talk. The conversation was more intimate than anything they'd shared. "It was in Deuteronomy, chapter thirty."

"Ahhh." Clay's face was only inches from hers, their voices such that only the two of them could hear. "'I set before you life and prosperity, death and destruction.'"

She hesitated, allowing their eyes to carry on a conversation of their own. "'Choose life.'" Tears built up in her eyes. "Jake wrote me a note in the margins. 'Jamie, if you ever get the chance, choose life.'"

He felt her pain. It was written in his eyes and across the canvas of his heart, a place she could see clearly in this moment. "You miss him."

"I do." She used her shoulder to wipe a single tear. This wasn't a time for crying; she was happy, really. Happy because this—standing here with Clay this way, talking about Scripture—was what God wanted from her. For her. This was life; attention on the living. "I miss him, but he's never coming back." She sniffed. "If he were here, he'd tell me not to live my life in a memorial. He'd want me to start living again."

"I'm sorry, Jamie." His eyes shone, though she didn't think it was from the cold. "I'm sorry."

She wasn't sure which of them moved first, but slowly, as if drawn by a force neither of them could control, they came together. Their lips met in a gentle, soft kiss, one that was still building even as she drew back.

His breath was warm against her cheeks, and as though it was destined from the first time they were together on this very boat, his hand left hers and took gentle hold of her jaw, his fingers spreading along the side of her face. "Jamie . . . is it okay?"

"What?" She breathed the word against his face, so close his skin was touching hers. Her heart was doing somersaults; it was all she could do to remember to inhale.

"Is it okay if I kiss you? Really kiss you?"

The moment he breathed his question against her lips, she was his. She moved closer, giving him permission to do what she'd been imagining and fearing, desiring and dreading, every day since they met. They kissed, and it was something from a dream. Her tears came again because she was kissing someone other than Jake— something she'd never done in all her life. And because it didn't feel wrong and shameful, but sad and wonderful, impossible and right. God had answered her prayers not with quiet holy whispers but with Clay Miles. With this man standing there kissing her, putting his arms around her and holding her close, the way she wanted him to hold her forever.

He pulled back, catching his breath. "Jamie . . ." He looked at her, his eyes full of questions. Was she okay? Was it all right? Was it what she wanted?

"I'm fine, Clay. I am." She closed the distance between them and kissed him this time, full on his mouth, silencing his doubts the only way she knew. This time when they drew apart, she laughed. Not loud or hard, but with an abandon that expressed the joy welling within her. She found his eyes and searched his soul. "God brought you into my life for a reason." Her heart grew suddenly heavy; she felt the corners of her mouth fall. "I just wish we had more time."

He took her hands again. His eyes sparkled with something, maybe anticipation. "Funny you should ask."

"Funny why?" She loved how she felt, warm and safe and appreciated. The captain made his announcement. They were a few minutes from shore.

"Because I've been praying about us too."

"You have?"

He leaned in and kissed her, his lips tender against hers. "Yes, I have. I even talked to my brother back in Los Angeles. Everyone's in agreement."

She giggled. "About what?"

"About you joining us for Thanksgiving."

"In LA?" In a split instant, the idea bridged the gap between despair that he was leaving so soon and hope that maybe—just maybe—they'd find a way to see each other again. "You want me to come to LA for Thanksgiving."

"No." Clay's face got serious, but his eyes still danced. A huge grin spread over his face. "Not just you, crazy. You and Sierra." His words came faster. "Thanksgiving's always at my brother's house. He said he and his wife would love to have the two of you. You could fly in a few days before, and I could take you to the beach. I don't know, maybe take Sierra to Disneyland, that kind of thing. Make a week out of it."

He sounded like a kid talking about spring break, but she was as caught in the wave of enthusiasm as he. She thought for a moment. It was possible, wasn't it? She had Jake's father, but he'd understand if they didn't head upstate for the holiday this once. Besides, she and Sierra hadn't been on a vacation since Jake died. "You're serious? You really want us to come?"

"Of course." His eyebrows were raised halfway up his forehead. "It'll be great, Jamie. Say you'll come."

She laughed again. She'd laughed more those past two weeks than in the past three years combined. "I have to make my orange salad; it's Sierra's favorite."

"That's the nice thing about California in November." He frowned at the sky and shivered. "Oranges are in season."

Everything was happening so fast, but Jamie didn't mind. That was the strangest part of all. They walked off the ferry together and Clay admitted he didn't have to be at work until noon. The captain had changed the schedule at the last minute because of a big drug bust going on that morning in Chinatown.

They held hands as they headed across Battery Park, toward the line of waiting cabs. Jamie kept her steps slow; she didn't want the morning with Clay to end any sooner than it had to. "Why are you coming in so early?"

He stopped, faced her, and took both her hands in his. "I came to find you." He kissed her, just long enough to make her breathless again. "I had to tell you about Thanksgiving."

"Clay . . ." Her heart sang inside her. How had God done this? Brought a man into her life who was everything she needed, everything she hadn't even known she was looking for. "You came in early just for that?"

"Yep." They started walking again, their hands linked. "And now you're stuck with me. I might as well do my waiting at St. Paul's." His voice was upbeat. "Besides, I never finished looking at the memorial tables. Remember? I started on the last wall."

"True." They reached the curb and she hailed a cab. "Maybe it'll be slow and we can find somewhere to talk." Anywhere in the chapel would be comfortable. Aaron Hisel was working a later shift so there wouldn't be any need to explain Clay's presence or why they were together.

Traffic was busier than usual, and by the time they walked through the doors, one of the other volunteers waved Jamie down. A small crowd of people stood around her. "Help!" she mouthed.

Jamie nodded, and gave Clay a helpless smile. "I'll be back."

"Okay. No big deal." He squeezed her hand before letting it go. "I'll look around."

For the flash of an instant Jamie realized that for the first time Clay would see a picture of Jake—because it was still set up next to Sierra's letter at the first table near the door. Not that he'd know he was looking at Jake. And whereas the idea had bothered her the first time Clay came with her to the chapel, now it was something she'd come to accept, that one day Clay would see Jake. A part of her wanted him to see the man she'd loved since she was a girl. It would be one way of blending her worlds, life before Jake and life after him.

She joined the other volunteer and answered questions for ten minutes before Clay caught her attention. He was staring at the picture of Jake, staring at him with an odd intensity. Did he know? How could he? There was no way he could know that the man in the picture was her husband.

Then again . . . The letter next to the photo was signed *Sierra*. How many little girls named Sierra would've lost a firefighter father? She started to excuse herself, head back toward him, when he looked straight at her. Forty feet separated them, but even from that far away she could see his face.

It was ashen.

She slowed, suddenly afraid. Why did Clay look that way? Had he changed his mind about her, maybe decided she must not be ready for something new? His eyes were wide, his mouth open, looking like a person in shock.

"Jamie . . ."

Though she couldn't hear him, she could read her name on his lips.

Her heart skittered about, warning her that something—something she couldn't understand—had in a moment's time gone very wrong. She closed the distance between them, her eyes moving from Clay to the photo of Jake, and back again. "Clay?" She remembered to breathe. "What is it?"

"Is that . . . that's your husband, right?"

She let her eyes find Jake's. The clear blue eyes and short dark hair, the chiseled features of the man who loved her and promised her a lifetime. "You saw Sierra's note."

He nodded, his face still pale. For a long time he said nothing, just looked at Jake, realization coming into his expression.

Jamie relaxed. His reaction was understandable. Here was the picture of a man Jamie never would've left, of Sierra's father. And his likeness—in some cruel twist of senseless hatred—was not gracing the home where Jamie and Sierra lived, but a table in St. Paul's Chapel.

Of course Clay looked shocked. This was probably the first time he'd felt the terrorist attacks personally. She just needed to talk to Clay the way she'd talked to so many other visitors at St. Paul's. She would grieve with him, and they would come away richer for the experience. She was about to take his hand, when he turned to her.

"Jamie." The fear in his eyes was worse than before. "He looks exactly like my brother."

"Like your—" His words hit her in slow motion, each one ramming into her heart and kicking her in small circles until she had to brace herself against the table to keep from falling to the floor. She could feel the blood leaving her face, feel her knees trembling. Her eyes were locked on his, searching for some sort of explanation. He was kidding, or maybe his brother had dark hair or blue eyes. Not an exact replica, certainly. Because God never would've brought this marvelous man into her life only to have it all end in some cruel joke.

Words gathered in her throat but she couldn't say them. She searched Clay's eyes, his face. Bits of conversations came rushing back and she sifted through them for a sign. He couldn't be Eric's brother; it wasn't possible. Sure, he was from California, but that didn't mean anything. His name was Clay Miles, not—

The impossible breathed its hot breath against the nape of her neck. She moved back a few steps, leaning against one of the white pillars. "What's . . ." Her words were scratchy. It took everything to complete the question. "What's your last name?"

He looked as devastated as she felt. He moved closer, leaving only a foot between them. "Clay Michaels."

No! No, it wasn't true. His name was Clay Miles, not Michaels. The spinning in her head got worse and nausea swept over her. "No." She looked away. Navigating with her hands, she made it around the pillar and dropped into the first pew. Then she leaned her forearms on the back of the seat in front of her and hung her head.

She felt him move into the pew and ease into the space beside her. "Jamie, look at me. Talk to me." Anguish was raw in his voice, mixed with shock.

It took everything to lift her head. This wasn't happening; it couldn't be. "You . . . you told me your name was Clay Miles."

"No, Jamie." Alarm joined the emotions burning in his eyes. He lowered his brow, concentrating. "I told you my name on the ferry. We were outside in the stairwell; it was loud."

He was right. She could picture the moment, standing before him, the horn sounding when he told her his name. No wonder there'd been something familiar about him. He had his brother's eyes.

Clay was still watching her, staring at her, caught in the middle of a nightmare that couldn't possibly be true. "So you're the one." His words were slow, full of disbelief. "Of all the people in this city, how could you be the one?"

"I'm sorry, Clay. I can't . . ." She didn't finish her sentence; she didn't need to. The look on Clay's face told her he understood. That because of his relationship to Eric, she and Clay could never move forward.

She closed her eyes and lifted her face. *God . . . why? Of all people, why him?* If only she'd heard him right the first time, heard him say Clay Michaels. She would've known instantly why he looked familiar. They would've figured out their strange connection, talked about it for the rest of the ferry ride, and gone their separate ways.

"Jamie, nothing has to change." Clay leaned closer, his eyes wide, imploring her. "You don't have to come back for Thanksgiving if you don't want to; your time with Eric has nothing to do with this."

She shook her head. "I can't." She met his eyes and willed him to understand. Looking at Eric again would be like looking at Jake. She couldn't carry on even a friendship with Clay if it meant spending time with Eric. It'd be like trying to ignore Jake's ghost in the room.

Clay looked at his watch and pursed his lips. "I have to go." He put his hand on hers. "Jamie, please. We'll talk about this. Nothing's changed."

Jamie wanted to cry. She leaned toward him and slipped her arms around his neck. "Go, Clay." She couldn't tell him good-bye, couldn't bear it. A part of her was dying, the part that was connected to the man in her arms.

He stroked her back. She could feel his heart pounding against her shoulder. "I'll call you as soon as I'm done today."

The walls were up. His words no longer penetrated her heart the way they had before. She drew back and nodded. There was wetness on her cheeks, and for the first time she noticed. She was crying. He used his knuckle to wipe the tears from her cheeks. Then he stood and backed out of the pew, his eyes on her the entire time. "I'll call."

She didn't argue. She wanted to be alone, to gather her feelings and stop the dizziness in her head. To look in the mirror and convince herself that the impossible had happened. Eric Michaels's brother really had come to town, saved her life, and made her feel things she hadn't felt since Jake.

"Don't, Jamie, please." He stopped. "This doesn't have to mean anything. Nothing's changed." His eyes told her he was desperate for her to see things his way, that even though this was a twist, a strange coincidence, it didn't need to mean the end of what they'd started.

"Go." She held up her hand, her eyes locked on his until he walked through the doors.

When he was gone, she knew it was too late. What they'd found was gone. If they'd figured it out that first morning, they could've spared themselves all of this. Because while she might be ready to start living again, ready to face a future without Jake, she couldn't start a relationship with Eric's brother.

Not if it meant seeing Eric again.

After all they'd been through, Jamie knew the only way she'd ever move on was to let him go. Bid him good-bye and never look back, not for anything.

Not even his brother, Clay.

TWENTY-ONE

Sue Henning would know what to do.

Jamie picked up Sierra at school and headed straight for her friend's house. She had barely survived the day, convinced it all had to be some sort of bad joke. As long as she'd lived she'd never believed in love at first sight. Until she met Clay.

Their first meeting was like some sort of cosmic metaphor. She, alone and vulnerable, unaware of the dangers that surrounded her. Him, looking out for her, rushing to her rescue, protecting her the way she still needed protecting. He loved God and his country and *The Lion King*. What more could she ask?

Crazy girl, she'd told herself a hundred times that day. She didn't even know him, didn't know his faults other than one: he was impulsive.

The thing was, she'd never been quick with her decision-making. But she'd been drawn to him in a way that kicked common sense out the door. So much so that this morning when he'd asked her about Thanksgiving in California, the idea had seemed practical. Logical, even.

But that was before she knew about Eric.

She gritted her teeth as she rounded the corner to Sue's house. Why would God allow it? Why let them meet, why light the fire in her long-cold heart only to snuff it out this way? *God . . . You promised You'd see me through this.*

The thought hung in the stale air of her car. A few feet away, Sierra turned and looked at her. "Did you cry today, Mommy?"

Jamie sniffed and shot her daughter a quick glance. "Of course not," she lied.

"Then how come your eyes are puffy?" Sierra's knobby knees stuck out from her woolen jumper, the uniform she wore to school.

Poor Sierra. She was still a little girl, her feet not quite touching the floor. She deserved a man like Clay in her life.

"Mommy, how come? How come your eyes are puffy?"

"Mrs. Henning says Katy's looking forward to seeing you."

Sierra stared out the car window. "What about Clay? Will we see him today?"

Her words hit her like so many rocks. "I don't think so."

The conversation stalled. Jamie turned into Sue's driveway. Anger welled up in her, anger at God for letting this insane thing happen. She cared about Clay, could easily love him. But being around Eric Michaels would be like being around Jake. Maybe she hadn't heard God about choosing life. Maybe He wanted her to choose her old life, with Jake's memory, her obsession with helping the victims of September 11, her work at St. Paul's.

Maybe she was never supposed to do anything more than thank Clay Michaels.

Sue was waiting out front, arms crossed, leaning against the door frame. Even from fifteen feet away Jamie could read her; she was worried.

Sierra jumped out, waved hello to Sue, and ran inside calling Katy's name. Jamie felt tired and old, battered by the turn of events. She dragged herself up the walkway and met Sue's gaze. Jamie hadn't told her anything except the basics. She'd met someone on the ferryboat, a police officer from California. He was the reason she hadn't called in a few weeks.

But now things had gone terribly wrong.

"I still can't believe you didn't call sooner." Sue's words were quiet, muffled by the icy breeze outside. They entered the house and went into the living room. Sue had two cups of tea already poured, waiting.

Jamie sat down across from Sue and clasped her hands. "I wanted to tell you." She barely lifted her shoulders. "I guess I didn't know how. I still can't believe it myself."

"Do you . . . do you have feelings for him?"

"I did." Jamie felt tears in her eyes. She swallowed hard and found her voice again. "I've seen him every day since I met him. Whenever he isn't training or sleeping, he's been with Sierra and me." Jamie told Sue how he'd taken them to *The Lion King* and shared a number of dinners with them. "It was all happening so fast, but it felt real. For the first time since Jake, it felt real."

Sue frowned. "So where's the problem? Jamie, it's been three years. You're allowed to care about someone else."

"You haven't."

"But I would." Sue's voice grew soft. "If God brought someone into my life, I would. I've thought about it lately."

Jamie still hadn't gotten to the most important part, but now she had this to consider. Sue would care about someone else? Date someone else? She'd been thinking about it lately? Maybe they'd both been thinking about it, too afraid to tell the other that they couldn't imagine being alone for the rest of their lives. Even if the idea was unthinkable in light of the men they'd lost.

Sue took a sip of her tea. "What's so bad, Jamie? If it's guilt that's stopping you, let it go. Jake would want you to let it go."

Jake's words filled her heart: *Choose life, Jamie. Whenever you can, choose life.* She closed her eyes. "You don't know the whole story." She blinked and searched her friend's face. "It's the worst thing, Sue. You won't believe it."

Worry colored the fine lines on Sue's forehead. "If he hurt you, he's not the guy you made him out to be."

Jamie shook her head. "No, nothing like that." She slid to the edge of the sofa, her heart beat fast and hard against the wall of her chest. "You remember Eric Michaels?"

Sue squinted. "Eric Michaels?"

"Yes." Jamie exhaled hard. What did she expect? She'd seldom talked about Eric, just telling everyone—even Sue—the straight facts. The man she'd thought was Jake was really a businessman from Los Angeles, a man suffering from amnesia, one who looked enough like Jake to pass for him. She kept her answers short, and Sue had always known better than to ask. Now she had to revisit that time again—something she'd never wanted to do.

Sue shook her head. "The name's familiar, but I can't figure out why."

"He's the man who lived with me, the one I thought was Jake."

A knowing look filled her face. "Oh, right. Okay." The frown was back. "Why bring him up?"

Jamie felt the blood leaving her face, felt herself reacting to the news as if she were hearing it for the first time again. Her tone was pinched, scratchy. "Clay's his brother."

Seconds passed while Sue processed the news. "Clay, the police officer you met on the ferry, is Eric Michaels's brother?" Her eyebrows lifted and she lowered her chin. "That's impossible."

"That's what I thought." She stood and walked to the window, her back to her friend. The girls were upstairs, playing in Katy's room. Outside the trees were bare, a light snow had fallen the night before, and everything was the color of winter. "It's true, Sue. Clay's his brother. We found out this morning." She looked over her shoulder at Sue. "He saw Jake's picture. A few minutes before he had to leave for his shift."

"Oh, Jamie." Sue's expression relaxed, but her face was taut, pale. "I can't believe it."

"I told him I couldn't see him tonight." She faced the window again. "I can't see him ever again."

Sue was quiet. After a while, Jamie returned to the sofa and drank down half her tea. "I already miss him. I can't believe this is happening." She set her cup down. "There's nothing you can do to help, but I had to tell you."

A minute passed, and then Sue stood and crossed the room to the fireplace. Next to it was a bookshelf, and from a place in the back she pulled out a small urn. Jamie had one like it—given to them by the city. The urn held a few cups of debris and ash from the collapsed Twin Towers.

With slower steps, Sue carried it back to the coffee table and set it down on a spot between them both. She leveled her gaze at Jamie. "You know why they gave us those urns?"

Where on earth was her friend going with this? She didn't want to look at the urn or think about what might've been inside. The ashy remains of any of the two thousand victims. Jamie had kept hers out of respect for the lives lost that day. But it was hardly a reminder of Larry or Jake. "No." She shook her head. "Mine's tucked away somewhere; I don't look at it."

"I keep mine out." She angled her head and looked at the detail on the small container. "It's a reminder of something that might be easy to forget otherwise."

"What?" Jamie still didn't know what the urn had to do with her situation, the one she was battling that day.

"That Larry's not coming home." Sue's voice cracked. "It reminds me that every terrible thing about September 11 really happened. That my husband and your husband were two of the heroes, two of the men who ran up the stairs when everyone else was running down." She sniffed and pressed her finger to her lip. Sue rarely broke down, and this would be no exception. "Larry's gone. When his name is on my lips, when I jump up to ask his advice about something or wonder what he might want for dinner, I remember the urn and it's all real again. He's gone and he's not coming home."

Jamie leaned closer. "I already know that about Jake." She pressed her fingers against her chest. "I'm the one who's been dating these past two weeks. I don't need an urn to remember the truth about Jake. He's gone; I get that."

"Yes." Sue's voice was even, her eyes unwavering. "But there is something you have trouble remembering."

"What?" She didn't come here for a lecture from Sue. "What do I have trouble remembering?"

Sue's voice slipped to a whisper. "That Eric Michaels wasn't Jake. That you didn't lose Jake the day Eric left on an airplane back to California. You lost him in the terrorist attacks, same as the rest of us."

Jamie felt her breath catch. She couldn't breathe, couldn't inhale for the emotions strangling her. She wanted to tell Sue she already knew that about the timing, that she'd lost Jake when the Twin Towers collapsed, same as the other firefighter widows. But she couldn't. Because what Sue had just said made her feel raw and hurt and aching inside.

"Jamie . . ." Sue's voice was a little louder now, filled with compassion. "Do you understand what I'm saying?"

Her head was spinning, her heart bleeding from wounds that still weren't healed. "Not really."

"So *what* if Eric and Clay are brothers? What does it matter?"

Jamie's heart rate doubled. Panic seized her by the neck and threatened to strangle her. "What does it matter? If Clay and I got close, I'd have to see Eric again." Tears blurred her vision, spilling from a well so deep Jamie barely acknowledged its presence. "I can't do that, Sue, I can't."

Sue wouldn't let up. "Why?"

"Because every time I saw him, I'd feel like I was with Jake."

This time Sue waited, and when she spoke her words were slow, measured. "Eric isn't Jake; he never was." She drew her feet up beside her on the sofa. "I wonder, Jamie. Have you ever worked through the memories you made with that man and told yourself that every single one of them was with a stranger? Have you allowed yourself to take Jake's name off each of those days you and Eric had together?"

Jamie felt the nausea rise inside her, felt her head swimming. She'd done that, hadn't she? Her head knew Jake hadn't come home, that he'd died right beside his best friend when the South Tower collapsed.

But did her heart know? Or had she, by suppressing details of that time, by never taking it out and spreading the memories on a table and examining them, allowed her heart to believe that Jake *had* come home. That she'd been given some sort of reprieve, a mulligan, a time with Jake, that none of the other survivors got to have with their loved ones.

Was that why she never talked about Eric? Maybe a part of her wanted to believe the man in her house hadn't been Eric at all, but Jake. At least until he'd taken the blood test and they'd known he was someone else.

Jamie stood and realized she was shaking. She needed to be alone, needed to think through this, to shine a light on the darkest corners of her heart. "Can you watch Sierra for a while? I need to go to the beach."

"It's winter, Jamie. It'll be freezing."

"That's okay. I have a coat in the car." The place where she and Jake liked to go was just a few miles from Sue's house. Cold weather wouldn't matter, not when she had so much to work through. "Can you watch her?"

"Yes." Sue stood and came to her. "Can I say something before you go?"

"Go ahead." Jamie's teeth were clattering, not because she was feeling the effects of winter, but because she was about to go places she hadn't gone in three years.

Their eyes locked, and Sue looked as serious as Jamie could remember seeing her. "Maybe God brought Eric into your life so he could become the man *he* needed to be. He was different when he went home, right? Isn't that what you told me?"

Jamie looked at the floor near her feet. "Yes."

"He wasn't supposed to replace Jake." Sue put her hand on Jamie's shoulder. "He was supposed to learn from him. Learn the value of faith and family and friendship."

"Then what about Clay?" Jamie lifted her eyes. "Why would God let me have feelings for Eric's brother?"

"Because." Sue gave her shoulder a gentle squeeze. "Maybe Eric's brother was the man you needed. Not because of Jake or Eric or anyone else. Just because of Clay." She hesitated. "Maybe that was part of God's plan too."

TWENTY-TWO

It was almost dusk when Jamie walked across the sand to the spot where she and Jake had set out their chairs and towels so many times before. This time she brought nothing with her, just pulled her long coat tight around her and eased down to the sand. Her eyes found a pale blue section of sky. "God . . . what is this feeling in my heart?"

When she remembered the three months after the terrorist attacks, one day stood out as changing everything. The day they went to the hospital and discovered the man living with her didn't have Jake's blood type. From that point on, Jamie had grieved. No longer could she spend every moment teaching the man in the downstairs bedroom how to be Jake, how to think like him and pray like him and father like him. How to love like him.

From that point on she knew a stranger was living with her, and it was up to her to care enough to help him find his way home. She had understood, hadn't she? When she said good-bye at LaGuardia she was saying good-bye to a nice man, a stranger named Eric Michaels. Jake was already dead.

But what about those twelve weeks when he'd *been* Jake to her in every way but one? When she longed for him and took him to church and held his hand?

A breeze rolled off the water and brushed against her cheeks. Could it be that she still savored memories of that time as if he wasn't a stranger at all but Jake?

She pulled her knees up to her chin and stared at the harbor. Had she done the thing Sue asked? Had she consciously told herself the truth about those weeks? That Jake hadn't been with them, hadn't sat beside her at the breakfast table, or cooked up blueberry pancakes for Sierra?

A deep ache began within her, and with it came a realization: if she could admit the truth about Eric, her fears about seeing him again were unfounded. If she could admit he'd never been Jake. Not for the first few days after the terrorist attacks. Not for the first few weeks or months.

Not at all.

"God," her voice took wind. "I was mad at You ... but it wasn't Your fault, was it?"

She looked up. If only God would give her a sign, something to tell her He was still on her side. A single seagull soared into view and dipped toward the ocean. For a moment, Jamie felt sorry for the bird, making his way through a late winter afternoon alone, without a friend or a mate.

But almost at the same time, she saw another seagull swoop down and join the first. Jamie blinked against the cold air and felt the burn of moisture in the corner of her eyes. The bird wasn't alone, after all.

But she was, and all because she had believed in some dark hall-way of her heart that Eric really was Jake; that she hadn't lost her husband in the collapse of the Twin Towers, but three months later. And yet, Eric wasn't Jake. No matter how much he looked like him or learned to act like him, he never could be.

Her heart splintered, and she bowed her head. "I'm sorry, God. I'm so sorry."

Remorse filled her. Remorse and guilt and understanding.

Remorse, because she'd never had Jake a minute past the time when he told her good-bye and headed off for work September 11; guilt, because how dare she believe another man to be Jake—even under the strangest circumstances; and understanding, because Sue was right. Jamie realized that now.

She'd never gone through the memories of those twelve weeks one at a time and painted in Eric's name, his face and likeness. She'd been okay with keeping that time locked up in her heart, protected from scrutiny so she didn't have to admit to herself that Jake had never been a part of any of it.

The sky was getting darker, colder. If she was going to unlock that time in her life and give it a proper burial, she needed to move quickly.

She started with the afternoon of September 11, the moment she got the call from Sergeant Riker. Jake was alive, he told her. Alive and hurt and at Mount Sinai Medical Center. After a day of desperate fear and worry, the news gave Jamie permission to breathe again.

The memory filled in, and she pictured herself responding to the amazing news. The telephone receiver fell slowly to her lap as she screamed her husband's name. He was alive! Relief, like a gust of air, filled a room where she'd been suffocating. Jake hadn't been in the South Tower after all. He was alive! Just like he'd promised!

Jamie held her breath and looked out to sea.

She exhaled, shaking. Sergeant Riker went on to tell her that Captain Hisel was searching the rubble at Ground Zero when he found Jake beneath a fire truck.

Awe filled Jamie's mind now as she realized the truth. She'd never quite convinced herself that Aaron hadn't found Jake there that day. But now she didn't want to miss a moment, had to remove Jake from every one of the places where he didn't belong.

Eric Michaels had been coming down the stairs, escaping the building when the tower collapsed. The force had sent him—not Jake—underneath the fire truck. Which meant that the man Aaron Hisel saw and helped and sent to the hospital wasn't Jake, either.

The hurt was so bad. Jamie remembered, years ago, when Jake broke his arm playing football in high school. He hadn't wanted to wear a cast because it might limit his playing time. So he continued on with the pain, not telling his parents or anyone else how bad it was.

But then he began to notice a bend in his forearm, a bend and a bump that finally his family doctor spotted. By then only one thing could be done to fix the arm. Rebreak it and let it heal correctly.

That's exactly how she felt now.

She'd let her heart heal in the wrong position, believing at least on some level that those memories of late September, October, and November still involved Jake. Now—with a pain that knew no bounds, she was letting God break her heart again so that it might heal correctly.

Jamie wasn't sure she could continue. But she had no choice. She dug to another level, the moment she rushed into the hospital room, certain Jake had survived, the hours she'd held vigil at his bedside, the days of stroking his hand, whispering to him, and begging him to wake up.

Jake hadn't been there for any of it.

Not when Sierra saw him for the first time, and he remembered her name. Eric had merely run into Jake in the stairwell and by some bizarre series of events, he'd seen the inside of Jake's helmet. The place where he'd kept a photo of Sierra and her name written below it.

Eric saw it and remembered it that day in the hospital.

Jamie no longer felt the cold air around her. Her battered heart took up all her energy, her determination to remove Jake from those moments after September 11 wore on her, leaving gaping wounds at her very core.

She kept on, working through the homecoming from the hospital. The man who rode the ferry with her and sang with Sierra, the man who stared at their wedding portrait and gasped, convinced he was in the picture. All of it took place with Eric Michaels.

One at a time Jamie continued, dissecting memories, painstakingly removing Jake and placing Eric there instead. Halfway through the process, she felt drops of water on her arms. She was crying and she hadn't even known it. She'd been too absorbed in the matter at hand to acknowledge how much it all hurt.

When she finished—when she staggered to her feet, dusted off the sand, and peered through the dusky evening toward the water one last time—the hole in her heart was so big she felt hollow, as if people could see straight through her. She walked closer to the shore, close enough so she could bend down and get her fingers wet.

"Jake . . ." Her voice was hoarse, raspy. This was where she liked to come to connect with him, to touch the water where the two of them had played so often together.

But everything was different, maybe because she had a firm grasp on the truth. The water wasn't warm and inviting, it was freezing cold, the same way her empty heart felt. She stood and slipped her wet fingers deep into the pocket of her coat.

Now came the hardest part.

She took herself back further than before, back to the week and days and hours before September 11. Back to her life with her husband. The jet skiing with Sue and Larry and the little girls, the small ceramic figurine of an angel she'd painted for him the Sunday before the attacks, the hugging and laughing and lovemaking.

Though her head knew the truth since Eric's blood test, her heart needed to understand once and for all. *Those* were her final days with Jake. That Tuesday morning, waking up beside him, wanting him to stay and go to the zoo with her and Sierra, wishing he'd play hooky and skip work for the day.

And then watching him consider the idea and decide instead to go to work. Tomorrow, he'd told her. They could play together tomorrow. Then her promising to get Chinese food for dinner and one last kiss, a final quick good-bye. Hearing him head down the hall to Sierra's room, enjoying his laughter as Sierra asked him for butterfly kisses and Jake promised to play horsie with her when he got home.

That was the end, his final moments with them.

She straightened and let her coat ease open, let the wind off the water blow over her, taking with it the remaining shards of her denial. This should have been the hardest part, the time when she would turn away and head for the car, so hollow and empty she could barely support herself.

And she was empty, no doubt. But through her tears, she could feel God doing something inside her, knitting her broken heart back together again. Correctly this time. She turned and trudged through the sand, a grieving widow leaving the scene of a burial. But amid the pain and loss and acceptance working its way through her was something else, something she hadn't expected.

Hope.

Because the emptiness meant Eric was no longer living in her heart, masquerading as Jake. And if Eric wasn't living in her heart, then maybe someday she could handle seeing him again. Not as Jake's substitute, a man she had wanted to keep as her own even after she knew the truth about his identity. Next time—if there was a next time—she wouldn't see him as Jake Bryan's double.

But as Clay Michaels's brother.

TWENTY-THREE

Clay and his partner were five minutes from the scene of the crime.

A drug lord had been shot in the head in a busy alley on the lower East Side, and the trail was getting colder by the hour. The NYPD detective force had a good idea that the key suspect was an ex-con who headed up a rival drug ring, but so far they had no proof.

Four of the detectives-in-training—including Clay and his buddy—had been selected to conduct street interviews with the New York detectives. Fan out, talk to regulars at a few of the taverns, chat with the locals and street vendors. That type of investigation almost always netted witnesses or leads that would help in the investigation.

Clay had no idea how he'd stay focused.

"You're quiet." Joe was in the backseat with him; two NYPD officers were in the front seat holding their own conversation.

"Yeah." Clay stared out his window.

"Jamie again?"

Clay turned and met his friend's eyes. "Is it that obvious?" He hadn't told Joe all the details, just that something had gone wrong, and he and Jamie weren't speaking. Not that Clay hadn't tried.

"Yep, it is." Joe pursed his lips and stared straight ahead. "As obvious as it is for me."

"I think Wanda will come around." Clay swallowed thoughts of his own heartache and thought of his partner. Joe hadn't seen Wanda in a few days, either. Ever since his breakdown after seeing Wanda's little boy—the one who looked exactly like the child they lost.

"She doesn't know what to say; I don't either. I told her I was sorry, but it's not enough. It's like she doesn't believe it."

Clay waited. They were almost at the alley, the one where the murder had taken place. "I still say she'll come around." He looked at his friend. "You belong together."

"Same as you and Jamie." Joe was the office cutup, dry and never missing a chance to get a laugh. Until now. Now his voice was quiet, even tender. "I've watched you after you've been with her, man. She's got you good. You can take a few days off from talking to her, but that won't change a thing. Your kind of gotcha doesn't go away ever."

Clay narrowed his eyes. Every inch of his heart ached for Jamie, but he couldn't do a thing about it. He'd called her twice a day each day since that terrible morning. Now he was leaving in a few days, and they hadn't even had a chance to say good-bye. Could that have been God's plan? Let them meet and feel something for each other that they'd never felt with anyone else, only to find out it was all for nothing?

The hardest part was Eric.

Clay had called him that Monday night, the day he'd found out the truth. Eric had answered the phone, upbeat. Maybe a little too upbeat. "So, little brother, how're you doing?"

"Been better." An awkward silence played over the phone line. That's when Clay knew; with a sixth sort of brotherly sense, he knew. Eric had been worrying about this since their last phone call, worrying that maybe by some horrible twist of fate, Clay's Jamie was actually Jamie Bryan.

"Yeah, well, training's almost done." Eric cleared his throat. "Hey, uh, tell me, Clay. What's the name of that girl you're seeing? The one you met on the ferry. You know, from Staten Island?"

"Why didn't you ask me the first time I called?" Clay tried to keep the bitterness from his voice. It wasn't Eric's fault. A sad chuckle eased through his lips. "You guessed it, right?"

Shock crept into Eric's tone. "What's her name, Clay?"

"Jamie Bryan." Clay stared at the ceiling of his hotel room. "That's her, right? The woman you lived with."

It was, of course.

Eric could no more believe the strange coincidence than Clay or Jamie could. What were the odds that Clay would go to New York

City and fall in love with the woman who for three months had played the role of Eric's wife?

Before the phone call ended, Eric tried to tell Clay it didn't matter, that they could all get past the strangeness of having Jamie Bryan around for Thanksgiving. But Clay could hear the doubt in his brother's voice. Eric didn't want a reunion with Jamie anymore than she wanted one with him.

And so Clay had lost again; lost to his brother twice.

This time so much worse than with Laura. Back in high school, he'd had a shot at dating Laura long before Eric entered the picture. But he hadn't been sure, hadn't been bowled over the way he wanted to be. Really, it was only after Eric started dating Laura that Clay became more interested.

Then, after September 11, when it looked like Eric was dead, Clay was convinced God had a plan for Laura and him to finally wind up together. But even then his feelings for her were more along the lines of brotherly love and deep concern.

Yes, he was attracted to Laura.

But he was blown away by Jamie Bryan.

The police car pulled over just outside the alley, and the detective at the wheel turned off the engine. "It's four o'clock." He looked at the other men in the car. "We have an hour before dusk, and that's about all we want. You know the routine." He grinned, his eyes hard and focused. "Get in, get the information, and get out. People know what happened." He patted his holster. "Be aware of your weapon, especially as the sun starts to set. The killer's loose. If it's the man we think it is, then his cronies are probably still around. It's no secret that they're packing more than dime bags of weed." He gave them a final look and nodded at his partner in the passenger seat. "We'll take the west side. Stay in pairs."

They climbed out of the car, and the detective and his partner crossed the alley. All four men were uniformed, armed, and carrying pens and notebooks. Joe turned to Clay and raised his eyebrow. "Man, you know what time it is?"

Clay fell in step beside him. "Late and getting later."

This time Joe shook his head. "Nope. Time to forget the women for a while."

The first establishment was a shoddy strip bar with no windows—typical for a back alley entrance. Though the shooting took place at the opposite end of the alleyway, they would try everyone they could find in a hundred-yard radius.

Clay pushed the door open and took a few seconds for his eyes to adjust to the darkness. He was immediately hit by a thick wall of cigarette smoke.

Joe nudged him. "Cockroach trap." He kept his voice low. "Buncha dirty old bugs who can't stand the light."

"That's for sure." Clay could see better now, but not much. The blue smoke was thick inside, and a heavy beat, loud and pulsing, filled the air. Neon lights spun and roved around a dimly lit stage where someone was dancing. Clay didn't look; he never did. Instead, when his job took him to places like this, he remembered Scriptures that spoke of evil being done in the darkness, and how the darkness can't stand the light.

Once, when he was a kid, Clay stumbled onto his father's *Playboy* magazine collection. Even back then something in his spirit had reeled at the idea. Made him sick to his stomach. His father looked at naked women? Women other than his mother?

As he got older, his faith solidified the feelings he'd had as a boy. Women dancing in a place like this didn't interest him. They made him sad, sorry for whatever experience had led the dancer through the doors in the first place.

The bartender was staring at them. He was bald with a single thick hoop earring and a tight T-shirt. He grunted at them. "Can I help you?"

Joe took the lead. "Guess you heard about the murder." He strolled toward the bar. "The one at the other end of the street?"

The bartender picked up a wet glass and buffed it with a dish towel. He never took his eyes from Joe's. "Well, Officer." His voice was measured. "Can't say that I did."

Clay shifted his weight, studying the man. He knew something, no doubt. But as they'd expected, he wasn't talking. People didn't simply open up and start spilling details to detectives. They had to be coaxed.

Joe had a reputation for brilliant coaxing.

"Right." He sat down and patted the stool next to him.

Clay took that seat and glanced at the few patrons sitting alone at dark tables. Joe would ask the questions; he would cover. "We'll take a couple of waters."

The bartender scowled. He grabbed two glasses, filled them with water and slid them across the bar. "I don't know nothing, okay? Now get outta here before you hurt business."

Joe leaned on the bar and glanced around the room. "Business isn't exactly booming."

"We've been down a bit, so?" He snapped his towel at the glass and glared at Joe. "Crime goes up, business goes down, okay?"

Joe's smile faded. "Cut the line." He leaned in, a snarl in his tone. "You heard about the murder. You probably know who did it. We didn't come here for ice water, okay?"

"I told ya, I don't know nothin'." The bartender's accent was so thick he was hard to understand.

"Fine." Joe settled back onto his stool. "We'll stay all day."

Clay leaned his forearms on the bar. "We could always get the inspector. He'd love a look around here, don't you think?"

"Great idea." Joe started to stand.

"Wait!" The man blinked three times and ran his tongue along his lower lip. He dried a few more glasses, but his hands shook so hard he finally stopped. An exaggerated huff came from him, loud enough that a few patrons turned and looked. "Listen." He braced himself against the bar, his voice a whisper. "The dead guy was a crack dealer. His boys hang out down the street. At the Top Hat." He lowered his head a little. "Their rivals come from ten, eleven blocks south. They wanted to expand and the guys down the street wouldn't give." He straightened and Clay noticed his lip. It was covered with a fine layer of sweat beads. "I swear that's all I know. I ain't never seen any of 'em in here."

"Okay." Joe didn't miss a beat. "But you know who did it, who was the shooter, right?"

"Not his name, no." He gave a quick shake of his head. "Just where his boys come from."

Clay didn't believe him; he doubted Joe did either. But it was a start. If they were going to interview people down at the Top Hat, they needed to get going. Joe must've thought the same thing. He jotted something down in his notebook. Took the man's name and the bar's phone number.

Outside, they headed down the street. "Amazing," Joe turned to him and grinned, "how much a person can remember when they want a cop to leave 'em alone."

"You did good."

Joe shrugged. "I figured the Top Hat was the place. That's what the guys at briefing said this morning."

Already dusk was falling; shady types lurked near doorways and talked in a cluster as they leaned against the occasional dumpster. Clay squinted at the opposite side of the street. The other pair of detectives were nowhere around.

"Get the feeling all eyes are on us?" Joe raised his eyebrows. He spoke from the side of his mouth, just loud enough for Clay to hear.

"No question." Clay kept his pace brisk. He wasn't worried, just aware. The situation could easily become dangerous.

They reached the Top Hat and spoke to three people. After going round and round with each of them, they came away with a possible shooter name—the one that matched the name of the man the NYPD detectives already suspected. They also had a tip from a homeless man who refused to give his name. He said the shooter was working with two other guys, and that they were all still in the area.

They left the Top Hat at dusk, though the shadows along the alley made it seem darker. Again the other detectives were not in sight. "Better head back to the squad car." Joe motioned toward the opposite end of the street.

Clay's caution grew. Though the establishments where they'd conducted interviews had front entrances on a busier street, the murder occurred in the alley. Any information they might get would have to come from there, but like most big-city alleys, it was intersected by even smaller alleyways. And in the shadowy darkness, as they passed the smaller alleys, Clay kept one hand on his revolver.

"We got some good stuff," Joe whispered. Voices carried, and neither of them wanted to be heard talking about the interviews they'd done that afternoon.

"Yeah." Clay looked across the alley again, his eyes darting up and down the length of it. "I was hoping for something—"

A form jumped out from a dark doorway, and Clay felt a hand clamp on to his arm and jerk him off his feet before he had time to pull out his gun. Joe had been grabbed as well.

"Shut up!" A voice hissed at them. The smell of alcohol and old tobacco filled the tight space. "I've got a gun! Don't move."

Next to him, Joe stopped scuffling and grew still. "We're police. Don't do something stupid."

A different voice laughed at them, and the sound was anything but humorous. Clay blinked and tried to make out their faces. Two Asian-American men, both young and high as kites.

"That's right, Superman; you're finished."

His partner kicked Clay's leg. "You didn't think you could come snoopin' around without an official welcome, did you?" His snort was half laugh, half nervous energy. "We'll lose business because of you jerks."

Business? The pieces came rushing together. They were drug dealers; maybe part of a ring. And now they were wanted in a murder.

In a rush of movement, Joe pulled his gun and pushed the guy who claimed to be armed. "Up against the wall!" His voice was loud, stern. He pulled away enough to get his hand on his revolver, but as he did, both men lunged at him.

Clay pulled his own gun free when a gunshot exploded through the small, cramped space. Joe slumped against the door frame and inched down. His eyes found Clay's and his mouth formed the word, "Help!"

"Joe!" Clay grabbed hold of his friend, stopping him from sliding all the way to the ground.

Both men stepped back and stared at Joe. "Now you did it!" one of them snarled. He pushed his buddy aside and ran down the alley, toward the Top Hat.

"I . . . I didn't mean it. I didn't shoot him; I swear it." Before the last word was out, the second man turned and followed after his friend.

"Backup!" Clay shouted over his shoulder. Where were the other detectives? *God, let them hear me. Please . . .* "I need backup. Officer down!"

His hands were shaking so hard he could barely use them. But he kept one set of fingers firmly around Joe's arm, and with the other he yanked his cell phone from his shirt pocket and dialed 911.

"911. What's your emergency?"

Clay gritted his teeth. The other detectives had to be close. *Come on, God . . . please let Joe be okay.* "Officer down!" He gave his location. "I need emergency backup."

Clay heard screeching tires in the distance and then footsteps, lots of them, running hard and growing closer. NYPD detectives ran up, breathless. "We called for help. Four cars have a bead on the suspects." Clay grabbed a quick breath. "An ambulance will be here any minute."

"Clay . . ." Joe's voice was fading. His eyes were open, but they looked frozen, in shock. He gasped for breath and stared hard at Clay. "Tell . . . tell Wanda I . . . I love her."

"Keep him upright." One of the detectives moved in along the other side of Joe and held that arm. "He's losing a lot of blood."

Something caught Clay's eyes and he saw it was a red stain on the door frame, a smeary blood trail caused by Joe's body sliding down it. Joe'd been shot clear through the abdomen just beneath his flak jacket. He had blood at the corners of his mouth and near his nose, and his eyes were closing. His breathing was labored and slow.

"Joe!" Clay gave him a shake. It was okay; he was going to be okay. He had to be okay. "Hang in there. Wanda wants you to tell her yourself, man. Come on!"

Sirens drew closer, but would the ambulance even matter? Joe was bleeding to death; he had maybe a few minutes by the looks of it. Clay hung his head. "God . . . please stop the bleeding. Make it stop, God . . ." His prayer was loud enough for the other detectives to hear, but even as Clay prayed, Joe closed his eyes and his head fell forward.

"No!" Clay tightened his grip on Joe's shoulder. His heart raced and he wanted to shake something. No, Joe couldn't die. "God, don't let him die, please!"

The ambulance sped up and slammed to a stop a few feet away. Clay stayed beside Joe as he was placed on the stretcher, as the men loaded him into the back. He would go with him, of course. Travel in the back to the hospital and stay with him until they found a way to save his life. "Joe, hang on!" Clay shouted the words, in case Joe could hear him.

One of the other detectives grabbed Clay's shirt and pulled him back from the scene. "You can't go with him."

"Why? He needs me there." He jerked away and took a step toward the ambulance.

"Stop!" It was the other officer, the lead detective.

"I'm going with him!" Clay spun, breathless. The paramedics were closing the door; if he waited another few seconds it would be too late.

"You can't, Michaels." The detective's expression changed. "The medic told me they're doing CPR; they need all the space they can get."

"CPR?" Clay felt the ground beneath him turn to liquid.

The detective motioned toward the NYPD squad car, fifty yards away. "Come with us; we'll get you there just as fast."

He was in the squad car, the other detectives driving him to the emergency room, when he figured out what to do next. He grabbed his phone and dialed Jamie's number.

She picked up on the second ring. "Clay . . . I'm glad you called."

"Jamie." He hesitated, not sure how to tell her. "Joe's been shot. I'm . . . I'm not sure he's going to make it."

Her gasp was sharp, and he could picture her face. Beautiful, terrified. "What happened?"

"We were doing street interviews." He didn't want to tell her the other details—not yet. He closed his eyes and pinched the bridge of his nose. The detective at the wheel had the siren on, making the best time possible to the hospital. "Pray, Jamie. Please." He told her what hospital they were headed for. "And call Wanda, okay?"

"Clay . . . are you all right?"

Her voice was balm for his soul, but he couldn't think about her that way; not now. He opened his eyes and stared at the city street ahead of them. The hospital wasn't far away. "Just pray."

As he hung up he realized something that ripped him apart inside, something that made him turn and lean his head against the car window. If they were doing CPR on Joe Reynolds, then he wasn't breathing. Which meant there was another reason they hadn't wanted Clay in the ambulance. Not so much because they had to start CPR.

But because they might have to stop it.

TWENTY-FOUR

It took Jamie twenty minutes to board the ferry for Manhattan.

Her first call had been to Wanda, and as she'd expected, her friend was terrified, too scared to speak. She was able to say only that she was on her way to the hospital and that she wanted Jamie to meet her there.

Next she called a neighbor, who was more than willing to take Sierra for the evening. Before she did that, she told Sierra that Clay's friend had been hurt and she needed to be with him. Sierra didn't say much, but her eyes shone. A strange mixture of fear and hope.

Jamie thought she knew why.

She hadn't seen or spoken about Clay in days, and Sierra wasn't happy about the fact. Now, though, if Jamie was going to the hospital to meet him—even for a sad reason—then maybe she would get to see Clay again.

Even so, they didn't talk about Clay. Every second counted, and she wanted to be at the hospital when Wanda arrived. She took time to do just one thing before she left. She went to her bedroom dresser, where she kept Jake's Bible, and she lifted her left hand.

She'd always believed she would know. That when it was time for her wedding ring to come off, she wouldn't have any doubts. She studied the ring. Jake, her marriage to him, their days of loving and laughing and making a life together, would always be a part of her. But the ring . . .

It was time.

She worked it off her finger, held it in her hand a moment, then opened the lid on a small blown-glass box. With careful fingers, she set her wedding ring inside the box, and shut the lid.

Her hand seemed empty. She ran her thumb over the bare spot, the pale indented circle at the base of her finger. It would bear for a very long time the proof that Jake's ring had been there. Much as her heart would forever bear proof of Jake himself.

She took a quick step back, then left the room. She ran Sierra over to the neighbor's, then headed toward the ferry. The news was still working its way through her, convincing her that this latest, terrible thing really had happened. That Joe had been shot and critically wounded on the streets of Manhattan.

Jamie parked and made her way to the line for the ferry. Once aboard, she crossed to the opposite side, so she'd be first off when the boat docked. It was dark, the sky providing a cloud cover that kept temperatures from dropping too much. She found a place outside, near the railing, and stared at the skyline.

God ... let him live. Guide the doctors and be with Wanda. Please, Father.

Peace wrapped its arms around her and she leaned into it.

Tragedy used to scare her to death. The news of it almost as much as the event itself. That was something else the terrorist attacks had taught her—how to handle bad news. Nothing could be as terrible as coming into the health club lobby that awful Tuesday morning and seeing the World Trade Center in flames on television.

She was anxious, lifting her voice to God every few minutes on Joe's behalf. But she was calm at the core, convinced that survival was possible—even in the face of great loss. And so it wasn't only thoughts of Joe that filled her mind as the boat sliced through the harbor. It was thoughts of Clay and Jake and Sierra and life.

And of her epiphany on the beach.

It wasn't that she'd avoided life all this time. She hadn't chosen death over life, not at first. Working at St. Paul's had been her way of choosing to live. It was that or crawl into bed and never get up again.

But after two years of volunteering, after hearing the stories of loss and praying with grieving relatives and letting strangers cry on her shoulder, Jamie had grown. She no longer needed a reason to get out of bed in the morning. God gave her that just by sending the morning, by giving her another day with Him.

Whether she spent that day with Sierra or the people at St. Paul's, she no longer felt like one of the walking dead, the empty-eyed grievers who still colored the Manhattan landscape. Rather she was excited about life, about what God wanted to do with her and through her as long as she drew breath. It only made sense that she'd outgrown her time at Ground Zero. She could find purpose at St. Paul's, but she couldn't move on there.

She looked at the sky and saw Jake's image, his face smiling at her, giving her that knowing look. The one that told her he knew what she needed to do, and she knew it too. Now all she had to do was make the decision.

"Choose life, right, Jake?" Tears blurred her eyes. "Even with someone new. That's what you want me to do, isn't it?"

His eyes were as clear as if he were standing in front of her, clear and blue and filled with a love that she hadn't understood when he was alive. "Jake . . ."

The image held for a moment longer. Then it faded and blurred and became night sky. Yes, that's exactly what he would want her to do. Him and God Almighty.

See, I set before you now life and prosperity, death and destruction . . . Choose life!

That was why God brought Clay into her life in the first place. That she might be moved forward in the healing process, past the point of St. Paul's and toward the possibility of new life.

New love.

Just the thought of Clay made her breath catch in her throat. As desperate as the situation was, she felt a little bit like Sierra. Frightened and filled with concern, but with eyes that shone with hope. Because in a very little while she would see Clay again. And at some point, she'd tell him about her day, how she'd figured things out on a cold lonely beach, and how wrong she'd been before.

How much she needed him.

But what about Joe? What if he didn't make it? Clay had sounded desperately worried. She wanted to be with Clay, to pray with him and help him believe everything would work out. She pressed into the railing, urging the boat to move faster.

They needed to sit by Joe and coax him to hold on, because with God Almighty calling the shots, life—with all its painful turns and gut-wrenching losses—still had tremendous hope even in the simplicity of a sunrise.

Jamie had made the choice to choose life. Now, where Joe was concerned, she would pray for it.

The boat pulled up to the dock, and Jamie had a cab in record time. She was still praying for Joe when they arrived at the hospital and she paid the driver. Now that she'd come this far, she couldn't wait to find Clay, and she ran into the lobby and down the hall toward the emergency room.

Clay was the first person she saw.

He had his back to her, his arms crossed, head hung. He wore his uniform, and next to him sat two detectives, talking to a third uniformed officer with a notepad. Their conversation was hushed, relegated to the far corner of the waiting room.

Jamie made her way closer, and when she was halfway there, Clay turned. His eyes found hers, and her heart skipped. How could she have considered leaving this man, losing him, just because his brother was Eric Michaels? The entire situation seemed ludicrous now. After all, if Eric made her uncomfortable, she could keep her distance from him.

But she couldn't keep her distance from Clay. Not a minute longer.

In as much time as it took him to look at her she understood that, understood it to the core of her being. He came to her, and they met in the middle, falling into an embrace that was seeped in sorrow and relief. Sorrow over Joe; relief that despite the strange circumstances, they'd found their way back together.

Clay held her for a long time, his arms around her waist, hers around his neck. Being with him like this was better than she could've dreamed. She closed her eyes and savored it. Life. Bubbling through her and filling her with a sort of joy that left her speechless. *God . . . I don't want him to ever let go. Please, God.*

She opened her eyes. The officers had looked away. The waiting room offered little privacy, but at least the others weren't watching. She pressed her face against Clay's, still relishing the feel of his arms around her waist. "How is he?"

"Alive." Clay drew back. He searched her eyes. "They're operating, but it doesn't look good. The bullet messed up his insides pretty good." His cheeks were red and blotchy, his expression pained. "They told us to expect the worst."

Jamie felt her heart sink to her ankles. "No . . ." She shook her head and tightened her grip on Clay's arms. "We can't give up."

"I know." Determination filled his eyes. "I've been praying."

"Me too." She paused. This wasn't the time, really. But she had to tell him, had to share what had happened to her that day. "Clay, there's something I want you to know."

Concern filled his face. Clearly he expected her to say that though she had come, it was only as a show of support because of Joe. Not because she'd changed her mind about Clay or the situation with Eric.

"Relax. It's a good thing."

He studied her, his brow knit together. "Good?"

"Yes." She felt the corners of her mouth lift some. She eased her thumb along the fine lines in his forehead. "Sierra and I would like to spend Thanksgiving with you and your family." Even with the sadness and pain in her heart because of Joe, she felt her eyes dance a little. "If we're still welcome, that is."

"What about Eric?" He moved his hands up to her shoulders and studied her. As if she might vanish if he didn't hold on to her. "You're okay with him? Dinner's at his house."

"God showed me something today." She looped her hands around the back of his neck. "I lost Jake on September 11; he was never alive after that." A wave of sorrow came over her, but she rode it out. "Every memory I have from that point on wasn't with Jake; it was with Eric. A stranger who came to our house to learn how to be the kind of father and family man God wanted him to be."

Clay nodded, studying her, making sure she believed the words she was saying. "You mean it?"

"Yes." She hugged him for a long while before pulling back and finding his eyes. "Eric was never Jake, and if he wasn't Jake, then what's the problem? He's just a nice guy who looks a lot like my husband."

For a moment, Clay's mouth hung open. Then he shook his head. "I prayed for this, Jamie. That you'd understand about Eric. But when you didn't take my calls, I—"

"Shhh." She held her finger up to his lips. "I understand." They released their hold on each other, and she led him to a pair of seats a few yards away from the other officers. When they sat down, she wove her fingers between his. "We need another miracle tonight. Let's pray for Joe."

Clay held her eyes a moment, then bowed his head and began to pray. He begged God for the same things Jamie had been asking for. That Joe would live; that he would have no lasting effects from the terrible gunshot wound.

When the prayer was over, they spotted Wanda. She was just entering the emergency room, frantic fear scrawled across her face. Right away she saw them and she started to cry. "Jamie!"

She stood and met her friend, holding her even when her legs buckled. Clay was on his feet, helping ease Wanda into a chair, but she was unstable. Dizzy from the shock. When she was seated between them, she leaned forward, clearly trying to fight what must've been a consuming panic. "How is he? Can I see him?"

Clay gave her the update, and when he got to the part about his chances, Wanda broke down, weeping, clinging to both of them.

"I . . . I waited too long!" She could barely breathe for the sobs. "I can't . . . lose him now." She looked at Jamie, her expression frozen in regret. "I love him, Jamie. I love him."

They stayed that way most of the night, long after the other detectives reported that the suspects had been arrested, along with four other men—all part of the drug ring responsible for the murder in the alley, as well as a host of other unsolved crimes. Once they'd delivered that news, the other detectives said their good-byes and their condolences.

And still the three of them stayed, Jamie and Clay on either side of Wanda, taking turns holding her while she cried, comforting her and listening to her talk about Joe and how much she'd missed him and how come she couldn't have told him so sooner.

"Pride, that's what it was." She came up with this conclusion sometime around four in the morning. "I would've called him back the day he left if it weren't for my cursed pride."

Jamie shot a look at Clay as relief made its way through her. *Thank You, God . . . that it's not ten years from now and me saying those words about Clay.*

The night wore on, and twice doctors reported no change. Joe was still in critical condition, still on life support, his body trying to adjust to the massive blood loss and internal injuries. Jamie was exhausted, but they had to hold on. News could come at any minute.

The group grew quiet, lost in their own prayers and thoughts. Sometime around seven that morning, Clay was pacing along the window area, and Wanda had her face in her hands when a doctor entered the waiting room.

He was grinning.

All three of them were on their feet, meeting the doctor. Only Clay could find the words to speak. "How is he?"

"I'm amazed, really. A half hour ago his vital signs had a sudden improvement. We took him off life support, and he's doing well." The doctor gave a shake of his head. "*Very* well. Almost as if someone breathed life into him."

"Oh my . . ." Wanda lifted her fingers slowly to her mouth. Her eyes found Clay's and then Jamie's. "For the past hour I changed my prayer. I told God if he'd let Joe live, I'd spend the rest of my days by that man's side, following the Lord together, the way we should have from the beginning."

Chills ran down Jamie's arms.

The doctor gave Wanda a knowing nod. "I've seen this kind of thing too often to doubt it. God still works miracles today; I'm convinced." He paused. "You've been here all night. You can come in and see him if you'd like. He's trying to come around."

"Oh, thank God!" Wanda hugged the doctor. "He's giving me one more chance!"

Jamie rubbed her arms to ward off another series of chills. How was it possible? Two hours ago Joe barely clung to life, and now he was breathing on his own, waking up? The power of God at work in their presence was enough to drop her to her knees.

Instead she took Clay's hand and the three of them followed the doctor to Joe's room. He was hooked to half a dozen machines, and he had tubes running into his nose and arms. But otherwise he looked well. His midsection was bandaged and a light sheet covered him to his waist.

Wanda looked at the doctor. "Can I . . . can I touch him?"

Joe moved his lips and made a weak attempt at clearing his throat. "Doc . . ." His voice was scratchy. "That's my Wanda." He struggled, wincing from the pain. "You better . . . tell her yes."

"Joe!" She framed his face with her hands and kissed him square on the mouth. "I'm sorry! It wasn't all your fault, it was mine." She was crying again, crying and smiling and holding on to Joe the same way Jamie had hung on to Clay hours earlier. Her words spilled out almost too fast to understand. "I should've gone after you when Jimmy died, and instead I made a stupid mistake and lost you. I lost you, but it was my pride." She took a quick breath. "My pride, I tell you. It kept me from calling when I should've, and now it almost kept me from telling you the most important thing, because Joe Reynolds, I have pride something fierce! But guess what?"

He blinked and his eyes opened just enough to see her. "You won . . . the speed-talking award?"

She stopped and sat a bit straighter. Then her eyes lit up, and she looked at Jamie and Clay. "He's gonna be fine! If he's got his humor, he's gonna be just fine."

The slits in Joe's eyes grew wider. He looked around the room, wincing again as he shifted himself higher on his pillow. "Michaels?"

"I'm here." Clay took a step forward.

"Tell me they got those punks." His words were slow, but he was coming back a little more every few minutes.

Clay smiled and Jamie moved in beside him. "Got 'em good, buddy. Real good."

"Attempted murder?" He managed a weak smile.

Jamie understood. *Attempted* murder, because Joe had every intention of surviving the shooting. She felt something warm work its way through her, and she knew what it was. Blessed assurance. The certainty that God had indeed worked not just one miracle in their midst by bringing her to the understanding that she could see Clay again. But He'd worked the miracle of Joe's life as well.

Clay took another step closer and put his hand on Joe's knee. "More than that." He looked at Jamie. "The guys were wanted for a bunch of drug deals and one other murder. They were part of a ring."

"Scary." Jamie felt the blood leave her face.

"Yeah." Clay gave her a look that told her he'd known this information all night, but hadn't wanted to share it until now.

Jamie looked at the floor near her feet, too shocked to speak. Fear tap-danced around Jamie but didn't touch her. It could have been Clay just as easily. She met his eyes and looped her arm through his. "I'm so glad they caught them."

Joe gave a slow nod and looked at Jamie. He shifted his gaze to Clay. "What else they get 'em for?"

"Besides attempted murder?" Clay grinned at his friend. "Homicide in the alley killing and a number of drug charges."

Joe lifted his head a few inches off the pillow. "They were the killers?"

"Not sure which one was the shooter, but the police think one of 'em is their guy."

"Okay, then ask the doc . . . when I can leave." His voice was still scratchy, his words still slow. He smiled at Wanda. "That news calls for a party."

"No parties." Wanda kissed him on the cheek. The mood changed as she grew quiet, searching his eyes. "You have to get better, Joe. And when you go back to L.A. you have to take me and the kids with you." Her voice was softer, not the hysterical weeping or giddy excitement from earlier, but a deep warmth that filled the room. "I love you, Joe Reynolds. God gave me the chance to tell you. This time I'm not going to miss it."

Clay shifted and pulled Jamie into another embrace. Not as desperate as the one they'd shared when she first arrived at the hospital, but one of joy and contentment.

He whispered close to her ear. "I think we should leave them alone."

"Me too." Jamie stifled a giggle and let herself get lost in Clay's eyes. "Besides, you have a call to make."

"I do?" He nuzzled his nose against hers.

"Yes." Now that Joe was doing better, she allowed herself to be lost in the feelings he stirred in her. She wanted to kiss him, wanted it as much as she wanted her next breath. But they had other details to take care of first.

"Okay, Miss Jamie." He held her closer, a lazy smile hanging on his lips, his eyes filled with desire. "Who do I have to call?"

"Your brother, so you can tell him the news. Sierra and I are coming for Thanksgiving."

TWENTY-FIVE

Jamie was nervous.

Whatever she told herself or Clay or Sue or anyone else, her stomach was tight and her heart raced even when she was sitting still. For three years she had accepted she would never see Eric Michaels again, and now, in a few days, she was about to do just that. The level of anxiety over the matter hit her again the Wednesday morning before Thanksgiving. She was about to have dinner with Eric and his wife; the idea still seemed like something from a dream.

Or a nightmare.

The flight took forever, and Jamie tried not to think about Eric. There were more pressing matters. How fast the plane could fly, for instance. Only two days had passed since she'd been with Clay, but she couldn't wait to see him. It seemed forever before the plane finally circled over Burbank and came in for a smooth landing.

"I'm excited, Mommy. I've never seen California." Sierra squeezed Jamie's hand as they stepped off the plane and onto the jetway.

"I think you'll like it." Jamie grinned at her. They held hands as they headed down the concourse toward security. She spotted Clay just as his eyes found her through the crowd.

"Look!" Sierra let go of her hand and did a few jumps. "It's Clay! Can I go see him?"

Jamie laughed, her eyes still locked on his. "Just don't knock anyone down."

She took off toward Clay, her red backpack bouncing, and when she reached him, she threw her arms around his waist. He stooped down and handed her a long-stemmed white rose. Then he gave her a red one and nodded toward Jamie.

"Mommy!" Sierra ran the few feet that separated them and handed the flower over. "Here! It's from Clay."

Jamie stopped and took the rose. She looked at Clay and thanked him with her eyes. A few seconds later she and Sierra were at his side. He leaned close and kissed Jamie. "I missed you." He spoke the words low, near her ear. "Two days felt like forever."

"I know." Her cheeks burned, but she didn't chide herself. So what if she felt like a schoolgirl in Clay's presence? She refused to feel guilty or ashamed. God had brought him into her life, everything about him was a blessing from God. The feelings he stirred in her heart were something everyone should be so blessed to feel.

The three of them went to the baggage area, where they found Jamie's suitcase and Sierra's duffel bag, then they headed for Clay's Jeep. As they walked, Sierra rattled on about Wrinkles staying with the neighbor and how she'd explained the trip to the cat so the cat wouldn't worry about her.

"But did you take the dress-up clothes to the neighbor's house?" Clay tried to look serious. "What will Wrinkles do without his fancy socks for a whole week?"

Sierra giggled and skipped along between them. "You're silly, Clay."

"Only with my jester hat."

By the time Jamie and Sierra checked in to their hotel, and the three of them found lunch, the day was almost over. They spent the afternoon touring Hollywood and Malibu Beach.

Every hour or so Jamie remembered that the meeting with Eric was coming. But for the most part her anxiety didn't interfere with the day.

They had dinner at Gladstone's on the beach and were back at the hotel by nine o'clock. Clay walked them to their door and made sure they got inside safely. Sierra was digging through her duffel bag looking for her nightgown when Clay bid them good-bye.

Before he left, Jamie stepped just into the hallway, pulled the door partially shut behind her, and smiled at him. "I can't believe we had dinner on the beach in November."

"I told you." He raised an eyebrow at her. "California's not too bad." His arms circled her waist and drew her close.

"Mmmm." She looked deep into his eyes. "I'm beginning to see that."

He searched her face, and it was clear what he was thinking before he said it. "Are you okay? About tomorrow?"

"Yes." Her smile eased. It was the truth. She was nervous, yes. But not enough to stop her from going ahead with the meeting. "I'm fine."

"Good." He took one hand from her waist and slid his fingers along the side of her face. "I'm so glad you came, Jamie."

"Me too." He was going to kiss her, and she could hardly wait. But just as he moved closer, a split second before his lips touched hers, Sierra opened the door.

"Hey, guys!" She had her nightgown in her hands. At the sight of the two of them, she giggled.

Jamie exhaled her frustration, then shook her head with a laugh. "Did you need something, dear?"

She giggled again. "My toothbrush."

"On that note . . ." Clay took a step back and chuckled. "Guess I better get going." He winked at Sierra and gave Jamie a look that would make it hard to fall asleep later. "I had a wonderful day."

"Me too." Sierra grinned at him, clearly happy that the two of them had been hugging.

"I think we all did." Jamie hoped he could read her eyes, that given the chance she would've spent as long as he liked kissing him in the hallway. But once again the moment would have to wait.

Clay left, and Sierra was asleep in fifteen minutes. But not Jamie. She lay there, staring at the ceiling, half the time wondering what she was doing, the other half wishing morning would come.

She wasn't sure when she drifted to sleep, but when she woke the next morning, she sat straight up, overcome by a burst of anxiety that made her head spin and left her sick to her stomach. Once as a young girl she visited Six Flags with her parents on a day when there were no lines. Ten rides on the giant wooden roller coaster and she wasn't sure she'd ever feel normal again.

That's how she felt now.

She looked at Sierra, sleeping in the other bed. Maybe they shouldn't have come; she hadn't told Sierra the truth about Eric, that he was Clay's brother. Now it might feel rushed, forced. She wasn't sure why she'd waited so long. Maybe because the news would be difficult for Sierra; maybe because it would be too difficult for herself.

She glanced at her suitcase. She could still do it. Grab her clothes, stuff them inside, wake Sierra, and catch a cab to the airport. It wasn't too late.

The air in the hotel room was stuffy. Jamie stood, went to the window, and opened the drapes. She pressed her forehead against the cool glass and realized she was holding her breath. No wonder the air felt stuffy; she wasn't getting any of it.

She exhaled.

As she did so, she found a point of balance again. She was here because she wanted to be, because the strength of her feelings for Clay Michaels wouldn't be denied. Maybe they would wind up friends, Internet pen pals who kept in touch from opposite sides of the country. Or maybe one day they'd be something much more.

But Eric?

She took in a slow breath and stared at the already busy Ventura Boulevard, just beyond the parking lot. Eric was a nice man with an uncanny resemblance to Jake. But Eric wasn't Jake, nor was he some ex-lover she needed to avoid. He'd never belonged to her, not even when she thought she was married to him.

So what was the problem? Why the nervous stomach and—

"Mommy?"

Jamie spun around and found a quick smile. "Good morning, honey." She crossed the room and sat on the edge of Sierra's bed. "Happy Thanksgiving."

She rubbed her eyes and gave Jamie a sleepy grin. "What time is Clay coming?"

"In a few hours."

It was time to tell Sierra the truth. Jamie brushed her daughter's bangs with her fingertips and felt a lump in her throat. Sierra had been just four when the terrorist attacks hit. Chances were she wouldn't recognize Eric if they passed on the street.

"I like when you play with my hair, Mommy." Sierra leaned back into the pillow, a dreamy look on her face.

"I like it too."

Jamie studied her daughter. No, Sierra might not recognize Eric, but what if something serious did come of Jamie's relationship with Clay? One day she would have to know the truth. The same way she'd needed the truth about Eric not being Jake. Sierra deserved to know who Eric was.

Jamie cleared her throat. "Honey, I have something to tell you." She brushed her knuckles against Sierra's cheek. "Something about Clay's brother."

Sierra made a face. "Clay's brother? We're having dinner at his place today, right?"

"Yes." Fear was making a logjam of her throat. Jamie swallowed hard. "Sweetie, this is sort of a strange thing." She uttered a soft laugh. "I don't really believe it myself, but here's the deal. Remember the man who looked like Daddy? The one in your picture on your dresser?"

Sierra leaned up on her elbows, more interested than before. "My second daddy, the one with his own family."

"Right, well—" she pursed her lips, searching for the words— "that man is Clay's brother." She hesitated. "Isn't that strange?"

"Clay's brother is Mr. Michaels, the man we thought was Daddy?" Sierra sat all the way up now, her eyes wide.

"Yes." Jamie slumped. Clearly Sierra thought about Eric; otherwise she wouldn't have remembered his name. She clenched her fists. "I'm sorry, honey. I didn't know about this when I met Clay that day on the ferryboat. I just found out a little while ago."

"They're brothers?" Sierra looked toward the window, eyes distant.

"Yes." Jamie braced herself for what was ahead. Sierra might break down and cry, even be afraid to see the man again. Or maybe she would be confused, unwilling to go to the Thanksgiving dinner.

Instead Sierra turned her eyes back to Jamie and clapped her hands. "So I get to see Clay *and* Mr. Michaels, all in one day?"

Once again Jamie couldn't draw a breath. She was too intent on her daughter, waiting for the bad reaction she'd been dreading. "You're . . . you're not upset?"

"No." Sierra's eyes danced. "Remember, Mommy? I told you I wanted to see him again, the man I thought was my daddy." She grinned. "Now I get to." Her feet slid over the edge of the bed and she hopped onto the floor. "It's going to be the bestest Thanksgiving Day ever."

"But he's not your daddy." Jamie searched her daughter's eyes. "You understand that, right?"

Sierra's smile faded. "Daddy died in the Twin Towers." She paused, thoughtful. "Mr. Michaels might look like him, but he isn't him. I know that."

Jamie exhaled. All that worry, all the dread, and of the two of them, her daughter had the best grip on the situation. Jamie felt herself relax, and almost at the same time she looked at the clock. "Yikes." She tousled Sierra's long golden hair. "We'd better get ready."

Anxiety played with Jamie's mind while she showered and did her hair, even into the final minutes before Clay arrived. But the moment she saw him, her fears faded. They hugged, and his eyes held the questions she'd been asking herself all morning.

"I'm fine." She grabbed her purse and Sierra's hand. "Let's go have Thanksgiving dinner." She grinned at her daughter. "Sierra says it's going to be the bestest one yet."

They left the room happy and laughing and looking forward to the day. Because no matter how strange or bizarre the situation was, no matter how uncomfortable she might feel in Eric's house, meeting his wife, watching him with his family, it didn't matter.

Her feelings for Clay Michaels were stronger.

Eric looked out the window for the fifth time in as many minutes. His heart thudded deep within him, the way it did every time he stopped moving. They would be there any minute, Clay and Jamie and Sierra.

He understood his pounding heart. It simply wouldn't believe it was possible. Clay went to New York City and met Jamie Bryan? The woman he'd learned to love in those terrible days after September 11? The woman he'd worked so hard to put out of his mind?

There had been no wavering in Clay's voice when he called. His feelings for Jamie were strong and certain. Yes, she'd struggled with the idea that the two of them were brothers. She hadn't planned on seeing him again, any more than he'd planned on seeing her. But apparently she'd reached some sort of resolution in her mind, because she had flown to Los Angeles with Sierra, and now—at any time—she would be there.

Jamie Bryan. Walking into his world.

The last time they were together they'd had an emotional intimacy that was typically reserved for married couples. And why not? For more than two months they both believed they were married.

And what about Sierra?

It had killed him to tell her good-bye. He remembered it still, his last morning with her, curling her hair and holding back tears as she chattered about her little friend. Katy, wasn't it? And how nice it was that Mommy was going to church with them. And he had told her that next week maybe Mommy should curl her hair, that Mommy might do an even better job than him.

Eric pushed the memories away and stared out the window, searching for Clay's Jeep.

They'd told Josh the facts, that his uncle Clay had met up with the woman Eric had lived with. They'd told their son about Eric's time in New York before. But the blank look on Josh's face the other day told Eric that at eleven years old, his son still didn't quite understand. He seemed content that his parents were happy; nothing else mattered.

Josh was upstairs getting ready now; same with Laura.

A car pulled onto their street, but it was too small to be Clay's. Eric had to watch for them, had to see them pull up. Because unless he saw it for himself, he wouldn't believe it. Jamie Bryan? About to walk through his door? Not just Jamie, but Sierra. Sweet little Sierra, the little girl who captured his heart from the moment he woke up in a New York hospital with amnesia.

She would be . . . how old? Seven, at least.

The memories stirred in his soul, lifting and falling and taking wind like the last remains of autumn's fallen leaves.

Had it been three years since that final good-bye? He could see it all, feel the emotions from that day. The way he'd hugged Sierra in the entryway of her home, hours before his flight back to Los Angeles. He and Jamie had agreed to keep up the facade, pretending he was her daddy. She was too young to understand anything different. And so, in keeping with the act, he bid her good-bye the way he might've any other time. He played with her curls and at her request he promised to give her a horsie ride that night when he returned.

Only he never returned. Because by then he'd figured out who he was and where he belonged. Two hours later he stood in LaGuardia Airport telling Jamie good-bye, hugging her, holding her. Thanking her for helping him find his way back. They held hands until the last minute, when Laura appeared in the distance with a stream of passengers.

What he'd told Clay several weeks earlier had been right on. His physical healing, and the transformation in his life, had been only part of the miracle. The other part was that he'd been able to leave Jamie.

He felt someone behind him and he turned. "Laura."

Her expression was pained. "Do you have to stand there waiting like that?" Her voice was soft, defeated. "She'll be here soon enough."

"Hey." He pulled away from the window and faced her. A quiet warmth filled his tone. "Laura ... don't be like that. This isn't my fault."

"It isn't anyone's fault. That's just it." She hugged herself tight. "Fault doesn't change how I feel."

He ran his knuckle along her brow. "How do you feel?"

"Scared." Her answer was quick, pointed. "Sometimes scared to death."

"Ah, Laura ..." His heart went out to her. Of course she was anxious. The whole situation was too strange to believe. He brushed a piece of her blonde hair off her face and touched his lips to hers. "Clay met a woman and fell in love. The woman happened to be Jamie Bryan. It has nothing to do with you and me, okay? Don't be afraid."

"I'm trying not to, Eric." She looked straight to his heart. "You lived with her for three months. I keep thinking ..." She hesitated and lifted her hands. "I don't know. I keep thinking you must've been in love with her." Defeat colored her eyes again. "I picture you spending that much time with another woman and I can't help but wonder what it was like. Not just the physical stuff, but the emotional connection."

He ached for the pain in her eyes. This was the road they never traveled, the one that took him back in time to Jamie Bryan. He'd been honest with her from the beginning, but once he'd shared the details, he locked them away in a place he never intended to go again. Over the years, when she expressed doubts about that time in his life, he quickly dismissed them.

But now . . .

"Laura." He took gentle hold of her shoulders. "I kept nothing from you. Yes . . ." He swallowed, praying she would believe him. Grateful it was the truth. "We kissed a few times, but nothing more. Neither of us wanted to be intimate unless I remembered."

"But you must've loved her, Eric. Or at least felt like you loved her."

This was the hard part. What was love, really? Eric leaned against the windowpane. "I thought I was her husband; I allowed myself to *believe* I loved her." He hung his head and rubbed the muscles in his neck. When he looked up he exhaled hard. "I thought it was the right thing, Laura. Whatever it was, God used it for good. But you know how I feel. I left Jamie planning to never look back."

She held his eyes for a long time. Then she nodded, her expression still troubled, but less doubtful. "Okay." She leaned up and kissed his cheek. "Maybe it's a bad case of morning sickness." She blew a wisp of hair off her forehead. "Anyway, Josh is still in the shower. I have to finish my makeup." She bit her lip. "I don't want to be out here when they pull up."

He waited until she was gone, then he turned around and looked out the window. If only the memories weren't so vivid. How many times after they knew the truth about his blood type, and before he realized who he was, had she looked in his eyes and told him what she was feeling.

That sometimes she hoped he would stay forever and never find his way back.

He drew in a sharp breath and sat on the edge of the windowsill.

After he left her, it was all he could do to put her out of his mind. God had given him the best way. He prayed for her. It wasn't something he talked about with anyone but God, but it was the least he could do. The least and the most.

Daily, hourly sometimes, he prayed that Jamie and Sierra would survive the loss of first Jake, and then him, his presence in their lives. That Jamie would grow strong in her new faith and lean on Christ when she wasn't sure she could make it through another day. And that ultimately, one day—if her heart allowed it—she might find someone else to love.

That was the most amazing part. All those prayers, all that time when he asked God to take care of Jamie, he still could hardly let himself believe this was the answer he'd prayed about. His own brother? A chill passed over his arms. *God ... Your ways are so far beyond ours. Get us through this day, please. Let it be okay with everyone. For Clay's sake ... and Jamie's.*

Be still ... and know that I am God.

What? Eric stood up. He leaned against the window frame and closed his eyes. The response was so quick, so clear. Often when he prayed, he had a sense, a knowing that the Lord wanted him to do one thing or another. But this time ...

The answer had been audible. Maybe not in the way most people might hear it. But no question someplace in his soul Eric had *heard* the words. *Be still and know that I am God.* It was a verse he'd learned first from Jake Bryan's Bible. During his days of amnesia, it had taught Eric he couldn't rush God, couldn't force himself to remember. Rather, he was to be still and let God do the work.

Now God was calling him to that again. Be still and wait; and know that whatever happened that day, God was in control.

His mouth was dry, his heart heavy with the weight of his memories. He went to the kitchen, put the kettle on, and grabbed a mug. A cup of coffee would help clear the cobwebs. After a few minutes the water came to a boil, and just as he poured his cup, he heard a knock at the door and the sound of it opening.

"Eric?" Clay's happy voice didn't sound forced, but it wasn't quite natural either.

No wonder. Clay couldn't help but feel the strain of the situation, same as the rest of them. "Coming." He left his coffee on the counter and headed for the front door.

Clay was just walking through the door. "Jamie's getting something from the car." He stepped inside.

Behind him came Sierra. A taller, older version of Sierra.

She saw him and there was a flicker of recognition. "Hi, Mr. Michaels." Her chin stayed tucked close to her chest, her eyes shy and nervous.

Eric's throat was thick. Too thick to speak. She was different now, not the same sprite she'd been as a four-year-old. This Sierra was more mature, touched by sorrow. He held out his arms. "Hi, Sierra."

With slow, uncertain steps she came and hugged him. Then she looked into his eyes and smiled. "My mom told me about when you lived with us." Her eyes softened and in them was a hint of the Sierra he'd so easily loved as a daughter. "I understand now."

"Sierra understands a lot." Clay stood a few feet away, his eyes damp.

At the sound of Clay's voice, Sierra lit up, skipped across the room, and took Clay's hand. Suddenly she was just a taller version of the girl Eric had known. "We have to tell him about Wrinkles and the jester hat, okay?"

Eric blinked. What was this? Sierra barely remembered him, but Clay . . . clearly she was taken with him. A strange sort of pain seared Eric's heart, but only for an instant. This was what he had prayed for. It was right. The little Sierra, the one he gave butterfly kisses to, was gone forever. She had never belonged to him in the first place, but to her father, Jake Bryan.

And by the way things looked, this new Sierra belonged to Clay.

Footsteps sounded in the doorway, and Eric felt his heart stand still. Jamie walked in, looking exactly as he remembered her, and her eyes found his. In her hands was a thick bouquet of orange and yellow flowers. She hesitated. "These are for you and Laura." Her voice was thick.

He remembered enough to know she was on the verge of tears. His eyes looked deep into hers, to the places they'd shared together. "Thanks." There was a sound from upstairs. "Laura'll be down in a minute."

"Good. I'm anxious to meet her."

Eric shifted his weight. He wasn't sure what to do, whether to go to her the way he wanted to, tell her he was so glad she'd survived the past few years. Or whether to keep his distance.

In the end she made the first move. She set the flowers down near the door and erased the years between them in a single heartbeat. Her arms came around his neck and he held her. It was not a hug borne of passion, but of pain. A hug that allowed them to say everything they couldn't voice, everything that only the two of them would ever understand. And for a handful of seconds, they were the only two in the room.

When he took a step back, her eyes were bright with tears. But she uttered a sound that was mostly laugh. "Can you believe this?" She laughed again and wiped at her eyes.

"No." He cleared his throat, trying to push his words past his emotions. "I knew I wouldn't believe it until you walked through the door."

"Me neither." She took his hands, squeezed them once and let go. "It's amazing."

"It is." And that's when he noticed it. There was something different about her. Something in her easy smile, a depth in her eyes. Then it hit him.

She was at peace.

In their short time together, he'd never seen her like this. First, because she was so determined to help him remember that he was Jake; next, because of the doubts that eventually crept in; and finally because she had to help him find his real identity. Even in the end, when she'd found faith in Christ and strength enough to let him go, even when she told him good-bye at LaGuardia, she wasn't at peace. Not like she was now.

He returned her smile. As strange as things were, this . . . this meeting again was going to be okay. He could feel it in his soul.

The moment changed. Memories faded and yesterday melted away. Eric took another step back and felt himself being brought back to the present. The entire exchange with Jamie had taken no more than a few seconds, and now he turned his attention to Clay. "Hey, brother. Glad you're here." He shook Clay's hand and grinned. "You know Laura's turkeys."

"Okay, I heard my name." Laura was at the top of the stairs, with Josh behind her. Her voice sounded as bright and sunny as she looked. Gone were the doubts and fears from her eyes. In their place was the confidence Eric loved. Confidence and cheerfulness and an underlying determination that she would not play victim that day.

She took the stairs with a spring in her step, hugged Clay, and then smiled first at Sierra, then at Jamie. "I'm Laura." She put her hand on Jamie's shoulder. "I'm glad you could come."

Whatever Laura had done upstairs must've involved more than makeup and mirrors. For this sort of transformation, she probably spent most of the time on her knees. Eric's love for her swelled. *You go, Laura. Thata girl.*

Jamie picked up the flowers and handed them to her. "These are for you." She gave Laura a warm smile. "Thanks . . . for making us feel welcome."

"Well—" she returned the smile, utterly genuine—"I imagine God brought us together to be friends."

"Yes." Jamie's eyes were wet again. "I think so too."

Laura turned to Josh. "This is Josh, he's eleven."

"Hi." Jamie shook his hand. "You have a nice home here." She smiled at Clay and reached for Sierra's hand. "This is my daughter, Sierra."

Laura put her hands on her knees and stooped down. "Sierra. What a pretty name." She angled her head. "I'm glad you're here."

Sierra returned to her place by Clay. "Thank you."

From where he stood, Eric watched the whole thing, beaming. He looked around the room at Clay and Sierra, Jamie and Laura and Josh and suddenly Laura looked at him, a look that lingered. Her eyes sparkled and in her smile he saw something. It wasn't an act. Laura was okay. Despite all the worry she was going to be fine.

In fact, they all were.

TWENTY-SIX

He was still the mirror image of Jake.

From the moment she walked through Eric Michaels's door, that was what surprised Jamie most of all. She had expected him to look different, as if maybe now that his injuries were completely healed, now that his burns had faded from his face and arms, he would have his own look.

An Eric Michaels look.

But the resemblance between him and Jake was uncanny, amazing. Same face and build, same dark hair and blue eyes. When she walked through the door and saw him, it was all she could do to keep from gasping. She had wanted to run to Clay, take his hand, and lean on him for support, but she had to deal with the man standing before her.

Seeing Eric was like seeing a ghost.

Within her, though, she felt God at work, felt Him leading her through the moment, giving her perspective, and reminding her of the truth. Eric wasn't Jake. That truth came quick and served as a lead rope while she blindly walked through those first few minutes.

It wasn't until she met Laura that the swirling emotions in her heart settled. Laura was wonderful. Kind and upbeat, content with the situation in a way that was surprising. Jamie had wondered several times how difficult it must've been for her, how strange she would've felt if the tables were turned. If Jake had disappeared for three months only to resurface a victim of amnesia and having lived with another woman all that time.

But Laura seemed at ease, warm and welcoming. She was pretty, fair skinned with blonde hair and sparkling eyes. Their son, Josh, was a mix between his mother and father. He had her coloring and wider cheekbones rather than Eric's chiseled face. But what struck Jamie the most about him was his easy smile, his comfortable expression. If this boy had been neglected by Eric before September 11, it was impossible to tell now. He was obviously a happy, well-adjusted child. For some reason, that struck a chord of hope in Jamie.

Because in a very clear way, Josh Michaels's life was different because of what God did through Jake. The words in Jake's journal, and the power of the highlighted sections in Jake's Bible, had changed Eric. In the process, they'd changed Josh too.

It was part of Jake's legacy, really. Seeing that in person was far more powerful than she'd ever imagined.

Despite the dozens of thoughts and memories and observations fighting for position in Jamie's mind, she felt comfortable at the Michaels' home. The morning flew by, and Jamie found the most comfortable place—the spot next to Clay. Clay, not Eric, had captured her heart. She knew that now. Otherwise she never would've been able to sit at a table opposite the man who had lived with her and played the role of her husband, a man who so easily could've been Jake, and want nothing more than to savor every minute with Clay.

"I can't believe this is November." Jamie leaned just enough so that her arm occasionally brushed against Clay's. "It feels like summer."

"Sometimes I wish we had seasons." Laura gripped the arms of her chair and angled her face toward the sun. "But I don't wish it for long." She held her hands out with palms up as if she were weighing something. "Let's see . . . eight degrees on Thanksgiving Day or eighty degrees . . . piles of snow and ice or green grass and sunscreen." She grinned at Jamie. "I'll take Southern California."

Eric was inside peeling potatoes. Jamie, Clay, and Laura sat around the backyard patio table, watching the kids toss a Frisbee. Sierra hadn't played with one before, and more than once the plastic disc hit her in the head, but not hard enough to hurt her.

"Clay, guess what?" Sierra giggled in their direction. "I think I need the jester hat. You know why?"

"Why?" Clay leaned forward, his eyes dancing the way they did whenever he and Sierra teased each other. There was no denying how much he cared for her.

"'Cause then the Frisbee would hit the hat instead of my head."

Clay chuckled. "Or maybe a helmet might help." He stood and jogged out to Sierra's side. "Here, let me show you how to catch it." With his hand up in front of his face, he nodded to Josh. "Okay, bucko, show me what you got!"

Grinning, Josh flung it four times as hard as before. "Take that!"

The phone rang, and Eric must've answered it in the house. He came to the door, opened the screen, and handed it to Laura. "It's Gina." His eyes caught Jamie's for a minute, and he gave her a hesitant smile, checking, maybe, to see if she and Laura were still hitting it off.

Jamie gave him a knowing look. Yes, she was fine. Laura was easy to be around. Eric looked out at the yard. "Way to throw it, Josh. Uncle Clay won't last; he wears down easy." Eric winked at his brother. "Hey, Clay, if he wears you out come join me in the kitchen." Then he turned, shut the door, and disappeared into the house.

Jamie sat back in her chair. Laura's conversation seemed deep, as if maybe the Gina woman, whoever she was, had troubling news. Clay was caught up in what had now become Frisbee golf. Jamie stood and stretched, then went to the edge of the patio and called out to Clay. "I'm going to make some tea. Want some?"

"No, thanks." He grinned at her. "Tell Eric I'm beating his son."

She laughed and raised her eyebrows in Laura's direction. *Tea?* she mouthed the word.

Laura covered the phone again. "No, thanks." Her words were barely a whisper. "My friend's son is in the hospital." She frowned. "Sorry about this."

Jamie gestured that it didn't matter; Laura could take as long as she liked. Then she went inside and when the kitchen came into view she stopped. Eric was working over the pot of potatoes, and from the back . . .

She gritted her teeth and kept walking. He wasn't Jake. She drew a quick breath. "Clay says to tell you he's beating your son."

Eric turned around. "Is that right?" He nodded to the pot, his eyes brimming with laughter. "I'm almost done, and then we'll see who wins at Frisbee golf."

She took the teakettle from the stove, careful not to brush against him or get in his way. "Want some tea?" She filled it with water, brought it back, and set it on the burner next to the potatoes.

"No, thanks." He was peeling the last one, cutting it into chunks, and dropping it into the pot. He turned the burner on to the highest level and put the lid on; then he did the same for the adjacent burner, the one with the teakettle.

They were suddenly out of busy things to do.

She leaned against the kitchen island and he stood opposite her, a few feet away. "You doing okay?"

Just like that he could still speak to the deepest part of her. "Yes." Her eyes held his and for a moment neither of them spoke. "Thanks for not pretending."

"Not pretending?" He narrowed his eyes, seeing straight to her soul.

"That we were strangers, that we never ..."

"Never had that time together?" His tone was soft, understanding.

"Yes." She looked at the floor and then back up at him. "Thanks for that."

He bit his lip, as though considering whether to say whatever was on his mind or not. "Wanna see something?"

"Okay." She'd hoped they'd have this, time alone to acknowledge the past and let it find its proper place.

She followed him to a small room off the entryway. "This is my office." He held open the door and let her go in first. The place was spacious with shelves and cupboards and a countertop that lined one wall. "I do most of my work from home now."

"Good for you, Eric." A sad smile tugged at the corners of her lips. "Jake taught you that."

"He did." Eric crossed the room and opened a cupboard at the far end, then looked back at her. "Come here."

She came closer, and he pulled something off the top shelf that made her heart skitter into a strange rhythm. It was the book she'd made him, the one she'd given him at LaGuardia the day they said good-bye. The cover—faded and weathered from use—read, "In Case You Ever Forget." Inside were photocopies of key entries from Jake's journal, special sections of highlighted Scripture that Eric came to love during his time with her and Sierra.

Tears blurred her eyes. With trembling hands she took the book from Eric. "You still have it."

He looked over her shoulder at it. "I read it all the time."

She sniffed and turned, lifting her eyes to him. "You still have his mannerisms, his way of helping out and laughing at himself." A single tear slid onto her cheek and she struggled to find her voice. She stroked her hand along the cover of the handmade book. Then she handed it back to him. "I . . . I understand things better now."

He put the book back, closed the cupboard, and rested against the wall. "About us?"

"Mmmhmm." She dabbed at her cheek and blinked back the tears that stood in line. "God brought us together so we'd both find Him." She searched his eyes. He understood what she was saying; she still knew him well enough to see that. "You were never supposed to replace Jake."

"No." He went to her then and hugged her, letting her know he still cared. Regardless of how right he'd been to go home to Laura, in some way that involved their souls, he still cared about her. "I was never him."

"Exactly." She drew back first and crossed her arms. She'd imagined this conversation with Eric, and always she pictured her heart breaking. Instead, all she felt were deep peace and hope because the truth about Eric's identity was clearer now than it ever had been. She led the way back to the office door. "Your wife is lovely. You seem very happy. Josh too."

He fell in step beside her and a glow lit up his eyes. "We are. In fact—" he hesitated—"Laura's pregnant. Just a couple months."

Jamie wasn't sure what to feel. She was excited for Eric and his family, thrilled for them. But oh, how she would've liked that for herself and Jake—another child. Something she would never have. She found her smile. "Congratulations."

"We haven't told Clay yet. Laura wanted to announce it tonight."

It was yet another bit of Jake's legacy, that Eric would come home from New York ready to love his wife and son, able to rebuild what he'd lost over the years to the point that now they were expecting another child. Jamie felt her own desire to have another child easing. Instead her heart sang for Eric and Laura. "I won't say a word."

"I know what you're thinking; that it's because of what I learned from Jake. What God let me learn. You're right, Jamie." He glanced toward the cupboard one more time as they left the room. "What God taught me because of Jake will stay with me forever." He stopped and looked at her again. "Always. God's plan in all this is . . ." He chuckled and raked his fingers through his hair. "Well, it's more than I can understand." He paused. "Even now, with you and Clay."

"Yes." She felt her cheeks get hot. The way she cared about Eric's brother was getting stronger every day. And now, alone with Eric, she could hardly wait to get back to Clay. She bit the inside of her lip. "He's . . . he's wonderful."

"He's more than that." Eric stuck his hands in his pockets and gave her a pointed look, his eyebrows raised. "He's in love with you. I've been watching. I've never seen my brother like he is with you."

Butterflies scattered in Jamie's stomach. "Really?" She felt like a high school girl being told that the guy she had a crush on liked her too. The corners of her mouth lifted. "Me too, Eric. I can't believe how fast I'm falling."

"I know; I see it." He looked deep at her one last time, seeing to the places he'd known back when she was at the lowest point in her life. "I prayed for this, Jamie. That you'd find someone one day." He chuckled. "Who would've thought it would be my very own brother?"

"I know." Jamie let her head fall back against the hallway wall. "I read something in Jake's Bible, something I hadn't caught before."

"What?"

"It was in Deuteronomy. It talks about God setting before His people life and death, blessings and destruction." She paused. "Then it says to choose life." Her eyes were dry now. "Jake wrote something beside it. A note to me. He told me, 'Jamie, as often as you have the chance, choose life.'"

"And that's what you're doing with Clay." Eric reached out and touched her shoulder. "You couldn't find a nicer guy than my brother."

"I know." She meant it. With her whole heart.

Eric led the way from the room, and when they reached the kitchen, he turned and grinned at her. "I guess that means there's only one question left." He chuckled. "How do you feel about California?"

They both laughed as they returned to the kitchen. The kettle was boiling, and they slipped into easy conversation about the gravy and stuffing and the timing of pulling together a Thanksgiving dinner. It felt wonderful, talking this way with Eric, building something new with him, something casual and current. Something they could share without constantly revisiting the past.

Dinner was far more pleasant than Jamie had ever imagined. The tension was gone, and in its place was something new. A friendship that seemed to be setting a stage for the future. Jamie sat between Sierra and Clay, savoring the friendly banter between the two brothers. Clay was like Eric in many ways, but he was his own person, a man whose faith ran deep and true, clearly strengthened by the passing of time.

As for Eric, sitting across from him now at the table, Jamie saw that something was different about his eyes. He looked so much like Jake, she'd missed it at first, but now that she had time to watch him, to study him while he interacted with Clay and Laura and the rest of them, she could see it clearly.

He didn't have Jake's eyes.

Oh, they looked like Jake's at a glance. But deep within them were memories and emotions that were Eric's alone. Memories he hadn't had when he was living with her in Staten Island. She took a bite of fruit salad and felt herself relax even more.

"This is good turkey, Mrs. Michaels." Sierra beamed at Laura. "Maybe the bestest ever."

"Thank you, Sierra." Laura cast a quick smile at Eric. "I had help with it."

Jamie let her eyes rest on her daughter. Sierra was in her element. She was a people person, someone who loved being around big families. No wonder she was ready to have a second daddy, as she called it. The past three years had been little more than a healing time, a time to say good-bye to Jake and figure out a way to face the future without him.

Watching her, Jamie was convinced. Sierra, too, was ready to choose life.

They went around the table then, telling what they were thankful for. Josh was thankful for his family; Sierra, for her new friends;

and Laura, for the chance to be together. Clay looked at Jamie when he gave his answer. "I'm thankful for God's gift of new life." Under the table, he took hold of her fingers for a few seconds. "Not just once, but every day."

Eric looked around the room at each of them and gave a slow nod. "I'm thankful for answered prayers."

It was Jamie's turn. She massaged her throat, working out the lumps that had sprung up in the last minute or so. Then she looked at Clay and said, "I'm thankful God allows us the chance to choose life."

"On that note—" Eric leaned close to Laura, his eyes on hers— "we have an announcement to make."

Laura looked at Josh and then Clay. "We're going to have a baby!" Her face glowed.

"Seriously?" Clay was on his feet.

"Seriously." Eric laughed. "I know. I can't believe it myself."

Clay walked around the table and gave Eric a hearty hug, slapping him hard on the back. "I'm so happy for you." He held on for a few seconds and then he hugged Laura. "Congratulations." On the way back to his seat he gave Josh a light punch in the arm. "You're going to be a big brother, eh, Josh?"

"I guess." He flashed a lopsided grin at his parents. "I just found out this morning. It's kinda hard to believe."

Jamie leaned forward. "Congratulations, guys. That's wonderful."

Sierra wanted to know if Laura was having a girl baby or a boy baby, and Laura tried to explain that it was too soon to tell.

The conversation took wing, shifting from the idea of a little one running around the house to Josh's basketball abilities to Sierra's make-believe dress-up games and the meaning of the jester hat.

When they hit a lull, Eric held up his finger. "Wait!" He wiped his mouth with a napkin and uttered a quiet laugh. Then he looked at Laura. "Can I tell them about your run-in with the law?"

"What?" Clay's eyes got wide. "Laura Michaels had a run-in with the law? I've got to hear this."

"Sort of." Laura gave Jamie a weak smile, and then lifted her shoulders in Eric's direction. "Ah, go ahead and tell it."

Eric was immediately in his element, explaining how Laura had to go to the mall before Josh's basketball game, and on the way home she was in a big hurry. "Apparently she'd missed the on-ramp for the freeway and tried to make a sweeping U-turn across six lanes of traffic." He laughed and patted her hand. "But she still didn't have a bead on the on-ramp, so she straightened out and wound up in oncoming traffic. That's when she heard the siren."

"I was scared to death." She looked at Jamie for sympathy. "They changed that whole intersection. It's impossible to figure out which lane gets on to the freeway."

Jaime nodded, trying to look earnest, but wanting to laugh out loud.

"So then—" Eric winked at his wife—"when the officer pulls up behind her, she parks with her two right tires way up on the curb.

Laura raised her brow, her eyes dancing. "I wanted to stay out of traffic."

"So the officer comes up to the window, taps on it, and tells her, 'Ma'am, I have several concerns.'"

"Yes," Laura nodded. "That's right. Several."

Everyone was laughing now. Eric waited until he caught his breath to continue. "The officer was so flustered he didn't know what to do." Eric anchored his elbows on the table, his laughter getting the better of him. "So they call for backup and give her a sobriety test. My Laura, standing there near the Thousand Oaks Mall exit to the Ventura Freeway, getting a sobriety test." He grabbed at his sides, still laughing. "'The amazing thing is,' the officer told her, 'you really haven't been drinking.'"

The kids were smiling at each other and shrugging their shoulders. Josh was busy helping Sierra butter her dinner roll.

Clay stopped laughing long enough to turn to Laura. "So what'd they get you for?"

She shrugged. "Nothing. Isn't that great?" She smiled at them, triumphant. "After I passed the test, he told me to buy a map and be more careful."

"Glad it wasn't me." Clay leaned back in his chair and took a long breath. His eyes were damp from laughing so hard. "I would've ticketed you for sure."

"Why?" Laura was indignant. "For parking on the curb?"

"Nope." Clay exhaled long and loud. "For impersonating a drunk driver."

The laughter continued throughout the meal, but even as they chatted, Jamie kept glancing at Clay, sensing his nearness to her and thinking about Eric's question, the one that had been on her own heart for the last week or so. Especially during the days when she and Clay had been apart. It was a question that might have to be answered one of these days, so as they finished dinner and cut into dessert, as they continued talking over coffee and finally as Clay helped them gather their things and head for the car, Jamie let it play again and again in her mind.

How *did* she feel about California?

Twenty-Seven

Clay did everything he could to make the minutes last, but on Sunday afternoon he drove Jamie and Sierra back to the Burbank Airport. The trip had been better than either of them had hoped, and even Sierra was sad to leave. They had decided that he would help them in with their luggage and say a quick good-bye.

Their real good-byes were said the night before, in the hallway outside Jamie's hotel room. They'd gone to Disneyland that day, and Sierra had fallen asleep on the way home. Clay carried her up and set her on the nearest bed, and then he and Jamie snuck into the hallway.

For a while they did nothing but look at each other. Clay broke the silence first. "I'm trying to imagine how I'll get through a week without you." They were both leaning against the same wall, a few feet from each other. Clay reached out and took her hand. "What're we going to do?"

Jamie ran her thumb along the side of his hand, her eyes never leaving his. "I could cancel our flight." Her tone was light, half teasing.

"Forever?" He looked back at her hotel door. "Maybe live here for a year or so?"

"Right." She gave him a sad smile. "I had a wonderful time, Clay."

"Me too." He took a step closer. They hadn't kissed once since Jamie had been in California, and Clay was almost glad. She needed to sort through her feelings, figure out how to act around Eric—and how she felt about Clay outside of the routine they'd found on the East Coast.

But now that everything had worked out, now that she was comfortable around Eric, and after a day of holding hands through Disneyland, Clay didn't want to wait another minute. He closed the gap between them and took her into his arms, hugging her the way he'd known he wouldn't get to at the airport. "Jamie," he whispered her name near the side of her face. "I'll miss you so much."

She drew back first, searching his eyes. "When will I see you again?"

"I don't know." He brought his hand up along her cheek and worked his fingers into her hair. "I'll come for Christmas, maybe, how about that?"

Her eyes lit up. "Really, Clay?"

"Yes." He kissed first one cheek, then her other, never breaking eye contact. "If I can wait that long."

"Clay . . ." She hugged him closer, clinging to his shoulders as if she were desperate to find a way to keep from leaving him. She pressed her cheek against his and suddenly, with an intensity that had been building since she stepped off the plane the day before Thanksgiving, the mood between them changed.

Their lips met, and they kissed. Slowly at first, and then with an intensity that seemed to take both of them by surprise. "Jamie . . ." He was breathless. "If we spend much more time like this, I know I won't last a month."

"Maybe that's a good thing. That way you'll come to New York sooner." She framed his face with her hands and kissed him in a way that left no doubts about her feelings. When she pulled away, she looked straight to his soul. "God brought us together, don't you think so?"

"Yes." He stroked her hair, memorizing the look in her eyes.

"Then why does it feel like everything's going to change after tomorrow?"

He brought his lips to hers once more. "We'll be three thousand miles apart, but nothing's going to change. Nothing." His breathing was shaky, his body on fire for the way she made him feel. "Christmas is a month away, okay?"

"Okay."

They kissed one last time and then said good-bye.

Clay had been restless all night, dreading the airport scene. He kept telling himself the same thing he'd told her. Christmas was only a month away. But now, as he turned his Jeep into the airport parking lot, December 25 felt like a lifetime away. The three of them were quiet as they walked into the concourse and Jamie checked her bags with the attendant.

Boarding passes in hand, they found a place near a concession stand where they were out of the flow of traffic. Sierra took the lead. "Bye, Clay." She hugged his waist and gave him a teary smile. "Thanks for a fun time." She glanced at Jamie, and then crooked her finger in his direction. "C'mere. I wanna tell you a secret."

"Okay." He bent down so she could whisper whatever she wanted to say. "What's the secret?"

She cupped her hands over her mouth and pressed them on either side of his ear. "I wish you were my second daddy, Clay. Wouldn't that be great?" She leaned back, her eyes dancing. Then she came in close again. "But don't tell Mommy, 'cause she told me telling you that might make you confused."

Clay's heart soared, but he checked his reaction. Grinning at Jamie, he whispered back at Sierra. "Can I tell you a secret?"

Sierra nodded.

"I wish I were your second daddy too."

Sierra jumped back, her eyes big. "Really?" This time her voice was almost too loud. She clapped her hands and did a little circle dance. Then she hugged him again and her excitement faded as quick as if someone had thrown a bucket of water on her. She crooked her finger at him again, and once more he bent close to her. Her words were slow and sad. "Yeah, only you can't be my second daddy because we don't live in the same place."

He looked at Jamie and she gave him an understanding smile. They had time; if Sierra needed this private conversation with him, he had Jamie's approval. He cupped his hands over her ear and whispered back to her. "Let's pray about that. And maybe one day there won't be so much space between us, okay?"

Sierra took a step back. Her expression was still sad, but a smile played on the corners of her lips. "Okay, Clay." She hugged him one last time. "Good-bye."

He ran his hand along the back of her head. "Good-bye, Sierra."

She pointed to a drinking fountain a few feet away. "Can I get a sip, Mommy?"

"Sure, sweetie." Jamie looked at Clay. "I guess this is good-bye."

"No." Clay came to her, hugging her, and giving her a brief kiss. "It's only see ya later."

Tears formed a shiny layer over her eyes and she nodded. Sierra returned and stood at her side. "See ya later, Clay."

He watched them go. They went through security and waved one last time before heading down the hallway toward their gate. Only when he got back to his car did he realize how badly he was going to miss her, how much he wanted her in his life. Because that's when he noticed something that hadn't happened to him as far back as he could remember.

His cheeks were wet.

TWENTY-EIGHT

The weeks of December took forever to fall off the calendar.

Jamie continued volunteering at St. Paul's, but only once a week. Twice she worked a shift with Aaron Hisel, but their friendship wasn't what it had once been. At the end of the second shift, he approached her in the break room upstairs and stuffed his hands in his pockets.

"There's someone else, right?" His tone wasn't angry or defensive, but matter-of-fact. "I saw you with him once at the café."

Jamie thought about denying it, but it was impossible. He was right, and more so every day. She ran her tongue along her lower lip and prayed for the right words. "Yes, Aaron. There is."

He looked at the floor near his work boots and gave a slow nod. "I thought so." His eyes found hers again and he shrugged. "I guess it never would've worked anyway. The whole faith thing, you know? We never would've agreed about it." He paused. "I've thought about it, Jamie. I can't believe in God. I'm not ready, not even for you."

Her heart sank. "I'm sorry, Aaron." She touched his shoulder. "I can only tell you what I've told other people here, people who can't get past September 11." She hesitated. "God believes in you, even if you don't believe in Him. He'll keep calling to you the way He's been calling to all of us since the beginning of time. Since Adam and Eve hid from Him in the garden." She let her hand fall to her side. "One of these days, I know you'll hear Him, and then you'll understand. Without Him, nothing makes sense. Nothing at all."

His lips lifted in a crooked smile. "Maybe." He took a step back. His eyes told her he was uncomfortable, ready to end the conversation. "If that ever happens, you'll be the first to know."

"I'll be praying."

She hadn't seen him again after that. The days continued to pass slowly, until even Sierra seemed irritable.

"How many days, Mom?" she asked over dinner one night.

"Twelve. He'll be here in twelve days."

She set her fork down and frowned. "That's too long. Can't we call him and tell him to come sooner?"

"He works, Sierra. He's in training."

"But he could do training here, right, Mommy?"

The conversations were the same every night, and once in a while Jamie let Sierra have a turn on the phone when Clay called. When Jamie took over again, she and Clay talked about their days. Later, when Sierra was in bed, they talked about their feelings, about where things were headed and how they could solve the problem of the distance between them.

Jamie was still thinking about California, but she couldn't fathom leaving Staten Island. She'd grown up there. It was where she'd played with Jake as a child, where she'd gone to high school and buried her parents after their car accident. It was where she'd gotten married.

Clay wasn't opposed to moving, but his detective training had just begun. He needed to put in at least a year to finish and get grounded in the job before looking at another department. Once in a while they would agree that maybe the timing was wrong, maybe they were supposed to be good friends, an encouragement to each other and nothing more.

But as soon as she'd imagine that possibility, she'd lay in bed, sick at the thought of being apart from Clay. She could pack her bags tomorrow, couldn't she? So what if she'd lived all her life on the East Coast? That only meant she was ready for change, right? She would move to the moon to be with Clay, wouldn't she?

The options were confusing, and since the answers didn't come easy, she and Clay did their best to stay away from the hard questions.

Finally it was eight days before Christmas. Sierra was in bed, and Jamie was on the phone with Clay, telling him about Sierra, how neither of them could wait until he arrived. His flight was due in on Thursday, December 23.

"I have an idea." Clay sounded more upbeat than usual. "Tomorrow's Saturday. Take Sierra into Manhattan. You haven't done that yet, right?"

"Not yet." Jamie flopped onto her bed and considered the idea. "We haven't had time, really, with Sierra in school."

"And all the hours on the phone." Clay chuckled.

Jamie rolled onto her back and stared at the ceiling. "Manhattan, huh?"

"Yes. Do it, Jamie. Spend the day there; you'll both have a good time."

By the end of the phone call, Jamie agreed with Clay. A day in Manhattan, shopping on Fifth Avenue and taking in the Christmas lights, would do both her and Sierra good. When she told Sierra the next morning, her daughter jumped up and down. "What a great idea, Mommy. We'll wear our red gloves and pretty scarves and buy presents for Katy and Mrs. Henning and Clay and everyone we know!"

They set off after breakfast. Snow had fallen a few days before, so the scene was like something from a storybook. Crowded streets, bustling with shoppers looking for the perfect gift before time ran out. They bought Sue Henning a sweater at Bergdorf's and at FAO Schwartz they found Katy a stuffed Nala—like the one Clay had brought for Sierra.

For Clay, Sierra picked out a pair of woolly socks, so his feet wouldn't get cold when he was riding around in his police car. Jamie bought him a new Bible—something he'd talked about one of the days they were together in Los Angeles. The store was able to engrave his name on it while Jamie and Sierra had lunch together. She found a few other items before leaving the bookstore.

They were on their way out when Jamie looked at her watch. "Well, sweetie, I think it's time to head back."

Sierra looked alarmed. "But, Mommy, we haven't been in all the stores yet."

"Honey, we wouldn't have time for all the stores if we stayed here two days straight."

"I know but . . ." Sierra licked her lips. "What time is it?"

Jamie stared at her daughter. Usually by now Sierra would be tired, more than ready to go home. "It's three o'clock."

Immediately, Sierra took her hand. "Please, Mommy . . . please can we stay longer? What about that big store down there with the Christmas tree on top, please?"

"Sierra . . ." Jamie's feet hurt. She wanted to play the parent card and call it a day. But maybe Sierra was getting old enough that a day in the city couldn't last long enough. Maybe it was a sign that she was growing up. She bit her lip and searched Sierra's face. "It'll be dark soon."

Sierra jumped up and down. "That's right! That's why I want to stay; so I can see the lights!"

A chill wind passed over them and Jamie pulled her coat tighter. She made a silly face at Sierra and took her hand. "All right, missy. One more store, but that's it. Then we have to go."

It was four-thirty by the time they boarded the ferry and headed back to Staten Island. Jamie expected Sierra to be drained, but she was bouncing around the mostly empty ferryboat like a baby chimp.

"How long till we get back?" She did a skip number three feet in either direction of Jamie. "Come on, Mommy, how long?"

Jamie tried to get a bead on her daughter, but she wouldn't stand still long enough. "Sierra, what's gotten into you?"

"Happiness, Mommy. Happiness got in me today."

Jamie blinked at her daughter. She could hardly argue with that problem. "Shouldn't your happiness be toning down a little?" Jamie had packages stacked around her. Whatever Sierra lacked in exhaustion, she made up for it. The crowds and lights and Christmas music for hours on end had left her ready for bed.

"You didn't answer me, Mommy. How long till we get back?" Sierra twirled twice and did an impromptu tap number. "I want to take tap dancing lessons, is that okay? Katy said she's taking tap in third grade, so I wanna take them too, okay?" She tapped out a little rhythm again.

"Sierra!" Jamie's voice was half laugh, half exasperation. "Stand still for just a minute."

Sierra stopped moving. She stared at Jamie, breathless and at attention. "Yes, Mommy. Sorry."

"Okay." Jamie breathed out, tired just from watching her daughter. "I'll answer your first question first. We'll be back home in twenty minutes; second question, yes. I'll consider tap dancing lessons."

Sierra skipped around in a circle. "Goodie! Yes, it's the bestest day. I'm definitely happy, aren't you, Mommy?"

Jamie was about to order Sierra to stop again, but she couldn't. Suddenly looking at Sierra was like looking at the picture of herself. She'd been motionless for long enough, unable to hear the music of life let alone find the rhythm of it. But now she was dancing again. Just like Sierra. Jamie leaned back and smiled at her daughter.

Sierra was merely choosing life.

Fifteen minutes later they were off the ferryboat and in their car, headed home. It was dark by now, but that didn't stop Sierra. She grew more animated and talkative the closer they got to home. Jamie had long since given up the idea of curbing her enthusiasm. Instead she chuckled to herself and let Sierra carry on, bopping from a request for red hair bands to a curiosity about whether Wrinkles should get dress-up clothes in his stocking this year.

She talked all the way home, until they pulled in the driveway. Then, like a switch had been flipped, she fell silent. It wasn't until they stepped out of the car and headed up toward the front door that Jamie stopped short and gasped.

In the light from the street lamp, she saw . . .

It couldn't be. He wouldn't have come early and surprised her, would he? He stood up and her doubts vanished. She dropped her packages and ran to him.

"Clay!"

"I guess I got my dates mixed up." He grinned and took her into his arms. "Mmmm." He whispered into her ear. "I missed you."

"I can't believe you're here." Tears stung her eyes. It was the best surprise she'd had in years. Three years, to be exact. She drew back and raised her eyebrows at Sierra. "Did you know something about this, missy?"

Sierra giggled and clapped her hands. "I didn't say anything, Clay. I kept the secret."

Clay pulled back enough to give Sierra a high five. "Way to go!" He winked at her, the wink Jamie had come to love. "I knew I could trust you."

"You could, Clay. You could trust me a whole lot because I didn't even say anything about—"

Clay put his hand over her mouth and gave her a gentle pull back to the porch step.

Jamie stood a few feet away. Sierra and Clay were so good together. She put her hands on her hip. "Okay, what's up?"

Sierra pinched her lips into a straight line and did the zipping motion across them. She tried to speak, but with her words trapped in her mouth, it sounded like gibberish.

Clay put his arm around Sierra and whispered something to her. Then he took something from his coat pocket, something Jamie couldn't make out. A present of some kind, maybe. He nodded at Sierra, and she did the same.

It must've been a signal, because she jumped up and ran to Jamie. "Mommy! Come on." Sierra grabbed her hand and led her over to Clay. "It's time."

Jamie's heart was thudding hard inside her chest. What was this? Clay and Sierra had obviously planned this moment. She held her breath. It couldn't be what she was thinking, the thing she couldn't put into words even in her head.

Not this soon, God. I'm not ready.

Daughter, I am with you. I am with you.

The answer came quick and certain, echoing through her heart and reminding her to exhale. It was okay; God was with her. He was with her and whatever was coming, He was in control. She steadied her legs. "Okay." She forced a short laugh. "How come I'm the only one who doesn't know what's going on?" She stood in front of Clay now, trying to get his attention. The thing he'd taken out of his pocket was hidden under his arms.

Beside her Sierra giggled. She tugged on Jamie's arm. "Quiet, Mommy. Clay wants to ask us something."

Then, as if it were happening in slow motion, Clay pulled a small velvet box from his lap. He stood and came close enough that Jamie could smell his cologne, savor the way it mixed with the fresh soap smell he always had.

She looked at him, searched his eyes. "Clay?" It couldn't be happening, could it? Was she ready? Could she ever be ready?

Sierra bounced up on her toes a few times, but she had her mouth zipped again.

Jamie's head began to spin. She was just barely able to keep focused on Clay and the thing he was doing now. He was getting down on one knee in the crusty snow, his eyes shining, his gaze never leaving hers. And he was opening the box . . . and there inside was a brilliant white gold solitaire diamond ring.

"Jamie . . ." Clay searched her eyes, her face. He took the ring from the box, slipping the box back in his pocket. "The more I think about life, the more I'm convinced of one thing." He swallowed and shifted his position so that his other knee was in the snow now. "When you know what to do, and you know it's the most right thing in the world, then you should do it. Whether it's forgiving someone or loving someone." He stood and took a step toward her, his face intense, serious. "Or asking someone to marry you."

Sierra made a slight squeal.

Jamie heard herself suck in a quick breath, and her fingers came to her mouth. She expected to reel hard one way and then the other, fall to her hands and knees, maybe even faint. It was too soon, right? Wasn't that how she'd been feeling seconds ago?

But now . . . as she looked from the ring to Clay, she felt strangely centered. The spinning stopped and everything faded except the words he was saying.

"Life's a fragile thing." His expression sobered. "September 11 taught us that." His words were a gentle caress. "For those of us who remain—all of us touched by that day—we need to find strength and hope in Christ, and to do the thing He asks us to do. Choose life."

"Clay . . ." She felt like a person lost in the forest for weeks on end, a person who was only now seeing clear of the trees. In a single instant, everything she'd fretted about slipped behind her. Now all she saw ahead was a vista wide open and inviting. And if she walked toward it, she'd find a new life, a new home for her and Sierra.

She could see it all.

"Marry me, Jamie." A smile lifted his lips and with his free hand, he framed her face. "Come be my wife in California and start life over again. Trust me that I'll cherish you as long as I live, and that

I'll do everything I can to keep God at the center of us." He winked at Sierra. "All of us." He held the ring out to Jamie. "Say yes. Please, Jamie."

She circled her arms around his neck and felt the tears come. "Yes, Clay." The sound she made was half laugh, half cry. He was right; so what if they hadn't known each other for years? They weren't kids out of college, needing to figure each other out. They were adults who belonged together from the moment they first met; adults with faith at the center of everything, and a connection that rarely came around twice in a lifetime.

He drew back a few inches. Surprise and uncertainty fighting for position in his eyes. "You really will?"

Her head dipped back and she laughed out loud this time. She glanced at Sierra and pulled her into the embrace. Then she looked at Clay again. "Yes, I'll marry you."

"And we can move to California, right, Mommy? Because I think it would be the bestest thing to live with Clay *and* be near Disneyland."

They all laughed, and Jamie realized she had an answer for that question too. One that didn't feel painful or frightening or rushed because no matter how often she told herself she wasn't ready, she'd been thinking about it a long time. She locked eyes with Clay and grinned. Good thing his arms were around her, otherwise she would've floated away.

"Well?" The uncertainty was gone from his expression.

"Yes." Jamie said it once and the second time she practically shouted it. "Yes!" She tightened her grip on both Clay and Sierra. "I'll marry you, Clay, and I'll move right *into* Disneyland if you want." Her voice softened and a chill passed down her spine at God's provision, His perfect timing. "Sierra and I will be wherever you are, Clay. From now on."

The certainty in her heart was stronger than cement. It was sweet and sure and mingled with the sorrow of good-bye, because after today she would never again live in a memorial. In a little while, she would never again work in one. Her past—beautiful as it was— would simply be her past.

Her yesterdays belonged to Jake Bryan, where they would always belong.

But because of God's goodness, because He had led her to choose life, her future had a home that was calling to her. And not just her, but Sierra. A future suddenly bright and full and colored with happy expectations. A home together.

And maybe, one day, a home blessed with another child.

She would no longer be Jamie Bryan, except in her distant memories. Because her tomorrows would take her to a place where she had a new name, a name she was breathless to take on—Jamie Michaels.

The most amazing feeling flooded her. *Jamie Michaels.* The sound of it rang across the quiet places of her heart. Clay's touch on her hand made her turn. Through eyes blurred with happy tears, she leaned closer and kissed him. A kiss of joyful excitement over a future that was even now just beginning.

TWENTY-NINE

Sierra was almost finished packing.

Mommy had given her a big suitcase for her clothes and special things. Special things didn't go on the moving truck; they went with her on the airplane. Sierra got jumbles in her tummy whenever she thought of the moving truck, because it was coming in two days and then some mover guys would come into the house and take everything into the back of the truck.

Even their van!

But the jumbles and rumblies were extra moving around now that the truck was coming so soon. Because that meant they had to finish packing and do the thing Sierra didn't really want to do. Tell Katy and Mrs. Henning good-bye.

She'd already told her class friends good-bye. James jumped up and down and gave her a little punch in the arm when she told him she was getting a second daddy too. Just like he got a second daddy. Her teacher said the class would miss her, but she would have a wonderful life in California.

Sierra sat on her bed next to Wrinkles and studied her open suitcase.

It was true. She couldn't wait to get to California. They were going to live in something called a 'partment for a little while. Until summertime. That's when Mommy and Clay were getting married, and after that Sierra could call Clay the thing she wanted to call him.

Daddy.

A sad feeling came into her heart. But not her first daddy, because nothing could ever erase her first daddy's face from her heart. Clay would be her second daddy; just as nice and wonderful as her first daddy, but different.

She was running out of room in her suitcase, and she knew why. The helmet took up half the space. It was her first daddy's helmet, the one he wore when he was fighting fires. The one he was wearing when the Twin Towers fell down. She dropped to her knees next to the suitcase and patted the top of the helmet. It was big and strong looking, the way her first daddy had always looked.

The helmet made her remember some special times with that daddy. Times when he gave her horsie rides and curled her hair and did butterfly kisses and took her to church and sang songs with her. She looked around her room. Sometimes when she wanted to remember him she only had to move her eyes so they would see a special place. Like the chair she and Daddy sat in or the place on her bedroom floor where they used to play horsie.

So what about when she didn't have this house anymore?

Stinging happened in her eyes and she blinked. Wrinkles jumped off the bed and curled up next to her on the floor.

"Wrinkles, you know what?" Sierra stirred her fingers in the soft hair at the top of her cat's head. "Maybe I don't really want to move."

The cat yawned very big and did a few slow blinks. Probably he wasn't getting enough sleep.

Sierra looked at the place on the floor a little ways away, where she and Daddy used to play. At the same time, two hot little tears splashed down her cheeks. Then she looked at the helmet in her suitcase. And suddenly in her heart an idea started.

If she looked hard enough at her daddy's firefighter helmet, she could see him. She had always been able to see him. So maybe she didn't need her very own house to remember him. Maybe she could remember him even in a 'partment. And something else too.

Mommy said her first daddy would always be in her heart. Because in her heart she would always be that little girl with long yellow curlies walking into church, holding her daddy's hand.

And he would always be her hero.

She put her hand on the helmet and looked hard at it. Her first daddy wouldn't want her to stay in the old house if it meant not having Clay. Because Clay was very big and strong, just like Daddy was. And plus he liked *Lion King* just like her, and he even liked to play dress-up.

In California they would have other family too. Clay's family. And that meant she would get to see Mr. Michaels. Mommy said Mr. Michaels would be her uncle after they got married, and Josh—the nice boy who played Frisbee with her—would be her cousin.

So that was pretty nice. And after school was over and Mommy and Clay got married, they would all live in a house with a swimming pool! A real in-the-ground swimming pool!

She patted Wrinkles on the head. "We can get a little boat for you, Wrinkles. And you can go sailing while I swim, okay?"

Wrinkles closed his eyes, because he needed his rest. Mommy said he wouldn't sleep much in the plane because he had to be in a big box down with the luggage. Sierra hadn't told Wrinkles about that yet. Some things were better if they were surprises, actually. Plus also, Wrinkles might not want to go if he knew he was flying to California with the luggage.

Once more she looked at the helmet, and this time she picked it up and held it to her heart. She kissed the top of the helmet and then held it a little higher and gave it butterfly kisses, first with one set of eyelashes and then the other.

When she was done, she set the helmet back in her suitcase and a smile came to her face. Because she could still see him, her first daddy. Tall and nice and laughing, standing right beside her. And deep inside she could hear God telling her some good news. Yes, her daddy would always be there, the same way he was now. Whether they lived in Staten Island or California, he would be there.

Forever and ever and ever.

Jamie stood in the doorway and stared into her empty house.

The movers had come and were already headed west. She and Sierra had stayed one last night, and at four o'clock they would fly nonstop to Los Angeles. Now they had all day to say their good-byes.

The old house was first on the list.

"Okay, Sierra." Jamie glanced at her daughter, sitting on the front porch steps sticking her finger through the holes in Wrinkles's air carrier box. The For Sale sign was fifteen yards away, sticking out of the snow. "Come say good-bye to your house."

Sierra looked up. "I already did, Mommy. After the movers left yesterday." She bit her lip. "Can I stay out here with Wrinkles?"

Jamie gave her a sad smile. "Okay." She looked back through the front door. "I'll hurry."

She started upstairs with Sierra's room, the same room she and her sister had slept in as little girls. She welcomed the torrent of memories, little moments that formed the skeleton of her entire life. It was a small room with a single window. Nothing remarkable, except the fact that it had been hers since she was born.

Now it would belong to someone else. "Good-bye, little room." She stepped out and closed the door.

The next room would be hardest of all. Her bedroom. The place where her parents had slept so many years ago; the place where she and Jake had shared their love for nearly a decade.

Jamie worked the muscles in her jaw and squinted, blinded by the brightness of the past. This was why she needed to move, why she couldn't welcome Clay into her East Coast world. Because in this house, her memories were so alive they fairly breathed. She would take them with her, of course. They were woven into the fabric of who she was. But if she was to have new life, she would need new surroundings.

She closed her eyes, stepped back, and closed that door.

The rest of the house was easier, though the memories of all that had happened there—family dinners, birthday parties, movie nights, and a thousand other memories—were not. She floated through the rooms, hating the emptiness, allowing the image of those warm old walls to burn a forever impression in her mind.

Soon she was back at the front door, taking one last look. She breathed in slow—she would even miss the smell of it, the old wood and windows.

It smelled like home. The way home had always smelled.

Jamie had known this day would involve tears, and it was no surprise that they kicked into action now. She hesitated. *God . . . bless whoever comes here next, whoever lives here and loves here and laughs here the way we did. Bless them that they might feel Your Spirit and know You are in this place.*

Then, her eyes blurred, she stepped back, closed the door, and locked it.

Sierra looked up at her and immediately she understood. "Mommy, it's okay." She stood and gave her a hug around her waist. "California will be good too."

"I know it will." Jamie sniffed. She gave Sierra a sad smile and looked deep into her eyes. "Crying is okay, you know why?"

"Why?" Sierra's eyes were damp too. The day was bound to be hard for both of them.

"Because if you cry a lot when you say good-bye, it means you loved a lot." She stooped down and kissed Sierra's nose. "Do you understand that?"

"Yes, Mommy." Sierra lowered her brow, very serious. "Then today will be a lot of crying. Because I loved living here and being friends with Katy Henning a very lot."

At that moment, the Hennings' car pulled up. Sue was picking them up and taking them to lunch. After that, Jamie and Sierra would board the ferry to Manhattan, and from there catch a cab to the airport.

Sue climbed out of her pickup truck, and the moment their eyes met, Jamie saw she wasn't the only one affected. Sue was crying too. She crossed the yard, her eyes on Jamie the entire time. Sierra ran to the car to see Katy and little Larry, both buckled into the backseat.

"I'll miss you so much." Sue hugged her, expressing the sorrow Jamie knew had been building for both of them since she accepted Clay's proposal. Sue stepped back and dragged her hand across her cheeks. "I'm sorry; you don't need this. It's just . . ." Her features twisted as she gave a sideways nod of her head. "You're like a sister to me, Jamie. After all we've been through. The guys . . . our faith—" Two short sobs interrupted her. "I can't . . . imagine life without you."

"Oh, Sue." Jamie held her again. "I'll visit. I promise I will." She took her friend's shoulders and leaned back enough to see her eyes. "And you will too. Okay? This spring you fly out, and we'll take the kids to Disneyland, okay?"

Sue nodded, but still the tears poured down her face. She stared at Jamie's house for several seconds and then grabbed a suit-case with each hand. When the car was loaded and they drove off, the conversation lightened up. They spent the morning at the Henning house, talking about old times, remembering the friendship between Larry and Jake, how fun they were together, how well they embraced life right until the end.

They shared lunch together and cried again when Sue dropped them off at the ferry. Less, this time, because of their own sorrow than the sadness of seeing their daughters say good-bye.

Sierra hugged Katy tight. "Don't forget me, Katy. Best friends forever, okay?"

"Best friends forever." Katy ran to Sue's side and buried her face in her mother's jacket.

Both girls were crying too hard to say more than that. Jamie gave one last wave to Sue, and a look that told her this wasn't the end. That a friendship like theirs, forged out of the very best moments and the most horrifically painful ones, would not end simply because of a move.

Sue and her children turned then and headed back for their car; Jamie did the same, pulling their suitcases while Sierra clutched Wrinkles's carrier. Just before they boarded the ferry, Sierra stopped, stooped down, and spread her hand out on the ground.

"What're you doing, honey?" Jamie felt her tears drying in the winter wind. She pulled up and watched her daughter.

"Saying good-bye." Sierra stood and picked up Wrinkles again. "Good-bye to Staten Island."

The ferry ride felt faster than usual, and they found a cab without any wait. Jamie directed the driver to St. Paul's, promising to pay him extra if he'd wait while she and Sierra ran inside.

She'd had her last shift two weeks earlier, but it wouldn't be right to pass by the area without a final farewell. Someday she'd come to St. Paul's again, but once the new buildings were built—the ones that would stand where the Twin Towers had stood—the atmosphere at the chapel would change.

Items that formed the memorial inside the little church would be moved to the official memorial, the one planned for somewhere in the new construction. And St. Paul's would return to being only a nice little chapel in the middle of Manhattan's financial district. A landmark, yes, but not the mission it had been in the years after September 11.

Jamie wasn't sure she wanted to see St. Paul's that way.

Neither did most of the other volunteers, those who helped remove the pile of debris and those who served and offered their time. She was part of a community of people who would never enter St. Paul's without seeing the place lined with posters and pictures and letters, without seeing photographs of the dead and pews full of vacant-eyed firefighters, covered in soot and weary from the grim task of working the pile.

This . . . this final good-bye, was the last time the chapel would look the way she would always remember it.

She led Sierra by the hand, jogged lightly across the street, up the steps, and inside. The place was quiet, as usual. She turned to the first table, the one on the left of the front door, and immediately found Jake's picture.

Sierra stayed close at her side. "That's Daddy!"

"Yes." Jamie had always figured she would know when it was right to bring Sierra. But they'd run out of time, so right or not, this was the moment. "Remember when I would do my volunteer work?"

"Yes." Sierra looked at her, eyes wide.

"Well—" Jamie shifted her eyes back to Jake's picture—"this is where I would come."

"Oh." Sierra looked at the picture again too. Then she caught a quick breath and pointed. "That's my letter to Daddy!"

"Yep." Jamie put her arm around Sierra's shoulders and hugged her. "It'll stay with his picture for always."

Sierra thought about that for a minute. "I like that."

One of the other volunteers approached her then, an older woman who had connected often with Jamie. She knew why Jamie was there and she introduced herself to Sierra. "Want some cookies upstairs? I baked them this morning."

Sierra looked at Jamie. "Can I?"

"Yes." Jamie cast the woman a grateful look. "But only for a minute. The cab's waiting."

Sierra went off with the woman. Once she was gone, Jamie turned and found Jake's picture again. Sweet Jake, the man who had prayed for her and cherished her and written words that guided her way still. The man who had led her to God.

She looked deep into his eyes. So much of their time together she had worried about him, that he would lose his life fighting fires. What a waste of time. If she had it to do all over again, she would choose to love Jake, even knowing their time together would be short.

The lessons he'd taught her would live on, as would the memory of his love. Yes, the page was turning. She could feel it in her heart, feel the way St. Paul's didn't quite have the same hold on her as it once had. She didn't need a memorial to remember Jake, to honor him.

She would do that with her life.

The volunteer returned with Sierra, and Jamie hugged the woman. "Tell the others good-bye, okay?"

"I will." She pulled an envelope from her pocket. "Aaron Hisel told me to give this to you. He heard you were moving."

Jamie's heart sank. Aaron had been important in her life for a time, one of the reasons she'd been able to process the pain of losing Jake. She would miss him, even though their time together had ended long before she decided to marry Clay.

"Did . . . did he say anything?"

The woman smiled. "He wanted you to hear it from him."

Jamie nodded. She slipped the envelope in her coat pocket, said another quick good-bye, and led Sierra back outside. She walked to the corner and for a moment she stared at the empty sky, the place where the buildings had stood.

It would be good to get away from that part of the skyline, good to know she could drive to the market without catching a glimpse of the emptiness. Jake went into those towers because it was the right thing to do. She had no doubt that even until the last few seconds, he and Larry were helping people, probably praying with them and telling them about Jesus.

She didn't need St. Paul's or Ground Zero to remind her of that.

"That's where the Twin Towers were, right, Mommy?" Sierra squinted up, shading her eyes so she could see despite the glare from the snow and white cloudy sky.

"Yes." Even now she hated the past tense, hated how it reminded her that such an awful thing really had happened. "That's where they were."

Sierra looked at her and squeezed her hand a little tighter. "But that's not where Daddy is now. Daddy's in heaven." Her eyes were dry now, the trauma of good-bye already fading. She touched her fingers to her chest. "And his picture is right here." She angled her head, her eyes curious. "Do you think Daddy's happy that we're moving to California and marrying Clay?"

Jamie looked at her feet for a minute and then up at the empty skyline again. Jake's smile, the memory of it, flashed in her mind as big and bright as heaven itself. "Yes, Sierra. I think he's very happy."

The plane was halfway to Los Angeles when Jamie remembered Aaron's letter. Sierra was sleeping in the seat beside her, so she was careful not to wake her. She pulled out the envelope, opened it, and slid out the letter.

> *Dear Jamie,*
> *I won't make this long, but I promised you I'd tell you if some-thing changed. Well, something did.*

Jamie closed her eyes, her heart doing a double beat. What was this? Aaron couldn't be talking about the one thing they never agreed on, could he? She blinked and found her place.

> *One of the new guys at the station had a baby with a heart problem. The guy asked every one of us who believed to pray. You know me; I told him I couldn't pray because I didn't believe. But that night I asked God to show me He was real, let me know if I was wrong about the whole faith thing.*
> *And guess what happened?*
> *The new guy comes up to me the next day and says, "You don't have to believe in God, Hisel, He believes in you."*
> *The exact words you told me. And I don't know, I got chills and something happened inside me. Like I knew right then that God was real, and He was there. I'm not saying I have it all fig-ured out or any of it figured out, really. But the new guy's talking to me. He's buying me a Bible.*
> *I guess I just wanted you to know so you could keep praying for me. I already know Jake's praying. I'm happy for you, Jamie. Take care of yourself.*

Aaron

Jamie blinked back tears and read the letter again. Then she closed her eyes and let her head fall against the seat back. *God . . . You're so good, so faithful. I knew You'd get Aaron's attention, and now You have. You work all things out in Your timing.*

The hum of the jet soothed her, helped clear her mind.

She opened her eyes and looked out the window. Down below were clusters of lights, places where families gathered, sharing notes from a day of work or school. The way she and Clay and Sierra would be soon.

Joy rose up within her and warmed her heart. There was really nothing more to be sad about. She pictured Clay's face, the way he would look when they got off the plane and walked into his world once and for all. Thoughts of the future filled her head. It would be so good to see him and hold him and plan a wedding with him, so much fun unpacking her things and watching Sierra and Clay and Wrinkles play dress-up together.

Choose life. Jake's voice sounded in her soul once more, ringing with sincerity and faith, the way it had always done back when he was alive, when he was hers. *Choose life, Jamie. Choose life.*

She smiled at the sleeping form of their daughter. *I am, Jake. I'm choosing life.*

The jet engines hummed low in the background. She looked out the window, every mountain or field they passed taking them a little closer to California. Closer to Clay. A warm certainty settled in her chest, convincing her of what she'd known all along. With all its trials and tragedies, all its brokenhearted confusion, life was still the greatest choice of all. God-given life. That was her choice.

Now and always.

A NOTE FROM KAREN

Those of you who read *One Tuesday Morning* know that telling Jamie Bryan's story was something I had to do. That first book came to me almost complete on the afternoon of September 11, 2001, and it stayed in my heart until I wrote it for you.

It was the same way with this sequel.

Beyond Tuesday Morning is really the rest of the story, the way the rest of the story might play out for all those touched or changed by tragedy. Like Jamie, all of us will have the chance to choose life. For some of you, that might mean making a recommitment to a dying marriage or looking for ways to encourage your husband or wife.

Choosing life might mean taking time to play with your children. So often we get caught up in the business of raising a family—making vacation plans, buying a house, getting a job, doing housework, fixing up the yard—that we miss the point. Making time with your children and the people you love is definitely a way to choose life.

But the way that is illustrated in this book is vitally important.

I've heard it said that all of us are either leaving a trial, heading into one, or smack in the middle of one. Trials can vary from issues at work to the death of a loved one. In Jamie's case, she was willing to spend her life memorializing the years she'd had with Jake.

But ultimately it was God's Word, combined with words written by Jake, that helped her choose life.

Grief and sorrow are important stages, seasons that we must go through. To some extent we will never be fully rid of either—not when we're dealing with the loss of someone we loved. I hear from hundreds of you every week—mostly letters of encouragement and offers of prayer, for which I will forever be grateful. But once in a while you tell me of tragic events in your families or communities.

When I hear about a car accident or illness or loss, I always pray. I pray for hope and healing wherever possible.

And I pray for life.

Life is God's gift to us. With every sweet breath, we confirm the fact that God has us here for a reason, that He has a plan for our lives. I truly believe that the more we surrender our lives to Him, the more we trust Him with the days He gives us, the better off we'll be. There is such peaceful freedom, such uninhibited joy, in knowing that God Almighty is the reason we woke up today. If we have tomorrow, it's because He has more for us to do.

In that light, it's almost impossible to spend a day bemoaning our situation, unwilling to rejoice. Grief stays with us, but it need not stay *on* us. I think of the apostle Paul, chained in a Roman prison, rats nibbling at his knees. What was he doing? Singing . . . telling the jailors about Jesus . . . and writing letters to his friends back home, encouraging them to glorify God with their lives.

If you or someone you love is in a difficult situation, I pray this book has given you hope. But I also pray it sends you looking for the purpose God has for your life. Allow the possibility that whatever you're going through, this too shall pass. Not without pain, not without tears, but with possibility and trust in God.

Things are good on the home front. Kelsey is fifteen and in high school and has just finished cheering for the freshmen football team. Tyler, twelve, is being homeschooled so he can have more time for the arts he's so passionate about. He is very involved in Christian Youth Theater and will audition for all three of the musicals this year. Sean, Josh, EJ, and Austin have just completed a wonderful season of soccer. With Christmas behind us, we're settling in for a productive winter/spring season. We still do devotions every morning, and I am thrilled to see each of the kids gradually making decisions for Christ that are motivated by their own love for God, their own choices for life.

If you're a believer in Jesus Christ, I pray this book encourages you to keep on fighting the good fight. If you're not, then this may be the chance in a lifetime, the chance to call on Jesus as your Savior, to get to a Bible-believing church and find out about a relationship with the true God of the universe. Trusting Jesus for life is the very first step to choosing life. *Abundant* life. John 10:10 says that the thief comes to kill, steal, and destroy, but Jesus has come to give us life, life to the fullest measure.

Don't waste another day with the thief; rather make the choice to spend your life, from this day on, with the Giver of life. One of my favorite sections of Scripture is Hebrews 12, which encourages us to never give up, but to "run with perseverance the race marked out for us." The race of life. That's what God called Jamie Bryan to do.

It's what He calls each of us to do.

Until next time, I pray God keeps His mighty arms around you, that you feel the presence of His loving touch, His gentle hug, even on the darkest nights. May He bless you and yours and grant you life. Always life.

In His light and love,
Karen Kingsbury

P.S. My website, www.KarenKingsbury.com, has become a big part of my ministry. You can leave a prayer request, pray for other readers with specific needs, and meet prayer partners at the Prayer Ministry link. You can get involved in discussions about my books at the Reader Forum link, and you can see how God is using these books to affect the lives of other readers at the Guest Book link.

You can contact me at the website or at my email address: rtnbykk@aol.com. As always, I love hearing from you and look forward to your letters.

Even Now

Karen Kingsbury

Sometimes hope for the future is found in the ashes of yesterday.

Shane Galanter—a man ready to put down roots after years of searching. But is he making the right choice? Or is there a woman somewhere who even now remembers—as does he—those long-ago days and a love that hasn't faded with time?

Lauren Gibbs—a successful international war correspondent who gave up on happily-ever-after years ago—when it was ripped away from her. Since then, she's never looked back. So how come she can't put to rest the one question that haunts her: Why is life so empty?

Emily Anderson—a college freshman raised by her grandparents who's about to take her first internship as a journalist. But before she can move ahead, she discovers a love story whose tragic ending came with her birth. As a result, she is drawn to look back and search out the mother she's never met.

A young woman seeking answers to her heart's deep questions. A man and woman separated by lies and long years, who have never forgotten each other. With hallmark tenderness and power, Karen Kingsbury weaves a tapestry of lives, losses, love, and faith—and the miracle of resurrection.

Also available in unabridged audio CD.

Softcover: 0-310-24753-5

Pick up a copy today at your favorite bookstore!

ZONDERVAN®

GRAND RAPIDS, MICHIGAN 49530 USA

WWW.ZONDERVAN.COM

Three ways to keep up on your favorite Zondervan books and authors

Sign up for our *Fiction E-Newsletter*. Every month you'll receive sample excerpts from our books, sneak peeks at upcoming books, and chances to win free books autographed by the author.

You can also sign up for our *Breakfast Club*. Every morning in your email, you'll receive a five-minute snippet from a fiction or nonfiction book. A new book will be featured each week, and by the end of the week you will have sampled two to three chapters of the book.

Zondervan *Author Tracker* is the best way to be notified whenever your favorite Zondervan authors write new books, go on tour, or want to tell you about what's happening in their lives.

Visit *www.zondervan.com* and sign up today!